READER'S DIGEST
CONDENSED BOOKS

www.readersdigest.co.uk

The Reader's Digest Association Limited 11 Westferry Circus Canary Wharf London E14 4HE

Printed in France
ISBN 0 276 42739 4

READER'S DIGEST CONDENSED BOOKS

Selected and edited by Reader's Digest

CONDENSED BOOKS DIVISION

THE READER'S DIGEST ASSOCIATION LIMITED, LONDON

CONTENTS

A brilliant illusionist turns his hand to murder, and expert forensic criminologist Lincoln Rhyme, and his partner and lover Amelia Sachs, are brought in to help the investigation. As the death toll rises, they find themselves misdirected and wrong-footed at every turn by the magician's use of smoke and mirrors. Yet again, Deaver succeeds in weaving a page-turning story in which appearances are very often cleverly deceiving.

PUBLISHED BY
HODDER & STOUGHTON

When the body of a young girl is discovered beside a lake near a small Norwegian village, Inspector Konrad Sejer makes house-to-house enquiries. The victim appears to have had no enemies; her life was strikingly normal. Then, as Sejer probes deeper, he discovers that beneath the surface of the unremarkable community, passions run deep. A skilfully crafted crime novel from an author who is winning critical acclaim across Europe.

PUBLISHED BY HARVILL

PREY

page 281

Michael Crichton

Jack Forman loves his wife, Julia, but since she's been working for Xymos Technologies, she's been brittle and secretive, often disappearing abruptly to the company's remote base in the Nevada Desert. Jack decides he must see for himself what Xymos are up to. What he finds in their labs is a scientific breakthrough beyond any scientist's wildest dreams—and nightmares. A chilling, futuristic thriller from the author of *Jurassic Park*.

PUBLISHED BY HARPERCOLLINS

STREET BOYS

page 423

Lorenzo Carcaterra

In September 1943, the war in Europe is almost won. Naples has been evacuated, but the German army is moving in with orders to destroy what is left, expecting little resistance. Orphaned or hidden by parents, abandoned or lost, the children of Naples decide to fight back. Aided by a lone Allied soldier, they are determined to save their city—or die trying. Moving and passionately told, Carcaterra's story is based on true events.

PUBLISHED BY SIMON & SCHUSTER

THE VANISHED MAN

JEFFERY DEAVER

At a Manhattan music school, in the wake of a homicide, the police have their suspect surrounded, trapped inside a room. But when they force their way in, the room is completely empty—the killer has escaped.

As if by magic.

PART I: EFFECT

Saturday, April 20

CHAPTER ONE

Greetings, Revered Audience. Welcome.

Welcome to our show.

We have a number of thrills in store for you over the next two days as our illusionists, our magicians, our sleight-of-hand artists weave their spells to delight and captivate you.

Our first routine is from the repertoire of a performer everyone's heard of: Harry Houdini, the greatest escape artist in America, if not the world. Today we'll re-create a routine known as the Lazy Hangman.

In this trick, our performer lies prone on the belly, hands bound behind the back with classic Darby handcuffs. The ankles are tied together and another length of rope is wound round the neck, like a noose, and tied to the ankles. The tendency of the legs to straighten pulls the noose taut and begins the terrible process of suffocation.

Why is it called the Lazy Hangman? Because the condemned executes himself.

We begin in a moment . . . but first a word of advice:

Never forget that by entering our show you're abandoning reality. What you're absolutely convinced you see might not exist at all. What you know has to be an illusion may turn out to be God's harsh truth. What seems safe may be deadly. And the dangers you guard against may be nothing more than distractions to lure you to greater danger.

In our show what can you believe? Whom can you trust?

Well, Revered Audience, the answer is you should believe nothing.

And you should trust no one. No one at all.

Now, the curtain rises, the lights dim, the music fades, leaving only the sound of hearts beating in anticipation.

And our show begins . . .

THE BUILDING LOOKED as if it had seen its share of ghosts. Gothic, sooty, dark. On the Upper West Side. It dated from the Victorian era and had been a boarding school and later a sanatorium, where the criminally insane lived out their frazzled lives. The Manhattan School of Music and Performing Arts could have been home to dozens of spirits.

But none so immediate as the one that might be hovering here now, above the warm body of the young woman lying, stomach down, in the dim lobby outside a small recital room. Her eyes were still and wide but not yet glassy, her face was dark as plum from the constriction of the taut rope connecting her neck to her ankles.

Also present was the man who'd killed her, examining her carefully. He felt no urge to rush. Today was Saturday, the hour early. There were no classes in the school at weekends, he'd learned. The practice rooms were in a different wing of the building. He leaned closer to the woman, wondering if he could see some essence, some spirit rising from her body. He didn't.

'YOU'RE SURE IT WAS SCREAMING?'

'Yeah . . . No,' the security guard said. 'Maybe not screaming. Shouting. Upset. For just a second or two.'

'Anybody else hear anything?' Officer Diane Franciscovich continued. She was a portable, a beat cop in the Patrol Services Division, working out of the 20th Precinct.

The heavy guard, breathing hard, glanced at the tall, brunette policewoman and shook his head.

'Call for back-up?' asked Nancy Ausonio, another rookie patrol officer, shorter than her partner, blonde.

Franciscovich wasn't sure. Portables walking the beat in this part of the Upper West Side dealt mostly with traffic accidents, shoplifting and car theft. The two women officers, on their Saturday-morning watch, had been spotted on the sidewalk and motioned inside by the guard to help check out the screaming. Well, upset shouting. 'Let's hold off,' Franciscovich said. 'See what's going on.'

'Spooky place,' Ausonio offered.

Miles of dim corridors later, they had found nothing out of the ordinary. Then the security guard paused. Franciscovich nodded to a doorway in front of them. 'What's through here?'

'It's only—' the guard began.

Franciscovich pushed the door open.

Inside was a small lobby that led to the door of Recital Hall A. And near *that* door was the body of a young woman, trussed up, rope round her neck, hands in cuffs. A brown-haired, bearded man in his early fifties stood over her. He looked up.

The officers drew their weapons and Franciscovich sighted on the man with what she thought was a surprisingly steady hand.

'You, don't move! Put your hands in the air.'

The man did as he was told.

'Lie face down on the floor. Keep your hands in sight!'

Ausonio started forward to the girl. It was then that Franciscovich noticed that the man's right hand, over his head, was closed in a fist.

Pop . . .

She went blind as a flash of searing light filled the room. It seemed to come directly from the suspect's hand. Ausonio froze and Franciscovich went into a crouch, squinting to get her vision back, swinging the gun back and forth. Then she saw the killer running into the recital hall. He slammed the door shut. There was a thud as he moved a chair or table against it.

Ausonio dropped to her knees in front of the girl. With a knife she cut the rope off her neck, rolled her over and started CPR.

'Any other exits?' Franciscovich shouted to the guard.

'Only one—in the back, round the corner. To the right.'

'Hey,' she called to Ausonio, 'watch this door!'

She sprinted towards the door the guard had told them about, calling for back-up on her Motorola Handie-Talkie radio. She saw someone standing at the end of the corridor. Franciscovich drew a target on the man's chest.

'Lord,' croaked the elderly janitor, dropping his broom.

'You see somebody come out of that door?' Franciscovich shouted.

'No, ma'am.'

'How long you been here?'

'I don't know. Ten minutes, I'd guess.'

There was another thud from inside as the killer continued to blockade the door. Franciscovich sent the janitor into the main corridor with the security guard then eased up to the door. Gun held high, she tested the knob gently. It was unlocked. She stepped to the side so she wouldn't be in the line of fire if the perp shot through the wood.

'Nancy?' Franciscovich whispered into her Handie-Talkie.

Ausonio's voice, shaky, said, 'She's dead. I tried.'

'He's still inside. I can hear him.'

'I called for back-up. Let's go get him.'

'No,' Franciscovich said, 'we'll keep him contained until ESU gets here. Sit tight.'

Which is when she heard the man shout from inside, 'I've got a girl in here. Try to get in and I'll kill her!'

'You, inside,' Franciscovich shouted. 'Nobody's going to do anything. Don't worry. Just don't hurt anybody else.' She heard Ausonio call Central and report that the situation was now a barricade and hostage-taking.

A gunshot from inside.

'You think he shot her?' Ausonio asked on her radio.

'I don't know. How do I know?'

'Diane,' Ausonio whispered. 'We've gotta go in. Maybe she's wounded.' Then, shouting: 'You, inside!' No answer. 'You!'

'Maybe he killed himself,' Franciscovich offered. Then that terrible image returned to her: the door to the recital lobby opening, casting the pale light on the victim, her face blue and cold as winter dusk.

'We have to go in, Diane,' Ausonio whispered again.

'OK. We'll go in. Tell the guard we'll need lights inside the hall.'

A moment later Ausonio said, 'He'll turn 'em on when I say so. Ready. On three. You count it.'

'One . . . Wait. I'll be coming in from your two o'clock.'

'Go ahead.'

'One.' Franciscovich gripped the knob. 'Two. Three!' She shoved through the doorway just as the glaring lights came on. 'Freeze!' she screamed—to an empty room.

A glance to her left, the other doorway, where Nancy Ausonio stood, doing the same frantic scan of the room.

Franciscovich noticed about fifty folding chairs. Four or five of them were lying on their backs or sides. But they didn't seem to be a barricade; they were randomly kicked over. To her right was a low stage. On it sat a battered grand piano.

The room was essentially a sealed cube. No windows. The air-conditioning and heating vents were only six inches across. A wooden ceiling, not acoustic tile. No trap doors on the stage. No doors except the main one and the fire door that Franciscovich had used.

'Yo,' a loud voice called from the doorway.

They spun towards it, drawing targets on the empty lobby.

'Ambulance and some other officers just got here.' It was the security guard, hiding out of sight.

Heart slamming from the fright, Franciscovich beckoned him in.

He asked, 'Is it, uhm . . . I mean, you get him?'

'He's not here,' Ausonio said in a shaky voice.

'What?' The man peeked cautiously into the hall.

The women stood transfixed, trying vainly to figure out how the killer had escaped from a room from which there *was* no escape.

'HE'S LISTENING TO MUSIC.'

'I'm not *listening* to music. The music happens to be on.'

'Music, huh?' Lon Sellitto muttered as he walked into Lincoln Rhyme's bedroom. 'That's a coincidence.'

'He's developed a taste for jazz,' Thom explained to the paunchy detective. 'Surprised me, I have to tell you.'

'As I said,' Lincoln Rhyme continued petulantly, 'I'm working and the music happens to be playing. What do you mean, coincidence?'

Nodding at the flat-screen monitor in front of Rhyme's Flexicair bed, the young aide, dressed in a white shirt, tan slacks and purple tie, said, 'He's not working. Unless staring at the same page for an hour is work. He wouldn't let *me* get away with work like that.'

'Command, turn page.' The computer recognised Rhyme's voice and obeyed his order, slapping a new page of *Forensic Science Review* onto the monitor. He asked Thom acerbically, 'Say, you want to quiz me on what I've been *staring at*? The composition of the top five exotic toxins found in recent terrorist laboratories in Europe? And how 'bout we put some money on the answers?'

'No, we have other things to do,' the aide replied, referring to the various bodily functions that caregivers must attend to several times a day when their patients are quadriplegics like Lincoln Rhyme. 'If you'll excuse us for a moment, Lon.'

'Yeah, sure,' said the middle-aged detective and stepped into the corridor outside the first-floor bedroom of Rhyme's Central Park West town house. He closed the door.

Minutes later Thom let Sellitto back in. 'Coffee?'

'Yeah. Could use some. Too early to work on a Saturday.'

The aide left.

'Gotta bizarre case, Linc,' Sellitto said. 'Found a body a half-hour ago at a music school up the street. I'm case officer and we could use some help.'

Music school. I'm listening to *music*. A poor coincidence.

Sellitto ran through the facts: student killed, the perp got away through some kind of trap door that nobody could find.

'How's the scene?'

'Still pretty virgin. Can we get Amelia to run it?'

Rhyme glanced at the clock. 'She's tied up for another twenty minutes or so.'

'What's she doing?'

'Oh, something dangerous,' Rhyme said. 'What else?'

HER PALMS SWEATED and, beneath the fiery red hair shoved up under her dusty issue hat, her scalp itched. She remained still as a uniformed officer slipped up beside her against the tenement wall.

'OK, here's the situation,' the man said. He explained that just round the corner of the tenement was a vacant lot, in the middle of which was a getaway car that had crashed after a high-speed pursuit.

'Drivable?' Amelia Sachs asked.

'No. Hit a Dumpster and it's out of commission. Three perps. They bailed but we got one in custody. One's in the car with some kind of hunting rifle. He wounded a patrolman.'

'Condition?'

'Superficial.'

She asked, 'The third perp?'

'Hell, he made it to the ground floor of this building here.' Nodding towards the tenement. 'He's got a hostage. Pregnant woman.'

Sachs shifted her weight from one foot to the other, to ease the pain of the arthritis in her joints. She noticed her companion's name on his chest. 'The hostage-taker's weapon, Wilkins?'

'Handgun. Unknown type.'

'Where's our side?'

The young man pointed out two officers behind a wall at the back of the lot. 'Then two more in front of the building.'

She clicked on her Motorola and said, 'Crime Scene Five Eight Eight Five to Supervisor.'

A moment later: 'This is Captain Seven Four. Go ahead.'

'Ten-thirteen at a lot east of 605 Delancey. Officer down. Need back-up, EMS bus and ESU. Two subjects, armed. One with hostage. We'll need a negotiator.'

'Roger, we'll get back-up there as soon as we can.'

Wilkins shook his head. 'But we can't get a negotiator near the apartment. Not with the shooter still in the car.'

'I'm working on that,' Sachs replied.

She edged to the corner of the tenement and glanced at the car, with its nose against a Dumpster, doors open, revealing a man holding a rifle. She shouted, 'You in the car, you're surrounded. We're going to open fire if you don't drop your weapon. Do it now!'

He spun round. She ducked for cover. On her Motorola she called the two officers crouched in the back of the lot. 'You got a shot?'

'Probably through the door.'

'No, don't shoot blind. Go for position.'

She saw the men move to a flanking position. One officer said, 'I've got a shot. Should I take it?'

'Stand by.' She shouted, 'You in the car. You have ten seconds or we'll open fire. Drop your weapon.' She repeated this in Spanish.

To the two officers she radioed, 'Give him twenty. Then you're green-lighted.'

At close to the ten-second mark, the man dropped the rifle and stood up, hands in the air. 'No shoot, no shoot!'

'Keep those hands up. Walk to the corner of the building.'

When he got to the corner Wilkins cuffed and searched him. Sachs said to the suspect, 'The guy inside. Who is he?'

'I don't gotta tell you—'

'Yeah, you do gotta. Because if we take him out, which we *are* going to do, you'll go down for felony murder. Now, is that man in there worth forty-five years in Ossining?'

The man sighed.

'Come on,' she snapped. 'Name, address, family, what he likes for dinner, his mother's first name, he have relatives in the system—you can think of all kinds of real helpful stuff about him, I'll bet.'

As the man finally spoke, Sachs scribbled down the details.

Her Motorola crackled. The hostage negotiator and the Emergency Services Unit had just shown up. She handed her notes to Wilkins. 'Get those to the negotiator.'

She read the rifleman his rights, wondering if she had handled the situation the best way she could.

Five minutes later the supervising captain walked round the corner of the building. He smiled. 'The H-T released the woman. No injuries. We've got three collared. The wounded officer'll be OK.'

Sachs was surveying the lot, where the perps' car rested against the Dumpster. She said to Wilkins, 'You said *three* perps?'

'That was the report from the jewellery store they hit.'

'Look at the getaway car,' Sachs snapped, pulling out her Glock.

All the doors were open. *Four* men had bailed.

Dropping into a crouch, she aimed her gun towards the only possible hiding place: a cul-de-sac behind the Dumpster.

'Weapon!' she cried, almost before she saw the motion.

Everyone around her turned as the large, T-shirted man with a shotgun jogged out of the lot, making a run for the street.

Sachs's Glock was centred on his chest. 'Drop the weapon!' she ordered.

He hesitated then grinned and began to swing it towards the officers.

She pushed her Glock forward.

And said, 'Bang, bang . . . You're dead.'

The shotgunner stopped and laughed. 'Damn good. I thought I was home free.' He strolled over to the cluster of fellow cops beside the tenement.

The 'hostage', played by a Latina policewoman, joined them too. 'Nice work, Amelia.'

Pleased with her performance, Sachs nonetheless kept a solemn face, like a student who'd just aced an important exam.

Which was, in effect, exactly what had just happened.

Amelia Sachs was pursuing a new goal. Her father, Herman, had been a portable all his life. Sachs now had the same rank, but after the September 11 attacks she'd decided she wanted to do more for her city. So she'd submitted the paperwork to be promoted to detective sergeant. Sachs wanted to be more than a detective; she wanted rank too. In the NYPD one becomes a detective on the basis of merit and experience. To become a sergeant, though, the applicant goes through an arduous triathlon of exams: written, oral and—what Sachs had just endured—an assessment exercise.

The captain, a soft-spoken veteran, was the primary assessor for the exercise and had been taking notes on her performance.

'OK, Officer,' he said, 'we'll write up our results and they'll be attached to your review. But let me say a word unofficially.' Consulting his notebook. 'Your threat assessment regarding civilians and officers was perfect. Calls for back-up were timely and appropriate. Your deployment of personnel negated any chance the perpetrators would escape from the containment situation and yet minimised exposure. And getting the personal information from the one suspect for the hostage negotiator was a nice touch. Then, at the end, well, frankly, we never thought you'd determine there was another perp in hiding.' The officialese vanished and he smiled. 'But you nailed him.'

Then he asked, 'You've done the written and orals, right?'

'Yessir. Should have the results any day now.'

'My group'll complete our evaluation and send that to the board with our recommendations. You can stand down now.'

'Yessir.'

The cop who'd played the bad guy with the shotgun wandered up to her. He was a good-looking Italian, half a generation out of the Brooklyn docks, she judged, and had a cocky smile.

'I gotta tell ya—I've done a dozen assessments and that was the best I ever seen, babe.'

She laughed in surprise at the word. There were certainly cavemen left in the department but they tended to be more condescending than openly sexist. Sachs hadn't heard a 'babe' or 'honey' from a male cop in at least a year.

'Let's stick with "Officer", you don't mind.'

'No, no, no,' he said, laughing. 'You can chill now. The AE's over. When I said "babe", it's not like it's a part of the assessment. You don't have to, you know, deal with it official or anything. I'm just saying it 'cause I was impressed. And 'cause you're a pretty girl. And I'm a guy. You know what that's like . . . So.'

'So,' she replied and started away.

He stepped in front of her, frowning. 'Hey, hold on. This isn't going too good. Look, let me buy you a coffee. You'll like me when you get to know me.'

'Don't bet on it,' one of his buddies called, laughing.

Which is when Sachs's pager beeped and she looked down to see Lincoln Rhyme's number on the screen. The word URGENT appeared after it.

'Gotta go,' she said.

'Well, how 'bout a phone number?' the Babe Man asked.

She made a pistol with her index finger and thumb and aimed it at him. 'Bang, bang,' she said. And trotted towards her yellow Camaro.

THIS IS A SCHOOL?

Wheeling a large black crime scene suitcase behind her, Sachs walked through the dim corridor. A half-dozen cops stood near a double doorway at the end of the hall. Dishevelled Lon Sellitto was talking to a guard. Through the open doorway she glimpsed a light-coloured form. The victim.

To the crime scene tech she said, 'We'll need lights.' The young man nodded and headed back to the rapid response vehicle, a station wagon filled with forensic collection equipment.

Sachs studied the young blonde, lying on her back ten feet away, belly arched up because her bound hands were underneath her. Even in the dimness Sachs noted the deep ligature marks on her neck.

'Who was first officer?'

A tall woman with short brunette hair, her name tag reading D. FRANCISCOVICH, said, 'We were.' A nod towards her blonde partner: N. AUSONIO.

The two patrol officers gave their account. Finding the perp, a flash of light, his disappearing, a barricade. Then he was gone.

'You said he claimed to have a hostage?'

'That's what he said,' Ausonio offered. 'But everybody in the school's accounted for. We're sure he was bluffing.'

'Victim?'

'Svetlana Rasnikov. Twenty-four. Student.'

Sellitto said to Sachs, 'Bedding and Saul are interviewing everybody in the building here this morning.'

She nodded towards the scene. 'Who's been inside?'

Sellitto said, 'The first officers. Then two medics and two ESU. They backed out as soon as they cleared it.'

'The guard too,' Ausonio said. 'But only for a minute.'

'Good,' Sachs said. 'Witnesses?'

Ausonio said, 'There was a janitor outside the room.'

'He didn't see anything,' Franciscovich added.

Sachs said, 'I still need to see the soles of his shoes for comparison. Could one of you find him for me?'

'Sure.' Ausonio wandered off.

From the black suitcase, Sachs extracted a white Tyvek jumpsuit. She donned it, pulling the hood over her head. Then gloves. The outfit was standard issue for all forensics techs at the NYPD; it prevented substances—trace, hair, epithelial skin cells and so on—from sloughing off and contaminating the scene. The suit had booties but she still did what Rhyme always insisted on—put rubber bands on her feet to distinguish her prints from the victim's and the perp's.

Mounting the earphones on her head and adjusting the stalk mike, she hooked up her Motorola. She called in a land-line patch and a moment later she heard the low voice of Lincoln Rhyme in her ear.

'Sachs, you there?'

'Yep. It was just like you said—they had him cornered and he disappeared.'

The tech returned with tall lamps on tripods. Sachs set them up in the lobby and clicked the switch.

There's a lot of debate about the proper way to process a scene. Before his accident, however, Lincoln Rhyme had run most scenes alone and he insisted that Amelia Sachs do the same. He believed that a crime scene searcher working alone is better able to forge a mental relationship with the victim and the perpetrator.

It was into this difficult state of mind that Amelia Sachs now slipped as she gazed at the body of the young woman. Near the body were a spilt cup of coffee, sheet music and a piece of the woman's silver flute, which she'd apparently been in the act of assembling when the killer flipped the rope round her neck.

'I'm at the body, Rhyme,' she said as she snapped digital pictures of the corpse.

'Go ahead.'

'She's on her back—but the respondings found her on her abdomen. They turned her over to give her CPR. Injuries consistent with strangulation.' Sachs now delicately rolled the woman back onto her belly. 'Hands are in some old-fashioned handcuffs. Her watch is broken. Stopped at exactly eight o'clock. Doesn't look accidental. It's nice. A Seiko. Why break it? Why not steal it?'

'Good question. Might be a clue, might be nothing.'

Which was as good a slogan for forensic science as any, Sachs reflected.

'One of the respondings cut the rope round her neck. She missed the knot.' Knots can reveal a great deal of information about the person who tied them.

Sachs then used a tape roller to collect trace evidence—recent forensic thinking was that the portable vacuum cleaner picked up too much trace. Most crime scene teams were switching to rollers. She bagged the trace and used a vic kit to take hair combings and nail scraping samples from the woman's body.

Sachs said, 'I'm going to walk the grid.' The phrase came from Rhyme's preference for searching a crime scene. The grid pattern is the most comprehensive method: back and forth in one direction, then turning perpendicular and covering the same ground again.

She began the search, looking for dropped objects, rolling for trace, taking electrostatic prints of shoeprints and digital photos.

'Officer?' Sellitto called. 'Just wondering . . . you want some backup in there?'

'Nope,' she said, silently thanking him for reminding her that a missing murderer was last seen in this room. Another of Lincoln Rhyme's crime scene aphorisms: Search well but watch your back.

She tapped the butt of her Glock to remind herself exactly where it was in case she needed to draw fast—the holster rode slightly higher when she wore the Tyvek jumpsuit—and continued the search.

'OK, got something,' she told Rhyme a moment later. 'In the lobby. About ten feet away from the victim. Piece of black cloth. Silk, I mean, it *appears* to be silk. It's on top of a part of the vic's flute so it has to be his or hers.'

The lobby yielded nothing else and she entered the performance space itself. There was no hiding place where a perp could be, no hidden doorways or exits.

'Rhyme, this is strange . . . There's a burnt string tied round the chairs that are lying on the ground. Fuses too, it looks like. I smell nitrate and sulphur residue. The reportings said he fired a round. But it's not the smell of smokeless powder. Ah, OK . . . it's a little grey firecracker. Maybe that was the gunshot they heard . . . Hold on. There's something else. It's a small green circuit board, with a speaker attached to it. About two inches by five.'

She bagged everything, then left by the fire door and electrostaticked and photographed the footprints she found there. Finally she took control samples to compare against the trace found on the victim and where the unsub—for 'unknown subject'—had walked. 'Got everything, Rhyme. I'll be back in a half-hour.'

'And the trap doors, secret passages everybody's talking about?'

'I can't find any.'

She returned to the lobby and found Franciscovich and Ausonio by the doorway. 'You find the janitor?' she asked.

Ausonio shook her head. 'He had to take his wife to work. I left a message with maintenance for him to call.'

Her partner said solemnly, 'Hey, Officer, we were talking, Nancy and me? And we don't want this scumbag to get away. If there's anything more we can do, you know, to follow up, let us know.'

Sachs understood exactly how they felt. 'I'll see what I can do.'

Sellitto's radio crackled and he took the call. Listened for a moment. 'Bedding and Saul've finished interviewing the wits.'

Sachs and Sellitto returned to the front of the school and joined the two men in the main lobby. Bedding and Saul were detectives from the Big Building who specialised in post-crime interviewing of witnesses.

'We talked to the seven people here this morning,' Bedding said. 'Plus the guard.'

'Nobody knew the victim very well,' added Saul. 'When she got here this morning she walked to the recital room with a friend. The friend didn't see anybody inside. They stood in the lobby for five, ten minutes talking. The friend left around eight.'

'So,' said Rhyme, who'd overheard on the radio, 'he was inside the lobby waiting for her.'

'The victim,' Saul said, 'had come over here from Georgia—that's the Russia Georgia—about two months ago. She was kind of a loner.'

'All the other students were in practice rooms today,' Beddings added. 'None of them heard anything or saw anyone they didn't know.'

'Why wasn't Svetlana in a practice room?' Sachs asked.

'Liked the acoustics better in the hall, her friend said.'

'Husband, boyfriend, girlfriend?' Sachs asked. Rule number one in homicide investigations: the doer usually knows the doee.

'None that the other students knew.'

'How'd he get into the building?' Rhyme asked and Sachs relayed the question.

The guard said, 'Only door's open is the front one.'

'And he'd have to walk past you, right?'

'And sign in. *And* get his picture took.'

Sachs glanced up. 'There's a security camera, Rhyme.'

They gathered behind the desk. The guard punched buttons and played the tape. Bedding and Saul had vetted seven of the people. But they agreed that one person—a brown-haired, bearded older man in jeans and bulky jacket—hadn't been among them.

'That's him,' Franciscovich said. 'That's the killer.'

Nancy Ausonio nodded.

On the tape he signed the register then walked inside.

'Did you get a look at him?' Sachs asked the guard.

'Didn't pay no attention,' he said defensively. 'If they sign I let them in. That's all I gotta do.'

'We've got his signature, Rhyme. And a name. They'll be fake but at least it's a handwriting sample. Which line did he sign on?'

Sachs picked up the sign-in book with latex-clad fingers. They ran the tape, fast forward, from the beginning. The killer was the fourth person to sign the book. But in the fourth slot was a woman's name.

Rhyme called, 'Run the tape again. Count the people who signed.'

They watched nine people fill in their names—eight students, including the victim, and her killer.

'Nine people sign, Rhyme. But there are eight names on the list.'

Rhyme: 'Ask the guard if he's sure the perp signed. Maybe he faked it.'

She put the question to the placid man.

'Yeah, he did. I saw it. I don't always look at their faces but I make sure they sign.'

'Well, bring me the sign-in book with everything else and we'll have a look at it here,' Rhyme said.

CHAPTER TWO

And now, Revered Audience, we'll take a short intermission. Relax. Our next act will begin shortly . . .

THE MAN WALKED ALONG Broadway on the Upper West Side of Manhattan. When he reached one street corner he stopped, as if he'd forgotten something. He pulled his cellphone off his belt and lifted it to his ear. As he spoke, he gazed around him casually. He was not, however, actually making a call. He was looking for any sign that he'd been followed.

Malerick's present appearance was very different from his incarnation when he'd left the music school. He was now blond and beardless and wearing a jogging outfit. Had passers-by been looking they might have noticed a few oddities in his physique: leathery scar tissue peeked over the top of his collar and along his neck, and two fingers—little and ring—of his left hand were fused together. But no one *was* looking. Because his gestures and expressions were natural, and—as all illusionists know—acting naturally makes you invisible.

Content that he hadn't been followed, he turned the corner down a cross street and continued along the tree-lined sidewalk and up the stairs to the apartment he'd rented a few months ago.

AS I WAS SAYING, our next act will begin shortly.

For now, Revered Audience, gossip about the illusion you've just seen, try to guess what's next on the bill.

THESE WORDS and dozens more looped automatically through Malerick's mind. *Revered Audience* . . . He spoke to this imaginary assembly constantly. A white noise of words, in that broad theatrical intonation a greasepainted ringmaster or Victorian illusionist would use. Patter, it was called—a monologue directed to the audience to give them information they need to know to make a trick work, to build rapport. And to disarm and distract them at times too.

After the fire, Malerick cut off most contact with fellow human beings, and his imagined Revered Audience slowly replaced them, becoming his constant companions. It gave him intense comfort, knowing that he hadn't been left completely alone in life after the tragedy three years ago.

The apartment had come lightly furnished: inexpensive couches and armchairs, a dining-room table currently set for one. The bedrooms were packed with the tools of the illusionist's trade: props, ropes, costumes, latex moulding equipment, wigs, bolts of cloth, a sewing machine, paints, squibs, make-up, circuit boards, batteries, flash paper and cotton, fuses . . . a hundred other items.

He made herbal tea and sat at the dining-room table. He was pleased with this morning's act. He'd killed the first performer easily. Never a clue he'd been waiting in the corner, under the black silk, for a half-hour. The surprise entrance by the police—well, that had shaken him. But like all good illusionists Malerick had prepared an out, which he'd executed perfectly.

He finished his tea and took the cup into the kitchen, washed it carefully and set it in a rack to dry. He was meticulous in all his ways. His mentor, a fierce, obsessive, humourless illusionist, had beaten that discipline into him.

The man now put on the videotape he'd made of the site of the next performance. Though he virtually had it memorised, he was now going to study it again. His mentor had also beaten into him—sometimes literally—the importance of the 100:1 rule. You rehearse one hundred minutes for every one onstage.

As he watched the tape he pulled a velvet-covered performing table towards him. Not watching his hands, Malerick practised some simple card manoeuvres: the False Dovetail Shuffle, the Three-Pile False Cut; then some trickier ones: the Reverse Sliparound, the Glide.

He ran through some of the card tricks that had been in Harry Houdini's early repertoire. Most people think of Houdini as an escapologist but the performer had actually been a well-rounded magician. Houdini had been an important influence in his life. When he first started performing, in his teens, Malerick used as a performing name 'Young Houdini'. The 'erick' portion of his present name was both a remnant of his former life—his life before the fire—and a homage to Houdini himself, who'd been born Ehrich Weiss. As for the prefix 'Mal', Malerick had picked it because it came from the Latin root for 'evil', which reflected the dark nature of his brand of illusion.

He now studied the tape, measuring angles, noting windows and the location of possible witnesses, blocking out his positions as all good performers do. And as he watched, the cards in his fingers riffled together in lightning-fast shuffles that hissed like snakes. Watching this performance, an audience would shake their heads, half-convinced that reality had given way to delusion, that a human being couldn't possibly do what they were observing.

But the card tricks Malerick was now performing absently were not miraculous at all; they were carefully rehearsed exercises in dexterity and perception, governed by mundane rules of physics.

'HEY, THERE.'

The young woman sat down beside the bed. 'So. How you feeling, Mom?' Kara adjusted the down pillow under her mother's head. Then sat and sipped coffee from the Starbucks container.

Her hair was boyish, currently auburn-purple, having been pretty much every colour of the spectrum at some point in her years in New York City. Today she wore black stretch pants and a dark purple top and, though she was not much over five feet, flat shoes.

'I've got a show tomorrow. One of Mr Balzac's little things. But this time he's letting me go on solo.' Kara continued talking about what she planned for the next day. As she spoke she studied her mother, the skin oddly smooth for a woman in her seventies and as healthy pink as a baby's, hair mostly grey but with plenty of defiant wiry black strands. The staff beautician had done it in a stylish bun. 'Anyway, Mom, it'd be great if you could come too.'

Kara, now sitting on the edge of the chair, realised that her fists were clenched, her body a knot of tension. The woman was hardly a human being at all. At most a child, sleeping with her eyes open.

Her mother hadn't said a single word today. Or during yesterday's visit. She'd lain in some kind of waking coma. Some days she was like that. On others, she might be fully awake but babbling scary nonsense that only attested to the success of the invisible army moving relentlessly through her brain, torching memory and reason.

But once in a rare while, there'd be a fragile moment of clarity, just like in the days before the cerebral haemorrhage. At moments like that Kara would convince herself that her mother was improving. The doctors said that there was virtually no hope for this, of course.

A glance at her watch. Late for work. Mr Balzac would *not* be happy. Kara walked into the hallway.

A large black woman in a white uniform lifted a hand in greeting.

'Kara!' A broad smile in a broad face. 'She still awake?'

'Hi, Jaynene. No. She was out when I got here.'

'Oh, I'm sorry.'

'Was she talking before?' Kara asked.

'Yep. Just little things. Couldn't tell if she was with us or not.'

'I've gotta get to work,' Kara told the nurse. 'Hey, I'm doing a show tomorrow. At the store. Remember where it is?'

'Sure do. What time?'

'Four. Come on by. Hey, bring Pete.'

The woman scowled. 'Girl, th'only way that man'll see you on Sunday is if you're playing the half-time show for the Knicks or the Lakers an' it's on network TV.'

ONE HUNDRED YEARS AGO a successful financier might have called this place home. Or a prosperous shop owner, or possibly a politician.

The present owner of the Central Park West town house, however, didn't know or care about its provenance. Nor would the Victorian furnishings that had once graced these rooms appeal to Lincoln Rhyme at all. He enjoyed what surrounded him now: a disarray of sturdy tables, swivel stools, computers, scientific devices. And wires and cables everywhere, covering much of the room, some tidily coiled and connecting pieces of machinery, some disappearing through holes cut into the century-old lath-and-plaster walls.

Lincoln Rhyme himself was largely wireless now. Advances in infrared and radio technology had linked a microphone on his wheelchair—and on his bed upstairs—to environmental control units and computers. He drove his Storm Arrow wheelchair with his left ring finger on a state-of-the-art touchpad, but all the other commands, from phone calls to email to slapping the image from his compound microscope onto computer monitors, could be accomplished by using his voice.

Rhyme heard the front door slam.

There was the erratic beat of footsteps in the front hall and the parlour. One of the visitors was Amelia Sachs, he knew; for a tall woman she had a light footfall. Then he heard the distinctive clump of Lon Sellitto's big, out-turned feet.

'Sachs,' he muttered, as she entered the room, 'was it a big scene?'

'Not so big.' She frowned at the question. 'Why?'

His eyes were on the grey milk crates containing evidence she—and several other officers—carried. 'I was just wondering because it seemed to take a long time to search the scene.' When Rhyme was bored he grew testy. Boredom was the biggest evil in his life.

Sachs, however, was impervious to his sourness. She said merely, 'We've got ourselves some mysteries here, Rhyme.'

'Give me the scenario. What happened?'

'The respondings heard a shot inside the hall then they did a kick-in. Went in through the only two doors. He was gone.'

Sellitto consulted his notes. 'The patrol officers put him in his fifties, medium build, a beard, brown hair. A janitor didn't see anybody go in or out of the room. The school's gonna call with his name and number. I'll see if I can refresh his memory.'

'What about the vic? What was the motive?'

Sachs said, 'No sexual assault, no robbery.'

Sellitto added, 'She hasn't got any present or recent boyfriends. Nobody in the past that'd be a problem.'

'She was a full-time student?' Rhyme asked.

'Full-time, yeah. But she did performing on the side.'

Rhyme recruited his aide, Thom, to act as a scribe, as he often did, jotting down the evidence on one of the large whiteboards in the lab.

There was a knock on the door and Thom disappeared momentarily into the hallway. Into the room walked Mel Cooper, a slim, balding lab technician whom Rhyme, then head of NYPD forensics, had met some years ago. With degrees in maths, physics and chemistry, Cooper was top-notch at physical evidence analysis. He was based in the NYPD crime lab in Queens but he often worked with Rhyme when the criminalist was consulting on an active case.

Greetings all round and then Cooper shoved his thick, Harry Potter glasses high on his nose and squinted at the crates of evidence. 'What do we have here?' he asked softly.

Sellitto ran through the scenario of the killing for him as Cooper donned latex gloves. Rhyme wheeled up. 'What's *that*?' He was gazing at the green circuit board with a speaker attached.

'The board I found in the recital hall,' Sachs said. 'The unsub put it there—I could tell by his footprints.'

Rhyme was the first to admit that some subjects were beyond his realm of expertise. Clues like computers, cellphones and this curious device he farmed out to the experts.

'Get it downtown. To Tobe Geller,' he instructed.

The FBI had a talented young man in its New York computer crimes office and Rhyme knew that if anyone could tell him what the device was Geller could. Sachs handed the bag to Sellitto, who in turn gave it to a uniformed policeman for transport downtown.

They turned next to the pyrotechnic items found at the music school: the fuses and the firecracker.

Sachs had figured out one mystery, at least. The killer, she explained, had leaned chairs backwards on two legs, holding them in that position with cotton string. He'd tied fuses to the middle of the strings and lit them. After a minute the flame in the fuse hit the string and burned it in half. The chair tumbled to the floor, making it sound like the killer was still inside. He'd also lit a fuse that ultimately set off the squib they mistook for a gunshot.

'Can you source any of it?' Sellitto asked.

Cooper shook his head. 'Generic fuse—untraceable—and the squib's destroyed.' The string also turned out to be generic, impossible to source.

'There was a flash too,' Sachs said. 'When the officers saw him with the victim he held up his hand and there was a brilliant light. Like a flare. It blinded them.'

'Any trace?'

'None that I could find.'

'Let's move on. Footprints?'

Cooper pulled up the digitised NYPD database on shoe-tread prints. After a few minutes of perusal, he said. 'Shoes are slip-on black Ecco brand. Appear to be a size ten.'

'Trace evidence?' Rhyme asked.

Sachs picked several plastic bags out of a milk crate. Inside were strips of adhesive tape, torn off the trace pick-up roller. 'These are from where he walked and next to the body.'

Cooper extracted the adhesive tape rectangles, one by one. Most of the trace adhering to them was dust that matched Sachs's control samples, meaning that it was found naturally at the crime scene. But on several of the pieces of tape were fibres that Sachs had found only in places were the perp had walked or on objects that he'd touched.

''Scope 'em.'

The tech lifted them off with a pair of tweezers and mounted them on slides. He put them under the stereo binocular microscope and hit a button. The image popped onto the large flat-screen computer monitor for everyone to see. The fibres appeared as thick greyish strands.

Fibres are important forensic clues because they're common and can be easily classified. Rhyme noted immediately that these weren't viscose rayon or polymer based and therefore had to be natural. 'Look at the cell structure. I'm betting it's excremental.'

'Whatsat?' Sellitto asked. 'Excrement?'

'Excrement, like *silk*. It comes from the digestive tract of worms. Dyed grey. Processed to a matt finish. Was the perp wearing grey?'

'No,' Sellitto reported.

'The vic wasn't either,' Sachs said.

'Ah,' Cooper said, peering into the eyepiece, 'might have a hair here.' On the screen a strand of brown hair came into focus.

'Human hair,' Rhyme called out. 'But it's fake.'

'Fake?' Sellitto asked.

'Well,' Rhyme said impatiently, 'it's real hair but it's from a wig. The end's not a bulb. It's *glue*. Might not be his, of course, but it's worth putting on the chart.'

Cooper continued his examination and found that two adhesive squares revealed a minuscule bit of dirt and some plant material.

''Scope the plant material first, Mel.'

In analysing crime scenes in New York, Lincoln Rhyme had always placed great importance on geologic, plant and animal evidence—because only one-eighth of the city is actually on the North American mainland; the rest is situated on islands. This means that minerals, flora and fauna tend to be more or less common to particular boroughs and even neighbourhoods within them, making it easier to trace substances to specific locations.

An image of a reddish twig and a bit of leaf appeared on the screen.

'Good,' Rhyme announced. 'It's a red pignut hickory. You hardly ever find them in the city. The only places I know of are Central and Riverside Parks. And . . . oh, look at that. That little blue-green mass? Lichen, right? And I'd vote for *Parmelia conspersa*.'

'Could be,' the tech said cautiously.

'And it's most abundant in Central Park . . . We've got two links to the park. Now, let's look at the dirt.'

Cooper mounted another slide. The image in the microscope wasn't revealing and Rhyme said, 'Run a sample through the GC/MS.'

The gas chromatograph/mass spectrometer is a marriage of two chemical analysis instruments, the first of which breaks down an unknown substance into its component parts with the second determining what each of those parts is.

The results of Cooper's analysis showed that the dirt Sachs had recovered was impregnated with an oil. The database, though, reported only that it was mineral based—not plant or animal.

Rhyme commanded, 'Send it to the FBI. See if their lab people've run across it.' Then he squinted into a plastic bag. 'That's the black cloth you found?'

Sachs nodded. 'It was in the corner of the lobby where the victim was strangled.'

'Was it hers?' Cooper wondered. He examined it carefully. 'Silk.'

Rhyme observed that even though it could be folded into a tiny wad it opened up to be quite large, about six by four feet.

'We know from the timing he was waiting for her in the lobby,' he said. 'I'll bet he hid in the corner with that cloth draped over him. He'd be invisible.'

Cooper found several flecks adhering to the black cloth. He touched one with a fine probe. The material was springy.

Rhyme suggested, 'Rubber of some kind. Run it through the GC.'

While they waited for the results the doorbell rang.

Thom stepped out of the room to open the door and returned with an envelope. 'Latents,' he announced.

'Ah, good,' Rhyme said. 'Fingerprints are back. Run them through AFIS, Mel.'

The powerful servers of the FBI's automated fingerprint identification system would search digitised images of friction ridges—fingerprints—throughout the country, in federal and state databases.

'How do they look?' Rhyme asked.

'Pretty clean.' Sachs held up the photos for him to see. The first thing Rhyme noticed was that the killer had two deformed fingers on the left hand—the ring and little fingers. They were joined, it seemed, and ended in smooth skin, without prints.

Ironic, Rhyme thought, the unsub's left ring finger is damaged; mine is the only extremity below my neck that can move at all.

Then he frowned. 'Hold off on the scan for a minute, Mel . . . Notice anything unusual about them, Sachs?'

She said, 'Not really . . . Wait.' She laughed. 'All his fingers—they're the *same*.'

'He must be wearing some kind of glove,' Cooper said, 'with fake friction ridges on them.'

The results from the GC popped onto a computer screen. 'OK, I've got pure latex . . . and what's this?' Cooper pondered. 'Something the computer identifies as an alginate.'

'It's a powder you mix with water—to make moulds,' Rhyme said. 'Dentists use it for crowns and dental work. Maybe our doer had just been to the dentist.'

Cooper continued to examine the screen. 'Then we have minute traces of castor oil, propylene glycol, cetyl alcohol, mica, iron oxide, titanium dioxide, coal tar and some neutral pigments.'

'Some of those are found in make-up,' Rhyme said.

'Hers?' Cooper asked Sachs.

'No,' the policewoman answered. 'I took swabs of her skin. She wasn't wearing any.'

'Well, put it on the board. We'll see if it means anything.'

Turning to the rope, the murder weapon, Mel Cooper looked up from where he was slumped over a porcelain examining board. 'It's a white sheath of rope round a black core. They're both braided silk—real light and thin—which is why it doesn't look any thicker than a normal rope even though it's really two put together.'

'It's getting mysteriouser,' Sachs said.

'Yup,' Rhyme confirmed, disconcerted. 'And the knot?'

'Tied by an expert but I don't recognise it,' Cooper said.

A call came in from Tobe Geller at the Computer Crimes Unit at New York's FBI headquarters. 'This is fun, Lincoln,' he said.

'Glad we're keeping you amused,' Rhyme murmured. 'Anything *helpful* you might be able to tell us about our *toy*?'

'It's a digital audio recorder. Your unsub recorded something on it, stored the sounds on a hard drive then programmed it to play back after some delay. We don't know what the sound was—he built in a wiping program so that it destroyed the data.'

Rhyme muttered, 'When he said he had a hostage it was just a recording. It was to make us think he was still in the room.'

'That makes sense. It'd mimic a human voice.'

'There's nothing left on the disk?'

'Nope. Gone for good.'

Rhyme sighed in frustration and it was left to Sachs to tell Geller how much they appreciated the help.

The team then examined the victim's wristwatch. It yielded no evidence except the time it was broken. Perps occasionally broke watches or clocks at crime scenes after they'd set them to the wrong time to mislead investigators. But this was stopped at the actual time of death. What should they make of that?

Rhyme looked over the bag containing the sign-in book. 'The missing name in the book.' He mused, 'Nine people signed but there are only eight names in the log . . . I think we need an expert here.' Rhyme ordered into the microphone, 'Command, telephone. Call Kincaid, comma Parker.'

A moment later the laid-back voice of one of the country's pre-eminent document examiners came on the line. 'Kincaid residence.'

'Parker, it's Lincoln.'

'Hey, Lincoln. So, what's up?'

'I need some help. Perp was seen writing his name on a security desk sign-in book.'

'And you need the handwriting analysed?'

'The problem is we don't *have* any handwriting.'

'And you're sure the writer wasn't faking?'

'Positive. A guard saw ink going on paper.'

'Anything visible now?'

'Nothing. So how'd he pull that off?'

'He Ex-laxed it,' Kincaid announced. 'Used disappearing ink. We call it Ex-laxing in the business.'

'Can you buy this stuff anyplace in particular?'

'Hm,' Kincaid considered. 'Most likely toy stores or magic shops. Entertainers use it.'

Entertainment, Rhyme thought grimly, looking at the board on which were taped pictures of poor Svetlana Rasnikov.

'OK, well, that's helpful, Parker.' After he disconnected the call Rhyme said grumpily, 'The more we learn, the less we know.'

Bedding and Saul called in and reported that Svetlana's part-time job wasn't likely to have produced any stalkers; she led sing-alongs at kids' birthday parties.

A package arrived from the Medical Examiner's office which contained the old handcuffs the victim had been restrained with. They were antique, heavy and made of unevenly forged iron.

Cooper brushed the mechanisms but found no significant trace. The fact they were antique, though, would limit the sources they might have come from. Rhyme told Cooper to photograph them and print out pictures that they could show to dealers.

Sellitto received a phone call. He listened for a moment then, looking bewildered, said, 'Impossible . . . You're sure? . . . Yeah, OK. Thanks.' Hanging up, the detective glanced at Rhyme. 'That was the administrator of the music school. There *is* no janitor. The cleaning staff doesn't work on Saturday. And none of 'em look like the guy the respondings saw.'

'Oh, damn,' Rhyme snapped. 'It was him! The janitor looked different from the perp, right?'

Sellitto consulted his notebook. 'He was in his sixties, bald, wearing grey overalls.'

'*Grey* overalls!' Rhyme shouted. 'That's the silk fibre.'

'What are you talking about?' Cooper asked.

'Our unsub killed the student. Then when he was surprised by the respondings he blinded them with the flash and ran into the performance space, set up the fuses and the digital recorder to make them think he was still inside, changed into the janitor outfit and ran out the second door.'

'How the hell could he've done it?' Sellitto asked. 'There's no way.'

'No way?' Rhyme mused cynically as he wheeled closer to the whiteboard on which Thom had taped the print-outs of the digital photos Sachs had taken of the footprints. He examined the perp's footprints and then the ones that she had lifted in the corridor near where the janitor had been.

'Shoes,' he announced.

'They're the same?' Sellitto asked.

'Yep,' Sachs said, walking to the board. 'Ecco, size ten.'

Rhyme asked, 'OK, what do we have? A perp in his late forties, early fifties, medium build, medium height and beardless, two deformed fingers—and that's *all*.' Then Rhyme frowned. 'No,' he muttered darkly, 'that's *not* all we know. He had a change of clothes with him, murder weapons . . . He's an organised offender. He's going to do this again.'

Sachs nodded her grim agreement.

Rhyme wondered: What ties this all together? The black silk, the make-up, the costume change, the disguises, the flashes and the pyrotechnics. The disappearing ink.

Rhyme said, 'I think our boy's got some magic training.'

Sellitto nodded. 'OK. But whatta we do now?'

'Seems obvious to me,' Rhyme said. 'Find our own.'

'Our own what?' Sellitto asked.

'Magician. What else?'

'DO IT AGAIN.'

She'd done it eight times so far. 'Again?'

The man nodded. And so Kara did it again.

The Triple Handkerchief Release is an audience-pleaser. It involves separating three different-coloured silks that seem hopelessly knotted together. Kara felt good about how the trick had gone.

David Balzac didn't, however. 'Your coins were talking,' he sighed, meaning that a trick was clumsy and obvious. The older man with a white mane of hair and tobacco-stained goatee shook his head.

They stood on a small stage in the back of Smoke & Mirrors, the store that Balzac had bought after he'd retired from the international magic and illusion circuit ten years ago. The place sold magic supplies and rented costumes and props. Every week the store also presented free, amateur magic shows. A year and a half ago Kara, doing freelance editing, had finally worked up her courage to try it. Afterwards, the Great Balzac had told her she could be a great illusionist—with the proper training—and proposed that she come and work in the shop in exchange for his being her mentor and teacher.

Balzac had been a headliner in Las Vegas for years. He'd toured the world and knew virtually every major illusionist alive today. Illusion was Kara's passion and this was a chance of a lifetime. She accepted on the spot.

At the first session her guard was up; she knew what 'mentor' might entail, especially when he was a divorcé and she was an attractive woman forty years younger than he. The lesson indeed turned out to be upsetting—though for an entirely different reason.

He tore her to shreds. Then they got back to work. And so began an eighteen-month love-hate relationship that kept her up until the early hours of the morning practising, practising, practising.

Friends sometimes asked her where her love of illusion came from. An A student, gymnast and school-choir singer, she started on the path of entertainment by attending a Penn and Teller performance in Cleveland with her grandparents, followed a month later by a family trip to Vegas exposing her to flying tigers and fiery illusions.

That's all it took. Which is not to say there wasn't any motive that set—and kept—her on this course. No, what drove Kara could be found in the blinks of delighted surprise on the faces of the audience. Over the past year and a half with David Balzac, though, she sometimes felt she'd lost whatever talent she'd once had.

But just as she'd be about to quit he'd nod and offer the faintest of smiles. Several times he actually said, 'That was a tight trick.'

At moments like that her world was complete.

Much of her life, though, blew away like dust as she spent more time at the store, handling the books and inventory. Then about a year ago her mother's condition had begun to worsen and only-child Kara spent her little remaining free time with her. An exhausting life. But she could handle it for now. In a few years Balzac would pronounce her fit to perform and off she'd go with his blessing.

Kara did the three-silk trick again. *Wshhhhhh* . . . the entangled silks separated and flew into the air like triumphant flags.

'Ah,' Balzac said. A faint nod.

She put the trick away and stepped behind the counter in the business area of the store to log in the merchandise that had arrived in

Friday's afternoon shipment. Balzac returned to his desk.

'You hear that the Cirque Fantastique's in town?' she called. 'Opens tonight.'

The old illusionist grunted.

'You going to go?' she persisted. 'I think we should go.'

Cirque Fantastique—a competitor to the older Cirque du Soleil—was part of the next generation of circuses. It combined traditional circus routines, ancient *commedia dell'arte* theatre, contemporary music and dance, avant-garde performance art and street magic.

But David Balzac was old school: Vegas, Atlantic City, *The Late Show*. 'Why change something that works,' he'd snap.

Kara loved Cirque Fantastique, though, and was determined to get him to a performance. But before she could convince him to go the front door opened and an attractive, red-headed policewoman walked in and asked for the owner.

'That's me. I'm David Balzac.'

The officer said, 'We're investigating a case involving someone who might've had training in magic. We're hoping you can help us.'

'You mean, somebody's running a scam or something?' Balzac asked. He sounded defensive. Magic has often been linked to crooks.

'Actually,' the policewoman said. 'The case is a homicide.'

CHAPTER THREE

'I have a list of items we found at a crime scene,' Amelia Sachs told the store owner, 'and was wondering if you might've sold them.'

David Balzac took the sheet she handed him and read it as Sachs looked over Smoke & Mirrors. The black-painted cavern of a store in Manhattan's Chelsea neighbourhood smelt of mould and chemicals—plastic too, the petrochemical body odour from the hundreds of costumes that hung like a limp crowd from nearby racks. The grimy glass counters were filled with card decks and wands and phoney coins and dusty boxes of magic tricks.

He tapped the list. 'We sell some of this, sure. But so does every magic store in the country. Toy stores too.'

'How about these?' Sachs showed him the printout of the handcuffs.

'I don't know anything about escapology.'

The young woman with striking blue eyes and black fingernails looked at the picture. 'They're Darbys,' she said. 'Regulation Scotland Yard handcuffs from the nineteenth century. Houdini's favourites.'

'Where could they've come from?'

Balzac rocked in his office chair. 'We wouldn't know.'

Sachs offered him the list again. 'You did say you sold *some* of these products. Do you have records of customers?'

'I meant, products like them. And, no, we don't keep customer records. Sorry. Wish we could be more help.'

'I wish you could be more help too,' Sachs said. 'Because, see, this guy killed a woman and escaped by using magic tricks. And we're afraid he's going to do it again.'

Giving a frown of concern, Balzac said, 'Terrible . . . You know, you might try East Side Magic and Theatrical. They're bigger than us.'

'We have another officer over there now.'

'Ah, there you go.'

Sachs let a moment pass, silent. Then: 'Well, if you can think of anything else, I'd appreciate a call.' She nodded farewell to the young woman and glanced at a cardboard cup she was sipping from. 'Hey, there anyplace around here to get some decent coffee?'

'Fifth and Nineteenth,' she replied.

'Good bagels too,' Balzac said, helpful now that there was no risk, or effort, involved.

Outside, Sachs found the recommended coffee shop, walked inside and bought a cappuccino. She leant against a narrow mahogany bar in front of the window, sipping the hot drink and watching the Saturday-morning populace here in the Chelsea neighbourhood—salespeople from the clothing stores in the area, commercial photographers, rich yuppies who lived in the massive lofts, poor artists, lovers young and lovers old, a wacky notebook scribbler or two.

And one magic-store clerk, now entering the shop.

'Hi,' said the woman with short, reddish-purple hair, carrying a battered faux zebra-skin bag over her shoulder. She ordered a large coffee, filled it with sugar and joined Sachs.

Back at the store the policewoman had asked about a venue for coffee because of a conspiratorial glance the assistant had shot Sachs; it seemed she'd wanted to say something out of Balzac's presence.

The woman said, 'The thing about David is—'

'He's uncooperative?'

'Yeah. Anything outside his world he doesn't trust or want any part of. He was afraid we'd have to be witnesses or something. I'm not supposed to be distracted.'

'From what?'

'From the profession.'

'Magic?'

'Right. See, he's sort of my mentor more than my boss.'

'What's your name?'

'Kara—it's my stage name but I use it most of the time.'

'So,' Sachs said, 'why'd you give me that look back at the store?'

'David's right about that list. You can buy those props anywhere. But about the Darbys. Those are rare. You should call the Houdini and Escapology Museum in New Orleans. It's the best in the world. Can you tell me what happened? With that murder?'

Normally circumspect about an active case, Sachs knew they needed help and gave Kara an outline of the killing and the escape.

'Oh, that's horrible,' the young woman whispered.

'Yeah,' Sachs replied softly. 'It is.'

'The way he disappeared? There's something you ought to know, Officer—Do I call you officer? Or are you a detective?'

'Amelia's fine.'

Kara sipped her coffee. 'You know what illusion is?' she asked.

'David Copperfield,' Sachs replied, shrugging. 'Houdini.'

'Copperfield, yes. Houdini, no—he was mainly an escapologist. Well, illusion's different from sleight of hand. Like . . .' Kara held up a quarter in her fingers. She closed her palm and when she opened it again the coin was gone.

Sachs laughed. Where the hell had it gone?

'That was sleight of hand. Illusion is tricks involving large objects or people. What the killer did is a classic illusionist trick. It's called the Vanished Man. In magic we use "vanish" to mean "to make disappear". Like, "I just vanished the quarter."'

'Go on.'

'Basically the trick involves the illusionist getting out of a locked room. The audience sees him step into this little room onstage—they can see the back because of a big mirror behind it. They hear him pound on the walls. The assistants pull the walls down and he's gone. Then one of the assistants turns round and it's the illusionist.'

'How does it work?'

'There was a door in the back of the room. The illusionist covers himself with a large piece of black silk so the audience can't see him in the mirror and slips through the back door just after he walks inside. There's a speaker built into one of the walls to make it sound like he was inside all the time and a gimmick that hits the walls and sounds like he's pounding. Once the illusionist's outside he does a quick change behind the silk into an assistant's costume.'

Sachs nodded. 'That's it, all right.'

The Vanished Man . . .

Sachs was recalling that the killer had changed disguises to become an older man, recalling, too, Balzac's lack of cooperation. She asked, 'Where was Mr Balzac at eight this morning?'

'Here. I mean, in the store. He got in early because some friend of his is in town doing a show and he needed to borrow some equipment. I called to tell him I'd be late.'

Sachs nodded. 'Can you take time off work? We're really afraid this person's going to kill someone else. Please. Just for a few hours.'

'Oh, no way. He won't let me. You don't know David.'

'What I know is that I'm not letting anybody else get hurt if there's any way I can stop it.'

Kara finished her coffee and absently played with the cup. 'Using our tricks to kill people,' she whispered in a dismayed voice.

Sachs said nothing and let silence do the arguing for her.

Finally Kara grimaced. 'My mother's in a home. Mr Balzac knows that. I guess I could tell him I have to go check on her.'

'We really could use your help.' Sachs then glanced down. 'Hey, one thing: what happened to that quarter?'

'Look under your coffee cup,' the girl replied.

Sachs lifted up the cup. There sat the coin.

'LINCOLN, MEET KARA.'

She'd been warned, Rhyme could see, but the young woman still blinked and gave him the Look, the one he knew so well, and the Smile. It was the famous don't-look-at-his-body gaze, accompanied by the oh-you're-handicapped-I-never-noticed grin.

The spritely young woman walked further into the parlour lab in Rhyme's town house. 'Hi. Amelia asked me if I could help with this case of yours. Nice to meet you.' The eyes remained rooted in his.

OK, Kara. Don't worry. You can give the gimp your insights then get the hell out. He said how pleased he was to meet her too.

Kara was the only magician lead they'd snared. None of the employees at the other shops in town had been any help.

She was introduced to Lon Sellitto and Mel Cooper. Thom nodded and offered refreshments.

'Maybe coffee?' she asked.

'Coming up,' the trim blond aide said, and headed for the kitchen.

'Officer Sachs', Rhyme said to Kara, 'told us that you had some information you thought might help.'

'I think I might.'

'Hey, what're we calling him?' Sellitto tapped the evidence whiteboard. Until the identity of the unsub was learned, many law enforcers gave perps nicknames. 'How 'bout the "Magician"?'

'No, too tame,' Rhyme said, looking at the pictures of the victim. 'How 'bout, "Conjurer"?'

The detective wrote the words on top of the chart. *The Conjurer*.

'Now let's see if we can make him appear,' Rhyme said.

Sachs said, 'Tell them about the Vanished Man.'

Kara described the illusionist's trick that sounded almost identical to what the Conjurer had done at the music school. She added the discouraging news that most illusionists would know it.

Rhyme asked, 'Give us some idea about how he does the tricks. Techniques. So we know what to expect if he targets somebody else.'

'You want me to tip the gaff, huh?'

'Tip the—?'

'Gaff,' Kara said, then explained: 'See, all magic tricks are made up of the effect and the method. The *effect* is what the audience sees. You know: the girl levitating, the coins falling through a solid tabletop. The *method* is the mechanism of how the magician does it—wires holding up the girl, palming the coins then dropping identical ones from a rig under the table.'

Effect and method, Rhyme reflected. Kind of like what I do: the effect is catching a perp when it seems impossible. The method is the science and logic that let's us do it.

Kara continued, 'Tipping the gaff means giving away the method of a trick. Like I just did—explaining how the Vanished Man worked. Mr Balzac, my mentor, he's always hounding magicians who tip the gaff in public and give away other people's methods.'

Thom carted a tray into the room. He poured coffee for those who wanted some. Kara dumped sugar into hers and sipped it fast.

They went over each item of evidence with Kara, who studied it carefully and said that there were hundreds of sources for most of the items. The rope was a colour-changing rope trick, sold in magic stores across the country. The knot was one Houdini used in his routines when he planned to cut through the rope to escape; it was virtually impossible for a bound performer to untie.

'Even without the cuffs,' Kara said softly, 'that girl never had a chance of getting away.'

The castor oil in the make-up, Kara continued, meant that he was using very realistic theatrical cosmetics and the latex was, as Rhyme had suspected, probably from the fake finger cups, which were also popular magician's tools. The alginate, Kara suggested, wasn't from dental work but was used to make moulds for latex casting, probably for the finger cups or the bald cap he'd worn in his janitor disguise. The disappearing ink was more of a novelty.

Only a few things were unique, she explained: the circuit board, for instance. But he'd made that himself. The Darby handcuffs too were rare. Rhyme ordered someone to check out the escapology museum that Kara had mentioned. Sachs suggested they take the responding officers, Franciscovich and Ausonio, up on their offer to help. Rhyme agreed and Sellitto arranged it through the head of the Patrol Services Division.

'How about his escape?' Sellitto asked. 'What's the deal where he changed into janitor clothes so fast?'

'"Protean magic" it's called,' Kara said. 'Quick change. It's one of the things I've been studying for years. It can be amazing. And, see, true quick-change artists don't just change clothes. They're actors too. They hold themselves differently, speak differently. He'll prepare everything ahead of time. The clothes are breakaway—they're held together with snaps or Velcro. And they're made of silk or nylon, real thin, so we can wear layers of them.'

'Silk?' Rhyme asked. 'We found grey silk fibres. The officers on the scene reported that the janitor was wearing a grey uniform. The fibres were abraded—sort of buffed to a matt finish.'

Kara nodded. 'So they'd look like cotton or linen. We also use shoe coverings. Wigs, of course. To alter a face the most important thing is the eyebrows. Change those and the face is sixty, seventy per cent different. Then add some prostheses: latex strips and pads you put on with spirit gum. Quick-change performers study the basic facial structures of different races and genders. A good protean artist knows the proportions of a woman's face versus a man's and can change gender in seconds.

Rhyme wanted specific suggestions. 'Is there anything you can tell us that'll help us find him?'

She shook her head. 'I can't think of anything specific. But I do have some general thoughts.'

'Go ahead.'

'Well, the fact he used the changing rope and the finger cups tells me he's familiar with sleight of hand. That means he'll be good at picking pockets, hiding guns or knives. Getting people's keys and IDs. He also knows quick change and it's obvious what kind of problem *that'll* be for you. But more important—the Vanished Man routine, the fuses and squibs, the disappearing ink, the black silk means he's a classically trained illusionist.'

'Why's that important for us?'

'Because illusion is more than physical technique. Illusionists study audience psychology and create whole routines to trick them—not just their eyes but their minds too. Their point is to make you believe in your heart that everything you see is one way when it's the opposite. There's one thing you'll have to keep in mind. Never forget it.'

'What?' Rhyme asked.

'Misdirection . . . Mr Balzac says it's the heart and soul of illusion. You've heard the expression that the hand is quicker than the eye? Well, it's not. The eye is always quicker. So illusionists *trick* the eye into not noticing what the hand is doing. There are lots of rules he's been drumming into me—like, the audience doesn't notice the familiar but are drawn to novelty. They don't notice a series of similar things but focus on the one that's different. They ignore things that stand still but they're drawn to movement. You want to make something invisible? Repeat it four or five times and pretty soon the audience is bored and their attention wanders. That's when you zing 'em.

'OK, now there're two kinds of misdirection. First, *physical* misdirection. Watch.' Kara stepped near Sachs and stared at her own right hand as she lifted it very slowly and pointed to the wall. Then she dropped her hand. 'See, you looked at my arm and where I pointed. Perfectly natural reaction. So you probably didn't notice that my left hand's got Amelia's gun.'

Sachs gave a jump as she glanced down and saw that, sure enough, Kara's fingers had lifted the Glock partway out of the holster.

'Careful there,' Sachs said, reholstering the pistol.

'So, that's *physical* misdirection. The second kind of misdirection is *psychological*. This is harder. Audiences aren't stupid. They know you're going to try to trick them. I mean, that's why they've come to the show, right? So we try to reduce or eliminate the audience's suspicion. The most important thing in psychological misdirection is to act naturally. As soon as you do something in an unnatural way, the audience is onto you. OK, I say I'm going to read your mind and I do this.' Kara put her hands on Sachs's temples and closed her eyes.

She stepped away and handed Sachs back the earring she'd just plucked from the policewoman's left ear.

'I never felt a thing.'

'But the audience'd know instantly how I did it—because touching someone while you're pretending to read minds isn't natural. But if I say part of a trick is for me to whisper a word so that nobody else can hear.' She leaned closer to Sachs, with her right hand over her own mouth. 'See, that's a natural gesture.'

'You missed the other earring,' Sachs said, laughing.

'But I vanished your necklace. It's gone.'

Sachs looked around her for the jewellery and then at Kara, who offered her empty right hand. 'Vanished,' she repeated.

'But,' Rhyme said, 'I *do* notice that your left hand's in a fist behind your back. Which is a rather *unnatural* gesture. So I assume the necklace is there.'

'Ah, you're good,' Kara said. 'But not at catching moves, I'm afraid.' She opened her left hand and it too was empty.

'Keeping my left fist closed? Well, that was the most important misdirection of all. I knew you'd spot it and it would focus your attention on my left hand. And as soon as you did that your mind snapped shut and you stopped considering any other explanations for what had happened. And when you were staring at my left hand that gave me the chance to slip the necklace into Amelia's pocket.'

Sachs reached inside and pulled the chain out.

Cooper applauded. Rhyme gave an impressed grunt.

Kara nodded towards the evidence board. 'So, that's what *he's* going to do, this killer. Misdirection. He'll use your suspicions—and your intelligence—against you. In fact, he *needs* your suspicions and intelligence for his tricks to work. Mr Balzac says that the best illusionists'll rig the trick so that they'll point directly at what they're going to do. But you won't believe them. You'll look in the opposite direction. When that happens, you've had it.' She glanced at the clock. 'I really have to get back now . . . Oh, one thing you might want to do? There's a circus in town. The Cirque Fantastique. They have a quick-change act. You might want to check it out.'

Sachs nodded. 'They're setting up across the street in Central Park.'

Kara started for the door.

'Wait,' Rhyme said.

She turned.

'I'd like you to stay. Work with us on the case. At least for today. You could go with Lon or Amelia to talk to the people at the circus.'

'Oh, no. I can't really.'

Rhyme said, 'We could use your help.'

'You know, Linc,' Sellitto said uneasily, 'better not to have too many civilians on a case. There *are* regs on that.'

'Didn't you use a psychic one time?' Rhyme asked drily.

'*I* didn't hire her. Somebody at HQ did.'

'And then you had the dog tracker and—'

'You keep saying "you". No, *I* don't hire civilians. Except you. Which gets me into enough shit.'

'Ah, you can never get into enough shit in police work, Lon.' Rhyme glanced at Kara. 'Please. It's very important.'

Kara hesitated. 'You really think he's going to kill someone else?'

'Yes,' he replied, 'we do.'

The girl finally nodded. 'If I'm going to get fired, at least it'll be for a good cause.' She looked over the evidence chart. 'You do this in all your cases? Write down all the clues and things you've learned?'

'That's right,' Sachs confirmed.

'Here's an idea—most magicians specialise. Like the Conjurer doing both quick-change and large-scale illusion? That's unusual. Let's write down his techniques. That might help narrow down the number of performers it could be.'

'Yeah,' Sellitto said, 'a profile. Good.'

The young woman grimaced. 'Mr Balzac was going to be out of the store today with that friend of his . . . Oh, man, he's not going to like this.' She looked around the room. 'There a phone I can use? You know, one of those special ones?'

'Special one?' Thom asked.

'Yeah, in private. So there's nobody around to hear you lie to your boss.'

SACHS AND KARA were making their way to the huge white tent of the Cirque Fantastique through Central Park.

Noticing two lovers kissing on a bench, Kara asked, 'So, he's more than your boss?'

'Lincoln? That's right.'

'I could tell . . . How'd you meet?'

'A case. Serial kidnapper. A few years ago.'

'Is it hard, him being that way?'

'No, it's not,' Sachs replied simply.

'Can they do anything for him, the doctors?'

'There's some surgery he's been thinking about. It's risky, though, and it probably wouldn't do any good. He decided not to last year and hasn't mentioned it since. So the whole thing's been on hold for a while. He may change his mind at some point. But we'll see.'

'You don't sound like you're in favour of it.'

'I'm not. A lot of risk and not much gain. To me, it's a question of balancing risks. Sometimes the risk is worth it, sometimes it's not. But if he wants to go ahead with the surgery, I'm with him. That's the way we work.'

Then Sachs explained that he'd been undergoing a series of treatments that involved electronic stimulation of his muscles and a battery of exercises that Thom and some physical therapists had been administering. 'Lincoln doesn't talk about it but sometimes he just disappears and has Thom and the PTs work on the exercises. I don't hear from him for a few days.'

'Another sort of vanished man, hm?' the young woman asked.

'Exactly,' Sachs replied, smiling.

They were silent for a moment, then Kara continued, 'Most of the guys I meet are interested in two things. A one-night romp in the hay. Or else the opposite—wooing then settling down in the 'burbs . . . You ever get wooed?'

'Sure,' Sachs said. 'It can be creepy. Depending on the wooer, of course.'

'You got it, sister. So hay-romping or wooing and 'burb-settling . . . they're both a problem for me. I don't want either. Well, a romp now and then. Let's be realistic.'

They walked closer to the glowing tent. The young woman's eyes lit up as she gazed at it.

'This the sort of place you'd like to work?' Sachs asked.

'Oh, man, I'll say. This is my idea of heaven.'

'You should audition here.'

'You're kidding,' Kara replied. 'I'm nowhere near ready. Your act has to be perfect. You have to be the best.'

'Why?'

'For the audience,' Kara explained. 'Mr Balzac's like a broken record: Every breath you take on stage is for your *audience*. Illusion can't be just OK. You can't just satisfy—you have to thrill.'

Sachs jumped at a loud crack above her. She looked up and saw two large banners, thirty or forty feet high, snapping in the wind. On one was painted the name CIRQUE FANTASTIQUE. On the other was a huge drawing of a thin man in a black-and-white chequered bodysuit. He was holding his arms forward, palms up, inviting his audience inside. He wore a black, snub-nosed half-mask, the features grotesque. It was a troubling image. She thought of the Conjurer, hidden by masks of disguise. His motives and plans hidden too.

Kara noticed Sachs's gaze. 'It's Arlecchino,' she said. 'In English, that's "Harlequin". You know *commedia dell'arte*?'

'No,' Sachs said.

'Italian theatre. It lasted from the mid-sixteenth century for a couple of hundred years. The Cirque Fantastique uses it as a theme. There were a dozen or so continuing characters that all the *commedia dell'arte* troupes used in their plays. They wore masks to show who they were playing.'

Sachs turned away to see a guard approaching, looking over her uniform. 'Help you, Officer?'

She asked to see the manager. The man explained that he was away but did they want to talk to an assistant? Sachs said yes and a moment later a short, thin, harried woman arrived.

'Yes, I can help you?' she asked in an indeterminate accent.

Sachs said, 'We're investigating a series of crimes in the area. We'd like to know if you have any illusionists or quick-change artists appearing in the show.'

'We have that, yes, of course,' she said. 'Irina and Vlad Klodoya.'

Kara nodded. 'I know about them. They're Ukrainians who were with the Circus of Moscow a few years ago.'

'Have they been here all morning?'

'Yes. They rehearsed until about twenty minutes ago. Now they are shopping.'

'OK,' Sachs said. 'What we're going to do is have a couple of police officers parked outside. If you hear about anyone bothering your employees or the audience, acting suspicious, tell the officers right away.' This had been Rhyme's suggestion.

'I will tell everyone, yes. But can you tell me what is this about?'

'A man with some illusionist experience was involved in a homicide earlier today. There's no connection to your show that we know of but we just want to be on the safe side.'

They thanked the assistant, who offered a troubled farewell.

Sachs called Rhyme's phone and got Thom. She gave him the Ukrainian performers' names. 'Have Mel or somebody run them through NCIC and the State Department.'

'Will do.'

She disconnected the call and they started out of the park.

Another loud snap behind her—the banners again, flapping in the breeze, as the playful Harlequin continued to beckon passers-by into his otherworldly kingdom.

Refreshed, Revered Audience? Relaxed?

Good, because it's time now for our second routine.

You may not know the name P. T. Selbit but if you've been to any magic shows at all or seen illusionists on television you're probably familiar with tricks this Englishman made popular in the early twentieth century. One of my favourites was a routine Selbit introduced in 1922. The title says it all: 'The Idol of Blood, or Destroying a Girl'.

Today, I'm delighted to present to you an updated variation of Selbit's most renowned illusion. It's known as . . .

Ah, but no . . . No, Revered Audience. I think I'll keep you in suspense for the moment.

Enjoy our next routine. I know of one person who certainly won't.

CHAPTER FOUR

The play had ended at midnight, then there'd been drinks at the White Horse, home at three. Then the plumbing had started banging at eight thirty. How many hours' sleep was that then?

Tony Calvert decided it was better not to know too much about the degree of his exhaustion. At least he was working on Broadway.

He closed his big yellow make-up case and glanced in the mirror by the door. He looked better than he felt. A make-up stylist knows hundreds of ways to make the weary look alert.

Calvert pulled on his leather jacket, locked the door and started down the hallway of his East Village apartment building a few minutes before noon. As always, he used the back exit, which deposited him in the alleyway behind the building. Starting for the sidewalk he noticed something down one of the cul-de-sacs leading off the alley.

He squinted into the dimness. An animal. A cat, apparently injured. It was lying on its side, mewing faintly.

He moved slowly over the cobblestones so he wouldn't spook the animal. Crouching, he set his make-up case down and reached out carefully. He touched the cat but then drew his hand back in shock. The animal was ice-cold and emaciated—he could feel stiff bones beneath the skin. Had it just died? He touched it again. Wait, they weren't *bones* under the skin. They were rods.

Then he glanced up and saw someone ten feet away. Calvert gasped. A man was crouching . . . But, no, he realised. It was his *own* image, reflected from a full-length mirror sitting at the end of the dark alley. Then Calvert watched himself slowly falling forward—as the mirror pivoted to the cobblestones and shattered.

The bearded, middle-aged man hiding behind it charged forward, swinging a large piece of pipe.

Calvert grabbed the make-up case and thrust it towards the attacker, deflecting the blow. The young man struggled to his feet and started to run. The assailant started after him but slipped on the slick cobblestones and went down hard.

'Take the wallet!' Calvert pulled his billfold from his pocket and flung it behind him. But the man ignored it and rose. He was between Calvert and the street; the only escape was back into the building.

Keys! he thought. Get them now! Fishing them out of his jeans. If I don't get the door unlocked on the first try, I'm dead.

Calvert slammed hard into the metal door and, a miracle, slid the key home instantly, turning it fast. The latch opened. He pulled the key out and leapt through the doorway, slamming the steel door shut behind him. It locked automatically.

He ran to his apartment. This door too he opened fast. He leapt inside, swinging it shut after him and locking it.

Hurrying into the kitchen, he seized the phone and dialled 911. A moment later a woman's voice said, 'Police and fire emergency.'

'A man just attacked me! He's outside. I locked the doors. But you have to send the police! He could still be in the alley!'

Calvert felt a sudden breeze against his face.

The 911 operator asked, 'Hello, sir, are you there?'

Calvert spun towards the door and cried out, seeing the bearded man with the pipe calmly unplugging the phone line from the wall.

'What?' he whispered, noting the scars on the man's neck, his deformed hand. 'What do you want?'

The assailant ignored him and looked around—first at the kitchen table then at the large wooden coffee table in the living room. Something about it seemed to please him.

THE SERGEANT was out of the first squad car before it had braked to a stop. Only six minutes had elapsed since the 911 call came in. Even though the call had been cut off, Central knew which building and apartment it had been placed from, thanks to caller ID.

He sent one of his men round to the back to cover the service door and the rear windows and told another to stay in the front. The third officer trotted with the sergeant towards the lobby.

This was Alphabet City, its name courtesy of the north–south avenues here—A, B, C. It was improving but was still one of the most dangerous neighbourhoods in Manhattan. If they were lucky the perp would be armed only with a knife.

Well, they got one break at least—they didn't have to find somebody to let them through the security door. An elderly woman, listing against the weight of a shopping bag that sprouted a huge pineapple, was on her way out. Blinking in surprise, she held the door open for the two cops and they hurried inside, answering her question about their presence with a noncommittal, 'Nothing to be concerned about, ma'am.'

Apartment 1J was on the ground floor towards the back. The sergeant rapped hard with his big knuckles. 'Police. Open the door.'

No response from inside. He tried the knob. More luck. It was unlocked. The sergeant shoved the door open, and both men stood back, waiting. Finally the sergeant peeked round the corner.

'Oh, Christ on earth,' he whispered when he saw what was in the centre of the living room.

THE SECRET to successful protean magic—quick change—is making distinct but simple changes to your appearance and demeanour while simultaneously distracting your audience with misdirection. And no change was more distinctive than turning yourself into a seventy-five-year-old woman.

Malerick had known the police would arrive quickly. So after the brief performance in Calvert's apartment he did a fast change into a high-necked blue dress and a white wig. He pulled his elasticised jeans above the hemline of the dress, revealing opaque support hose. The beard came off and he applied a heavy base of eccentric-lady rouge. Several dozen strokes with a thin sienna pencil gave him septuagenarian wrinkles. A change of shoes.

As for the misdirection, he'd found a shopping bag and filled the bottom with newspaper—along with the pipe and the other weapon he'd used for his routine—and added a large fresh pineapple from Calvert's kitchen. If he met anyone as he left the building they'd focus on the pineapple.

Now, a quarter of a mile from the building, still dressed as the woman, he eased into a dim alley. With one tug the dress, held together by tiny Velcro dots, came off. This garment and the wig went under a foot-wide elastic band he wore round his stomach.

He tugged his trouser cuffs down, took make-up removal pads

from a small plastic bag in his pocket and wiped his face until the rouge and wrinkles were gone, checking with a pocket mirror. The pads he dropped into the shopping bag with the pineapple, which he in turn placed in a green garbage bag and then discarded.

Back on the street, heading for one of the West Side subways.

And what did you think of our second act, Revered Audience?

He himself thought it had gone well. Malerick had studied the fine art of lock-picking for years. It was one of the first skills his mentor had taught him. It can be time-consuming to push aside the locking pins one at a time, though, so Malerick had mastered a technique called 'scrubbing', in which you move the pick back and forth quickly, brushing the pins out of the way. It had taken Malerick less than thirty seconds to scrub open the locks in both the back door and the apartment door of Calvert's place.

Pausing outside the subway he bought a *New York Times* and flipped through it as he studied passers-by. Again, it seemed that no one had followed him. He trotted down the stairs to catch the train. The next routine would be a difficult one—and he had to make some preparations. He didn't dare risk disappointing his audience.

'It's bad, Rhyme.'

Amelia Sachs was speaking into the stalk mike as she stood in the doorway of apartment 1J, in the heart of Alphabet City.

Earlier that morning Lon Sellitto had ordered all dispatchers to call him with news of any homicide in New York City. When a report came in about this killing they concluded that it was the work of the Conjurer. The mysterious way the killer had gained access to the man's apartment was one clue. The clincher, though, was that he'd smashed the victim's wristwatch—just as he'd done with the student's at the first killing that morning.

One thing that was different was the cause of death. Which had prompted Sachs's comment to Rhyme. While Sellitto gave commands to the detectives and patrol officers in the hall, Sachs studied the unfortunate vic—a young man named Anthony Calvert. He lay on his back in the middle of the coffee table in the living room, spread-eagled, hands and feet tied to the legs of the table. His abdomen had been sawn completely through down to his spine.

Sachs now described the wound to Rhyme.

'Well,' said Lincoln Rhyme unemotionally. 'Consistent. I'd say he's keeping with the magic theme. Cutting someone in half.' His voice rose as he called across the room, presumably to Kara. 'That's a magic trick, right? Cutting somebody in half?' A pause and then he was addressing Sachs again. 'She said it's a classic illusionist trick.'

Sachs noticed a major blunt-object trauma to Calvert's temple. That wound hadn't bled much, which suggested that his heart had stopped beating soon after the skull had been crushed.

'Rhyme, looks like the cutting was post-mortem.'

The sight of the victim gripped her hard and wouldn't let go. But this was as she wanted it. Death, she felt, deserved a moment of stillness. Sachs allowed this so that her heart would resist hardening to stone, a process that happened all too frequently in her calling.

A sergeant and a uniformed officer joined Sellitto in the doorway. 'Been talking to the neighbours,' one of them said. 'The vic was a nice, quiet guy. Everybody like him. Gay but not into rough trade or anything. Hadn't been seeing anybody for a while.'

Sachs nodded then said into her mike. 'Doesn't sound like he knew the killer, Rhyme.'

'We didn't think that likely now, did we?' the criminalist said. 'The Conjurer's got a different agenda—whatever the hell it is.'

'What line of work?' she asked the officers.

'Make-up artist. We found his case in the alley. He was on his way to work.'

An Asian-American detective from the 9th Precinct, which covered this part of town, walked up to the doorway, hanging up his cellphone. 'How 'bout this one, huh?' he asked breezily.

'How 'bout it,' Sellitto muttered. 'Any idea how he got away? The vic called nine-one-one himself. Your respondings must've got to the scene in ten minutes.'

'Six,' the detective said.

A sergeant said, 'We rolled up silent and covered all the doors and windows. When we got inside, the body was still warm. We did a door-to-door but no sign of the doer.'

'Wits?'

The sergeant nodded. 'The only person in the halls when we got here was this old lady. She was the one let us in. When she gets back we'll talk to her. Maybe she got a look at him.'

'She left?' Sellitto asked.

The detective said, 'It's OK. We left cards under everybody's door. One of 'em had to be hers. She'll call us back.'

'No, she won't,' Sachs said, sighing. 'That was the doer.'

'She was, like, seventy years old. And carrying a big bag of groceries. A pineapple—'

'Look,' Sachs said and pointed to the kitchen counter, on which were two spiky leaves. Next to them was a little card on a rubber band, courtesy of Dole, offering recipes for fresh pineapple.

Hell. They'd *had* him—he was inches away from them.

'And', Rhyme's voice said in her ear, 'he probably had the murder weapon in the grocery bag.'

She repeated this to the increasingly sullen detective from the 9th, then suited up in the Tyvek overalls and ran the scenes—the apartment, the hallway and the alleyway (where she found the strangest bit of evidence she'd ever come across: a toy black cat).

She was heading for her car when Sellitto stopped her.

'Hey, hold on, Officer.' He hung up his phone. 'I've gotta meet with the captain and dep com about the Conjurer case. But I need you to do something for me. We're going to add somebody to the team. I want you to pick him up.'

THE BRIDGE OF SIGHS. This was the aerial walkway connecting the criminal courts to the Manhattan Detention Center on Centre Street in downtown Manhattan.

Amelia Sachs crossed the bridge now, on her way to Detention—still known informally as the Tombs, a nickname inherited from the original city jail located across the street. Here, Sachs gave her name to a guard, surrendered her Glock and entered the secure lobby on the other side of a noisy electrical door. It groaned shut.

A few minutes later the man she was here to pick up came out of a nearby prisoner interview room. Trim, in his late thirties, with thinning brown hair and a faint grin moulded into his easy-going face. He wore a black sports jacket over a blue dress shirt and jeans.

'Amelia, hey there,' came the drawl of Detective Roland Bell.

Two men who'd also been in the prisoner interview room joined them. One was in a suit, a detective she'd met before. Luis Martinez, quiet, with careful eyes.

The second man wore khaki slacks and a black shirt under a faded windcheater. He was introduced to Sachs as Charles Grady, though Sachs knew him by sight; the assistant district attorney was a celebrity among New York law enforcers. The lean, middle-aged Harvard Law grad had remained in the DA's office long after most prosecutors had fled to more lucrative pastures. Grady, however, was content to stay in the prosecutor's office and pursue his passion, which he described simply as 'putting bad guys in jail'.

And which he happened to be damn good at. His conviction

record was one of the best in the history of the city.

Bell was here thanks to Grady's current case. The state was prosecuting a forty-five-year-old insurance agent who lived in a small rural town in upstate New York. Andrew Constable was known less for writing homeowner's policies, though, than for his local militia group, the Patriot Assembly. He was charged with conspiracy to commit murder and hate crimes and the case had been moved down here on a change-of-venue motion.

Then a few days ago Grady had received a call from the FBI. Agents had learned that a serious attempt on Grady's life might be imminent. At that point the decision was made to call Roland Bell.

The soft-spoken North Carolina native's official assignment was working Homicide and other major crimes with Lon Sellitto. But he also headed up an unofficial division of NYPD detectives known as SWAT, which wasn't the same famous acronym that everyone knows; this version stood for the 'Saving-the-Witness's-Ass Team'.

Bell had, as he expressed it, 'This sorta knack for keeping people alive other people want dead.' The result was that, in addition to his regular investigation caseload with Sellitto and Rhyme, Bell ended up doing double duty running the protection detail.

But now Grady's bodyguards were in place and the brass downtown had decided that more muscle was needed on the Conjurer team; Bell was a logical choice.

'So that was Andrew Constable,' Grady said to Bell, with a nod towards the interview room. 'He what you expected?'

'Was thinkin' he'd be more of a blueprint bigot,' Bell drawled. 'But that fella, he's fair mannerable.'

Grady grimaced. 'Gonna be hard to get a conviction.'

Bell said, 'We got another situation needs looking into. I'll leave my team with you and your family. But I'll be a phone call away.'

'Thanks, Detective,' Grady said.

Luis Martinez noticed Grady start for the door and was instantly at the prosecutor's side. 'You want to wait here for a minute, Charles?' The bodyguard left the secure area, retrieved his pistol from the guard who oversaw the lockbox behind the desk and looked over the hallway and bridge carefully.

It was then that a soft voice sounded behind Sachs. 'Hello, miss.'

She turned and saw Andrew Constable standing next to a huge guard. The prisoner was quite tall, his posture completely erect. His pepper-and-salt hair was wavy and thick. His short, round lawyer stood next to him.

Constable continued, 'Are you part of the team looking out for Mr Grady?'

'It's not my case,' Sachs said dismissively.

'Ah, no? Was just going to tell you I honestly don't know anything about any threats to Mr Grady. I wouldn't hurt Mr Grady. One of the things that made this country great is playing fair.' A laugh. 'I'll beat him at trial. Which I *will* do—thanks to my brilliant young friend here.' A nod towards his lawyer. Then a look of curiosity at Bell. 'Detective, I was wondering if you might have some interest in what my Patriots have been doing up in Canton Falls. I don't mean that crazy conspiracy nonsense. I mean what we're really about.'

'How d'you mean, sir?' Bell asked stiffly.

The expected allusion to the detective's Southern roots didn't materialise. He said, 'States' rights, working folk, local government versus federal. You should go to our web site, Detective.' He laughed. 'People expect swastikas. They get Thomas Jefferson.' When Bell said nothing the prisoner shook his head. Then he looked abashed. 'Sorry. Sometimes I just can't stop myself—all this preaching. Get a few people around me and look what happens.'

The guard said, 'Lessgo.'

'All right then,' the prisoner responded. A nod to Sachs, one to Bell. He shuffled down the hall to the faint clink of the shackles on his legs. His lawyer nodded to the prosecutor and left the secure area.

A moment later Grady, Bell and Sachs followed, and joined Martinez.

The policewoman said, 'Doesn't seem like a monster.'

Grady said, 'Some ATF folk working undercover on a weapons sting upstate found out about this plot we think Constable was behind. Some of his people were going to lure state troopers to remote areas of the county on fake nine-one-one calls. If any of them were black they were going to kidnap, strip and lynch 'em.'

Sachs blinked in shock. 'Are you serious?'

Grady nodded. 'And that was just the start of it. They were hoping that if they murdered enough troopers the blacks'd rise up in revolt. That'd give the whites around the country the chance to retaliate and wipe them out. They were hoping the Latinos and Asians would join the blacks, and the white revolution could take them out too.'

'In this day and age?'

'You'd be surprised.'

Bell nodded to Luis. 'He's in your care now. Stay close.'

'You bet,' the detective responded. Grady and the slim bodyguard left the Detention lobby while Sachs and Bell retrieved their weapons from the check-in desk. As they returned to the courthouse portion of the Criminal Courts building, walking over the Bridge of Sighs, Sachs told Bell about the Conjurer and his victims.

Bell winced. 'Motive?'

'Don't know.'

'What's the perp look like?' Bell asked.

'Little dicey on that part too.'

'So nobody's got a look at him, huh?'

'Actually a lot of people have. Except the first time they did, he was a dark-haired, bearded male in his fifties. Next time he was a bald janitor in his sixties. Then he was a woman in her seventies.'

'I'm good,' Bell said, shaking his head and tapping the automatic pistol on his hip. 'But I need a target.'

THE EVIDENCE from the second scene had arrived and Mel Cooper was arranging it on examining tables in Rhyme's parlour.

Sellitto had just returned from a tense meeting with the deputy commissioner and the mayor about the Conjurer case. Rhyme had heard that the Ukrainian illusionists with the Cirque Fantastique had no record. Police stationed at the tent reported no suspicious activity.

A moment later Sachs strode into the room, accompanied by Roland Bell. Greetings and introductions all round.

Bell hadn't been told about Kara and she answered his querying glance with: 'I'm like him.' A nod towards Rhyme. 'Sort of consultant.'

'Nice to meetcha,' Bell said, and blinked to see her absently rolling three coins back and forth over her knuckles simultaneously.

As Sachs went to work on the evidence with Cooper, Rhyme asked Sellitto, 'Who was he, the vic?'

'Anthony Calvert. Thirty-two. Make-up artist on Broadway.'

'Any connection with the student at the music school?'

'Doesn't seem to be,' Sellitto answered.

Sachs stepped to the whiteboard and taped up the digital print-outs of the body. Rhyme wheeled closer and studied the gruesome images.

'And the weapon was?' Roland Bell asked.

'Looks like a crosscut saw,' Cooper said, examining some close-ups of the wounds.

Rhyme was suddenly aware of an odd hissing sound from nearby. He turned to see Kara behind him. The sound was her frantic breath. She was looking at the pictures of Calvert's body, transfixed, tear-filled eyes wide in shock. She turned away from the board.

Rhyme knew then, seeing the pain in her face, that this was it for her. She'd reached the end. His life—crime scene work—entailed this type of horror; her world didn't.

Sachs started towards her but Rhyme shook his head: he knew they were losing the girl and that they had to let her go.

Except that he was wrong.

Kara took a deep breath—like a high diver about to plunge off the board—and turned back to the pictures, a determined look in her eyes. She finally nodded. 'P. T. Selbit,' she said.

'That's a person?' From Sachs.

Kara nodded. 'A British illusionist who did that same routine in the 1920s. It's called Sawing a Woman in Half. This is the same, tied down, spread-eagle. The only difference is he picked a man for the performance.' She blinked at the benign word. 'I mean, murder.'

Rhyme asked, 'Would only a limited number of people know it?'

'Nope. Anyone with knowledge of magic history'd be aware of it.'

Rhyme said to Sachs: 'OK, tell us what happened at Calvert's.'

'Looks like the vic left through his building's back entrance—like he always did, the neighbours said. He walked past an alley and saw that.' She pointed to the black toy cat in a plastic bag.

Kara looked it over. 'It's an automaton. Like a robot. We'd call it a feke. F-E-K-E. A prop that the audience is supposed to think is real.' She pushed a switch and suddenly it started to move, giving off a realistic-sounding meow.

'The vic must've seen the cat, maybe thought it was hurt,' said Sachs. 'That's how the Conjurer got him into the cul-de-sac.'

'Source?' Rhyme asked Cooper.

'Sing-Lu Manufacturing in Hong Kong. I checked the web site. The toy's available in hundreds of stores around the country.'

Rhyme sighed. 'Too common to trace' was the theme of the case, it seemed.

Sachs continued. 'So Calvert checked it out. The perp was hiding somewhere and—'

'The mirror,' Rhyme interrupted. A glance at Kara, who nodded.

'Illusionists do a lot with mirrors. You aim them just right and you can vanish whatever or whoever's behind them completely.'

Sellitto continued, 'Now, this is the crazy part. Calvert got back into his apartment then called emergency. He told them the attacker was outside the building and the doors were locked. But then the line went dead. Somehow the Conjurer got inside.'

'He must've had the vic's keys.'

'No,' Kara said. 'He picked the lock.'

Rhyme shook his head. 'Two doors in sixty seconds?'

Kara sighed. 'Yeah, in sixty seconds. And it's important. It tells us something else about him: locked doors don't mean anything to him.'

Rhyme glanced at Sellitto, who said, 'Working Larceny I busted a dozen burglars and none of 'em could get through locks that fast.'

'Mr Balzac has me practising lock-picking ten hours a week,' Kara said. 'I could open your front door in thirty seconds, the deadbolt in sixty. And I don't know how to scrub a lock. If the Conjurer does he could cut that time in half.'

Rhyme grudgingly accepted Kara's assessment. He nodded and said to Thom, 'OK, put down on the chart that our boy's a master lock-picker too.'

Sachs continued, 'No sign of whatever the Conjurer used to knock him out. He took that with him too.'

The report from Latents came in. But Rhyme could see that the prints were from the finger cups.

Turning to the trace Sachs had collected at the scene, they found the same mineral oil they'd recovered at the music school that morning and more of the latex, make-up and alginate.

Rhyme asked Sachs, 'You said he smashed Calvert's watch?'

'Yep. At noon exactly. A few seconds after.'

'And the other victim was at eight. He's on a timetable, looks like. And probably has somebody lined up for four this afternoon.'

Less than three hours from now.

'Got some shoes,' Sachs said, lifting a bag out of a cardboard box.

'His?'

'Probably. They're the same Ecco brand we found at the music school—same size, too.'

'He left 'em behind. Why?' Sellitto wondered.

Rhyme suggested, 'Probably thought that we knew he was wearing Eccos at the first scene and was worried the respondings'd notice them on an elderly woman.'

Mel Cooper said, 'We've got some good trace in the indentation between the upper and sole.' He scraped the material out.

''Scope it, Mel,' Rhyme ordered.

The workhorse of tools in a forensic lab is the microscope. This one was a stereo binocular microscope, which the tech had used to examine the fibres from the first scene. These instruments have relatively low magnification and are used for examining three-dimensional objects like insects and plant materials.

The image popped onto the computer screen.

'OK, let's walk through it,' Rhyme said.

Hundreds of shapes scrolled past, some dark, some red or green, some translucent. Rhyme felt, as he always did when looking through the eyepiece of a microscope, that he was a voyeur, examining a world that had no idea it was being spied upon.

And a world that could be very revealing.

'Hairs,' Rhyme said. 'Animal.' He could tell this by the number of scales.

'Dog, I'd say,' Cooper offered. Rhyme concurred.

'What's that long stuff?' Sellitto asked.

Rhyme glanced at it. 'Dried grass. But I don't recognise that other material. GC it, Mel.'

Soon the chromatograph/spectrometer had spat out its results.

'Dead bacterial matter, partially digested fibre and grass. It's *doggy do*,' Rhyme said. 'What else from the scene?'

'Zip,' Sachs said. 'That's it.'

Rhyme resumed scanning the evidence charts. Enigmas to unravel and not much time in which to do it. They had less than three hours to stop the Conjurer before he found his next victim.

CHAPTER FIVE

The well-known Hammerstead Riding Academy on the Upper West Side is still in its original structure, built in 1885. Ninety horses reside there, some privately owned and some for rent, and one of these latter was now being led down a ramp from his stall by a groom, a red-headed teenage girl, to a waiting rider.

Cheryl Marston felt the same thrill she did every Saturday at this time when she saw the tall, feisty horse with the mottled rump of an appaloosa. 'Hey, Donny Boy,' she called, her pet name for the animal, whose real name was Don Juan di Middleburg. 'See you in an hour,' she told the groom, swinging up onto Donny Boy.

A touch to the ribs and they were on their way. Out onto 86th Street, the shod feet clopping loudly on the asphalt, drawing everyone's attention to the gorgeous animal and, high atop him, the thin-faced, serious woman dressed in jodhpurs, red jacket and black velvet helmet, out of which dangled a long blonde French braid.

Crossing into Central Park, Marston glanced south and saw in the distance the office building in Midtown where she practised corporate law. She felt the sun-warm, loam-scented air on her face as Donny Boy trotted along the dark path, surrounded by early jonquils and forsythia and lilacs.

For half an hour she circled the reservoir slowly. She enjoyed a brief canter then slowed to a trot as they came to the sharper turns in the more deserted northern part of the park, near Harlem.

She wasn't sure exactly how it occurred. She'd slowed to make a turn through a narrow gap between two stands of bushes when a pigeon flew directly into Donny Boy's face. Whinnying, he skidded to a stop so fast that Marston was nearly thrown off. Then he reared and she almost went backwards over his rump.

'Whoa, Donny,' she cried, trying to pat his neck.

He kept rearing, crazed. Sharp rocks jutted from the ground on either side of them. If Donny Boy lost his balance on the uneven ground he could go down hard—possibly with her under him.

'Donny!' she called breathlessly. But he reared again, edging towards the rocks. His feet were clattering on the stones and she felt the huge muscles quiver in panic as he sensed his balance go.

Then, from nowhere, a man in a jogging suit stepped from the bushes. He jumped forward, grabbing bit and bridle.

'No, get back!' Marston shouted. 'He's out of control!'

The slim man was looking not at her but into the eyes of the horse. Speaking words she couldn't hear. Miraculously the appaloosa was calming. The rearing stopped. The man pulled the horse's head down, close to his and said a few more words.

Finally he stepped back. 'Are you all right?' he asked her.

'I think so.' Marston inhaled deeply.

'What happened?'

'A bird spooked him. Flew into his face.'

A close examination. 'Looks OK to me. You might want to have a vet look at him. But I don't see any cuts.'

'What did you do?' she asked. 'Are you . . .?'

'A horse whisperer?' he replied, laughing. 'Hardly. But I ride a lot.'

'I don't know how to thank you.'

'You rent from Hammerstead? Or is he yours?'

'Hammerstead. I ride him every week.'

Calm now, Marston examined the man more closely. He was a handsome man in his early fifties. He had a trim beard and thick eyebrows that met above the bridge of his nose. On his neck—and chest too—she could see what looked like bad scarring and his left hand was deformed. Though none of that mattered to her, considering he liked horses. Cheryl Marston, divorced for the last four of her thirty-eight years, realised that they were both sizing each other up.

He gave a faint laugh. 'I was . . . I was just wondering if it'd be out of line to ask if you want to get some coffee.'

'Not out of line at all,' she responded, pleased by his straightforward attitude. 'I'm going to finish my hour. I've got about twenty minutes left . . . Got to get back up on the horse, so to speak. How's that fit with your schedule?'

'Twenty minutes is perfect. I'll meet you at the stable.'

'Good. Oh, you ride English or Western?'

'Bareback, mostly. I used to be a pro.'

'Really? Where?'

'Believe it or not,' he answered shyly, 'I rode in the circus.'

A FAINT DING resounded from Cooper's computer, indicating he'd received an email.

'From our friends on Ninth and Pennsylvania.' He decrypted the FBI message. 'The results from the oil. Brand name Tack-Pure. Used to condition saddles, reins, equestrian-related products.'

Rhyme spun his Storm Arrow around. 'The manure on the shoes.'

'What about it?' Sachs asked.

'It's not from dogs. It's from *horses*! Dogs are carnivores. They don't eat grass and hay . . . All right, let's think. Other evidence placed him in Central Park . . . And the hairs. You know that area, the dog knoll? That's in the park too.'

'It's right across the street,' Sellitto pointed out. 'Where everybody walks their dogs.'

'Kara,' Rhyme asked, 'does the Cirque Fantastique have horses?'

'No,' she said. 'No animal acts at all.'

'OK, that lets the circus out . . . What else could he be up to? The dog knoll's right next to the bridlepath in the park, right? Maybe he rides or's been checking out riders. One of them could be a target.'

Sellitto said, 'There's a stable someplace around here, isn't there?'

'Find out,' Rhyme called. 'And get some people over there.'

Sachs glanced at the clock. It was 1.35pm. 'Well, we've got some time. Two and a half hours till the next victim.'

'Good,' Sellitto said. 'I'll get surveillance teams set up in the park and around the stable. If they're in place by two thirty that'll be plenty of time to spot him.'

Rhyme noticed Kara frowning. 'What is it?'

'You know I was telling you about misdirection?'

'I remember.'

'Well, there's also *time* misdirection. That's tricking the audience by making them think something's going to happen at one time when it really happens at another. Like, an illusionist'll repeat an act at regular intervals, but then shorten the time between the intervals. The audience isn't paying attention and they completely miss whatever he's doing. You can spot a time misdirection trick because the illusionist always lets the audience know what the interval is.'

Rhyme asked, 'So you don't think we have until four?'

Kara shrugged. 'He knows you've found the watches. He knows you're smart. If I were him I'd be going after the next victim right now.'

'That's good enough for me,' Rhyme said. 'Forget surveillance. Lon, get ESU into the park. In a big way.'

Cooper looked up from his computer. 'Got the stable. Hammerstead Riding Academy.'

Bell, Sellitto and Sachs started for the door.

SHE WAS CAUTIOUS, Malerick observed, as befitted any woman who'd just been picked up by a man in Manhattan, even if that stranger was shy, friendly and able to calm rearing horses.

Still, Cheryl Marston was relaxing little by little.

After the vet had examined Donny Boy and declared him in good health, Malerick and his next unwitting performer strolled to this restaurant just off Riverside Drive. The woman now chatted with 'John' about her life in the city, her early love of horses.

For his routine in Central Park today to snare Cheryl Marston, Malerick had drawn on the work of Howard Thurston, a popular illusionist in the early twentieth century, who specialised in animal acts. Malerick had captured a pigeon, then stroked the bird until it was hypnotised. As Cheryl Marston approached he'd flung the pigeon hard into the horse's face. Donny Boy's rearing had nothing to do with the bird, though, but was caused by an ultrasonic pitch generator, set to a frequency that stung the horse's ears. As Malerick stepped out of the bushes to 'rescue' Cheryl he shut the generator off and by the time he grabbed the bridle the horse was calming.

Now the equestrian was growing less cautious as she learned how much they had in common. Or *appeared* to.

This illusion was due to Malerick's use of *body*-reading. He was noting subtle changes in Cheryl's poses, facial expressions and gestures in response to comments he made. Some told him he was straying from her thoughts, others that he was on the mark.

He mentioned, for instance, a friend who'd been through a divorce and he could see easily that Cheryl had too—and had been on the receiving end. So he added that he was divorced too and that his wife'd had an affair and left him.

'*I* gave up a boat,' she said grimacing, 'just to get away from that son of a bitch. A twenty-four-foot sailboat.'

Neither John nor Cheryl had children. Both had cats, divorced parents and a love of tennis. A match made in heaven . . .

Almost time, he thought. Even if the police had some leads they'd be thinking he wouldn't kill again until 4.00pm; it was now just after two. Still, he was eager to get on with the next part of the routine.

Malerick picked up his spoon. As he tapped it absently on the tabletop Cheryl glanced at it. A fraction of a second. But it gave Malerick enough time to empty a capsule of tasteless powder into her coffee as he reached for the sugar with his other hand.

After a few moments Malerick could see that the drug was having its effect; her eyes were slightly unfocused. She didn't sense anything was wrong, though. That was the good thing about the famous date-rape drug Rohypnol: you didn't know you'd been drugged. Not until the next morning.

He smiled at her. 'Hey, you want to see something fun?'

'Fun?' she asked drowsily. She blinked, smiling broadly.

He paid the bill. 'I just bought a boat.'

She laughed in delight. 'A boat? I love boats. What kind?'

'Sailboat. Thirty-eight feet. My wife and I had one,' Malerick told her sadly. 'She got it in the divorce.'

'John, no, you're kidding me!' she said, laughing groggily. 'My husband and I had one! He got *ours* in the divorce.'

'Really?' He laughed and stood. 'Let's walk down to the river. You can see it from there.'

'I'd love to.' She rose unsteadily and took his arm.

He steered her through the doorway. The dosage seemed right. She was submissive and forgetful but she wasn't going to pass out. They now headed towards Riverside Park. He stopped at his car, a stolen Mazda, and took out a heavy gym bag. From inside the bag came a loud clank of metal. Cheryl glanced at it, began to speak but then seemed to forget what she was going to say.

'Let's go this way.' Malerick led her across a pedestrian bridge over the parkway and down into an overgrown, deserted strip of land on the riverbank. He gripped her firmly round the back and under the arm. 'My boat's down there.'

'Really?' she asked, adding that she and her ex-husband had had one. But she'd lost it in the divorce.

THE RIDING ACADEMY was a slice of old New York. Smelling powerful barn scent, Amelia Sachs looked through an archway into the interior of the woody old place at the horses. Atop them, the riders looked stately in their tan jodhpurs, black or red riding jackets, velvet helmets.

A half-dozen uniformeds stood outside the lobby. More officers were in the park, under the command of Lon Sellitto, deployed around the bridlepath, looking for their elusive prey.

Sachs and Bell walked into the office and the detective flashed his gold shield to the woman behind the counter. She asked uneasily, 'Yes? Is there a problem?'

'Ma'am, do you use Tack-Pure to treat leather?'

'Yessir, we do.'

'We found traces at the scene of a homicide today,' Bell said. We think the suspect might be stalking one of your employees or a rider.'

'No! Who?'

'That's what we're not sure about. And we're not sure of the suspect's appearance either. All we know is he's average build. Around fifty years old. White. Might have a beard and brown hair. Fingers on his left hand might be deformed. What we need is for you to talk to your employees, regular customers too, and see if they've noticed anybody fitting that description.'

'Of course,' she said uncertainly.

Bell took several of the uniformed patrol officers and disappeared through a doorway. 'We'll do a search,' he called to Sachs.

The policewoman glanced at the clock—2.00pm. She radioed in to Central and had the transmission patched into Rhyme's phone. The criminalist came on the line. 'Sachs, Lon's teams haven't seen anything in Central Park. Any luck with you?'

'The manager's interviewing staff and riders here at the academy. Roland and his team are searching the stables.' She noticed the manager with a cluster of employees. One girl, a round-faced redhead, suddenly began to nod.

'Hold on, Rhyme. May have something.'

The manager beckoned Sachs over and the teenage groom said, 'This rider comes in every Saturday. Cheryl Marston.'

Rhyme shouted into Sachs's ear, 'At the same time? Ask her if she comes in at the same time every week. People with regular habits are easier to target.'

Sachs relayed the question.

'Oh, yeah,' the girl said. 'She's like clockwork.'

'And what about her?'

'Today she comes back from a ride. About a half-hour ago. And what it is she hands off her horse to me and she wants the vet to check him out because a bird flew into his face and spooked him. So, we're looking him over and she's telling me about this guy who calmed Donny down. She's all excited 'cause she's going to have coffee with him. I saw him waiting for her. And I'm like, what's wrong with his hand? It looked like he only had three fingers.'

'That's him!' Sachs said. 'Do you know where they were going?'

She pointed west. 'I think that way.'

'Get a description,' Rhyme called.

The girl explained that he had a beard and his eyebrows were odd. 'All kind of grown together.'

To alter a face the most important thing is the eyebrows.

'Wearing?' she asked.

'A jogging jacket and sweatpants. Running shoes.'

AND NOW WE TURN to escapology, my friends.

We'll see what is perhaps Harry Houdini's most famous escape. He was bound, hung by his heels and submerged in a tank of water. He had only a few minutes to try to bend upwards from the waist, release his ankles and open the locked top of the chamber before he drowned.

The tank was, of course, 'prepared'. The bars apparently intended to keep the glass from shattering were handholds that let him pull himself up to reach his ankles. The locks on his feet and the top of the tank had hidden latches that would instantly release his ankles and the lid.

Our re-creation of the famous escapologist's popular feat, needless to say, doesn't offer such features. And I've added a few variations of my own. All for your entertainment, of course.

And now, courtesy of Mr Houdini, the Water Torture Cell.

BEARDLESS AND DRESSED in chinos and a white shirt, Malerick wrapped chains round Cheryl Marston.

They were hidden from view by thick bushes, near the Hudson River, next to a stagnant pool of water, which at one time had been a tiny inlet for dinghies. Landfill and debris had sealed it and created this pond about ten feet in diameter. On one side was a rotting pier on which was a rusty crane that had been used for lifting boats out of the water. Malerick now swung a rope over the crane, caught the end and began tying it to the chains holding Cheryl's feet.

'No, no, nooooo,' she whispered groggily. 'It hurts. Please!'

Malerick pressed duct tape over her mouth. Then he braced himself, took a good grip and pulled down on the rope, which lifted the lawyer's feet and began dragging her towards the brackish water.

ON THIS GLORIOUS spring afternoon a busy crafts fair filled the large central square of West Side College between 79th and 80th Streets.

Sachs and Bell jogged up and down the streets, looking through the fair, the restaurants and the alleys.

Nothing. Until, desperate minutes later, a break.

The two cops walked into Ely's Coffee Shop near Riverside Drive. Sachs gripped Bell's arm, nodding towards a black riding hat and a leather crop next to the cash register.

Sachs ran to the manager, a swarthy Middle Easterner. 'Did a woman leave those here?'

'Yeah, ten minutes ago. She—'

'Was she with a man?'

'Yeah. She forgot the hat and that whip.'

'Do you know where they went?' Bell asked.

'I hear him say he going to show her his boat. But I hope he took her home.'

'How do you mean?' Sachs asked.

'The woman, she was sick. Couldn't walk steady. Seem drunk but all they drank was coffee. And she was fine when they got here.'

'He drugged her. We've gotta look for her,' she said to Bell.

'If he said boat, let's go west. The Hudson.'

COUGHING AND CHOKING, Cheryl was hauled out of the greasy pond, upside-down, spinning lazily, held by a rope looped over a crane jutting over the water.

Her skull throbbed as the blood settled in her head. What was going on? This man studying her with pleasant curiosity as she died. Not understanding how he could treat her this way. A man so nice to horses yet so cruel to her.

He looked down at her, then played out the rope, lowering her into the disgusting pond again. Cheryl gave up. She inhaled through her nose to let comforting death into her lungs.

'THERE!' AMELIA SACHS cried.

She and Bell ran towards the thick cluster of bushes and trees on the edge of the Hudson River. A man in chinos and a white shirt was holding a rope that arced over a small rusting crane. The other end disappeared below the surface.

'Hey,' Bell called, 'you!'

He had brown hair, yes, but the outfit was different. No beard, either. And his eyebrows didn't seem that thick. Sachs couldn't see if the fingers of his left hand were fused together.

As they jogged closer he looked up in apparent relief. 'Help me,' he cried. 'There's a woman in the water!'

Bell and Sachs sprinted through the brush. 'Don't trust him,' she called breathlessly to Bell.

The man pulled harder and a woman's body emerged. She was wrapped in chains. They closed the distance fast, Bell calling on his Handie-Talkie for back-up and medics.

'Help me! I can't pull her up alone!' the rescuer called to Bell and Sachs. His voice was a gasp, out of breath from the effort. 'This man, he tied her up and tried to kill her!'

Sachs drew her weapon and trained it on the man.

'Hey, what're you doing?' he asked in shock. 'I'm trying to save her!'

She still couldn't see his left hand; it was enclosed by his right.

'Keep your hands on that rope, sir,' she said.

'I didn't do anything!' He was wheezing—an odd sound. Maybe it wasn't exertion but asthma.

Staying clear of her line of fire, Bell grabbed the crane and swung it towards the muddy shore. When the woman was in arm's reach he tugged her towards him, as the man holding the rope let out slack until she was lying on the ground. She lay on the grass, limp. The detective pulled the tape off her mouth and began to give her CPR.

Sachs saw the victim stirring . . . Yes! They'd got to her in time. Then she noticed something. Sitting nearby was a wad of shiny navy-blue cloth. It could be the jogging jacket.

The man's eyes followed hers and he saw it too.

Several people had gathered nearby, drawn by the commotion. Suddenly a man's panicked voice shouted, 'Yo, lady, look out! That guy in the jogging suit—to your right! He got a gun!'

Sachs crouched, spinning to her right, squinting for a target. 'Roland, look out!'

Bell dropped to the ground, beside the woman, and looked in the same direction as Sachs, his Sig in his hand.

But Sachs saw nobody in a jogging suit. Oh, no, she thought. Ventriloquism. She turned back fast to see a brilliant fireball explode from the rescuer's hand. It hovered in the air, blinding her.

'Amelia!' Bell called. 'I can't see anything. Where is he?'

A fast series of gunshots sounded from where the Conjurer had been standing. Sachs aimed at the sound of the shooting. Bell did too. They both squinted for targets but the killer was gone by the time her vision returned; she found herself aiming at a cloud of faint smoke—from more of the explosive squibs.

Then, to the east, she saw the Conjurer on the other side of the parkway. He leapt up the wide stairway that led to the nearby college and vanished into the crowd at the crafts fair, like a copperhead disappearing into tall grass.

THEY WERE EVERYWHERE. Dozens of police. All searching for him.

Gasping from the sprint, Malerick leaned against the cool limestone of one of the college's classroom buildings. He looked behind him, west, the direction he'd come from. Already the police had cut off that entrance. On the north and south sides of the plaza were tall concrete buildings. The windows were sealed and there were no doors. His only exit was east, on the other side of a football-field-size expanse of fair booths and dense crowds.

He made his way in that direction. But he didn't dare run. Because illusionists know that fast attracts attention. He glanced at the goods for sale, nodded in pleasure at a guitarist's performance, laughed at a balloon-tying clown. He did what everyone else did. Easing east. Wondering how the police had found him. It was as if they'd *anticipated* he'd kidnap someone in that part of the city. How?

Ahead of him was the east stairway leading from the square down to Broadway. Only another fifty feet to freedom, forty.

But then he saw flashing lights. A half-dozen uniformed officers jumped out of their cars, climbed the stairs and merged into the crowd. Then he saw the policewoman with the steely eyes and red hair, who'd tried to arrest him at the pond, at the top of the stairs.

What to do? Malerick thought desperately. He had one remaining quick-change outfit left under what he now wore.

The trim, brown-haired cop who'd been giving Cheryl Marston CPR now crested the stairs.

Malerick walked to the row of Porta-Potties, stepped inside one of the fibreglass boxes and executed a change. In thirty seconds he was out again, a ponytailed biker with a beer gut, wearing a baseball cap, a greasy denim Harley-Davidson shirt and dirty black jeans.

He picked up an old newspaper in his left hand to obscure his fingers, then moved towards the east side of the fair again.

The stairway that led down to Broadway was about thirty yards wide and the police had managed to close off much of it. They were now stopping all adults who left the fair and asking for IDs.

The red-haired policewoman was only feet from him. She spoke into her radio. 'Five Eight Eight Five. Requesting a land-line patch to Lincoln Rhyme.' A moment later: 'We're at the fair, Rhyme. He *has* to be here . . . He couldn't've got out before they sealed the exits. We'll find him. If we have to frisk everybody we'll find him.'

Malerick eased through the crowd.

SACHS SCANNED the people near her again—an elderly couple, a biker in a Harley shirt, two European women bargaining with a vendor. A man was walking away, limping. He couldn't be the Conjurer. Or could he? She was at sea.

Sachs heard a voice over her radio. 'RMP Four Seven to all available officers on that ten-twenty-four by the river. Suspect just broke through perimeter at the east side of the street fair. Is now on West End approaching Seven-eight Street, heading north on foot . . . Wearing jeans, blue shirt with Harley-Davidson logo. Dark hair, braid, black baseball cap. Can't see any weapons . . . I'm losing him.'

The biker! And I was three feet from him!

Sachs caught sight of Roland Bell, frowning as he pressed the headset of his Motorola closer to his ear. They caught each other's eye and he nodded in the direction of the pursuit.

Ignoring her painful arthritis, she leapt down the stairs two at a time after Bell.

HE'S FAST. BUT I'M FASTER.

Patrolman Lawrence Burke sprinted out of Riverside Park onto West End Avenue, only twenty feet behind the perp, some biker asshole in a Harley shirt.

Running round pedestrians, broken field, exactly the way he used to do in high-school football. 'Yo, you! Hold it!' Burke gasped.

The guy skidded to the left, down an alley. The cop took the turn. From three feet away he launched himself into the air, remembering to aim high and use the guy's body for padding when they went down.

'Jesus,' the biker gasped as they crashed to the cobblestones. 'I didn't do anything! Why were you chasing me?'

'Shut up!' Burke muttered, and cuffed him. He used a plastic restraint on his ankles too. Nice and tight. He frisked the man carefully and found a wallet. There was no ID inside, only money.

'I'm going to sue you! If you think I did something, you're way wrong, mister.'

But then Burke tugged up the guy's shirt and T-shirt and blinked. His chest and abdomen were real badly scarred. But even stranger was a bag round his waist. Burke expected a stash, but no, all that the guy was hiding was a pair of jogging pants, a turtleneck, chinos, white shirt and a cellphone. And make-up.

Burke pushed the button on his Motorola. 'Portable Five Two One Two to Central. I've got the perp in that ten-two-four in custody, K.'

'Location?'

'Block and a half east of West End, K. Hold on a minute. I'll get the cross street.' Burke walked to the mouth of the alley to look for the street sign and wait for his fellow cops to show up.

SACHS AND BELL continued quickly up West End towards where Patrolman Burke had radioed that he'd collared the killer. They turned the corner onto 88th Street.

Bell noted an alleyway. 'There,' he said, pointing.

The alley was empty.

'He said Eighty-eighth, right?' Sachs asked.

Bell called on his Motorola, 'Portable Five Two One Two, what street are you on, K?'

Sachs squinted down the alley, 'Oh, no.'

Running forward, she found, resting on the cobblestones, a pair of handcuffs, open. Next to them was a plastic hog-tie, severed.

'He got out of the cuffs and cut the restraint.' Sachs looked around.

Bell called in a 10-39, escaped suspect, with an officer missing or in pursuit. He asked the dispatcher if there'd been any transmissions from Burke but was told that there'd been none.

Sachs walked the length of the alley. But neither she nor Bell found any sign of either the officer or the perp.

What a terrible day. Two dead this morning. And now a police officer was missing.

Bell said, 'You search the scene here, Amelia. I'm going to go interview the victim. See if she can tell us anything.'

A crime scene bus was parked on 88th Street. Sachs walked to it and began to collect her equipment to run the scenes. The coffee shop, the pond and the alley.

SACHS WALKED THE GRIDS, took digital photos and released the scenes to Latents and Photo. She then returned to the fair, where she met Roland Bell. He'd interviewed Cheryl Marston at the hospital. She gave a good description. She also recalled that he'd stopped at a car. She remembered the make and the first few letters of the tag.

The Department of Motor Vehicles had reported that a car matching the description—a 2001 tan Mazda 626 had been stolen from White Plains airport a week ago. Sellitto put out an emergency vehicle location request to all law enforcement agencies in the metro area.

Bell was concluding his narrative about Cheryl Marston's harrowing ordeal when a patrol officer interrupted. 'Just got a report—radio motor patrol spotted him on Central Park West around Ninety-second. They went after him but he drove over the kerb into the park. The RMP got stuck on the embankment.'

Sachs nodded to the evidence crates. 'Get all this to Rhyme,' she called and ten seconds later she was in the seat of her Camaro and had the big engine rattling. She snapped the race-car harness on and pulled the canvas straps snug.

Skidding onto Central Park West, heading north, Sachs pitched the blue flasher onto the dash and plugged it into the cigarette lighter outlet. The brilliant light began rotating and as she hurtled forward she slapped the horn in time to the flash.

A clatter through the headset of her Motorola, which lay on the front passenger seat. She pulled it on.

''Lo?' she called, dispensing with the requisite police radio codes.

'Amelia? Roland here,' Bell called. He'd also given up on standard communication protocols. 'He drove out of the park on Central Park North. It was less'n a minute ago. He's going north.'

A new voice in her headset. 'Sachs, we've got him!'

'Where, Rhyme?'

He'd turned westbound on 125th Street, the criminalist explained. 'Near Fifth Avenue.'

'I'll try to block him. But get me some back-up,' she called.

Sachs honked her way into the busy intersection at 125th Street. She parked crosswise, blocking the two westbound lanes. She jumped out of her car, Glock in hand. Several cars were stopped in the eastbound lanes. Sachs shouted to the drivers, 'Out! Police action. Get out of those cars and under cover.' The drivers did as they were told. Now all the lanes of 125th Street were blocked.

In the distance Sachs saw the Mazda weaving frantically through traffic as it sped west towards her impromptu roadblock. The

Conjurer didn't notice the blockade until he was past the street that he could've taken to avoid her. He skidded to a halt. Behind him a garbage truck making a turn braked hard. The driver saw what was happening and bailed, leaving the truck to block him from the rear.

Sachs leaned over the hood of the Camaro and centred the blade sight on the windshield.

So here he was at last, the Conjurer. She could see his face, his blue Harley shirt. Beneath a black cap his fake braid whipped back and forth as he looked desperately for some way to escape.

But there wasn't any.

'You! In the Mazda! Get out of the car and lie down on the ground!'

No response. Come on, you son of a bitch, she thought. Put the goddamn car in drive. Give me an excuse . . .

If he just tried to speed past her she'd take out the fan blades or a tyre and try to capture him alive. But if he drove towards her or aimed for the sidewalk, endangering someone else, then she'd drop him.

And then Sachs saw a slow-moving mass of yellow ease behind the Mazda. A school bus, filled with children, pulled away from the kerb into traffic, the driver unaware of what was happening. It stopped at an angle between the Mazda and the garbage truck.

Even a direct hit might not stop the slug, which could careen into the bus after it passed through its target.

Sachs looked through the windshield of the Mazda. She could see the faint motion of the Conjurer's head as he glanced up and to his right, locating the bus in the rearview mirror.

He then looked back towards her and she had the impression that he smiled, deducing that she couldn't fire now.

The raw squeal of the Mazda's front tyres filled the street as he floored the pedal and headed towards Sachs at fifty miles an hour.

As the Mazda headed straight at her, Sachs ran to the sidewalk to try for a cross-fire shot.

Lifting the Glock, she aimed at the dark form that was the Conjurer's head, leading him by three or four feet. But beyond him were dozens of store windows and apartments and people crouching on the sidewalk. There was simply no way to fire even a single round safely. She lowered the gun, shoulders slumped, as she watched the Mazda streak straight for the Camaro.

Oh, not the car . . . No!

Thinking of when her father had bought her the '69 muscle car, a junker, and how together they'd rebuilt much of the engine and suspension, added a new transmission, and stripped it, to goose the horsepower skyward. This vehicle and a love of policing were his essential legacies to his daughter.

Thirty feet from the Camaro the Conjurer turned the wheel hard to the left, towards Sachs. She leapt aside and he turned the other way. The Mazda skidded, cutting diagonally towards the kerb. At a glancing angle, it slammed into the passenger door and right front fender of the Camaro, spinning it in a circle over two lanes onto the far sidewalk.

The Mazda went back into the street and turned north. Sachs glanced at the Camaro. The side was a mess, the front end too, but the torn fender wasn't binding on the tyres. Yeah, she could probably catch him. She jumped in and fired up the engine.

Amelia Sachs was doing sixty in eight seconds. The Camaro wobbled like crazy but it drove more or less straight. The Conjurer wasn't half the driver she was, and slowly she closed the gap. Then he turned into a side street. She skidded round the corner and stopped.

No sign of him.

The only escape route was a short dead end, terminating in a wall of bushes. Beyond that, she could see the elevated Harlem River Drive, beyond which was just a bank leading down to the river.

Then a voice crackled. 'All units in the vicinity of Frederick Douglass and One-five-three Street, be advised, we have a ten-five-four.

Car accident with probable injuries.

'Vehicle has gone into the Harlem River. Mazda or Toyota. Late model. Beige.'

Sachs sped her Camaro to the end of the cul-de-sac and parked on the sidewalk as an ambulance and Emergency Services Unit truck arrived and rocked slowly through the brush, which had been crushed by the speeding Mazda. She followed, walking carefully over the rubble. As they broke from the vegetation she saw a cluster of decrepit shanties and lean-tos. Dozens of homeless, mostly men.

Apparently the Conjurer, expecting to find a road on the other side of the bushes, had gone through the brush fast. She saw the panicked skid marks as he slid uncontrollably through the slick muck, careened off a shack, then went into the river.

Two ESU officers helped the residents of the shack out of the wreckage—they were unhurt—while others scanned the river for any sign of the driver. She radioed Rhyme and Sellitto and told them what had happened.

Sachs approached several men who were talking excitedly in Spanish. They held fishing rods; this was a popular place to catch bluefish. They said the car had sped through the bushes fast and gone straight into the river. They'd all seen a man wearing a hat in the driver's seat and were positive he hadn't jumped out.

More police cars were arriving, TV crews too, turning their cameras on what was left of the shack and on a police boat, off the stern of which two wet-suited divers were rolling backwards into the water.

Now that the emergency activity had shifted to the river itself, the land-side operation became Amelia Sachs's. She had little crime scene equipment in the Camaro but she did have plenty of yellow tape, with which she now sealed off a large area of the riverbank.

When the rapid response vehicle arrived she carried one of the crime scene suitcases to the perimeter of the scene and was opening it when she heard an accented voice call out urgently, 'My God, what happened? Is everyone all right?'

Near the TV crews a well-coiffed Latino man in jeans and a sports jacket pushed forward through the crowd. He squinted in alarm at the damaged shack and then began to run towards it.

'Hey,' Sachs called. He didn't hear her.

The man ducked under the yellow tape, tramping over the Mazda's tyre treads and possibly obliterating anything that the Conjurer might have thrown from the car or had fallen out—maybe even destroying the killer's own footprints if he *had* bailed, despite what the fishermen believed they'd seen.

She checked out his left hand and could see that the ring and little finger weren't fused together. So he wasn't the Conjurer but who the hell is he? Sachs wondered. And what was he doing in *her* crime scene?

The man was now wading through the wreckage of the shack, grabbing planks and sheets of wood and corrugated metal, flinging them over his shoulder.

'Hey, you!' she called. 'Get the hell out of there!'

He shouted over his shoulder, 'There could be somebody inside!'

Angry now, she snapped, 'This's a crime scene! You can't be in there.'

'There could be somebody inside!' he repeated.

'No, no, no. Everybody's out. They're OK.' She gestured to two nearby patrol officers. 'Get him out.'

Sachs disgustedly watched the officers' footprints adding to the slow erosion of her crime scene. They grabbed the intruder by the arms. He called to her, 'Listen, Officer, I'm Victor Ramos—this is *my* neighbourhood, not yours.'

'Cuff him,' she said. 'Then get him the hell out of here.'

The officers ratcheted the cuffs on the red-faced man and he was led, fuming and cursing, out of the scene. 'Want we should book him?' one officer called.

'Naw, just put him in time-out for a while,' she shouted, and watched him being deposited in the back of a squad car.

Sachs then dressed in the Tyvek outfit and waded into the scene. She took her time and searched carefully. After this harrowing, day-long pursuit Amelia Sachs was accepting nothing at face value.

THE RED BALL couldn't possibly move from Kara's outstretched right hand to the spot behind her ear. But it did. How? Rhyme wondered.

She and the criminalist were in the downstairs lab of his town house, waiting for Amelia Sachs and Roland Bell. As Mel Cooper was setting the evidence out on examination tables Rhyme was being treated to his own sleight-of-hand show.

'Where do you live?' he asked Kara.

'The Village.'

'Your accent?' he asked.

'Midwest. But I've been here since I was eighteen. Went to school in Bronxville.'

'Sarah Lawrence, drama,' Rhyme deduced.

'English.'

'And you liked it here and stayed.'

'Well, I liked it once I got out of the 'burbs and into the city. Then after my father died my mother moved here to be closer to me.'

'Where does she live?'

'She's in a care facility, Upper East Side.'

'Is she very sick?'

'Nothing serious. She'll be fine.' Kara absently rolled the red balls over her knuckles and into her palm.

Rhyme glanced towards the door. No sign of Thom. 'Do me a favour.'

'Sure.'

'I need some medicine.'

Kara noticed some pill bottles against the wall.

'No, over on the bookcase.'

'Ah, gotcha. Which one?' she asked.

'The one on the end. Macallan, eighteen years.' He whispered, 'And probably the quieter you poured it, the better.'

'Hey, you're talking to the right person. The French magician Robert-Houdin said there were three skills you needed to master to be a successful illusionist. Dexterity, dexterity and dexterity.' In a moment a healthy dose of the smoky whisky had been poured into his tumbler—indeed silently and almost invisibly. Thom could have been standing nearby and would never have noticed. She slipped the straw into the cup and fitted it into the holder on his chair.

'Help yourself,' he said.

Kara shook her head and gestured towards the coffeepot—which she alone had nearly drained. 'That's my poison.'

Rhyme sipped the Scotch. He tilted his head back and let the burn ease into the back of his mouth then disappear.

'I've got a confession,' Kara said.

'Yes?'

'When I first saw you I had this thought.'

Oh, yes. The Look. Served up with the Smile.

She said, 'I thought, what an amazing illusionist you are.'

'Me?' a surprised Rhyme asked.

Kara nodded. 'You're all about perception and reality. People see you can't move. They probably think you've got mental problems or you're slow. Right?'

This was true. People who didn't know him often spoke slower and louder, explained the obvious in simple terms.

'An audience'd be convinced that you couldn't possibly be behind the illusions they were seeing. Half of them'd be obsessing with your condition. The other half wouldn't even look at you. That's when you'd hook 'em . . . Anyway, there I was meeting you and I wasn't sympathetic and didn't ask you how you were doing. I was just thinking, damn, what a performer you'd be. That was pretty crass, and I had a feeling you picked up on it.'

This delighted him completely, 'Believe me, I don't do well with sympathy. Crass scores a lot more points.'

She lifted a newly filled coffee cup. 'To the famous illusionist, the Immobilised Man.'

Then they heard the front door open and the voices of Sachs and Sellitto.

LON SELLITTO ASKED, 'First of all, do we think he's dead?'

'Bring me his corpse,' Rhyme said, 'and I'll believe it.'

He was encouraged about one thing, though: that it was after 4.00pm and they'd had no reports of a homicide or disappearance.

'What about Larry Burke?' Rhyme asked.

Sellitto shook his head. 'We've got dozens of people out searching. I'm thinking he might be in that car went into the river.'

'They haven't brought it up yet?'

'They haven't *found* it yet. Water's black as night and, with that current, a diver was telling me a car could drift a half-mile before it hit the bottom.'

'Let's get back to the evidence,' Rhyme said. 'What do we have?'

'Nothing in the restaurant,' Sachs said, grimacing. 'The staff had cleaned the table and mopped the floor.'

'How 'bout the pond? Where you nailed him.'

'We found some things there,' Sachs said. 'He blinded us with more of that flash cotton and then set off some squibs.'

'All right,' Rhyme sighed. 'What else is there?'

'Chains. Two lengths.' He'd wrapped these round Cheryl Marston. There were no manufacturer's markings.

The gym bag that the killer had collected from the car, presumably containing the chains and rope, was unbranded and had been made in China. Cooper inverted the bag above an examining tray. A bit of white powder drifted out. The substance turned out to be Rohypnol.

'Date-rape drug of choice,' Sachs told Kara.

There were also tiny pellets of a sticky translucent material inside.

'I don't recognise it,' Cooper said.

But Kara looked it over and said, 'Magician's adhesive wax. Maybe he had an open capsule of the drug stuck to the palm of his hand. When he reached over her drink or coffee he tipped it in.'

Within the bag Cooper also found some tiny metallic shavings and a circular black mark—as if from some residue on the bottom of a small bottle. An examination through the microscope revealed the metal was probably brass and there were unique machining patterns on the metal. But any deductions were beyond Lincoln Rhyme.

'Send some pictures down to our friends in the Bureau,' he said.

Cooper took the images and emailed them to Washington. The black stains turned out to be permanent ink. But the database couldn't identify what kind specifically.

'What's that?' Rhyme asked, looking towards a plastic bag containing some navy-blue cloth.

'We were lucky there,' Sachs said. 'That's the jogging jacket he was wearing when he picked up the Marston woman. We found some things in the pockets.'

The first item they examined was a press pass for one of the big cable TV networks. The reporter's name was Stanley Saferstein and the photo on the pass revealed a thin, brown-haired man with a beard. Sellitto called the network. It turned out that Saferstein was one of their senior reporters. His pass had been stolen last week.

The jacket also contained a grey plastic hotel key-card. Rhyme was delighted. Even though there was no hotel name on it, he assumed it would have codes in the magnetic strip to tell them which hotel and room it belonged to.

Cooper found the manufacturer's name in small type on the back of the card. 'APC Inc., Akron, Ohio.'

In a few minutes the team was on the speakerphone with the president of APC himself. Rhyme explained the situation to him and described the key.

'Ah, that's the APC-42. It's our most popular model. I'm afraid you'll just have to start calling hotels and see who uses grey ones. We have that information here someplace but it could be a day or two.'

After they hung up, Rhyme decided he wasn't content to wait for APC so he had Sellitto send the key to Bedding and Saul with instructions to start canvassing hotels.

Roland Bell returned from the scenes on the West Side and was briefed on what the team had learned so far. They then returned to the evidence and found the Conjurer's running jacket contained something else: a restaurant bill from a place called the Riverside Inn in Bedford Junction, New York. The bill revealed that four people had eaten lunch on Saturday, April 6—two weeks ago.

Sachs shook her head. 'Where's Bedford Junction?'

'Way upstate, I do believe,' Mel Cooper said.

'There's a phone number on the receipt,' Bell drawled. 'Long shot, but who knows?'

It *was* a long shot—too long. The manager and the waitresses there had no idea who might have been in on that Saturday.

'I don't like it,' said Sachs. 'What's he doing with three other people?'

Sellitto added, 'Pattern doers are almost always loners.'

Kara disagreed. 'But he's an illusionist, remember? They always work with other people. You've got volunteers from the audience. Then assistants onstage that the audience knows are working with the performer. And then there are confederates too—people who're working for the illusionist but the audience *doesn't* know it. They might be disguised as stagehands, members of the audience, volunteers. In a good show you're never quite sure who's who.'

'Let's look at what you found where Burke collared him.'

The first item was the officer's handcuffs.

Rhyme studied them carefully. 'I see fresh scratches in the hole. I'd say it was picked . . .'

'But Burke would've frisked him,' Sachs pointed out. 'Where'd he get a pick?'

'Could've been hidden anywhere,' Kara said. 'His hair, his mouth.'

'Mouth?' Rhyme mused. 'Hit the cuffs with the ALS, Mel.'

Cooper donned goggles and shone an alternative light source on the cuffs. 'Yep, we've got some tiny smears and dots around the keyhole.' This meant, Rhyme explained to Kara, the presence of bodily fluid, saliva most likely.

'Houdini did that all the time. Sometimes he'd let somebody from the audience check his mouth. Then just before he did the escape his wife'd kiss him—she was really passing a key from her mouth to his.'

Sachs had also found a tiny piece of serrated-edge metal.

'Yeah, it's his too,' Kara said. 'Another escapologist tool. A razor saw. Probably used it to cut through those plastic bands on his ankles.'

'Would that've been in his mouth too? Wouldn't it be dangerous?'

'With practice it's pretty safe.'

'At the riverside, Sachs, you find anything?'

'Just skid marks in the mud.'

Sellitto asked Bell, 'What about the vic, the Marston woman?'

The detective summarised his interview with her: Cheryl Marston had described the Conjurer as slim, strong, bearded, scars on neck and chest. 'Oh, and she confirmed his fingers *were* deformed, like we thought. Fused together, she said. And he picked the alias "John".'

Useless, Rhyme assessed.

'One thing she said,' Bell added. 'It was like he could read her mind.'

'Body-reading,' Kara said. 'He'd say something and then check out her reactions. That'd tell him a lot about her.'

'Then he drugged her and took her to the pond. Dunked her upside-down.'

'It was a variation of the Water Torture Cell routine,' Kara explained. 'Houdini. One of his most famous.'

'And his escape from the pond?' Rhyme asked Sachs.

'At first I wasn't sure it was him,' she said. 'His clothes were different and his eyebrows too. But he distracted me, used ventriloquism. I was looking right at his face—I never saw his lips move.'

Kara said, 'I'll bet he picked words that didn't have any *b*'s or *m*'s or *p*'s. Probably no *f*'s or *v*'s either.'

'You're right. I think it was something like, "Yo, look out, on your right, that guy in the jogging suit's got a gun." Perfect black dialect.' She grimaced. 'I looked away—the same direction he looked. Then he set off that flash cotton and I got blinded. He got me cold.'

Kara said, 'Don't take it too hard. Hearing's the easiest sensation to fool.'

Sachs continued, 'While Roland and I were still blinded from the flash he took off and slipped into the crafts fair. I saw him fifteen minutes later—this biker, wearing a Harley shirt. He was right *there* in front of me.'

'Man,' Kara said, 'his coins definitely don't talk.'

'What's that?' Rhyme asked. 'Coins?'

'Oh, an expression magicians use. Literally it means you can't hear any clinking when you do coin tricks but we use it to mean somebody's really good. We'd also say he's got "tight tricks".'

Walking to the whiteboard reserved for the magician profile, she picked up the marker and added to it, commenting, 'So, he does close-in and mentalism and even ventriloquism. And animal tricks. We knew he does lock-picking—from the second murder—but now we know he's an escapologist too. What kind of magic *doesn't* he do?'

HARRY HOUDINI was renowned for his escapology but there were many great escapologists who preceded him and were his contemporaries. What set Houdini apart was the challenge. His show involved an invitation to anyone to dare Houdini to escape from a device that the challenger himself provided. He thrived on these challenges.

And so do I, Malerick thought, walking into his apartment now, after his escape from the Harlem River. But he was still badly shaken up by the events that afternoon. When he'd been performing regularly, before the fire, there was often an element of danger in the routines. Real danger. His mentor had beaten into him that if there was no risk how could you possibly hope to engage your audience? But what a series of challenges this particular act had turned out to be; the police were far better than he'd expected.

There was something that he needed to do now. He drew the shades and placed a candle on the mantelpiece, next to a small inlaid wooden box. He struck a match and lit the candle. Then sat on the sofa. He controlled his breathing. Inhaled slowly, exhaled.

Concentrating on the flame, drifting into a meditation. Praying for the spirit of his soul mate to appear, to send him a sign. Malerick used the candle for this communication because it was fire that had taken his love away from him.

And then the candle flickered! Yes, he saw it. The flame moved a fraction closer to the inlaid box. Very possibly it was a sign that the soul of his dead beloved was hovering near.

'Are you there?' he whispered. 'Are you?'

Breathing so very slowly, afraid that his exhalation would reach the candle and make it shiver, Malerick wanted proof positive that he was not alone.

Finally the candle burned itself out.

It was now time to get ready for the next act.

Fire and illusion are soul mates.

Fire, Revered Audience, is the devil's toy and the devil has always been linked to magic. Fire destroys and it creates. Fire transforms.

It's at the heart of our next act, one I call the Charred Man.

'WHERE'S THE FOOD?' Sellito asked, looking out of Rhyme's parlour window. Sachs and Kara had gone up the street to pick up some takeout from a nearby Cuban restaurant.

But the food meant nothing to Thom. He took Rhyme's blood pressure and found the results high. 'I don't like it,' he said. 'Time for bed.'

'It's nine thirty-eight, Thom,' Rhyme pointed out. 'We have a killer on the loose who keeps changing his mind about how often he wants to kill people. I have work to do.'

'No, you don't. If you don't want to call it a night, all right. But we're going upstairs to take care of some things and then you're taking a nap.'

'This is crip abuse,' Rhyme muttered. But he understood the danger. When a quad sits too long in one position or is constricted in the extremities or, as Rhyme loved to put it so indelicately in front of strangers, needs to piss or shit and hasn't for a while—there was a risk of autonomic dysreflexia, a soaring of the blood pressure that could result in a stroke, leading to more paralysis or death. So Rhyme acquiesced to a trip upstairs. It was moments like this—disruptions of 'normal' life—that infuriated him most about his disability.

In the bedroom upstairs Thom took care of the necessary details. 'OK. Two hours' rest.'

'One hour,' Rhyme snapped.

Thom conceded, 'One hour. If you sleep.'

The aide left, closing the door behind him. Rhyme closed his eyes, trying to figure out the Conjurer's motive, what the bits of evidence might mean: the brass, the hotel key, the press pass, the ink . . . Finally his eyes sprang open. Sleeping was out of the question.

He felt a breeze tickle his cheek and was angrier yet at Thom—for leaving the air conditioning on. When a quad's nose runs, there damn well better be somebody nearby to wipe it. He summoned up the climate control panel on the monitor. But the screen told him that the air conditioner was off.

There! He felt it again, a definite waft of air on his other cheek, his right one. He turned his head quickly. Was it from the windows? No, they too were closed.

Then he noticed the door. Oh, no, he thought, chilled to his heart. The door to his bedroom had a bolt on it—a latch that could be closed only by someone in his room. Not from the outside.

It was locked.

Another breath on his skin. Hot, this time. Very close. He heard a faint wheeze too and gasped as a hand appeared suddenly in front of his face, two fingers deformed, fused together. The hand held a razor blade, the sharp edge aimed towards Rhyme's eyes.

'If you call for help,' said the Conjurer in a breathy whisper, 'if you make a noise, I'll blind you. Understood?'

Lincoln Rhyme nodded.

The blade in the Conjurer's hand vanished. One moment it was in his fingers, aimed at Rhyme's face; the next, it was gone.

The man—brown-haired, beardless, wearing a policeman's uniform—walked around the room, examining the books, the CDs. He returned to Rhyme. 'Well,' he said in a throaty whisper, looking over the Flexicair bed. 'You're not what I expected.'

'The car,' Rhyme said. 'In the river? How?'

'Oh, that?' he said dismissively. 'I was never *in* the car. I escaped before it went in the water . . . A simple trick: a closed window—so the witnesses would see mostly glare—and my hat on the headrest.'

'So they weren't skid marks from braking,' Rhyme said. 'They were skid marks from accelerating. You put a brick on the accelerator.'

'A brick wouldn't've looked natural when the divers found the car; I wedged it down with a shoe.' The Conjurer looked Rhyme over closely. 'But you never believed I was dead.'

'How did you get into the room?'

'I was here first. I slipped upstairs ten minutes ago. I was downstairs too in your war room, or whatever you call it.'

'You brought that evidence in?' Rhyme recalled being vaguely aware of a patrolman carting in a box of evidence.

'That's right. I was waiting outside. This cop came up with a couple of boxes. I said hello and offered to help. Nobody ever stops you if you're in a uniform and you seem to have a purpose.'

'And you've been hiding up here—covered up with a piece of silk that was the colour of the walls.'

'You caught on to that trick, did you?'

Rhyme frowned, looking at the man's uniform. It seemed genuine. His heart suddenly sank. He knew where it had come from. Larry Burke, the officer who'd arrested the Conjurer near the street fair. 'You killed him . . . You killed him and stole his clothes.'

The Conjurer shrugged. 'Reverse.'

Rhyme asked in a whisper, 'Where's his body?'

'On the West Side.'

In his heart Lincoln Rhyme would always be a cop. And there is no bond closer than that between fellow police officers. He struggled to remain calm and asked casually, 'How did you find me?'

'At the crafts fair. I got close to that red-headed policewoman. Anyway I heard her talking to you on her radio. She mentioned your name. Then it just took a little research to find you. You're famous.'

'Famous? A freak like me?'

'Apparently.'

Rhyme shook his head and said slowly. 'I'm old news. The chain of command passed me by a long time ago.'

The word 'command' zipped from Rhyme's mouth through the microphone mounted to the headboard into the voice-recognition software in his computer. 'Command' was the latch word that told the computer to be prepared for instructions. A window opened up on the monitor, which he could see but the Conjurer could not. *Instruction?* it asked silently.

'Chain of command?' the Conjurer asked. 'What do you mean?'

'I used to be in charge of the department. Now, sometimes the young officers, they won't even return my telephone call.'

The computer seized the last two words of the sentence. Its response: *Whom would you like to call?*

Rhyme sighed. 'I'll tell you a story. I needed to get in touch with an officer the other day. A lieutenant. Lon Sellitto.'

The computer reported: *Dialling Lon Sellitto.*

And I told him—'

A sudden frown from the Conjurer. He stepped forward quickly, swinging the monitor away from Rhyme's face and looking it over. Then he grimaced, ripped the phone lines from the wall and unplugged the computer. With a faint pop it went silent.

Rhyme pressed his head back into the pillows, expecting the razor blade to appear. But the killer seemed more impressed than angered.

'You know what that was, don't you?' he asked, smiling coldly. 'Classic verbal misdirection. That was good. What you were saying was natural—until you mentioned the name. Telling me the name *wasn't* natural. It made me suspicious. But up to then you were good.'

The Immobilised Man . . .

'I'm good too, though.' The Conjurer smiled and stepped back. He glanced across the room into the shadows on the far wall. 'Now, Revered Audience, let's begin our routine with some prestidigitation. I'll be assisted by a fellow performer here.' These words were spoken in an eerie, theatrical tone.

The killer's hand rose and he displayed the glistening razor blade. He tugged at the waistband of Rhyme's sweatpants and underwear and tossed the blade down towards his naked groin.

Rhyme stared at the front of his pants, waiting for blood to appear.

The Conjurer smiled. 'But maybe the blade's not there . . . Maybe it's someplace else.' He reached into his mouth and pulled out the steel rectangle. Then he removed three more blades from his mouth.

Rhyme glanced at the alarm clock. Thom had left only fifteen minutes ago. He asked, 'Those people you killed? What was the point?'

'They weren't *all* killed,' the Conjurer pointed out angrily. 'You ruined my performance with the equestrian by the Hudson River.'

'Well, *attacked* then. Why?'

'It was nothing personal,' he said and broke into a coughing spell. 'It was more what they represented than who they were.'

The Conjurer looked at the door. 'We don't have much time.' He walked slowly round Rhyme's bed, breathing hard. 'There's a trick called the Burning Mirror. My favourite. It starts out with an illusionist looking vainly in the mirror. He sees a beautiful woman on the other side of the glass. She beckons and he steps through. We see they've changed places. The woman's now on the front side of the mirror. But there's a puff of smoke and she becomes Satan.

'Now the illusionist is trapped in hell, chained to the floor. Flames begin to shoot up from the floor around him. Just as he's about to be engulfed by flames he gets out of the chains and leaps through the fire at the back of the mirror to safety. The devil vanishes. The illusionist shatters the mirror with a hammer. Then he pauses and snaps his fingers. There's a flash of light and, you've probably guessed, he's become the devil . . . The audience loves it . . . But I know that part of everyone's mind is rooting for the performer to die.' He paused. 'And, of course, that *does* happen from time to time.'

'Who *are* you?' Rhyme whispered.

'Me?' The Conjurer leaned forward and passionately rasped, 'I'm the Wizard of the North. I'm the greatest illusionist who ever was.

I'm Houdini. I'm the man who can escape from the burning mirror. From handcuffs, chains, locked rooms, shackles, ropes, *anything* . . .' He eyed Rhyme closely. 'Except . . . except you. You're too good. I had to stop you before tomorrow afternoon . . .'

'Why? What's happening tomorrow afternoon?'

The Conjurer didn't answer. He looked into the gloom. 'Now, Revered Audience, our main act—the Charred Man. Look at our performer—no chains, no handcuffs, no ropes. Yet he can't escape.'

A small grey object appeared in the Conjurer's hand and the killer slapped a piece of duct tape over Rhyme's mouth. He then shut out all the lights in the room except a nightlight. He returned to Rhyme's bed and held an index finger up and flicked his thumb against it. A three-inch point of flame rose from the digit.

'Fire . . . Isn't it fascinating? Probably the most compelling image in illusionism. It's the perfect misdirection. Everyone watches flame. I could do anything with my other hand and you'd never notice. For instance . . .' Rhyme's bottle of Scotch appeared in the man's grip. He took a sip of liquor and held the flaming finger in front of his lips, looking directly at Rhyme, who cringed. But the Conjurer smiled, turned aside and blew the flaming spray towards the ceiling, stepping back slightly as the stream of fire vanished into the darkness.

Rhyme's eyes flickered to the wall in the corner of the room.

The Conjurer laughed. 'Smoke detector? I got that earlier.' He set the bottle down.

Suddenly a white handkerchief appeared. It was soaked in gasoline. The Conjurer draped the handkerchief round Rhyme's neck. Then he walked towards the door, silently opened the deadbolt and then the door, looked out.

Rhyme's nose detected another scent mixed with the gasoline. What was it? A rich, smoky scent . . . Oh, Scotch. It was overpowering. There was Scotch everywhere. And Rhyme understood with dismay what the man was doing. He'd poured a stream of liquor from the door to the bed, like a fuse. The Conjurer flicked his finger and a white fireball flew from his hand into the pool of single malt.

The liquor ignited and blue flames raced along the floor. Soon the fire would climb up the bedclothes and begin devouring his body, which he wouldn't feel, and then his face and head, which he horribly would. He turned to the Conjurer but the man was gone. Smoke began to sting Rhyme's eyes and fill his nose.

Soon the blue and yellow flames began lapping at the blankets at the foot of Lincoln Rhyme's bed.

CHAPTER SIX

A diligent NYPD police officer, perhaps hearing an odd noise, perhaps seeing an unlocked door, stepped into a West Side alleyway. Fifteen seconds later another man emerged, dressed in a lightweight maroon turtleneck, tight jeans, baseball cap.

No longer in the role of Officer Larry Burke, Malerick began walking purposefully up Broadway. He paused at a basement cocktail lounge, glanced inside. He decided this would be a good place in which to hide out temporarily.

He found a stool at the bar and ordered a Sprite and a turkey sandwich. Looking around: the arcade games with their electronic soundtracks, the room smoky and dark. The liquor-induced laughter and hum of pointless conversation. All of which transported him back to the world of his youth in the city built from sand.

Las Vegas is a mirror surrounded by glaring lights. It's a dusty, hard place where the cheery illumination of the Strip fades fast just a block or two from the neon. And everywhere the dusty, endless, beige desert. This was the world that Malerick was born into.

Father a blackjack dealer and mother a restaurant hostess, they were two of the army of Vegas service people. Like many Vegas children left on their own by parents working long and irregular shifts—and like children living in bitter homes everywhere—their son had gravitated to a place where he found some comfort.

And that place for him was the Strip.

The Strip was his refuge. The magic shops specifically. Las Vegas is known among performers around the world as the Capital of Magic. The boy found that these shops were places where performing and apprentice magicians hung out to share stories and tricks.

It was in one of these that the boy learned something important about himself. He might be skinny and timid but he was miraculously dexterous. The men working in these places—clerks in magic stores are usually aspiring or retired magicians themselves—would show him palms and pinches and drops and conceals and he'd pick them up instantly. One of these clerks lifted an eyebrow and said about the thirteen-year-old, 'A born prestidigitator.'

The boy had never heard the word.

'A French magician made it up in the nineteenth century,' the man explained. '"Presti" as in presto, fast. "Digit" as in finger. Prestidigitation—fast fingers. Sleight of hand.'

He'd leave school every afternoon and head directly to his favourite store, where he'd sop up method. At home he practised constantly. One of the shop managers would hire him occasionally to put on demonstrations.

He could still picture his initial step up onto the stage. From that day on, Young Houdini—his first stage name—would talk his way onstage at any opportunity. What a joy it was to mesmerise his audience, delight them. Scare them too. He liked to scare them.

Finally he got busted—by his mother. The woman eventually realised that the boy hardly spent any time at home and raided his room to find out why. 'I found this money,' she snapped, rising from her dinner and waddling into the kitchen one evening to confront him as he walked in the back door. 'Explain.'

'It's from Abracadabra.'

'Who's *that*?'

'The store? By the Tropicana. I was telling you about it—'

'You stay off the Strip.'

'Mom, it's just a store. That magic store.'

'Where you been? Drinking? Let me smell your breath.'

'Mom, no.' Backing away, repulsed by the massive woman in the pasta-sauce-stained top, her own breath horrific. 'I was just at the store. I do a little show. People give me tips sometimes.'

'Show? What kind of show?'

'Magic.' He was frustrated. He'd told her this months before. 'Watch.' He did a card trick for her.

'That was good,' she said, nodding. 'But for lying to me I'm keeping this money.'

'I didn't lie!'

'You didn't tell me what you're doing. That's the same as lying.' With some effort she stuffed the money into a jeans pocket sealed closed by her belly. Then she hesitated. 'OK, here's ten back. If you tell me something. You ever seen your father with Tiffany Loam?'

'I don't know . . . Who's that?'

'You know. That waitress from the Sands was over here with her husband a couple months ago for dinner. She was in that yellow blouse. Did you see them? Driving out to the desert yesterday?'

'I didn't see them.'

She examined him closely and decided he was telling the truth. 'If you *do* see them you let me know.'

And she left him for her spaghetti, coagulating on a TV tray in the living room.

One day, performing a show, the boy was surprised to notice a slim, unsmiling man enter the store. All the magicians and clerks in the store fell silent. He was a famous illusionist appearing at the Tropicana. He was known for his temper and his dark, scary illusions.

After the show the illusionist gestured the boy over. 'Do some more.' Nodding at a velvet table.

The boy did, nervous now.

'Let me see your hands,' the illusionist said.

Young Houdini held his palms up and the man touched them, stroked them with his thumbs. It felt to the boy that there was an electric current running between them.

'You've got the hands to be great,' he whispered to the boy. 'You've got the drive and I *know* you've got the cruelty . . . But you don't have the vision. Not yet.' A razor blade appeared and he used it to slice through a piece of paper, which began to bleed. He crumpled the paper and then opened it up. There was no slash and no blood. He handed it to the boy, who noticed that on the inside was an address, written in red ink.

'Come see me,' he whispered, his lips brushing the boy's ear. 'You have a lot to learn. And I have a lot to teach.'

Young Houdini couldn't work up the courage to go to see him. Then, at his fifteenth birthday party, his mother flew into a rage and flung a platter of fettucini at her husband.

The boy decided he'd had enough. The next day he went to visit the illusionist, who agreed to be his mentor. The timing was perfect. In two days the man was starting an extensive tour of the United States. He needed an assistant. Young Houdini ran away from home to work as a magician.

SHE HEARD THE SIRENS when they were two blocks from Rhyme's. The sound seemed to be coming from the direction of his town house.

Of course it wasn't, Amelia Sachs decided.

But then, the flashing lights, blue and red, *were* on Central Park West, where his place was located. Too much of a coincidence.

Come on, girl, she reassured herself. It's your imagination, stoked by the horror of the Conjurer's murders. Forget it.

Shifting the large shopping bag containing garlicky Cuban food to the other hand, she and Kara continued down the busy pavement.

The young woman sipped her double Cuban coffee, to which, she said, she'd become addicted at first taste. 'I'll tell you, I love finds like this. It's the little things in life, don't you think?'

But Sachs had lost the thread of the conversation. Another ambulance sped by. The vehicle braked to a fast stop at the corner next to Rhyme's building.

Heart pounding, Sachs dropped the bag and began sprinting.

As she turned the corner she looked up and gasped in shock. Smoke was drifting out of Rhyme's bedroom.

Sachs ducked under the police line and ran towards the cluster of fire-fighters in the doorway. She leapt up the front steps.

'No, Amelia!' Lon Sellitto's gruff voice cut through the hallway.

She turned, panicked, thinking that he wanted to stop her from seeing Lincoln's burnt corpse. If the Conjurer had taken Lincoln from her he was going to die. Nothing in the world would stop her.

'Lon!'

The detective embraced her. 'No, no, it's OK. Thom brought him down to the guest room in the back. This floor.'

Thom, grim-faced, joined them. 'He's all right, Amelia. No burns, some smoke inhalation. It'll be OK.'

'What happened?' she asked the detective.

'The Conjurer,' Sellitto muttered. 'He killed Larry Burke. Stole his uniform. That's how he got in. Somehow he snuck up to Rhyme's room. He set a fire round his bed. Somebody saw the smoke from the street and called nine-one-one. And Dispatch called me. Thom and Mel and I got most of it out before the trucks got here.'

She asked Sellitto, 'I don't suppose we got him.'

A bitter laugh. 'Whatta you think? He vanished. Thin air.'

'LINCOLN!' Sachs walked fast into the guest room, sat on the bed and hugged him hard. He lowered his head against her hair. She was crying. He'd only seen tears in her eyes perhaps twice since he'd known her.

'No first names,' he whispered. 'Bad luck, remember.'

'You're OK?'

'Yes, I'm fine,' he said, still in a whisper, troubled by the illogical fear that if he spoke louder the particles of smoke would somehow puncture and deflate his lungs.' Search the scene. There's got to be something that he's left behind. There was that handkerchief he put round my neck. And he had some razor blades.'

Sachs said she would and left the room.

Twenty minutes later she returned. 'Didn't find much,' she

reported. 'Got that handkerchief and a couple of footprints. He's wearing a new pair of Eccos.'

'Well, search again. You missed things. You must have.'

'Forget the crime scene. It's toast—so to speak. I'm going to interview the witness.' Sachs stepped to the doorway, called down the hall to Lon Sellitto: 'You have your tape recorder?'

'Sure.' He ambled in and handed it to her. 'There's a wit?'

Rhyme said, 'Well, who the hell is it?'

'You,' she said, pulling a chair close to the bed.

'Me? Ridiculous.'

'No. Not ridiculous.' She examined Sellitto's small recorder, checked the tape and clicked it on.

'This is NYPD Patrol Officer Amelia Sachs, interviewing Lincoln Rhyme, witness in a ten-twenty-four assault and ten-twenty-nine arson at 345 Central Park West. The date is Saturday, April 20th.' She set the recorder on the table near Rhyme. 'Now,' she said. 'Description.'

A look at the ceiling. 'He was medium-built, male, approximately fifty to fifty-five years of age, wearing a police officer's uniform. No beard. Scar tissue and discoloration on his neck and on his chest.'

'You could see his chest?'

'Excuse me,' he said with bright sarcasm. 'Scar tissue at the base of his neck *presumably* continuing down to his chest. Little and ring fingers of his left hand were fused together. He had . . . *appeared* to have brown eyes.'

'Good,' she said. 'We didn't have his eye colour before.'

'And we may not now if he's wearing contacts,' he snapped.

Sachs continued, 'Now. What did he say?'

'Sachs,' he said sardonically, 'don't you think I might've been a little spooked and confused?'

She touched his hand. 'I know you don't trust witnesses. But they do see things . . This is *my* speciality, Rhyme. I'll walk you through it. Just like you walk me through the grid. We'll find something important.' She rose, walked to the door and called, 'Kara?'

A moment later the young woman appeared.

Sachs explained that she wanted Kara to listen, she might recognise something the killer had said that could be helpful to them. The policewoman sat down again. 'Let's go back there, Rhyme. Tell us what happened.'

He began, running through the events as he remembered them. 'It was like he was pretending he was performing a show and I was a fellow performer. I *do* remember one thing. He's got asthma. Or at least he sounded winded. He was gasping for breath a lot, whispering.'

'Good,' Sachs said. 'I'd forgotten he sounded that way at the pond after the Marston assault. What else?'

'That's about it. He was either burning me or threatening to slice me up . . .'

'Come on, Rhyme, go on back there. Now, how do you tell he's here at first? Did you hear anything?'

'No, I felt a draught. He was blowing on my neck and cheek.'

'Just to . . . Why?'

'To scare me, I guess. It worked, by the way.' Rhyme closed his eyes. 'He threatened to blind me if I tried to call for help.'

'How did he get in?'

'He walked in with the officer who brought some evidence from the afternoon scenes.'

'Shit,' Sellitto said. 'From now on we check IDs—everybody who walks through the friggin' door. I mean, *everybody*.'

'What else is he saying?' Sachs continued.

'I don't know,' Rhyme muttered. He was angry with Sachs because she was pushing him. She had to understand how hard it was for him to go back to the flames, to the smoke that threatened his lungs—

Wait. Smoke . . . Lincoln Rhyme said, 'Fire. I think that was what he talked about the most. Seemed like he was obsessed with it. There was an illusion he mentioned. The . . . right, the Burning Mirror.'

Rhyme and Sachs glanced at Kara, who was nodding. 'I've heard of it. But it's rare. Takes a lot of set-up and it's pretty dangerous. Most theatres' owners won't let performers do it nowadays.'

'I told you he was acting as if he were giving a performance? He kept talking to somebody. "My *something* audience."'

'An imaginary audience.'

'Right. Hold on . . . I think it was "respected audience". Talking to them directly.'

Sachs frowned. A glance at Kara, who shrugged. 'We always talk to the audience. It's called patter. In the old days performers would say things like "my esteemed audience".'

Sachs leaned closer to Rhyme. 'Let's say this is your bedroom. You're in the Flexicair. Where was *he* standing?'

'There. Near the foot of the bed, facing me. One thing . . . He was talking about the victims. He said he killed them because of what they *represented*.'

Sachs was frowning. 'There's something wrong. You're using *your* language, not his. Murderers *never* think of the people they kill as "victims". They never humanise them. At least a pattern doer like the Conjurer wouldn't. Did he talk about any of them specifically? How about Cheryl Marston?'

Rhyme closed his eyes, shook his head. 'I don—'

And then the word came to him.

'Equestrian. He called her the equestrian.'

'Excellent!' she said.

Rhyme felt a burst of unreasonable pride.

'How 'bout the others?'

'No, she was the only one he referred to.'

Sellitto said, 'So he thinks of the vics as people doing a particular thing—that may or may not be their jobs. Whatta we *do* with that?'

Sachs replied, 'We don't know yet, Detective. But it's a step closer to figuring him out.' To Rhyme, 'Can you think of anything else?'

'Nope,' he said. 'I think that's it.'

'OK. Good, Rhyme.'

But he recognised the tone in her voice. She wasn't finished.

She continued, 'You weren't gagged the whole time, were you?'

'No, just at the end.'

'That means *you* took part in an *exchange*. Think about it, Rhyme.'

Sure enough, her question jogged something in his mind. 'I remember!' he said. 'I asked him who he was.'

'Good question. And he said?'

'He said he was a wizard . . .' Rhyme struggled to go back to that hard place. 'It reminded me of *The Wizard of Oz* . . . The Wicked Witch of the West.' He frowned. Then he said, 'Yeah, got it. He said he was the Wizard of the North.'

'Does that mean anything to you?' Sachs asked Kara.

'No.'

'He said he could escape from anything. Except, he didn't think that he'd be able to escape from us. Well, from me. That's why he came. He said he had to stop me before tomorrow afternoon.' Rhyme sighed. 'I really think that's it, Sachs.'

Sachs clicked the tape recorder off then leaned forward and with a tissue wiped the sweat off his forehead.

Sellitto asked about the likelihood of some food since his anticipated Cubano sandwich hadn't survived the trip back to the town house. As Thom vanished into the kitchen, Sachs handed Kara the notes she'd taken and asked if she'd write down anything she thought was relevant on the magician profile board. Kara went into the lab.

A few minutes later Mel Cooper walked in. He held up a plastic bag. 'This's all the evidence from the Mazda.' The bag contained what seemed to be a single folded sheet of the *New York Times*.

Rhyme asked him, 'Can you see the date?'

Cooper examined the soggy paper. 'Two days ago.'

'Then it has to be the Conjurer's,' Rhyme noted. 'The car was stolen before then. Can you read anything on it?'

'Nope. And I don't want to unfold it yet. Too wet.'

'OK, get it over to the document lab.'

Cooper arranged for a messenger to take the sample to the NYPD crime lab in Queens and then disappeared into Rhyme's lab.

A few minutes later Kara returned carrying fresh coffee. She said to Sachs, 'I was writing on the board? And I got an idea. So I made a phone call. I think I found out his real name.'

'Whose?' Rhyme asked.

'Well, the Conjurer's.'

The faint ring as Kara stirred the sugar into her coffee became the only sound in the room.

'You've got his *name*?' Sellitto asked. 'Who is he?'

'I think it's a man named Erick Weir. W-E-I-R. He was an illusionist. I called Mr Balzac and I gave him the profile and told him some of the things he'd said to Lincoln. He told me it sounded like Weir.'

'Why?' Sachs asked.

'Well, he'd be about the same age. Early fifties. And Weir was known for dangerous routines. Sleights with razor blades and knives. He's also one of the few people who's ever done the Burning Mirror. And remember I said most magicians specialise? It's really unusual to find one performer who's good at so many different tricks—illusion and escape and protean and sleight, even ventriloquism and mentalism? Well, Weir did all of them. And he was an expert on Houdini. Some of what he's been doing this weekend are Houdini's routines or are based on them.

'Then that thing he also said—about being the Wizard. There was a magician in the nineteenth century, John Henry Anderson. That's what he called himself—the Wizard of the North. He had bad luck with fires. David told me that Weir was badly burned in a circus fire.'

'The scars,' Rhyme said. 'The obsession with fire.'

'And maybe his voice wasn't asthma,' Sachs suggested. 'The fire might've damaged his lungs.'

'When was Weir's accident?' Sellitto asked.

'Three years ago. The circus tent he was rehearsing in was destroyed and Weir's wife was killed. They'd just got married.'

It was a good lead. 'Mel!' Rhyme shouted, forgetting his concerns about imperilling his own lungs. '*Mel!*'

Cooper stepped back into the room. 'Feeling better, I hear.'

'Lexis/Nexis search, ViCAP, NCIC and state databases. Details on an Erick Weir. W-E-I-R. Performer, illusionist. He may be our perp.'

'You found his *name*?' the tech asked, impressed.

A nod towards Kara. '*She* found his name.'

After a few minutes Cooper returned with a number of print-outs. 'Not much,' he said. 'Erick Albert Weir. Born Las Vegas, October 1950. Virtually no early history. He worked for various circuses and casinos as an assistant then he went out on his own as an illusionist and quick-change artist. Married Marie Cosgrove three years ago. Just after that he was appearing in the Thomas Hasbro and The Keller Brothers circus in Cleveland. During a rehearsal a fire broke out. The tent was destroyed and he was badly burned and his wife was killed. No mention of him after that.'

'Track down Weir's family.'

Sellitto called some Homicide task force detectives in the Big Building and put them on the job.

'A few other things,' Cooper said, flipping through the print-outs. 'A couple of years before the fire Weir was arrested and convicted of reckless endangerment in New Jersey. A member of the audience was badly burned when something went wrong onstage. In another show the manager found out Weir was using a real gun and real bullets in an act. Weir wouldn't change the routine so the manager fired him.' More reading. 'In an article I found the names of two assistants who were working with him at the time of the fire. One's in Reno and one's in Las Vegas. I got their numbers from the Nevada State Police.'

'It's earlier their time,' Rhyme pointed out, glancing at the clock. 'Dig up the speakerphone, Thom.'

Thom vanished. A moment later he returned with the phone, plugged it in, set the unit close to Rhyme on the bedside table.

Sellitto dialled a number. The recorded voice of Arthur Loesser's wife answered and told them that the family wasn't home but please leave a message. Sellitto did so then he dialled the other assistant.

John Keating answered and Sellitto explained they were in the middle of an investigation and had some questions for him.

A pause, then a man's nervous voice rattled out of the tiny speaker. 'OK. I guess it's OK.'

Sellitto asked, 'You used to work for a man named Erick Weir, didn't you?'

'Mr Weir? Well, uh-huh. I did. Why?' The voice was edgy.

'We just have some general questions,' Sellitto said. 'Have you had any contact with him lately?'

The words clattered like marbles on metal. 'I hadn't heard from Mr Weir for years. I thought he was dead. There was a fire in Ohio. He got burned. Real bad. He disappeared. But then maybe six or seven weeks ago he called.'

'From where?' Rhyme asked.

'I don't know. He didn't say. I didn't ask.'

Rhyme asked, 'What did he want?'

'He wanted to know if I still kept up with anybody at the circus where the fire happened. The Hasbro circus. Hasbro's not even in business any more. After the fire the owner folded it and it became a different show. Why would I keep up with anybody there?'

Sachs continued, 'Can you tell us anything about him in general. Other friends, places he liked to go, hobbies.'

'Sure,' came the voice, snappy. 'There *was* nothing else. He was totally absorbed in the profession.'

She asked, 'Well, what about his frame of mind? How he thought about things?'

A long pause. 'Fifty minutes, twice a week for three years I've been trying to figure him out and I can't. Ever since the fire. And he still hurts me. I—' Keating broke into a harsh laugh. 'You catch that? I said "hurts". I meant to say "haunts". How's that for Freudian?'

Rhyme said, 'We heard his wife was killed in the fire. Do you know anything about her family?'

'Marie? No, they'd only gotten married a week or two before the fire. They were really in love. We thought she'd calm him down. But we never got to know her.'

'Can you give us the names of anybody who might know something about him?'

'Art Loesser was first assistant. I was the second. They called us "Erick's boys". Everybody did.'

Rhyme said, 'We have a call in to Loesser. Anyone else?'

'The only one I can think of is the manager of the Hasbro circus at the time. Edward Kadesky's his name. He's a producer in Chicago now, I think. Look, I should go.'

After they hung up, Sachs walked to the speakerphone to hit the disconnect button. 'Brother,' she muttered.

'Well, at least we've got a lead,' Rhyme said. 'Track down Kadesky.'

Mel Cooper disappeared for a few minutes and when he returned he had found Kadesky Productions on South Wells Street in Chicago. Sellitto placed a call and, not surprisingly, being late Saturday night, got the answering service. He left a message.

Sellitto said, 'He's messed up his assistant's life. He's unstable. He's injured people. But what's making him tick?'

Sachs looked up at this. 'Let's give Terry a call.'

Terry Dobyns was an NYPD psychologist. Sellitto placed a call to Dobyns at home.

'Terry.'

'Lon. You've got speakerphone echo. Let me deduce that Lincoln's there too.'

'Yep,' Rhyme confirmed. He had a fondness for Dobyns, the first person he saw when he woke up after the accident in which he broke his spine.

'Sorry it's late,' Sellitto offered. 'But we need some help with a multiple doer.'

'This the one in the news?'

'Right. We're at a loss. And he's told Lincoln that he's going to start up again tomorrow afternoon.'

'He *told* Lincoln? Over the phone? A letter?'

'In person,' Rhyme said.

Sellitto and Rhyme gave the man a run-down on Weir.

Dobyns asked a number of questions. He fell silent for a moment, then he finally said, 'I see two forces at work in him. Is he still performing?'

'No,' Kara said. 'He hasn't performed since the fire.'

'Public performing', Dobyns said, 'is such an intense experience, that when it's denied someone who was successful the loss is profound. The fire basically eradicated the man he had been.'

The Vanished Man, Rhyme reflected.

'That in turn means he's now motivated not by ambition to succeed or to please his audience or a devotion to his craft but by anger. And that's aggravated by the second force: the fire deformed him and damaged his lungs.'

'So he wants to get even?'

'Yes, but not necessarily in a literal sense. Fire quote "murdered" him—his old persona—and by murdering someone else he feels better; it reduces the anxiety that the anger builds up in him.'

'Why these victims?'

'There's something about them that's tapped into his anger. I don't know what it could be—not yet, not without more data.'

'One other thing, Terry. He also seemed to be talking to an imaginary audience . . . Wait, I thought it was "respected" audience. But I just remembered—it was "revered".'

' "Revered",' the psychologist said. 'That's important. After his career and his loved one were taken away from him he shifted his reverence, his *love*, to an audience—an impersonal mass. People who prefer groups can be dangerous to individual human beings. And in Weir's case it's even more dangerous because he's not talking to *real* audiences, only his imaginary one. This suggests to me that actual people have no value to him at all. This guy's going to be a tough one.'

'Thanks, Terry.'

'Go to bed,' Thom said to Rhyme after they hung up.

'All right, all right,' Rhyme conceded. He was tired. And, though he wouldn't admit it, the fire had scared him badly.

The team departed for their respective homes.

Sachs disappeared up the stairs. 'I'm showering,' she called.

Ten minutes later Rhyme heard her walk downstairs. But she didn't join him right away. From different parts of the house came thuds and creaks, muted words with Thom. Then finally she returned to the guest room. She was wearing her favourite pyjamas—black T-shirt and silk boxers—but she had two items that were atypical of her sleep gear. Her Glock pistol and her issue flashlight.

'That guy gets into places too damn easy,' she said, setting both on the table next to her. 'I checked every square inch of the house, balanced chairs against all the doors and told Thom if he hears anything to give me a shout—but to stay put. I'm in the mood to shoot somebody but I'd really rather it wasn't him.'

PART II: METHOD

Sunday, April 18

CHAPTER SEVEN

Sunday morning passed in frustration as the search for Erick Weir stalled. The team learned that after the fire in Ohio the illusionist had remained in the burns unit of a local hospital for several weeks and then left without officially checking out. There was a record that he sold his house in Las Vegas not long after but no record of him buying another.

No reports from the Violent Criminal Apprehension Program or the National Crime Information Center. The officers tracking down Weir's family found only that both parents were deceased, that he was an only child and that no next of kin could be located.

Late in the morning Weir's other assistant, Art Loesser, returned their call from Las Vegas. The man wasn't surprised to learn that his former boss was wanted in connection with a crime and echoed what they'd learned already: that Weir was one of the world's greatest illusionists but that he took the profession far too seriously and was known for his dangerous illusions and hot temper. Loesser still had nightmares about being his apprentice.

'When did you last see him?' Sachs asked. She was in plain clothes today—jeans and a forest-green knit blouse.

'In the hospital, the burns unit. All he'd talk about was getting even with anybody who'd ever hurt him. Then he disappeared.'

But then, the former protégé explained, Weir had called out of the blue about two months ago. Loesser's wife had taken the call. 'He didn't leave a number and said he'd call back but he never did.'

'He didn't tell your wife what he might be calling about?'

'She said he sounded odd, agitated. He was whispering, hard to understand. I remember that from after the fire. His lungs had been damaged. Made him even scarier.'

Tell me about it, Rhyme thought.

'He asked if we'd heard anything about Edward Kadesky—the producer of the Hasbro show when the fire happened. That was it.'

Loesser couldn't provide any other information and they hung up.

Thom let two policewomen into the lab. Sachs nodded a greeting and introduced them to Rhyme. Diane Franciscovich and Nancy Ausonio, the respondings at the first murder, who had been given the assignment of tracking down the antique handcuffs.

'The handcuffs are Darbys, like you thought,' Ausonio said. 'They're pretty rare—and expensive. But we've got a list—'

'Oh my God, look.' Franciscovich was pointing to the evidence chart, where Thom had written: *Perp's identity: Erick A. Weir.*

Ausonio flipped through the sheets she held. 'Erick Weir placed a mail order for a pair of the cuffs from Ridgeway Antique Weapons in Seattle last month.'

'Address?' Rhyme asked excitedly.

'Post office box in Denver. But the lease lapsed.'

'Method of payment?' Sachs asked.

'Cash.'

Rhyme said, 'At least we've got a confirmation that this is our boy.'

He thanked the officers and Sachs walked them to the door just as Kara arrived, armed with a large coffee cup.

Sellito was delivering a monologue about weight-loss techniques to Roland Bell when he was interrupted by another phone call.

'Lincoln?' the voice crackled through the speakerphone. 'Bedding here. We think we've narrowed the key down to three hotels: the Chelsea Lodge, the Beckman or the . . . what is it?'

'Or the Lanham Arms,' his partner, Saul, supplied.

'Right. They're the only ones using this colour Model 42. We're at the Beckman now. Thirty-four and Fifth.'

'Say, gentlemen?' Bell said into the phone.

'Hey there, Roland. Recognised the accent.'

'You said the Lanham Arms. Where is that?'

'East Seventy-five. Near Lex.'

'Something familiar 'bout the name. Can't quite place it.'

'That's next on our list.'

They left the duo to it.

Cooper's computer beeped and he read an incoming email. 'FBI lab in Washington . . . Finally got a report on the brass shavings in the Conjurer's gym bag. They say the markings suggest they're consistent with a clock mechanism.'

'It's a detonator,' Sachs said solemnly.

'A gas bomb?' Cooper asked, nodding towards the handkerchief Weir had left last night, which had been soaked in gasoline.

'He's got a supply of gas and he's obsessed with fire.'

Rhyme noticed the hour was approaching 12.00. The next victim was going to die soon. But when? A shudder of frustration and anger started at the base of his skull and vanished into his stony body. They had to *move*. But he could come to no conclusions based on the evidence they had. And the day dragged on, slow as an IV drip.

A fax arrived. Cooper read it. 'From the document examiner in Queens. They opened up the newspaper that was in the Mazda. No notations and nothing circled. Those're the headlines.'

He taped it to the board.

ELECTRICAL BREAKDOWN CLOSES POLICE STATION

PARENTS PROTEST POOR SECURITY AT GIRLS' SCHOOL

MILITIA MURDER PLOT TRIAL OPENS MONDAY

SPRING ENTERTAINMENT FOR KIDS YOUNG AND OLD

GOVERNOR, MAYOR TO MEET ON NEW WEST SIDE PLAN

'One of those is significant,' Rhyme said. But which one?

Sellitto's phone rang. As he took the call, everyone stared at him, anticipating another death. But apparently the news wasn't bad. The detective lifted an eyebrow in pleasant surprise and said into the receiver, 'Really? Well, that's not far away. Could you come over here?' He then gave Rhyme's address and hung up.

'Who?'

'Edward Kadesky. The manager of the circus in Ohio, the one where Weir was burned. He's in town. He got the message from his service in Chicago and he's coming over.'

THE MAN WAS STOCKY, of medium height. Silver beard and wavy hair to match. Rhyme, suspicious after Weir's visit last night, greeted Edward Kadesky then asked for identification.

Kadesky complied and offered Sellitto his Illinois driver's licence. Mel Cooper took a look at both the picture and the circus producer and then nodded to Rhyme. The tech had already gone online with Illinois Department of Motor Vehicles and obtained the licence particulars and a picture of the man.

'Your message said this was about Erick Weir?' Kadesky asked.

Rhyme said, 'He's a suspect in a series of homicides.'

'No! Who did he kill?'

'Some local residents. A police officer too,' Sellitto explained. 'We were hoping you could give us information that'd help find him.'

'I haven't heard about him since just after the fire. He blamed me for it, you know . . . It was three years ago. Weir and his assistants were doing the illusion and quick-change acts in our show. Oh, they were good. I mean, astonishing. But Weir scared people. He was a little dictator. And those assistants of his—we called them the Moonies. He had them indoctrinated. Illusion to him was like a religion. Sometimes people got hurt in rehearsal or during the show. Weir couldn't've cared less. He thought magic worked best when there was some risk.' The producer laughed grimly. 'But we can't have that in the *entertainment* business, now, can we? One Sunday morning before the matinée I told the stage manager to let him go.'

'That was the day of the fire?' Rhyme asked.

Kadesky nodded. 'The manager found Weir rigging the stage with propane lines for an illusion of his. The Burning Mirror. He told him what we'd decided. But Weir kept right on rigging the trick. I went down to the stage. He lost it and grabbed me. A propane line was loose. We fell into some metal chairs and, I guess, a spark ignited the gas. He was burned and his wife was killed. The whole tent was destroyed. We talked about suing him but he snuck out of the hospital and disappeared.' The producer looked at his watch. The time was 1.45. 'You know, my show starts in fifteen minutes . . . I think it'd be a good idea to get a few more police cars over there. With Weir around and everything that happened between us.'

'Over where?' Rhyme asked.

'To my show.' He nodded towards Central Park.

'That's *yours*?' The Cirque Fantastique?'

'Right. I assumed you knew that. Cirque Fantastique *is* the old Hasbro and Keller Brothers circus.'

Rhyme glanced at Kara, who was shaking her head. 'Mr Balzac never told me that when I called him last night.'

Rhyme said, 'So this is in effect the same show Weir was fired from.'

'Technically, yes. The acts are very different. But a lot of the same people are in this production. I—'

'*That's* what Weir's doing here,' Rhyme announced. 'Your show's his target. Cirque Fantastique.'

Scanning the evidence again. Applying facts to the premise.

'Damn dogs! Look at the chart. The animal hairs and Central Park dirt are from the dog knoll! Right outside the window.' A fierce nod towards the front of his town house. 'He wasn't there to check out Cheryl Marston on the bridlepath; he was checking out the *circus*. The newspaper, the one in his Mazda—look at that headline: "Entertainment for Kids Young and Old". Call up the paper—see if there's information about the circus in it. Thom—call Peter! Hurry.'

The aide was good friends with a *New York Times* reporter. He grabbed the phone and placed the call. It took less than a minute to find the answer: 'The circus was the feature of the story. All sorts of details—hours, acts, bios of employees. Even a sidebar on security.'

Rhyme snapped, 'He was doing his research . . . And the press pass? That'd give him access to backstage.' Rhyme squinted at the evidence chart. 'Yes! I get it now. The victims. What did they represent? Jobs in the circus. A make-up artist. A horseback rider . . . And the first victim! Singing and entertaining kids—like a clown.'

'And the murder techniques themselves,' Sachs pointed out. 'They were all magic tricks.'

'Yep. He's after your show. Terry Dobyns said his motive was ultimately revenge. Hell, he's planted a fuel bomb.'

'My God,' Kadesky said. 'There are two thousand people there! And the show's starting in ten minutes.'

At two in the *afternoon* . . . 'The Sunday matinée,' Rhyme added. 'Just like in Ohio three years ago.'

Sellitto grabbed his Motorola and called the officers stationed at the circus. There was no answer. The detective frowned and placed a call on Rhyme's speakerphone.

'Officer Koslowski here,' the man answered a moment later.

Sellitto identified himself. 'Why isn't your radio on, Officer?' he barked.

'Well, Detective, we were told to stand down. Some detective came by a half-hour ago and told us we weren't needed any more. Said we could take the rest of the day off.'

'Describe him.'

'Fifties. Beard, brown hair.'

'Where'd he go?'

'No idea. Walked up to the car, flashed his shield and dismissed us.'

Sellitto slammed the disconnect. 'It's happening . . .' He shouted to Sachs, 'Get the Bomb Squad there.' Then he called Central and had Emergency Services and fire trucks sent to the circus.

Kadesky ran towards the door. 'I'll evacuate the tent.'

'I want more plain-clothes officers in the park,' Rhyme said. 'I have a feeling the Conjurer's going to be there.'

'Be there?' Sellitto asked.

'To watch the fire. He wouldn't miss this for the world.'

HE WASN'T WORRIED so much about the fire itself. As Edward Kadesky sprinted the short distance from Rhyme's apartment to the tent of the Cirque Fantastique he was thinking that with fire retardants, circus tent fires proceed fairly slowly. No, the real danger is the panic, the stampede that tramples and crushes and suffocates.

Saving people in a circus disaster means getting them out of the facility without panic. Traditionally, to alert the employees that a fire has broken out the ring master would send a subtle signal to the band leader, who would then launch into the John Philip Sousa march, *Stars and Stripes Forever*. The workers were then supposed to calmly lead the audience through designated exits. The tune had been replaced over the years by far more efficient procedures.

Edward Kadesky ran into the tent and saw 2,600 people eagerly awaiting the opening of his show.

His young, brunette assistant noticed and instantly joined him. 'What?' she whispered.

He told her what he'd learned.

'How do we handle it?' she asked tersely.

He considered this for a moment then gave her instructions.

She nodded and walked first to the lighting man and then to the band leader to deliver Kadesky's instructions.

Kadesky glanced at the orchestra, nodded. A drumroll began.

As he strode, smiling, into the middle of the ring the audience fell silent. He stopped and the drumroll ceased. A moment later two fingers of white illumination—the main spots—targeted him. He lifted a cordless microphone and began to speak. 'Good afternoon, ladies and gentlemen, welcome to the Cirque Fantastique.' Calm, pleasant, commanding. 'We have a wonderful show for you today. And to begin I'm going to ask your indulgence. We have a special performance outside the tent. So I'm going to ask you to hold on to your ticket stubs and step outside into Central Park. Find space anywhere nearby. If you can see the buildings on Central Park South you'll be able to watch the act just fine.'

The crowd began murmuring excitedly. What could he mean? Were there daredevils doing high-wire acts on the skyscrapers?

'Now, lower rows first, in an orderly manner.'

The house lights went up. The audience chatted as they rose and ambled towards the exits to safety. But Kadesky was thinking. It was now 2.10. When was the bomb set to go off? Probably not right away. Weir would give the latecomers a chance to arrive and take their seats—to cause the most injuries. And where was it?

Smiling broadly, Kadesky continued to tell people what a delightful act awaited them outside. Suddenly loud music interrupted him. He glanced at the bandstand. The musicians had left—as ordered—but the band leader stood over the computer console that controlled the prerecorded music they sometimes used. Their eyes met and Kadesky nodded in approval. The leader, an old veteran of circus life, had put on a tape and turned the volume up. The tune was *The Stars and Stripes Forever*.

WEARING A BELLHOP'S UNIFORM that closely matched those worn by the staff at the Lanham Arms Hotel, Malerick walked along its fourteenth floor hallway. He carried a room service tray on which was a domed plate cover and a vase containing a huge red tulip.

Only one thing set him apart from the other bellhops at the Lanham: under the dome was not a plate of eggs Benedict but a loaded Beretta automatic pistol, equipped with a sound suppressor, and a leather pouch of lock-picking and other tools.

He wondered what sort of excitement was unfolding inside the white tent of the Cirque Fantastique—the place to which he'd spent the past few days directing the police with the clues he'd left at the sites of the murders. Or *mis*directing them, he should say.

Misdirection and ruse were the keys to successful illusion and there was no one better at it than Malerick, the man who materialised like a struck match, who disappeared like a snuffed flame.

The man who vanished himself.

The police would be frantic, of course, looking for the gasoline bomb. But there was no bomb.

At the end of the hallway Malerick observed that he was alone. Quickly he set the tray on the floor near a doorway and lifted the cover. He slipped the black pistol and pouch into a zippered pocket. Moving fast, he raised the window. He stepped carefully onto the twenty-inch-wide ledge, 150 feet above the ground.

After a stroll of only fifteen feet he came to the corner of the hotel and stopped, looking at the building next door to the Lanham Arms.

This, an apartment building facing East 75th Street, had no ledges but did have a fire escape, six feet away from where he now stood. Malerick took a brief running start and leapt over the gap, easily reaching the fire escape and vaulting over the railing.

He climbed up two flights and paused at a window on the sixteenth floor. A glance inside. The corridor was empty. He placed the gun and the tool kit on the window ledge then stripped off the bellhop's uniform, revealing beneath it a grey suit, white shirt and tie. The gun went into his belt and he used the tools to open the window lock. He hopped inside.

Malerick then walked down the corridor towards the apartment he sought. Stopping at the door, in three seconds he'd scrubbed the lock open. In five, the deadbolt. A moment later he was inside the hallway of the apartment. Malerick eased the door shut silently.

On the walls of the hallway were some portraits and a clumsy watercolour of New York painted by a child. The artist's signature was 'Chrissy': Christine Grady, the daughter of New York assistant district attorney Charles Grady. The man whose apartment this was.

The man Malerick was being paid $100,000 to kill.

THE BRASSY MUSIC from the tent stopped and Edward Kadesky stepped outside. The Bomb Squad and a dozen firemen had scoured the tent and found no device. A tarp-covered box had turned out to contain toilet paper. The trailers and supply trucks held nothing either.

Sachs, one of the first officers to have arrived, frowned. They'd been wrong? How could that be? It seemed that all the evidence had come together and pointed directly to the Cirque Fantastique as the Conjurer's target.

MALERICK PAUSED, listening to the voices he heard from the living room and kitchen of the apartment. He knew his way around; he'd been here once before briefly—disguised as a maintenance man—but that had been basic reconnaissance.

Now, Malerick hung a fake NYPD badge round his neck. He glanced in a mirror. Yes, he was in role, looking like a detective here to protect a prosecutor against whom death threats had been made.

And now, Revered Audience, the real show is about to begin . . .

Malerick turned the corner of the corridor and strode into the living room.

'HEY, HOW'S IT GOING?' the man in the grey suit asked, startling Luis Martinez, the quiet, slim detective working for Roland Bell.

Martinez was sitting on the couch, a Sunday *New York Times* in his lap. He glanced at the newcomer's badge and ID. 'You the relief?'

'That's right.'

'How'd you get in? They give you a key?'

'Got one downtown.' He was speaking in a throaty whisper, like he had a cold.

'Lucky you,' Luis muttered. 'We've gotta share one. Pain in the ass.'

'Where's Mr Grady?'

'In the kitchen,' Luis said. He frowned. 'I don't think I know you.'

'Name's Joe David,' the man said. 'Usually work over in Brooklyn. This is my first rotation here. Bodyguard detail.'

'OK, how 'bout your last, too?' Luis dropped the newspaper and leapt up, drawing his Glock and pointing it at the man he knew was Erick Weir. He shouted, 'He's *here*!'

Two officers waiting in the kitchen—Bell and Lon Sellitto—shoved through another doorway. They grabbed Weir's arms and pulled a silenced pistol from his belt.

'Down, now, now!' Sellitto shouted, his gun pressed into the man's face. And what an expression was on it! Luis thought. He'd seen a lot of surprised perps over the years, but this guy took the prize.

'Where the hell d'he come from?' Sellitto asked breathlessly.

Bell was calling others on his Handie-Talkie. 'Heaven help me—he got inside . . . I don't know how.'

Two uniformed officers hurried in from the hallway, where they'd been hidden near the elevator. 'Looks like he jemmied the window on this floor,' one of them said. 'You know, at the fire escape.'

Bell glanced at Weir and he understood. 'The ledge from the Lanham? You jumped?'

Weir said nothing but that had to be the answer.

Sellitto donned latex gloves and patted him down. The search yielded burglary tools and various props. The oddest were the fake fingertips, glued on tightly. Sellito pulled them off and deposited them into a plastic evidence bag.

'Any ID?' Bell asked.

Sellitto shook his head. 'FAO Schwarz.' The name of the toy store was used to mean low-quality fake NYPD badges and ID card.

'How did you figure it out?' Weir asked.

Sellitto supplied an answer of sorts. 'There's somebody who'd love to answer that question in person. Come on, we're going for a ride.'

LOOKING OVER the double-handcuffed killer standing in the doorway of his lab, Lincoln Rhyme said, 'Welcome back.'

'But . . . the fire.' Dismayed, the man looked towards the stairway that led up to the bedroom.

'Sorry we ruined your performance,' Rhyme said coldly. 'I guess you couldn't quite escape from me after all, could you, Weir?'

He hissed, 'That's not my name any more. Weir's who I *used* to be.'

Rhyme recalled psychologist Terry Dobyns's observation that the fire had 'murdered' Weir's old persona. 'What are you calling yourself?'

'That's between me and my audience.'

Ah, yes, his revered audience.

'How'd you find me?' the man wheezed. 'I led you to . . .'

'To the Cirque Fantastique? You did.' When Rhyme had outthought a perp he was pleased to chat. 'You mean you *misdirected* us there. I was looking over the evidence and I got to thinking the whole case seemed a bit too easy.'

'Easy?' Weir coughed briefly.

'After everyone ran off to look for gas bombs at the circus I got this sense that some of the clues had been planted—the shoes you left at the second victim's apartment had dog hairs and dirt and vegetation common to Central Park. It occurred to me that a smart perp might've ground the dirt and hairs into the shoes and left them at the scene so we'd find them and think about the dog knoll next to the circus. And all the talk of fire when you came to see me last night.'

'But I tried to kill you,' Weir wheezed. 'If I'd told you those things to lead you off I'd need you to be alive.'

Rhyme laughed. 'You didn't try to kill me at all. You wanted to make it look that way to give what you told me credibility. The first thing you did after you set the fire in my bedroom was to call nine-one-one from a payphone. I checked with Dispatch. The man who called said he could see the flames from the phone kiosk. Except that it was round the corner. You can't see my room from there.'

Weir closed his eyes as he realised the depth of his mistake.

Rhyme stared at the evidence board. 'All of the victims had jobs or interests reflecting performers in the circus—the musician, make-up artist, horseback riding. And the murder techniques were magic tricks too. But if your motive really was to destroy Kadesky you'd have led us *away* from Cirque Fantastique, not towards it. That meant you were leading us away from something else. What? At the third scene, by the river, we surprised you—you didn't have time to pick up your jacket with the press pass and hotel key-card in the pocket, which meant that those couldn't've been planted clues.

'The hotel key-card was from one of three hotels—one of them was the Lanham Arms—Detective Bell thought it sounded familiar and checked his logbook. It turned out that he had coffee with Charles Grady in the lobby bar to talk about the security detail for his family a week ago. Roland told me that the Lanham was right next door to Grady's apartment. Then the press pass? I called the reporter you stole it from. He was covering the Andrew Constable trial and had interviewed Charles Grady several times . . . We found some brass shavings and assumed the worst, that they were from a bomb timer. But they might've just come from a key or a tool.'

Sachs took up the narrative. 'Then the *New York Times* page we found in your car we hauled out of the river? It had an article about the circus, yes. But there was also an article about Constable's trial.'

Rhyme continued. 'The restaurant bill was in your jacket too.'

'What bill?' Weir asked, frowning.

'From a restaurant in Bedford Junction, two Saturdays ago.'

'I don't know what you're talking about.'

Rhyme continued. 'Bedford Junction turns out to be the town next to Canton Falls, where Constable lives.'

'Who's this Constable you keep talking about?' Weir asked quickly. But Rhyme could see signs of recognition in his face.

Sellito took over. 'Was the militiaman Jeddy Barnes one of the people you had lunch with?'

'I don't know who you mean.'

'You know about the Patriot Assembly, though?'

'Just what I've read about in the paper.'

'We don't believe you,' Sellito said.

'Believe what you like,' Weir snapped. He had a coughing fit. When it ended he was looking across the room. 'And who are you?'

'I'm an illusionist,' Kara said defiantly.

'One of us,' Weir mocked. 'And you're what? A consultant or something? Maybe after I'm released I'll visit you. Maybe I'll vanish you.'

Sachs snapped, 'Oh, you ain't getting released in this lifetime, Weir.'

Rhyme said, 'Well, I answered your "how". How 'bout you answer my "why"? We thought it was revenge against Kadesky. But it turns out you're after Grady. What are you? Some kind of hit-man illusionist?'

'Revenge?' Weir asked, furious. 'What good is revenge? Will it take the scars away and fix my lungs? Will it bring my wife back? . . . You don't understand! The only thing in my life, the only thing that's *ever* meant anything to me is performing. Illusion, magic. The fire took that away from me. I don't have the strength to perform. My hand's deformed. My voice is ruined. Who'd come to see me? I can't do the one thing that God gave me talent for. If the only way I can perform is to break the law, then that's what I'll do.' He looked around and laughed. 'You really think you can keep me in prison?'

Sellitto said to Rhyme and Sachs, 'I'll take him downtown.'

Rhyme said, 'Hold on. When he got away from Larry Burke after the crafts fair he slipped the cuffs.'

'Right.'

'We found saliva, remember? Take a look in his mouth. See if he's got a pick or key hidden there.'

Sellitto pulled on the latex gloves that Mel Cooper offered. 'Open up. You bite me and I'll vanish your balls.'

The Conjurer opened his mouth and Sellitto shined his flashlight into it, fished around a bit. 'Nothing.'

Kara said, 'Check his teeth. Wiggle them. Especially the molars.'

The Conjurer sighed. 'Right top molar. Right on my side.'

Sellitto reached in and pulled. His hand emerged with a fake tooth. Inside was a small piece of bent metal.

The detective said, 'He can actually use that?'

Kara examined it. 'Oh, he could open a pair of regulation handcuffs in about four seconds with that.'

Rhyme thought of something. 'You have a feeling when he helped us find the pick in his tooth that might've been misdirection?'

Kara nodded. 'You're right.'

Sellitto searched again. He found a second lock pick in a similar fake tooth on the lower left jaw. 'I'm gonna make sure they put you someplace real special,' the detective said ominously. He then shackled Weir's feet with two more sets of cuffs.

'I can't walk this way,' Weir complained.

'Baby steps,' Sellitto said coldly. 'Take baby steps.'

CHAPTER EIGHT

The man got the message at the diner on Route 244, which because he didn't have a phone in his trailer—didn't want one, didn't trust 'em—is where he took and made all his calls.

Hobbs Wentworth was a bear-sized man with a thin red beard round his face and a fringe of curly hair. The word 'career' was one that nobody in Canton Falls, New York, had ever associated with Hobbs, which wasn't to say he didn't work like an ox. He'd give a man his money's worth, as long as the job was outdoors, didn't require too much calculating and his employer was a white Christian.

A lifelong resident of Canton Falls, he liked it here. There was plenty of good hunting land, virtually none of it posted. Hobbs had lots of opportunities to do the things he enjoyed. Like telling Bible stories in Sunday school, which he had a flare for.

Having finished one of those classes now, he walked into Elma's Diner. The waitress walked up to him.

'Hey, Hobbs.' She handed him a slip of paper. On it were the words: *Call me—JB*. She asked, 'That Jeddy Barnes? Sounded like him.'

He ignored her question. As he went to the payphone, his mind went back to a lunch at the Riverside Inn over in Bedford Junction. It'd been him and Frank Stemple and Jeddy Barnes from Canton Falls and a man named Erick Weir, who Barnes later took to calling Magic Man, because he was a professional conjurer.

Barnes had puffed up Hobbs's day ten times by saying to Weir when Hobbs arrived, 'Meet the best shot we got in the county.'

Hobbs poked his fork into the daily special as Barnes and Stemple told him how they'd met Weir. He was like a mercenary, which Hobbs knew all about, being a subscriber to *Soldier of Fortune*.

Barnes had been reluctant to even meet with Weir at first. But Weir had been right up front. He'd told them that he personally didn't believe in their militia causes—his interest was only in making money. Which suited everybody just fine. Magic Man had laid out his plan then shook their hands and left.

Hobbs was supposed to 'stay on call' in case he was needed.

He punched in Barnes's number and heard an abrupt 'Yeah?'

'S'me.'

Because of the state police all over the county looking for Barnes after the raids against Andrew Constable's Patriot Assembly a few months ago, they kept conversations over the phone to a minimum.

Barnes said, 'You gotta do what we talked about at lunch.'

'Go to the lake and take the fishing gear with me? When?'

'Now. Right away.' Barnes hung up abruptly.

Hobbs ordered a coffee and a bacon and egg sandwich to go.

When the food was ready he pushed outside. He had one stop to make—his trailer. Then he'd pick up the old junker Dodge registered to somebody who didn't exist and speed down to the 'lake', which didn't mean any lake at all, it meant a place in New York City.

Just like the 'fishing gear' he was supposed to take with him sure didn't mean a rod and reel either.

BACK IN THE TOMBS. On one side of the floor-bolted table sat a grim-faced Joe Roth, Andrew Constable's pudgy lawyer. Charles Grady was on the other side, flanked by Roland Bell. Amelia Sachs stood.

The door opened and Constable's guard led the prisoner into the interview room, recuffed his hands in front of him. Then he swung the door closed and returned to the corridor.

'It didn't work,' was the first thing Grady said to him.

'What didn't . . . ?' Constable began.

'This is about Erick Weir,' Grady said. The prosecutor explained about the attempt on his family's life by the former illusionist.

'No, no, no . . . I didn't have anything to do with this. I've told you all along, Charles, there are some people I've known in the past who've gone way overboard with things. They see you and the state as the enemies—working with the Jewish people and the African-Americans or whoever—and they're twisting my words around and using me as an excuse to come after you.'

'Let's not play games here, Charles,' Roth said. 'If you've got something to connect my client to the break-in of your apartment, then—'

'This Weir killed two individuals yesterday—and a police officer. That makes it capital murder.'

Constable winced. His lawyer added bluntly, 'Well, I'm sorry about that, Charles. But I notice you haven't charged my client. Because you don't have any evidence linking him to Weir, right?'

Grady ignored this. 'We're negotiating with Weir right now about turning state's evidence.'

Sachs remained silent, as did Bell. It wasn't their job to argue with suspects. The detective was here to keep an eye on Grady and see if he could learn more about the attempt on the DA's life and any other possible future attacks. Sachs was here to see if she might learn more about Constable and his partners to help solidify the case against Weir.

Constable shook his head. 'Look, it makes no sense for me to try and kill you. The trial'd go on, only I'd have a murder charge slapped on me. Why'd I want to do that?'

'Because you're a bigot and a killer and—'

Constable said heatedly, 'I've put up with a lot, sir. I was arrested, humiliated in front of my family. And you know what my only crime is?' He levelled his gaze to Grady. 'Asking hard questions.'

'Andrew,' Constable's lawyer touched his arm. But with a loud jangle the prisoner pulled it away. He was indignant and wouldn't be stopped.

'I'm asking if you don't agree that when government gets to be too big it loses touch with the people. Look at what's happened in Washington. They let terrorists walk right into our country, and we don't dare offend 'em by keeping 'em out or forcing 'em to be finger-printed and carry ID cards . . . And let me ask you, why don't we all just admit that there're differences between races and cultures? I've never said one race is better or worse than any others. But I do say you get grief if you try to mix them.'

Grady said, 'Before you play the persecution card, Andrew, whatta you do with the fact that Erick Weir had lunch with three other people in Bedford Junction two weeks ago. Which is two clicks from the Patriot Assembly meeting hall in Canton Falls and about five from your house.'

Constable glanced at his lawyer, who shook his head.

Grady said, 'Well, Joe, I'm about at the end of the line here. All I've been hearing is he didn't do this, he didn't do that. If that's the case'—he turned directly to Constable—'prove it. Get me the names of the people who tried to kill me and my family, then we'll talk.'

A consultation between client and attorney.

Roth finally said, 'My client's going to make some phone calls.'

The prosecutor stood up. 'If I don't hear from you by nine tonight we go to trial tomorrow as planned.'

IT WASN'T MUCH OF A STAGE. When David Balzac had retired from the illusionist circuit and had bought Smoke & Mirrors he'd torn out the back half of the store to put in the small theatre. He held free shows here—every Sunday afternoon and Thursday night—so that his students could experience what performing was really like.

Kara knew that practising at home and performing onstage were night and day. Something inexplicable happened when you got up in front of people.

Now, approaching 4.00pm on Sunday, people were entering the theatre. Kara was confident of her routine. And now, for the last few minutes before curtain time, she didn't think about her tricks but gazed at the audience, enjoying this momentary peace of mind.

She peeked through the curtain again. Most of the chairs were filled. She was pleased when Jaynene from the nursing home arrived, her huge figure blocking the back doorway momentarily.

Then just after four o'clock one final member of the audience entered—someone she never in a million years would have expected to come see her show.

'IT'S ACCESSIBLE,' Lincoln Rhyme commented wryly to Sachs and Thom, driving his glossy Storm Arrow to a spot halfway down the aisle in Smoke & Mirrors and parking. An hour ago he'd surprised Sachs and Thom by suggesting they drive down to the store in his van to see Kara's performance.

As he looked around the shabby theatre he noticed a heavyset black woman glance at him. She rose slowly and joined them. She asked Rhyme if they were the police officers Kara'd been helping out. He said yes and introductions were made. Her name turned out to be Jaynene and she was a nurse working at Stuyvesant Manor, the ageing care facility where Kara's mother lived.

Rhyme said, 'Kara told me she's sick. Is she doing better?'

'A bit, yes,' the woman said.

There was a story behind this, Rhyme sensed.

Then the lights dimmed and the crowd fell silent. A white-haired man climbed up onstage.

Ah, Lincoln Rhyme deduced, the infamous mentor, David Balzac. He didn't identify himself but looked out over the audience. 'Today, ladies and gentlemen, I'm pleased to present one of my most promising students. She's going to treat you to some of the more esoteric illusions in the history of our profession. Don't be surprised'—a demonic look that seemed directed at Rhyme himself—'or *shocked* at anything you see today. And now, ladies and gentlemen . . . I give you . . . Kara.'

Rhyme had decided to come and pass this hour by being a scientist. He'd enjoy the challenge of spotting the mechanics of Kara's illusions.

The young woman walked out onstage, wearing a tight black bodysuit with a cut-out in the shape of a crescent moon on her chest, under a shimmery, see-through drape, like a translucent Roman toga. She moved like a dancer. There was a long pause while she examined the audience slowly. Finally: 'Change,' she said in a theatrical voice. 'Change . . . How it fascinates us. Alchemy—changing lead and tin into gold . . .' She held up a silver coin. Closed it in her palm and opened it an instant later to reveal a gold coin, which she flung into the air; it turned into a shower of gold confetti.

Applause from the audience and murmurs of pleasure.

'There's a book,' Kara said, a serious expression on her face, 'written thousands of years ago by the Roman writer, Ovid. The book is called *Metamorphoses*. Like "metamorphosis"—when a caterpillar becomes a . . .' She opened her hand and a butterfly flew out.

She continued, '*Metamorphoses* . . . It's a book about change. About people becoming other people, animals, trees, objects. Some of Ovid's stories are tragic, some enthralling but all of them have one thing in common.' A pause and then she said in a loud voice, 'Magic!' With a burst of light and a cloud of smoke she vanished.

For the next forty minutes Kara mesmerised the audience with a series of illusions and sleight-of-hand tricks based on a few of the poems in the book. As for catching her moves, Rhyme gave up on that completely. After a long ovation she left the stage. Five minutes later the young woman emerged in jeans and a white blouse.

Sachs nodded at Kara, who joined them.

'Hey, this is great,' she said. 'I never thought I'd see you guys here.'

'What can I say?' Sachs offered. 'Fantastic.'

'Excellent,' Rhyme said.

'Kara,' Sachs said, 'you *have* to try out for the Cirque Fantastique.'

Kara laughed in reply. Rhyme could tell she didn't want to pursue the issue. But then she added lightly, 'I'm right on schedule. There's no hurry. A lot of people make the mistake of jumping too fast.'

'Let's get some food,' Thom suggested. 'I'm starving. Jaynene, you come too.'

The nurse said she'd love to and suggested a new place near the Jefferson Market.

Kara demurred, saying that she had to stay and work on some of the routines she'd slipped up on. She hugged Sachs and said goodbye. They exchanged phone numbers. Rhyme thanked her again. 'We couldn't've caught the Conjurer without you.'

He started to pilot the Storm Arrow towards the front of the store. As he did he saw Balzac's eyes watching. The illusionist then turned to Kara as she joined him. Immediately, in his presence, she was a very different woman, timid and self-conscious.

Metamorphosis, Rhyme thought.

DOWNSTAIRS IN THE TOMBS the two officers, both with a firm grip on the prisoner's arms, let him shuffle to the booking station.

Doesn't look so scary to me, Department of Corrections Officer Linda Welles thought. No, she didn't quite know why they were making all this fuss about this skinny old guy, Weir, Erick A.

Watch his hands all the time. Don't take the shackles off.

Despite Detective Sellitto's concerns, fingerprinting and mugshots went without incident. Welles and Hank Gersham, a large male DOC officer, gripped Weir and started down the long corridor to intake.

A moment later the prisoner moaned and slumped against Welles.

'Cramp,' he gasped. 'It hurts . . . The shackles!' His left leg was straight out, quivering.

Hank asked her, 'Undo him?'

Welles hesitated. Then said, 'No. Get him on the floor.'

They eased Weir down and Welles began to massage his stiff leg. Then she noticed that Weir's cuffed hands, still behind his back, had slid to his side and that his slacks had been pulled down a few inches.

She saw a Band-Aid had been peeled away from his hip and—what *was* that? She realised it was a slit in the skin.

It was then that his palm hit her in the nose, popping the cartilage.

A key! He'd had a key or pick hidden in that little crevice of skin.

Her partner reached out fast but Weir rose even faster and elbowed him in the throat. The man went down, gasping. Weir clamped a hand on Welles's pistol and tried to pull it from her holster. She struggled to control it with both hands. Blood from her broken nose made her choke.

'Help me!' she cried, coughing blood. 'Somebody, help!'

At the end of the corridor a door opened and someone came running. But the hallway seemed to be ten miles long. They rolled to the floor, Weir's eyes inches from hers, the muzzle of the gun turning slowly towards her.

No way in hell, Welles thought, furious. She planted her foot against the wall and shoved hard. Weir went over backwards and she fell on top of him. The pistol went off with a stunning explosion.

Then Welles realised that she was no longer wrestling for the weapon. It was in her hand alone. She leapt to her feet.

The bullet had struck the prisoner directly in the side of the head, leaving a horrible wound. On the wall behind him was a spatter of blood, brain matter and bone. Weir lay on his back, glazed eyes staring at the ceiling. Blood flowing down his temple.

Shaking, Welles wailed, 'Look what I did! Help him, somebody!' She broke down in wrenching sobs.

'CONSTABLE'S GOT SOME INFORMATION,' the defence lawyer's voice came crisply through the phone. 'Made some calls to Canton Falls. Looks like some former Patriot Assembly members have gone rogue.'

'You know Weir's dead?' Charles Grady asked.

'Yep . . . I really believe Andrew didn't have anything to do with trying to hurt you, Charles.'

Grady asked, 'And he's got solid information?'

'He does, yes,' Roth said. 'He wants to meet you face to face. How soon can you get down to Detention?'

'A half-hour. I'll leave now.' Grady hung up.

Luis, the still-eyed bodyguard, said, 'I'll go with you.'

After Weir's death Lon Sellitto had cut back the protection team to one officer.

'No, you stay here with my family, Luis. I'd feel better.'

SACHS'S WAR-TORN yellow Camaro SS pulled to a stop outside 100 Centre Street. She tossed the NYPD placard onto the dash then climbed out. She nodded to a crime scene crew standing beside their rapid response vehicle. 'Where's the scene?'

'Basement in the back. The corridor to intake.'

'Sealed?'

'Yep.'

'Whose weapon?'

'Linda Welles, DOC. She's pretty shook up. Bastard broke her nose.'

Sachs grabbed a suitcase and started for the front door of the Criminal Courts building. The other crime scene techs followed suit.

An accidental shooting involving an officer and a suspect who'd tried to escape? Pro forma. Still, the event was a homicide and required a crime scene report for the Shooting Incident Board.

A guard checked their IDs and led the team through a maze of corridors into the basement. Finally they came to a yellow police line tape across a closed door. Here, a detective was talking to a uniformed officer, her nose stuffed with tissue.

Sachs introduced herself and asked Linda Welles what had happened.

'It took him two, three seconds. All the cuffs. Just like that, they were open. He didn't get my key. He had a pick or key or something on his hip. You'll see.' She nodded towards the corridor where Weir's body lay. 'There's a cut in his skin. Under a Band-Aid.'

Sachs supposed that he'd cut himself to create a hiding place.

'Then he grabbed my weapon. I tried to keep control and I couldn't.' Welles touched her nose gently and began to cry.

'*We* collared and searched him at the takedown,' Sachs said kindly. 'And we missed the key too.' Pulling on latex gloves, she asked for the woman's Glock. She took it, slipped the clip and ejected the round in the chamber. Everything went into a plastic evidence bag.

The crime scene team set up shop outside the door to the corridor where the shooting had occurred, opening the suitcases and arranging evidence-collection equipment, supplies and cameras. Sachs dressed in the white Tyvek suit, fitted the microphone over her head and asked for a radio patch to Lincoln Rhyme's phone. Ripping down the police tape, she opened the door.

'Oh, damn,' she spat out.

'Hello to you too, Sachs,' Rhyme said acerbically through her headset.

'I don't believe it, Rhyme. The ME took the body before I could process it.' The corridor was bloody but empty.

The rule in crime scene work was that emergency medics could enter a scene to save an injured person but, in a homicide, the body had to remain untouched by everyone, including the doctor from the Medical Examiner's office, until it had been processed by forensics.

'Problem, Amelia?' one of the techs called from the doorway.

'The ME got the body before we processed it. What happened?'

The crewcut young tech frowned then said, 'Uhm, well, the doc's outside. He was waiting to move the body after we were finished.'

The chill went straight to her soul. 'Rhyme, you don't think—'

He barked out, 'What do you see, Sachs? What's the blood spatter look like?'

She ran to where the shooting had happened and studied the bloodstain on the wall. 'It doesn't look normal for a gunshot, Rhyme.'

'Brain matter, bone?'

'Grey matter, yeah. But it doesn't look right either.'

'Do a presumptive blood test.'

She sped back to the doorway, grabbed the catalytic blood kit then returned to the corridor and took a swab from the wall. A moment later she had the answer. 'I don't know what it is but it's definitely not blood. Rhyme, he faked the shooting.'

'Call security. Have them seal the exits.'

Sachs yelled, 'It's an escape—have the exits sealed.'

A detective called back, 'They've notified the guards at all the exits. But this isn't a lock-down corridor. As soon as we closed the doors here he could've stood up and wandered anywhere. He's probably on the subway to Queens.'

'Get an escape bulletin out now,' Sachs said, leaving the issue of pursuit in the detective's hands and turning back to her own area of expertise. For the search of the crime scene, which was supposed to be a brief formality, had now become a matter of life and death.

'IT WAS AN OUT,' Kara said. The young woman had been whisked back to Rhyme's town house a few moments ago.

'An out?' the criminalist asked. 'What's that?'

'It means an alternative plan. All good illusionists have one or two back-ups for every routine. If you screw up, you have an escape plan to save the trick.'

'How'd he do it?'

'Explosive squib behind a blood bladder hidden in his hair.'

'What about the eyes?' Rhyme asked. 'The wits said his eyes were open. He never blinked. And they looked glazed.'

'He might've used eyedrops that lubricate the surface. You can keep them open for ten or fifteen minutes.'

Rhyme sighed. Then snapped, 'Where the hell's the evidence?' He looked from the door to Mel Cooper, as if the slim technician could make the delivery from the Detention Center materialise on command.

It turned out there were *two* crime scenes downtown: one was the corridor where the phoney shooting had occurred. The other was in a janitor's closet off a connected corridor in the courthouse basement. There, one of the search teams had found the fake wound appliance, clothes and other things hidden in a bag.

Thom answered the door chime and Roland Bell hurried into the laboratory. 'Can't believe it,' he said breathlessly. 'He's rabbited?'

'Sure has,' Rhyme muttered darkly. 'ESU's scouring the place. Amelia's down there too.'

Bell drawled, 'I'm thinking it's time to get Charles and his family into a safe house.'

Sellitto said, 'Absolutely.'

Bell pulled out a cellphone and placed a call. 'Luis? It's Roland. Listen here, Weir's escaped . . . No, no, he wasn't dead at all. Faked it. I want Grady and his family in a safe house till . . . *What?*'

Everyone's attention swivelled to Bell. 'By himself?'

Bell turned to Sellitto. 'Luis said you called and had the baby-sitting team stand down.'

'Called who?'

'Called Grady's house. You told Luis to send everyone but him home.'

'Why would I do that?' Sellitto asked. 'He did it again. Just like sending the guards at the circus home.'

Bell said to the team, 'It gets worse—Grady's on his way down-town by himself to meet with Constable about some plea bargain.' Into the phone he said, 'Keep the family together, Luis. And call the others on the team. Get 'em back right now. I'll try and find Charles.' He hung up and dialled another number. 'No answer.' He left a message: 'Charles, this is Roland. Weir's escaped. As soon as you hear this, get next to an armed officer you know personally, then call me.' He hung up and shook his head. 'Missed this one by a mile.'

'One thing I know,' Rhyme said. 'He's not leaving town. He's enjoying this.'

'THANK YOU, SIR. Thank you.'

The guard hesitated at these gentle words as he ushered the man who'd spoken them—Andrew Constable—into the interview room atop the Tombs in Lower Manhattan.

A moment later Joseph Roth came into the room.

'Hi, Joe. Grady's agreed to negotiate?'

'Yeah. Should be here in ten minutes, Andrew. You have names?'

Constable said, 'You bet I have names. Friends. Used to be, at least. That lunch at the Riverside Inn? Some of them *did* hire that man Weir to kill Grady. There's a lot of Patriots going to cooperate to the hilt. Don't worry.'

'Good,' Roth said, looking relieved. 'I think things are going to work out.'

'Thanks, Joe. I'm glad I hired you.'

'I have to tell you, Andrew, I was surprised at first, you hiring a lawyer that was Jewish. You know, with what I heard about you.'

'But then you got to know me.'

'Then I got to know you.'

They were interrupted by a guard at the door. He motioned Roth outside and they had a brief conversation.

When the lawyer returned he said, 'We're supposed to sit tight here for a bit. Weir's escaped. He may still be in the building.'

'Is Grady safe?'

'I don't know.'

The prisoner sighed in disgust. 'You know who's going to come off the heavy? Me, that's who. I'm sick and tired of this crap. I'm going to find out where Weir is and what he's up to.'

'You? How?'

'I'll have everybody I can muster up in Canton Falls track down Jeddy Barnes. Maybe they can convince him to let us know where Weir is and what he's doing. Between you and me, Joe, I don't care about Grady. This is for me. Giving 'em Weir and Jeddy's head on a platter—maybe at last everybody'll believe I'm on the up and up. Now let's make some phone calls and get to the bottom of this mess.'

HOBBS WENTWORTH didn't get away from Canton Falls often.

Dressed like a janitor, wheeling a cart containing push brooms, mops and his 'fishing gear' (that is, his Colt AR-15 semiautomatic assault rifle), Hobbs Wentworth realised that life in the big city had changed quite a bit in the past twenty years, the last time he'd been here. And he noted that everything he'd heard about the slow cancer eating away the white race was true.

There were more Japanese people—or Chinese, who could tell?—than in Tokyo. And Hispanics *everywhere* in this part of New York City, like mosquitoes. And ragheads and Indians too.

But God had given Hobbs Wentworth the blessed role of freedom fighter. Because Jeddy Barnes and his friends knew that Hobbs had one other talent aside from teaching Bible stories to children. He killed people. And he did it very, very well.

And now he was going to add a prosecutor to his list.

He pushed the cart through the nearly empty underground parking garage off Centre Street and paused at one of the doors, looking as if he was about to start his night shift as a janitor. After a few minutes the door opened and a woman stepped out. She smiled but pulled the door shut firmly behind her and said, sorry, she couldn't let him inside with security being what it was.

A minute later he dumped her body into the cart. He slid her ID through the electronic reader and the door clicked open.

He now took the elevator to the second floor, rolling the cart in front of him, the woman's body obscured by garbage bags. Hobbs found the office that Mr Weir had decided would be the best one to use. The door was locked but the big man simply kicked his way inside.

Hobbs took his gun from the cart, mounted the 'scope and sighted on the street below. He couldn't miss.

When Grady appeared Hobbs would shoot five rounds at him through the sealed window. The first bullet would shatter the glass and might be deflected but the rest would kill the prosecutor.

WHERE? WHERE WAS WEIR? Trotting along Centre Street, Roland Bell looked into the cars he passed, looked at trucks on the street, in alleyways, gun ready but not drawn. Bell had decided it made the most sense for them to hit Grady here on the street, before he entered the building, where there was a better chance of escaping alive. He doubted that these people were suicidal—that didn't fit the profile. In the moment between the time Grady parked his car and stepped out until he walked into the massive doors of the Criminal Courts building, the killer would go for his shot. And an easy one it would be—there was virtually no cover.

Where was Weir? And, just as important, where was *Grady*?

His wife had said he'd taken the family car, not the city one. Bell had put out an emergency vehicle location request for the prosecutor's Volvo but no one had spotted it.

Bell turned slowly, surveying the streets, revolving like a lighthouse. His eyes rose to the building across the street, a government office building, a new one, with dozens of windows facing Centre Street. Bell had been involved in a brief hostage-taking in the building and he knew that it was practically deserted now, on Sunday. A perfect place to hide and wait for Grady. But then the street would be a good vantage point too—for a drive-by, say.

Where, where?

'I'M DOING A DOOR-TO-DOOR, Rhyme. The last wing of the basement.' Sachs was in the Tombs now, working her way through the corridors. 'OK, I'm going silent, Rhyme. I'll call you back.'

Rhyme and Cooper returned to the evidence. In the corridor on the way to intake in the Tombs, Sachs had recovered fragments of beef bone and grey sponge—to simulate skull and brain matter—as well as samples of the fake blood. Weir had used his jacket or shirt to wipe as much as he could from the floor and the handcuffs but Sachs had run the scene as methodically as ever and she'd recovered enough of a sample for analysis.

The janitor's closet where he'd done his quick change yielded more—a paper bag in which he'd hidden the bloody squib and bladder, and what he'd been wearing when they'd collared him at Grady's: the grey suit and a pair of Oxford businessman's shoes. Cooper had found substantial trace evidence on these items, including thick nylon fibres and more fake blood.

The fibres turned out to be charcoal-grey carpet. Some phoney blood was paint. Cooper sent the chemical composition analysis and photos down to the FBI, with an urgent request for sourcing.

Then an idea occurred to Rhyme. 'Kara,' he called, seeing the girl sitting next to Mel Cooper, rolling a quarter over her fingers as she stared at the computer image of a fibre. 'Can you help us out with one thing?'

'Sure.'

'Could you go over to the Cirque Fantastique and find Kadesky? Tell him about the escape and see if there's anything else he can remember about Weir. Anything that'll give us an idea of what he might really look like.'

'Maybe he's got some old clippings or pictures of him in costume,' she suggested.

He told her that was a good idea and then returned again to the evidence chart.

THE CIRQUE FANTASTIQUE was coming alive, an hour before that night's performance. Inside the backstage portion of the tent Kara found a friendly employee. She explained what she was doing there—that a former illusionist wanted for murder had been identified as someone Mr Kadesky had worked with a long time ago and they needed to talk to him. The woman invited Kara to wait until the producer returned from dinner. She gave Kara a pass to sit in one of the VIP boxes and then left on another errand.

ROLAND BELL was standing in one of the canyons of downtown Manhattan: Centre Street between the grimy, towering Criminal Courts building, crowned by the Bridge of Sighs, and the nondescript government office building across the street from it.

Still no sign of Charles Grady. No sign of Weir.

He turned and found himself looking right at Charles Grady, who was strolling up the street. The detective sprinted towards him calling, 'Charles! Get down! Weir's escaped!'

Grady crouched on the sidewalk, between two parked cars. 'What happened?' he shouted. 'My family!'

'I've got people with them,' the detective called.

'But Weir—'

'Faked the shooting in Detention.'

Bell finally reached Grady and stood over him, his back to the dark windows of the government office building across the street.

'Just stay right where you are, Charles,' Bell said. 'We'll get out of this fine.' And pulled his Handie-Talkie off his belt.

HOBBS WENTWORTH watched his target below him—the prosecutor cowering on the pavement behind a man in a sports jacket, a cop obviously.

The cross hairs of Hobbs's 'scope poked around the officer's back, searching unsuccessfully for an unprotected shot at Grady. Well, he had to do something pretty soon. The cop was talking on his radio. There'd be a hundred others here in a minute.

All right. He'd shoot the cop in the thigh. Most likely, the cop would fall backwards, exposing the prosecutor. He'd give the cop a moment or two longer to step out of the way.

The cop continued to huddle over the prosecutor.

Well, that's it, Hobbs thought. He centred the cross hairs on the cop's leg and began to apply pressure on the trigger.

THE MUFFLED CRACK of a gunshot resounded through the canyon of the street. Bell jumped.

'Gunshot!' Charles Grady cried. 'Are you hit?'

'Just stay down,' Bell said, dropping into a crouch. He spun around, lifting his gun and squinting hard at the government building across the street. He was counting furiously.

'Got the location,' he said finally into his radio. 'I make it the second floor, fifth office from the north end of the building.'

A moment later an armoured Emergency Services van pulled up and five seconds after that Bell and Grady were inside it, squealing away from the attempted hit.

Bell had concluded that the best way to try to hit Grady would be from the office building across the street. Bell had remained in the open as bait because of something he knew about this particular building from the hostage situation he'd run there: the windows, as in many of the newer government buildings here, couldn't be opened and were made from bombproof glass.

He'd taken the chance of luring the sniper into shooting, in the hope that a bullet would spider the window and reveal the man's location.

And his idea had worked.

'ESU Four to Bell. Scene is secure. K.'

'Roger, that.' Bell responded, 'Where'd he hit himself, K?'

Bell had spotted the shooter's location not because of cracked glass but because of a large spatter of blood on the window. The ESU officer explained that the slug that the man had fired had ricocheted off the glass, shattered and struck the shooter himself in a half-dozen places, and severed a large artery or vein. The man had bled out by the time the ESU team arrived.

'Tell me it's Weir, K,' Bell said.

'Sorry. Somebody named Hobbs Wentworth.'

SITTING IN THE INTERVIEW ROOM with Andrew Constable, Joseph Roth looked uneasy. They'd just learned that a man with a rifle had made an attempt on Grady's life in front of the building a few minutes ago. But it hadn't been Weir. The lawyer said, 'I'm worried that Grady'll be too spooked to deal with us.' Moving his finger over the sheet of names and numbers that Constable's associates in Canton Falls had provided in response to their questions about what Weir might have planned, Roth said, 'You think anybody here'll know something specific about Weir?'

Constable leaned forward and looked at the list. Then at his lawyer's watch. 'I doubt it,' he said.

'You . . . You doubt it?'

'See this first number? It's the dry-cleaner on Harrison Street in Canton Falls. The next one's the Baptist church. And those names?'

'Right,' Roth said. 'Jeddy Barnes's associates.'

Constable chuckled. 'Gosh no. They're all made up.'

'I don't understand.'

Constable whispered, 'Of course you don't, you pathetic Jew,' and slammed his fists into the side of the lawyer's face.

Andrew Constable was a strong man and paunchy Joe Roth was no match for him. Constable pinned him against the table then struck him hard in the throat.

The prisoner began pummelling the bleeding man with his cuffed fists locked together. In a moment Roth was unconscious. Constable propped him up at the table, his back to the door. If one of the guards happened to glance in, it would look as if he were reading the papers, head down. He'd kill the lawyer later. For now, for a few minutes at least, he needed this innocent-looking tableaux.

A few minutes—until he was free.

Which was the whole point of Erick Weir's plan.

Constable's best friend, Jeddy Barnes, second-in-command of the Patriot Assembly, had hired Weir not to kill Grady but to break the prisoner out of the notoriously secure Manhattan Detention Center, and transport him to freedom into the New England wilderness, where the Assembly could resume its mission to rid the land of blacks, gays, Jews, foreigners—the 'Them' that Constable railed against in his weekly lectures at the Patriot Assembly.

It occurred to Constable that he ought to have a weapon so he lifted a metal pencil from the lawyer's shirt. The sharp point would make a fine stabbing implement. Then he sat back, across from Roth, thinking about the plan created by Weir. It was a masterpiece. It began with Weir carefully planting the idea with the police that there was a conspiracy to kill Grady. The cops'd stop looking for any other crimes—such as the planned jail break.

Weir himself would then intentionally get caught during an attempt to kill Grady and be taken to Detention.

Meanwhile, Constable was supposed to do some misdirection of his own. He'd disarm his captors by being the voice of reason, pleading his innocence by offering to incriminate other conspirators.

When Grady arrived, Hobbs Wentworth would try to kill the prosecutor but whether he succeeded or not didn't matter; the important thing was that Hobbs would divert the police from the Detention Center. Then Weir—who was roaming free in the building after faking his own death—would sneak up here and break Constable out.

Then, right on schedule, Constable heard the buzz of the outer door. His chariot to freedom had arrived.

The door to the interview room swung open. But it was the red-headed officer who'd picked up Detective Bell yesterday.

'Injury here,' she shouted as she glanced at Roth. 'Call EMS!'

Behind her one guard grabbed a phone and the other hit a red button on the wall, sending a klaxon alarm braying.

What was going on? Where was Weir?

Constable glanced back at the woman to see the pepper spray—the only permissible weapon in Detention—in her hand. He thought fast and began moaning loudly, holding his belly. 'I've been stabbed!'

The woman frowned and looked around the cell as Constable

slumped to the floor, thinking: When she gets closer he'd stab towards her face with the pencil. Weir had to be close by.

Come on, honey. A little closer.

'Your lawyer?' she asked. 'Is he stabbed too?'

'Yes! It was some black prisoner.'

Just a few more feet . . .

Constable looked up to find his target.

And saw the nozzle of the pepper spray, a foot away from his eyes. She pushed the button and the stream shot him square in the face.

AMELIA SACHS put the pepper spray canister away.

Having noticed the shiv half-concealed in Constable's hand, she thoroughly enjoyed hearing the vicious bigot squeal like a pig as she sprayed him. She stepped aside as the two floor guards grabbed the prisoner and dragged him out.

Joseph Roth was breathing but unconscious and badly hurt. Soon an emergency medical service team arrived and went to work on him.

Sachs went outside. She called Rhyme to tell him what had happened. Then she added, 'Constable was expecting him, Rhyme.'

'Expecting Weir?'

'I think so. He was surprised when I opened the door. I could tell he was waiting for somebody.'

'So that's what Weir's up to—breaking Constable out?'

'That's what I think.'

'Damn misdirection,' he muttered. 'He's had us focused on the plot to kill Grady.' Then he added, 'Unless the *escape* is misdirection and Weir's job really *is* to kill Grady.'

She considered this. 'That'd work too.'

'And no sign of Weir anywhere?'

'None. I'm going to keep hunting.'

LINCOLN RHYME turned from gazing out of the window at the evening sky and wheeled back to the evidence chart.

The frustration seared him. Rhyme had long ago accepted that with his condition he would never physically capture a perp. But he could at least out-think the criminals he pursued.

Except that with Erick Weir, the Conjurer, he couldn't.

Bell had returned with Charles Grady to the town house, where the Grady family was now packing up to go to a safe house.

Sachs, Sellitto and ESU were scouring the Detention Center and courts. Kara was at the Cirque Fantastique interviewing Kadesky. A

Physical Evidence Response Team was searching the scene of the office building where Hobbs Wentworth had shot himself, and technicians in Washington were still analysing the fibre and fake-blood paint found by Sachs at the Detention Center.

What else could Rhyme do?

Only one thing. He decided to try something he hadn't done for years. Rhyme began to walk some grids.

This search started at the intake of the Manhattan Detention Center and took him through winding corridors, lit with algae-green fluorescence. Around corners. Into closets and furnace rooms, trying to follow the footsteps—and discern the thoughts—of Erick Weir.

The walk was, of course, conducted with his eyes closed and took place exclusively in his mind. Still, it seemed appropriate that he should engage in a pursuit that was imaginary when the prey he sought was a vanished man.

THE STOPLIGHT CHANGED to green and Malerick accelerated slowly.

As he picked his way through the Sunday-evening traffic, he was amused to think of Constable's growing dismay and panic as he waited for Weir to sneak him out of the building—an event that, of course, was never going to happen.

The trial would go on and Andrew Constable—as confused as Jeddy Barnes and Hobbs Wentworth and everyone else—would never know how they'd been used.

The police, too, would be floating in a soup of confusion, having no idea what was actually going on.

Well, what's been going on for the past two days, Revered Audience, is a sublime performance featuring the perfect combination of physical and psychological misdirection.

Physical—by directing the police towards Charles Grady's apartment and the Manhattan Detention Center.

Psychological—by shifting suspicion away from what Malerick was really doing and towards the motives that Lincoln Rhyme believed he'd figured out: the hired killing of Grady and the orchestration of Andrew Constable's escape.

What he was really up to had nothing to do with the Constable case. All the clues he'd left so obviously—the illusionist-trick attacks on the first three victims, who represented aspects of the circus, the shoe with the dog hairs and dirt ground into it, the references to the fire in Ohio and the connection with the Cirque Fantastique . . . all those had convinced the police that his intent couldn't really be revenge against Kadesky because that, as Lincoln Rhyme had told him, was too obvious. He *had* to be up to something else.

But he wasn't.

Now, dressed in a medical technician's uniform, he eased the ambulance he was driving through the service entrance of the tent housing the Cirque Fantastique.

He parked under the box seats scaffolding, climbed out and locked the door. None of the stagehands, police or security guards paid any attention to him or the ambulance. After the bomb scare earlier in the day, it was perfectly normal for an emergency vehicle to be parked here—perfectly *natural*, an illusionist would note.

Look, Revered Audience, here is your illusionist, centre stage yet completely invisible. He's the Vanished Man, present but unseen.

The vehicle wasn't an ordinary ambulance at all, but a feke, one he'd bought some months ago and fixed up. In place of medical equipment it now held a dozen plastic drums containing a total of 700 gallons of gasoline, attached to a simple detonation device, which would soon spark the liquid to life, sending the deadly flood erupting into the audience of more than 2,000 people.

Among whom would be Edward Kadesky.

See, Mr Rhyme, when we talked before, during our Charred Man act? My words were just patter. Kadesky and the Cirque Fantastique destroyed my life and my love and I'm going to destroy him. Revenge *is* what this is all about.

Ignored by everyone, the illusionist now walked casually out of the tent and into Central Park. He'd change into a new disguise and return under cover of night, finding a good vantage spot to enjoy the finale of his show.

FAMILIES, FRIENDS, couples, children were slowly entering the tent, filling the bleachers and box seats, slowly changing from individuals into that creature called an *audience*.

Kara turned away from the sight and stopped a security guard. 'I've been waiting for a while. You have any idea when Mr Kadesky'll be back? It's really important.'

No, he didn't know.

She turned back to the brightly lit interior of the huge circus tent. Looking at all the magic around her, feeling the excitement, the anticipation . . . Oh, what she wouldn't give to be standing in the prep tent right now.

She wondered, *Am* I good enough? But Balzac's firm voice looped through her mind: *Not yet, not yet, not yet* . . . She had to have confidence in him. Besides, there was her mother . . .

Kadesky's assistant appeared and gestured towards her. 'He just called. He was doing a radio interview. He'll be here soon. That's his box in the front. Why don't you wait there?'

Kara nodded, walked to the seat the woman indicated and sat down.

Thud. A loud drum resonated through the tent. The lights went down, plunging them into darkness. The crowd was instantly silent.

Thud . . . thud . . . thud. The crisp drum beat sounded slowly.

A brilliant spotlight shot into the centre of the ring, illuminating Arlecchino, dressed in his black-and-white-chequered bodysuit, wearing his matching half-mask. Holding a long sceptre high in the air, the harlequin looked around mischievously. He stepped forward and began to march round the ring as a procession of performers appeared behind him. Other *commedia dell'arte* characters, as well as spirits, fairies, princesses, princes and wizards. Some walking, some dancing, some cartwheeling slowly like gymnasts underwater.

Faces masked, faces painted white or black or silver or gold, faces dotted with glitter. Solemn, regal, playful, grotesque, the parade was hypnotic. And its message was unmistakable: whatever existed outside the tent was invalid here. Your heart was now beating in time to the crisp drum, and your soul was no longer yours; it had joined this unearthly parade as it made its way into the world of illusion.

We come now to the finale of our show, Revered Audience.

It's time to present our most celebrated—and controversial—illusion. A variation on the infamous Burning Mirror.

I have to warn you, Revered Audience, that the most recent attempt to perform this trick resulted in tragedy.

I know, because I was there.

So, please, for your own sake, spend a moment looking around the tent and consider what you will do should disaster strike . . .

But on reflection, no, it's too late for that.

Malerick had returned to Central Park and was standing about fifty yards from the glowing white tent of the Cirque Fantastique.

Bearded once more, he was dressed in a jogging suit and a high-necked sweatshirt. Tufts of damp blond hair poked from under a Chase Manhattan 10K Run for the Cure cap. Faux sweat stains—out of a bottle—attested to his present persona: a minor financial executive at a major bank out for his Sunday night run. He'd stopped for a breather and was absently looking at the circus tent.

He saw two figures just outside the large service doorway through which he'd driven the ambulance not long before. A man and a young woman. Speaking to each other, ear close to mouth so they could converse over the sound of the music.

Yes! One of them was Kadesky. He'd been worried that the producer might not be present at the time of the explosion. The other was that girl he'd seen in Lincoln Rhyme's. The young woman with the reddish-purple hair.

Kadesky pointed inside and together they walked in the direction he'd indicated. Malerick estimated that they had to be no more than ten feet from the ambulance. A look at his watch. Almost time.

And now, my friends, my Revered Audience . . .

Exactly at 9.00pm a spume of fire shot from the doorway of the tent. A moment later the silhouette of the flames rolled across the glowing canvas as they consumed the bleachers, the audience, the decorations. The music stopped abruptly, replaced by screams, smoke began to pour from the top of the tent.

Malerick leaned forward, mesmerised by the horror of the sight.

He waited a few moments longer but he knew that soon hundreds of police would fill the park. He eased towards the sidewalk, then looked back to see, half obscured by smoke, the huge banners in front of the tent. On one of them masked Arlecchino, the Harlequin, reached outwards, holding up his empty palms.

Look, Revered Audience, nothing in my hands.

Except that, like a sleight-of-hand artist, the character *was* holding something. And only Malerick knew what it was.

The coy Harlequin was holding death.

PART III: TIPPING THE GAFF

Sunday, April 21 to Thursday, April 25

CHAPTER NINE

Amelia Sachs's Camaro hit ninety on the West Side Highway. So the killer had tricked them with yet another genius's touch. Neither Charles Grady's death nor Andrew Constable's escape was Weir's goal. The killer had been after what they'd rejected yesterday as being too obvious—the Cirque Fantastique.

As she'd been about to kick in one of the few remaining hiding spots in the basement of the Manhattan Detention Center, Glock high, Rhyme had called her and told her the situation. Everybody was needed and Rhyme wanted her uptown as fast as possible.

'I'm on my way,' she'd said.

MALERICK WANDERED SLOWLY out of the park, jostled by people running the opposite way, towards the fire.

At the corner of Central Park West and a cross street, he collided with a young Asian woman. She asked, 'You know what happened?'

Malerick thought, Yes, indeed I do: the man and the circus that destroyed my life are dying. But he frowned and said gravely, 'I don't know. But it seems pretty serious.'

He continued west, beginning what would be a circuitous journey back to his apartment, during which he'd execute several quick changes and make absolutely certain no one was following him.

His plans called for him to stay there tonight then in the morning leave for Europe, where he'd resume performing—under his new name. Not a soul on earth, other than his revered audience, knew 'Malerick', and that's who he'd be to the public from now on.

And now the show closes, Revered Audience, as they always do.

I hope I've given you excitement and joy. I hope I've brought wonder to your hearts as you joined me in this netherworld where life is transformed to death, death to life and the real to the unreal.

I bow to you, Revered Audience . . .

SAFELY BACK AT HIS APARTMENT, Malerick lit a candle and settled into the couch. He kept his eyes fixed on the flame. Tonight, vengeance complete, he *knew* that it would shudder, that he would receive a message.

The candle flickered. Yes!

But the shuddering wasn't a message from the supernatural spirit of a loved one long gone but from the gust of cool April evening air that filled the room when the half-dozen police officers in riot gear broke the door in. They flung the gasping illusionist to the floor, where the red-haired policewoman rested a pistol against the back of his head and gave a recitation of his rights.

THEIR ARMS TREMBLING against the weight of both Lincoln Rhyme and his Storm Arrow wheelchair, two sweating ESU officers carried their burden up the stairs into the building and deposited the criminalist in the lobby. He manoeuvred his chair into the Conjurer's apartment and parked next to Amelia Sachs.

Rhyme watched as Bell and Sellitto carefully searched the astonished killer. Rhyme had suggested they borrow a doctor from the Medical Examiner's office to help in the search. It turned out to be a good idea; the MD found several slits in the man's skin. They looked like small scars but could be pulled open. Inside were tiny metal tools.

'X-ray him at the Detention infirmary,' Rhyme said.

When the Conjurer was triple cuffed and double shackled, two officers pulled the man into a sitting position on the floor. He gazed at Rhyme in shock. The criminalist was examining a bedroom in which was a huge collection of magician's props and tools.

'How?' the Conjurer whispered.

Sachs said, 'There wasn't a lot of evidence but it suggested what you were really going to do. In the closet—the one in the basement of the Criminal Courts building—we found the bag with your change of clothes in it, the fake wound. There was some dried red paint on the shoes and your suit. And carpet fibres.'

'I thought the paint was fake blood.' Rhyme shook his head. 'But the FBI's paint database identified it as automotive paint used exclusively for emergency vehicles. The fibres were automotive too—they were from heavy-duty carpet installed in General Motors ambulances.'

Sachs: 'So Lincoln deduced that you'd bought or stolen an old ambulance and fixed it up. Then he remembered the bits of brass—what if they actually *were* from a timer, like we'd thought originally? And, since you'd used gasoline on the handkerchief in Lincoln's apartment, well, that meant that, possibly, you were going to hide a gas bomb in a fake ambulance.'

Rhyme offered, 'Then I simply used logic—'

'He played a hunch is what he's sayin',' Bell chided.

'Logic, I was saying. Kara had told us about pointing your audience's attention towards where you *don't* want them to look. That's what you did . . . And I have to say it was a brilliant idea. Not a compliment I give very often . . . You wanted revenge against Kadesky for the fire that ruined your life. And so you created a routine just like you'd create an illusion for the stage, with layers of misdirections. The first misdirection: you "forced"—Kara told us that's the word illusionist's use, right?'

The killer said nothing.

'First, you *forced* the thought on us that you were going to destroy the circus for revenge. But I didn't believe it—too obvious. And our suspicion led to misdirection two: you planted the newspaper article about Grady, the restaurant receipt, the press pass and the hotel key to make us conclude you were going to kill him . . . Oh, the jogging jacket by the Hudson River? You left that at the scene intentionally.'

Weir nodded.

'At that point, we think you've been hired to kill Charles Grady . . . We've figured you out. There go our suspicions . . . To an *extent*.'

The Conjurer managed a faint smile. '"An extent",' he wheezed.

'So you hit us with misdirection number three. You made us think that you got arrested intentionally to get inside the Detention Center not to kill Grady but to break Constable out of jail. By then we'd forgotten completely about the circus and Kadesky.'

Bell asked, 'But why go to the trouble to set up Constable?'

Sellitto answered, 'Obviously—to misdirect us away from the circus so he'd have an easier time getting the bomb there.'

'Actually, no, Lon,' Rhyme said. 'There was another reason.'

At these words, or perhaps at the tone in Rhyme's voice, the killer turned towards the criminalist, who could see caution in his eyes—real caution, if not fear—for the first time that night.

Gotcha, Rhyme thought. He said, 'See, there was a *fourth* misdirection.'

'Four?' Sellitto said.

'That's right . . . He's not Erick Weir,' Rhyme announced.

'Not Weir?'

'That', Rhyme continued, 'was the whole point of what he did this weekend. He wanted revenge against Kadesky and his circus. Well, it's easy to get revenge if you don't care about escaping. But he wanted to stay out of prison, keep performing. So he did an *identity* quick change. He became Erick Weir, got himself arrested this afternoon, fingerprinted and then escaped.'

Sellitto nodded. 'So after he killed Kadesky and burned down the circus everybody'd be looking for *Weir* and not for who he really is.' A frown. 'And who the hell *is* he?'

'Arthur Loesser, Weir's protégé.'

The killer gasped softly as the last shred of anonymity—and hope for escape—vanished.

'But Loesser called us from out west,' Sellitto pointed out.

'No, he didn't. I checked the phone records. The call came up "No caller ID" on my phone because he placed it through a prepaid long distance account. He was calling from a payphone on West Eighty-Seventh Street. The message on his voicemail in Vegas was fake.'

'Just like he called the other assistant, Keating, and pretended to be Weir, right?' Sellitto asked.

'Yep. He had to leave a trail that Weir'd resurfaced. Like ordering the Darby handcuffs in Weir's name.'

Rhyme looked over the killer. 'How's the voice?' he asked sardonically. 'The lungs feel better now?'

'You know they're fine,' Loesser snapped. The whisper and wheezing were gone.

Rhyme nodded towards the bedroom. 'I saw some poster designs in there. The name on them was "Malerick". That's you now, right?'

He nodded. 'I hated my old name, I hate anything about me from before the fire. It was too hard to be reminded of those times. Malerick's how I think of myself now . . . How did you catch on?'

'After they sealed the corridor in Detention, you wiped the floor and the cuffs,' Rhyme explained. 'When I thought about that I couldn't figure out why. The only answer I could come up with was that you wanted to get rid of your fingerprints. But you'd just been printed; why would you be worried about leaving them in the corridor?' Rhyme gave a shrug, suggesting that the answer was painfully obvious. 'Because your real prints were different from the ones on the card that'd just been rolled and filed at the Detention Center.'

'How the hell d'he manage that?' Sellitto asked.

'Amelia found traces of fresh ink at the scene. That was from his being printed tonight. The trace wasn't important in itself but what was significant was that it matched the ink we found in his gym bag at the Marston assault. That meant he'd come in contact with fingerprint ink before today. I guessed that he stole a blank fingerprint card and printed it at home with the real Erick Weir's prints. He must've had it hidden in his jacket lining tonight—we were looking for weapons and keys, not pieces of cardboard—and then after they rolled his prints he distracted the technicians and swapped the cards. Probably flushed the new one or threw it out.'

Loesser grimaced in anger, a confirmation of Rhyme's deduction.

'Department of Correction sent over the card they had on file and Mel processed it. The rolled prints were Weir's but the latents were Loesser's. He was in the AFIS database from when he was arrested with Weir on those reckless endangerment charges in New Jersey. We checked the DOC officer's Glock too. She took that with her and he didn't get a chance to wipe it down. Those prints came back a match for Loesser too.'

'But', Sellitto pointed out, 'he'd be younger than Weir.'

'He *is*.' Rhyme nodded towards Loesser's face. 'The wrinkles are just latex appliances. Loesser's twenty years younger than Weir so he had to age. The latex must be uncomfortable.'

'You get used to it.'

'Sachs, let's see what he really looks like.'

She peeled off the beard and wrinkles around his eyes and chin. He was clearly much younger. The structure of his face was different.

'The fingers too.' Rhyme nodded at the killer's left hand.

To make the fusing of the fingers credible they'd been bound together with a bandage then covered in thick latex.

Rhyme said, 'Pretty close to a perfect crime: a perp who made certain that we charged somebody else. We'd know Weir was guilty, we'd have positive ID. But he'd disappear. Loesser would go on with his life and Weir would be gone for ever. The Vanished Man.'

'But there's one problem,' Sellitto pointed out. 'What do you mean Weir'd be gone for ever? There's no way he'd get away.'

Rhyme said, 'Why do you think I made those strapping young officers carry me up the stairs, Lon?' He glanced up at the fireplace. 'I think I've found our perp.' On the mantel sat an inlaid box and a candle. 'That's Erick Weir, right? His ashes.'

Loesser said softly, 'That's right. He wanted to get out of the burns unit in Ohio and go back to his house in Vegas before he died. I snuck him out and drove him home. He lived another few weeks. I bribed a night-shift operator at a mortuary to cremate him.'

'And the fingerprints?' Rhyme asked. 'You rolled his prints after he died to make the fake fingerprint card?'

A nod.

'So you've been planning this for years?'

Passionately Loesser said, 'Yes! His death—it's like a burn that doesn't stop hurting.'

Bell asked, 'All of this for revenge? For your boss?'

'Boss? He was more than my *boss*,' Loesser spat. 'You don't understand. I think about Mr Weir every hour of the day. Mr Weir may've made my life hell sometimes but he saw what was inside me. He cared for me. He taught me how to be an illusionist . . .' A cloud filled the man's face. 'And then he was taken away from me. Because of Kadesky. He and that damn business of his killed Mr Weir . . . And me too. Arthur Loesser died in that fire.' He looked at the box and in his face there was an expression of sorrow and hope and such odd love that Rhyme felt a chill start down his neck until it disappeared into his numb body.

Loesser looked back at Rhyme. 'Well, you may've caught me. But Mr Weir and I won. The circus is gone, Kadesky's gone.'

'Ah, yes, the Cirque Fantastique, the fire.' Rhyme shook his head gravely. 'Think back a little. Earlier tonight. You're in Central Park, watching the flames, the smoke, listening to the screams . . . You figure you better leave—we'll be looking for you soon. A young woman, an *Asian* woman bumps into you. You go separate ways.'

'What the hell are you talking about?' Loesser snapped.

'Check the back of your watchband,' Rhyme said.

With a clink of the cuffs Loesser turned his wrist over.

On the band was a small black disk. Sachs peeled it off. 'GPS tracker. We used that to follow you here.'

'But who—? Wait! It was that illusionist, that girl! Kara!'

Rhyme said, 'We spotted you in the park but we were afraid you'd get away. You *do* have a tendency to do that, you know. So I asked Kara to do a little disguise of her own. She's good. When she bumped into you she taped the sensor to your watch.'

Sachs continued, 'We might've been able to take you down on the street but you've been just a little too good at escaping. Anyway, we wanted to find your hidey-hole.'

'But that means you knew *before* the fire!'

'Oh,' Rhyme said dismissively, 'your ambulance?' The bomb squad found it and rendered it safe in about sixty seconds. They replaced it with another one so you wouldn't think we'd caught on. We knew you'd want to watch the fire. We got as many undercover officers as we could into the park, looking for a male about your build who'd watch the fire but then leave not long after it started. A couple of them saw you and we had Kara nail you with the chip. And presto—' Rhyme smiled at his choice of word. 'Here we are.'

'But the fire . . . I *saw* it!'

Sachs said, 'What you saw was smoke from a couple of smoke grenades we mounted on the top of the tent. The flames? From a propane burner at the stage door. Then they backlit a couple more burners in the ring and projected the shadows of the flames onto the side of the tent.'

'I heard screams,' he whispered.

'Oh, Kara thought we could have Kadesky tell the audience they were taking an intermission from the show so a movie studio could shoot a scene about a fire in a circus. He had everybody start screaming on cue. They loved it.'

'No,' the Conjurer whispered. 'It was—'

'—an illusion,' Rhyme said to him. 'It was all an illusion.'

Some sleight of mind from the Immobilised Man.

'I'd better run the scene here,' Sachs said.

'Sure, sure, Sachs. What *was* I thinking of?'

With multiple cuffs and shackles binding him and two officers on either side the killer was led out of the door.

Lon Sellitto's phone rang. 'She's right here . . .' A glance at Sachs. 'You want to talk to her . . .?' Then he shook his head at her and continued to listen, looking grave. 'OK, I'll tell her.' He hung up.

'That was Marlow,' he said to Sachs.

The head of Patrol Services. What was up? Rhyme wondered, seeing the troubled look on Sellitto's face.

Sellitto continued speaking to Sachs, 'He wants you downtown tomorrow morning at ten. It's about your promotion.' Sellitto then frowned. 'He wanted me to tell you something about your score on the test. What was it?' The detective snapped his fingers. 'Oh, yeah, now I remember. He said you got the third-highest score in the history of the department.' He looked at Rhyme. 'You know what this means, don'cha. Now there'll be no living with her.'

GERALD MARLOW was head of the NYPD's Patrol Services Division. Now, Monday morning, Amelia Sachs stood more or less at attention in front of him. They were in Marlow's corner office high up in the Big Building, One Police Plaza, downtown.

Marlow glanced up from the file he'd been reading. 'So, Herman Sachs's daughter.'

'That's right.'

Marlow said, 'OK, Officer. Here it is. You're in trouble.'

It hit her like a physical blow. 'I'm sorry, sir?'

'A crime scene on Saturday, by the Harlem River. Car went into the water. You ran it?'

'Yes, that's right.'

'You placed somebody under arrest at the scene,' Marlow said.

'Not really arrest. This guy went under the tape and was digging around in a sealed area. I had him escorted out and detained.'

'Detained, arrested. The point is he was in custody for a while.'

'Sure. It was an active scene.'

'Well, the guy? He was Congressman Victor Ramos.'

The captain opened a New York *Daily News*. 'Let's see. Ah, here.' A centrefold featured a large picture of the man in cuffs at the scene.

Marlow offered, 'He claimed he was looking for survivors.'

'Survivors?' she barked, laughing. 'EMS cleared the shack and I sealed it. The only living things in that place were the lice.'

The captain's grimace, containing shreds of sympathy, faded. The emotion was replaced by his bureaucratic façade. 'Do you know for a fact that there was any evidence Ramos destroyed that would've been relevant to collaring the suspect?'

'Doesn't make a difference, sir. It's the procedure that's important.' She was struggling to keep calm.

'Trying to work things out here, Officer,' he said sternly. Then repeated. 'Do you know for a *fact* that evidence was destroyed?'

She sighed. 'No. We *were* after a cop-killer, Captain. Does that count for anything?'

'To me. To a lot of people, yeah. To Ramos, no.'

She nodded. 'OK, what kind of firestorm are we talking?'

Marlow's lips tightened. 'Ramos checked on you. Found out about the sergeant's exam. He pulled strings. He got you flunked.'

'He did *what*? I had the third-highest exam in the history of the department.' She laughed bitterly. 'Isn't that right?'

'Yes. But you need to pass the assessment exercise too.'

'I did fine on it.'

'The preliminary results were good. But in the final report you flunked. One of the officers in the exercise wouldn't pass you.'

'Wouldn't pass me? But I . . .' Her voice faded as she pictured the handsome officer with the shotgun stepping out from behind the Dumpster. The man she'd snubbed.

Bang, bang . . .

The captain read from a piece of paper. 'He said you didn't quote "display proper respect for individuals in a supervisory position".'

'So Ramos tracked down somebody willing to dime me out.' Then she looked carefully at Marlow. 'What else, sir?'

'Ramos is trying to get you suspended. He's going for suspension without pay.' This punishment was usually reserved for officers accused of crimes.

'What'd the grounds be?'

'Insubordination, incompetence.'

'I can't lose my shield, sir.' Trying not to sound desperate. Feeling heartsick.

'There's nothing I can do about your flunking the exam, Amelia. That's in the board's hands. But I'll fight the suspension.'

'Can I speak freely, sir?'

'You have to know I feel bad about this, Officer. Say what you want.'

'If he tries for suspension, sir, my next call'll be to the PBA lawyers. I'll light this one up.'

And she would. Though she knew how non-rank cops who fought discrimination or suspensions through the Patrolmen's Benevolent Association were unofficially red-flagged. Many of them found their careers permanently sidetracked even if they won technical victories.

Marlow held her steady gaze as he said, 'Noted, Officer.'

So it was knuckle time. Her father's expression. About being a cop.

Amie, you have to understand: sometimes it's a rush, sometimes you get to make a difference, sometimes it's boring. And sometimes, not too often, thank God, it's knuckle time. Fist to fist. You're all by your lonesome, with nobody to help you. And I don't mean just the perps. Sometimes it'll be you against your boss. Could be you against your buddies too. You gonna be a cop, you got to be ready to go it alone.

'Well, for the time being you're still on active duty.'

'Yessir. When will I know?'

'A day or two.'

Walking towards the door she stopped, turned back. 'Sir?'

Marlow glanced up.

'Ramos was in the middle of my crime scene. If it'd been you there, or the mayor, or the president himself, I would've done exactly the same thing.'

'That's why you're your father's daughter, Officer, and why he'd be proud of you.'

CHAPTER TEN

Thom let Lon Sellitto into the front hallway, where Lincoln Rhyme sat in his chair, grumbling at construction workers to mind the woodwork as they carted refuse downstairs from the repair work currently going on in his fire-damaged bedroom.

Sellitto said, 'Hey, Linc. We've got to talk.'

The criminalist noted the tone—and the look in Sellitto's eyes. What *now*? he wondered.

'It's about Amelia.' Sellitto cleared his throat.

Rhyme's heart undoubtedly gave an extra slam in his chest. He never felt it, of course. Thinking: Bullet, car crash.

'She washed out. The sergeant's exam.'

The explanation was pure Sachs, it turned out. She'd ordered somebody out of an active crime scene and, when he wouldn't leave, had him cuffed.

'The guy turned out to be Victor Ramos.'

'The Congressman.' Lincoln Rhyme knew about Ramos: an opportunistic politico. 'She can fight it. She *will* fight it.'

'And you know what happens to street cops who take on brass. Odds are, even if she wins, they'll send her to East New York. Hell, they'll send her to a *desk* in East New York.' Sellitto paced around the room. 'One thing,' he said softly, a whiff of conspiracy in his voice. 'There's this guy I know.'

'Yeah?'

'Yeah. He's got serious wire all over the Big Building.'

'I don't know,' Rhyme said. 'If she made sergeant that way, well, *she* wouldn't be the one making it.'

The detective replied, 'You know what this promotion means to her, Linc.'

Yeah, he did.

ALL TRACES OF THE FIRE in the bedroom had been 'vanished', as Thom had put it. Now, night, the room dark, Rhyme lay in his Flexicair bed, staring out of the window. He'd dozed off ten minutes ago only to be woken by a loud burst of applause from the circus tent.

'They should have a curfew on that,' Rhyme grumbled to Sachs, lying beside him in bed.

'I could shoot out their generator,' she replied, her voice clear.

She apparently hadn't got to sleep at all. Her head was on the pillow next to his, lips against his neck, on which he could feel the faint tickle of her hair and the smooth cool plane of her skin. He relished the closeness.

Sachs always adhered to Rhyme's firm rule that those walking the grid not wear scent because they might miss olfactory evidence at crime scenes. But she was off duty at the moment and he detected on her skin a pleasant, complex smell, which he deduced to be jasmine, gardenia and synthetic motor oil.

They were alone in the apartment. They'd shipped Thom off to the movies and had spent the evening with some new CDs, two ounces of sevruga caviar and copious Moët.

Sachs looked up at his face in the dim light. 'You heard about the sergeant's exam?'

A hesitation. Then: 'Yep,' he replied. He'd scrupulously avoided bringing up the matter; when Sachs was prepared to discuss something she would. Until then the subject didn't exist.

'You know what happened?' she asked.

'Not all the details. I assume it falls into the category of a quasi-corrupt, self-interested government official versus the overworked heroic crime scene cop. Something like that.'

A laugh. 'Pretty much.'

'I've been there myself, Sachs.'

'Did Lon talk to you about pulling strings for me?'

He chuckled. 'He did, yeah. You know Lon.'

Sachs asked, 'And what'd you say about that?'

Rhyme said, 'I said no. I wouldn't let him do it. I told him you'd make rank on your own or not at all.'

He believed that her arm round his chest gripped him tighter. 'What you told him, Rhyme, that means more to me than anything.'

'I know that.'

'It could get ugly. Ramos's going for suspension. Twelve months off duty, no pay. I don't know what I'll do.'

'You'll consult. With me.'

'A civilian can't walk the grid, Rhyme. I'll go crazy.'

'We'll get through it.'

'Love you,' she whispered. His response was to inhale her flowery Quaker State scent and tell her that he loved her too.

Sachs curled up against him and was soon asleep.

But not Rhyme. As he lay listening to the music from the circus and the voice of the MC some ideas began to form in his mind.

Which were, not surprisingly, about the circus.

LATE THE NEXT MORNING Thom walked into the bedroom to find that Rhyme had a visitor. 'Hi,' he said to Jaynene Williams, the nurse from Stuyvesant Manor.

'Thom.' She shook his hand.

The aide, who'd been shopping, was clearly surprised to see someone there. Thanks to the computer, the environmental control units and CCTV, Rhyme was, of course, perfectly capable of calling someone up, inviting them over and letting them inside when they arrived.

'No need to look so *shocked*,' Rhyme said caustically. 'I *have* invited people over before, you know.'

'Blue moon comes to mind,' Thom said. 'Coffee all round.'

After the aide had gone to make the coffee, Rhyme said, 'There's a problem. I think you can help. I'm hoping you can.'

Jaynene eyed him cautiously. 'Maybe.'

'How long have you known Kara?' he asked.

'Kara? Little over a year. Since her mother came to Stuyvesant.'

'That's an expensive place, isn't it?'

'Painfully,' Jaynene said.

'Does her mother have insurance?'

'Medicare is all. Kara pays for most of it herself.' She added, 'As best she can. She's current now but she's in arrears a lot of the time.'

Rhyme nodded. 'I'm going to ask you one more question. Think about it before you answer. I need you to be completely honest.'

'Well,' the nurse said. 'I'll do the best I can.'

THAT AFTERNOON Roland Bell was in Rhyme's living room. They were talking about the evidence in the Andrew Constable case.

Charles Grady had decided to delay the man's trial in order to include additional charges against the bigot—attempted murder of his own lawyer, conspiracy to commit murder and felony murder. He was also going for the death penalty against Arthur Loesser for the murder of Patrol Officer Larry Burke, whose body had been found in an alley on the Upper West Side.

Amelia Sachs now walked through the doorway, looking frazzled after an all-day meeting with lawyers arranged through the Patrolmen's Benevolent Association about her possible suspension. She was supposed to have been back hours ago and, glancing at her face, Rhyme deduced that the results of the session were not good.

He himself had some news—about his meeting with Jaynene and what had happened after that—and had tried to reach her but had been unable to. Now, though, there was no time to brief her because another visitor appeared.

Thom ushered Edward Kadesky into the room. 'Mr Rhyme,' he said. He nodded to Sachs. He shook Roland Bell's hand. 'Your message said there's something more about the case.'

Rhyme nodded. 'This morning I did some digging, looking into a few loose ends. Ends I didn't know were loose.'

Sachs frowned. The producer too looked troubled. 'Weir's assistant—Loesser. He hasn't escaped, has he?'

'No, no. He's still in Detention.'

The doorbell rang again. A moment later Kara stepped through the doorway into the room. She looked around, ruffling her short hair, which had lost its purple sheen and was now ruddy as a freckle. 'Hi,' she said to the group, blinking in surprise when she saw Kadesky.

The criminalist said to Kara, 'Thanks for coming by. I want to know a few more details about the night that the Conjurer drove the ambulance bomb into the circus.'

The young woman nodded. 'Anything I can do to help.'

'The show was scheduled to start at eight, wasn't it?' Rhyme asked Kadesky.

'That's right.'

'You weren't back from your radio interview yet when Loesser parked the ambulance in the doorway?'

'No, I wasn't.'

Rhyme turned to Kara, 'But you were there?'

'Yeah. I saw the ambulance drive in. I didn't think anything about it at the time.'

'Where did Loesser park the ambulance, exactly?'

'It was near the main bleachers,' she said.

'Not under the expensive seats though?' Rhyme asked Kadesky.

'No,' the man said.

Bell asked, 'Lincoln, what are you getting at?'

'What I'm getting at is Loesser parked the ambulance so that it would do the most damage and yet still give a few people in the box seats a chance to escape. How did he know that?'

'I don't know,' the producer responded. 'He probably checked it out ahead of time.'

'He *might've* checked it out earlier,' Rhyme mused. 'But he also would be reluctant to be seen doing reconnaissance around the circus—since we had officers stationed there. So, isn't it possible that someone on the *inside* might've told him to park there?'

'Inside?' Kadesky asked, frowning. 'Are you saying somebody was helping him? No, none of my people would do that.'

Rhyme turned to Kara. 'You were *in* the box seat area?'

She nodded.

'Near the exit row?'

She looked around the room awkwardly, 'I guess. Yeah, I was.'

'I'm asking because I remember something *you* told us, Kara. About people who're involved in an illusionist's act. There's the *assistant*. Then there's the *volunteer* from the audience. Then there's someone else: the *confederate*. Those are people who are actually working with the magician but seem to have nothing to do with him.'

Kadesky said, 'Right, lots of magicians use confederates.'

Rhyme turned to Kara and said sharply, 'Which is what *you've* been all along, haven't you?'

The young woman gasped.

'No!' Kadesky said. 'Her?'

Rhyme continued. 'She needs money badly and Loesser paid her fifty thousand to help him. Balzac's in on it too.'

'Kara?' Sachs whispered. 'No. I don't believe it.'

Tearfully the young woman said, 'Amelia, I'm so sorry . . . But you don't understand . . . Mr Balzac and Weir were friends. They performed together for years. Loesser told him what he was going to do and Mr Balzac forced me to help him. But, you have to believe me, I didn't know they were going to hurt anybody. Mr Balzac said it was just an extortion thing—to get even with Mr Kadesky. By the time I realised Loesser was killing people it was too late. He said if I didn't keep helping him I'd go to jail.' Suddenly she leapt for the door.

'Stop her, Roland!' Rhyme shouted.

Bell tackled her. They tumbled into the corner of the room. Bell managed to cuff her, then used his Motorola, as Sachs looked on in dismay, to call for a prisoner transfer.

Rhyme sighed. 'I tried to tell you earlier, Sachs. I couldn't get through on the phone. I wish it weren't true. But there you have it. They gulled us like we were their audience.'

The policewoman whispered, 'I just . . . I don't see how she did it.'

Rhyme said, 'She manipulated the evidence, lied to us, planted fake clues . . . Roland, go over to the whiteboards. I'll show you.'

Bell went to the whiteboards and as he pointed out items of evidence Rhyme explained how Kara had used it to fool them.

Moments later Thom called, 'There's an officer here.'

A policewoman walked through the doorway and joined Sachs and Kadesky, surveying them through stylish glasses. In a Hispanic accent, she asked Bell, 'You called for prisoner transport, Detective?'

Bell nodded to the corner. 'She's over there.'

The woman glanced at Kara's prone form and said, 'OK, I'll take her downtown.' She hesitated. 'But I got a question first.'

'Question?' Rhyme asked, frowning.

The officer sized up Kadesky. 'Could I see some identification, sir?'

'You want my ID *again*? I did that the other day.'

'Sir, please.'

Huffily the man withdrew his wallet. Except that it wasn't his.

He stared at a battered zebra-skin billfold.

The policewoman said, 'I'm sorry, sir. You're under arrest for pickpocketing.'

'There's some mistake.' Kadesky opened up the wallet and stared.

Then he barked an astonished laugh, held up the driver's licence picture for everyone to see. It was Kara's wallet.

There was a handwritten note inside. *Gotcha.*

'This is . . .' Kadesky said, studying the policewoman closely. 'Wait, is this *you*?'

The 'officer' laughed and removed the glasses then her cop cap and the brunette wig beneath it, revealing the short reddish hair once again. With a towel that Roland Bell, now chuckling hard, handed her she wiped the dark-complexion make-up off her face and peeled away the thick eyebrows. She then took her wallet back from the hands of the astonished Kadesky and handed him his, which she'd dipped when she'd ploughed by him in her 'escape' towards the door.

Sachs and Kadesky were staring at the body lying on the floor.

Kara walked over and lifted the lightweight frame in the shape of a person wearing clothing that resembled the jeans and windcheater she'd been in. The arms of the outfit ended in what turned out to be thin latex hands, hooked together with Bell's handcuffs, which Kara had escaped from and then relatched on the phoney wrists.

When Sachs and the others had turned away—misdirected by Rhyme towards the chart—Kara had escaped from the cuffs, unfurled the body frame and then silently slipped out of the door to do the quick-change in the hallway.

She folded up the device, which compressed into a package the size of a small pillow—she'd had it hidden under her jacket when she'd arrived.

Kadesky was shaking his head. 'You did the whole escape *and* the quick change in less than a minute?'

'Forty seconds.'

'So the point of this is, I assume,' said Kadesky cynically, 'that you want an audition?'

Kara hesitated and Rhyme shot a prodding glance towards her.

'No, the point is, this *was* the audition. I want a job.'

Kadesky studied her. 'It was one trick. You have others?'

'Plenty.'

'How many changes have you done in one show?'

'Forty-two. Thirty characters. During a thirty-minute routine.'

'Forty-two set-ups in half an hour?' the producer asked, eyebrows raised. He thought for a few seconds. 'Come see me next week. I'm not cutting back my current artists' time in the ring. But I could use an understudy. And maybe you can do some shows at our winter location in Florida.'

Rhyme and Kara exchanged glances. He nodded firmly.

'OK,' the young woman said to Kadesky. She shook his hand.

Kadesky glanced at the spring-loaded wire form that had fooled them. 'You made that?'

'Yep.'

'You might want to patent it.' Then nodding, he left the room.

Sachs laughed. 'Damn, you had me going.'

It had started last night, Rhyme explained, lying in bed, listening to the music from Cirque Fantastique. His thoughts segued to Kara, how good her performance at Smoke & Mirrors had been.

Recalling her lack of self-confidence and Balzac's sway over her.

Recalling too what Sachs had told him about her mother's illness had prompted Rhyme's invitation to Jaynene the next morning.

'I'm going to ask you one more question,' Rhyme had said. 'Think about it before you answer. And I need you to be completely honest.'

The query was: 'Will her mother ever come out of it?'

'No. She needs to be cared for, sure. But not at our place. She's paying for rehab and recreation, medical intervention. Short-term care. Kara's mom could be anywhere. Sorry to say it but all she needs is maintenance at this point.'

'What'll happen to her if she goes to a long-term home?'

'She'll keep getting worse until the end. Just the same as if she stayed with us. Only it wouldn't bankrupt Kara.'

After Jaynene left, Rhyme called Kara. She'd come over and they'd had a talk. The conversation had been awkward. Confronting a heartless, multiple killer was easy compared with intruding on the tender soul of someone's life.

'When I saw you perform at the store I was impressed,' Rhyme had said. 'And it takes a lot to impress me. You should be on the stage.'

'I'm not ready yet. I'll get there eventually.'

After a thick pause Rhyme said, 'The problem with that attitude is that sometimes you *don't* get there eventually.' He glanced down at his body. 'Sometimes things . . . intervene. And there you are, you've put off something important. And you miss it for ever.'

'But Mr Balzac—He's only thinking what's best for me.'

'No, he's not. He's *not* thinking of *you*. Look at Weir and Loesser. And Keating. Mentors can mesmerise you. Thank Balzac for what he's done, stay friends, send him tickets for your first Carnegie Hall show. But get away from him now—while you can.'

'I'm not mesmerised,' she'd said, laughing, but Rhyme sensed that she was considering just how much she was under the man's thumb.

He continued, 'We've got some juice with Kadesky—after everything we've done. Amelia told me how much you like the Cirque Fantastique. I think you should audition.'

'Even if I did, I have a personal situation. My—'

'Mother,' Rhyme'd interrupted. 'I had a talk with Jaynene. I think you should put your mother someplace that'll give her what she needs—care and companionship. Not what *you* need. Not a rehab centre that's going to bankrupt you . . . If there's something you know you're made to do in life, that has to take priority over everything else. Get a job with Cirque Fantastique. You have to move on.'

She'd shaken her head. 'Look, Lincoln, even if I decided to, do you know how many people'd die for a job at Cirque Fantastique?'

Finally he'd smiled. 'Well, now, I've been thinking about that. The Immobilised Man has an idea for a routine.'

Rhyme now finished telling Sachs the story.

Kara said, 'We thought we'd call the trick the Escaping Suspect. I'm going to add it to my repertoire.'

'And Balzac?' Sachs asked. 'He wasn't really involved?'

Rhyme nodded at Kara. 'Pure fiction.'

Kara offered to run up the street to get the Cuban takeout they'd missed the other day. But before they could decide on the order they were interrupted by Rhyme's ringing phone. A moment later Sellitto's voice came on the speakerphone. 'Linc, you busy?'

'Depends,' he grumbled. 'What's up?'

'No rest for the wicked . . . We need your help again. We got a weird homicide.'

'All right, all right,' the criminalist grumbled.

Though the translation of Lincoln Rhyme's gruff demeanour was simply how pleased he was that boredom would be held at bay for at least a little while longer.

THE HOMICIDE was indeed a weird one.

A double murder in a deserted part of Roosevelt Island—that narrow strip of apartments, hospitals and ghostly ruins in the East River. Since it's not far from the United Nations, many diplomats and UN employees live on the island. Two of these individuals—junior emissaries from the Balkans—had been found murdered, their hands bound, each shot in the back of the head twice.

There were several curious things that Amelia Sachs had turned up when she'd run the scene. And strangest of all was the fact that each man was missing his right shoe. 'Both of them the *right* shoe,

Sachs,' Rhyme said, looking at the evidence board, in front of which he sat and she paced. 'What do we make of that?'

But the question was put on hold by Sachs's ringing cellphone. It was Captain Marlow's secretary, asking if she could come down to his office. Several days had passed since she'd learned about Victor Ramos's action against her. There'd been no further word about the suspension.

Sachs disconnected and, with a tightlipped smile towards Rhyme, she said, 'This is it. Gotta go.'

A half-hour later Sachs was in Captain Gerald Marlow's office.

Marlow looked at her in a fatherly way. It was as if the punishment to which she'd been sentenced was so severe that she needed the buffer of paternal kindness. 'People like Ramos, Officer, you're not going to beat 'em. Not on their turf. You won the battle, cuffing him at the scene. But he won the war.' He rummaged through the piles of paperwork on his desk, apparently looking for something.

Within her, the disappointment formed into a rock.

'Right,' the captain said, finally finding what he wanted, a large envelope with a piece of paper stapled to it. He read it quickly. 'Let's get on with it, Officer. Let me have your shield.'

She dug into her pocket. 'How long?'

'A year, Officer,' Marlow said. 'Sorry.'

Suspended for a year, she thought in despair.

'That's the best I could do.' Marlow held out his hand.

Dismay pooling around her, drowning her, she handed him the battered leather case containing the silver shield and ID card.

Badge Number Five Eight Eight Five . . .

Behind him the captain's phone rang and he spun round to answer it. As he talked to the caller, something about the Andrew Constable trial, it seemed, the captain placed the interoffice envelope in his lap. He pinched the phone in the crook of his neck, turned back to face Sachs and continued his conversation as he unwound the red thread that was twisted round the clasps to keep the envelope sealed.

Droning on about the new charges against Constable, raids up in Canton Falls. Oh, Rhyme, Sachs thought What're we going to do? We'll get through it, he'd said. But life isn't about getting through. Getting through is losing.

Marlow finally got the envelope opened and dropped her shield into it. He then reached in and extracted something wrapped in tissue paper.

'Don't have time for a ceremony. We'll do something later.'

This latter message was whispered and it seemed to Sachs he was speaking to her.

Marlow unwrapped the tissue, revealing a gold NYPD badge.

Whispering again, to her. 'Kept your old number, Officer.' He held up the badge, which glistened brilliant yellow. The numbers were the same as her Patrol ID: 5885. He slipped the badge into her leather shield holder. Then he found something else in the yellow envelope: a temporary ID, which he also mounted in the holder. Then handed it back. The card identified her as Amelia Sachs, detective third grade.

Marlow hung up. 'OK, Officer, you'll need to get your picture taken for your permanent ID.'

'But, I'm not suspended?'

'No, you made detective. Didn't they call you?'

'Nobody called me. Except your secretary. What happened?'

'I told you I'd do what I could. I did. I mean, let's face it—there was no way I was letting you go on suspension. Can't afford to lose you.' He hesitated, looked at his tide of paperwork. 'Not to mention, it would've been a nightmare to go up against you in a PBA suit.'

'But the year? You mentioned something about year.'

'That's the *sergeant's exam* I was talking about. You can't take it again until next April. It's civil service and there was nothing I could do about that. But reassigning you to the Detective Bureau, that's discretionary. Ramos couldn't stop that. You'll report to Lon Sellitto.'

She stared at the golden shield. 'I don't know what to say.'

'You can say, "Thank you very much, Captain Marlow. I've enjoyed working with you in Patrol Services all these years. And I regret I will no longer be doing so." '

'I—'

'That's a joke, Officer. I do have a sense of humour despite what you hear. Oh, you're third grade, you might've noticed.'

'Yessir.' Struggling to keep the grin off her face.

'If you want to make it all the way to first grade and sergeant I'd think hard about who you arrest—or *detain*—at crime scenes.'

'Noted, sir.'

OUTSIDE, ON CENTRE STREET, Amelia Sachs walked round her yellow Camaro, examining the damage to the side and front end from the collision with Loesser's Mazda in Harlem.

She decided she'd take the car to a shop in Astoria, Queens, one she'd used before, where the mechanics were talented, more or less honest and had a reverence for power wheels like this.

Pulling out of the police lot, she also made another decision. She thought that since the shop would have to replace a quarter of the Chevy's sheet metal, and it would need repainting anyway, she'd pick a different hue. Fire-engine red was her immediate choice. This shade had a double meaning to her. Not only was it the colour her father always said that muscle cars ought to be but it would also match Rhyme's own sporty vehicle, his Storm Arrow wheelchair. This was just the sort of sentiment that the criminalist would appear wholly indifferent to, while privately pleasing him no end.

Yep, she reflected, red it would be.

She thought about dropping the Chevy off now but, on reflection, decided to wait. At the moment she wanted to get back home, to Lincoln Rhyme, to share the news with him about the alchemy that had transformed her badge from silver to gold—and to get back to work unravelling the thorny mysteries that awaited them: two murdered diplomats, and a couple of missing shoes.

Both of them right.

JEFFERY DEAVER

Author Jeffery Deaver has a reputation for creating cunning narrative twists and conjuring up endings which surprise the reader. 'I love to trick my audience with "sleights of hand" in my plots,' he explains, 'the same way illusionists do in their shows. So I thought it would be natural to write a book about illusion itself.'

The Vanished Man was inspired by a visit Deaver made to the *Big Apple Circus* several years ago. 'I was blown away by the quick-change act and I thought, what a scary thing if a criminal could change appearances and become a whole different person in a matter of seconds.'

The more Deaver looked into the subject, the more fascinated he became. 'All of the illusions and tricks described in the book are real, though naturally I've varied them somewhat, as in my story the Conjurer is trying to actually destroy lives and cause havoc, while most of the danger in a real performance is, of course, illusionary.'

As is often the case with his books, Deaver put in months of research before he began writing. Having trained as a lawyer before becoming a full-time author, he sees a lot of common ground between the two professions. 'For me a thriller is a very carefully structured story. I spend eight months outlining and researching the novel before I begin to write a single word of the prose. The skills I use to do that are the same I used when practising law, researching and structuring a legal document or case. The difference is that writing novels is a lot more fun than practising law!'

Jeffery Deaver, who has homes in Virginia and California, is divorced and has no children, just a very large German Shepherd dog, Gunner, who is more than happy to run the author's life.

DON'T LOOK BACK

KARIN FOSSUM

Beneath the imposing Kollen Mountain in Norway lies a small village where children run in and out of each other's houses and play in the streets without fear.

At police headquarters, Inspector Konrad Sejer usually has nothing more serious to investigate than stolen bicycles, joy-riding and petty theft.

Until an fifteen-year-old girl is found murdered.

CHAPTER ONE

Ragnhild opened the door cautiously and peered out. Up on the road everything was quiet, and a breeze that had been playing among the buildings during the night had finally died down. She turned and pulled the doll's pram over the threshold.

'We haven't even eaten yet,' Marthe complained.

'I have to go home. We're going out shopping,' Ragnhild said.

'Shall I come over later?'

'You can if you like. After we've done the shopping.'

She began to push the pram towards the front gate. It was heavy going, so she turned it round and pulled it instead.

'See you later, Ragnhild.'

The door closed behind her. Ragnhild started off across the street in the direction of the garages. She heard a neighbour close his garage door. He smiled at her. A big black Volvo stood in the driveway, rumbling pleasantly.

'Well, Ragnhild, you're out early, aren't you? Isn't Marthe up yet?'

'I slept over last night,' she said. 'On a mattress on the floor.'

'I see.'

He locked the garage door and glanced at his watch: 8.06am. A moment later he turned the car into the street and drove off.

Ragnhild pushed the pram with both hands. She had reached the downhill stretch, which was rather steep, and she had to hold on tight so as not to lose her grip. She was wearing a red track suit with Simba the Lion across the chest, with a green anorak over it. Her hair was thin and blonde, and not very long, but she had managed to pull it into a topknot with an elastic band. She was six and a half, but small for her age.

She met no one on the hill, but as she approached the intersection she heard a car. So she stopped, squeezed over to the side, and waited as a van with its paint peeling off wobbled over a speed bump. The driver rolled down his window and stared at her.

'Are you going up the hill with that pram?' he asked.

She nodded. 'I live in Granittveien.'

'It'll be awfully heavy. What have you got in it, then?'

'Elise,' she replied, lifting up the doll.

'Excellent,' he said with a broad smile and scratched his head.

His eyes are funny, she thought, really big and round as a ball. They were set wide apart and were pale blue, like thin ice. His mouth was small with full lips, and it pointed down like the mouth of a fish.

'I can drive you up there,' he said. 'There's room for your pram in the back.'

Ragnhild thought for a moment. She stared up the street, which was long and steep.

'Mama's waiting for me,' she said. A bell seemed to ring in the back of her mind, but she couldn't remember what it was for.

'You'll get home sooner if I drive you,' he said.

That decided it. Ragnhild was a practical little girl. She wheeled the pram behind the van and the man hopped out. He opened the back door and lifted the pram in with one hand.

'You'll have to sit in the back and hold on to the pram. Otherwise it'll roll about,' he said, and lifted in Ragnhild too.

He climbed into the driver's seat and released the brake.

He was finally over the last bump, and he shifted to second gear. The little girl sat on the floor of the van steadying the pram. A very sweet little girl, he thought. Red and cute in her track suit, like a ripe little berry. He whistled a tune and felt on top of the world, enthroned behind the wheel in the big van with the little girl in the back. Really on top of the world.

THE VILLAGE LAY in a valley, at the end of a fiord, at the foot of a mountain, and the roads that led there were indescribably bad. Konrad Sejer traced the main highway in the road atlas with a fingertip. They were approaching a roundabout. Police Officer Karlsen was at the wheel.

'Now you have to turn right onto Gneisveien, then left at

Feltspatveien. Granittveien is off to the right. A cul-de-sac,' Sejer said. 'Number five should be the third house on the left.'

Karlsen manoeuvred the car into the housing estate and over the speed bumps. They approached the house, trying to steel themselves, thinking that perhaps the girl might even be back home by now. It was 1.00pm, so she had been missing for five hours. Their unease was growing steadily. Both of them had children of their own; Karlsen's daughter was eight, Sejer had a grandson of four.

Number five was a low, white house with dark blue trim. A large verandah with a prettily turned railing ran round the building. The house sat almost at the top of the ridge, with a view over the whole village, which was surrounded by farms and fields. A patrol car that had come on ahead of them was parked next to the letterboxes.

Sejer went first, ducking his head as he entered the living room. It took them only a second to see that the child was still missing. The panic was palpable. On the sofa sat the girl's mother, a stocky woman in a gingham dress. Next to her, with a hand on the mother's arm, sat a woman officer. The mother was using what little strength she had to hold back her tears. The slightest effort made her breathe hard, as was evident when she stood up to shake hands with Sejer.

'Mrs Album,' he said. 'Someone is out searching, is that correct?'

'Some of the neighbours. They have a dog with them.'

She sank back onto the sofa. He sat down in the armchair facing her and leaned forward, keeping his eyes fixed on hers.

'We'll send out a dog patrol. Now, you have to tell me all about Ragnhild. Who she is, what she looks like, what she's wearing.'

No reply, just persistent nodding. Her mouth looked stiff and frozen.

'Have you called every possible place where she could be?'

'There aren't many,' she murmured. 'I've called them all.'

'Does she have brothers or sisters?'

'She's our only child.'

He tried to breathe without making a sound. 'First of all,' he said, 'what was she wearing? Be as precise as you can.'

'A red track suit,' she stammered, 'with a lion on the front. Green anorak with a hood.' She spoke in fits and starts, her voice threatening to break.

'And Ragnhild herself? Describe her for me.'

'About four foot tall. Thirty-five pounds. Very fair hair.'

She went over to the television, where a number of photos were hanging on the wall beside it. Most of them were of Ragnhild, one was of Mrs Album in national costume, and one of a man in the field uniform of the Home Guard, presumably the father. She chose one in which the girl was smiling and handed it to him. Her hair was almost white. The mother's was jet black, but the father was blond. Some of his hair was visible under his service cap.

'What sort of girl is she?'

'Trusting,' she gasped. 'Talks to everybody.' This admission made her shiver.

'That's just the kind of child who gets along best in this world,' he said firmly. 'We'll have to take the picture with us.'

'I realise that.'

'Tell me,' he said, 'where do the children in this village go walking?'

'Down to the fiord. To the beach or to Horgen's Shop. Or to the top of Kollen. Some go up to the reservoir or walking in the woods.'

He looked out of the window and saw the black firs.

'Has anyone at all seen Ragnhild since she left?'

'Marthe's neighbour saw her when he was leaving for work. I know because I rang his wife.'

'Where does Marthe live?'

'In Krystallen, just a few minutes from here.'

'What's the neighbour's name?'

'Walther,' she said, surprised. 'Walther Isaksen.'

'Where can I find him?'

'He works at Dyno Industries, in the personnel department.'

Sejer stood up, went over to the telephone and called information, then punched in the number and waited.

'I need to speak with one of your employees immediately. The name is Walther Isaksen.'

Mrs Album gave him a worried look from the sofa.

'Konrad Sejer of the police,' Sejer said curtly. 'I'm calling from number five, Granittveien, and you probably know why.'

'Is Ragnhild still missing?'

'Yes. But I understood that you saw her when she left Marthe's house this morning.'

'I was just shutting my garage door.'

'Did you notice the time?'

'It was six minutes past eight. I was running a little late.'

'You left her at six minutes past eight and drove straight to work?'

'Yes.'

'Did you pass any cars along the way that appeared to be driving towards the village?'

The man was silent for a moment. Sejer waited.

'Yes, actually, I did pass one, just before the roundabout. A van, I think, ugly and with peeling paint. Driving quite slowly.'

'Who was driving it?'

'A man,' he said hesitantly.

'MY NAME IS RAYMOND.' He smiled.

Ragnhild looked up, saw the smiling face in the mirror, and Kollen Mountain bathed in the morning light.

'Would you like to go for a drive?'

'Mama's waiting for me.' She said it in a stuck-up sort of voice.

'Have you ever been to the top of Kollen?'

'One time, with Papa.'

'Shall we drive up to the top?'

'I want to go home,' she said, a bit uncertain now.

'Just a short ride?' he asked.

His voice was thin. Ragnhild thought he sounded so sad. She got up, walked forward to the front seat and leaned over.

'Just a short ride,' she repeated. 'Up to the top and then back home right away.'

He backed into Feltspatveien and drove back downhill.

'What's your name?' he asked.

'Ragnhild Elise.'

He rocked a little from side to side and cleared his throat.

The van was out on the main highway now; he drove in second gear down to the roundabout and passed through the intersection with a hoarse roar. Ten minutes later he turned left, up into the wooded mountainside. On the way they passed a couple of farms with red barns and tractors parked here and there. They saw no one. The road grew narrower and peppered with holes. 'This is where I live,' he said suddenly and stopped.

'With your wife?'

'No, with my father. But he's in bed.'

'Hasn't he got up?'

'He's always in bed.'

She peered curiously out of the window and saw a peculiar house. It had been a hut once, and someone had added on to it, first once, then again. The separate parts were all different colours. Next to it stood a garage of corrugated iron. But Ragnhild wasn't interested in the house; she had her eye on something else.

'Bunnies!' she said faintly.

'Yes,' he said, pleased. 'Do you want to look at them?'

He hopped out, opened the back, and lifted her down. He had a peculiar way of walking; his legs were almost unnaturally short and he was severely bow-legged. His feet were small. His wide nose nearly touched his lower lip, which stuck out a bit. Ragnhild thought he wasn't that old, although when he walked he swayed like an old man. He wobbled over to the rabbit hutches and opened them.

Ragnhild stood spellbound. 'Can I hold one?'

'Yes. Take your pick.'

'The little brown one,' she said, entranced.

'That's Påsan. He's the nicest.'

He opened the hutch and lifted out the rabbit. A chubby, lop-eared rabbit, the colour of coffee with a lot of cream. It kicked its legs vigorously but calmed down as soon as Ragnhild took it in her arms. For a moment she was utterly still. She could feel its heart pounding against her hand, as she stroked one of its ears cautiously. It was like a piece of velvet between her fingers. Its nose shone black and moist like a liquorice drop. Raymond stood next to her and watched. He had a little girl all to himself, and no one had seen them.

'THE PICTURE,' SEJER SAID, 'along with the description, will be sent to the newspapers. Unless they hear otherwise, they'll print it tonight.'

Irene Album fell across the table sobbing. The others stared wordlessly at their hands, and at her shaking back. The woman officer sat ready with a handkerchief. Karlsen scraped his chair a bit and glanced at his watch.

'Have you had any luck getting hold of your husband?'

'He's in Narvik on manoeuvres,' she said.

'Don't they use mobile phones?'

'They're out of range.'

'The people who are looking for her now, who are they?' Sejer wanted to know.

'Boys from the neighbourhood. One of them has a phone.'

Sejer spoke to her as softly and clearly as he could.

'What you fear the most has probably *not* happened. Do you realise that? Children get lost all the time, just because they're children. But as a rule they turn up just as suddenly as they disappeared. Generally'—he took a breath—'they're quite all right.'

'I know,' she said, looking at him. 'But she's never gone off like this before.'

'She's growing up and becoming more adventurous,' he said. God help me, he thought. I've got an answer for everything.

'This is a small village,' he went on. 'Has she ever been given a ride by one of the neighbours?'

'Yes, that happens sometimes. There are about a hundred houses on this ridge, and she knows almost everyone.'

Another bout of sobbing took hold. As she wept, the others sat still and waited. The phone rang. A sudden ominous jangle. Sejer lifted the receiver.

'Hello? Is Irene there?'

It sounded like a boy. 'Who's calling?'

'Thorbjørn Haugen. We're looking for Ragnhild.'

'You're speaking with the police. Do you have any news?'

'We've been to all the houses on the whole ridge. Every single one. A lot of people weren't home, though we did meet a lady in Feltspatveien. She said that this morning a lorry had backed into her farmyard and turned round. She lives in number one. A kind of van, she thought. And inside the van she saw a girl with a green jacket and white hair pulled into a topknot on her head.'

'Do you know what time it was?'

'It was eight fifteen.'

'Can you come over to Granittveien?'

'We'll be right there, we're at the roundabout now.'

Sejer hung up. 'Someone saw her,' he said slowly. 'She got into a van.'

'I'M HUNGRY,' Ragnhild said suddenly. 'I have to go home.'

Raymond looked up. Påsan was shuffling about on the kitchen table and licking up the seeds they had scattered over it. They had fed all the rabbits. Ragnhild now realised that it was getting late.

'You can have a slice of bread.'

'I have to go home. We're going shopping.'

'We'll go up to Kollen first, then I'll drive you home afterwards.'

'Now!' she said firmly. 'I want to go home now.'

Raymond thought desperately for a way to stall her.

'All right. But first I have to go and buy some milk for Papa, down at Horgen's Shop. You can wait here, then it won't take as long.'

He stood up and looked at her. Her eyes were clear and blue and her eyebrows were dark, surprising beneath her white fringe. He sighed heavily, walked over to the back door and opened it.

Ragnhild really wanted to leave, but she didn't know the way home so she would have to wait. She padded into the little living room with the rabbit in her arms and curled up in a corner of the sofa. They hadn't slept much last night, she and Marthe, and she quickly grew sleepy. Soon her eyes closed.

It was a while before he came back. For a long time he sat and looked at her, amazed at how quietly she slept. Not a movement, not a single little sigh. He looked anxiously out of the windows and down the hall to his father's bedroom. Then he stood up and poked her lightly on the shoulder.

'We can go now. Give me Påsan.'

For a moment Ragnhild was completely bewildered. She got up slowly and stared at Raymond, then pulled on her anorak and followed him out of the house. The pram was still in the back of the van. Raymond looked sad, but he helped her climb in, then got into the driver's seat and turned the key. Nothing happened.

'It won't start,' he said, annoyed. 'I don't understand it. It was running a minute ago. This piece of junk!'

He went on trying the ignition and stepping on the accelerator; but it kept up a complaining whine and refused to catch.

'We'll have to walk.'

'It's much too far!' she whined.

'No, not from here. We're on the back side of Kollen now, we're almost at the top, and from there you can look straight down on your house. I'll pull your pram for you.'

He put on a jacket that lay on the front seat, got out and opened the door for her. Ragnhild carried her doll and he pulled the pram behind him. It bumped a little on the potholed road. Ragnhild could see Kollen Mountain looming further ahead, ringed by dark woods. For a moment they had to pull off to the side of the road as a car passed them noisily at high speed. The dust hung like a thick fog behind it. The road grew steeper, ending in a turning space, and the path, which went round to the right of Kollen, was soft and dusty. The sheep had widened the path, and their droppings lay as thick as hail. After a few minutes there was a lovely glistening visible through the trees.

'Serpent Tarn,' Raymond said.

She stopped next to him, stared out across the lake and saw the water lilies, and a little boat that lay upside-down on the shore.

Ragnhild followed the bank of the tarn with her eyes, a wavy yellow line of rushes, except for one place where what might be called a beach broke the line like a dark indentation. Raymond let go of the pram, and Ragnhild stuck a finger in her mouth.

THORBJØRN STOOD fiddling with the mobile phone. He was about sixteen, and had dark, shoulder-length hair held in place with a bandanna. He stared hard at Sejer.

'What you have discovered is important,' Sejer said. 'Do you remember her name and address?'

'Helga Moen at number one.' He almost spoke in a whisper as he printed the words on the pad that Sejer gave him.

'Sit down, Thorbjørn.'

He nodded to the sofa where there was room next to Mrs Album. The woman officer stood up slowly. For the first time she ventured to make a suggestion.

'Mrs Album,' she asked, 'why don't we make everyone some coffee?'

The woman nodded weakly, got up and followed the officer out to the kitchen. A tap was turned on and there was the sound of cups clattering. Sejer motioned Karlsen over towards the hallway. They stood there muttering to one another.

Sejer opened the door to get some fresh air. And there she stood. In her red jogging suit, on the bottom step with a tiny white hand on the railing.

'Ragnhild?' he said in astonishment.

A HAPPY HALF-HOUR LATER, as their car sped down Skiferbakken, Sejer ran his fingers through his hair with satisfaction. His lined face looked peaceful, not closed and serious as it usually did. Ragnhild was sitting safely at home on her mother's lap with two thick slices of bread in her hand.

The moment when the little girl stepped into the living room was etched into the minds of both officers. The mother, hearing her thin little voice, rushed in from the kitchen and threw herself at Ragnhild, lightning fast. Ragnhild's thin limbs and the white sprout of hair stuck out through her mother's powerful arms. And there they stood. Not a sound was heard, not a single cry from either of them. And then, finally, with a sobbing laugh:

'*You terrible child!*'

Karlsen turned onto the main road and picked up speed.

'I've been thinking,' Sejer cleared his throat, 'about taking a week's holiday. I have some time off due to me.'

'What will you do with it? Go skydiving in Florida?'

'I thought I'd air out my cabin on Sand Island.'

Sejer caught sight of the village church off to the left, a little white wooden building a bit off the road between green and yellow fields, surrounded by lush trees. A beautiful little church, he thought; he should have buried his wife in a spot like that. Of course, it was too late now. She had been dead more than eight years and her grave was in the cemetery in the middle of town, right by the busy high street, surrounded by exhaust fumes and traffic noise.

'Do you think the girl was all right?' Karlsen asked.

'She seemed to be. I've asked the mother to ring us when things calm down a bit. Six hours,' Sejer said thoughtfully, 'that's quite a while. Must have been a charming lone wolf.'

'He evidently has a driving licence, at least. So he isn't a total hermit.'

'We don't know that, do we? That he has a driving licence?'

'No, damn it, you're right,' Karlsen said. He braked abruptly and turned into the petrol station.

'I need something to eat,' Sejer said. 'Are you coming?'

They went into the shop and Sejer bought a newspaper and some chocolate. He peered out of the window and down to the fiord.

'Excuse me,' said the girl behind the counter, staring nervously at Karlsen's uniform. 'Nothing has happened to Ragnhild, has it?'

'Do you know her?' Sejer put some coins on the counter.

'No, I don't know her, but I know who they are. Her mother was here this morning looking for her.'

'Ragnhild is all right. She's back at home.'

She smiled with relief and gave him his change.

'Are you from around here?' Sejer asked. 'Do you know most people?'

'I certainly do. There aren't many of us.'

'If I ask you whether you know a man, maybe a little odd, who drives an old, ugly van with its paint peeling off, does that ring a bell?'

'That sounds like Raymond,' she said, nodding. 'Raymond Låke.'

'What do you know about him?'

'He works at the Employment Centre. Lives with his father in a cabin on the far side of Kollen. Raymond has Down's syndrome. He's about thirty, and very nice.'

'Does Raymond have a driving licence?'

'No, but he drives anyway. It's his father's van. He's an invalid, so he probably doesn't have much control over what Raymond does. The sheriff pulls him over now and then, but it doesn't do much good. He never drives above second gear. Did he pick up Ragnhild?'

'Yes.'

'Then she couldn't have been safer,' she smiled. 'Raymond would stop to let a ladybird cross the road.'

Sejer and Karlsen both grinned and went back outside.

'Do you think someone with Down's syndrome can be a good driver?'

'No idea,' Karlsen said. 'Anyway, Ragnhild certainly let herself be charmed.'

'I think the rabbits helped.'

They got into the car and Karlsen drove on. Sejer settled his grey head against the headrest and closed his eyes.

CHAPTER TWO

After the quiet of the countryside the city seemed like a filthy, teeming chaos of people and cars. Sejer stared down at the street from the chief's office. He had put in his holiday request, and now he was sitting in Holthemann's office waiting for the reply. It was a formality: Holthemann would never dream of turning down Konrad Sejer, but the chief did like everything done by the book.

The telephone rang. Sejer said a prayer that his holiday wouldn't be snatched from under his nose.

'Yes, he's here,' Holthemann said. 'Put the call through.'

Sejer took the receiver from him. It was Mrs Album.

'Is everything all right with Ragnhild?' he asked.

'Yes, she's fine. But she told me something very odd. I had to ring you, I thought it sounded so peculiar.'

'What is it about?'

'This man she was with, his name is Raymond, by the way, she remembered it afterwards. They walked up the far side of Kollen and past Serpent Tarn, and there they stopped for a while.'

'Yes?'

'Ragnhild says there's a woman lying up there.'

He blinked in surprise. 'What did you say?'

'That there's a woman lying up at the lake. Quite still and with no clothes on.' Her voice was anxious and embarrassed at the same time.

'I'll look into it. Don't mention this to anyone. We'll be in touch.'

He hung up and in his mind he closed up his seaside cabin. The scent of sea spray and cod sprats vanished abruptly. He smiled at Holthemann.

'You know, there's something I have to take care of first.'

KARLSEN WAS OUT on patrol so he took Jacob Skarre with him instead, a young, curly-haired officer about half his age, cheerful and optimistic. They parked again by the letterboxes in Granittveien and had a brief talk with Irene Album. Ragnhild clung like a burr to her mother's dress. Her mother pointed and explained, saying they had to follow a signposted path from the edge of the woods facing the house, uphill to the left past Kollen. It would probably take them twenty minutes, she said.

The tree trunks were marked with blue arrows, indicating the way. They eyed the sheep droppings balefully, stepping out into the heather now and again, but persevered upwards. The path grew steeper and steeper. Skarre was panting a little, while Sejer walked easily. The forest was so thick that they were walking in semidarkness. They had been climbing for exactly seventeen minutes when the forest opened up and the sunlight shone through. Now they could see the water. A mirrorlike tarn, no bigger than a large pond. For a moment they scanned the terrain, following the yellow line of the reeds with their gaze, and caught sight of something that looked like a beach a little further away. They set out towards it.

It could hardly be called a beach, but was more like a muddy patch with four or five large stones, just enough to keep the reeds out. A woman lay in the mud and dirt. She was on her side with her back to them, a dark anorak covering her upper body. Otherwise she was naked. Blue and white clothes lay in a heap next to her.

Sejer approached carefully. 'Don't move,' he said in a low voice.

Skarre obeyed. Sejer was at the water's edge. He balanced himself on a rock a little way out in the tarn so he could see the woman from the front. He didn't want to touch anything, not yet. Her eyes were half-open and fixed on a point out in the lake. Her mouth stood open; above it and extending up over her nose was a yellowish bit of foam, as if she had vomited. He placed two fingers over her carotid artery. The skin felt as cold as he had expected.

On her ear lobes and on the side of her neck he found some faint purple marks. He went back the same way. Skarre stood waiting, his hands in his pockets, looking puzzled.

'Totally naked under her jacket,' Sejer said. 'No visible external injuries. I should say about eighteen to twenty years old.'

Then he telephoned headquarters and requested an ambulance, forensics, photographer and technicians. When he'd finished he looked around for something to sit on, choosing the flattest stone. Skarre sank down next to him. They settled down to wait.

SIX MEN CAME TRAMPING out of the woods. Their voices died out except for a few faint coughs when they caught sight of the men by the water. A second later they saw the dead woman.

Sejer stood up and gestured. 'Stay on that side!' he shouted.

They did as he ordered. They all recognised his grey shock of hair.

'Take pictures from both sides,' Sejer said to the photographer. 'I'm afraid you'll have to go out in the water, because I need pictures from the front without moving her.'

'Mountain lakes like this are usually bottomless,' the photographer said sceptically.

'There's a rowing boat over there. We can use that.'

While the photographer was working, the others stood still and waited. One of the technicians was already working further up the shore, searching through the area, which proved to be free of litter.

'Unbelievable,' he said. 'Not so much as a burnt match.'

'He probably cleaned up after himself,' Sejer said.

'But it looks like a suicide, don't you think?' the technician said.

'She's stark naked,' Sejer replied.

'Yes, but she must have done that herself. Those clothes were not pulled off by force, that's one thing for certain.'

Sejer looked at her. He could understand how the technician had come to that conclusion. It really did look as if she had lain down herself; her clothes were piled carefully next to her, not thrown about. They were muddy but seemed undamaged. Only the jacket that covered her torso was dry and clean. He stared at the mud and dirt and caught sight of what looked like shoe prints. 'Look at these,' he said to the technician.

The man squatted down and measured all the prints several times. 'This is hopeless. They're filled with water.'

'Take pictures anyway.'

The photographer took several shots of the prints. Then he got into the old rowing boat to take the rest.

Sejer went down to the water, took off his shoes and socks and placed them on a rock, rolled up his trousers and waded out. He stood a few feet from her head. She had a pendant round her neck. He fished it out carefully with a pen he took from his inside pocket.

'A medallion,' he said in a low voice. 'There's something on it. An H and an M. Get a bag ready.'

He bent over and loosened the chain, then he removed the jacket.

'The back of her neck is red,' he said. 'An ugly blotch, as big as a hand.'

Snorrason, the medical examiner, waded out in his gumboots and inspected in turn the eyeballs, the teeth, the nails. He cautiously touched the foam above her mouth with a wooden spatula. It seemed solid and dense, almost like a mousse.

Sejer nodded to her mouth. 'What's that?'

'I think it's a fluid from the lungs, containing protein.'

'Which means?'

'Drowning. But it could mean other things.' Snorrason rolled her carefully onto her stomach. 'A big, well-built woman in healthy condition. Broad shoulders. Good musculature in upper arms and thighs and calves. Probably played sports.'

'Do you see any sign of violence?'

Snorrason inspected her back and the backs of her legs. 'Apart from the reddening of the neck, no. Someone may have grabbed her hard by the back of the neck and pushed her to the ground. Obviously while she was still clothed. Then she was pulled up again, carefully undressed, laid in place, and covered with the jacket.'

'Any sign of sexual assault?'

'Don't know yet.'

Sejer nodded to the men with the stretcher and stood watching them with his arms crossed. For the first time in a long while he raised his eyes and looked up. The sky was pale, and the pointed firs stood round the tarn like raised spears. Of course they would figure it out. He made himself a promise. They'd figure everything out.

THE MISSING PERSONS list lay before Sejer on the table. Four names: two men and two women, both born before 1960 and therefore not the woman they had found by Serpent Tarn. It was 6.00pm, and there wasn't much more that could be done until they had the woman's identity. He grabbed his leather jacket from the back of the chair and took the lift down to the ground floor.

He headed for his car in the car park, an elderly ice-blue Peugeot 604. He drove slowly through the town to his flat. Skarre had promised to call as soon as the woman was reported missing.

As he fumbled with his key in the lock he heard the thump as his Leonberger, Kollberg, jumped down from the forbidden spot on the armchair. Sejer lived in a block of flats, the only one in town that was thirteen storeys high, so it looked out of place in the landscape. It loomed in the sky above the surrounding buildings. When he'd moved in twenty years ago with Elise, it was because the flat had an excellent floor plan and, situated on the thirteenth floor, a spectacular view. Inside, the flat was cosy and warm, with wood panelling. The furniture, old and of solid sandblasted oak, had belonged to his parents. For the most part, the walls were covered with books, and in the little remaining space he had hung a few favourite photographs. One of Elise, several of his grandson, Matteus, and his daughter, Ingrid.

The rules in this apartment society, in which the families were stacked on top of one another, were strict. It was forbidden to shake rugs from the balcony, and Kollberg shed hair like crazy. But the apartment was clean and tidy and reflected what was inside him: order and simplicity. The dog had a corner in the kitchen where dried food was always scattered about with spilt water; this corner indicated Sejer's one weak point: his attachment to his dog was an emotional one.

He braced his legs to receive Kollberg's welcome, which was overwhelming. He took him out for a quick walk behind the building, gave him fresh water, and was halfway through the newspaper when the phone rang. He felt a slight tension as he picked up the receiver. Someone might have called in; maybe they had a name to give him.

'Hi, Grandpa!' said a voice.

'Matteus?'

'I have to go to bed now. It's night-time.'

'Did you brush your teeth?' he asked, sitting down on the telephone bench. He could see before him the little mocha-coloured face and pearly white teeth.

'Mama did it for me.'

He chatted to his grandson for a long time, with the receiver pressed to his ear so that he could hear all the little sighs and lilts in the lively voice. Finally he exchanged a few words with his daughter. He heard her resigned sigh when he told her about the body they had found, as if she disapproved of the way he had chosen to spend his life. She sighed in exactly the same way as Elise had done. He didn't mention her own involvement in Somalia, wracked by civil war.

IT WAS ALMOST MIDNIGHT when Sejer's phone rang for the second time. He was dozing in his armchair with the newspaper on his lap. Twenty minutes later he was in his office.

'They arrived in an old Toyota,' Skarre said. 'I was waiting for them outside. Her parents.'

'What did you say to them?'

'Probably not the right things. I was a little stressed. They called first, and half an hour later they drove up. They've already gone.'

'To the morgue?'

'Yes. They brought along a photo. The mother knew exactly what she had been wearing. The anorak wasn't hers.'

'Are you kidding?'

'Incredible, isn't it? He left us a clue, free of charge.'

'Who is she, by the way?'

Skarre looked at his notes. 'Annie Sofie Holland.'

'Annie Holland? What about the medallion?'

'Belonged to her boyfriend. His name is Halvor.'

'Where is she from?'

'Lundeby. They live at number twenty, Krystallen. It's the same street where Ragnhild Album stayed overnight. An odd coincidence.'

'And her parents? What were they like?'

'Shattered,' he said in a low voice. 'Nice, decent people. She talked nonstop, he was practically mute.'

Sejer put a Fisherman's Friend lozenge in his mouth.

'She was only fifteen,' Skarre continued. 'A high-school student.'

'That can't be right!' Sejer shook his head. 'I thought she was older. Are the photos ready?' he asked as he sat down.

Skarre handed him a folder from the file. The photos had been blown up to eight by ten inches.

'This doesn't look like a sex crime. This is different.' Sejer leafed through the stack. 'She's laid out too nicely. No bruises or scratches, no sign of resistance. Sex offenders don't do things like that, they show off their power. They cast their victims aside.'

'But she's naked.'

'Yes, I know.'

'So what do you think the pictures are telling us? At first glance.'

'I'm not really sure. That jacket is arranged so protectively over her shoulders,' Sejer said.

'How long do you think we have to wait for the report?'

'I'll breathe down Snorrason's neck as effectively as I can.' Sejer crunched the lozenge with his teeth, went over to the sink and filled a paper cup with water. 'What about the Hollands?' he asked. 'Do they have any other children?'

'Another daughter. Older.'

'Thank God for that.'

'Is that supposed to be some kind of consolation?' Skarre said.

'For us it is,' Sejer said gloomily.

'There are two ways to reach Serpent Tarn,' Skarre said. 'By the marked path that we took, or the road on the far side, which was the way that Ragnhild and Raymond went. If anyone lives along that road, don't you think we should pay them a visit later today?'

'It's called Kolleveien. I don't think there are many houses, I checked on the map at home. Just a few farms. But of course if she was taken to the lake by car, they must have come that way.'

'I feel sorry for her boyfriend.'

'I guess we'll find out what kind of guy he is.'

'If a man takes a girl's life,' Skarre said, 'by holding her head under water until she's dead, but then he pulls her out and proceeds to lay out her body, this suggests something along these lines: "I didn't really mean to kill you, it was something I was forced to do." It makes me think it was a way of asking for forgiveness, don't you agree?'

Sejer downed the water and crushed the paper cup flat. 'I'll talk to Holthemann in the morning. I want you on this case.'

'He's assigned me to the Savings Bank case,' Skarre stammered, surprised. 'Along with Gøran.'

'But you're interested?'

'Interested in a murder case? It's like a Christmas present. I mean, it's a big challenge. Of course I'm interested.'

LIKE GRANITTVEIEN, Krystallen was a cul-de-sac. The houses stood close together, twenty-one in total. From a distance, they looked like terraced houses, but as Sejer and Skarre walked down the street, they could see that narrow passageways ran between each building. The houses were three storeys high, tall with pitched roofs, and identical. The colours complemented each other: deep red, dark green, brown, grey. One stood out; it was the colour of an orange.

Sejer could almost feel the neighbours' eyes on the back of his neck as he and Skarre stood at the front door of number twenty. He tried to calm his breathing, which was faster than normal. This sort of thing was such an ordeal for him that many years ago he had fashioned a series of set phrases which now, after much practice, he could utter with confidence.

Ada and Eddie Holland, Annie's parents, obviously hadn't done a thing since coming home the night before—not even slept. The mother was sitting in a corner of the sofa, the father was perched on the armrest. He looked numb. The woman hadn't yet taken in the catastrophe; she gave Sejer an uncomprehending look, as if she couldn't understand what two police officers were doing in her living room. This was a nightmare, and soon she would wake up. Sejer had to take her hand from her lap.

'I can't bring Annie back,' he said in a low voice. 'But I hope that I can find out why she died.'

'We're not thinking about why!' shrieked the mother. 'We're thinking about who did it! You have to find out who it was and lock him up! He's sick.' She was breathing hard, gasping for air.

Her husband patted her arm awkwardly.

'First we have to ascertain that someone really did take her life,' Sejer said.

'If you think she took her own life, you'd better think again,' the mother said. 'That's impossible. Not Annie.'

'I need to ask you about a few things. I need to know what kind of girl Annie was. Tell me whatever you can.' And at the same time, he thought, what are they supposed to say to that? The very best, of course, the sweetest, the nicest. Someone totally special. The very dearest thing they had.

They both began to sob. The mother from deep in her throat, a painfully plaintive wail; the father soundlessly.

Ada Holland shifted her eyes past Skarre and Sejer.

'Let's start at the beginning,' Sejer said. 'What time exactly did she leave home?'

The mother answered, staring at her lap, 'At twelve thirty.'

'Where was she going?'

'To Anette Horgen's house. A schoolfriend. Three of them were doing a project.'

'And she never got there?'

'We rang them at eleven last night, since it was getting awfully late. Anette was in bed. Only the other girl had turned up. I couldn't believe it . . .' She hid her face in her hands.

'Why didn't the girls ring you to talk to Annie?'

'They assumed she didn't feel like coming over,' she said, stifling her sobs. 'Thought she'd just changed her mind.'

'Was she going to walk over there?'

'Yes. It's three miles and she usually rides her bike, but it needs repairing.'

'Where does Anette live?'

'They have a farm and a general store: Horgen's Shop.'

Sejer nodded, hearing Skarre's pen scratching across the page.

'She had a boyfriend?'

'Halvor Muntz.'

'Had it been going on for long?'

'About two years. He's older. It's been on again, off again, but it's been going fine lately, as far as I know.'

Ada Holland didn't seem to know what to do with her hands; they fumbled over each other, opening and clenching.

'Do you know if it was a sexual relationship?' he asked lightly.

The mother stared at him, outraged. 'She's fifteen years old!'

'You have to remember that I didn't know her,' he said.

'There was nothing like that,' she said.

'I don't think that's something we would know,' the husband ventured at last. 'Halvor is eighteen. Not a child any more.'

'I would have known!'

'But you're not much good at talking about things like that!'

The mood was tense. Sejer made his own assumption.

'If she was going to work on a school project, she must have taken a schoolbag along.'

'A brown leather bag. Where is it?'

'We haven't found it.' So we'll have to send out the divers, he thought. 'What kind of girl was she? Open? Talkative?'

'Used to be,' the husband said.

'What do you mean?' the mother said. 'She was at a difficult age. Sølvi was the same. Sølvi is her sister,' she added.

'So she was not open and talkative?'

'She was quiet and modest,' the mother said. 'Meticulous and fair-minded. Had her life under control.'

'But she used to be more lively?'

'They make more of a fuss when they're young.'

'What I need to know,' Sejer said, 'is when she changed?'

'At the normal time. When she was about fourteen. Puberty,' she said, as if to explain.

He nodded, staring at the father.

'There was no other reason for the change?'

'What would that be?' the mother said quickly.

'I don't know.' Sejer sighed a little and leaned back. 'But I'm trying to find out why she died.'

The mother began shaking so violently that they almost couldn't understand what she said. '*Why* she died? But it must be some . . .'

She didn't dare say the word. 'Was she . . .' Another pause.

'We don't know, Mrs Holland. Not yet. These things take time.'

He looked round the room, which was neat and clean. Wreaths of dried flowers above the doors, lace curtains. Photographs. Crocheted doilies. He stood up and went over to a photograph on the wall.

'That was taken last winter.'

The mother came over to him. He was amazed every time he saw a face again that he had seen only devoid of life or lustre. The same person and yet not the same. Annie had a wide face with a large mouth and big grey eyes. Thick, dark eyebrows. She had a shy smile. At the bottom edge of the picture he saw the collar of her shirt and a glimpse of her boyfriend's medallion. Pretty, he thought.

'Was she involved in sports?'

'Used to be,' the father said in a low voice.

'She played handball,' the mother said sadly. 'But she gave it up. She was running a lot. At least twenty miles a week.'

'Why did she stop playing handball?'

'She's had so much homework lately.'

'Was she good? At handball?'

'Very good,' said the father softly. 'She was the goalkeeper. She shouldn't have stopped. She never really explained why she did.'

Sejer sat down again. 'Did she do well at school?'

'Better than most. I'm not boasting, it's just a fact,' the father said.

'May I see her room?'

The mother got up and led the way, taking short, shuffling steps. Her husband stayed seated on the armrest, motionless.

The room was tiny, but it had been her own little hideaway. Just enough space for a bed, desk and chair. He looked out of the window and stared straight across the street at the neighbour's porch. The orange house. The room was full of trophies, certificates and medals; and there were a few pictures of Annie. One picture of her in her goalie's uniform with the rest of the team, and another of her standing on a windsurfing board, looking in fine form. On the wall over the bed she had several photos of little children, one of her pushing a pram, and one of a young man. Sejer pointed.

'Her boyfriend?'

The mother nodded.

'Did she work with children?'

He pointed to a picture of Annie holding a blond toddler.

'She baby-sat for all the children on the street.'

'So she liked children?'

She nodded again.

'Did she keep a diary, Mrs Holland?'

'I don't think so,' she said as she led the way back to the living room. The husband was still perched on the armrest. He looked as if he was about to collapse.

'What about her sister?'

'She's flying home today. She's in Trondheim visiting my sister.'

Mrs Holland sank onto the sofa and leaned against her husband. Sejer went to the window and stared out.

'You live close to your neighbours here,' he said. 'Does that mean you know each other well?'

'Quite well. Everyone talks to each other.'

'And everyone knew Annie?'

She nodded wordlessly.

'We'll have to go door to door. Could you lend us a few photos?'

The father got up and went over to the shelf under the television. 'We have a video,' he said. 'From last summer.'

'They don't need a video,' the mother said. 'Just a photo of her.'

'I'd be glad to have it.' Sejer took the video from the father and thanked them. 'You said she ran twenty miles a week?' Sejer said. 'Did she go alone?'

'No one could keep up with her,' the father said.

'So she made time to run twenty miles a week in spite of her school work. Maybe it wasn't her homework that made her give up handball after all?'

'She could run whenever she liked,' said the mother. 'Sometimes she'd go out before breakfast. But if there was a game, she had to show up. She couldn't make her own plans. I don't think she liked being tied down. She was very independent, our Annie.'

'Any other interests?' Sejer asked. 'Aside from running?'

'Film and music and books and things like that. And she loved little children,' the father said.

Sejer asked them to make a list of everyone who knew Annie. Friends, neighbours, teachers, family members. When they were done, the list had forty-two names.

'Are you going to talk to everyone on the list?' the mother asked.

'Yes, we are. And this is just the beginning. We'll keep you informed of our progress,' he said.

SEJER DROVE while Skarre read through his notes.

'I asked the father about the handball business,' he said. 'While the two of you were in the girl's room.'

'And?'

'He said that Annie was very promising. The team had a terrific season; they made it to the finals. He couldn't understand why she gave it up. It made him wonder if something had happened.'

'We should find the coach, whoever he or she is. Maybe that would give us a lead.'

'It's a man,' Skarre said. 'He'd been calling for weeks, trying to persuade her to come back. The team had big problems after Annie left. No one could replace her. His name is Knut Jensvoll, and he lives at number eight, Gneisveien, down the hill from here.'

'Thanks,' Sejer said, raising an eyebrow. 'I'm sitting here thinking about something,' he continued. 'The fact that Annie might have been killed at exactly the time when we were on Granittveien, a few minutes away, worrying about Ragnhild.'

RAYMOND SPREAD BUTTER on a piece of thin flatbread. He was concentrating hard so that it wouldn't break, with his tongue sticking out of his mouth. He had four pieces of flatbread stacked on top of each other with butter and sugar in between; his record was six.

The kitchen was small and cosy, but now it was messy after his efforts with the food. He had a slice of bread prepared for his father too. White bread with the crust cut off, spread with bacon fat from the frying pan. After they had eaten he would wash the dishes, and then sweep the kitchen floor. He was about to pour coffee into his father's mug when he heard a car pull up by the front door. To his terror he saw it was a police car. He stiffened, backed away from the window and ran into a corner of the living room. Maybe they were coming to put him in prison. Then who would take care of Papa?

Car doors slammed in the courtyard and he heard voices. He wasn't sure whether he had done something wrong. It wasn't always that easy to know. For safety's sake he didn't budge when they knocked on the door, but it was clear that they weren't intending to give up; they knocked and knocked and called his name. Maybe his father would hear them. After a while it grew quiet. He was still in the corner of the living room, beside the fireplace, when he caught sight of a face at the window. A tall, grey-haired man was waving at him. The man looked friendly enough, but that was no guarantee of his being nice. Raymond ran to the kitchen, but there was a face there too. Fair, curly hair and a dark uniform. He stood there, rocking a little. After a while he went out to the hall and looked anxiously at the key in the lock.

'Raymond!' one of them called. 'We just want to talk. We won't hurt you.'

'I wasn't mean to Ragnhild!' he shouted.

'We know that. That's not why we're here. We just need a little help from you.'

Still he hesitated, before finally opening the door.

'May we come in?' the taller one said. 'We have to ask you a few questions.'

'All right. I wasn't sure what you wanted. I can't open the door to just anyone.'

'No, you certainly can't,' Sejer said, looking around him. 'But it's good if you open the door when it's the police.'

'We'll sit in the living room then.'

Raymond walked ahead of them and pointed to the sofa. They sat down and studied the room, rather small and square with the sofa, table and two chairs.

'Is your father home?' Sejer began.

'He's in bed. He doesn't get up any more, he can't walk.'

'So you take care of him?'

'I make the food and clean the house, just so you know!'

'Your father's pretty lucky to have you.'

Raymond gave a big smile, in that uncommonly charming manner characteristic of people with Down's syndrome. An uncorrupted child in a robust body.

'You were so nice to Ragnhild yesterday, and you took her home,' Sejer said. 'That was a kind thing to do.'

'She's not so big, you know!' he said, trying to sound grown-up.

'No, she isn't. So it was good she had you with her. But when she came home, she had a story to tell, and we thought we'd ask you about it, Raymond. I'm talking about the girl the two of you saw at Serpent Tarn.'

Raymond stared at him anxiously. 'I didn't do it!' he blurted out.

'We don't think you did. That's not why we're here. Let me ask you about something else instead. I see you have a watch.'

'Yes, I have a watch.' He showed it to them. 'It's Papa's old one.'

'Can you tell me what time it is now?'

Raymond looked at his watch. 'It's just after ten past eleven.'

'That's right.' Sejer nodded and glanced over at Skarre, who was assiduously taking notes.

'Did you look at it when you took Ragnhild home? Or, for instance, when you were standing by Serpent Tarn?'

'No.'

'Can you guess what time it might have been?'

'Now you're asking me hard questions,' he said.

'It's not easy to remember everything, you're right about that. I'm almost finished. Did you see anything else up by the lake—I mean, did you see any people up there? Besides the girl?'

'No. Is she sick?' he said suspiciously.

'She's dead, Raymond.'

'Too soon, I think.'

'That's what we think. Did you see a car or anything driving by the house here in the daytime? Or people walking past? While Ragnhild was here, for example?'

He thought for a long time. 'Well, yes, one car. Just as we were leaving. It zoomed past, like a regular racing car.'

'Going up or down?'

'Down.'

Zoomed past here, Sejer thought. But what does that mean to someone who never drives above second gear?

'Did you recognise the car? Was it someone who lives up here?'

'No, they don't drive that fast.'

Sejer did some mental calculations. 'Ragnhild was home a little before two, so it might have been around one thirty, right? It didn't take you very long to go up to the lake, did it?'

'No.'

'What kind of car was it?' Sejer asked and then held his breath. A car sighting would be something to go on. A car in the vicinity of the crime scene, driving at high speed at a specific time.

'Just an ordinary car,' Raymond said, pleased.

'An ordinary car?' Sejer said. 'What do you mean, exactly?'

'Not a truck, or a van or anything. A normal car.'

'I see. A normal car. Are you good at recognising makes?'

'Not really.'

'What kind of car does your father have?'

'A Hiace,' he said proudly.

'Do you see the police car outside? Can you see what kind it is?'

'That one? You just told me. It's a police car.'

'What about the colour of the car, Raymond? Did you notice the colour?'

He tried hard to remember but gave up, shaking his head. 'It was so dusty. Impossible to see the colour,' he muttered.

'But could you tell us whether it was dark or light?'

'In between. Maybe brown or grey or green. A dirty colour.'

'Fine. I understand.'

'There was something on the roof,' he said suddenly. 'A long box. Flat and black.'

'A ski-box maybe?' Skarre suggested.

Raymond hesitated. 'Yes, maybe a ski-box.'

Skarre smiled and made a note, delighted at Raymond's eagerness.

'Good observation, Raymond. Did you get that, Skarre? So your father is in bed?'

'He's waiting for his food now, I think.'

'We didn't mean to hold you up. Could we say hello before we go?'

'Sure, I'll show you the way.'

He walked across the living room, and the two men followed. At the end of the hall he stopped and opened a door very gently. In the bed lay an old man, snoring.

'We won't disturb him,' Sejer said. They thanked Raymond and went out to the courtyard. He trotted after them.

'We might come back again. You've got nice rabbits,' Skarre said.

'That's what Ragnhild said. You can hold one if you want.'

'Another time.'

They waved and then jolted off along the bumpy road. Sejer drummed on the steering wheel in annoyance.

'That car is important. And the only thing we've got to go on is "something in between". But a ski-box on the roof, Skarre! Ragnhild didn't say anything about that.'

'Everyone under the sun has a ski-box on their car.'

'I don't.'

They drove down the highway until they came to a small country shop on the left-hand side of the road. They parked and went inside. A bell rang above their heads, and a man wearing a blue-green nylon smock appeared from the back room. 'Is it about Annie?' he asked.

Sejer nodded.

'Anette feels so terrible,' he said, sounding shocked. 'She rang Annie today. All she heard was a scream on the other end of the line.'

A teenage girl appeared in the doorway. Her father put his arm round her shoulders.

'We're letting her stay at home today.'

Sejer went over and shook hands. 'Do you live next to the store, Mr Horgen?' he asked.

'Five hundred yards from here, down by the shore. We can't believe what's happened.'

'Did you see anything unusual in the area yesterday?'

He thought for a moment. 'A group of boys came in and each bought a Coke. Otherwise only Raymond Låke. He came in around midday and bought milk and flatbread. He lives with his father up near Kollen. We don't have many customers.'

He kept patting his daughter on the back as he talked.

'And a motorcycle stopped here too. Must have been between twelve thirty and one o'clock. Stopped for a minute and then left. A big bike with large saddlebags. Might have been a tourist.'

'A motorcycle? Can you describe it?'

'Oh, dark, I think. Shiny and impressive. He was sitting with his back to me, wearing a helmet. Reading something.'

'Did you see the number plates?'

'No, sorry.'

'Do you remember seeing a brown, grey or green car with a ski-box on the roof?'

'No.'

'What about you, Anette?' Sejer said, turning to the daughter. 'Is there anything you can think of that might be important?'

'I should have called her,' she said.

'You can't blame yourself for this, you couldn't have done anything to prevent it. Someone probably picked her up on the road. Can you think of anyone she might have met along her route? Had she mentioned any new acquaintances?'

'Oh, no. She had Halvor, you know.'

'I see. Well, please call if you think of anything. We'd be happy to come over again.'

They thanked Anette and her father, then left.

Sejer shut the car door. 'Thorbjørn thought they went past Serpent Tarn at about twelve forty-five, when they were searching for Ragnhild. At that time, the body wasn't there. Raymond and Ragnhild saw the body at approximately one thirty. That gives us a window of forty-five minutes. That almost never happens. A car drove past them at high speed just before they left. An ordinary car, sort of in between, not old, not new. A dirty colour, not light, not dark.'

He slammed his hand against the dashboard.

'Not everybody is a car expert,' Skarre said with a smile.

'We'll ask him to come forward. Whoever it was that drove past Raymond's house between one and one thirty yesterday, at high speed. Possibly with a ski-box on the roof. We'll also put out a description on the motorcycle. If no one comes forward, I'm going to have to put pressure on Raymond and Ragnhild about that car.'

'How are you going to do that?'

'Don't know yet. Maybe they can draw. Kids are always drawing.'

AFTERWARDS THEY ATE in the cafeteria at the courthouse. Sejer mopped up the last scraps on his plate with a piece of bread, then carefully wiped his mouth with his napkin.

'We'll start with Krystallen. We'll take one side each, but we'll wait until after five, when people are home from work.'

'What should I be looking for?' Skarre said.

'Irregularities. Anything at all out of the ordinary. Turn on the charm and get them to talk.'

'We'd better talk to Eddie Holland by himself.'

'I thought of that.'

'Annie's sister must be home by now. We need to talk to her too.'

When they had finished their food, they went over to the forensics department, but no one could tell them anything significant about the blue anorak that had covered the body.

'Imported, from China. Sold by all the discount chains. The importer said they'd brought in two thousand jackets. A packet of butterscotch in the right pocket. Otherwise nothing.'

'The size?'

'Extra large. But the sleeves must have been too long. The cuffs were folded back.'

They drove back to Krystallen. There was more traffic now and the pavements were teeming with children, some with doll's prams, others on a variety of vehicles: tricycles, tractors, and one home-made go-cart with a mangy flag flapping in the wind. When the police pulled up next to the letterboxes, the colourful tableau froze. Almost everyone realised that something had happened, but they didn't know what.

Sejer and Skarre presented their questions at every house, each taking one side of the street. Time after time they had to watch disbelief and shock flood the frightened faces. Everyone had known Annie well.

Skarre went first to the orange house, number nine. It belonged to a bachelor called Fritzner, who was in his late forties. In the middle of the living room was a little red boat with full white sails. In the bottom of the boat lay a mattress and lots of cushions, and a bottle holder was fastened to the gunwale. Skarre stared at it, intrigued.

Fritzner didn't know Annie well, but he said that occasionally he had offered her a lift into town. He liked Annie. She'd been a good handball goalie, he said.

Sejer moved on down to number six, the home of a Turkish family. The Irmaks were just about to eat when he rang the bell. The man of the house, a stately figure wearing an embroidered shirt, rose from the table and stretched out a hand. Sejer told him that Annie Holland was dead, and that it seemed that someone had murdered her.

'No!' he said, horrified. 'It can't be true. Not that pretty girl in number twenty, not Eddie's daughter!'

The wife had seen Annie leave. She thought it must have been around 12.30pm.

'Has she ever been to your house?'

'Yes. She came on the day we moved in, with a flower in a pot. As a welcome from them.'

When Sejer left, they thanked him for his visit and said he was welcome to come again. On the street he paused for a moment and stared straight across at Skarre, who was just coming out of number nine. They nodded to each other and went on their separate ways.

'DID YOU FIND many locked doors?' Skarre asked.

'Only two. Johnas in number four and Rud in number eight.'

'I got notes from all of mine.'

'Any immediate thoughts?'

'That she knew everybody and had been in and out of their houses for years. And that she was well liked by everyone.'

They rang the Hollands' bell. A young woman opened the door. She was obviously Annie's sister; they were alike, and yet they were different. Her hair was just as blonde as Annie's, but it was darker at the roots. Her eyes were outlined with black mascara, trapped inside, very pale blue and uncertain. She wasn't big and tall like Annie, or sporty and muscular. She was wearing lavender stretch pants and a white blouse that was unbuttoned halfway down.

'Sølvi?' Sejer said.

She nodded and offered him a limp hand, then led the way inside and at once sought refuge next to her mother. Mrs Holland was sitting in the same corner of the sofa as before. She looked sombre and strained. Eddie Holland was not in evidence.

After half an hour of conversation it became clear that the two sisters hadn't been especially close. Each had led her own life. Sølvi had a cleaning job at a beauty parlour and had never played sports. Sejer thought that in all likelihood she had been preoccupied with herself, and with her appearance. She was older than Annie, but her face had a naive look to it. Sølvi looks like her mother, he thought, while Annie takes after her father.

'Do you know whether Annie had made any new friends recently? Met any new people?'

'She wasn't interested in meeting people,' Sølvi answered.

'Do you know whether she kept a diary?'

'Oh, no, not Annie. She wasn't like that. She was different from other girls, more like a boy. Didn't even use any make-up. Hated getting dressed up. She wore Halvor's medallion, but only because he pestered her about it. It got in the way when she went running.'

'Do you know her friends?'

'They're younger than me, but I know who they are.'

'Who do you think knew her best?'

'She spent time with Anette.'

'Do you think she would ever hitchhike?'

'Never. Neither would I,' she said. 'But we often can catch a ride when we walk along the road. We know just about everybody.'

'Do you think she seemed unhappy about anything?'

'Not unhappy. But she wasn't exactly jumping with joy either. She wasn't interested in much. Just school and running.'

'And Halvor, perhaps?'

'I'm not really sure. She seemed indifferent about Halvor too.'

Sejer saw an image in his mind's eye of a girl turned slightly away with a sceptical look on her face, a girl who did as she pleased, who went her own way, and who had kept all of them at a distance. Why?

'Your mother says she used to be livelier,' he said.

'Oh, yes, she used to be more talkative.'

Sejer cleared his throat. 'This change,' he said, 'did it happen suddenly, do you think? Or was it gradually, over a long period of time?'

'I'm not sure. She just became different.'

'Can you say anything about when that happened, Sølvi?'

She shrugged. 'Last year some time. She broke up with Halvor and right after that she stopped playing handball. Plus she was growing so tall. She grew out of all her clothes and got so quiet.'

'Do you mean angry or sullen?'

'No. Just quiet. Disappointed, in a way.'

Sejer nodded. 'Do you know whether Annie and Halvor had a sexual relationship?'

She turned bright red. 'I'm not sure. You'll have to ask Halvor.'

'I will.'

CHAPTER THREE

Halvor's hands shook as he pulled photos out of a yellow Kodak envelope. He was a slender young man with narrow shoulders. He had a small mouth, and one corner was stretched taut—when he smiled, which happened rarely, it refused to turn upwards. Close up, it was possible to see the scar from the stitches; it extended from the right side of his mouth to his temple. His hair was brown, cut short and soft, and his sideburns were sparse.

Slowly, he shuffled through the pictures. He had looked at them countless times before. But now they had acquired a new dimension. Now he was searching them for signs of what was to happen later on, things that he hadn't known when he'd taken them. Annie on the end of the diving board, erect as a pillar in her black bathing suit. Annie asleep in the green sleeping-bag. Annie on her bike, her face hidden by her blonde hair.

'Halvor!' cried his grandmother from the window. 'There's a police car outside!'

'Yes,' he said in a low voice.

'Why are they coming here?' She turned to look at him, suddenly anxious.

'It's because of Annie.'

'What's wrong with Annie?'

'She's dead. They're coming here to interrogate me. I knew they would come. I've been waiting for them.'

'Why are you saying that Annie's dead?'

'Because she *is* dead!' he shouted. 'She died yesterday. Her father called me.'

'Yes, but why?'

'How should I know. All I know is that she's dead.'

He hid his face in his hands. His grandmother collapsed like a sack of flour into her chair, looking even paler than usual. Things had been so peaceful for so long. But it couldn't last, of course it couldn't.

Someone knocked loudly on the door. Halvor gave a start, shoved the photos under the tablecloth, and went to open the door. There were two of them. They stood on the porch for a moment and looked at him. It wasn't hard to guess what they were thinking.

'Are you Halvor Muntz?'

'Yes.'

'We've come to ask you some questions. Do you know why?'

'Her father called last night.' Halvor nodded over and over. Sejer caught sight of the old woman in the chair and said hello to her.

'Is there somewhere we can talk in private?'

'My room's the only place.'

'Well, if it's all right with you . . .'

Halvor led the way out of the living room, through a cramped little kitchen, and into his bedroom. The two men cleared a place to sit on a sagging sofa, Muntz sat down on the bed.

'Is she your grandmother? The woman in the living room?'

'Yes, my father's mother.'

'And your parents?'

'They're divorced.'

'Is that why you live here?'

'I was allowed to choose where I wanted to live.'

Sejer looked around, searching for pictures of Annie, and found a small one in a gold frame on the bedside table. Next to it stood an alarm clock and a statue of the Madonna and child. A stereo and CD player. A wardrobe, a pair of trainers. Beside the window stood a desk with a good computer. From the window he looked out onto the courtyard, where he could see their Volvo parked in front of the shed, an empty kennel, and a motorcycle covered with plastic.

'You ride a motorcycle?' he began.

'When it's running. It doesn't always start. I have to get it fixed, but I don't have the money right now.'

'Do you have a job?'

'At the ice-cream factory. Been there two years.'

The ice-cream factory, Sejer thought. For two years. So he must have left at the end of middle school and gone to work. It was clear that he wasn't athletic—a little too thin, a little too pale. Annie was much fitter in comparison, training diligently and working hard at school, while this young man packed ice cream and lived with his grandmother. Sejer didn't think it added up.

'When did you last see Annie?'

'On Friday. We went to the movies, the seven o'clock show.'

'What did you see?'

'*Philadelphia*.'

'And then?'

'We ate at the Kino Pub and took the bus back to her house. Sat in her room and listened to music. I took the bus home at eleven.'

'And you didn't see her again?'

He shook his head.

'And you didn't talk to her on the phone or anything?'

'Oh, yes,' he said at once. 'She called me the next evening.'

'What did she want?'

'Nothing.'

'She was a very quiet girl, wasn't she?'

'Yes, but she liked to talk on the phone.'

'What did you talk about?'

'We talked about all sorts of things.'

Sejer smiled. Halvor stared out of the window the whole time, as if he wanted to avoid eye contact. Perhaps he felt guilty, or maybe he was just shy. He felt a sad empathy for him. His girlfriend was dead, and probably he had no one to talk to except his grandmother. And maybe, Sejer thought, he's our killer.

'And yesterday you were at your job, as usual? At the factory?'

Halvor hesitated. 'No, I was at home. I wasn't feeling too good.'

'Your grandmother can confirm all this, of course?'

'Yes.'

'And you didn't go out at all during the day?'

'Just for a short while.'

'Even though you were sick?'

'We have to eat! It's not easy for Grandmother to get to the shops. She has arthritis,' he said.

'OK, I understand. Can you tell us when you went out?'

'Around eleven o'clock, I guess.'

'On foot?'

'On my motorcycle.'

'Which store did you go to?'

'The Kiwi shop in town.'

'So your bike started OK yesterday?'

'Actually, it always starts if I keep at it long enough.'

'How long were you out?'

'Maybe an hour.'

'Do you have a licence to drive a car?'

'No.'

'How long were you together, you and Annie?'

'A couple of years.' He kept on staring out at the courtyard.

'Do you think it was a good relationship?'

'We split up a few times.'

'Was she the one who wanted to break up?'

'Yes.'

'Did she say why?'

'Not really. But she wasn't always enthusiastic. Wanted to keep things on a friendship basis.'

'And you didn't?'

He blushed and looked down at his hands.

'Was it a sexual relationship?'

He coloured even more and shifted his glance back to the courtyard. 'Not really.'

'Not really?'

'Like I said. She wasn't very enthusiastic.'

'But the two of you gave it a try? Is that right?' Sejer sounded extremely kind as he asked the question.

'Yes, sort of. A couple of times.' His face was now so strained that it had lost all expression.

'Do you know whether she'd had sex with anyone else?'

'I have no idea, but it's hard for me to imagine that she did.'

'So you and Annie were together for two years. She broke up with you several times, she wasn't particularly interested in having sex with you—and yet you continued the relationship? You aren't exactly a child, Halvor. Are you really so patient?'

'I guess I am.'

'Do you think you knew her well?'

'Better than a lot of people.'

'Did she seem unhappy about anything?'

'Not exactly unhappy. Maybe more sad.'

'Is that something different? Being sad?'

'Yes,' he said. 'When someone is unhappy, he still hopes for something better. But when he gives up, sadness takes over.'

Sejer listened with surprise to this explanation.

'When I met Annie two years ago, she was different,' he said. 'Joking and laughing with everybody. The opposite of me.'

'And then she changed?'

'All of a sudden she grew so tall. And then she became quieter. Not as playful any more. I waited, thinking that it might pass, that she'd be her old self again. Now there's nothing left to wait for.'

He clasped his hands and stared at the floor; then he made an effort to meet Sejer's gaze. His eyes were as shiny as wet stones. 'I don't know what you're thinking, but I didn't hurt Annie.'

'We're not thinking anything. We're talking to everyone. Did Annie drink or take drugs?'

'Don't make me laugh! You're way off the mark.'

'Well,' Sejer said, 'I didn't know her.'

'I'm sorry, but it just sounded so ridiculous.'

'What about you?'

'It would never occur to me.'

Good heavens, Sejer thought. A sober, hard-working young man with a steady job.

'Do you know any of Annie's friends? Anette Horgen, for instance?'

'A little. But we were mostly alone. Annie sort of wanted us to keep to ourselves.'

'Why was that?'

'Don't know. But she's the one who decided.'

'And you did what she wanted?'

'It wasn't difficult. I don't care much for crowds myself.'

Sejer nodded sympathetically. Maybe they had been compatible after all. 'Do you know whether Annie kept a diary?'

Halvor hesitated for a moment, then shook his head. 'I don't think so,' he muttered. 'She never mentioned one.'

'Do you own a blue anorak, Halvor?'

'No.'

'What do you wear when you go outdoors?'

'A denim jacket. Or a padded jacket if it's cold.'

'Will you call the station if you happen to think of anything, anything at all, that you think might explain Annie's death?'

'Yes.'

Sejer stood up. 'We'll be in touch.' In the living room the old woman was sitting in a rocking chair, wrapped warmly in a blanket. She gave them a frightened look as they passed. Outside stood the motorcycle covered with plastic. A black Suzuki.

'Are you thinking the same thing I am?' Skarre asked as they drove off.

'Probably. He didn't ask us a single question. Someone has murdered his girlfriend, and he didn't seem the least bit curious. But that might not mean anything.'

'It's still strange.'

'Maybe it didn't really sink in until right now, as we drove away.'

'Or maybe he knows what happened to her. That's why it didn't occur to him.'

'The anorak we found would be too big for Halvor, don't you think?'

'The sleeves were turned up.'

They needed a break. They drove back, putting the village behind them and leaving its residents to their shock and their own thoughts. In Krystallen people were dashing across the street, phones were ringing. Annie's name was on everyone's lips. The first tiny rumours were being conceived in the glow of candles, and then spreading like weeds from house to house.

Raymond, meanwhile, was preoccupied with other things. He was sitting at the kitchen table, gluing pictures into a book. He didn't notice the man staring at him intently through the window.

HALVOR CLOSED THE DOOR to the kitchen and switched on his computer. He logged on to the hard drive and stared pensively at the rows of files: games, tax forms, address lists. But there was one other thing. A file labelled 'Annie'. To open it he had to enter a password. He had no idea what password she had chosen or what the file might contain. He double-clicked anyway and immediately received the message: 'Access denied. Password required.'

He was determined to open it. This was all he had left of her. What if there was something about him in there, something that might be dangerous? Maybe it was some kind of diary. It's an impossible job, he thought. He tried to relax. He sat for a moment and stared at the file. Perhaps it contained something that would explain why she was the way she was. So damned inscrutable. He decided to begin with numbers—birth dates, social security numbers. Of course she might have chosen a word. It was going to be a tedious job.

SEJER AND SKARRE had taken over the lecture room in the courthouse. The video had been rewound to the beginning and they had closed the curtains. Skarre was ready with the remote control.

'What in the world is that?'

Skarre leaned forward. 'Someone running. Could be the New York Marathon. Maybe he gave us the wrong tape.'

'I don't think so. Stop there. I saw some islands and skerries.'

The picture settled and focused on two women in bikinis.

'Sølvi and her mother,' Sejer said.

Sølvi was lying on her back with one knee bent. Her mother was partially covered by a newspaper. Now the lens turned towards the shoreline further away, and a tall, blonde girl came walking along from the right. She was carrying a windsurfing board on her head and was facing away from the camera. They could hear the roar of the waves, quite loud, suddenly pierced by the sound of her father's voice.

'Smile, Annie!'

She finally turned round, and for several seconds she stared straight at Sejer and Skarre. Her blonde hair was caught by the wind and fluttered around her ears, a quick smile flitted across her lips. Skarre looked into her grey eyes and felt the goose bumps rise on his arms as he watched the long-legged girl striding into the waves.

'That board isn't for beginners,' he said.

Sejer didn't reply. Annie was still walking out into the water. Then she stopped, got onto the board, grabbed the sail with strong hands and found her balance. The board made a 180-degree turn and picked up speed. The men were silent as Annie sailed out. Her father followed her with the camera. They became the father's eyes now, watching his own daughter through the lens. Through the images they could feel his pride, what he must have felt for her.

The rest of the video flickered past. Annie and her mother playing badminton. The family gathered round the table, playing Trivial Pursuit. When it had finished, Sejer stood up with some effort.

'Put the tape in the file,' he said.

'She was good at windsurfing,' Skarre said with awe.

The phone rang before Sejer could reply. Skarre picked it up, grabbing a notepad and pencil at the same time. Sejer read along as he wrote: *Henning Johnas, 4 Krystallen. 12.45pm. Horgen's Shop. Motorcycle*.

'Can you come down to the station?' Skarre said. 'No? Then we'll come to you. Thanks for calling. That's fine.' He hung up.

'One of the neighbours. Henning Johnas. He lives at number four. Just got home and heard about Annie. He picked her up at the roundabout yesterday and let her out near Horgen's Shop. He says there was a motorcycle there. It was waiting for her.'

Sejer perched on the edge of the table. 'That motorcycle again, the one Horgen saw. And Halvor has a motorcycle,' he said. 'Why couldn't the man come here?'

'His dog is about to have puppies.'

JOHNAS STUCK HIS HAND under the dog's stomach and pressed gently. She was breathing hard and her tongue was hanging out of her mouth, a moist pink tongue. She lay very still and let him touch her. It wouldn't be long now.

'Good girl, Hera,' he said, petting her.

He sank down onto the floor. He would have liked to sit there like that until it was all over, just listening to her breathe. Then the doorbell rang, one brief, shrill ring. He got up and opened the door.

Sejer gave him a firm, dry handshake. The man radiated authority. The younger officer was different. He had a thin, boyish hand with slender fingers. Johnas invited them in.

'How's it going with your dog?' Sejer asked. A nice-looking Doberman lay on a black and crimson Oriental rug. Surely nobody would let a bitch in labour lie on a genuine Oriental rug?

'It's her first time. Three pups, I think. But it'll go fine. There's never any trouble with Hera.'

He looked at them and shook his head. 'I'm so upset about what happened that I can't concentrate on anything.'

Johnas glanced at the dog as he talked, running a powerful hand over the top of his head, which was bald. A fringe of brown curls ringed his skull and he had unusually dark eyes. A man of average build, possibly in his late thirties, with a powerful torso and a few extra pounds round his waist.

'You don't want to buy a pup, do you?'

'I've got a Leonberger,' Sejer said. 'And I don't think he'd forgive me if I came home with a puppy in tow.'

Johnas directed them to the sofa and pulled the coffee table out so the two men could slip past. 'I met Fritzner by the garage this evening, as I was coming back from a trade fair in Oslo. He told me about it. I don't think it's really sunk in yet. I shouldn't have let her out of the car, I shouldn't have done that.'

'Where were you headed at twelve thirty when you picked up Annie?'

'I was going to work. I have a carpet shop,' he explained. 'Downtown, on Cappelens Gaten.'

'That's rather late in the day, isn't it?'

'Yes, well, people need milk and bread in the morning, but Persian carpets come later.' He gave an ironic smile.

Sejer nodded. 'Annie was going over to Anette Horgen's to work on a school assignment. Did she mention that to you?'

'A school assignment?' he said. 'No, she didn't mention it.'

'But she had a book bag with her?'

'Yes, she did. She was going to Horgen's Shop, that's all I know.'

'What did you see?'

'Annie came running down the steep slope at the roundabout, so I pulled over into the bus-stop and asked her if she wanted a lift. I let her out at the shop and drove off. I saw the motorcycle parked next to the shop. The last I saw of her, Annie was heading towards it.'

'What kind of bike was it?' Sejer asked.

'I don't know much about bikes. For me it was just chrome and steel.'

'What about the colour?'

'Aren't all bikes black?'

'Definitely not,' Sejer said.

'It wasn't bright red, at any rate, I would have remembered that.'

'Was it a big, powerful bike, or a smaller one?' Skarre said.

'I think it was big.'

'And the motorcyclist?'

'There wasn't a lot to see. He was wearing a helmet. There was something red on the helmet, that much I remember. He was probably a young guy.'

Sejer nodded. 'Do you know her boyfriend? Could it have been him?' he asked.

Now Johnas frowned as if on his guard. 'I don't know him but I've seen them together in the street. I can't say if it was him. I don't even want to suggest that.'

'The motorcycle is important,' Sejer said. 'Another witness saw it too.'

Johnas shook his head sharply. 'All I saw was someone wearing a leather outfit and a helmet. It could have been anybody. I have a seventeen-year-old son; it could have been him. I wouldn't have recognised him in that get-up. Do you see what I mean?'

'Yes, I see,' Sejer said. 'You've answered my question anyway. It could have been her boyfriend.'

Johnas swallowed hard.

'What did you and Annie talk about in the car?'

'She didn't say much. I passed the time talking about Hera.'

'Did she seem anxious or nervous?'

'Not at all. She was the same as always.'

Sejer looked around the living room and noticed that it was sparsely furnished, as if Johnas hadn't finished decorating. But there were plenty of carpets, both on the floor and on the walls, big Oriental carpets that looked expensive. Two photographs hung on one wall; one was of a boy about two years old, the other was of a teenager.

'Are those your sons?' Sejer pointed, to change the subject.

'Yes,' Johnas said. 'But not recent photographs.' He went back to petting the dog, stroking her black, silky-soft ears and damp snout. 'I live alone now,' he added. 'Finally found myself an apartment in town, on Oscarsgaten. This place is too big for me. I haven't seen much of Annie lately. I think she was upset when my wife left. And there weren't kids to take care of any more.'

They thanked him and paused a moment at the door. 'We'll probably be back; I hope you understand.'

'Of course. If the puppies come tonight, I'll be home for a few days.'

Hera whined plaintively, lying there on her Oriental rug. Skarre gave her a long look and then reluctantly followed his boss.

CHAPTER FOUR

Ragnhild Album bent over the paper and started drawing. The notebook was new, and she had opened it reverently to the first untouched page. A car in a cloud of dust might not, in a sense, be worthy of the task that was going to rob the notebook of its chalk-white purity. The box held six crayons. Sejer had been out shopping: one box for Ragnhild and one for Raymond. Today she had two pigtails on top of her head, pointing straight up like antennae.

'I like the way you've fixed your hair today,' he said.

'With this one,' said her mother, tugging on one pigtail, 'she can get her daddy in Narvik, and with the other she gets her grandmother, who lives way up north on Svalbard.'

He had to laugh.

'She says it was just a cloud of dust,' she went on, anxiously.

'She says it was a car,' said Sejer. 'It's worth a try.'

He put his hand on the child's shoulder. 'Close your eyes,' he said, 'and try to picture it. Then draw it as best you can. And not just any old car. You should draw the car that you and Raymond saw.'

'I know,' she said impatiently.

He ushered Mrs Album out of the kitchen and into the living room so Ragnhild could draw in peace. Mrs Album went over to the window and looked at the blue mountains in the distance.

'Annie took care of Ragnhild for me lots of times,' she said. 'She had a natural talent with children.'

'Do you know her sister too? Sølvi?'

'I know who she is. But she's only her half-sister.'

'Oh?'

'Didn't you know that?'

'No, I didn't.'

'Everyone knows,' she said. 'It's not a secret or anything. They're very different. For a while they had difficulties with her father. Sølvi's father, I mean. He lost his visitation rights, and apparently he's never got over it.'

'Why?'

'The usual trouble. Drunk and violent. That's the mother's version, of course, but Ada Holland is hard to take, so I'm not sure how much is true.'

'But Sølvi is over twenty-one, isn't she? And can do what she wants?'

'It's probably too late. I dare say that things have probably gone sour between them. I've been thinking a lot about Ada,' she said. 'She didn't get her little girl back, the way I did.'

'I'm done!' came a shout from the kitchen.

They went in to have a look. Ragnhild was not looking especially pleased. A grey cloud filled most of the page, and out of the cloud stuck the front end of a car, with headlights and bumper. It looked as if it had a big grin with no teeth. The headlights were slanted.

Sejer stared at the drawing. 'What about the colour, Ragnhild?'

'Well, it wasn't really grey. It was a colour that doesn't exist.'

'What do you mean?'

'Well, I mean a colour that doesn't have a name.'

'Ragnhild,' he said, 'can you remember if the car had anything on the roof?'

She stared at him, thinking hard. 'Yes!' she exclaimed. 'A little boat.'

'I don't know what I would have done without you,' Sejer said, smiling, as he flicked his fingers at her antennae.

She blushed shyly, put the lid on the box, closed up the notebook and slid them over to him.

'No, they're yours to keep.'

She opened the box at once and went back to drawing.

'ONE OF THE RABBITS is lying on its side!' Raymond was standing in the doorway to his father's room, rocking back and forth uneasily.

'Which one?'

'Caesar. The giant Belgian.'

'Then you'll have to kill it.'

Raymond got so scared that he farted. But the little release didn't make any difference in the stale air of the room.

'But it's breathing so hard!'

'We're not about to feed rabbits that are dying, Raymond. Put it on the chopping block. The axe is behind the door in the garage.'

Raymond went outside and plodded dejectedly across the courtyard towards the rabbit cages. He stared at Caesar for a moment through the netting. It's lying there just like a baby, he thought, rolled up like a soft little ball. Its eyes were closed. He took a grip on the scruff of its neck and lifted it out. It kicked halfheartedly.

Afterwards he slumped in his chair at the kitchen table. In front of him lay an album with pictures of the national soccer team and birds and animals. He was looking very depressed when Sejer arrived. He was wearing nothing but track-suit bottoms and slippers when he came to the door. His hair stood up from his head, his belly was soft and white.

'Hello, Raymond.' Sejer gave a deep bow to appease him a bit. 'Have I come at a bad time?'

'Yes, because I was just working on my collection and now you're interrupting me.'

'That can be awfully annoying. I can't imagine anything worse. But I wouldn't have come if I didn't have to, I hope you realise that.'

'Yes, of course, yes.'

He relaxed a little and went back to the kitchen. Sejer followed him and put the drawing materials on the table.

'I'd like you to draw something for me,' he said. 'A car.'

'A car?' Now Raymond looked suspicious.

'The car that you and Ragnhild saw. The one that was driving fast.'

'You keep on talking about that car.'

'That's true, but it's important.'

'But I told you it was driving too fast to see properly.'

'You noticed that it was a car, didn't you? Not a boat or a bike. Or a caravan of camels, for instance.'

'Camels?' He laughed heartily. 'That would have been funny, seeing a bunch of camels going down the road! There weren't any camels. It was a car. With a ski-box on the roof.'

'Draw it,' Sejer commanded.

Raymond gave in. He sank onto a chair at the table and stuck his tongue out, like a rudder. His drawing looked like a piece of crispbread on wheels.

'Could you colour it too?'

Raymond opened the box, carefully examined all the crayons, and finally selected the red one. Then he concentrated hard, trying not to colour outside the lines.

'Red, Raymond?'

'Yes,' he said brusquely, and kept on colouring.

'So the car was red? Are you sure? I thought you said it was grey.'

'I said it was red.'

Sejer pulled a stool out from under the table, and thought carefully before he spoke. 'You said you couldn't remember the colour. But that it might have been grey, like Ragnhild said.'

Raymond scratched his stomach, looking offended. 'I remember things better after a while, you know. I told him that yesterday, the man who was here, I told him it was red.'

'Who was that?'

'Just a man who was out walking and stopped in the courtyard. He wanted to see the rabbits. I talked to him.'

Sejer felt a faint prickling on the back of his neck. 'Was it someone you know?'

'No.'

'Can you tell me what he looked like?'

Raymond stuck out his lower lip. 'No,' he said.

'Don't you want to tell me?'

'It was just a man. And you won't like what I say, anyway.'

'Please tell me. I'll help you. Fat or thin?'

'In between.'

'Dark or light hair?'

'Don't know. He was wearing a cap.'

'Is that right? A young man?'

'Don't know.'

'Older than me?'

Raymond glanced up. 'Oh, no, not as old as you. Your hair is grey.'

Thanks a lot, thought Sejer.

'I don't want to draw him.'

'You don't have to. Did he come by car?'

'No, he was walking.'

'When he left, did he head down the road or up towards Kollen?'

'Don't know. I went in to see to Papa. He was really nice,' he said.

'I'm sure he was. What did he say to you, Raymond?'

'That I had great rabbits.'

'Go on.'

'Then we talked about the weather. And how dry it's been. He asked me if I'd heard about the girl at the tarn and if I knew her.'

'What did you tell him?'

'That I was the one who found her. He thought it was too bad the girl was dead. And I told him about you, that you had been here and asked me about the car. "The car," he said, "that noisy one that's always driving too fast on the roads around here?" Yes, I told him. That's the one I saw. He knew which one it was. Said it was a red Mercedes. I must have been mistaken when you asked me before, because now I remember. The car was red.'

'Did he threaten you?'

'No, no, I don't let anyone threaten me. A grown man doesn't let people threaten him. I told him that.'

'What about his clothes, Raymond. What was he wearing?'

'Just ordinary clothes.'

'Brown clothes? Or blue? Can you remember?'

Raymond gave Sejer a confused look and hid his face in his hands. 'Stop bothering me so much!'

Sejer let Raymond sit for a moment and calm down. Then he said, in a very soft voice, 'But the car was really grey or green, wasn't it?'

'No, it was red. I told the truth, and there's no use threatening me. Because the car was red, and that pleased him.'

Sejer picked up the drawing. 'How's your father?' he asked.

'He can't walk.'

'I know. Let's go and see him.'

He stood up and followed Raymond down the hall. The room was in semi-darkness, but there was more than enough light for Sejer to make out the old man standing next to the bedside table, wearing an old undershirt that was much too big. His knees were shaking perilously. He was just as gaunt as his son was round and stout.

'Papa!' cried Raymond. 'What are you doing?'

'Nothing, nothing.' He fumbled for his false teeth.

'Sit down. You'll break a leg.'

Raymond helped him get back into bed and handed him his teeth. The man avoided Sejer's gaze and stared up at the ceiling. Sejer went over and stood in front of him, looking towards the window that faced the courtyard and road. The curtains were almost completely drawn, letting in only a minimum of light.

'Do you watch what goes on out on the road?' he asked.

'You're from the police?'

'Yes. You have a good view if you open the curtains.'

'I never do that. Unless it's overcast.'

'Have you noticed any strange cars around here, or motorcycles?'

'Could be. Police cars, for instance.'

'Anyone on foot?'

'Hikers. They head up to Kollen, come hell or high water.'

'Did you know Annie Holland?'

'I know her father from my days at the garage. He delivered cars, when there were any.'

'Annie Holland is dead.'

'I know that. I do read the paper, just like anybody else.'

'A man was out in the courtyard here yesterday, talking to Raymond. Did you see him?'

'I heard them mumbling out there. Raymond may not be so quick-witted,' he said sharply, 'but he has no idea what malice is. Do you understand? He's so good-natured that you can lead him by a piece of string. But he does what he's told.'

Sejer looked into the colourless eyes. 'I know that,' he said. 'So you weren't tempted to pull the curtain aside a bit?'

'No.'

'What if I told you that there's a chance that the man in the courtyard is mixed up in the murder of the Holland girl—would you then realise how serious this is?'

'Even then. I didn't look outside, I was busy with the newspaper.'

Sejer looked around the small room and shuddered. The room didn't smell good, it needed to be cleaned. The window should have been opened and the old man needed a hot bath. He went out to get some fresh air, drawing in deep breaths. Raymond trotted after him and stood with his arms crossed as Sejer got into his car.

'Have you had your van fixed, Raymond?'

'Papa says I need a new battery. But I can't afford it right now. I don't drive on the roads,' he said quickly. 'Almost never.'

'That's good. Go on back inside, you'll catch cold.'

'Yes,' he said, and shivered. 'And I gave my jacket away.'

'That wasn't so smart, was it?' Sejer said.

'I felt I had to,' he said sadly. 'She was lying there with nothing on.'

'What did you say?' Sejer looked at him in astonishment. The jacket on the body belonged to Raymond! 'Did you spread it over her to cover her?'

'She wasn't wearing any clothes at all,' he said, kicking at the ground with his slipper.

Sejer stared into his eyes, the eyes of a child as pure as spring water. But he had muscles as heavy as Christmas hams. Involuntarily Sejer shook his head.

'That was a kind thought,' Sejer said. 'Did you talk to each other?'

Raymond looked at him in surprise. 'You said she was dead!'

Afterwards, when Sejer was gone, Raymond slipped out and peeped into the garage. Caesar was lying in a far corner under an old jumper, and he was still breathing.

SKARRE FINISHED GOING over the statements. He smiled with satisfaction. Life was good. It would soon be summer. And there stood his boss, waving a Krone ice-cream bar at him. He put the papers quickly aside and took it.

'The anorak that was spread over the body belongs to Raymond,' Sejer said.

Skarre was so startled that his ice cream slid sideways.

'But I believe him when he says that he put it there on his way back, after he took Ragnhild home. He spread it over her nicely because she was naked. But . . . it's his jacket. We'll have to keep an eye on him. I told him that unfortunately he couldn't have it back right away, and he was so disappointed that I promised to give him one of my old ones. Find anything exciting?' he asked.

Skarre tore the paper wrapper off his ice-cream bar. 'I've run checks on all of the Hollands' neighbours. They seem decent people for the most part. But I found something else. Have a look at this.' He leafed through the statements and pointed.

'Knut Jensvoll, eight Gneisveien. Annie's handball coach. He served time for rape. Did eighteen months at Ullersmo Prison.'

Sejer bent down to look. 'He may have managed to keep that quiet. Better watch what you say when we're out there.'

Skarre nodded and licked his ice cream. 'Maybe we should bring in the whole team. Perhaps he's tried something on some of the girls. How did you get on?'

Sejer sighed and pulled the drawings from his inside pocket.

'Ragnhild says the ski-box was a boat. And Raymond's drawing is pretty funny. But what's more interesting is that a man who was in Raymond's courtyard yesterday seems to have tried to convince him that the car was red.'

Skarre's eyes grew big. 'What? Could he describe—'

'Something in between,' Sejer said laconically. 'Wearing a cap. I didn't dare push him too hard, he gets so upset.'

'I call that fast work.'

'I call it bold, more than anything else,' Sejer said. 'But now we're talking about someone who knows who Raymond is. He was seen. He wanted to find out what Raymond saw. So we have to focus on the car. He must be very close to us, for God's sake.'

'But to go to Raymond's house, that's pretty reckless. Do you think anyone else might have seen him?'

'I went to every house nearby. No one saw him.'

'What about the old man?'

'He says he heard them outside, but wasn't tempted to look out of his window.'

They ate their ice creams in silence.

'Shall we forget about Halvor? And the motorcycle?'

'Absolutely not.'

'When do we bring him in?'

'Tonight.'

'Why wait?'

'It's quieter at night. You know, I talked to Ragnhild's mother while the girl was drawing. She said that Sølvi isn't Holland's daughter. And the biological father lost his visitation rights, apparently because of drunkenness and violence.'

'Sølvi is twenty-one, isn't she?'

'She is now. But evidently there have been years of conflict.'

'What are you getting at?'

'In a sense he lost his child. Now his ex-wife, with whom he has a strained relationship, is going through the same thing. Maybe he wanted revenge. It's just a thought.'

Skarre gave a low whistle. 'Who is he?'

'That's what you're going to find out as soon as you're done with your ice cream. Then come to my office. We'll leave the moment you locate him.'

Sejer left. Skarre punched in the Hollands' phone number and licked his ice cream as he waited.

'I don't want to talk about Axel,' Mrs Holland said. 'He just about destroyed us, and after all these years we're finally rid of him. If I hadn't taken him to court, he would have destroyed Sølvi.'

'I'm only asking you for his name and address. This is just routine, Mrs Holland.'

'He never had anything to do with Annie.'

'Please give me his name, Mrs Holland.'

Finally she gave in. 'Axel Bjørk. I can also give you his address.'

Skarre took notes, and thanked her. Then he switched on his computer and did a search for 'Bjørk, Axel'. He found the man with no trouble and began reading.

'God damn it all!' he exclaimed. He clicked on 'Please Print', picked up the page and crossed the corridor to Sejer's office.

'I've got him. He's got a record, of course.'

Skarre sat down opposite Sejer and put the sheet of paper on the blotting pad.

'Well, let's have a look. Bjørk, Axel, born 1948.'

'A former police officer,' said Skarre quietly.

Sejer didn't react. He read slowly through the report.

'We're no better than anyone else, now are we, Skarre? We'll have to hear the man's side of the story. So, we're going to have to take a trip to Oslo. He obviously does shift work, so there's a chance that we'll find him at home.'

THEY FOUND THE NAME Bjørk on the second floor of a block of flats. They rang the bell and waited.

Bjørk's face in the half-open doorway was a study of muscles, nerves and tics that made his dark face shift from one expression to another in seconds. The last expression, which stuck, was a bitter smile.

'Well,' he said, opening the door wide. 'If you hadn't turned up, I wouldn't have a particularly high opinion of modern detective work. Come on in. Is this the master and his apprentice?'

They ignored his remark and followed him down a short corridor. The smell of alcohol was unmistakable.

Bjørk's apartment was a tidy little place comprising a spacious living room with a sleeping alcove and a small kitchen. On the wall above an old desk hung a picture of a little girl, about eight years old. Her features hadn't changed much over the years. It was Sølvi.

They caught sight of a German shepherd dog, lying perfectly still in a corner, staring at them with watchful eyes. It hadn't moved or barked when they came into the room.

'What have you done with that dog?' Sejer said. 'Something I obviously haven't managed to do with mine. He charges at people as soon as they set a foot in the door.'

'If that's the case, you're too attached to him,' he said curtly. 'You shouldn't treat a dog as if it's the only thing you have in the world.'

He studied Sejer with narrowed eyes, aware that the rest of the conversation wasn't going to proceed in so friendly a tone. His hair was cut short, but unwashed and greasy, and he hadn't shaved in a while.

'So,' he said, 'you want to know whether I knew Annie, right?' He wriggled the words out of his mouth like a fishbone. 'She'd been here several times, with Sølvi. Then Ada found out and put a halt to any kind of visiting. Sølvi liked coming here. I don't know what Ada has done to her, but it looks a lot like brainwashing. Now she's not interested any more. She's let Holland take over.'

He rubbed his jaw. 'Maybe you were thinking that I killed Annie to take revenge? Let me assure you I didn't. I have nothing against Eddie Holland, and I wouldn't want even my worst enemy to lose a child. But I admit that the thought did cross my mind, of course, that now she knows what it feels like to lose a child. But now my chances of contacting Sølvi are even slimmer. Ada will keep close tabs on her. And I would never put myself in that situation.'

Sejer sat motionless and listened. Bjørk's voice was angry and sharp as acid.

'Where was I at the time in question? She was found on Monday, wasn't she? Some time in the middle of the day, if I remember rightly. So here's my answer: in my apartment, no alibi. Most likely I was drunk, I usually am when I'm not at work. Do I get violent? Absolutely not. It's true that I hit Ada, but she was asking for a good smack in the face. She knew that if she got me to cross the line, she would have something to take to court. I hit her once, with my fist. It was pure impulse, the only time in my whole life that I've actually hit someone. I hit her hard and broke her jaw, and Sølvi was sitting on the floor and saw it all. Ada had set the whole thing up. She put Sølvi's toys on the floor in the living room so that she would be sitting there, watching us, and she had filled the refrigerator with beer. Then she started arguing, she was very good at that. And she didn't give up until I exploded. I walked right into the trap.'

Beneath the bitterness there was a kind of relief, perhaps because someone was finally listening.

'How old was Sølvi when you divorced?'

'She was five. Ada had already taken up with Holland, and she wanted Sølvi to herself.'

'You were suspended?'

'I started drinking too much. Lost my wife and child, my job and my house, and the respect of nearly everybody.'

'What did the two of you fight about?' Skarre asked.

'We fought about Sølvi.' He crossed his arms and stared out of the window. 'Sølvi is a little different, she's always been like that. Ada always wanted to protect her. She's not very independent, may even be a little slow. Abnormally obsessed with boys. Ada wants her to find a husband as fast as possible, someone who will take care of her. I've never seen anyone steer a girl so wrongly. I tried to explain that what she needs is exactly the opposite—she needs self-confidence. She needs physical exercise, needs to get her hair mussed up without panicking. Right now she slouches around in a beauty salon, looking at herself in the mirror all day.'

'How do you make your living now?'

Bjørk stared at Sejer with a gloomy expression. 'I'm sure you already know that. I work for a private security company. Run around at night with a dog and a torch.'

'When was the last time the girls were here?'

'Some time last autumn. Annie's boyfriend was here too.'

'So you haven't seen the girls since then?'

'No.' He got up suddenly and went over to stand by the window with his back to them, pulling himself up to his full height.

'Do you own a motorcycle, Bjørk?' Sejer asked.

'No, I don't,' he said. 'I had one when I was younger. I only have the helmet left.'

'What kind of helmet?'

'It's hanging in the hallway.'

Skarre peered into the corridor and caught sight of the helmet. It was a full helmet, all black, with a smoke-coloured visor.

'A car?'

'I only drive the Peugeot from the security company.'

He suddenly looked worn out. 'This is goddamned awful,' he said and turned round. 'I hope for Eddie's sake that you find the bastard who did it, I really do.'

'For Eddie's sake? Not for Ada's?'

'No,' he said fervently. 'Not for Ada's sake.'

CHAPTER FIVE

Bardy Snorrason stuck a hand under the steel handle and pulled Annie's body out of the wall. The drawer slid almost soundlessly on well-oiled runners. He handled the misfortune and deaths of others with the utmost respect, and figured that those who came after him would do the same with his own body when that day arrived. Nothing in his thirty years as a medical examiner had given him cause to think otherwise.

It took him two hours to go through all the points. The picture gradually took on familiar signs as he worked. He read his notes into a Dictaphone. Later, his assistant would translate them into precise terminology for the written report.

After he'd been through everything, he put the top of the skull back in place, pulled the skin over it, and filled the empty chest cavity with crumpled newspaper. Then he sewed the body back up. He was very hungry. He needed to have some food before he started the next one, and he had four sandwiches and a Thermos of coffee waiting for him in the canteen.

He caught sight of someone through the translucent glass in the door. The person stopped and stood motionless for a moment, as if wanting to turn round. Snorrason pulled off his gloves and smiled. There weren't many people of such a towering height.

Having pulled on the mandatory plastic coverings over his shoes, Sejer opened the door. He had to duck a little as he came in. He cast an indifferent glance at the trolley, where Annie's body was now wrapped in a sheet.

'I've just finished,' Snorrason said. 'She's over there.'

Now Sejer gave the body on the trolley a look of greater interest. 'So I'm in luck.'

'That's questionable.'

The medical examiner began washing his hands, scrubbing his skin and fingernails with a stiff brush for several minutes. Then he pulled out a chair and slid it towards the chief inspector.

'There wasn't much to discover here.'

'Don't destroy all my hopes straight away. Surely there must be something?'

Snorrason pushed aside his hunger pangs and sat down.

'It's not my job to determine the value of what we find. But usually we do find something. She seems so untouched.'

'Presumably he was a strong, healthy individual. He had the benefit of complete surprise. And he removed her clothing afterwards.'

'Presumably. But she wasn't assaulted. She's not a virgin, but she wasn't sexually assaulted, or mistreated in any other way. She simply drowned. Her clothes were taken off after her death, all the buttons are in place on her shirt, none of the seams are ripped.'

'Maybe he just wanted us to believe that he's a sex offender.'

'Why would he want to do that?'

'To hide his real motive. And that could mean there's something behind all this that could be traced, that it wasn't an impulsive act by a disturbed individual. And besides, she must have gone with him willingly. She must have known him, or he must have made an impression on her. And from what I understand, it wasn't easy to make an impression on Annie Holland.'

He opened a button in his jacket and leaned towards Snorrason. 'Go ahead. Tell me what you found.'

'A fifteen-year-old girl,' the examiner said, intoning like a minister, 'height five foot eight inches, weight one hundred and forty-three pounds, minimum of fat; for the most part the fat had been converted into muscle due to hard exercise. Her lung capacity was excellent, which would indicate that it took a long time for her to lose consciousness.'

Sejer looked down at the worn linoleum.

'How long does it actually take?' he asked softly. 'How long does it take for an adult to drown?'

'Anywhere from two to ten minutes, depending on the physical condition. If she was in as good a condition as I think, it most likely took closer to ten.'

Up to ten minutes, Sejer thought. Think of all he could do in ten minutes.

'No traces of alcohol or other chemicals in her blood. No irregularities in the brain. She has never been pregnant. And,' Snorrason sighed and fixed his gaze on Sejer, 'she never would have been.'

'What? Why not?'

'She had a large tumour in her left ovary that had started spreading to her liver. Malignant.'

Sejer stared at him. 'Are you saying that she was seriously ill?'

'Yes. Are *you* saying that you didn't know?'

'Her parents didn't know either.' He shook his head in disbelief. 'Otherwise they would have said something, wouldn't they? Is it possible that she might not have known herself?'

'Well, you'll need to find out if she had a doctor, and whether it was known. But she would have felt pain in her abdomen. The truth is, she would have been dead in a matter of months.'

The news made Sejer completely lose track of why he was there. It took him a minute to collect himself.

'Should I tell them? Her parents?'

'You'll have to make that decision yourself. But they're going to want to know what I have discovered.'

'It'll be like losing her all over again.'

'Yes, it will.'

'What about her clothes?'

'Soaked through with muddy water, except for the anorak, which I sent over to you. But she had a belt with a buckle. The lab found fingerprints on it. Two different ones. One of them was Annie's.'

Sejer narrowed his eyes. 'And the other?'

'Unfortunately, it's not complete; but it should be useful in eliminating people.'

Sejer stood up. 'When can I get this in writing?'

'I'll let you know. And what about you? Have you found a lead?'

'No,' he said. 'Not a thing. I can't see any reason in the world why anyone would kill Annie Holland.'

HALVOR BROODED as he sat in front of the screen. The door to the living room stood open in case his grandmother called. He leaned his chin on his hands and stared at the screen. 'Access denied. Password required.' He was hungry, but like so much else right now, that had to take low priority.

Annie probably hadn't used a number password, Halvor thought. She would have come up with something more imaginative. He switched his thinking to the books she'd read and talked about. Titles, characters in the books, things they'd said. He had plenty of time. He felt so close to Annie as he worked. Finding the password would be like finding his way back to her. He scratched the corner of his mouth with a sharp fingernail and suddenly remembered Annie's enthusiasm for the book *Sophie's World.* And since her name was Annie Sofie, he typed in the title. Nothing happened. His stomach growled, and a throbbing in his temples signalled a headache.

AT POLICE HEADQUARTERS, Sejer sat reading a stack of pages covered with text and stapled at one corner. The initials BCH, standing for Bjerkeli Children's Home, kept popping up. Halvor's childhood made for depressing reading. According to the child welfare authorities, his mother spent most of her time in bed, fragile and whimpering, with frayed nerves and an ever-growing armoury of sedatives in reach. Halvor had certainly been through the wringer, Sejer thought. Impressive that he could hold down a steady job and take care of his grandmother on top of everything else.

It seemed that his father's alcohol problem and his mother's delicate nerves had marked the family from the outset. Halvor and his brother bumbled around in the house, getting their own food, when there was any. Their father was usually in town, first drinking up his salary cheque and later his welfare payments. A few kind neighbours helped out as best they could, in secrecy behind their father's back. As the years passed, he became more and more violent. The boys would retreat to their room and lock the door. They grew thinner and quieter.

Gradually their father lost his grip on reality. One night he came bursting into the room where the two boys slept. On that night, as so often, the younger brother was asleep in Halvor's bed. Their father had a knife. Halvor saw it gleaming in his hand. They could hear their mother whimpering, terrified, downstairs. Suddenly he felt the sharp pain of the knife as it struck his temple; he flung himself away and the knife sliced through his cheek, splitting it in half. His father's eyes could suddenly see what was real again: the blood on the pillow and the younger boy screaming. He raced down the stairs and into the yard. Hid in the woodshed.

Sejer finished reading the report on the Muntz family, locked up the office and walked down the hall with Skarre. The boys had done well at Bjerkeli. Halvor graduated from the ninth grade. The younger brother was put into a foster home, and then Halvor was all alone. After a while he chose to move in with his grandmother. He was used to taking care of someone.

'From what you say, it's strange that the boys turned out all right, in spite of everything,' said Skarre, shaking his head.

'Maybe we don't know how Halvor has turned out,' said Sejer bluntly. 'It remains to be seen.'

Skarre nodded, fiddling with his car keys. They got into the car and Skarre started the engine and pulled away from the parking space. He drove slowly, because the road was unbelievably bad, buckled by frost, narrow and meandering across the landscape. It was still chilly, as if someone had waylaid summer. Birds huddled under shrubbery, regretting their return home.

From a distance the house didn't look inviting. Little windows high up on the wall. Faded grey clapboard weatherproofing. The courtyard overgrown with weeds.

HALVOR'S HEADACHE was getting worse and his eyes were sore from staring at the flickering screen. It was finally night-time. His grandmother had been sitting alone for a long time. Eventually he got up, almost reluctantly, to get something to eat. He left the monitor on and went out to the kitchen. His grandmother was watching a programme about the American Civil War on television. She was cheering for the ones in blue uniforms because she thought they were more handsome. Halvor poured cornflakes into a bowl and sprinkled them liberally with sugar. He carried the bowl into the dining room. The spoon shook in his hand. His blood sugar was low.

Through the dining-room window Halvor saw a faint light. Then he heard the sound of a car and some of his milk dribbled down his chin. The headlights flickered through the dim light of the room. Moments later, they were standing in the doorway, looking at him.

'We need to have a little talk,' said Sejer. 'You'll have to come with us, but you can finish eating first.'

He wasn't hungry any more, but then he hadn't thought he was going to get off easily. He went calmly out to the kitchen and carefully rinsed the bowl under the tap. He slipped into his room and turned off the monitor, muttered something into his grandmother's ear, and followed them out of the house.

'I'M TRYING TO PUT together a picture of Annie,' Sejer said. 'Who she was and how she lived. I want you to tell me everything about what kind of girl she was. And why she'd withdrawn from everyone.'

'I have no idea,' Halvor answered. He studied Sejer's blotting pad.

'You were an important part of Annie's landscape,' Sejer said. 'That's actually what I'm getting at. I'm trying to map out the area that was hers.'

'So that's what you're doing?' said Halvor drily. 'You're drawing a map?'

'Perhaps you have a better idea?'

'No,' he said.

'Your father is dead,' Sejer said abruptly. He searched the young face in front of him. 'He took his own life. But you said that your parents were separated. Is it hard for you to talk about that?'

'I suppose so.'

'Is that why you concealed the truth from me?'

'It's not exactly something to boast about.'

'I understand. Can you tell me what you wanted from Annie?' he said. 'Since you were waiting for her at Horgen's Shop on the day she was murdered.'

His surprise seemed genuine. 'I'm sorry, but you're really on the wrong track!'

'A motorcyclist was observed in the vicinity at a crucial moment. You were out riding around. It could have been you.'

'You'd better check that person's eyesight as soon as possible.'

'I will. Do you want something to drink?'

'No.'

Silence. Halvor listened. Someone was laughing nearby; it all seemed so unreal. Annie was dead, and people were making noise and behaving as if nothing had happened.

'Did you get the impression that Annie wasn't well?'

'What?'

'Did you ever hear her complain of pain, for example?'

'Nobody was as healthy as Annie. Are you saying she was sick?'

'Unfortunately, I'm not allowed to divulge certain information to you, even though the two of you were close. She never mentioned anything of the kind?'

'No.'

'How are you spending your time at the moment?'

'Trying to find out what happened,' he blurted out.

'Do you have any leads for us?'

'I'm searching my memory.'

'I'm not sure that you're telling me everything you know.'

'I didn't do anything to Annie. You think I did it, don't you?'

'To be honest, I don't know. You're going to have to help me, Halvor. It sounds as if Annie had undergone some sort of change in personality. Do you agree?'

'Yes.'

'Someone might change drastically if they lose someone close to them; or if they experience serious trauma, or suffer a serious illness. Another thing that can lead to a change in personality is drug abuse. Or a brutal assault, such as rape. Does any of this sound familiar?'

'I think she had a secret,' Halvor said at last. 'Something that had upset her whole life. Something she couldn't ignore.'

'Are you going to tell me that you don't know what it was?'

'Yes. I have no idea.'

Sejer hid his face by leaning his head on his hands. 'Why don't we have a Coke?' he said. 'The air is so dry in here.'

Halvor nodded and relaxed a bit. But then he grew tense again. Maybe this was some kind of tactic, this first small glimpse of sympathy from the grey-haired inspector. The door closed behind him, and Halvor took the opportunity to stretch his legs. Sejer came back and poured some Coke into two plastic cups.

'Do you know Knut Jensvoll?'

'The coach? I know who he is. I went to handball matches with Annie once in a while.'

'Did you like him?'

Halvor shrugged. 'I thought he chased after the girls too much.'

'Annie too?'

'He didn't dare. She didn't let anyone get too close.'

'But I don't understand it, Halvor.' Sejer shoved his plastic cup aside and leaned forward. 'Everyone speaks so well of Annie—about how strong and independent and sporty she was. Didn't let anyone get too close, as you say. And yet she went with someone deep into the woods, to the lake. Apparently of her own free will. And then,' he lowered his voice, 'she let herself get killed.'

Halvor gave him a frightened look, as if the absurdity of the situation finally dawned on him, in all its horror.

'Someone must have had power over her,' he said.

'But was there anyone who had power over Annie?'

'Not as far as I know. I didn't, that's for sure.'

Sejer drank his Coke. 'A damn shame she didn't leave anything behind. A diary, for example.'

Halvor bent his head over his cup and took a long gulp.

'But could it be true?' Sejer said. 'That someone actually had some kind of hold over her? Someone she didn't dare defy? Could Annie have been mixed up in something dangerous that she needed to keep secret? Could someone have been blackmailing her?'

'Annie was very law-abiding. I don't think she would have done anything wrong.'

'A person can do lots of wrong things and still be law-abiding,' Sejer said. 'One act doesn't describe a whole person.'

Halvor noted those words, carefully storing them away.

'Annie was a quiet girl, who liked to be in control of her life. But think carefully, Halvor. Did she also seem scared of something?'

'Not exactly scared. More closed down. Sometimes almost angry.'

'But you can't think of a single person who knew Annie and might have wanted to harm her?'

'Not one,' Halvor said. 'I've thought over and over about everything that happened, and I can't make sense of it. It must have been a madman.'

YES, SEJER THOUGHT, it could have been a madman. He drove Halvor home, manoeuvring the car right up to the front steps.

'I suppose you have to get up early,' he said kindly. 'It's late.'

'I usually don't have any trouble getting up.'

Halvor liked him and didn't like him. It was confusing.

He climbed out, opened the front door cautiously, hoping his grandmother was asleep. To make sure, he peered into her room and heard her snoring. Then he sat down in front of the monitor again and continued where he had left off. He scratched the back of his neck and typed 'Annie Holland', because it suddenly occurred to him that he hadn't tried the simplest possibility. 'Access denied'. He shoved his chair back a little from the desk, stretched, and put his hand on the back of his neck again. It prickled, as if something on his neck was annoying him. There was nothing there, but the feeling continued. A sudden impulse made him stand up and draw the curtains. He had a strong sense that someone was watching him, and the feeling made the hairs on his head stand on end. Swiftly, he turned off the light.

Outside he heard retreating footsteps, as though someone were running away. He peered through a crack in the curtains but couldn't see anyone. He switched off the computer, tore off his clothes, and climbed under the covers. He lay in bed, quiet as a mouse, and listened. Then, after several minutes, he heard a car start up.

KNUT JENSVOLL WAS WORKING with an electric drill, trying to put up a shelf where he could leave his wet trainers to dry after exercising. When he stopped for a moment, he heard the doorbell. He peered out of the window and saw Sejer looming on the top step. He'd had a feeling they might come. He took a moment to gather his thoughts, smoothed down his clothes and his hair.

One thought was uppermost in Jensvoll's mind: had they found out about the rape? That had to be the reason why they were here. Once a criminal, always a criminal; that was a maxim he knew well.

'Police. Can we come in?'

Jensvoll nodded. He cast a worried glance at Skarre, who was fishing a notebook out of his jacket. Jensvoll was close to fifty, but his body was firm and muscular. He had good colour in his face, a thick mane of red hair, and an elegant, neatly trimmed moustache.

'I take it this has something to do with Annie?' he said.

Sejer nodded.

'I have never been so shocked in my life. I knew her well, so I think I have good reason to say that. But it's been a while since she left the team. That was a tragedy because no one could replace her.'

'Yes, it's a real tragedy,' Sejer said, somewhat more acidly than he had intended. 'When did you last see Annie?'

Jensvoll had to think about it.

'Two or three weeks ago, maybe. At the post office, I think.'

'Did you talk to her?'

'Just said hello. She wasn't particularly talkative of late.'

'Why did Annie stop being a goalkeeper?'

'If only I knew.' He shrugged. 'I'm afraid I pressured her hard to change her mind, but it didn't do any good. She was fed up with it. Well, I don't really believe that, but that's what she said. Wanted to run instead, she said.'

He was still waiting for them to drag the skeleton out of the closet; he had no hope that it would be avoided.

'Do you live alone here?'

'I was divorced a while ago. Now I'm on my own, and I like it this way. Don't have a lot of time to spare after I finish my job and sports practice. I also coach a boys' team and I play on an Old Boys team.'

'You didn't believe her when she said she was tired of it—so what do you think the real reason was?'

'I have no idea. But she had a boyfriend, and those kinds of things take up time. He wasn't especially athletic, by the way, a pipe cleaner with skinny legs. Pale and slight, like a lima bean. He came to the matches once in a while, sat on the bench and never said a word. He wasn't the right type for her; she was a lot tougher than that.'

'They were still together.'

'Is that right? Well, each to his own.'

Sejer nodded, keeping his thoughts to himself. 'Where were you last Monday between eleven in the morning and two in the afternoon?'

'On Monday? You mean . . . on that day? At work, of course.'

'And this can be confirmed by the warehouse where you work?'

'I'm out driving a lot. We do home delivery, you see.'

'So you were in your vehicle? Alone?'

'Part of the time I was in my truck. I delivered two wardrobes to a house on Rødtangen—that much, at least, they can confirm.'

'When were you there?'

'Between one and two o'clock, I think.'

'Be a little more precise, Jensvoll.'

'Hmmm . . . I suppose it was closer to two o'clock.'

Sejer did the calculation in his head. 'And the hours before that?'

'Well, I was in and out. I overslept. And I grabbed a half-hour at the tanning salon. We manage our own time, pretty much.'

'Where were you, Jensvoll?'

'I got a late start that day,' he said. 'A couple of us were out on the town on Sunday night. I didn't get home until one thirty.'

'Who were you with?'

'A friend. Erik Fritzner.'

'Fritzner? Annie's neighbour?'

'Yes.'

'So . . .' Sejer nodded to himself and stared at the coach. 'Do you think Annie was an attractive girl?'

'Of course. You've seen her photo.'

'Yes, I have,' Sejer said. 'She wasn't just nice to look at, she was quite grown up for her age. Mature, in a way, more than most teenage girls. Don't you agree?'

'Yes, I suppose so. Although I was more concerned with her expertise in the goal.'

'Of course. That makes sense. Otherwise? Did you ever have any conflicts with the girls?'

'What type of conflicts?'

'Any kind,' Sejer said deliberately, 'regardless of type.'

'Naturally I did. Teenage girls are quite volatile.'

'What about Annie? Did you ever have a disagreement with her?'

Jensvoll crossed his arms and nodded. 'Well, yes, I did. On the day she called me and wanted to quit the team. I said a few desperate words that I should have held back. Maybe she took it as a compliment—who knows? She hung up on me and handed in her team uniform the next day. Done with it.'

'And that's the only time the two of you had a falling-out?'

'Yes, that's right. The only time.'

Sejer nodded to Skarre. The conversation was over. They walked to the door, Jensvoll following. A good deal of suppressed frustration was about to get the better of him.

'Come on, be honest,' he said, annoyed, as Sejer was opening the door. 'Why are you pretending that you haven't looked at my record? That's why you're here, isn't it? I know what you're thinking.'

Sejer turned round and stared at him.

'Do you have any idea what would happen to my team if that story got out around here? The girls would be locked in their rooms and the whole athletics programme would collapse.' His voice grew louder as he talked. 'And if there's one thing this place needs, it's a good sports programme. The ones who aren't involved sit in pubs and buy dope. Just so you're aware what you'll be starting if you publicise what you know. And besides, it was eleven years ago!'

'I haven't said a word about it,' Sejer said quietly. 'And if you keep your voice down, maybe we can prevent it from getting out.'

Jensvoll shut up at once and blushed bright red. He retreated back to the hall, and Skarre shut the door behind them.

'If we had enough personnel,' Sejer said, 'I'd put a tail on him.'

Skarre gave him an astonished look. 'Why's that?'

'Probably just to be unpleasant.'

FRITZNER LAY on his back in the dinghy, sipping a beer. After each sip he took a drag on his cigarette. He was completely absorbed by the book on his lap, propped against his knees. After a while he put down the beer and went to the living-room window. From there he could look down into Annie's bedroom. The curtains were drawn, even though it was only early afternoon.

He looked down the road and saw a police car by the letterboxes. There was the young officer with the curly hair. Probably going to the Holland house to give them the latest news. Suddenly, the officer turned left and entered his own front garden. Fritzner frowned.

Skarre said hello and then went over to the window, just as Fritzner had done.

'You were looking down at Annie's bedroom,' he said.

'Yes, I was.'

Fritzner continued. 'Actually, I'm a dirty old man, so I stood here often, gaping and drooling, hoping to catch a little peek. But she wasn't exactly the exhibitionist type. She would draw the curtains before she took off her jumper.'

He had to smile when he saw Skarre's expression.

'If you lived here, right across the street from Annie, you would have cast an eye at her house now and then. That's not a crime, is it?'

'No, I don't believe it is.'

'Have you discovered anything?' Fritzner said.

'Of course. We have silent witnesses. Everyone leaves something behind.'

Fritzner stood there for a moment, thinking. Looked at Skarre out of the corner of his eye and then seemed to make up his mind. He pulled his hand out of his pocket and held out something. 'I wanted to show you this.'

Skarre peered at it. It looked like a hairband, covered with material, blue, with beads sewn on.

'It's Annie's,' Fritzner said, staring at him. 'I found it in the car. On the floor in front, stuck between the seat and the door. It was just a week ago that I gave her a lift into town. She dropped it in the car.'

'Why are you giving this to me?'

He took a long, deep breath. 'I could have kept it. Burned it in the fireplace, not said a word. It's to show you that I'm playing with a clean deck.'

'I never thought otherwise,' Skarre said.

Fritzner smiled. 'Do you think I'm stupid?'

'Possibly,' said Skarre, smiling back. 'Maybe you're trying to trick me. Maybe you're such a conniving person that this whole sweet confession has been staged. I'll take the hairband with me. And take you into consideration to a greater extent than before.'

Fritzner turned pale. Skarre couldn't resist laughing at him.

'I WONDER IF SØLVI might have a little problem,' Eddie Holland said, putting a plump finger to his forehead. 'Not something that would show up in a scan or anything, she's learned what she needs to learn here in the world, she's just a little slow. A little one-sided, perhaps. You mustn't talk to Ada about this,' he said.

'Would she deny that Sølvi has a problem?' Sejer asked.

'She says that if they can't find anything, then it must not be there. People are just different, she says.'

Sejer had called him to his office. Holland still seemed lost in a vast darkness. The district prosecutor had given his verdict that Annie Holland could be buried and it was barely twenty-four hours since the funeral.

'I have to ask you about a few things,' Sejer said. 'If Annie had met Axel Bjørk on the road, would she have got into his car?'

The question made Holland gape in surprise. 'That's the most monstrous thing I've ever heard,' he said.

'A monstrous crime has been committed. Just answer my question.'

'Sølvi's father,' he said. 'Yes, I suppose so. Why wouldn't she?'

'What kind of relationship do you have with him?'

'We don't have a relationship.'

'But you've talked to him?'

'Barely. Ada has always stopped him at the door. Claimed that he was trying to force his way in.'

'What do you think about that?'

'I thought it was pretty stupid. He didn't want to ruin things for us. He just wanted to see Sølvi once in a while.'

'What about Sølvi? Did she want to see him?'

'I'm afraid Ada wrecked any desire she might have had. She can be very harsh. I think Bjørk has given up. You see, it's not easy to go against Ada,' he said. 'Not that I'm afraid of her, or anything,' he gave a brief, ironic laugh. 'But she gets so upset.'

'You're one of the people who knew Annie best,' Sejer said after some reflection. 'She had undergone a change in behaviour and I had the impression that it might have been due to something more than just puberty. Can you confirm that?'

'Ada says—'

'But what do *you* say?' Sejer interrupted, held his gaze. 'She rejected Halvor, quit the handball team, and then withdrew into herself. Did something out of the ordinary happen at that time?'

'Have you talked to Jensvoll?'

'Yes, we have.'

'Well, I heard rumours. Just something that Annie mentioned. That he was once in prison. A long time ago. I don't know why.'

'Did Annie know?'

'So he *was* in prison?'

'That's correct, he was. But I didn't think anyone knew about it. We're checking everyone around Annie, to see whether they had an alibi, but no one is yet a suspect in the case.'

'There's a man who lives up on Kolleveien,' Holland said, 'who's not all there. I've heard that he's tried things with girls around here.'

'We've talked to him too,' Sejer said patiently. 'He was the one who found Annie.'

'Yes, that's what I thought.'

'He has an alibi.'

Sejer thought about Ragnhild and didn't tell Holland that his alibi was a six-year-old child. 'Why do you think she stopped baby-sitting?'

'I think she just grew out of it.'

'But I understand that she really loved taking care of children. That's why I think it's a little strange.'

'For years she did nothing else,' Holland said. 'First she'd do her homework and then she'd go outside to see if anyone on the block needed a ride in a pushchair. And if there was a fight going on, she'd calm everybody down. She had authority.'

'A diplomatic personality, in other words?'

'Exactly. She liked to work things out. She was a kind of middleman. But in a way, she seemed to lose interest in that too. She didn't get involved in things the way she used to.'

'When was this?'

'Some time last autumn.'

'What happened last autumn?'

'I've already told you. She didn't want to be part of the team any more, didn't want to be with other people the way she used to do.'

'But why?'

'I don't know,' Holland said in despair.

'Try to look beyond yourself and your immediate family, Eddie,' said Sejer quietly. 'Beyond Halvor and the team and the problems with Axel Bjørk. Did anything else happen in the village at that time? Anything that might not have been directly related to you?'

Holland threw out his hands. 'Well, yes. Although it doesn't have anything to do with this. One of the children she baby-sat for died in a tragic accident. That didn't help matters. Annie didn't want to take part in anything after that. The only thing she thought about was putting on her trainers and running away from home and the street.'

Sejer could feel his heart take an extra beat.

'What did you just say?' He leaned his elbows on the table.

'One of the children she took care of died in an accident. His name was Eskil.'

'Did it happen while Annie was baby-sitting for him?'

'No, no! Annie was extremely careful when she was caring for children. Didn't let them out of her sight for an instant.'

'How did it happen?'

'At his house. He was only about two years old. Annie took it really badly.'

'And when did this happen?'

'Last autumn, I told you. About the time that she withdrew from everything.'

'When exactly did this death occur, Eddie?'

'I think it was in November.'

'Did it happen before or after she left the team?'

'I don't remember.'

'Then we'll keep going until you do. What kind of accident was it?'

'Something got caught in his throat and they couldn't get it out.'

There was a long silence.

'Tell me about Annie, about how she reacted.'

Holland straightened up in his chair and paused to think. 'I don't remember the date, but I remember the day, because we overslept. I had the day off. Annie was late for her bus, but came home early from school because she wasn't feeling well. I didn't dare tell her right away. She went to her room to lie down. I sat in the living room, dreading having to tell her. Finally I went to her room and sat down on the edge of her bed.'

'Go on.'

'She was stunned,' he said thoughtfully. 'Stunned and frightened.

Turned away and pulled the covers over her head. Afterwards she didn't show much of her feelings; she grieved in silence. She didn't want to go to the funeral either.'

'Did she visit his grave later?'

'Oh, yes, several times. But she never went to their house again.'

'But she must have talked to the parents?'

'I'm sure she did. They were separated after a while. It's difficult to find each other again after a tragedy like that. Annie was never the same. I think she realised that we're all going to die sooner or later. I remember the same feeling when I was a boy, when my mother died. That I was going to die too. And my father, and everyone I knew.'

His gaze seemed fixed on something far away, and Sejer listened with both hands resting on his desk.

'We have more to talk about, Eddie,' he said after a while. 'But there's something you should know first.'

'I don't know if I can stand to hear anything else.'

'I can't keep it from you. Not with good conscience.'

'What is it?'

'Annie had a tumour in her left ovary,' Sejer said in a low voice.

'A tumour?'

'About as big as an egg. Malignant. It had spread to her liver.'

Now Holland's whole body grew rigid. 'They must be mistaken,' he said. 'Nobody was healthier than Annie.'

'She had a malignant tumour in her ovary that had started to spread to her liver,' Sejer repeated. 'There was a high chance that her illness would have led to death.'

'So you're saying she would have died anyway?' Holland's voice had an aggressive edge to it.

'That's what the medical examiner said.'

'Am I supposed to be happy that she didn't have to suffer this?' he screamed, a drop of spit striking Sejer on the forehead. Holland hid his face in his hands. 'No, no, I didn't mean that,' he said, his voice choking, 'but I don't understand what's happening. How could there be so many things I didn't know about?'

'Either she didn't know herself, or else she concealed the pain and purposely decided not to consult a doctor. There's no mention of it in her medical records.'

'It probably doesn't say anything at all in them,' Holland said. 'There was never anything wrong with her.'

'There's also one thing I want you to do,' Sejer said. 'I want you to talk to Ada. We need to have her fingerprints. We found two prints on Annie's belt buckle. One of them was Annie's. One of them might be your wife's. If it's not hers, then it belongs to the killer. He undressed her. He must have touched the buckle.'

Holland nodded wearily. Nothing seemed to be standing still any more. Sejer's face was flickering slightly.

'Please ask your wife to come here. She should ask for Skarre.'

CHAPTER SIX

Halvor ate his pork sausage and boiled cabbage at the counter in the kitchen. Afterwards he cleaned up and put a blanket over his grandmother, who was dozing. He went to his room, drew the curtains, and sat down in front of the monitor. This was how he spent most of his spare time now. He had tried out a lot of the music that he knew Annie liked, typing in titles and the names of musicians she had in her stack of CDs. The task seemed insurmountable, but the important thing was not to give up. He sat there until midnight, then dragged himself to bed and turned off the light. He didn't hear the footsteps outside going back and forth. As he waited to fall asleep, he thought about Annie.

Outside, the courtyard was dark and quiet. The entrance to the empty kennel gaped like an open, toothless mouth, but it wasn't visible from the road, and a thief might think there was a dog inside. Behind the kennel stood the shed with a modest woodpile, his bicycle, and a pile of newspapers. In the far corner, behind a foam mattress, lay Annie's schoolbag.

HE HAD RUN OUT to Bruvann and back, eight miles. Had tried to stay below the pain threshold, at least on the home stretch. Elise used to pour an ice-cold beer and hand it to him when he came out of the shower. Now no one stood waiting for him, except for his dog, who lifted his head expectantly when Sejer opened the door and let the steam out. He got dressed and then found a bottle of beer for himself, snapped off the cap and put it to his lips. The doorbell rang as he was half-done with the bottle. He raised an admonishing finger at the dog and went to open the door. Outside stood Skarre.

'I was in the neighbourhood,' he said.

He looked different. His curls were gone, sheared off close to his scalp. His hair had acquired a darker sheen, making him look older.

'Nice haircut,' Sejer said. 'Come on in.'

Kollberg came leaping over, as he always did.

'He's a little overzealous,' Sejer said. 'But he's good-natured.'

'He'd better be, at that size. He's like a wolf.'

'He's supposed to look like a lion. That's what the chap who mixed the breeds and created the first Leonberger intended. He was from Leonberg in Germany and wanted to create a town mascot.'

'A lion?' Skarre studied the big animal and smiled. 'No, I'm not that gullible.' He took off his jacket and hung it in the hall. 'Did you have a talk with Holland today?'

'I did. What have you been doing?'

'I visited Halvor's grandmother.'

'Did you?'

'She served me coffee and *lefse* flatbread, along with all the misery of her old age.'

Sejer led the way into the living room, where they both sat down. 'How old is she?'

'She's eighty-three. And she's obviously not all there.'

'Do you want a beer?'

'OK, thanks.'

Sejer went into the kitchen and Skarre stared at the shelf next to the stereo. 'You have a lot of CDs. Have you counted them?'

'Approximately five hundred,' Sejer replied. He re-emerged carrying a beer, which he handed to Skarre before sitting down again.

Skarre drank deeply. 'What did Holland say?'

'Annie knew Jensvoll had been in prison. Maybe she knew why.'

'Go on.'

'And one of the children she often baby-sat for died in an accident. It happened in November, at about the same time everything got so difficult. Annie wouldn't go to the funeral, and she didn't want to baby-sit any more. After that she left the handball team, temporarily broke up with Halvor, and withdrew into herself. So it happened in that order. The child died. Annie withdrew from everyone.'

'So that's the reason for the change in her?'

'Possibly. But she also had cancer. Even though she may not have known about it herself, it could have changed her. But I was hoping to find something else. Something we could use.'

'What about Jensvoll?'

'I have a hard time believing that a man would commit murder just to guarantee silence about a rape that took place eleven years ago, and which he's done time for. Unless he tried it again and the whole thing went wrong . . . Do you have time to take a drive?'

'Of course. Where are we going?'

'To Lundeby church.'

'Why there?'

'I'm not sure. I'd like to snoop around.' Sejer downed some beer, then asked, 'What else did Halvor's grandmother give you? Aside from the *lefse* and a lecture on decay?'

'She says Halvor has been holed up in his room. Sometimes he sits in front of his computer all evening and well into the night.'

'What do you think he's doing?'

'I have no idea. Maybe he's writing a diary.'

'In that case, I'd like to read it.'

'Are you going to bring him in again?'

'Certainly.'

They finished their beers and got to their feet. On their way out Skarre caught sight of a photo of Elise, with her dazzling smile.

'Your wife?' he said.

'The last one she had taken.'

'She looks like Grace Kelly,' Skarre said. 'How did an old grouch like you ever capture such a beauty?'

Sejer was so taken aback by this impudence that he actually stuttered as he answered mildly, 'I wasn't an old grouch back then.'

THE CAR CRUNCHED over the gravel road to Lundeby church. It was floodlit and stood in the pink-coloured light with solemn self-possession. They shut the car doors and headed for the graves.

Annie had been laid to rest at the edge of the cemetery, down near a field of barley. The flowers had faded and were beginning to decay. The two officers stared at them, each lost in his own thoughts. Then they began to read the inscriptions on the other headstones. Two rows beyond Annie's grave, Sejer found what he was looking for. A small headstone, rounded on top, with a beautifully etched inscription. Skarre bent down and read what it said. '"Our beloved Eskil"?'

Sejer nodded. 'Eskil Johnas. Born August 4th, 1992, died November 7th, 1994.'

'Johnas? The carpet dealer?'

'The carpet dealer's son. He got something caught in his throat and choked to death. After he died the marriage fell apart. Johnas has another son who lives with the boy's mother.'

'He had pictures of the boys on the wall,' Skarre said, sticking his hands in his pockets. 'What's that little hollow on the top?'

'Someone must have stolen something from the headstone. Maybe there was a bird or an angel. There often is on a child's grave.'

'Strange that they haven't replaced it. It looks almost neglected.'

They turned and looked down at the fields surrounding the cemetery. Lights from the nearby rectory flickered piously in the blue dusk. 'The mother moved to Oslo and it's a long way from there.'

'It would only take Johnas two minutes.'

'Johnas can see the church from his living-room window,' Sejer said. 'Maybe he thinks that's enough.'

'His dog must have had her pups by now.'

Sejer didn't answer.

'Where are we headed next?'

'I don't really know, but this little chap is dead.' He glanced down at the grave again and frowned. 'And Annie became a different person afterwards. Why would she take it so hard?'

'And how could anyone steal from a grave?' asked Skarre, as they started back to the car.

'The fact that you can't comprehend it is a good sign,' Sejer said, plucking a leafy twig from the windscreen.

'I would have bought another bird,' Skarre said, 'and had it properly attached to the headstone. If it was my child.'

Sejer started up the old Peugeot and let the engine run as he sat in silence for a moment.

'I would too.'

HALVOR WAS AT HIS COMPUTER. He hadn't thought it would be easy, because his life had never been easy. It might take months, but that didn't frighten him. Often he simply sat and stared at the screen. He didn't care about anything else any more. Finding the password had become an excuse for staying in the past and avoiding the future.

What he had shared with Annie was, of course, too good to last; he should have known that. He had often wondered where it was leading and how it would end.

His grandmother said nothing, although she did have her opinions; like that he should do something useful, such as raking the courtyard or cleaning up the shed. That was what most people did in the spring. Every time she mentioned it, he nodded distractedly, and then went back to what he was doing. Eventually she gave up. With much effort she managed to tie the laces on a pair of trainers and limp outside with a crutch under one arm. She crossed the courtyard and opened the door to the shed. Maybe the old garden furniture could be put in front of the house as decoration. She fumbled for the switch on the wall and turned on the light.

ASTRID JOHNAS OWNED a wool shop on the west side of Oslo. She was sitting at a knitting machine and working on something soft and angora-like, perhaps for a newborn baby. Sejer walked across the room and cleared his throat, stopping beside her to admire her work with a slightly awkward expression on his face.

'I'm making a blanket,' she said, smiling. 'To put in a baby's pram. I make them on commission.'

He stared at her, at first with some surprise. She was a good deal older than her former husband. But, more than that, she was astonishingly beautiful, and for a moment her beauty took his breath away. Hers was not the gentle, restrained beauty that his wife, Elise, had possessed, but rather a dark beauty evident at first glance.

'Konrad Sejer,' he said. 'From the police.'

'I thought so.' She gave him a smile. 'Sometimes I wonder why it's always so easy to tell, even when you're not wearing a uniform.'

He blushed and wondered whether he might have acquired a different posture or a way of dressing after so many years in the police force, or whether she was simply more astute than most people.

She stood up and turned off her work lamp. 'Come into the back room. I have a small office where I eat my lunch.' She moved in a very feminine way. 'This whole thing with Annie is so awful.'

She pointed to a chair. He stared at her, slowly overcome by an almost forgotten sensation.

'I knew Annie well. She spent a lot of time at our house and took care of Eskil. We had a son who died last year,' she said.

'I know.'

'You've talked to Henning, of course. Unfortunately, we lost contact with her afterwards; she didn't come to see us any more. At that age it's not easy to know what to say. Have you any idea who might have done it?'

'No,' he said. 'At the moment we're just gathering information.'

'I'm afraid I won't be of much help.' She looked down at her hands. 'I knew her well; she was a lovely girl, much smarter and nicer than most girls her age.' There was a pause. 'What is it you want to know?'

He said nothing, studying her. She had a trim, slender figure and dark eyes. All her clothes were knitted, like one big advertisement for her shop. An attractive red suit with a straight skirt and fitted jacket.

A simple, straight hairstyle. Some years younger than Sejer, with the first hint of fine lines at her eyes and mouth. Her son Eskil must have been born towards the end of her youth.

'I'm not looking for anything in particular,' he said. 'So Annie came to your house to baby-sit Eskil?'

'Several times a week,' she said. 'No one else wanted to baby-sit for him; he wasn't easy to deal with. He was so full of energy, up and down, always restless. Hyperactive, I guess it's called.' She gave a rather helpless laugh. 'This isn't an easy thing to admit, but he was a difficult child. To be quite frank, Annie was one of the few who could handle him. She came over a lot. Henning and I were always so worn out, and it was a blessing whenever she appeared in the doorway, smiling and offering to baby-sit. We have another son, Magne. But he was too old to go out pushing a pram.'

She shifted her position in the chair. Talking about her son seemed to make her uneasy. Her eyes were on everything except Sejer's face.

'How old was Eskil when he died?' Sejer asked.

'Only twenty-seven months,' she whispered, and seemed to flinch.

'Did it happen while Annie was baby-sitting him?'

She glanced up. 'No, thank God. I kept on saying how lucky that was.'

Another pause. He took a new approach. 'But . . . what kind of accident was it?'

'I thought you talked to Henning,' she said.

'I did,' he said. 'But he didn't go into detail.'

'Eskil got some food caught in his throat. I was upstairs in bed. Henning was in the bathroom shaving and didn't hear a thing. But Eskil couldn't scream anyway, with the food caught in his throat. He was strapped to his chair with a harness, the kind children have at that age. He was sitting there eating his breakfast.'

'I know them. I have a daughter and a grandchild,' he said.

She swallowed and then went on. 'Henning found him hanging in the harness, blue in the face. It took the ambulance more than twenty minutes to arrive, and by then there was no hope.'

'And you were asleep the whole time, is that right?'

Suddenly she looked him straight in the eye. 'I thought you wanted to talk about Annie?' She crossed her arms.

'Yes. What concerns me is Annie's reaction to the accident,' he said. 'The fact that she reacted so strongly.'

'That's not so strange, is it?' she said, her voice a little sharp. 'They were very attached to each other.'

'I suppose it's not so strange. I'm just trying to find out who she was. What she was like.'

'I'm not trying to be uncooperative, but it's not easy to talk about this.' She looked directly at him again. 'But . . . you're looking for a sex criminal, aren't you?'

'I'm not sure.'

'You're not? Well, that's what I assumed straight away, since it said that she was found naked.' Now she was blushing as she fidgeted with her fingers. 'What else could it be?'

'That's the question. As far as we know, she had no enemies. But if the motive wasn't sex, then the question is: What was it?' Sejer paused for a moment. 'How long were you married to your husband?'

She gave a start. 'For fifteen years. I was pregnant with Magne when we got married. Henning—he's a lot younger than I am,' she said. 'Eskil was actually a kind of afterthought.'

'So your older son, Magne, is getting on for seventeen now?'

She nodded.

'Does he have contact with his father?'

She gave him a look of dismay. 'Of course he does! He often goes to Lundeby to visit old friends.'

'Do you go out to Eskil's grave very often?'

'No,' she said. 'But Henning tends to it. It's difficult for me. As long as I know it's being looked after, I can bear it.'

He thought about the neglected grave. Then the door opened and a young man came into the shop. Mrs Johnas glanced up.

'Magne! I'm in here!'

Sejer turned and studied her son. He bore a strong resemblance to his father, although he was much more heavily built. He paused in the doorway, apparently reluctant to talk. His expression was stony; it suited his black hair and the bulging muscles of his upper arms.

'I must get going, Mrs Johnas,' Sejer said, standing up.

He nodded to mother and son, and was gone. Mrs Johnas stared after him and then gave her son an agonised look.

'He's investigating Annie's murder,' she said. 'But all he wanted to talk about was Eskil.'

Outside the shop, Sejer paused for a moment. A motorcycle was parked next to the entrance; perhaps it belonged to Magne Johnas. A big Kawasaki. Leaning on the motorcycle, with her bottom against the seat, was a young woman. She didn't notice him because she was concentrating on her nails. She was wearing a short red leather jacket covered with studs, and she had a cloud of blonde hair that reminded him of angel's hair, the kind they used to put on the Christmas tree when he was a child. Then she looked up.

He smiled. 'Hello, Sølvi,' he said, and headed across the street.

SEJER DROVE SLOWLY, ordering his thoughts in neat rows. Eskil Johnas. A difficult child who few but Annie could handle. And who suddenly died, all alone, harnessed to his chair. He thought of his own grandson and shivered as he headed for Halvor's house.

Halvor Muntz was standing in the kitchen, running water over some spaghetti. He kept forgetting to eat. He didn't hear the car pull up outside because the water was gushing out of the tap. But he heard his grandmother slam the door, mutter something to herself and shuffle across the floor in her Nike trainers. On the counter stood a bottle of ketchup and a bowl of grated cheese. His grandmother was groaning in the living room.

'Look what I found in the shed, Halvor!'

Something fell to the floor with a thud. He looked into the room.

'An old schoolbag,' she said. 'With books inside.'

Halvor took two steps forward and then stopped abruptly.

'That's Annie's,' he whispered.

'Did she leave it here?'

'Yes,' he said quickly, moving to pick it up. 'I'll put it in my room for the time being and take it over to Eddie later.'

His grandmother looked at him, and an anxious expression spread over her wrinkled face. Suddenly, a familiar figure appeared in the dimly lit room. Halvor felt his heart sink; he stiffened and stood as if frozen to the spot, with the bag dangling from one strap.

'Halvor,' Sejer said. 'You'll have to come with me.'

Halvor swayed and had to take a step sideways in order not to fall. The ceiling was moving towards him, soon he would be crushed against the floor.

'You can take the bag to Annie's house on the way,' his grandmother said nervously, twisting her wedding ring, which was much too big, round and round. Halvor didn't reply. The room was starting to swirl around him, and sweat poured out of him as he stood there shaking, with the bag in his hand. It wasn't very heavy. Inside it were a novel and a notebook—along with Annie's wallet, which contained a picture of him from the previous summer when he looked tanned and handsome, with his hair bleached by the sun. Not as he looked now, with sweat on his forehead and his face chalk-white with fear.

THE MOOD WAS TENSE. Normally he had no trouble staying the course and taking whatever came his way. Now he felt caught off guard.

'You realise that this was necessary?' Sejer said.

'Yes.'

Halvor raised one leg and studied his trainer.

'Annie's schoolbag was found in the shed at your house, which directly connects you with the murder. Do you understand what I'm saying?'

'Yes. But you're wrong.'

'Since you were Annie's boyfriend, you were a suspect. The problem was that we couldn't charge you with anything. But now your grandmother has done the job for us. I'm sure you hadn't expected that, Halvor, since she isn't very mobile. All of a sudden she decides to clean out the shed. Who would have thought that would happen?'

'I have no idea where it came from! She found it in the shed, that's all I know. Someone's trying to frame me.'

'What do you mean by that?'

'Someone must have put the bag there. I heard someone sneaking around outside my window the other night.'

Sejer smiled sadly.

'Go ahead and sneer,' Halvor said, 'but it's true. Someone put it there, someone wants me to take the blame.' He gave the chief inspector a stubborn stare.

'I've always thought that the killer knew her,' Sejer said. 'I think he knew her well. Maybe as well as you did?'

'I didn't do it! Listen to me! I didn't do it!' He wiped his brow and tried to calm down.

'We'll see. Finding the bag also gives us reason to do a closer check on your motorcycle and gear and helmet. And the house you live in. Is there anything you need before we continue?'

'No. Do I have to stay here tonight?'

'I'm afraid so.'

'For how long?'

'I don't know yet.' He looked at the boy's face across the table and changed tactics. 'What have you been writing on your computer, Halvor? You sit in front of the monitor for hours, often long into the night. Can you tell me what you've been doing?'

Halvor looked up. 'Have you been spying on me?'

'In a way. We've been spying on a lot of people lately. Are you writing a diary?'

'I just play games. Chess, for example.'

'With yourself?'

'With the Virgin Mary,' he said.

Sejer blinked. 'I would advise you to tell me what you know. You're keeping something from me, Halvor, I'm sure of that. Were there two of you? Are you covering up for someone?'

Halvor remained silent.

'If we end up charging you, I'm afraid we may have to confiscate your computer.'

'Go ahead,' he said. 'But you won't be able to get in!'

'Because you've put a password on it?'

Halvor's mouth was dry, but he didn't want to beg for a Coke.

'So I assume that it contains something important, since you've made sure that no one could find it.'

'There's nothing important. Just things I scribble when I'm bored.'

Sejer stood up. 'You look thirsty. I'll get us a couple of Cokes.'

Sejer left and the office closed in around Halvor. Far off in the distance he could hear a siren. Otherwise there was a steady hum in the big building. Sejer came back with two bottles and an opener.

'I'm going to open the window a little. OK?'

Halvor nodded. 'I didn't do it.'

Sejer found two plastic cups and poured the Coke. Foam spilled over the sides.

'There was no reason for me to do it.'

'It's not immediately clear to me either why you would do it.' Sejer sighed and took a drink. 'But that doesn't mean that you didn't have a reason. Sometimes our feelings can run away with us—that's often the simple answer. Has that ever happened to you?'

Halvor didn't reply.

'Do you know Raymond, who lives on Kolleveien?'

'The guy with Down's syndrome? I see him in the street once in a while.'

'Have you ever been to his house?'

'I've driven past. He has rabbits.'

'Ever talk to him?'

'Never.'

'Did you know that Knut Jensvoll, who was Annie's coach, once served time for rape?'

'Annie told me that.'

'Did anyone else know?'

'I have no idea.'

'Did you know the boy she used to baby-sit for? Eskil Johnas?'

Now he looked up, startled. 'Yes. He died.'

'Tell me about him.'

'Why?'

'Just do as I ask.'

'Well, he was sweet . . . and funny.'

'Sweet and funny?'

'Full of energy.'

'Difficult?'

'A bit of a handful, maybe. Couldn't sit still. I think he took medication for it. I went along a few times when Annie took care of him. She was the only one who could handle him.' He emptied his cup and wiped his mouth.

'Did you know his parents?'

'I know who they are.'

'How about the older son?'

'Magne? I know what he looks like.'

'Did he ever show any interest in Annie?'

'Just the usual. Long looks whenever she walked past.'

'What did you think about that, Halvor? The fact that other boys were giving your girlfriend the once-over?'

'First of all, I was used to it. Second, Annie wasn't interested.'

'And yet she went off with someone. There's an exception here, Halvor.'

'I realise that.'

Halvor was tired. He closed his eyes. The scar at the corner of his mouth shone like a silver cord in the light from the lamp. 'There was a lot about Annie that I didn't understand. Sometimes she'd get angry for no reason, or irritated, and if I asked what was the matter, she'd get even worse and snap at me, saying that it's not always easy to understand everything in this world.' He gasped for breath.

'So you have a feeling that she knew something? That something was bothering her?'

'I don't know. I guess so. I told Annie a lot about myself. Almost everything. So she should have known that it wasn't dangerous to confide in someone.'

'But your own confidences couldn't have been exactly earth-shaking. Maybe hers were worse?'

Nothing could have been worse. Nothing in the world.

'Halvor?'

'There was something,' he said in a low voice as he opened his eyes again, 'that had locked Annie up tighter than a sealed drum.'

CHAPTER SEVEN

Something had locked Annie up tighter than a sealed drum.

The sentence was so delicately formulated that Sejer realised he believed it. Or was it simply that he *wanted* to believe it? In any case, there was the schoolbag, hidden. The strong feeling that Halvor was keeping something concealed. Sejer stared at the pavement ahead of him and arranged several ideas in his mind. Annie liked to baby-sit for other people's children. The boy she chose to take care of was particularly difficult, and he had died. She could never have had children of her own, and she didn't have long to live. She had a boyfriend at whom she occasionally snapped; she broke off with him and then took him back. As if she didn't really know what she wanted. He could see no connections between this set of facts.

He stuck his hands in his pockets and headed across the car park, got into his car and carefully manoeuvred it out to the street. Then he drove to the next county, the community where Halvor had spent his non-existent childhood. Back then the community police department was in an old villa, but now he found it located in a new shopping centre. He was lost in thought when the community officer came into the reception area. The man was in his late forties, thin, and had barely concealed curiosity in his blue-green eyes.

'It's good of you to take the time,' Sejer said, following the community officer down the corridor.

'You mentioned a homicide. Annie Holland?'

Sejer nodded.

'I've been following the case in the papers. I assume that you have someone in the spotlight who you think I might know?'

He pointed to a chair.

'Well, yes. We do have someone in custody. He's just a boy, but what we found at his house gave us no choice but to arrest him.'

'And you would have preferred to have a choice?'

'I don't think he did it.' Sejer gave a little smile at his own words.

'I see. That happens sometimes.'

The community officer folded his hands and waited.

'In December 1992 you had a suicide here in your district. Two brothers were subsequently sent to the Bjerkeli Children's Home, and the mother ended up in the psychiatric ward of the Central

Hospital. I'm looking for information on Halvor Muntz, born 1976, the son of Torkel and Lilly Muntz.'

The community officer recognised the names, and at once he looked anxious.

'You dealt with the case, didn't you?'

'Yes, unfortunately, I did. Halvor, the older boy, called me at home. It happened at night. I didn't want to go out there alone, so I took along a new recruit. When it came to Halvor's family, we never knew what we might find. We drove out to the house and found the mother on the sofa in the living room, huddled under a quilt, and the two boys upstairs. Halvor didn't say a word. Next to him in bed was his little brother, who wouldn't even open his eyes. There was blood everywhere. We checked the boys, saw that they were still alive, and breathed a sigh of relief. Then we started searching. The father was lying inside a rotting sleeping-bag. Half of his head was blown away.'

He stopped, and Sejer could almost see the images like shadows in his pupils.

'It wasn't easy to get anything out of the boys. They clung to each other and refused to say a word. But after a lot of coaxing, Halvor told us that his father had been drinking heavily since morning and had started smashing up the house. The boys had spent most of the day outside, but when night fell, they had to come in because it was cold. Halvor woke up to find his father bending over the boys' bed with a bread knife in his hand. He stabbed Halvor and then seemed to come to his senses. He rushed out and Halvor heard the door slam, and then they heard him struggling with the door to the shed. After a little while they heard a shot. Halvor didn't dare go out to investigate; he tiptoed down to the living room and called me. But he guessed what had happened. Told us he was afraid that something was wrong with his father. The Child Welfare Service had been trying to take custody of those kids for years, but Halvor had always refused. After that night, he didn't object.'

'How did he take it?'

The community officer got up and paced the room.

'It was hard to tell what he was feeling. Halvor was a very closed sort of child. But to be honest, it definitely wasn't despair. It was more a sort of determination, maybe because he could finally start a new life. His father's death was a turning point.'

He fell silent again.

'It wasn't until later that we started to think about things.' He went back to his chair. 'The father was lying inside a sleeping-bag. He had taken off his jacket and boots, had even rolled up his sweater and stuck it under his head. I mean, he had really settled in for the night. Not,' he said, taking a breath, 'not to die. So it occurred to us afterwards that someone might have helped him on his way to eternity.'

Sejer shut his eyes. 'You mean Halvor?'

'Yes,' the community officer said sombrely, 'I mean Halvor. He could have followed his father out, watched him fall asleep, stuck the shotgun inside the sleeping-bag, into his father's hands, and pulled the trigger.'

The information made Sejer freeze. 'What did you do?'

'Nothing.'

The community officer threw out his hands in a helpless gesture. 'We didn't do anything at all. We didn't find anything that could connect him to it, nothing concrete. The wound was typical for a suicide. A 16-calibre shotgun, fired at close range, with the entrance wound under the chin and the exit wound at the top of the skull. No other fingerprints on the shotgun. No suspicious footprints outside the shed.'

'But you talked to him?'

'We brought them in for questioning, but we didn't get anywhere. The younger brother was only about six; he couldn't confirm or deny the timing. The mother was full of Valium, and none of the neighbours heard the shot. Their house was quite isolated. But fortunately there were a number of contraindications.'

'Such as?'

'If Halvor was the one who fired the shot, he would have had to lie down next to his father, with the shotgun pressed to his chest and the muzzle up under his chin. Would a fifteen-year-old be able to think that clearly, with his cheek sliced open?'

'It's not impossible. Someone who lives in a house with a psychopath has to learn a lot of tricks. Halvor's a bright kid.'

'Were they sweethearts? Halvor and the Holland girl?'

'Sort of,' Sejer said. 'I'm not happy about your theory, but I'm going to have to take it into consideration.'

'So you're going to make it public?'

'If you give me a copy of the case file, that would be great. But it's probably impossible now, after so much time, to prove anything. I don't think you need to worry.'

The community officer stared sadly out of the window.

'I've probably damaged Halvor's case by telling you this. He deserved better. He's the most considerate boy I've ever met. He took care of his mother and brother all those years, and I've heard that he's been living with old Mrs Muntz now, and taking care of her.'

'That's right.'

'So he finally found a girlfriend. And it ends up like this? How's he doing? Is he keeping his head above water?'

'Yes, he is. But perhaps he didn't expect anything from life other than repeated catastrophes.'

'If he killed his father,' the community officer said, looking Sejer straight in the eye, 'then it was in self-defence. He saved the whole family. It was him or them. I have a hard time believing that he would kill for any other reason. So it would not be fair to use this as evidence against him. Give him the benefit of the doubt.'

'We have a departmental meeting later today, and we'll have to evaluate the charges. I'm afraid . . .'

'Yes?'

'I'm afraid I won't be able to convince the team to let him go free. Not after this.'

HOLTHEMANN LEAFED through the report and gave them a stern look. 'What about that character up on Kolleveien?' the department head asked. 'How thoroughly have you investigated him? Raymond Låke?'

'The jacket found on the body was his. And Skarre says that there are rumours about him.'

'Which rumours are you thinking of?' Sejer asked.

'That he drives around drooling over girls. There are also rumours about his father. That there's nothing wrong with him, that he just lies in bed reading porn magazines. Maybe Raymond has been reading the magazines on the sly and got inspired.'

'I think we're definitely looking for a local man,' Sejer said. 'And I also think he's trying to mislead us.'

'You believe Halvor?'

'I do believe him. There is also an as yet unidentified person who appeared in Raymond's yard and convinced Raymond that the car he saw was red.'

'A rather far-fetched story. Maybe he was just a hiker. Raymond doesn't have all his wits about him, does he?'

Sejer bit his lip. 'I don't think Raymond's smart enough to make up a story like that. I think someone really did speak to him.'

'And this is the man who allegedly sneaked past Halvor's window? And put Annie's bag in the shed?'

'It's possible, yes.'

'It's not like you to be so gullible, Konrad. Have you let a dimwit and a teenager win you over with their charms?'

Sejer felt uncomfortable. He didn't like to be reproached, but perhaps he was letting his instincts overshadow the facts. Halvor was the closest person to the victim. He was her boyfriend.

'Did Halvor give you any details?' Holthemann asked.

'He heard a car starting up. Possibly an old car, possibly with one cylinder out. The sound came from the main road.'

'There's a turning place there. Lots of cars stop.'

'I realise that. Let's release him. He's not going to run away.'

'After what you've told us, he might well be a killer. Someone who killed his own father in cold blood. It doesn't look good for him, Konrad.'

'But he loved Annie, he really did. Even though she never gave him much encouragement.'

'He probably got impatient and lost control. And if he blew his father's head off, that shows there's plenty of explosive material inside that young man.'

'If he did kill his father—and we don't know that for sure—it must have been because he had no choice. His whole family was being destroyed, after years of abuse and neglect. And he'd been stabbed in the face. I have no doubt that he would have been acquitted.'

'Quite possibly. But the fact remains that he might be capable of murder. Not everyone is. What do you think, Skarre?'

Skarre was shaking his head. 'I picture an older murderer,' he said.

'Why is that?'

'She was in extremely good physical shape. Annie weighed one hundred and forty-three pounds, and most of it was muscle. Halvor is only one hundred and thirty-eight pounds, so they were about the same weight. If Halvor really did shove her into the water, he would have encountered enough resistance so that Annie would have been marked by some outward signs of a struggle—such as cuts and scratches. But all indications are that the killer was bigger than she was and probably much heavier. From what I've seen, Annie was physically superior to Halvor. I don't mean that he couldn't have done it, but I think it would have been very difficult for him.'

Sejer nodded silently.

'OK,' Holthemann said. 'That sounds reasonable enough. But then we're left with nothing. Have we found anyone else who might have a motive?'

'Halvor doesn't have any apparent motive either.'

'He had the bag, along with a strong emotional attachment. I'm the one who has to take responsibility here, even though I don't particularly like it, Konrad. What about Axel Bjørk? Bitter and alcoholic, with a dangerous temper? Did you find anything there?'

'We have no evidence that Bjørk was in Lundeby on the day in question.'

'I see. From the report, you both seem more interested in the death of a two-year-old boy.' Now he smiled, though not in an obviously scornful way.

'Not in the boy himself,' said Sejer. 'More in Annie's reaction to the death. We've tried to work out the reason for the change in her personality; it might have something to do with the boy, or possibly the fact that she was ill. I was hoping to find something there.'

'Such as what?'

'I don't know. That's what is so difficult about this case; we have no idea what kind of man we're looking for.'

'An executioner, maybe. He held her head under water until she died,' Holthemann said harshly. 'There wasn't a scratch on her.'

'That's why I think they were sitting on the shore, side by side, talking. Completely at ease. Maybe he had some kind of hold over her. Suddenly he puts his hand at the back of her neck and throws her down on her stomach in the water. All in the blink of an eye. But the idea may have occurred to him earlier, maybe while they were in the car, or on the motorcycle.'

'He must have been wet and muddy,' Skarre said.

'No one saw a motorcycle on Kolleveien?'

'Only a car, going fast. But the owner of Horgen's Shop saw a motorcycle. He didn't see Annie. Johnas didn't see her get on the motorcycle either. He let her out, saw the motorcycle, and thought that she seemed to be heading towards it.'

'Do you have any other new leads?'

'Magne Johnas.'

'What about him?'

'Not much, actually. He looks full of anabolic steroids, and he had his eye on Annie for a while. She wasn't interested. Maybe he's the type who won't stand for that. He also went to Lundeby occasionally, to visit old friends, and he drives a motorcycle. He seems to have taken up with Sølvi instead. We can't rule him out, at any rate.'

Holthemann nodded. 'All right,' he said. 'If something doesn't happen soon, I'm going to have to charge Halvor. Why, for instance, would the murderer take Annie's schoolbag home with him?'

'If they arrived by car, they must have got out at the turning place, and then the bag would have been left in the car,' Sejer said. 'Afterwards it may have been too awkward to go back and throw it in the water.'

'Sounds reasonable.'

'One question,' Sejer said. 'If the fingerprint on Annie's belt buckle doesn't belong to Halvor, shouldn't we let him go?'

'Let me think about that.'

Sejer went over to the map on the wall, where the road from Krystallen was highlighted with red, traced via the roundabout, down to Horgen's Shop, and up Kolleveien to the lake. Several little green magnets marked the locations along the way where Annie had been seen. One was placed outside her house in Krystallen, one at the intersection of Gneisveien, where she crossed the street and took a detour, one was at the roundabout where she was seen by a woman as she got into Johnas's car. One was at Horgen's Shop. Johnas's car and the motorcycle outside the shop were also indicated. Sejer plucked off one of the Annie magnets, the one near Horgen's Shop, and put it in his pocket.

'What if she never got out of Johnas's car?' he said. 'What if it's that simple?' He took a few steps as his thoughts whirled. 'We've only had Johnas's word that she did.'

'As far as we know, he's a respectable businessman with an impeccable reputation,' Holthemann said. 'Also he was grateful to Annie for regularly freeing him from a difficult child.'

'Exactly. She knew him. And he had good feelings towards her.' Sejer closed his eyes. 'Maybe she was mistaken.'

'What are you saying?' Holthemann leaned forward.

'I'm wondering whether she might have made a mistake,' he repeated. 'She underestimated him. Thought she was safe.' He paused. 'Maybe they shared a secret.'

'A bed, for example?'

Sejer put the Annie magnet back in place and turned round with a doubtful look.

'It wouldn't be the first time,' Holtheman said, smiling. 'Some young girls have a thing for older men. Have you noticed it yourself, Konrad?'

'Halvor denies that there was another man.'

'Of course he does. He can't bear the thought.'

'A relationship that she might expose, is that what you mean?

Someone with a wife and children and a big salary?'

'I'm just thinking out loud. Snorrason says she wasn't a virgin.'

Sejer nodded. 'She and Halvor tried sex, but in my opinion every male in Krystallen should be a possible candidate. They watched her grow up and get more and more attractive. They gave her lifts, she took care of their children, went in and out of their houses; she trusted them. They're all grown men she knew well. There are twenty-one houses minus her own; that gives us twenty men. Fritzner, Irmak, Johnas and so on, it's a whole gang. Maybe one of them was lusting after her in secret.'

'Lusting after her? I thought that there had been no sexual assault.'

'Maybe he was interrupted.'

Sejer studied the map on the wall. The possibilities were piling up, but how could anyone have killed the girl yet left her otherwise untouched? Simply arranged her body nicely, thoughtfully, considerately, with her clothes next to her. He picked up the last Annie magnet. Pressed it hard between his fingers and then, almost reluctantly, put it back on the map.

KOLLBERG NEEDED TO PEE. Sejer walked the dog behind the apartment building, let him do his business in the bushes, and then took the lift back upstairs. Padded out to the kitchen and peered inside the freezer. A packet of sausages, a pizza, and a little package marked 'bacon'. He decided on eggs instead, four fried eggs with salt and pepper, and a sliced sausage for the dog. Kollberg gulped down his food and then stretched out under the table. Sejer ate his eggs and drank some milk, his feet nestled under the dog's chest.

The meal took him ten minutes. He had the newspaper spread out next to his plate. BOYFRIEND TAKEN INTO CUSTODY. He sighed, feeling annoyed. He didn't have much patience with the press and the way they covered life's miseries. He cleared the table and plugged in the coffeepot. Maybe Halvor had killed his father. Pulled on a pair of gloves, stuck the shotgun inside the sleeping-bag and pressed it into his father's hands, pulled the trigger, swept the ground in front of the shed door, and run back to the bedroom to his brother. Who felt such an intractable loyalty to Halvor that he wouldn't have said so even if Halvor had been out of his bed when the shot was fired?

Sejer took his coffee to the living room. When he'd finished, he took a shower and then leafed through a catalogue of bathrooms and fixtures. They were having a sale on bathroom tiles. He would fix up the bathroom. If Elise knew that he still hadn't got round to it . . . eight years with imitation marble was shameful.

He stood up and went to the kitchen to fetch his bottle of whisky. The doorbell rang as he was putting the top back on the bottle, having poured himself a glass.

It was Skarre, not quite as shy as he'd been the previous time. He had come on foot, but frowned when Sejer offered him a whisky.

'Do you have any beer?'

'I don't, but I can ask Kollberg. He sometimes has a small supply at the back of the fridge,' Sejer said, with a grin. He went out and then returned with a beer.

'Do you know how to put up bathroom tiles?' he asked.

'I certainly do. I took a course in it. The key is not to skimp with the preparations. Do you need help?'

'What do you think about these?' Sejer pointed to the brochure.

'Those are great. What do you have now?'

'Imitation marble.'

Skarre nodded sympathetically and raised his beer. Then he said, 'Halvor's fingerprints don't match the ones on Annie's belt buckle. Holthemann has agreed to release him for the time being.'

Sejer didn't reply. He felt a sense of relief, mixed with irritation. He was glad that it wasn't Halvor, but frustrated because they didn't have a suspect. He took a sip of his whisky.

'I was hoping you still had a few cards up your sleeve,' Skarre said. 'I can't believe that we haven't made any progress. Time is passing and Annie's file is getting older. And you're the one who's supposed to be giving advice.'

'What do you mean by that?'

'Your name,' Skarre said. 'Konrad means: "The one who gives advice".'

Sejer raised one eyebrow. 'How do you know that?'

'I have a book at home. I look up a name whenever I meet someone new.'

'What does Annie mean?' Sejer asked at once.

'Beautiful.'

'Good God. Well, at the moment I'm not living up to my name. But don't let that discourage you, Jacob. What does Halvor mean, by the way?' he asked with curiosity.

'Halvor means "the guard".'

He called me 'Jacob', Skarre thought with astonishment. For the very first time he used my Christian name.

THE SUN WAS LOW in the sky, slanting across the balcony and making a warm corner so they could take off their jackets. They were waiting for the grill to heat up. It smelt of charcoal and lighter fluid, along with lemon balm from Ingrid's planter-box which she had just watered.

Sejer was sitting with his grandson on his lap, bouncing him up and down until his thigh muscles began to ache.

Ingrid picked up her clogs from the floor of the balcony and banged them together three times. Then she put them down again.

'Why do you do that?'

'An old habit,' she said, smiling. 'From Somalia.'

'But we don't have snakes or scorpions here.'

'I can't help myself. And we do have wasps and garter snakes.'

'Do you think a garter snake would crawl into your shoe?'

'I have no idea.'

He hugged his grandson and snuggled his nose in the hollow of his neck.

'Bounce more,' Matteus said.

'My legs are tired. Why don't you find a book and I'll read to you instead?'

The boy hopped down and raced into the apartment.

'So how are things going otherwise, Papa?' Ingrid asked.

'Otherwise', he thought. What she means is 'in reality'. How was he feeling deep inside, in the depths of his soul? Or it could be a camouflaged way of asking whether anything had happened? Whether, for instance, he had found a girlfriend. He couldn't imagine anything like that.

'Fine, but what do you mean?' he said, trying to sound sufficiently guileless.

'I was wondering if perhaps the days don't seem so long any more.'

She was being terribly circumspect. It occurred to him that she had something on her mind.

'I've been busy at work,' he said. 'And besides, I have all of you.'

This last comment prompted her to start fidgeting with the salad servers. She tossed the tomatoes and cucumbers energetically. 'Yes, but you see, we're thinking of going south again. For another term. The last one,' she said quickly, looking more and more guilty.

'South?' He hung on to the word. 'To Somalia?'

'Erik has an offer. We haven't given them our answer yet,' she said. 'But we're giving it serious consideration. Partly because of Matteus. We'd like him to see the country and learn the language. If we leave in August, we'll be there in time for the start of the school year.'

Three years, he thought. Three years without Ingrid and Matteus. Home only at Christmas. Letters and postcards, and his grandson taller each visit, and a year older, such abrupt changes.

'I have no doubt that you're needed down there,' he said, making an effort to keep his voice steady. 'You're not thinking that my welfare should stop you from going, are you? I'm not ninety, Ingrid.'

She blushed a little. 'I don't like it that you're all alone,' she said.

'I have Kollberg, you know.'

'But he's just a dog.'

'You should be glad he doesn't understand what you're saying.' Sejer cast a glance at Kollberg, who was sleeping peacefully under the table. 'We do pretty well. I think you should go if that's what you really want to do. Is Erik tired of treating appendicitis and swollen tonsils?'

'Things are different there,' she said. 'We can be so much more useful.'

'What about Matteus? What will you do with him?'

'He'll go to the American kindergarten. And besides,' she said, 'he actually has relatives there that he's never met. I don't like that. I want him to know everything.'

'What do you mean by "know everything"?' he asked, thinking about Matteus's real parents and their fate.

'We won't tell him about his mother until he's older.'

'You should go!' he said.

She looked at him and smiled. 'What do you think Mama would have said?'

'She would have said the same thing. And then she would have had a good cry in bed later on.'

'But you won't?'

Matteus came running over with a picture book in one hand and an apple in the other. '"It was a dark and stormy night . . ." Doesn't that sound a little scary?' Sejer said.

'Ha!' his grandson snorted, climbing up onto his lap.

'The coals are hot,' Ingrid said. 'I'm going to put on the steaks.' She placed the pieces on the grill, four in all, and went inside to get the drinks.

'I have a green rubber python in my room,' Matteus whispered. 'Should we put it in her shoe?'

Sejer hesitated. 'I don't know. Do you think that's a good idea?'

'Don't you?'

'As a matter of fact, I don't.'

'Old people are such chickens,' he said. 'I'm the one she'll blame.'

'OK,' he said. 'I'll look the other way.'

Matteus hopped down, ran to get his snake, and then carefully stuffed it inside his mother's clog.

'You can keep reading now.'

Sejer cringed at the thought of the awful rubber snake and how it would feel against her toes. '"It was a dark and stormy night,"' he began again, and just at that moment Ingrid came back, carrying three bottles of beer and a Coke. He stopped and gave her a long look. Matteus did too.

'Why are you staring at me like that? What's wrong with you?'

'Nothing,' they said in unison, bending over their book. She set the bottles on the table, opened them, and looked around for her shoes. Picked them up, turned them upside-down, and knocked them together three times. Nothing happened. It's stuck in the toe, they thought gleefully. Then everything happened at once. Sejer's son-in-law, Erik, appeared in the doorway, Matteus jumped down from Sejer's lap and rushed across the room. Kollberg leapt up from under the table and wagged his tail so hard that the bottles fell to the floor, and Ingrid stuck her feet inside her shoes.

SØLVI STOOD IN HER ROOM, taking things out of a box. For a moment she straightened up and peered outside. Directly across the street, Fritzner was standing at his window, watching her. He had a glass in his hand. Now he raised it, as if offering a toast.

Sølvi turned her back on him at once. True, she didn't mind men looking at her, but Fritzner was bald. Imagining life with a bald man was as unthinkable as imagining life with a man who was fat. They had no place in her dreams. She looked up again. He was gone. He was probably sitting in his boat again, the weirdo.

She heard the doorbell ringing and went out to open the door.

'Oh!' she said. 'It's you! I'm cleaning up Annie's room. Come on in. Mama and Papa will be home in a minute.'

Sejer followed her through the living room to her own room, which was next to Annie's. It was quite a bit bigger, decorated in pastels. A photograph of her sister stood on her bedside table.

'I have inherited a few things from her,' she said with an apologetic smile. 'Some knick-knacks and clothes and things like that. And if I can persuade Papa, I want to knock down the wall to Annie's room so I'll have one big room.'

'That will be very nice,' Sejer said. He looked around. He had never seen a room with so many knick-knacks.

Sølvi bent down to a box on the floor and began pulling more things out of it. 'It's mostly books. Annie didn't have any make-up or jewellery or anything like that. Plus a bunch of CDs and cassettes.'

'Do you like to read?'

'Not really. But the bookshelves look nice when they're full.'

He nodded in agreement.

'Has something happened?'

'Yes, actually. But we don't know yet what it means.'

She took one more thing out of the box. It was wrapped in newspaper.

'So you know Magne Johnas, Sølvi?'

'Yes,' she said. 'He's living in Oslo now. Works for a gym.'

'Do you know if he and Annie once had something going? Before your time?'

'Annie just laughed at him,' she said, her tone almost plaintive. 'Not that Halvor was anything to boast about. At least Magne looks like a guy should. I mean, he has muscles and everything.'

She pulled away the newspaper wrapping, avoiding his eye.

'Do you think he might have been offended?' he asked carefully.

'He could have been. It wasn't enough for Annie to say no. Everybody keeps on talking about how wonderful and nice she was, and I don't mean to say anything bad about my half-sister. But she was often snide, and nobody dares talk about it. Because she's dead. I can't understand how Halvor could bear it. Annie was the one who decided on everything.'

'Is that right?'

'But she was nice to me. She was always nice.'

'How long have you and Magne been together?' he asked.

'Only a few weeks. We go to the movies and stuff like that.'

Her reply was a little too quick.

'He's younger than you, isn't he?'

'Four years,' she said reluctantly. 'But he's very mature for his age.'

'I see.'

She held something up to the light and squinted at it. A bronze bird sitting on a perch. A chubby little feathered creature with its head tilted. 'It's broken,' she said uncertainly.

Sejer stared in astonishment. The sight of the bronze bird struck him like an arrow at his temple. It was the sort of thing that was placed on the gravestone of a small child.

'I could roll up a lump of clay and make a stand for it,' Sølvi said.

A picture of a new Annie was taking shape, a more complex Annie than the one Halvor and her parents had presented to him.

'What do you think it's for?' he said.

Sølvi shrugged. 'No idea. Just some kind of decoration that's broken, I suppose.'

'You've never seen it before?'

'No. I wasn't allowed in Annie's room when she wasn't home.' She put the bird on her desk, and bent down to the box again.

'Has it been a long time since you saw your father?' he asked as he continued to stare at the bird. His brain was working in high gear.

'My father?' She straightened up and looked at him in confusion. 'You mean . . . my father who lives in Oslo?'

He nodded.

'He was at Annie's funeral.'

'You must miss him, don't you?'

She didn't answer. It was as if he had touched on something that she rarely examined properly.

'What do you call Eddie?' he asked.

'I call him Papa,' she said.

'And your real father?'

'I call him Father,' she said simply. 'That's what I've always called him. It's what he wanted, he was always so old-fashioned.'

Was. As if he no longer existed.

'I hear a car!' she said, sounding relieved.

Holland's green Toyota pulled up in front of the house. Sejer saw Ada Holland set one foot on the gravel.

'That bird, Sølvi, may I have it?' he said quickly.

'The broken bird? Sure, take it.'

She handed it to him with an inquisitive look.

'Thanks. I won't disturb you any longer,' he said, and left the room. He tucked the bird into an inside pocket and went back to the living room. He leaned against the wall and waited.

The bird. Torn from Eskil's headstone. In Annie's room. Why?

Holland came in first. He nodded and held out his hand. There was something resigned about him that hadn't been there before. Mrs Holland went to the kitchen to make coffee.

'Sølvi's going to have Annie's room,' Holland said. 'So it won't stand there empty. And we'll have something to keep us busy. I'm going to take out the dividing wall and put up new wallpaper. It'll be a lot of work.'

Sejer nodded.

'I have to get something off my chest,' Holland said. 'I read in the paper that an eighteen-year-old boy was taken into custody. Surely Halvor couldn't be the one who did this? We've known him for two years. But we just can't imagine Halvor as a murderer, we just can't, none of us can. Is Halvor the one in custody?'

'We've released him,' Sejer said.

'Yes, but why was he taken into custody?'

'We had no choice. I can't tell you any more than that.'

Mrs Holland came in with four cups and some cookies in a bowl.

'But has something else come up?'

'Yes. For the time being I can't say much.'

Holland gave him a bitter smile. 'Of course not. I imagine we'll be the last people to find out. The newspapers will know long before we do, when you finally catch the killer.'

'That's not true at all.' Sejer looked into his eyes, which were big and grey like Annie's. They were brimming with pain. 'But the press is everywhere, and they have contacts. Just because you read something in the paper doesn't mean that we've given them the information. When we make an arrest, you will be told, I promise you that.'

'Now that I think about it, I'm not sure that I even want to know.'

'What are you saying?'

Ada Holland was staring at him in dismay.

'It doesn't matter any more. It's like the whole thing was an accident. Something unavoidable.'

'Why do you say that?' she asked in despair.

'Because she was going to die anyway. So it doesn't matter.'

'It *does* matter,' Sejer said, stifling his anger. 'You have the right to know what happened. I'll find out who did it, even it turns out to be a very long process.'

'A very long process?' Holland smiled, another bitter smile. 'Annie is slowly disintegrating,' he said.

'Eddie!' Mrs Holland said in anguish. 'We still have Sølvi!'

'*You* have Sølvi.'

He stood up and left the room, disappearing somewhere in the house. Mrs Holland shrugged her shoulders dejectedly.

'Annie was a daddy's girl,' she said.

'I know.'

'I'm afraid that he'll never be the same again.'

'He won't. Right now he's getting used to being a different Eddie. He needs time. Perhaps it will be easier when we discover the truth.'

'I don't know whether I dare find out.'

'Are you afraid of something?'

'I'm afraid of everything. I imagine all kinds of things could have happened up there at the lake.'

'Can you tell me about it?'

She shook her head and reached for her cup. 'No, I can't. It's just things I imagine.'

'It looks as if Sølvi is managing all right,' he said, to change the subject.

'Sølvi is strong,' she said, suddenly sounding confident.

Strong, he thought. Yes, maybe that *is* the proper term. Perhaps Annie was the weak one. Things began whirling through his mind in a disquieting way. It's bad enough that Annie is dead and gone, Sejer thought. But now her family is falling apart.

Sølvi came in. 'Where's Papa?'

'He'll be right back,' Mrs Holland said. She sighed and turned back to Sejer. 'You keep talking as if he must have had a good reason for doing it.'

'Not a *good* reason. But the killer had a reason.'

Mrs Holland glanced at her daughter. 'What do you think, Sølvi?' she said. Softly, using a different tone than he'd heard her use before, as if for once she wanted to penetrate that blonde head of her daughter's and find an answer.

'Me?' Sølvi stared at her mother in surprise. 'For my part I've never liked Fritzner. I've heard that he sits in his dinghy in his living room and reads all night long, with the rowlocks full of beer.'

CHAPTER EIGHT

Skarre had turned off most of the lights in his office. Only the desk lamp was on, sixty watts forming a white spotlight on his papers. A gentle, steady hum came from the printer as it spewed out page after page. He heard a door open and someone come in. He was about to look up to see who it was, but just at that moment the pages tumbled off the printer. He bent down to get them, straightened up, and discovered that something was sliding into his field of vision, across an empty page. A bronze bird sitting on a perch.

'Where?' he said at once.

Sejer sat down. 'At Annie's house. Sølvi has inherited her sister's things, and this was among them, wrapped in newspaper. I went out to the cemetery. It fits like a glove.' He looked at Skarre. 'Someone could have given it to her.'

'Who?'

'I don't know. But if she went there and took it herself, really went there, under cover of darkness, and used some kind of tool to break it off the headstone, then that's quite an unscrupulous thing to do.'

'But Annie wasn't unscrupulous, was she?'

'I'm not entirely sure. I'm not sure about anything any more.'

Skarre turned the lamp away from the desk so that it made a perfect half-moon on the wall. They sat and stared at it.

'Jensvoll has resigned from his job as coach of the girls' team,' Skarre said. 'The rumours are starting to circulate. The rape conviction is hovering over the waters. The girls stopped showing up.'

'I thought that would happen. One thing leads to another.'

'Things are going to be tough for a lot of people now, until the murderer is caught. But that will happen soon, because you've got it all worked out, haven't you?'

Sejer shook his head. 'It has something to do with Annie and Johnas. Something happened between the two of them.'

'Maybe she just wanted a keepsake to remind her of Eskil.'

'If that was it, she could have knocked on the door and asked for a teddy bear or something.'

'Do you think he did something to her?'

'Either to her or maybe to someone else she had a relationship with. Someone she loved.'

'Now I don't follow you—do you mean Halvor?'

'I mean his son, Eskil. He died because Johnas was in the bathroom shaving.'

'But she couldn't very well blame him because of that.'

'Not unless there's something unresolved about the way he died.'

Skarre whistled. 'No one else was there to see what happened. All we have to go on is what Johnas said.'

Sejer picked up the bird again.

'So what do you think, Jacob? What really happened on that November morning?'

THE NEXT MORNING, memories flooded over him as he opened the double glass doors and took a few steps inside. The hospital smell, combined with the sweet scent of chocolate from the gift shop and the spicy fragrance of carnations from the flower stand.

Instead of thinking about his wife's death, Sejer tried to think about his daughter Ingrid on the day she was born. This enormous building held memories of both the greatest sorrow and the greatest joy of his life. Back then he had stepped through these same doors and noticed the same smells.

He was not arriving unannounced. It had taken him exactly eight minutes on the phone to locate the medical examiner who had overseen the autopsy of Eskil Johnas. He had made it clear in advance what he was interested in, so they could find the files and reports and get them out for him.

He noticed the hospital smell grow stronger as he walked along the corridor of the eighth floor. The examiner, who had sounded staid and middle-aged on the phone, turned out to be a young man. A stout fellow with thick glasses and soft, plump hands.

'I have to confess that I took a quick glance at the file,' the examiner said. 'A tragic case. A two-year-old boy. An accident at home. Left without supervision for a few minutes. Dead on arrival. We opened him up and found a total obstruction of his windpipe, in the form of food.'

'What type of food?'

'Waffles. We were actually able to unfold them, they were practically whole. Two whole, heart-shaped dessert waffles, folded together into one lump. It turned out that he was quite a greedy little fellow, and hyperactive too. I remember the autopsy clearly.'

'Two whole waffles shaped like hearts. Had he chewed them?'

'No, apparently not. They were both nearly whole.'

'Do you have children?'

'I have four,' he said happily.

'Did you think about them when you were doing the autopsy?'

'Well, yes, I suppose I did. Or I might have been thinking more about children in general, and how they behave.'

'Yes?'

'At that time my son had just turned three,' the examiner went on. 'And he loves dessert waffles. I'm forever scolding him, the way parents do, about stuffing too much food into his mouth at one time.'

'But in this case no one was there to scold the boy,' Sejer said.

'No. Because then, of course, it wouldn't have happened.'

Sejer didn't reply. Then he said, 'Can you picture your own son when he was about the same age with a plate of waffles in front of him? Do you think he would have picked up two of them, folded them in half, and stuffed both into his mouth at the same time?'

Now there was a long silence.

'Well . . . this was a special kind of child.'

'Where exactly did you get that information from? I mean, the fact that he was special?'

'I got it from his father. He was here at the hospital all day. The mother arrived later.'

'From what I've been told, the father was in the bathroom when the accident occurred, is that right?'

'That's right. He was shaving. The boy was strapped to his chair; that's why he couldn't get loose and run for help. When the father came back to the kitchen the boy was lying across the table. He had knocked his plate to the floor and it had broken. The worst thing was that the father actually heard the plate fall.'

'Why didn't he come running?'

'Apparently the boy broke things all the time.'

'Who else was home when it happened?'

'Only the mother, from what I understood. The older son had just left to catch a school bus and the mother was asleep upstairs.'

'And didn't hear anything?'

'I suppose there was nothing to hear. He didn't manage to scream.'

'Not with two heart-shaped waffles in his mouth. But she was woken eventually—by her husband, of course?'

'It's possible that he shouted or screamed for her. People react very differently in those kinds of situations.'

'But she didn't come with the ambulance?'

'She arrived later. First she went to get the brother from school.'

'How much later did they arrive?'

'Let's see . . . about half an hour, according to what it says here.'

'Can you tell me a little about how the father acted?'

'He was in shock. He didn't say much.'

'Was it the father who called the ambulance?'

'Yes, that's what it says here.'

The examiner leafed through the papers and then pushed his glasses up his nose. 'Do you suspect something . . . criminal?'

He had been holding back this question for a long time. Now he felt that he finally had the right to ask it.

'I can't imagine what that might be. What do you mean?'

'How could I have any opinion about that?'

'You opened up the boy and examined him. Did you find anything unnatural about his death?'

'Unnatural? That's the way children are. They do stuff things in their mouths.'

'But if he had a plate of waffles in front of him, and was sitting there alone and didn't need to worry that anyone was going to come and take them away, why would he stuff two pieces in his mouth at once?'

'Tell me something: where are you going with these questions?'

'I have no idea.'

The doctor sat there, thinking back to the morning when little Eskil lay naked on the porcelain table, sliced open from his throat down. To the moment when he caught sight of the lump in his windpipe and realised that it was waffles. Two whole hearts. One big sticky lump of egg and flour and butter and milk.

'I remember the autopsy,' he said. 'I remember it in great detail. Maybe by that I mean that I was actually surprised. No, I can't really say that. But,' he added suddenly, 'how did you come up with the idea that there might be something irregular about his death?'

'Well,' said Sejer, looking closely at the examiner, 'he had a baby sitter. Let me put it this way: some of the signals she sent out in connection with the death have made me wonder.'

'Signals? You can just ask her, can't you?'

'No, I can't ask her.' Sejer shook his head. 'It's too late.'

DESSERT WAFFLES for breakfast, Sejer thought. They must have been left over from the day before. He buttoned his jacket and got into his car. No one would wonder about it. Children were always putting things down their throats. As the medical examiner had said: they stuff things in. He started the car, crossed Rosenkrantzgaten, and drove down to the river, where he turned left.

Against his will he allowed the flickering pictures to force their way into his mind, pictures of the little boy with his throat full. The way he must have flailed and waved his hands, breaking the plate and fighting for his life without anyone hearing him. His father had heard the plate smash. Why hadn't he come running? Because the boy was always breaking things, said the examiner. But still—even I would have come running at once, he thought. Yet his father had finished shaving. He thought about Astrid Johnas, who had been lying in bed alone upstairs, with no idea what was going on.

MRS JOHNAS WAS HAVING her lunch break. She peered at him from the back room, a piece of crispbread in one hand, wearing the same red knitted suit as the time before. She looked uneasy. She put the food down on the paper it had been wrapped in and concentrated on her coffee instead.

'Has something happened?' she asked, taking a sip from her cup.

'Today I don't want to talk about Annie,' Sejer said. 'Today I want to talk about Eskil.'

'Excuse me?' Her full lips became narrower. 'I'm done with all that. I've put it behind me. And if you don't mind my saying so, the effort has cost me a great deal.'

'I'm sorry I can't be more considerate. There are a few details about the boy's death that interest me.'

'Why is that?'

'That's not something I have to tell you, Mrs Johnas,' Sejer said gently. 'Just answer my questions.'

She pushed her cup aside, put her hands in her lap and straightened her back. As if she needed to steel herself. 'I don't like it,' she said. 'Tell me what you want to know and then you'd better leave.'

'Just before he died,' Sejer said, looking at her, 'he knocked his plate to the floor and it smashed. Did you hear it?'

The question surprised her. She stared at him with astonishment. 'Yes,' she said.

'You heard it? So you were awake?' He studied her face, noted the little shadow that flitted over it, and then went on. 'You weren't sleeping? Did you hear the electric shaver?'

'I heard Henning go into the bathroom and the door slam.'

'And before that? Before he went there?'

She hesitated a little. 'Their voices, in the kitchen. They were having breakfast.'

'Eskil was eating dessert waffles,' he said cautiously. 'Was that usual in your house?' He added a warm smile to his question.

'He must have begged for them,' she said wearily. 'And he always got what he wanted. It wasn't easy to say no to Eskil because it would set off a volcano inside him. And Henning wasn't especially patient; he hated to hear him screaming.'

'So you heard him screaming?'

She reached for her cup. 'He was always making a great deal of noise,' she said, staring at the steam rising from her coffee.

'Were they having a fight, Mrs Johnas?'

She smiled faintly. 'They fought all the time. Eskil was begging for waffles. Henning had buttered some toast and he wanted him to eat it. You know how it is—we do all we can to get our kids to eat, so he must have got out the waffles, or maybe Eskil had caught sight of them. They were on the counter from the night before.'

'Could you hear any words? Anything they said to each other?'

'What are you driving at with all these questions?' she blurted out. Her eyes had darkened. 'You should talk to Henning about it. I wasn't there. I was upstairs.'

'Do you think he has anything to tell me?'

Silence. Her fear was growing.

'I can't speak for Henning. He's not my husband any more.'

'Was it the loss of your child that made your marriage difficult?'

'Not really. We would have split up anyway. We argued too much.'

'When Henning found Eskil at the table, what did he do? Did he call out to you?'

'He just opened the door to the bedroom and stood there staring. It struck me how quiet it was; there wasn't a sound from the kitchen. I sat up in bed and screamed.'

'Is there anything about your son's death that seems unclear to you?'

'What?'

'Have you and your husband gone over what happened? Did you ask him about it?'

Again Sejer saw a trace of fear in her eyes.

'He told me everything,' she said carefully. 'He was inconsolable. Blamed himself for what happened, thought he hadn't paid enough attention. And that's not an easy thing to live with.'

'But there's nothing about the death itself that you didn't understand, or that hasn't been resolved?'

Her shoulders began to shake. He sat still for a moment, waiting patiently. She was getting close to a confession. Something was bothering her, something she didn't dare think about.

'I heard them screaming at each other,' she whispered. 'Henning was furious; he had a fierce temper. I was lying in bed with a pillow over my head. I couldn't stand listening to them.'

'Go on.'

'I heard Eskil making a lot of noise, he might have been banging his cup against the table, and Henning was shouting and slamming drawers and cupboard doors.'

'Could you make out any words they said?'

Her lower lip began trembling. 'Only one sentence. Just before he rushed off to the bathroom. He screamed so loud that I was afraid the neighbours would hear him.'

'What did you hear? What did he say?'

The bell rang suddenly in the shop as the door opened and two women swept in. Mrs Johnas jumped up, about to head into the shop. Sejer stopped her by putting his hand on her shoulder.

'Tell me!'

She bowed her head, as if she were ashamed. 'It just about destroyed Henning. He could never forgive himself. And I couldn't live with him any more.'

'Tell me what he said!'

'I don't want anyone to know. And it doesn't matter any more. Eskil is dead.'

'But he's no longer your husband, is he?'

'He's Magne's father. He told me how he stood there in the bathroom, shaking with despair. He stood there until he calmed down; then he was going to go back and apologise for being angry. Finally he went back to the kitchen. You know the rest.'

'Tell me what he said.'

'Never. I'll never tell a living soul.'

THE UGLY THOUGHT that had taken root in his mind was beginning to sprout and grow. He had seen so much that it was rare for him to be surprised. Maybe it would have been convenient to be rid of a child like Eskil Johnas.

He collected Skarre from his office and took him down the corridor. 'Let's go and look at some Oriental carpets,' he said.

'Why?'

'I just came from Astrid Johnas's shop. I think she's tormented by some terrible suspicion, the same one that has occurred to me. That Johnas is partially to blame for the boy's death. I think that's why she left him.'

'But how was he to blame?'

'I don't know. But she's terrified by the idea. Something else has occurred to me. Johnas didn't say a single word about the boy's death when we talked to him.'

'That's not so strange, is it? We were there to talk about Annie, after all.'

'I think it's strange that he didn't mention it. He said there weren't any children to baby-sit any more because his wife had left him. He didn't mention that the boy Annie took care of had died.'

'He probably couldn't stand to talk about it. Forgive me for mentioning this,' Skarre said, lowering his voice, 'but you've also lost someone close to you. How easy is it for you to talk about it?'

Sejer was so surprised that he stopped in his tracks. He felt his face grow pale. 'Of course I can talk about it . . . If it's a situation where I felt it was appropriate or absolutely necessary. If other considerations were stronger than my own feelings.'

He started walking again.

'I see,' Skarre said, unperturbed. 'What did Mrs Johnas say?'

'They had a fight. She heard them screaming at each other. The bathroom door slammed, the plate smashed. Johnas had a bad temper. She says he blames himself.'

'I would too,' Skarre said.

'Do you have anything at all encouraging to say?'

'In a way. Annie's schoolbag.'

'What about it?'

'It had some kind of grease on it, most probably to wipe away any fingerprints.'

'So?'

'We've identified what it is. It's a special cream for dogs. Intended for injured paws.'

Sejer nodded. 'Johnas has a dog.'

'And Axel Bjørk has a German shepherd. And you have a lion. I'm just mentioning it,' Skarre said quickly, holding the door open. The chief inspector led the way, feeling rather confused.

AXEL BJØRK PUT the leash on his dog and let him out of the car. He cast a swift glance in both directions, saw no one, and headed across the square, fishing a master key out of his uniform. The dog waited while he fumbled with the lock; they had done this so many times before, in and out of the car, in and out of doors and lifts, thousands of different smells. Achilles followed faithfully.

The factory building was quiet and empty, no longer in operation, used only as a warehouse. Crates, boxes and sacks were piled up from floor to ceiling; the place smelt of cardboard and dust and mouldy wood. Bjørk didn't turn on the lights. Hanging from his belt was a torch, which he switched on as they walked through the dark hall. His boots rang hollowly on the stone floor.

They approached the machinery, a huge rolling machine. Bjørk squeezed himself in behind the iron and metal, pulling the dog with him. He fastened the leash to a steel lever and gave the command to sit. The dog sat down but stayed alert.

Bjørk slid down to the floor; a rustling noise from his nylon coveralls and the panting of the dog the only audible sounds. He took a bottle out of his pocket, unscrewed the top, and began drinking.

The dog waited, his eyes shining, his ears pricked. Bjørk stared into the dog's eyes, not a word passed his lips. The tension in the dark hall grew. He could feel the dog watching him, as he watched the dog. In his pocket he had a revolver.

HALVOR GRUNTED with displeasure. The hum of the monitor had started to annoy him. Spit it out, Annie, he thought. Talk to me!

He thought of the first movie they had seen together. A Bond film. He still remembered the title: *For Your Eyes Only*.

He typed the title into the computer and waited for a moment, but nothing happened. Got up impatiently and took a couple of steps. This was hopeless. He shoved any trace of guilt to the far corner of his mind. Halvor walked through to the living room and looked up the telephone listing for computer equipment, found the number he wanted and punched it in.

'Ra Data. Solveig speaking.'

'Hi. I'm calling about a locked file,' he stammered.

'You can't get in?'

'Er, no. I can't remember the password.'

'I'm afraid the technician has left for the day. But wait just a minute and I'll ask somebody.'

Halvor glanced over at his grandmother, who was reading the paper with a magnifying glass, and he thought, 'Annie should have known it was possible to do this.'

'Are you still there?'

'Yes.'

'Do you live far away?'

'On Lundebysvingen.'

'You're in luck. He can drop by on his way home. What's your address?'

He sat in his room and waited, his heart pounding in his throat, with the curtains open so that he could see the car when it arrived. It took exactly thirty minutes before the technician appeared in a white car with the Ra Data logo on the door. A surprisingly young man got out and glanced uncertainly at the house.

Halvor ran to open the door. The systems specialist turned out to be a nice guy, plump as a dumpling, with deep dimples. Halvor thanked him for taking the trouble. Together they went to his room.

The technician opened his briefcase and took out a stack of charts. 'Is it a numerical or alphabet password?' he asked.

Halvor turned bright red.

'Can't you even remember that much?' he asked in surprise.

'I've used so many different ones,' Halvor muttered. 'I change them regularly.'

'Which file is it?'

'That one.'

'"Annie"?'

He didn't ask any more questions. Halvor went over to the window and stood there, his cheeks burning with shame and nervousness. Behind him he heard the keys clacking rapidly. After what seemed like an eternity, the technician got up from the chair.

'OK, man, there it is!'

Halvor slowly turned round and stared at the screen. He took the invoice that was handed to him for signature.

'What? Seven hundred and fifty kroner?' he gasped.

'Per hour and any fraction thereof,' said the man with a smile.

His hands trembling, Halvor signed the dotted line at the bottom of the page and asked to have the bill posted to him.

'It was a numeric password,' said the expert, smiling again. 'Zero seven one one nine four. Date and year, right?'

His dimples got even deeper. 'But obviously not your birth date. In that case you wouldn't be more than eight months old!'

Halvor escorted him out and thanked him, then ran back and sat down in front of the monitor. A new command had appeared on the screen: PLEASE PROCEED.

He had to press his hand to his heart because it was beating so hard. The words scrolled into view and he started reading. Something had happened, Annie had written it down and finally he had found it. He read with his eyes wide, and a terrible suspicion slowly began to develop.

THE CARPET GALLERY was located in a quiet street. Outside stood a Citroën, the kind with slanted headlights. The car was covered with dust. Skarre went over and looked at it. The roof was cleaner than the rest of the car, as if something had been on top, protecting the surface. It was blue-green.

'No ski-box,' Sejer said.

'No, it's been removed. There are marks from the fastenings.'

They opened the gallery door and went in. A camera was aimed at them from a corner. Sejer stopped and peered into the lens. Everywhere lay great piles of carpets. A broad stone staircase led up to the floors above. Several carpets were spread out on the floor and some hung from poles on the walls. Johnas came down the stairs. His whole manner was unmistakably that of a salesman: friendly, slick, accommodating.

'Well, hello!' he said. 'Come on in.'

'You have a lot of space here,' Sejer said, looking around.

'Two whole floors, plus an attic. Believe me, this has been a big investment. Originally it was an old villa. Follow me, please.'

He pointed up the stairs and led them to what he called his office, but it was actually a spacious kitchen. They sat round the table.

'How did it go with the puppies?' Skarre asked him.

'Hera will get to keep one of them, and the other two are already spoken for. Now what can I do for you?' He smiled.

Sejer knew that his friendliness would quickly evaporate.

'Just a few questions about Annie. I'm afraid we need to go over the same ground again and again,' he said. 'You picked her up at the roundabout—is that right?'

Sejer's choice of words, his intonation, and the tiniest hint of doubt about his previous statement sharpened Johnas's attention.

'That's what I said before, and that's exactly what I did.'

'But she actually preferred to walk, didn't she?'

'Excuse me?'

'It took a little persuasion for you to get her into the car, is that correct?'

Johnas's eyes narrowed but he remained silent.

'She preferred to walk,' Sejer said. 'She declined your offer of a ride. Am I right?'

Johnas nodded and smiled. 'She always did that; she was so unassuming. But I thought it was too far to walk to Horgen's Shop.'

'So you persuaded her?'

'No, no . . .' He shook his head hard. 'I coaxed her a little.'

'So it wasn't that she didn't want to get into your car?'

Johnas heard quite clearly the extra stress on the words 'your car'.

'That's the way Annie was. A little aloof, maybe. Who have you been talking to?'

'Several hundred people,' Sejer said. 'And one of them saw her get into your car after a long discussion. You're actually the last person to see her alive, and we've got to focus on that, don't you agree?'

Johnas smiled back. 'I wasn't the last person,' he said. 'Whoever killed her was the last person.'

'It's proving rather difficult to get hold of him,' Sejer said with deliberate irony. 'And we have nothing to corroborate that the man on the motorcycle was waiting for Annie. The only thing we have is you.'

'I'm sorry? What are you getting at?'

'Well,' Sejer said, 'I'm trying to get to the bottom of this case and it's the nature of my job to doubt what people say.'

'Are you accusing me of lying?'

'I'm afraid that's what I have to think,' Sejer said. 'I hope you'll forgive me. Why didn't she want to get in?'

Johnas was visibly uneasy. 'Of course she wanted to get in!' He had shown the first sign of anger, and now controlled himself. 'She got in and I drove her to Horgen's.'

'No further than that?'

'No, as I told you, she got out at the shop. And after that,' he stood up to get a pack of cigarettes from the counter, 'I never saw her again.'

Sejer steered his interrogation onto a new track.

'You lost a child, Johnas. You know what it feels like. Have you talked to Eddie Holland about it?'

For a moment Johnas looked surprised. 'No, no, he's such a private person, I didn't want to bother him. Besides, it's not an easy thing for me to talk about either.'

'How long ago was it?'

'You've talked to Astrid, haven't you? Almost eight months.'

He slipped a cigarette out of the pack and lit up.

'People often try to imagine what it's like.' He stared at Sejer with weary eyes. 'They try to picture the empty bed and imagine themselves standing there and staring at it. And I did do that often. But that's only part of it. I got up every morning and went out to the bathroom, and there was his toothbrush under the mirror. The rubber duck on the edge of the bath.'

Johnas was speaking through clenched teeth.

'I threw things out, a little at a time, and it felt as if I was committing a crime. It haunted me every second of the day, and it haunts me still.' He fell silent, and his tanned face had turned grey.

'Not long ago we went over to the cemetery,' Sejer said. 'Has it been a while since you were there?'

'What kind of question is that?' Johnas asked, his voice hoarse.

'I just want to know if you realise that something has been removed from the grave.'

'You mean the little bird. Yes, it disappeared just after the funeral.'

'Do you know who took it?'

'Of course not!' he said, his voice sharp.

'Annie took it,' Sejer said lightly. 'We found it among her things. Is this it?'

He stuck his hand in his pocket and pulled out the bird. Johnas took it with trembling fingers. 'It looks like the one. But why—'

'We don't know. We thought you might be able to help us.'

'Me? Dear God, I haven't a clue. Why on earth would she take it? She wasn't exactly the type to steal things. Not the Annie I knew.'

'That's why she must have had a reason for doing it. A reason far more important than merely wanting to steal things. Was she angry with you?'

Johnas sat and stared at the bird, struck dumb with surprise.

He didn't know about this, thought Sejer, casting a glance at Skarre, who sat beside him with glass-blue eyes, studying the man's slightest movement.

'Well, I guess she had her secrets,' Johnas said.

'She took it hard—Eskil's death?'

'She couldn't make herself come to see us any more. I could understand it; I couldn't be around people either for a long time. Astrid and Magne left me, and so much happened all at once. An indescribable chapter,' he muttered.

'You must have talked to each other, though?'

'Just brief nods when we met on the street.'

'Did she try to avoid you?'

'She seemed embarrassed, in a way. It was difficult for all of us.'

'And what's more,' Sejer said, as if he had only just thought of it, 'you had a fight with Eskil right before he died. That must have made it even harder.'

'You keep Eskil out of this!' he said bitterly.

'Do you know Raymond Låke?'

'Everybody knows Raymond.'

'Just give me a yes or no answer.'

'I do *not* know him.'

'But you know where he lives?'

'Yes, I do. In that old shack of a house, though he must think it's just fine, since he looks so idiotically happy.'

'Idiotically happy?' Sejer stood up. 'I think idiots are just as dependent on other people's goodwill to feel happy as the rest of us are. And here's something you should never forget: even though he can't interpret his surroundings in the same way you can, there's nothing wrong with his vision.'

Johnas's face stiffened slightly. He escorted them out. As they went down the stairs to the ground floor, Sejer felt the camera lens like a laser beam on the back of his neck.

THEY WENT TO SEJER'S apartment to collect Kollberg, and let him stretch out on the back seat of the car. The dog is alone too much, Sejer thought, tossing him an extra piece of dried fish.

'Do you think he smells bad?'

Skarre nodded. 'You should give him a Fisherman's Friend lozenge.'

They drove towards Lundeby, turned off at the roundabout, and parked next to the letterboxes. Sejer walked along the street, fully aware that everyone could see him, all twenty-one houses. The house belonging to Johnas looked semi-vacant. The curtains were drawn in many of the windows. Slowly he walked back.

'The school bus leaves the roundabout at ten past seven every morning,' he said. 'All the kids in Krystallen going to school take it. So they leave home at about seven o'clock, in order to catch the bus. Magne Johnas had just left for school when Eskil got the food caught in his throat.'

Skarre waited.

'And Annie left a little later than the others. Holland remembered that they had overslept. She walked past his house, maybe while Eskil was sitting there eating breakfast.'

'Yes. What about it?' Skarre looked at Johnas's house. 'Only the windows to the living room and bedroom face the street. And they were in the kitchen.'

'I know, I know,' he said irritably. They kept on walking, approached the house, and tried to imagine that November day at seven in the morning. It's dark at that time in November, Sejer thought.

They stopped and stared at the house for a moment. The kitchen window was on the side, facing the neighbours' house.

'Isn't that a pathway between the houses?'

Skarre looked. 'Yes, it is. And someone's coming.'

A boy appeared between the two houses.

'It's Thorbjørn Haugen, the boy who helped search for Ragnhild.'

Sejer waited for him as he strode briskly along the path. Thorbjørn was tall, and he reached to the middle of the kitchen window.

'Taking a short cut?' Sejer asked.

'What?' Thorbjørn stopped. 'This path goes straight to Gneisveien.'

'Do most people take this route?'

'Sure, it saves you five minutes.'

Sejer took a few steps along the path and stopped outside the window. He was taller than Thorbjørn and had no trouble peering into the kitchen. There was no highchair there now. The house seemed practically uninhabited. November 7th, he thought. Pitch-black outside and brightly lit indoors. Anyone outside could look in, but those inside wouldn't be able to see out.

'Johnas gets a little cranky when we go this way,' Thorbjørn said. 'Says he's sick of this short cut past his house. But he's moving.'

'So all the young people use this short cut to catch the school bus?'

'Everyone who goes to the junior high and high school.'

Sejer nodded to Thorbjørn and turned back to Skarre. 'I remember something Holland said when we talked in my office. On the day Eskil died, Annie came home from school earlier than usual because she was sick. She went straight to bed. He had to go to her room to tell her about the accident.'

'Sick in what way?' Skarre wanted to know. 'I thought she was never sick.'

'He said that she wasn't feeling well.'

'You think she saw something, don't you? Through the window?'

'I don't know. Maybe.'

'But why didn't she say anything?'

'Maybe she didn't dare. Or maybe she didn't fully understand what she had seen. Maybe she confided in Halvor. I've always had the feeling that he knows more than he's telling us.'

'Konrad,' Skarre said, 'don't you think he would have told us?'

'I'm not so sure he would. He's an odd character. Let's go and have a talk with him.'

At that moment his mobile phone rang. He took it from his belt to answer it.

It was Holthemann. 'Axel Bjørk has shot himself in the head with an old Enfield revolver.'

Sejer had to lean against the wall for support. 'Did you find a suicide note?'

'Not on the body. They're searching his apartment. The man obviously had a guilty conscience about something, don't you think?'

'I don't know. He had a lot of problems.'

'He was an irresponsible alcoholic. And he had a grudge against Ada Holland.'

'He was mostly just unhappy.'

'Hatred and despair often look alike. People show whatever suits them best.'

'I think you're wrong. He had finally given up. And that must be why he put an end to it all.'

Sejer hung up and looked at Skarre. 'Axel Bjørk is dead. I wonder what Ada Holland will think now. Maybe the same as Halvor did when his father died. That it was a relief.'

CHAPTER NINE

Halvor sprang to his feet. His chair fell over and he turned abruptly towards the window, staring out at the deserted courtyard. He stood like that for a long time. So that's what happened. That's what Annie saw. He sat down again in front of the monitor and read it through from beginning to end. Within Annie's text was his own story, what he had confided to her, in deepest secrecy. The raging father, the shot in the shed, on December 13. It had nothing to do with Annie's death. He took a deep breath, highlighted the section and erased it from the document for all eternity. Then he inserted a floppy disk and copied the text. When he'd finished, he slipped quietly out of his room and went through the kitchen.

'What is it, Halvor?' his grandmother called as he came through the living room, pulling on his denim jacket. 'Are you going out?'

He didn't answer. He heard her voice, but the words made no impression on him.

'Where are you going? Are you going to the movies?'

He started buttoning his jacket.

'When are you coming back? Will you be home for supper?'

He stopped and looked at her, as if he had just noticed that she was standing there, right in front of him, and nagging at him.

'Supper?'

'Where are you going, Halvor? It's almost suppertime!'

'I'm going out to see someone.'

'Who is it? You look so pale. What did you say his name was?'

'I didn't say. His name's Johnas.'

Halvor's voice sounded unusually determined. The door slammed, and when she looked out of the window she could see him bending over his motorcycle, angrily trying to make it start.

THE CAMERA on the ground floor was not very well placed. There was too much glare on the lens, reducing the customers to vague outlines, almost like ghosts. He liked to see who his customers were before he went out to greet them. Upstairs, where the light was better, he could distinguish faces and clothing, and if they were regular customers, he could prepare himself before leaving the office, assuming an attitude appropriate for each one. He took another look at the screen. A lone figure was standing in the room. As far as he could see, it was a man, or maybe a teenager, wearing a short jacket. He walked quietly down the stairs. He had almost reached the bottom when he stopped.

'Good afternoon,' he said.

The young man was standing with his back turned, but now he turned round. In his eyes was suspicion, mixed with astonishment. He didn't say anything, simply stared.

Johnas recognised him. For a second or two he considered acknowledging the fact. 'Can I help you?'

Halvor didn't reply. He was scrutinising him. He knew that he had been recognised. Johnas had seen him many times. They had passed in the street when he had been with Annie. Now Johnas was on the defensive. Everything soft and dark about the man, the flannel and velvet and the brown curls, had hardened into a stiff shell.

'I'm sure you can,' Halvor said, approaching Johnas, who was still on the stairs with one hand on the banister. 'I want to buy a carpet.'

'Well!' Johnas said with a smile. 'I assumed as much. What are you looking for? Anything in particular?'

He's not looking to buy a carpet, Johnas thought. He can't afford one; he's after something else.

'Big or small?' he said, coming down the last step. The youth was more than a head shorter than he was and as slender as a piece of kindling.

'I want a carpet that's big enough to cover the whole floor.'

Johnas nodded. 'Come upstairs. That's where we have the biggest carpets.' He started walking up the stairs.

Halvor followed.

'What colour were you thinking of?'

Halvor stopped at the head of the stairs and looked round the room. He headed straight for a large carpet that hung on the wall.

'Two and a half by three yards,' Johnas said. 'An excellent choice, if I may say so.'

'You can have it deliverd, can't you?' Halvor said.

'Certainly. I have a delivery truck.'

'I'll take it.'

'Excuse me?' Johnas took a few steps closer and stared at him uncertainly. This young man was strange.

'It's almost the most expensive carpet I have—seventy thousand kroner.' He watched the boy closely as he said the price. Halvor didn't blink.

'I'm sure it's worth it.'

Johnas didn't like it. A nagging suspicion was creeping up his spine like a cold snake.

'Please wrap it for me,' Halvor said, crossing his arms.

Johnas hesitated. 'Forgive my rudeness—how will you pay for it?'

'Cash, if that's all right.'

He patted his back pocket. He was wearing faded jeans with frayed hems. Johnas stood in front of him, still dubious.

'Is there something wrong?' Halvor said.

'I know who you are,' Johnas said, deciding to take a firm stance. It was a relief to stop pretending.

'Do we know each other?'

Johnas nodded. 'Yes, we do, Halvor. Of course we know each other. I think you'd better go now.'

'Why? Is something wrong?'

'Let's cut the crap, right now!' Johnas said, tightlipped.

'I agree!' snarled Halvor. 'Take down that carpet, and do it fast!'

'Would it be too presumptuous of me to ask to see that you actually do have the money?'

Halvor shook his head. 'Of course not. I realise that it's impossible to know just from looking at people whether they have money these days.' He stuck his hand in his hip pocket and took out an old wallet, flat as a pancake. He poked his fingers inside and jingled some coins. Took out a few and put them on a mahogany drop-leaf table.

Johnas stared at him sceptically as the five-, ten-, and one-krone coins formed a little heap. 'All right, that's enough,' he said harshly. 'You've already taken up enough of my time. Now get out of here!'

Halvor looked at him. Things were starting to get dangerous, but he wasn't scared; for some reason he wasn't scared at all.

'I do have this,' he said suddenly, pulling something out of the slot for banknotes in his wallet. Johnas stared at him suspiciously, casting a dubious eye at what he was holding between two fingers.

'It's a disk,' Halvor said.

'I don't want a disk; I want seventy thousand kroner,' Johnas snapped, feeling fear begin to hack at his chest.

'Annie's diary,' Halvor said, waving the disk. 'She started keeping a diary a while ago. In November, as a matter of fact. We've been looking for it, several of us. You know how girls are: always having to confide things.'

Johnas was breathing hard.

'I've read it,' Halvor said. 'It's about you.'

'Give it to me!'

'Not until hell freezes over!'

Johnas gave a start. Halvor's voice had changed and deepened.

'I've made copies of it,' Halvor said. 'So I can buy as many carpets as I want. Every time I feel like having a new carpet, I'll just make another copy. Do you understand what I'm saying?'

'You hysterical little brat! What kind of institution did you escape from?'

Johnas steeled himself, and in a fraction of a second Halvor saw his torso swell up as he prepared to spring. Halvor dived to one side and saw the man miss his target and slide along the stone floor, slamming headfirst into the drop-leaf table. The coins scattered in all directions. Johnas was back on his feet in two seconds. A single glance at his dark face made Halvor realise that the battle was lost. He was much bigger. Halvor made for the stairs, but Johnas was after him at once, taking three or four steps, and then lunging forward. He rammed into Halvor's back at shoulder level. Instinctively the boy kept his head up, but his body struck the stone floor with great force. Halvor felt the man's breath on his face and his fists tightening round his throat.

'You're out of your mind!' he shouted. 'You're done for! I don't care what you do to me, but you're done for!'

Johnas was deaf and blind. He raised his clenched fist and took aim at the lean face. Halvor had been beaten before and knew what was in store for him. The knuckles struck him under the chin, and his jaw snapped like dry tinder. His lower teeth struck with powerful force against his upper teeth, and tiny bits of crushed porcelain mixed with the blood that came gushing out of his mouth. Johnas kept on pounding at him, striking out at random as Halvor flung his body from side to side. Finally, Johnas smashed his fist against the stone floor and howled, lurched to his feet and stared at his hand, panting. There was a great deal of blood. He stared at what was lying on the floor and took a long, deep breath. After a few minutes his heartbeat returned to normal and his mind cleared.

'HE'S NOT HERE,' said the grandmother surprised, when Sejer and Skarre appeared at her door. 'He was going out to visit somebody. I think his name was Johnas. He was all upset too, and he hadn't eaten anything. I don't know what's going on any more, and I'm too old to keep up with everything.'

The news made Sejer pound his fist twice against the door frame. 'Did he get a phone call or anything like that?'

'Nobody calls us. Annie was the only one who called every once in a while. He's been sitting in his room all afternoon, playing with his computer. Suddenly he stormed out and disappeared.'

'I'm sure we'll find him. You have to excuse us, but we're in a hurry.'

'Of all things,' he said to Skarre as he slammed the car door, 'this was the worst he could have done.'

'I DON'T SEE Halvor's motorcycle.'

Skarre jumped out. Sejer turned to Kollberg, who was still lying on the back seat, and took a dog biscuit from his pocket.

They pulled on the door, which swung slowly open, as they found themselves glaring defiantly at the video camera in the ceiling. Johnas saw them from the kitchen. For a moment he remained sitting, breathing calmly, as he blew on his injured knuckles. There was no rush. One thing at a time. Very calmly he stood up and proceeded to walk down the stairs.

'You're certainly getting around,' he said. 'It's beginning to border on harassment.'

'Do you really think so?'

Sejer loomed in front of him like a pillar. Everything looked presentable; there were no other customers in the gallery.

'We're looking for someone. We thought we might find him here.'

Johnas gave them an enquiring look, turned to look round the room, and threw out his hands. 'I'm the only one here. And I was just about to close up. It's late.'

'We'd like to take a look. Maybe he slipped inside when you weren't looking and is hiding somewhere. You never know.'

Sejer was trembling, and Skarre thought that he looked as if a great storm were gathering force under his shirt.

'I'm closing up now!' Johnas said.

They walked past him and up the stairs. Took a good look around. Went into the office, opened the door to the toilet, continued on up to the attic. No one in sight.

'Who did you expect to find here?'

Johnas was leaning against the banister, studying them with one eyebrow raised as they came down again. His chest was rising and falling visibly.

'Halvor Muntz.'

'And who is that?'

'Annie's boyfriend.'

'Why would he come here?'

'I'm not sure.'

Unperturbed, Sejer wandered round the gallery. 'But he hinted that he was coming here. He's been playing detective on his own, and I think we ought to put a stop to it.'

'I agree whole-heartedly,' Johnas said, with a condescending smile. 'But there hasn't been anyone here.'

Sejer kicked at the rolled-up carpets with the tip of his shoe. 'Does this building have a basement?'

'No.'

'Do you leave your carpets out?'

'Many of them, yes. But I put the most expensive ones in the vault.'

'I see.'

Suddenly Sejer caught sight of the small drop-leaf table, beneath which a handful of coins lay scattered. 'Are you always so careless with your small change?' he said.

Johnas shrugged. Sejer didn't like the fact that it was so quiet. He didn't like the expression on the carpet dealer's face. In a corner of the room he noticed a pink bucket with a scrubbing brush next to it. The floor was damp. 'Have you been washing the floor?' he asked.

'It's the last thing I do before I close up the shop. I save a lot of money by doing it myself.'

Sejer looked at him. 'Show us the vault.'

Johnas started heading down the stairs.

'It's on the ground floor. You can see it, of course, though naturally it's locked, and it would be impossible to hide inside.'

They followed him down to a corner under the stairs, where they saw a steel door. Johnas went over and twisted the dial of a combination lock back and forth. With every twist a tiny click was audible. He was using his left hand, a little clumsily, because he was right-handed.

'Is this boy so valuable that you think I would hide him in here?'

'Possibly,' said Sejer, staring at the clumsy left hand. Johnas gripped the handle of the heavy door and pulled with all his might.

'I'm sure it'd be easier if you used both hands,' Sejer said.

Johnas raised an eyebrow, as if he didn't understand. Sejer peered into the cramped space, which contained a small safe, two or three paintings leaning against the wall, and a number of rolled carpets stacked up on the floor like logs.

'That's all there is.' He gave them a belligerent look.

Sejer smiled. 'But he was here, wasn't he? What did he want?'

'Nobody's been here, except for you two.'

Sejer nodded and walked out of the vault. Skarre shot him an uneasy glance, but followed him out.

'If he happens to turn up, would you contact us immediately?' Sejer said. 'He's been going through a difficult time lately after all that's happened. He needs help.'

'Of course.'

The vault door slammed shut.

OUTSIDE THE GALLERY, Sejer signalled for Skarre to drive.

'Drive up the hill and pull into that driveway at the top. Do you see it?'

Skarre nodded.

'Park there. We'll wait until he leaves and then follow him. I want to see where he's going.'

They didn't have long to wait. No more than five minutes had passed before Johnas suddenly appeared in the doorway. He locked up, activated the burglar alarm, walked past the dirty blue-green Citroën, and disappeared down the driveway to a back courtyard. He was out of sight for a few minutes, then reappeared in an old Transit truck. Sejer could clearly hear the roaring of the engine.

'He would have a delivery truck,' Skarre said.

'With one cylinder gone. It's roaring like an old fishing boat. Let's get going, but be careful. Don't get too close.'

Johnas drove the big vehicle through town. He signalled and changed gear as he approached Oscarsgaten, and now they could clearly see him looking in his rearview mirror several times.

'He's stopping at the yellow building. Pull over, Skarre!'

Johnas jumped out of the truck, looked around, and then crossed the street with long strides. Sejer and Skarre stared at the door where he stood, fumbling with a key. He was carrying a toolbox.

'He's going up to his apartment. We'll wait here for the time being. As soon as he's inside, slip out and run over to his truck. I want you to look in through the back window.'

'What do you think he has in there?'

'I don't even dare guess what it might be. OK . . . Now! Hurry, Skarre!'

Bent double, Skarre ran along the pavement. He reached the back of the truck and put a hand on either side of his face to see better. Within seconds he turned and came sprinting back, threw himself into the driver's seat and slammed the door.

'A pile of carpets. And what looks like Halvor's motorcycle. Shall we go up?'

'Absolutely not. We're just going to sit here. If I'm right, he won't be long.'

'And then we'll keep following him?'

'That depends.'

'Is there a light on anywhere?'

'Not that I can see. There he is now!'

They ducked down and peered at Johnas, who had paused on the pavement to look up and down the street. Now he went over to the Transit truck, got in, started the engine, and began backing up. Skarre stuck his head up over the dashboard.

'What's he doing?' asked Sejer.

'He's backing across the street and parking right in front of the entrance. He's getting out. He's at the back door of the truck. Now he's opening it. Taking out a rolled-up carpet. He's putting it over his shoulder. He's swaying under the weight . . . he's going to fall over!'

Johnas teetered under the weight of the carpet. His knees seemed about to give way under him.

Sejer put his hand on the door handle. 'He's going back inside. He's probably trying to put it in the lift. Keep your eye on the front of the building, Skarre. See if he turns on a light!'

Kollberg started to whine.

'Be quiet, boy!' Sejer turned and patted the dog. They waited, peering at the façade of the building and the dark windows.

'There's a light on the third floor now. His apartment is there, right below that protrusion—can you see it?'

Sejer stared up at the wall. The yellow window had no curtains.

'Shouldn't we go up?' Skarre asked.

'Don't be too hasty. Johnas is clever. We should wait a bit.'

'Wait for what?'

'The light has gone off again. Maybe he's coming out. Get down, Skarre!'

They ducked down. Kollberg began to whine again.

'If you start barking, you won't get any food for a whole week!' Sejer whispered between clenched teeth.

Johnas came back outside. He got into the truck, slammed the door, and started the engine.

Sejer cracked open the door.

'Follow him. Keep a good distance. I'm going up to his flat.'

'How are you going to get inside?'

'I've taken a course in picking locks. Haven't you?'

'Of course, of course.'

'Just don't lose him! Don't move until you see him turn the corner, then follow him. When you see that he's headed for home, go to headquarters and get some back-up. Arrest him at his house. Don't give him a chance to change his clothes or put anything away, and don't say a word about this flat! If he stops along the way to dump the motorcycle, don't arrest him. Do you understand?'

'Yes, but why not?' Skarre asked.

'Because he's twice your size!'

Sejer grabbed Kollberg's leash and got out of the car, pulling the dog after him. He ducked down behind the car as Johnas put the truck in gear and drove off down the street. Skarre waited a few seconds and drove after him.

Sejer walked across the street, pushed a doorbell at random, and growled 'Police' into the intercom. The door buzzed and he stepped inside. Ignoring the lift, he dashed up the stairs to the third floor. There were two doors, but he automatically turned to the door facing the street, where they'd seen the lights. There was no name-plate. He peered at the lock: a simple latch. He opened his wallet in search of a credit card. He stuck the card into the crack, and the door slid open. He turned on the light.

He walked quietly from room to room, looking around. There was no furniture. A few cardboard boxes stood along the walls, labelled with a marker: Bedroom, Kitchen, Living Room, Hall. A couple of paintings. Several carpets, rolled up, lay beneath the living-room window. Kollberg sniffed at the air. The dog padded around on his own; Sejer followed, opening a cupboard here and there. The heavy carpet was nowhere in sight. The dog started whimpering and disappeared further into the apartment. Sejer followed.

Finally the dog stopped in front of a door. His fur stood on end.

'What is it, boy?'

Kollberg sniffed vigorously at the door, scraping at it with his claws. Sejer cast a glance over his shoulder, not exactly sure why, but he was suddenly gripped with a strange feeling. Someone was close by. He put his hand on the door handle and pressed down. Then he pulled the door open. Something struck him in the chest with great force. The next second was a chaos of sound and pain: snarling, growling and hysterical barking as a big animal dug its claws into his chest. Kollberg sprang and snapped his jaws just as Sejer recognised Johnas's Doberman. Then he hit the floor with both dogs on top of him. Instinctively he rolled onto his stomach with his hands over his head. The animals tumbled on to the floor while he looked around for something to use as a weapon but found nothing. He dashed through the open door into the bathroom, caught sight of a broom, picked it up, and ran back to where the dogs were standing just feet apart, growling and baring their teeth.

'Kollberg!' Sejer shouted. 'It's a bitch, damn it!' Hera's eyes shone like yellow lanterns in her black face. Kollberg put his ears back; the other dog stood there like a panther, ready to attack. Sejer raised the broom and took several steps forward while he felt sweat and blood running down under his shirt. Kollberg looked at him, paused, and for an instant forgot to keep an eye on the enemy, who rushed forward like a black missile, her jaws open. Sejer closed his eyes and struck. He hit Hera on the back of her neck and blinked in despair as the dog collapsed. She lay on the floor, whimpering. Sejer lunged forward, grabbed the dog's collar, and dragged the animal over to what had to be the bedroom. He opened the door, gave the dog a violent shove inside, and slammed the door. Then he fell against the wall and slid down to the floor, staring at Kollberg, who was still in a defensive position.

'Damn it, Kollberg. It's a bitch!' He wiped his forehead. Kollberg came over and licked his face. On the other side of the door they could hear Hera whining. For a moment Sejer sat with his face buried in his hands, trying to recover from the shock. He looked down at himself; his clothes were covered with dog fur and blood, and Kollberg was bleeding from one ear.

He got to his feet and trudged into the bathroom. On a blanket in the shower stall he suddenly caught sight of something black and silky soft that was crying pitifully.

'No wonder she tried to attack us,' he whispered. 'She was just trying to protect her puppies.'

The rolled-up carpet lay along one wall. He crouched down and stared at it. It was tightly rolled, covered with plastic, and taped up with carpet tape. He began tugging and pulling, the sweat still pouring off him. Finally he managed to get the tape off and began tearing at the plastic. He stood up and dragged the carpet into the living room. He bent down and gave the carpet a mighty shove. It unrolled, slow and heavy. Inside lay a compressed body. The face was destroyed. The mouth was taped shut, as was the nose, or what was left of it. Sejer swayed slightly as he stood there staring down at Halvor. He had to turn away and lean against the wall for a moment. Then he took the phone from his belt. He stood at the window as he punched in the number, fixing his eyes on a barge moving along the river. He heard the beep and a prolonged, melancholy ringing. Here I come, it was saying. Here I come, but there's no hurry.

'Konrad Sejer, fifteen Oscarsgaten,' he said into the phone. 'I need back-up.'

CHAPTER TEN

'Henning Johnas?' Sejer twirled a pen between two fingers and stared at him. 'Do you know why you're here?'

'What kind of a question is that?' Johnas asked hoarsely. 'Let me say one thing: there's a limit to what I'll stand for. If this has anything to do with Annie, then I have nothing more to say.'

'We're not going to talk about Annie,' Sejer said.

'I see.'

Sejer thought he registered a hint of relief flitting across the man's face. 'Halvor Muntz seems to have disappeared from the face of the earth. Are you still certain that you haven't seen him?'

'Absolutely positive. I don't know him.'

'You're sure about that?'

'You may not believe it, but I'm still quite clear-headed, in spite of repeated harassment from the police.'

'We were wondering what his motorcycle was doing in your garage. In the back of your truck.'

Johnas uttered a snorting sound of fear. 'Excuse me? What did you say?'

'Halvor's motorcycle.'

'It's Magne's motorcycle,' he said. 'I'm helping him repair it.'

He spoke quickly, without looking at Sejer.

'Magne has a Kawasaki. Besides, you don't know anything about motorcycles. Try again, Johnas.'

'All right, all right!' His temper flared and he lost his self-control, gripping the table with both hands. 'He came trotting into the gallery and started pestering me. Acting like he was on drugs, claiming that he wanted to buy a carpet. Of course he didn't have any money. I lost my temper. I gave him a slap. He ran off like the little brat he is, leaving behind his motorcycle and everything. I lugged it out to my truck and took it home with me. As punishment, he's going to have to come and get it himself. Beg me to give it back.'

'For just a slap, your hand certainly took a beating, didn't it?' Sejer stared at the flayed knuckles. 'The thing is that nobody knows where he is.'

'Then he must have taken off with his tail between his legs. He probably had a guilty conscience about something.'

'Do you have any suggestions?'

'You're investigating his girlfriend's murder. Maybe you should start there.'

'I don't think you should forget, Johnas, that you live in a very small place. Rumours spread fast.'

Johnas was sweating so heavily that his shirt was stuck to his chest.

'So what? I'm going to move,' he said.

'Could it be that you lose your temper rather easily, Johnas? Let's talk a little about that.' He twirled the pen some more. 'Let's start with Eskil.'

Johnas was lucky. He had just bent down to take his cigarettes out of his jacket pocket. He took his time straightening up.

'No,' he groaned, 'I don't have the strength to talk about Eskil.'

'We can take all the time we need,' Sejer said. 'Start with that day in November, from the moment you got up, you and your son.'

Johnas shook his head and nervously licked his lips. The only thing he could think about was the disk, which he hadn't had time to read. Maybe Sejer had taken it and read through everything that Annie had written. The thought was enough to make him feel faint.

'It's hard to talk about it. I've tried to put it behind me. Why are you so interested in an old tragedy?'

'I realise that it's hard. But try anyway. Tell me about Eskil.'

Johnas slumped forward and took a drag on his cigarette. He looked confused. His lips were moving, but not a sound came out. In his mind everything was clear, but now the room was closing in around him, and all he could hear was the breathing of the man across from him. He glanced at the clock on the wall. It was 6.00pm.

Eskil woke up with a gleeful shout at 6.00am. Tumbled around in our bed, hurling himself this way and that. Wanted to get up at once. Astrid needed to sleep some more, she hadn't slept well, and so I had to get up. He followed me into the bathroom, hanging on to my pyjama legs. His arms and legs were everywhere, and he talked nonstop, an endless stream of sounds and shouts. He wriggled around like an eel when I tried desperately to put his clothes on him. He didn't want to wear nappies. Didn't want to wear the outfit I found for him, kept on reaching for anything that wasn't nailed down, and finally climbed up on the toilet lid and began pulling things down from the shelf under the mirror. I lifted him down and was immediately swept up in the same old patterns. I scolded him, kindly at first, and shoved a Ritalin pill in his mouth, which he promptly spat out. I tried to get dressed, tried to make sure he didn't damage anything, didn't break anything. Finally we were both dressed. I lifted him up and carried him into the kitchen to put him in his chair. On the way across the room he suddenly threw his head back and hit me in the mouth. My lip split open and began to bleed. I strapped him in and buttered a piece of bread, but he didn't want it; he shook his head and threw the plate across the table while he screamed that he wanted sausage instead.

'Johnas?' Sejer said. 'Tell me about Eskil!'

Johnas shook himself and looked at the inspector. At last he made a decision. 'All right, if that's what you want. November 7th. A day like any other day, which means an indescribable day. He was a torpedo, he was destroying the whole family in his wake. Magne was getting worse and worse grades in school and couldn't stand to be home any more. He would go off with his friends every afternoon and evening. Astrid never got enough sleep; I couldn't keep regular hours at the shop. Every meal was a trial. Annie,' he said all of a sudden, smiling sadly, 'Annie was the only bright spot. She would come and get him whenever she had time. Then silence would descend on the house. We would collapse wherever we were sitting or lying and completely pass out. We were exhausted and desperate, and no one gave us any help. We were told quite clearly that he would never grow out of it. He would always have trouble concentrating, and he would be hyperactive the rest of his life. The whole family would have to put up with him for years to come. For years. Can you even imagine that?'

'And that day, you had a fight with him?'

Johnas laughed wildly. 'We were always fighting. We had no idea how to handle him. We screamed and shouted.'

'Tell me what happened.'

'Magne stuck his head in the kitchen and shouted goodbye. He went off to catch his bus with his bag over his shoulder. It was still dark outside. I buttered a piece of bread and put some sausage on it. Then I cut it up in little pieces, even though Eskil could easily have eaten the crust. The whole time he was banging his cup on the table, shouting and screaming, not with laughter or anger, just an endless stream of sounds. Suddenly he caught sight of the dessert waffles on the counter from the day before, and started nagging me for them. But even though I knew he would win, I said no. That word was like a red rag for him, so he refused to give up, banging his cup and rocking back and forth in his chair, which threatened to fall over. I stood at the counter with my back turned, shaking. Finally I stepped over and grabbed the plate, pulled off the plastic, and put the waffles in front of him. Tore off a couple of the hearts. I knew he wasn't going to eat them quietly. There was a lot more in store for me; I knew what he was like. Eskil wanted jam on them. Furious, my hands shaking, I spread raspberry jam on two of the hearts. That's when he smiled. I remember it so well, that last smile. He was pleased with himself. I couldn't stand the fact that he was so happy, while I was on the edge of a nervous breakdown. He picked up his plate and started slamming it against the table. He didn't want the waffles after all. They slid off the plate and onto the floor, so I had to find a cloth. I looked everywhere, but couldn't find one, so I picked up the waffles and folded them. He watched me with interest as I made a big lump. I was boiling inside, and some of the steam had to be let out, I didn't know how. Suddenly I bent over the table and stuffed the waffles in his mouth, pushing them in as far as they would go. I still remember his surprised look and the tears that sprang to his eyes.

'"Right now!" I shrieked at him. "Right now you're going to eat your goddamn waffles!"'

JOHNAS COLLAPSED like a broken stick. 'I didn't mean to do it!'

His cigarette was smouldering in the ashtray.

Sejer swallowed. He looked at Johnas. 'We have to accept the children we're given, don't you agree?'

'That's what they all said. Everyone who didn't know any better, and nobody knew. And now I'm going to be charged with abuse, resulting in death. I've charged and condemned myself long ago, and you can't make things any worse.'

Sejer looked at him. 'What exactly was the charge?'

'Eskil's death was entirely my fault. I was responsible for him.

Nothing can be excused or explained away. The only thing is that I didn't mean him to die. It was an accident.'

'It must have been terrible for you,' Sejer said. 'You didn't have anyone to go to with your despair. At the same time you probably feel that you've never been properly punished for what happened. Is that how it is?'

Johnas was silent. His eyes flitted around the room.

'First you lost your youngest son, and then your wife left you, taking your older son with her. You were left all alone, with no one.'

Now Johnas began to cry.

'And yet you've carried on. And you've expanded your business, which is thriving. It takes a lot of energy to start afresh the way you have.'

Johnas nodded. The words felt like warm water.

Sejer had taken aim; now he fired his shot.

'And then, after you had finally got a grip on things and your life was getting back to normal—then Annie popped up, didn't she?'

Johnas gave a start.

'Maybe she looked at you with accusing eyes when you met in the street. You must have wondered about that, about why she seemed so unfriendly. So when you caught sight of her running along with her schoolbag on her back, you had to find out what it was all about, once and for all, didn't you?'

A girl came running down the hill. She recognised me at once and pulled up short. Her face froze and she gave me a cold look.

She started walking again, taking swift strides, without looking back. Then I called out to her. I refused to give up, I had to find out what it was about. Finally she relented and got in, sitting with her arms wrapped around the bag that she held on her lap. I drove slowly, wanting to speak but not knowing exactly how to begin or whether I was about to do something that could be dangerous for both of us. So I kept on driving, and out of the corner of my eye I was aware of her tense figure, like one big trembling accusation.

'I need someone to talk to,' I started off, hesitantly, clutching the steering wheel hard in my hands. 'Things haven't been easy for me.'

'I know that,' she replied, staring out of the window, but suddenly she turned and looked at me for a brief moment.

'Can we drive somewhere and talk a little, Annie? It's hard to do in the car.'

My voice was thin and pleading; I saw that it touched her. She nodded slowly and seemed to relax a bit, settling back in the seat. After a while we passed Horgen's Shop, and I saw a motorcycle parked next to it. The driver was bending over the handlebars, studying something, maybe a map. I drove slowly and carefully up the bad road to Kollen and parked at the turning place. Annie suddenly looked worried. She left her bag on the floor of my car. I try to remember what I was thinking at that moment, but I can't. I remember only that we trudged up the overgrown path. Annie was tall and straight-backed beside me. She went with me down to the water and sat hesitantly on a rock.

'I saw you,' she said quietly. 'I saw you through the window. Right when you bent over the table. I ran away. Later Papa told me that Eskil was dead.'

'I knew you were accusing me,' I told her sombrely, 'because of the way you've been acting.'

I started to cry. I leaned forward and sobbed into my lap while Annie sat motionless at my side. She didn't say anything, but when I was done, I glanced up and saw that she had been crying too. I felt better than I had for a long time, I really did.

'What should I do?' I whispered then. 'What should I do in order to put this behind me?'

'Turn yourself in to the police, of course. And tell them the truth. Otherwise you'll never find peace!'

At that moment she looked at me. My heart turned to stone in my chest. I put my hands in my pockets, tried hard to keep them there. 'Have you told this to anyone?' I asked her.

'No,' she said. 'Not yet.'

'You should mind your own business, Annie!' I shrieked in desperation. Suddenly I felt as if I were rising up from the bottom, out of the darkness and into the light. A single paralysing thought occurred to me. That Annie was the only person in the whole world who knew about this. It was as if the wind had turned and was now roaring in my ears. Everything was lost. Her face wore the same astonished expression Eskil's face had. Afterwards I walked swiftly through the woods. I didn't turn round even once to look back at her.

JOHNAS STUDIED the curtains and the fluorescent light on the ceiling as he kept on shaping his lips to form words that wouldn't come. Sejer looked at him. 'We've searched your house and secured the forensic evidence. You will be charged with the negligent homicide of your own son, Eskil Johnas, and the premeditated murder of Annie Sofie Holland. Do you understand what I'm saying?'

'You're wrong!'

His voice was a fragile peep. Several burst blood vessels had given his eyes a reddish sheen.

'I'm not the one who will assess your guilt.'

Johnas was shaking so violently that he looked like an old man.

Sejer looked at him. 'But you didn't have to kill her, you know.'

'What are you talking about?' he said faintly.

'You didn't have to kill Annie. She would have died on her own if you'd just waited a little longer.'

'Are you joking?'

'No,' Sejer said. 'I would never joke about cancer of the liver.'

'You must be mistaken. Nobody was healthier than Annie. She was standing by the water when I stood up and left. I didn't dare tell you the first time, that she actually went all the way up to the lake with me. But that's what happened! She didn't want to drive back with me; she wanted to walk instead. Don't you see that someone must have turned up while she was standing there at the lake? A young girl, alone in the woods. It's crawling with tourists up at Kollen. Does it ever occur to you that you might be mistaken?'

'It does occur to me on rare occasions. But you have to understand that you've lost the battle. We found Halvor.'

Johnas grimaced, as if someone had stuck a needle in his ear.

'Sad, isn't it?'

THE NEXT DAY, Sejer sat motionless, his hands in his lap. He caught himself rubbing the spot above his wedding ring a few times. There wasn't much else to do. Besides, it was quiet and practically dark in the small room. Once in a while he glanced up and looked at Halvor's ruined face, which had been washed and tended to, but was still almost beyond recognition. His lips were slightly parted. Several of his teeth had been smashed, and the old scar at the corner of his mouth was no longer visible. But his forehead was still whole, and someone had combed back his hair so that the smooth skin was visible.

Sejer bowed his head and placed his hands carefully on the sheet. He heard only his own breathing and in the distance a lift creaking faintly. A sudden movement under his hands made him start. Halvor opened one eye and looked at him. The other was covered with a bandage. Sejer put a finger to his lips and shook his head. 'It's nice to see that smile of yours, but you mustn't say anything. The stitches will burst.'

'Thanks,' Halvor said indistinctly.

They looked at each other for a long time. Sejer nodded a few times, Halvor kept on blinking his green eye.

'The disk that we found at Johnas's place,' Sejer said. 'Is it an exact copy of Annie's diary?'

'Mm.'

'Nothing was erased?'

He shook his head.

'Nothing was changed or corrected?'

More shaking of his head.

'All right then,' Sejer said.

'Thanks.'

Halvor's eye filled with tears. He began sniffling.

'Don't fret!' Sejer said. 'The stitches will come out. And your nose is running. I'll find some tissues.'

He stood up and found some tissues by the sink, and gently dabbed at Halvor's face.

'I expect you found Annie difficult once in a while. But now you probably understand that she had her reasons. As a rule, we all do. And this was a huge burden for her to carry all alone. I know this may be a stupid thing to say,' he said, trying to comfort the boy because he felt such pity for him as he lay in bed, his face pulverised. 'But you're still young. Right now you've lost so much. Right now you feel as if Annie is the only one you would like to have near. But time will pass, and things change. Some day you'll think differently.'

Heavens, what a speech, he thought.

Halvor didn't reply. He stared at Sejer's hands lying on the covers, at the broad gold wedding band on his right hand. His expression was accusatory.

'I know what you're thinking,' Sejer said. 'That it's easy for me to talk, sitting here wearing a big wedding band. A really showy, ten-millimetre ring. But you see,' he said with a sad smile, 'it's actually two five-millimetre rings welded together.' He twisted the rings. 'She's dead,' he said. 'Do you understand?'

Halvor closed his eye and a little more blood and tears ran down his face. He opened his mouth, and Sejer could see the broken remains of his teeth. 'Mm solly.'

THE SUN WAS SHINING as Sejer and Skarre strolled down the street with the dog between them. Kollberg plodded along happily, with his tail held high like a banner.

Sejer had a bouquet of flowers in his hand, red and blue anemones wrapped in tissue paper. His jacket was slung over his shoulders. He strode along with his easy, supple gait while Kollberg hopped and leapt beside him. The dog walked at a surprisingly brisk pace.

Matteus was scurrying around, full of anticipation, a killer whale in his arms, made of black and white felt. His name was Willy, and he was almost as big as he was. Sejer's first impulse was to rush forward and lift him up, roaring out his great joy in a jubilant voice. That's the way all children ought to be greeted, with genuine, exuberant joy. But Sejer wasn't made that way. He took the boy carefully on his lap and looked at Ingrid, who was wearing a new dress; a butter-yellow summer dress with red raspberries. He wished her happy birthday and squeezed her hand. Before long they would be leaving for the other side of the globe, to heat and war, and they would be gone an eternity. He shook hands with his son-in-law while he held Matteus tight. They sat quietly and waited for the food.

Matteus never nagged. He was a well-mannered boy, blessedly free of defiant or contrary behaviour. The only thing Sejer didn't recognise from his own family was a tiny tendency for mischief. Matteus's daily life was all smiles and love, and his origins, about which they knew very little, seemed not to have given him genes that would manifest themselves in abnormal behaviour or drive family members out of their wits. Sejer's thoughts wandered. Back to when he himself was a child. For a long time he sat lost in memory. Finally he was listening. 'What did you say, Ingrid?'

He looked in surprise at his daughter and saw that she was brushing a lock of blonde hair away from her forehead as she smiled in that special way she had, reserved just for him.

'Coke, Papa? Do you want a Coke?'

AT THE SAME TIME, somewhere else, an ugly van bumped along the road in low gear. A big man, his hair sticking up, was hunched over the steering wheel. At the bottom of the hill he stopped to let a little girl, who had just taken two steps forward, cross the road. She stopped abruptly.

'Hi, Ragnhild!' he cried out.

She was holding a skipping rope in one hand, so she waved with the other.

'Are you out taking a walk?'

'I'm on my way home,' she said firmly.

'Listen to this!' Raymond said in a loud, shrill voice to be heard over the roar of the engine. 'Caesar is dead. But Påsan had babies!'

'But he's a boy,' she said.

'It's not easy to tell whether a rabbit is a boy or a girl. They have so much fur. But at any rate he had babies. Five of them. You can come and see them if you want.'

'They won't let me,' she said, disappointed, staring down the road and hoping vaguely that someone would appear to rescue her from such a spellbinding temptation. *Baby bunnies.*

'Do they have fur?'

'They have fur and their eyes are open. I'll drive you back home afterwards, Ragnhild. Come on, they're growing up so fast!'

She glanced down the road one more time, shut her eyes tight and opened them again. Then she dashed across and climbed in. Ragnhild was wearing a white blouse with a lace collar and tiny little red shorts. No one saw her get in. Everyone was in their back gardens, preoccupied with planting and weeding, tying up their roses and the clematis. Raymond felt so good in Sejer's old windbreaker. He put the van in gear. The little girl was sitting excitedly on the seat beside him. He whistled happily and looked around. Nobody had noticed them.

KARIN FOSSUM

Norwegian author Karin Fossum made her literary debut in 1974 with the publication of a collection of poems (under the name Karin Mathiesen), followed by two short story collections and a second collection of poems. Her major breakthrough came in 1995, with the publication of her first crime novel, *Evas øye* (Eve's Eye), destined to be the first in a series of Inspector Sejer mysteries. The novel met with critical acclaim in Norway and was subsequently published in sixteen European countries. In 1999 it was released as a feature film. Despite her track record, Fossum has never before been published in the UK.

She still clearly remembers the difficult early days, before she became established. 'There was a gap of many years between the publication of my first collection of poems and my first real success. My priority was to look after my two young daughters and I just had to focus on that. But I never lost my desire to be a writer.' In order to make ends meet, Fossum had to confine her writing to evenings, while working in a variety of jobs, including taxi driving and working in a residential home and a hospital. 'That period of my life seemed to last for a long time.'

Fossum admits that it isn't the details of police procedure and forensics that interest her as a novelist. 'I'm far more interested in what makes people tick and how we relate to one another in different situations,' she explains. She is especially interested in what motivates her series detective, Konrad Sejer. He is a strong, intuitive man who people trust and confide in but, Fossum says, appearances can be deceptive. 'At work, Sejer is the boss, in control, yet in his private life he is lonely and reserved. Often, people can be a success in one environment, but not in another.'

Her insight as a writer, combined with her storytelling ability, are sure to win Fossum many British fans, who will be pleased to know that Inspector Sejer is set to make another appearance on these shores in a new mystery.

MICHAEL CRICHTON

PREY

We watched the swarm hang there, rising and falling like it was breathing. The cloud had turned mostly black now, with just an occasional glint of silver. It had remained at the same spot for ten or fifteen seconds, pulsing up and down.

Suddenly the swarm rose up and began to move again.

It was tracking us.

Tracking its prey.

Day 1: 10.04am

Things never turn out the way you think they will.

I never intended to become a househusband. Stay-at-home husband, whatever you want to call it. But that's what I had become in the last six months. Now I was in Crate & Barrel in downtown San Jose, picking up some place mats; the woven oval ones that Julia had bought a year ago were getting pretty worn, and the weave was crusted with baby food. I found some yellow ones that looked really bright and appealing. They didn't have six on the shelf, and I thought we'd better have six, so I asked the salesgirl to look in the back and see if they had more. While she was gone my cellphone rang.

It was Julia. 'Hi, hon.'

'Hi, Julia. How's it going?' I said. I could hear machinery in the background, a steady chugging. Probably the vacuum pump for the electron microscope in her laboratory.

She said, 'What're you doing?'

'Buying place mats, actually. In Crate and Barrel.'

'Oh, that's good,' she said. I could tell Julia was completely uninterested in this conversation. Something else was on her mind. 'Listen, Jack, I'm really sorry, but I'm going to be late again.'

'Uh-huh . . .' The salesgirl came back with more yellow mats. Still holding the phone to my ear, I held up three fingers, and she put down three more mats. To Julia, I said, 'Is everything all right?'

'Yeah, it's just crazy like normal. We're broadcasting a demo by satellite today to the VCs in Asia and Europe, and we're having trouble with the satellite hook-up at this end. Anyway, I won't get back until eight at the earliest. Can you feed the kids and put them to bed?'

'No problem,' I said. And it wasn't. I was used to it. Lately, Julia had been working very long hours. Xymos Technology, the company she worked for, was trying to raise another round of venture capital—$20 million—to develop technology in what the company called 'molecular manufacturing', but which most people called nanotechnology. Nano wasn't popular with the VCs—the venture capitalists—these days. Too many VCs had been burned in the last ten years with products that were supposedly just around the corner, but then never made it out of the lab.

Not that Julia needed to be told that; she'd worked for two VC firms herself. Originally trained as a child psychologist, she ended up as someone who specialised in 'technology incubation', helping fledgling technology companies get started. Eventually, she'd stopped advising firms and joined Xymos, where she was now a vice-president.

'Listen, Jack, I want to warn you,' she said in a guilty voice, 'that Eric is going to be upset. I told him I would come to the game.'

'Julia, why? There's no way you can make that game. It's at three o'clock. Why'd you tell him you would?'

'I thought I could make it.'

I sighed. 'OK. Don't worry, honey. I'll handle it.'

'Thanks. Oh, and Jack? The place mats? Whatever you do, just don't get yellow, OK?' And she hung up.

I MADE SPAGHETTI for dinner because there was never an argument about spaghetti. By eight o'clock, the two little ones were asleep, and Nicole, who was twelve, was finishing her homework.

The littlest one, Amanda, was just nine months and was starting to crawl everywhere. Eric was eight; he was a soccer kid and liked to play all the time, when he wasn't dressing up as a knight and chasing his older sister around the house with his plastic sword.

When I first lost the job at MediaTronics, it was interesting to deal with sibling rivalry. And often, it seemed, not that different from what my job had been. At MediaTronics I had run a program division, riding herd over a group of talented young computer programmers. At forty, I was too old to work as a programmer myself any more; writing code is a young person's job. So I managed my team, who, like most in Silicon Valley, seemed to live in a perpetual crisis of crashed Porsches, infidelities, parental hassles and drug reactions, all superimposed on a forced-march work schedule with all-night marathons fuelled by cases of Diet Coke and Sun chips.

But the work was exciting, in a cutting-edge field. We wrote what are called distributed parallel-processing agent-based programs. These programs model biological processes by creating virtual agents inside the computer and then letting the agents interact to solve real-world problems. It sounds strange, but it works. For example, one of our programs imitated ant foraging (how ants find the shortest path to food) to route traffic through a big telephone network. Other programs mimicked the behaviour of swarming bees and stalking lions.

It was fun, and I would probably still be there if I hadn't taken on some additional responsibilities. In my last few months, I'd been put in charge of security, replacing a consultant who'd failed to detect the theft of company source code, until it turned up in a program being marketed out of Taiwan.

We knew it was our code, because the Easter eggs hadn't been touched. Programmers always insert Easter eggs into their code, little nuggets that don't serve any useful purpose and are just put there for fun. The Taiwanese company hadn't changed any of them. So the keystrokes Alt-Shift-M-9 would open up a window giving the date of one of our programmers' marriage. Clear theft. We sued.

The first thing I did as security officer was to monitor work station use. It was pretty straightforward; these days, eighty percent of companies monitor what their workers do at terminals.

Don Gross, the head of the company, was a tough guy, an ex-Marine. When I told him about the new system, he said, 'But you're not monitoring my terminal, right?' Of course not, I said. In fact, I'd set up the programs to monitor every computer in the company, his included. And that was how I discovered, two weeks later, that Don was having an affair with a girl in accounting and had authorised her to have a company car. I went to him and said that based on emails relating to Jean in accounting, it appeared that someone was having an affair with her, and that she might be getting perks she wasn't entitled to. I said I didn't know who the person was, but if they kept using email, I'd soon find out.

I figured Don would take the hint, and he did. But now he just sent incriminating email from his home, never realising that everything went through the company server. That's how I learned he was 'discounting' software to foreign distributors and was being paid large 'consultancy fees'. This was clearly illegal, and I couldn't overlook it. I consulted my attorney, Gary Marder, who advised me to quit.

'Quit?' I said. 'You think I should quit because *he*'s breaking the law? Is that your advice to me?'

'No,' Gary said. 'As your attorney, my advice is that if you are aware of any illegal activity you have a duty to report it. But as your friend, my advice is to keep your mouth shut and get out of there fast.'

I didn't think that was right. But now I found myself wondering if the code actually had been stolen. Maybe it had been sold. We were a privately held company, and I told one of the board members.

It turned out he was in on it. I was fired the next day for gross negligence and misconduct. Litigation was threatened; I had to sign a raft of Non Disclosure Agreements to get my severance package. My attorney handled the paperwork, sighing with each new document.

At the end, we went outside. I said, 'Well, at least that's over.'

He turned and looked at me. 'Why do you say that?' he said.

BECAUSE OF COURSE it wasn't over. In some mysterious way, I had become a marked man. My qualifications were excellent. But when I went on job interviews I could tell they weren't interested. Worse, they were uncomfortable. Silicon Valley is a small place. Word gets out. Eventually I found myself talking to an interviewer I knew slightly, Ted Landow. When the interview was over, I said, 'Ted, I've been on ten interviews in ten days. Tell me what you've heard about me?'

He sighed. 'Jack Forman. Troublemaker. Belligerent. Hotheaded. Not a team player.' He hesitated, then said, 'And supposedly you were involved in some kind of shady dealings. You were on the take.'

'*I* was on the take?' I said. I felt a flood of anger, and was about to say more, until I realised I was probably looking hotheaded and belligerent. So I shut up, and thanked him.

As I was leaving, he said, 'Jack, do yourself a favour. Give it a while. Things change fast in the Valley. Wait a few months . . .'

I knew he was right. After that, I stopped trying so hard. I began to hear rumours that MediaTronics was going belly up and there might be indictments. I smelt vindication ahead, but in the meantime there was nothing to do but wait.

I started taking the kids to school, picking them up, driving them to the doctor, the orthodontist, soccer practice. The first few dinners I cooked were disastrous, but I got better.

And before I knew it, I was buying place mats in Crate & Barrel. And it all seemed perfectly normal.

JULIA GOT HOME around nine thirty. I was watching the Giants game on TV, not really paying attention. She came in and kissed me on the back of my neck. She said, 'They all asleep?'

'Except Nicole. She's still doing homework.'

'Isn't it late for her to be up?'

'No, hon,' I said. 'We agreed. This year she gets to stay up until ten.'

Julia shrugged. We had undergone a sort of inversion of roles; she had always been more knowledgeable about the kids, but now I was. Sometimes I felt Julia was uncomfortable with that.

'How's the little one?'

'Her cold is better. Just sniffles. She's eating more.'

I walked with Julia to the bedrooms. She went into the baby's room, bent over the crib and kissed the sleeping child tenderly. Watching her, I thought there was something about a mother's caring that a father could never match. Julia listened to the baby's soft breathing and said, 'Yes, she's better.'

She checked on Eric, then she went into Nicole's room. Nicole was on her laptop, but shut the lid when Julia walked in. 'Hi, Mom.'

'You're up late.'

'No, Mom . . .'

'You're supposed to be doing homework.'

'I did it.'

'Then why aren't you in bed? I don't want you spending all night talking to your friends on the computer.'

'Mom . . .' she said, in a pained voice.

'Don't look at your father. We already know he'll do whatever you want. I'm talking to you, now.'

I put my arm around Julia's shoulder and said, 'It's late for everybody. Want a cup of tea?'

'Jack, I'm talking to Nicole. Please don't interfere.'

'Honey, we agreed she could stay up until ten. I don't know—'

'But if she's finished her homework, she should go to bed. I don't want her spending all day and night on the computer.'

'She's not, Julia.'

At that point, Nicole burst into tears and jumped to her feet crying, 'You always criticise me! I hate you!' She ran into the bathroom and slammed the door. That woke the baby, who started to cry.

Julia turned to me and said, 'If you would please just let me handle this myself, Jack.'

And I said, 'You're right. I'm sorry. You're right.'

IN TRUTH, that wasn't what I thought at all. I thought she was wrong.

Lately I had started to have the feeling that Julia had changed. She was different, somehow, tenser, tougher.

The baby was howling. I picked her up from the crib, hugged her, cooed at her, and simultaneously stuck a finger down the back of the diaper to see if it was wet. It was. I put her down on her back on top of the dresser and started to change her. Julia had gone downstairs.

I figured I would need to give the baby a bottle to get her to sleep again, so when I got her diaper on, I took her into the kitchen. The lights were low, just the fluorescents over the counter.

Julia was sitting at the table, drinking beer out of a bottle, staring into space. 'When are you going to get a job?' she said.

'I'm trying.'

'Really? When was your last interview?'

'Last week,' I said.

She grunted. 'I wish you'd hurry up and get one,' she said, 'because this is driving me crazy.'

I swallowed anger. 'I know. It's hard for everybody,' I said, watching her out of the corner of my eye.

At thirty-six, Julia was a strikingly pretty woman, petite, with dark hair and dark eyes, upturned nose, and the kind of personality that people called bubbly or sparkling. Unlike many tech executives, she was attractive and approachable. She made friends easily, and had a real gift for seeing the humorous side of life. She was famous for her equanimity; she almost never lost her temper.

Right now, of course, she was furious. Not even willing to look at me. Sitting in the dark at the round kitchen table, one leg crossed over the other, kicking impatiently while she stared into space. As I looked at her, I had the feeling that her appearance had changed, somehow, too. Of course she had lost weight recently, part of the strain of the job. A certain softness in her face was gone and it made her look harder, but in a way more glamorous. And her kicking foot made me notice she was wearing slingback high heels. The kind of shoes she would never have worn to work.

And then I realised that everything about her was different—her manner, her appearance, her mood, everything—and in a flash of insight I knew why: *my wife was having an affair.*

I had read somewhere that this was a syndrome. The husband's out of work, his masculine appeal declines, his wife no longer respects him, and she wanders. Was it really true? Or was I just tired, making up bad stories in my mind? I was probably just feeling inadequate, unattractive. These were probably my insecurities coming out.

But I couldn't talk myself out of it. I was *sure* it was true.

I had to turn away.

THE BABY TOOK the bottle, gurgling happily. In the darkened kitchen, she stared up at me with that peculiar fixed stare that babies have. It was sort of soothing, watching her. After a while she closed her eyes and her mouth went slack. I put her on my shoulder and burped her as I carried her back into her bedroom. I set her down in the crib and turned out the nightlight. As I turned to go, I saw Julia silhouetted in the doorway. She stalked forward. I tensed. She put her arms around me and rested her head on my chest.

'Please forgive me,' she said. 'You're doing a wonderful job. I'm just jealous, that's all.' My shoulder was wet with her tears.

'I understand,' I said, holding her. 'It's OK.'

I waited to see if my body relaxed, but it didn't. I was suspicious and alert. I had a bad feeling about her and it wasn't going away.

SHE CAME OUT of the shower into the bedroom, towelling her short hair dry. I was sitting on the bed, trying to watch the rest of the game. It occurred to me that she never used to take showers at night, just in the mornings before work. Now, I realised, she often came home and went straight to the shower before saying hello to the kids.

'How was the demo?' I said, flicking the TV off.

'The what?'

'The demo. Didn't you have a demo today?'

'Oh,' she said. 'Oh, yes. We did. It went fine, when we finally got it going. I have a dub of it. Do you want to see it?'

I was surprised. I shrugged. 'OK, sure.'

'I'd really like to know what you think, Jack.' I detected a patronising tone. I watched as she stuck a DVD in the player and came back to snuggle up with me on the bed. All very cozy, just like old times. I still felt uneasy, but I put my arm around her.

'OK, here we go,' she said, pointing to the screen. I saw black and white scramble, and then the image resolved.

The tape showed Julia in a large laboratory that was fitted out like an operating room. A man lay on his back on the gurney, an IV in his arm, an anaesthesiologist standing by. Above the table was a round flat metal plate about six feet in diameter, which could be raised and lowered, but was now raised. There were video monitors all around. And in the foreground, peering at a monitor, was Julia. There was a video technician by her side.

'This is terrible,' she was saying, pointing to the monitor. 'What's all the interference?'

'We think it's the air purifiers. They're causing it.'

'Well, this is unacceptable,' Julia shouted. 'I can't show the VCs an image of this quality. They've seen better pictures from Mars. Fix it.'

Beside me on the bed, Julia said, 'I didn't know they recorded all this. This is before the demo. You can fast forward.'

I pushed the remote, waited a few seconds and played it again.

Julia appeared on screen again, standing in front of the gurney.

'Hello to all of you,' she said, smiling at the camera. 'I'm Julia Forman of Xymos Technology, and we're about to demonstrate a revolutionary medical imaging procedure just developed here. Our subject, Peter Morris, is lying behind me on the table. In a few moments, we're going to look inside his heart and blood vessels with an ease and accuracy never before possible.'

She began walking around the table, talking as she went.

'Unlike cardiac catheterisation, our procedure is one hundred per cent safe. And unlike catheterisation, we can look everywhere in the body, at every sort of vessel, no matter how large or small. We can do this because the camera we put inside his vessels is smaller than a red blood cell. Quite a bit smaller, actually.

'Xymos technology can now produce these miniaturised cameras, and produce them in quantity—cheaply, quickly. It would take a thousand of them just to make a dot the size of a pencil point. We can fabricate a kilogram of these cameras in an hour.

'I'm sure you are all sceptical. We're well aware that nanotechnology has made promises it couldn't deliver. As you know, the problem has been that scientists could design molecular-scale devices, but they couldn't manufacture them. But Xymos has solved that problem.'

It suddenly hit me, what she was saying. '*What*?' I said, sitting up in bed. 'Are you kidding?' If it was true, it was an extraordinary development, a genuine technological breakthrough, and it meant—

'It's true,' Julia said quietly. 'We're manufacturing in Nevada.' She smiled, enjoying my astonishment.

Onscreen, Julia was saying, 'I have one of our Xymos cameras under the electron microscope, here'—she pointed to the screen—'so you can see it in comparison to the red blood cell alongside it.'

The image changed to black and white. I saw a fine probe push what looked like a tiny squid into position on a titanium field. It was a bullet-nosed lump with streaming filaments at the rear. It was a tenth of the size of the red blood cell.

'Our camera is one ten-billionth of an inch in length,' Julia said. 'Imaging takes place in the nose. Microtubules in the tail provide stabilisation, like the tail of a kite. But they can also lash actively and provide locomotion. Jerry, if we can turn the camera to see the nose. OK, there. Thank you. Now, from the front, you see that indentation in the centre? That is the miniature photon detector, acting as a retina, and the surrounding area is bioluminescent and lights the area ahead. Within the nose itself is a rather complex series of twisted molecules. That is our patented ATP cascade. You can think of it as a primitive brain, which controls the behaviour of the camera.'

'Where is the lens?' I asked.

'There is no lens.'

'How can you have a camera with no lens?'

'I thought you knew,' she said. 'You're responsible for that part.'

'Me?'

'Yes. Xymos got your team to write some agent-based algorithms to control a particle network.'

'Your cameras are networked? All those little cameras communicate with each other?'

'Yes,' she said. 'They're a swarm, actually.' She was still smiling, amused by my reactions.

'A swarm.' I was thinking it over, trying to understand what she was telling me. Certainly my team had written a number of programs to control swarms of agents, modelled on the behaviour of bees. Faced with new and unexpected conditions, the swarm programs didn't crash; they just sort of flowed around the obstacles and kept going.

But our programs worked by creating virtual agents inside the computer. Julia had created real agents in the real world. I didn't see how our programs could be adapted to what she was doing.

'We use them for structure,' she said. 'The program makes the swarm structure.'

Of course. It was obvious that a single molecular camera was inadequate to register any sort of image. Therefore, the image must be a composite of millions of cameras, operating simultaneously. That meant Xymos must be generating the equivalent of—

'You're making an eye.'

'Kind of. Yes.'

'But where's the light source?'

'The bioluminescent perimeter. Watch.'

MEANWHILE, the onscreen Julia was turning smoothly, pointing to the intravenous line behind her. She lifted a syringe out of a nearby ice bucket. 'This syringe,' she said, 'contains approximately twenty million cameras in isotonic saline suspension. At the moment they exist as particles. But once they are injected into the bloodstream, their temperature will increase and they will flock together to form a spherical shape with a small opening at one end. In effect the particles form an eye. And the image from that eye will be a composite of millions of photon detectors. Just as the human eye creates an image from its rods and cone cells.'

She gave a signal and the flat antenna was lowered until it was just inches above the waiting subject.

'This antenna will power the camera and pick up the transmitted image,' she said. She fitted the syringe with a needle and stuck it into a rubber stopper in the IV line. 'Here we go.'

She pushed the plunger down quickly, then withdrew the needle. 'Generally we have to wait about ten seconds for the shape to form, and then we should begin getting an image. Ah, here it is now.'

The scene showed the camera moving forward at considerable speed through what looked like an asteroid field. Except the asteroids were red cells, bouncy purplish bags moving in a clear, slightly yellowish liquid. An occasional much larger white cell shot forward, filled the screen for a moment, then was gone. What I was seeing looked more like a video game than a medical image.

'Julia,' I said, 'this is amazing.'

Beside me, Julia snuggled closer. 'I thought you'd be impressed.'

Onscreen, Julia was saying, 'We've entered a vein, so the red cells are not oxygenated. Right now our camera is moving towards the heart. You'll see the vessels enlarging as we move up the venous system . . . see the pulsations resulting from the ventricular contractions . . .'

I could see the camera pause, then move forward, then pause.

'We're coming to the right atrium, and we should see the mitral valve. There it is now. We are in the heart.' I saw the red flaps, like a mouth opening and closing, and then the camera shot through, into the ventricle, and out again.

'Now we are going to the lungs, where you will see what no one has ever witnessed before. The oxygenation of the cells.'

As I watched, the blood vessel narrowed swiftly, and then the cells plumped up and popped brilliantly red, one after another. It was extremely quick; in less than a second, they were all red.

'The red cells have now been oxygenated,' Julia said, 'and we are on our way back to the heart.'

I turned to Julia in the bed. 'This is really fantastic stuff,' I said.

But her eyes were closed and she was breathing gently.

She was asleep.

JULIA HAD ALWAYS TENDED to fall asleep while watching TV. Falling asleep during your own presentation was reasonable enough; after all, she'd already seen it. And it was pretty late. I decided I could watch the rest of the demo another time. I turned to switch off the TV, and as I did so I looked down at the time code running at the bottom of the image. Numbers were spinning, ticking off hundredths of a second. Other numbers to the left, not spinning. One of them was the date. I hadn't noticed it before, because it was in international format, with the year first, the day and the month. It read 02.21.09.

September 21.

Yesterday.

She'd recorded this demo yesterday, not today.

I turned off the TV and turned off the bedside light. I lay down on the pillow and tried to sleep.

DAY 2: 11.02AM

I was sitting in the paediatrician's waiting room for the baby's next round of immunisations. There were four mothers in the room, bouncing sick kids on their laps while the older children played on the floor. The mothers all talked to each other and studiously ignored me.

I was getting used to this. A guy at home, a guy in a setting like the paediatrician's office, was an unusual thing. It meant that there was probably something wrong with the guy, he couldn't get a job, maybe he was fired for alcoholism or drugs. Whatever the reason, it wasn't normal for a man to be in the paediatrician's office in the middle of the day. So the other mothers pretended I wasn't there.

Eventually we were ushered in. The doctor was very friendly, never asked why I was there instead of my wife. He gave two injections. Amanda howled. I bounced her on my shoulder, comforted her.

'She may have a little swelling, a little local redness. Call me if it's not gone in forty-eight hours.'

Then I was back in the waiting room, trying to get my credit card out to pay the bill while the baby cried. That was when Julia called.

'Hi. What're you doing?' She must have heard the baby screaming.

'Paying the paediatrician.'

'Bad time?'

'Kind of . . .'

'OK, listen, I just wanted to say I have an early night—finally! What do you say I pick up some dinner on my way home?'

'That'd be great,' I said.

BY FIVE THIRTY the kids were home, raiding the fridge. Nicole was eating a big chunk of cheese. I told her to stop; it would ruin her dinner. Then I went back to setting the table.

'When *is* dinner?'

'Soon. Mom's bringing it home.'

'Uh-huh.' She disappeared for a few minutes, and then she came back. 'She says she's sorry she didn't call, but she's going to be late.'

'What?' I was pouring water into the glasses on the table.

'She's sorry but she's going to be late. I just talked to her.'

'Damn.' It was irritating. I tried never to show my irritation around the kids, but sometimes it slipped out. I sighed. 'OK. Get your brother and get into the car,' I said. 'We're going to the drive-in.'

I LEFT THE TABLE set for dinner that night, a silent rebuke. Julia saw it when she got home around ten. 'I'm sorry, hon.'

'I know, you were busy,' I said.

'I was. Please forgive me?'

'I do,' I said.

'You're the best.' She blew me a kiss, from across the room. 'I'm going to take a shower,' she said, and headed off.

On the way down the landing, I watched as she looked into the baby's room and then darted in. A moment later, I heard her cooing and the baby gurgling. I walked down the landing after her.

In the darkened nursery, she was holding the baby up, nuzzling her.

I said, 'Julia . . . you woke her up.'

'No, I didn't, she was awake. Weren't you, little honey-bunny?'

The baby rubbed her eyes with tiny fists and yawned. She certainly appeared to have been woken.

Julia turned to me in the darkness. 'I didn't. Really. I didn't wake her up. Why are you looking at me that way? That accusing way.'

'I'm not accusing you of anything.'

The baby started to whimper and then to cry. Julia touched her diaper. 'I think she's wet,' she said, and handed her to me as she walked out of the room. 'You do it, Mr Perfect.'

After I changed the baby and put her back to bed, I heard Julia come out of the shower, banging a door. Whenever Julia started banging doors, it was a sign for me to come and mollify her. But I didn't feel like it tonight. I was annoyed she'd woken the baby and I was annoyed by her unreliability, saying she'd be home early and never calling to say she wouldn't. I was scared that she had become so unreliable because she was distracted by a new love. Or she just didn't care about her family any more. I didn't know what to do about all this, but I didn't feel like smoothing the tension between us.

I went back to the living room and sat down. I picked up the book I was reading and tried to concentrate but of course I couldn't.

When I finally went to bed, Julia was fast asleep. I slipped between the covers and rolled over on my side, away from her.

IT WAS ONE O'CLOCK in the morning when the baby began to scream. I groped for the light.

'What's the matter with her?' Julia said sleepily.

'I don't know.' I got out of bed, shaking my head, trying to wake up. I went into the nursery and flicked the light on.

The baby was standing up in her crib, howling. Tears were running down her cheeks. I held my arms out to her and she reached for me, and I comforted her. I thought it must be a nightmare.

She continued to scream, unrelenting. Maybe something was hurting her, maybe something in her diaper. I checked her body. That was when I saw an angry red rash on her belly, extending in welts round to her back and up towards her neck.

Julia came in. 'Can't you stop it?' she said.

I said, 'There's something wrong,' and I showed her the rash.

'Has she got a fever?'

I touched Amanda's head. She was sweaty and hot, but that could be from the crying. The rest of her body felt cool. 'I don't think so.'

I could see the rash on her thighs now. Was it on her thighs a moment before? I almost thought I was seeing it spread before my eyes. If it was possible, the baby screamed even louder.

'Jesus,' Julia said. 'I'll call the doctor.'

'Yeah, do.' By now I had the baby on her back—she screamed more—and I was looking carefully at her entire body. The rash was spreading, there was no doubt about it.

Julia came back and said she left word for the doctor. I said, 'I'm not going to wait. I'm taking her to the emergency room.'

'Do you want me to come with you?'

'No, stay with the kids.'

'OK,' she said. She wandered back to the bedroom.

The baby continued to scream.

'I REALISE it's uncomfortable,' the intern was saying. 'But I don't think it's safe to sedate her.' We were in a cubicle in the emergency room. The intern was bent over Amanda, looking in her ears with his instrument. By now her entire body was bright, angry red.

I felt scared. I'd never heard of anything like this before, a baby turning bright red and screaming constantly. And I didn't trust this intern, who seemed far too young to be competent. He couldn't be experienced; he didn't even look as if he shaved yet.

'She has no fever,' the intern said, ignoring the screaming, 'but in a child this age that doesn't mean anything. Under a year, they may not run fevers at all, even with severe infections.'

'Is that what this is?' I said. 'An infection?'

'I don't know. I'm presuming a virus because of that rash. But we should have the preliminary blood work back in—ah, good.' A passing nurse handed him a slip of paper. 'Uhh . . . hmmm . . .'

'Well?' I said, shifting my weight anxiously.

He was shaking his head as he stared at the paper.

'Well *what*?'

'It's not an infection,' he said. 'White cells counts all normal, protein fractions normal. She's got no immune mobilisation at all.'

'What does that mean?'

He was very calm, standing there, frowning and thinking. I wondered if perhaps he was just dumb.

'We have to widen the diagnostic net,' he said. 'I'm going to order a surgical consult, a neurological consult, we have a dermo coming, we have infectious coming. That'll mean a lot of people asking you the same questions, but—'

'That's OK,' I said. 'Just . . . what do you think is wrong?'

'I don't know. If it's not infectious, we look for other reasons for this skin response. She hasn't travelled out of the country?'

'No.' I shook my head.

'No recent exposures to heavy metals or toxins?'

'No, no.'

'Can you think of anything that might have caused this reaction?'

'No, nothing . . . wait, she had vaccinations yesterday.'

'What vaccinations?'

'I don't know,' I said irritably, 'whatever she gets for her age . . . You're the damned doctor—'

'That's OK, Mr Forman,' he said soothingly. 'I know it's stressful. If you just tell me the name of your paediatrician, I'll call him.'

I nodded. I wiped my hand across my forehead. I was sweating. I spelt the paediatrician's name for him while he wrote it down in his notebook. I tried to calm down. I tried to think clearly.

And all the time, my baby just screamed.

HALF AN HOUR LATER, she went into convulsions.

They started while one of the white-coated consultants was bent over her, examining her. Her little body wrenched and twisted. Her legs jerked spastically. Her eyes rolled up into her head.

I don't remember what I said or did then, but an orderly the size of a football player came in and pushed me to one side of the cubicle and held my arms. I looked past his huge shoulder as six people clustered round my daughter and a nurse stuck a needle into her forehead. I began to shout and struggle but the orderly explained it was just to start an IV, that the baby had become dehydrated. That was why she was convulsing.

The convulsions stopped in seconds. But she continued to scream.

SHORTLY BEFORE DAWN the huddled consultants announced that Amanda either had an intestinal obstruction or a brain tumour, they couldn't decide which, and they ordered an MRI scan. The sky was beginning to lighten when she was finally wheeled to the imaging room. The big white machine stood in the centre of the room. Amanda was strapped onto the board that rolled into its depths. My daughter was staring up at the MRI in terror, still screaming. The nurse told me I could wait in the next room with the technician. I went into a room with a glass window that looked in on the machine.

Amanda was now completely inside it. Her sobs sounded tinny over the microphone. The technician flicked a switch and the pump began to chatter; it made a lot of noise. But I could still hear my daughter screaming.

And then, abruptly, she stopped. She was completely silent.

I looked at the technician and the nurse. Their faces registered shock. We all thought the same thing, that something terrible had happened. My heart began to pound. The technician hastily shut down the pumps and we hurried back into the room.

My daughter was lying there, still strapped down, breathing heavily, but apparently fine. She blinked her eyes slowly, as if dazed. Already her skin was noticeably a lighter shade of pink, with patches of normal colour. The rash was fading right before our eyes.

'I'll be damned,' the technician said.

BACK IN THE EMERGENCY ROOM, they wouldn't let Amanda go home. They still thought she had a tumour or a bowel emergency, and they wanted to keep her in the hospital for observation. But the rash continued to clear, until an hour later it had vanished.

No one could understand what had happened, and the doctors were uneasy. But Amanda took a bottle of formula, guzzling it down hungrily while I held her. Then she fell asleep in my arms.

I sat there for another hour, then began to make noises about how I had to get my kids to school. And not long afterwards, the doctors announced another victory for modern medicine and sent us home. Amanda slept soundly all the way. The sky was almost light when I carried her up the driveway and into the house.

Day 3: 6.07AM

The house was silent. The kids were still asleep. I found Julia standing in the dining room, staring out of the window at the back yard.

I said, 'We're back.'

She turned. 'She's OK?'

I held out the baby to her. 'Seems to be.'

'Thank God,' she said, 'I was so worried, Jack.' But she didn't approach Amanda and didn't touch her. 'I felt awful. I couldn't sleep all night.' Her eyes flicked to my face, then away. She looked guilty.

'Want to hold her?'

'I, uh . . .' Julia shook her head. 'Not right now,' she said. 'I have to check the sprinklers. They're overwatering my roses.'

I watched her walk out into the back yard and stand looking at the sprinklers. She glanced back at me, then made a show of checking the timer box on the wall. I didn't get it. The gardeners had adjusted the sprinkler timers just last week. Maybe they hadn't done it right.

Amanda snuffled in my arms. I took her into the nursery to change her, then put her back in bed.

When I returned, I saw Julia in the kitchen, talking on her cellphone. This was another new habit of hers. She didn't use the house phone much any more. When I had asked her about it, she'd said it was because she was calling long distance a lot and the company paid her cellular bills.

I slowed my approach and walked on the carpet. I heard her say, 'Yes, damn it, of course I do, but we have to be careful now . . .'

She looked up and saw me coming. Her tone changed. 'OK, uh . . . look, Carol, I think we can handle that with a phone call to Frankfurt. Follow up with a fax and let me know how he responds.' And she snapped the phone shut. I came into the kitchen.

'Jack, I hate to leave before the kids are up, but something's come up at work.'

I glanced at my watch. It was a quarter past six. 'OK. Sure. I'll handle everything.'

'Thanks. I'll call you later.'

And she was gone.

I WAS SO TIRED I wasn't thinking clearly. The baby was still asleep, and with luck she'd sleep several hours more. My housekeeper, Maria, came at six thirty. The kids ate breakfast and I drove them to school, trying hard to stay awake.

Eric was sitting on the front seat next to me. He yawned.

'Sleepy today?'

He nodded. 'Those men kept waking me up,' he said.

'What men?'

'The men that came in the house last night. They vacuumed everything. And they vacuumed up the ghost.'

From the back seat, Nicole snickered. 'The *ghost* . . .'

I said, 'I think you were dreaming, son.' Lately Eric had been having vivid nightmares. I was pretty sure it was because Nicole let him watch horror movies with her, knowing they would upset him.

'No, Dad, it wasn't a dream,' Eric said, yawning again. 'The men were there. A whole bunch of them.'

'Uh-huh. And what was the ghost?'

'He was a ghost. All silver and shimmery. He didn't have a face.'

'Uh-huh.' By now we were pulling up at the school. The two kids piled out of the car, dragging their backpacks behind them.

I drove home again, hoping that I might get a couple of hours of sleep. It was the only thing on my mind.

MARIA WOKE ME UP around eleven, shaking my shoulder insistently. 'Mr Forman. Mr Forman. You see the baby, Mr Forman. She all . . .' She made a gesture, rubbing her shoulder and arm.

I was immediately awake. 'She's all what?'

'You see the baby, Mr Forman.'

I staggered out of bed and went into the nursery. Amanda was standing up in her crib, bouncing and smiling happily. Everything seemed normal, except for the fact that her entire body was a uniform purple-blue colour. Like a big bruise.

'Oh Jesus,' I said.

The thought that there was something wrong wrenched my stomach. I went over to Amanda, who gurgled with pleasure, stretching one hand towards me, grasping air, her signal for me to pick her up.

So I picked her up. She seemed fine, immediately grabbing my hair and trying to pull my glasses off, the way she always did. I felt relieved, even though her whole body looked bruised.

I decided I had to call the doctor in the emergency room. I dialled one-handed. I could do pretty much everything one-handed. I got right through; he sounded surprised.

'Oh,' he said. 'I was about to call you. How is your daughter feeling?'

'Well, she seems to feel fine,' I said, putting Amanda back in her crib while I talked. 'But the thing is—'

'Has she by any chance had bruising?'

'Yes,' I said. 'As a matter of fact, she has. That's why I was calling.'

'The bruising is all over her body? Uniformly?'

'Yes,' I said. 'Pretty much. Why do you ask?'

'Well,' the doctor said, 'all her lab work has come back, and it's all normal. Completely normal. We're still waiting on the MRI report, but the MRI's broken down. They say it'll be a few days.'

There was a pause. The doctor coughed.

'Mr Forman, I noticed on your hospital admissions form you said your occupation was software engineer.'

'That's right.'

'Does that mean you are involved with manufacturing?'

'No. I do program development.'

'May I ask where you work?'

'Actually, at the moment, I'm unemployed.'

'I see. All right. How long has that been?'

'Six months.'

'I see.' A short pause. 'Well, OK, I just wanted to clear that up.'

I said, 'Why are you asking me those questions?'

'Oh. They're on the form. It's an OHS enquiry. Office of Health and Safety.'

I said, 'What's this all about?'

'There's been another case reported,' he said, 'that's very similar to your daughter's. But it's a completely different situation. This case involved a forty-two-year-old naturalist sleeping out in the Sierras, some wild-flower expert. Anyway, he was hospitalised in Sacramento five days ago. And he had the same clinical course as your daughter—sudden unexplained onset, no fever, painful erythematous reaction.'

'And an MRI stopped it?'

'I don't know if he had an MRI,' he said. 'But apparently this syndrome—whatever it is—is self-limited. Very sudden onset and very abrupt termination.'

'He's OK now? The naturalist?'

'He's fine. A couple of days of bruising and nothing more.'

Then he asked me to call if there was any change in Amanda, I said I would and hung up.

I went back to the crib and picked Amanda up—and in an instant she had my glasses off. I grabbed for them as she squealed with pleasure. 'Amanda . . .' But too late; she threw them on the floor.

I blinked.

I don't see well without my glasses. I got down on my hands and knees, still holding the baby, and swept my hand across the floor in circles. I set the baby down and edged forward. Then I saw a glint of light underneath the crib. I retrieved the glasses and put them on.

In the process I found myself staring at the electrical outlet on the wall underneath the crib. A small plastic box was plugged into the outlet. I pulled it out. It was a two-inch cube, a surge suppressor by the look of it, an ordinary commercial product. A white label ran across the bottom, reading PROP. SSVT, with a bar code. It was one of those stickers that companies put on their inventory.

I turned the cube over in my hand. Where had this come from?

I got to my feet and looked round the room to see what else was different. To my surprise, I realised that everything was different—but just slightly. Amanda's nightlight had Winnie-the-Pooh characters printed on the shade. I always kept Tigger facing towards her crib, because Tigger was her favourite. Now, Eeyore faced the crib. Amanda's changing pad was stained in one corner; I always kept the stain bottom left. Now it was top right. And there was more—

The maid came in behind me. 'Maria,' I said, 'did you clean this room today?'

'No, Mr Forman.'

'But the room is different,' I said.

She looked around and shrugged. 'No, Mr Forman. The same.'

I read confusion in her face and this deepened when I showed her the cube in my hand. 'Have you seen this before?'

She shook her head. 'No.'

'It was under the crib.'

'I don't know, Mr Forman.' She inspected it, turning it in her hand. She shrugged and gave it back to me.

'OK, Maria,' I said. 'Never mind.'

She bent over to scoop up the baby. 'I feed her now.'

'Yes, OK.'

I left the room, feeling odd.

THERE WERE TIMES when the relentless pace of life at home seemed to defeat me, to leave me feeling washed out and hollow. Today, even though I knew I should really get the shopping done before I picked up the kids from school, I needed just to sit for a few hours.

I wondered idly if Julia was going to call me tonight with a different excuse. I wondered what I would do if she walked in one of these days and announced she was in love with someone else. I wondered what I would do if I still didn't have a job by then.

I wondered when I would get a job again. I turned the little surge suppressor over in my hand idly, as my mind drifted. I must have dozed briefly, because the next time I glanced at the clock it was almost time to go and pick up the kids.

ERIC DID HIS HOMEWORK in the car while we waited for Nicole to finish her play rehearsal. She came out in a bad mood; she had thought she was in line for a lead role, but instead the drama teacher had cast her in the chorus.

'Only two lines!' she said, slamming the car door. 'You want to know what I say? I say, "Look, here comes John now." And in the second act, I say, "That sounds pretty serious." Two lines!' She sat back and closed her eyes. 'I don't understand what Mr Blakey's problem is!'

'Maybe he thinks you suck,' Eric said.

'Rat turd!' She smacked him on the head. 'Stink-brain dimrod!'

'That's enough,' I said, as I started the car. I shot Nicole a glance in the rearview mirror. She looked on the verge of tears. I said, 'Honey, I'm really sorry you didn't get the part you wanted.'

'I don't care. Really. It's in the past. I'm moving on.' And then a moment later, 'You know who got it? That little suckup Katie Richards! Mr Blakey is just a dick!' And before I could say anything, she burst into tears.

I drove home, making a mental note to speak to Nicole about her language after dinner, when she had calmed down.

I WAS CHOPPING green beans when Eric came and stood in the kitchen doorway. 'Hey, Dad, where's my MP3 player?'

'I have no idea.' I could never get used to the idea that I was supposed to know where every one of their personal possessions was. Eric's Game Boy, his baseball glove, Nicole's tank tops . . .

'Well, I can't find it.'

'Have you looked?'

'Everywhere, Dad.'

'Uh-huh. You looked in your room?'

'All over.'

'Since you've already looked everywhere, I won't be able to find it either, will I?'

'Dad. Would you please just help me?'

The pot roast had another half-hour to go. I put down the knife and went into Eric's room. I looked in all the usual places, the back of his closet and under the piles of stuff on his desk. Eric was right. It wasn't in his room. We headed towards the family room. I glanced in at the baby's room as I passed by. And I saw it immediately. It was on the shelf beside the changing table. Eric grabbed it. 'Hey, thanks Dad!' And he scampered off.

There was no point in asking why it was in the baby's room. I went back to the kitchen and resumed chopping. Almost immediately:

'Daa-ad!'

'What?' I called.

'It doesn't work!' He came back to the kitchen, looking sulky. 'Amanda must have drooled on it or something, and she broke it.'

'You check the battery?'

He gave me a pitying look. ''Course, Dad. I told you, she broke it!'

I doubted his MP3 player was broken. These things were solid-state devices, no moving parts. And it was too large for the baby to handle. I held out my hand. 'Give it to me.'

We went into the garage and I got out my toolbox. Eric watched as I took the back cover off. I found myself staring at the green circuit board. It was covered by a fine layer of greyish dust, like lint, that obscured all the electronic components. I blew the dust away, hoping to see a loose battery connection, or something that would be easy to fix. I squinted at the chips, trying to read the writing. The writing on one chip was obscured, because there seemed to be some kind of—

I paused.

'What is it?' Eric said, watching me.

I swung my high-intensity lamp low and bent over the chip, examining it closely. The reason I couldn't read the writing was that the surface of the chip had been corroded. I understood now where the dust had come from. It was the disintegrated remains of the memory chip.

'Can you fix it, Dad?' Eric said. 'Can you?'

What could have caused this? The rest of the motherboard seemed fine. I wasn't a hardware guy, but I'd handled memory chips before, and I'd never seen anything like this.

'Dad? Can you fix it?'

'No,' I said. 'It needs another chip. I'll get you one tomorrow.'

'Cause she slimed it, right?'

'No. I think it's just a faulty chip.'

'Dad. It was fine for a whole year. She slimed it. It's not fair!'

As if on cue, the baby started crying. I went back inside the house. I would just have time to change Amanda's diaper and mix her cereal for dinner before the pot roast came out.

BY NINE, the younger kids were asleep and the house was quiet except for Nicole's voice, saying, '*That* sounds pretty serious. That *sounds* pretty serious. That sounds . . . *pretty serious*.' She was standing in front of the bathroom mirror, reciting her lines.

I'd had voicemail from Julia saying she'd be back by eight, but she hadn't made it. I wasn't about to call and check up on her. Anyway, I was too tired to work up the energy to worry about her.

After I'd done the cooking, fed the kids, played airplane to get the baby to eat her cereal, cleared the table, put the baby to bed and then cleaned up the kitchen, I was tired.

I flopped down on the bed and flicked on the TV.

There was only static, and then I realised the DVD player was still turned on. I hit the remote button and the disc in the machine began to play. It was Julia's demo, from three days before.

Julia was speaking to camera.

'The images you have seen are fleeting, but we can allow the camera to cycle through for as much as half an hour, and we can build up highly detailed composites of anything we want to see. When we are finished, we simply shunt the blood through an intravenous loop surrounded by a strong magnetic field, removing the particles, and then send the patient home.

'In the United States alone, more than thirty million people have diagnosed cardiovascular disease. Commercial prospects for this imaging technology are very strong. Because it is painless, safe and easy to administer, it will replace other imaging techniques and angiography and will become the standard procedure. Our per-test cost will be only twenty dollars. But at a mere twenty dollars, we expect worldwide revenues to exceed four hundred million dollars in the first year. And once the procedure is established, those figures will triple. Now, if there are questions . . .'

I yawned and flicked the TV off. It was impressive, and her argument was compelling. In fact, I couldn't understand why Xymos was having trouble getting their next round of funding.

But then, she probably wasn't having trouble. She was probably just using the funding crisis as an excuse to stay late every night. For her own reasons.

I stood up, and went to check the kids. Nicole was still up, emailing her friends. I told her it was time for lights out. Eric had kicked off his covers. I pulled them back up. The baby was still purple, but she slept soundly, her breathing gentle and regular.

I climbed into bed and, after a lot of tossing and turning, I finally fell into a restless sleep.

And I had a very strange dream.

SOME TIME DURING the night, I rolled over to see Julia standing by the bed, undressing. She was moving slowly, as if tired or very dreamy, unbuttoning her blouse. She was turned away from me, but I could see her beautiful face in the mirror. Her features looked more chiselled than I remembered, though perhaps it was just the light, and she appeared to be whispering something, or praying.

Then, as I watched, her lips turned dark red and then black. She didn't seem to notice. The blackness flowed away from her mouth across her cheeks and onto her neck. I held my breath. I felt great danger. The blackness now flowed in a sheet down her body until she was entirely covered, as if with a cloak. Only the upper half of her face remained exposed. Watching her, I felt a chill run deep into my bones. Then a moment later the black sheet slid to the floor and vanished.

Julia, normal again, finished removing her blouse and walked into the bathroom.

I wanted to get up and follow her, but heavy fatigue held me down on the bed, overwhelming my consciousness. Losing all awareness, I felt my eyes close and I slept.

DAY 4: 6.40AM

The next morning the dream was still fresh in my mind, vivid and disturbing. It felt utterly real, not like a dream at all.

Julia was already up. I got out of bed and walked round to where I had seen her the night before. I looked down at the rug, the bedside table. There was nothing unusual, nothing out of order. However disturbing my dream had been, it was still a dream.

But one part of it was true enough: Julia was looking more beautiful than ever. When I found her in the kitchen, pouring coffee, I saw that her face did indeed look more chiselled, more striking. Julia had always had a chubby face. Now it was lean, defined. She looked like a high-fashion model. Her body, too—now that I looked closely—appeared leaner, more muscular.

I said, 'You look great.'

She laughed. 'I can't imagine why. I'm exhausted.'

'What time did you get in?'

'About eleven. I hope I didn't wake you.'

'No. But I had a weird dream.'

'Oh yes?'

'Yes, it was—'

'Mommy! Mommy!' Eric burst into the kitchen. 'Nicole won't get out of the bathroom. She's been in there for an hour. It's not fair!'

'Go use our bathroom.'

'But I need my socks, Mommy. It's not fair.'

This was a familiar problem. Eric had a couple of pairs of favourite socks that he wore day after day until they were black with grime. For some reason, his other socks were not satisfactory.

'Eric,' I said, 'we talked about this, you must wear clean socks.'

'But those are my good ones! And she's been in there an hour, Dad. I'm not kidding. It's not fair.'

'Eric, go choose other socks.'

'Dad . . .'

I just pointed my finger towards his bedroom.

'Shees.' He walked off muttering about how it wasn't fair.

I turned back to Julia to resume our conversation. She was staring at me coldly. 'You really don't get it, do you?'

'Get what?'

'He came in talking to me, and you just took over.'

Immediately, I realised she was right. 'I'm sorry,' I said.

'This really is a problem, Jack. I don't think you are sorry. You keep shutting me out. Keeping me from my children—'

I took a breath. 'Julia, damn it, *you're never here*!'

A frosty silence. Then: 'I certainly am here. Don't you dare say that I'm not.'

'And when was the last time you made it for dinner, Julia? Not last night, not the night before. Not all week. You are *not* here.'

She glared at me. 'I don't know what kind of game you are playing, Jack, but I balance a very demanding job, a *very* demanding job, and the needs of my family. And I get absolutely no help from you.'

'What are you talking about?' I said, my voice rising still higher. I was starting to have a sense of unreality here.

'You undercut me, you sabotage me, you turn the children against me,' she said. 'I see what you're doing. Don't think I don't. And I must say it's a lousy thing to do to your wife.'

And she stalked out of the room, fists clenched. She was so angry, she didn't see that Nicole was standing back from the door, listening to the whole thing. And staring at me, as her mother swept past.

NOW WE WERE driving to school. 'She's crazy, Dad.'

'No, she's not.'

'You know that she is. You're just pretending.'

'Nicole, she's your mother,' I said. 'Your mother is not crazy. She's working very hard right now.'

Nicole snorted. 'I don't know why you put up with her.'

'And I don't know why you were listening to what is none of your business.'

'Dad, why do you pull that crap with me? It's not normal, what she's doing. I know you think she's crazy.'

'I don't,' I said.

From the back seat, Eric whacked her on the back of the head. 'You're the one who's crazy,' he said.

'Shut up, butt breath.'

'I don't want to hear any more from either of you,' I said loudly.

By then we were pulling into the driveway in front of the school. The kids piled out. Nicole jumped out of the front seat, turned back to get her backpack, shot me a look and was gone.

I DIDN'T THINK Julia was crazy, but something had certainly changed, and as I replayed that morning's conversation in my head, I felt uneasy for other reasons. A lot of her comments sounded like she was building a case against me.

Every father knew the legal system was hopelessly biased in favour of mothers. Even if she was absent.

I had worked myself into a fine lather when my cellphone rang. It was Julia. She was calling to apologise.

'I'm really sorry. I said stupid things today. I didn't mean it.'

'What?'

'Jack, I know you support me. Of course you do. I couldn't manage without you. You're doing a great job with the kids. I'm just not myself these days. I'm sorry I said those things, Jack.'

When I got off the phone I thought, I wish I had recorded that.

I HAD A TEN O'CLOCK meeting with my headhunter, Annie Gerard. We met in the sunny courtyard of a coffee shop on Baker. She had her laptop out and her modem plugged in.

'Got anything?' I said, sitting down opposite her.

'As a matter of fact I do. How about this? Chief research analyst for IBM, working on advanced distributed systems architecture.'

'Right up my alley.'

'I thought so, too. You're highly qualified for this one, Jack. You'd run a research lab of sixty people. Base pay two-fifty plus royalties on anything developed in your lab.'

'Sounds great. Where?'

'Armonk.'

'New York?' I shook my head. 'No way, Annie. Julia's got a job she likes, she's very devoted to it, and she won't leave it now.'

'People move all the time. Many of them have working wives, too.' Annie stared at me over the laptop screen. 'I think you better cut the crap, Jack. You're not in a position to be picky. You're starting to have a shelf-life problem.'

'Shelf life?' I said.

'You've been out of work six months now, Jack. Companies figure if it takes you that long to find a job, there must be something wrong with you. Pretty soon, they won't even interview. Not in San Jose, not in Armonk, not in Cambridge. You've got to talk to your wife. You've got to figure out a way to get yourself off the shelf.'

'But I can't leave the Valley. I have to stay here.'

'Here is not so good.' She flipped the screen up again. 'Whenever I bring up your name, I keep getting—listen, what's going on at MediaTronics, anyway? Is Don Gross going to be indicted?'

'I don't know.'

'I've been hearing that rumour for months now, but it never seems to happen. For your sake, I hope it happens soon.'

'I don't get it,' I said. 'I'm perfectly positioned in a hot field, multi-agent distributed processing, and—'

'Hot?' she said, squinting at me. 'Distributed processing's not hot, it's *radioactive*. Everybody in the Valley figures the breakthroughs in artifical life are going to come from distributed processing.'

'They are,' I said, nodding. In the last few years, artificial life had replaced artificial intelligence as a long-term computing goal. The idea was to write programs that had the attributes of living creatures—the ability to adapt, cooperate, learn, adjust to change. Most of these qualities were especially important in robotics, and they were starting to be realised with distributed processing.

Annie was tapping me on the hand. I blinked.

'Jack, did you hear anything I just said to you?'

'Sorry.'

'You're right. You are in a hot field. But that's all the more reason to worry about shelf life. You're at risk, Jack. So, will you talk to your wife? Please? Because otherwise I can't help you.'

I SAT AT MY DESK at home, trying to think what to do. I knew it was a waste of time even to bring up moving with Julia. She'd certainly say no—especially if she had a new boyfriend. But I had to ask. I had another hour and a half before I picked up the kids. I decided to call Julia and talk to her about it.

I was put through to Carol, her assistant. 'Carol, it's Jack.'

'Oh, hi, Mr Forman. How are you?'

'I'm fine, thanks.'

'Are you looking for Julia?'

'Yes, I am.'

'She's in Nevada for the day, at the fabrication plant. Shall I try to connect you there?'

'Yes, please.'

'One moment.'

I was put on hold. For quite a while.

'Mr Forman, she's in a meeting for the next hour. I expect her to call back when it breaks up. Do you want me to tell her anything?'

'No, thanks, Carol,' I said. 'Just ask her to call.'

'OK, Mr Forman.'

I hung up and stared into space. *She's in Nevada for the day.* Julia had said nothing to me about going to Nevada. I replayed the conversation with Carol in my mind. Was she covering? I couldn't be sure. I couldn't be sure of anything now. I began to feel depressed. It seemed like everything was wrong. I had no job, my wife was absent, the kids were a pain, I felt constantly inadequate dealing with them.

And then the baby began to cry.

DAY 5: 7.10AM

When I awoke the next morning, I saw that Julia's side of the bed was still made up, her pillow uncreased. She hadn't come home last night at all. I checked the telephone messages; there were none. Eric wandered in and saw the bed. 'Where's Mom?'

'I don't know, son.'

'Did she leave already?'

'I guess so . . .'

He stared at me, and then at the unmade bed. And he walked out of the room. He wasn't going to deal with it.

But I was beginning to think I had to. Maybe I should even talk to a lawyer. Except in my mind, there was something irrevocable about talking to a lawyer and I didn't want to believe my marriage was over.

That was when I decided to call my sister in San Diego. Ellen is a clinical psychologist, she has a practice in La Jolla. It was early enough that I figured she hadn't gone to the office yet. She sounded surprised I had called. I told her briefly about the things I'd been suspecting about Julia, and why.

'You're saying Julia didn't come home and she didn't call?'

'Right.'

'Did you call her?'

'Not yet.'

'How come?'

'I don't know.'

'Maybe she was in an accident, maybe she's hurt . . .'

'I don't think so. You always hear if there's an accident. There's other things going on, too. She's starting to say that I'm turning the kids against her. It's like she's trying to build a case against me.'

'Alienation of affection,' she said. 'Legal *cliché du jour*. Jack, you've got a problem. Why aren't you doing something?'

'Like what?'

'Like see a marriage counsellor. Or a lawyer.'

'Oh, jeez.'

'Don't you think you should?' she asked.

'I don't know. No. Not yet.'

A pause. 'Jack, I'm worried about you. Are you depressed?'

'No. Why?'

'Sleeping OK? Exercising?'

'Fair. Not really exercising that much.'

'Uh-huh. Do you have a job yet?'

'No.'

'Jack,' she said. 'You have to see a lawyer.'

'Maybe in a while.'

She sighed, a long exasperated hiss. 'OK. Listen, I'm taking a couple of days and coming up to see you.'

'Ellen—'

'Don't argue. I'm coming. You can tell Julia I'm going to help out with the kids. I'll be up there this afternoon.'

'But—'

'Don't argue.'

I CALLED JULIA to tell her that Ellen was coming up for a few days. Of course, I didn't reach Julia, so I left a longish message on her voicemail. Then I went to do the shopping because, with Ellen staying over, we'd need some extra supplies.

I was rolling my cart down the supermarket aisle when I got a call from the hospital. It was the beardless ER doctor again. He was calling to check on Amanda and I said her bruises were almost gone.

'That's good,' he said. 'Glad to hear it.'

I said, 'What about the MRI?'

The doctor said the MRI results were not relevant, because the machine had malfunctioned and had never examined Amanda. 'In fact, we're worried about all the readings for the last few weeks,' he said. 'Because apparently the machine was slowly breaking down. All the memory chips were being corroded, or something.'

I remembered Eric's MP3 player. 'Why would that happen?' I said.

'The best guess is it's been corroded by some gas that escaped from the wall lines, probably during the night. But the thing is, only the memory chips were damaged. The others were fine.'

THINGS WERE GETTING stranger by the minute. And they got stranger still a few minutes later, when Julia called all cheerful and upbeat, to announce that she was coming home in the afternoon and would be there in plenty of time for dinner.

'It'll be great to see Ellen,' she said. 'Why is she coming?'

'I think she just wanted to get out of town.'

I waited for her to explain why she hadn't come home. But all she said was, 'Hey, I got to run, Jack, I'll talk to you later—'

'Julia,' I said. 'Wait a minute.'

'What?'

I hesitated, wondering how to put it. I said, 'I was worried about you last night, when you didn't come home.'

'Honey, I called you. I got stuck out at the plant. Didn't you check your messages?'

'Yes . . . There was no message.'

'Well, I don't know what happened. I left a message on your cell.'

'Well, I didn't get it,' I said, trying not to sound like I was pouting.

'Sorry about that, honey, but check your service. Anyway listen, I really have to go. See you tonight, OK? Kiss kiss.'

And she hung up.

I CHECKED my cellphone. There was no message. No calls last night.

Julia hadn't called me. No one had called me.

I began to feel a sinking sensation. I felt tired, I stared at the produce on the supermarket shelves. I couldn't remember why I was there.

I had decided to leave the supermarket when my cellphone rang again. I flipped it open. It was Tim Bergman, the guy who had taken over my job at MediaTronics. 'Are you sitting down?' he said.

'No. Why?'

'I've got some pretty strange news. Don wants to call you.'

Don Gross, the guy who had fired me. 'What for?'

'He wants to hire you back.'

'He wants *what*? Why?' I said.

'We're having some problems with distributed systems that we've sold to customers.'

'Which ones?'

'Well, PREDPREY.'

'That's one of the old ones,' I said. 'Who bought that?'

Like most of our programs, PREDPREY had been based on biological models. It was a goal-seeking program based on predator/prey dynamics. But it was extremely simple in its structure.

'Well, Xymos wanted something very simple,' Tim said.

'You sold PREDPREY to Xymos?'

'Right. Licensed, actually. With a contract to support it. But it isn't working right, apparently. Goal seeking has gone haywire. A lot of the time, the program seems to lose its goal.'

'I'm not surprised,' I said, 'because we didn't specify reinforcers.' Reinforcers were program weights that sustained the goals; since the networked agents could learn as they went along, they might learn in a way that caused them to drift away from the goal. In fact, you could easily come to think of agent programs as children. The programs forgot things, lost things, dropped things.

It was all emergent behaviour. It wasn't programmed, but it was the outcome of programming.

'Well,' Tim said, 'Don figures you were running the team when the program was originally written, so you're the guy to fix it. Plus, your wife is high up in Xymos management, so your joining the team will reassure their top people.'

I wasn't so sure. 'Tim,' I said. 'I can't go back to work there.'

'Oh, you wouldn't be here. You'd be up at the Xymos fab plant. Hired as an off-site consultant. Something like that.'

'Uh-huh,' I said, in my best noncommittal tone. The last thing I wanted to do was go back to work for Don. But, on the other hand, if I agreed to work as a consultant, it would get rid of my shelf-life problem. After a pause, I said, 'Listen, Tim, let me think about it.'

'You want to call me back tomorrow morning?' he said, hinting.

'OK,' I said. 'Yes, tomorrow morning.'

'OF COURSE you told them yes,' Ellen said to me. She had just arrived and we were in the kitchen. Ellen looked exactly the same, still rail-thin, energetic, blonde, hyper. My sister never seemed to age. She was drinking a cup of tea from special organic tea bags that she had brought with her. That hadn't changed, either—Ellen always travelled around with her own teas, her own salad dressings, her own vitamins.

'No, I didn't,' I said. 'I said I'd think about it.'

'Are you kidding? Jack, you *have* to go back to work. You know you do.' She stared at me, appraising. 'You're depressed.'

'I'm not.'

'You should have some of this tea,' she said. 'All that coffee is bad for your nerves.'

'Tea has more caffeine than coffee.'

'And if it's a consulting job . . . wouldn't that be perfect?'

'I don't know,' I said.

'Really? What don't you know?'

'I don't know if I'm getting the full story,' I said. 'I mean, if Xymos is having all this trouble, why hasn't Julia said anything about it to me?'

Ellen shook her head. 'It sounds like Julia isn't saying much of anything to you these days.'

'I need to check around before I make a decision.'

'Check what, Jack?' Her tone conveyed disbelief. Ellen was acting like I had a psychological problem that needed to be fixed, and it was starting to get to me. My older sister, treating me like a kid again. 'Listen, Ellen,' I said. 'I've spent my life in this business, and I know how it works. There's two possible reasons Don wants me back. The first is the company's in a jam and they think I can help.'

'That's what they said.'

'Right. But the other possibility is that they've made an incredible mess of things and now it can't be fixed—and they know it.'

She frowned. 'So they want somebody to blame?'

'Right. I have to see if I can find out.'

'Which you will do by . . .'

'By making some calls. Maybe paying a visit to the fab building.'

'OK. That sounds right to me.'

'I'm glad I have your approval.' I couldn't keep the irritation out of my voice.

'Jack,' she said. She got up and hugged me. 'I'm just worried about you, that's all.'

'I appreciate that,' I said. 'But you're not helping me.'

'OK. Then what can I do to help you?'

'Watch the kids, while I make some calls.'

I FIGURED I WOULD first call Ricky Morse, one of the division heads at Xymos. I'd given him his first job, right out of college, and he'd rapidly moved into management. With his cheerful personality and upbeat manner, Ricky made an ideal project manager, even though he tended to underplay problems and give management unrealistic expectations about when a project would be finished. But he was so cheerful and appealing that everyone always forgave him. I had stayed friendly with Ricky and he was casual enough about information that he might tell me what was really going on at Xymos.

I called his office, but the receptionist said, 'I'm sorry, Mr Morse is not in the office.'

'When is he expected back?'

'I really couldn't say. Do you want voicemail?'

I left Ricky a voicemail message. Then I called his home number.

His wife answered. Mary was getting her Ph.D in French history alongside raising a young family. I imagined her studying, bouncing the baby, with a book open on her lap. I said, 'How are you, Mary?'

'I'm fine, Jack.'

'How's the baby?' I tried to sound casual. Just a social call.

'She's a good baby, Jack, thank God.'

I said, 'Actually, I'm looking for Ricky. Is he there?'

'No, Jack. He's been out at that fab plant in Nevada.'

'Oh, right.'

'Julia is there a lot, isn't she? What does she say about it?' I detected an uneasy tone.

'Well, not much. I gather they have new technology that's very hush-hush. Why?'

She hesitated. 'Maybe it's my imagination . . . But sometimes, when Ricky calls, he sounds kind of weird to me. I'm sure he's distracted and working hard, but he says some strange things. And he seems evasive. Like he's, I don't know, hiding something.'

'Hiding something . . .'

She gave a self-deprecating laugh. 'I even thought maybe he's having an affair. You know, that woman Mae Chang is out there, and he always liked her. She's so pretty.'

Mae Chang used to work in my division at MediaTronics. 'I hadn't heard she was at the fab plant.'

'Yes. A lot of people who used to work for you are there now.'

'Well,' I said. 'I don't think Ricky can be having an affair, Mary. It's just not like him. And it's not like Mae.'

'It's the quiet ones you have to watch out for,' she said, apparently referring to Mae. 'And I'm still nursing, so I haven't lost my weight yet, I mean, my thighs are as big as sides of beef.'

'Mary, I'm sure—'

'Is Julia OK, Jack? She's not acting weird?'

'No more than usual,' I said, trying to make a joke. I was feeling bad as I said it. For days I had wished that people would level with me about Julia, but now that I had something to share with Mary, I wasn't going to level with her. I was going to keep my mouth shut. I said, 'Julia's working hard, and she sometimes is a little odd.'

'Does she say anything about a black cloud?'

'Uh . . . no.'

'She mention a black cloak?'

I felt suddenly slowed down. Moving very slowly. 'What?'

'The other night Ricky was talking about being covered in a black cloak. It was late, he was tired, he was sort of babbling.'

'What did he say about the black cloak?'

'Nothing. Just that.' She paused. 'You think they're taking drugs out there? There's so much pressure, working around the clock.'

'Let me call Ricky,' I said.

It was a warm evening and we had dinner in the back yard. Julia got home on time and was charming and chatty, focusing her attention on my sister, talking about the kids, about school, about changes she wanted to make on the house. I was astonished by her performance. Even the kids were staring at her. Julia mentioned how proud she was of Nicole's big part in the forthcoming school play.

Nicole said, 'Mom, I have a *bad* part.'

'Oh, not really, honey,' Julia said.

'Yes, I do. I just have two lines.'

'And she says 'em in the bathroom, over and over,' Eric announced. 'About a billion gazillion times.'

'Shut up, weasel turd.'

'Oh. Well, anyway, I'm sure you'll be wonderful. And our little Eric is making such progress in soccer, aren't you, hon?'

'It's over next week,' Eric said, turning sulky. Julia hadn't made it to any of his games this fall.

Ellen wasn't saying anything, just nodding and listening.

For this particular evening, Julia had insisted on feeding the baby, and had positioned the high chair beside her. But Amanda was accustomed to playing airplane at every mealtime. She was waiting for someone to move the spoon towards her, saying, 'Rrrrrr-owwwww . . . here comes the airplane . . . open the doors!' Since Julia wasn't doing that, Amanda kept her mouth tightly shut.

'Oh well. I guess she's not hungry,' Julia said, with a shrug. 'Did she just have a bottle, Jack?'

'No,' I said. 'She doesn't get one until after dinner.'

'Well, I know that. I meant, before.'

'No,' I said. I gestured towards Amanda. 'Shall I try?'

'Sure.' Julia handed me the spoon and I sat beside Amanda and began to play airplane. 'Rrrrr-owwww . . .' Amanda immediately grinned and opened her mouth.

'Jack's been just wonderful with the kids,' Julia said to Ellen.

'I think it's good for a man to experience home life,' Ellen said.

'Oh, it is.' She patted my knee. 'You've helped such a lot, Jack.'

It was clear to me that Julia was too bright, too cheerful. She was keyed up, obviously trying to impress Ellen that she was in charge of her family. Ellen wasn't buying it, but Julia was so speedy she didn't notice. I began to wonder if she were on drugs. Was that the reason for her strange behaviour?

'And work,' Julia continued, 'is so incredible these days. Xymos is really making breakthroughs—the kind people have been waiting for more than ten years to happen. But at last, it's happening.'

'Like the black cloak?' I said, fishing.

Julia blinked. 'The what?' She shook her head. 'What're you talking about, hon?'

'Didn't you say something about a black cloak the other day?'

'No . . .' She shook her head. 'I don't know what you mean.' She turned back to Ellen. 'I have to tell you, it's really thrilling, Ellen.' She lowered her voice. 'And on top of it, we'll probably make a bundle.'

'Great,' Ellen said. 'But I guess you've had to put in long hours . . .'

'Not that long,' Julia said. 'All things considered.'

I saw Nicole's eyes widen. Eric was staring at his mother as he ate. But the kids didn't say anything. Neither did I.

'It's just a transition period,' Julia continued. 'All companies have these transitional periods.'

'Of course,' Ellen said.

The sun was going down. The air was cooler. The kids left the table. I got up and started to clear. Julia kept talking, then said, 'I'd love to stay, but I have to get back to the office for a while.'

At the door, she turned, blew me an air kiss and was gone.

Ellen frowned, watching her go. 'Just a little abrupt, wouldn't you say? Will she say goodbye to the kids?'

I shrugged. 'Probably not.'

Ellen shook her head. 'Jack,' she said, 'I don't know if she's having an affair or not, but—what's she taking?'

'Nothing, as far as I know.'

'She's on something. I'm certain of it.' Ellen shook her head. 'A lot of these hard-charging executives are on drugs.'

'I don't know,' I said.

She just looked at me.

I WENT BACK into my office to call Ricky, and from the office window I saw Julia backing her BMW convertible down the driveway. In the evening light I saw golden reflections on the windshield, streaking from the trees above. She had almost reached the street when I thought I saw a man sitting in the passenger seat beside her.

I couldn't see his features clearly through the windshield, with the car moving down the drive. When Julia backed onto the street, her body blocked my view of the passenger. But it seemed as if Julia was talking to him, animatedly. Then she put the car in gear and leaned back in her seat, and for a moment I had a brief, clear look. The man was backlit, his face in shadow, but from the way he was slouching I had the impression of someone young, maybe in his twenties. It was just a glimpse. Then the BMW accelerated and she drove off.

I thought: the hell with this. I ran outside and down the driveway. I reached the street just as Julia came to the stop sign to the end of the block, her brake lights flaring. She was probably fifty yards away, the street illuminated in low, slanting yellow light. It looked as if she was alone in the car, but I really couldn't see well. I felt a moment of relief, and of foolishness; my mind was playing tricks on me.

Then, as Julia made the right turn, the guy popped up again, like he had been bent over, getting something from the glove compartment. And in an instant all my distress came flooding back, like a hot pain that spread across my chest and body.

There *was* somebody in the car.

I trudged back up the driveway, feeling churning emotions, not sure what to do next.

'YOU'RE NOT SURE what to do next?' Ellen said. We were doing the pans at the sink, the things that didn't go in the dishwasher. Ellen was drying, while I scrubbed. 'You call her.'

'Uh-huh,' I said. 'So how do I put it? Hey, Julia, who's the guy in the car with you?' I shook my head.

She set down one of the pots with a bang. 'Jack. I understand that all this must be hard to accept.'

'It is, it is.' In my mind, I kept replaying the car backing down the driveway, over and over. I was thinking that there was something strange about the other person in the car, that I couldn't see the eyes, or the cheekbones or the mouth. In my memory, the whole face was dark and indistinct. I tried to explain that to her.

'It's not surprising.'

'No?'

'No. It's called denial. Look Jack, the fact is, you have seen the evidence. Don't you think it's time you believed it?'

I knew she was right. 'Yes,' I said. 'It's time.'

The phone was ringing. My hands were covered in soap suds. I asked Ellen to get it, but one of the kids had already picked it up.

'Jack,' Ellen said, 'you have to start seeing things as they really are and not as you want them to be.'

'You're right,' I said. 'I'll call her.'

At that moment Nicole came into the kitchen, looking pale.

'Dad? It's the police. They want to talk to you.'

DAY 5: 9.10PM

Julia's convertible had gone off the road about five miles from the house. It had plunged fifty feet down a steep ravine, cutting a track through the sage and juniper bushes. Then it must have rolled, because now it lay at an angle, wheels facing upwards. The sun was almost down and the ravine was dark. The three rescue ambulances on the road had their red lights flashing, and the rescue crews were already rappelling down on ropes. As I watched, portable floodlights were set up, bathing the wreck in a harsh blue glow.

'Is she hurt? Is my wife hurt?' I asked a motorcycle police officer.

'We'll know in a minute.' He was calm. He had a radio headset in his helmet, and he started talking in a low voice, using codewords.

I stood at the edge and looked down, trying to see. By now there were workers all around the car. A long time seemed to pass.

The cop said, 'Your wife is unconscious but she's . . . She was wearing her seat belt and stayed in the car. They think she's all right. Vital signs are stable. They say no spinal injuries but . . . '

'But she's all right?'

'They think so.' Another pause while he listened. When he turned back, he said, 'Yes. She's coming round. She'll be checked for internal bleeding at the hospital. They're getting her on a stretcher now.'

'Thank God,' I said, flipping open my cellphone. I called Ellen, told her to explain to the kids there was nothing to worry about, that Mom was going to be OK. 'Especially Nicole,' I said.

'I'll take care of it,' Ellen promised me.

I flipped the phone shut and turned back to the cop. 'What about the other guy?' I said.

'She's alone in the car.'

'No,' I said. 'There was another guy with her.'

He spoke on his headset, then turned back to me. 'They say no. There's no sign of anyone else.'

'Maybe he was thrown,' I said.

'They're asking your wife now . . .' He listened a moment. 'She says she was alone.' He looked at me and shrugged.

I turned away, looked over the edge of the road.

One of the rescue vehicles had extended a steel arm with a winch that hung over the ravine. A cable was being lowered.

A few minutes later the stretcher slowly rose into the air. I couldn't see Julia clearly, she was strapped down, covered in a silver space blanket. When the stretcher reached the level of the road the rescue workers swung it round and unclipped it from the line. Julia's face was swollen; her left cheekbone was purple and the forehead above her left eye was purple as well. She must have hit her head pretty hard. She was breathing shallowly. I moved alongside the stretcher. She saw me and said, 'Jack . . .' and tried to smile.

'Just take it easy,' I said.

She gave a little cough. 'Jack. It was an accident.'

'Of course it was.'

'It's not what you think, Jack.'

I said, 'What isn't, Julia?' She seemed to be delirious.

'I know what you're thinking.' Her hand gripped my arm. 'Promise me you won't get involved in this, Jack.'

I didn't say anything, I just walked with her.

She squeezed me harder. 'Promise me you'll stay out of it.'

'I promise,' I said.

She relaxed then, dropping my arm.

By now we were approaching the nearest ambulance. I got in first, then they slid the stretcher in and slammed the doors shut.

We started down the road, siren moaning.

At the hospital, the doctor's examination suggested Julia's injuries might be more extensive than they first thought, and they put her into intensive care. There was a lot to rule out: possible pelvic fracture, possible haematoma, possible fracture of a cervical vertebra.

But Julia was conscious, catching my eye and smiling at me from time to time, until she fell asleep. The doctors said there was nothing for me to do; they told me to go home and get some rest. I left the hospital a little before midnight.

I took a taxi back to the crash site, to pick up my car. It was a cold night. The police cars and rescue ambulances were gone. In their place was a big flatbed tow truck, which was winching Julia's car up the hill. A skinny guy smoking a cigarette was running the winch.

'Nothing to see,' he said to me. 'Everybody's at the hospital.'

I said it was my wife's car.

He asked me for my insurance card. I got it out of my wallet and handed it to him. He said, 'I heard your wife's OK.'

'So far.'

'You're a lucky guy.' He jerked his thumb, pointing across the road. 'Are they with you?'

Across the street a small white van was parked. The sides bore no markings, but low on the front door I saw SSVT UNIT.

I said, 'No, they're not with me.'

'Been here an hour,' he said. 'Just sitting there.'

I couldn't see anyone inside the van; the front windows were dark. I started across the street towards it, but when I was about ten feet away the engine started and the van roared off down the highway.

As it passed me, I had a glimpse of the driver. He was wearing a shiny suit of some kind, like silvery plastic, and a tight hood of the same material. I thought I saw some funny, silver apparatus hanging round his neck. It looked like a silver gas mask, but I wasn't sure.

As the van drove away, I noticed the rear bumper had two green stickers, each with a big X. That was the Xymos logo. But it was the licence plate that really caught my eye. It was a Nevada plate.

That van had come from the fabrication plant, out in the desert.

I frowned. It was time for me to visit the fab plant, I thought.

I pulled out my cellphone and dialled Tim Bergman. I told him I had considered his offer and I would take the consulting job.

Day 6: 7.12am

With the vibration of the helicopter, I must have dozed off for a few minutes. I opened my eyes. I was sitting in the front of the helicopter, alongside the pilot. The helicopter was flying east, into the glare of low morning sun. Beneath my feet I saw mostly flat terrain, with low clumps of cactus, juniper, and the occasional scraggly Joshua tree.

The pilot was flying alongside the power-line towers that marched in single file across the desert, a steel army with outstretched arms.

'Xymos Molecular Manufacturing is dead ahead,' he said. 'You can just see it now.'

Twenty miles in front of us, I saw an isolated cluster of low buildings silhouetted on the horizon.

When we got closer, the pilot pointed out the different buildings. 'That first concrete block, that's power. Walkway to that low building, that's the residences. Next door, fab support, labs, whatever. And then the square, windowless three-storey one, that's the main fab building. Over to the right, that low flat shed, that's for parking, with external storage beyond. Cars have to be under shade here or you get a first-degree burn if you touch your steering wheel.'

'So how many people live in this facility?' I said.

'The residences can take twelve,' the pilot said. 'But they've generally got about five to eight. Doesn't take a lot to run the place. It's all automated, from what I hear. I've never been inside. We've been told not to get out of the helicopter.'

The pilot turned the stick in his hand, the helicopter banked and started down. Once we had landed, I opened the plastic door in the bubble cockpit and got out. The blast of heat made me gasp.

'This is nothing!' the pilot shouted, over the whirr of the blades. 'This is almost winter! Can't be more than a hundred and five!'

'Great,' I said, inhaling hot air. I reached into the back for my overnight bag and my laptop, turned and moved away, crouched beneath the blades. I came to the edge of the pad where the concrete ended abruptly in a dirt path that threaded among the clumps of cholla cactus towards the blocky white power building fifty yards away. There was no one to greet me—in fact, no one in sight at all.

Looking back, I saw the pilot waving to me as he rose into the air. I waved back, then ducked away from the swirl of spitting sand. The helicopter circled once and headed west. The sound faded.

The desert was silent except for the hum of electrical power lines. I turned in a slow circle, wondering what to do now.

'Hey! Hey, you!'

I looked back. A door had cracked open in the white power block. A man's head stuck out. He shouted, 'Are you Jack Forman?'

'Yes,' I said.

'Well, what the hell you waiting for, an engraved invitation? Get inside, for Chrissake.'

And he slammed the door shut again.

That was my welcome to the Xymos Fabrication Facility.

Things never turn out the way you expect.

I STEPPED into a small room, with smooth, dark grey walls on three sides. It took my eyes a moment to adjust to the relative darkness. Then I saw that the fourth wall directly ahead of me was entirely glass, leading to a small compartment and a second glass wall. The glass walls were fitted with folding steel arms, ending in metal pressure pads, like you'd expect to see in a bank vault.

Beyond the second glass wall I could see a burly man in blue trousers and a blue work shirt, with the Xymos logo on the pocket. He was clearly the plant maintenance engineer. He gestured to me.

'It's an airlock. Door's automatic. Walk forward.'

I did, and the nearest glass door hissed open. A red light came on. In the compartment ahead, I saw grillework on floor, ceiling and both walls. I hesitated.

'Looks like a damn toaster, don't it?' the man said, grinning. 'But don't worry, it'll just blow you a little. Come ahead.'

I stepped into the glass compartment, and the glass door behind me hissed shut. The pressure pads sealed with a thunk. I felt a slight discomfort in my ears as the airlock pressurised. The man in blue said, 'You might want to close your eyes.'

I closed my eyes and immediately felt chilling spray strike my face and body from all sides. I smelt a stinging odour like acetone, or nail-polish remover. I began to shiver; the liquid was really cold.

The first blast of air came from above my head, a roar that quickly built to hurricane intensity. I stiffened my body to steady myself. My clothes flapped and pressed flat against my body. The wind increased, threatening to tear the bag from my hand. Then the air stopped for a moment and a second blast came up from the floor, lasting only a few moments. Then with a *whoosh* the vacuum pumps kicked in and I felt a slight ache in my ears as the pressure dropped, like an airplane descending. Then silence.

A voice said, 'That's it. Come ahead.'

I opened my eyes. The liquid they'd sprayed on me had evaporated; my clothes were dry. The doors hissed open before me. I stepped out and the man said, 'I'm Vince Reynolds,' but he didn't hold out his hand. 'You call me Vince. And you're Jack?'

I said I was.

'OK, Jack,' he said. 'They're waiting for you, so let's get started. We got to take precautions, because this is an HMF, that's high magnetic field environment, so . . .' He picked up a cardboard box. 'Better lose your watch.'

I put the watch in the box.

'And the belt.'

I took my belt off, put it in the box.

'Any other jewellery? Piercings? MedicAlert?'

'No.'

'How about metal inside your body? Old injury, bullets, shrapnel? No? Any pins for broken arms or legs, hip or knee replacement? No?'

I said I didn't have any of those things.

'Well, you're still young,' he said. 'Now, how about in your bag?' He made me take everything out and spread it on a table, so he could rummage through it. I had plenty of metal in there: a can of shaving cream, razor, a pocket knife, blue jeans with metal rivets . . .

He took the knife but left the rest. 'You can put your stuff back in the bag,' he said. 'Now, here's the deal. Your bag goes to the residence building, but no farther. OK? There's an alarm at the residence door if you try to take any metal past there. But do me a favour and don't set it off, OK? 'Cause it shuts down the magnets as a safety procedure and it takes about two minutes to start 'em up again. Pisses the techs off, especially if they're fabbing at the time.'

I said I would try to remember.

'The rest of your stuff stays right here.' He nodded to the dozen wall safes behind me, each with an electronic keypad. 'You set the combination and lock it up yourself.' He turned aside so I could do that.

'I won't need a watch?'

He shook his head. 'We'll get you a watch.'

'And my laptop?' I said.

'It goes in the safe,' he said. 'Unless you want to scrub your hard drive with the magnetic field.'

I put the laptop in with the rest of my stuff and locked the door. I felt strangely stripped, like a man entering prison.

WE ENTERED the power plant. Beneath blue halogen lamps, I saw huge metal tubs ten feet high, and fat ceramic insulators thick as a man's leg. Everything hummed. I felt a distinct vibration in the floor. There were signs all around with jagged red lightning bolts saying WARNING: LETHAL ELECTRICAL CURRENTS!

'You use a lot of power here,' I said.

'Enough for a small town,' Vince said.

We came to another door, with a keypad, and Vince punched in numbers quickly. The door clicked open. 'All the doors are keyed the same. Oh six, oh four, oh two.'

Vince pushed the door wide and we stepped into a covered passageway connecting the power plant to the other buildings. It was stifling hot here, despite the roar of the air conditioner.

At the end of the corridor was another door, and Vince had me punch in the code myself. The door clicked open.

I faced another airlock: a wall of thick glass with another wall beyond. Behind that second wall I saw Ricky Morse in jeans and a T-shirt, grinning and waving cheerfully to me. Over an intercom speaker, he said, 'I'll take it from here, Vince.'

Vince waved. 'No problem.' He slapped me on the back, jerked his thumb towards the interior of the building. 'Lots of luck in there.' Then he turned and walked back the way he'd come.

'It's great to see you,' Ricky said. 'You know the code to get in?'

I said I did. He pointed to a keypad. I punched the numbers in. The glass wall slid sideways. I stepped into another narrow space with metal grilles on all four sides. The wall closed behind me.

A fierce blast of air shot up from the floor, puffing up my trouser legs. Almost immediately it was followed by blasts of air coming from both sides, then from above. Then a *whoosh* of vacuum. The glass in front of me slid laterally and I stepped out.

'Sorry about that.' Ricky shook my hand vigorously. 'But at least we don't have to wear bunny suits,' he said. I noticed that he looked strong, healthy. The muscles in his forearms were defined.

I said, 'You look good, Ricky. Working out?'

'Oh, you know. Not really.' He led me briskly down a short hallway. 'So. How's Julia?'

'She hit her head pretty badly. She's in the hospital for observation. But she's going to be all right.'

'Good. That's good.' He nodded quickly, continuing down a corridor. Despite Ricky's apparent good health I was noticing now that he seemed nervous, edgy. 'Who's taking care of the kids?'

I told him that my sister was in town.

'Then you can stay awhile? A few days?'

I said, 'I guess. If you need me that long.' Ordinarily, software consultants don't spend a lot of time on site.

Ricky glanced over his shoulder at me. 'Did Julia tell you about this place?'

'Not really, no.'

'The last few weeks, she came out almost every day. Stayed over a couple of nights, too.' He opened the far door and waved me through. 'This is our residential module, where everybody sleeps and eats.'

The air was cool after the passageway. A series of doors opened off the hallway. One of them had my name on it, written on a piece of tape. 'Home sweet home, Jack.'

The room was monastic—a small bed, a desk just large enough to hold a work-station monitor and keyboard. Above the bed, a shelf for books and clothes. All the furniture had been coated with smooth-flowing white plastic laminate—no nooks or crannies to hold stray particles of dirt. There was no window in the room either.

Ricky said, 'Dump your gear and I'll give you the tour.'

Still keeping his brisk pace, he led me into a lounge with a couch and chairs around a coffee table, and a bulletin board. All the furniture here was the same flowing plastic laminate. 'To the right is the kitchen and the rec room with TV, video games, so forth.'

We entered the small kitchen, where a man and a woman were eating sandwiches. 'I think you know these guys,' Ricky said, grinning. And I did. They had been on my team at MediaTronics.

Rosie Castro was dark, thin, exotic-looking, and sarcastic; she wore baggy cargo shorts and a T-shirt tight across her large breasts, which read YOU WISH. Independent and rebellious, Rosie had been a protégée of Robert Kim at MIT, working on natural language programming. She was brilliant at it.

I said, 'Still wearing those T-shirts, Rosie.'

'Hey. Keeps the boys awake,' she said, shrugging.

'Actually, we ignore them.' I turned to David Brooks, stiff, formal, obsessively neat, and almost bald at twenty-eight. He blinked behind his glasses. 'They're not that good, anyway,' he said.

Rosie stuck her tongue out at him.

David was an engineer, with an engineer's lack of social skills. He shook my hand enthusiastically. 'Glad you're here, Jack.'

I said, 'Somebody's going to have to tell me why you're all so glad to see me.'

Rosie said, 'Well, it's because you know more about the multi-agent algorithms that—'

'I'm going to show him around first,' Ricky said, interrupting. 'Then we'll talk.'

David looked at his watch. 'Well, how long will that take?'

'I said, Let me show him around, for Christ's sake!' Ricky snarled. I was surprised; I'd never seen him lose his temper before.

'OK, Ricky. You're the boss.'

'That's right, I am,' Ricky said, still visibly angry. 'So let's get back to work.' He looked into the games room. 'Where are the others?'

'Fixing the perimeter sensors.'

'You mean they're *outside*?'

'No, no. They're in the utility room. Bobby thinks there's a calibration problem with the sensor units. He's taking care of it.'

It was then that my cellphone beeped. Surprised, I pulled it out of my pocket. I turned to the others. 'Cellphones work?'

'Yeah,' Ricky said, 'we're wired here.' He went back to his argument with David and Rosie.

I STEPPED into the corridor. A Dr Rana from the hospital was calling.

'Mr Forman, I understand you accompanied your wife to the hospital last night. Yes? Well then you know the seriousness of her injuries, or should I say her potential injuries. We really do feel that she needs to have a thorough workup for pelvic fracture, cervical fracture and for subdural haematoma.'

'Yes,' I said. 'That's what I was told last night. Is there a problem?'

'Actually, there is. Your wife is refusing to have an MRI.'

'She is?'

'Last night, she allowed us to take X-rays, but X-rays are limited in what we can see, and it is important for her to have an MRI, but she says she doesn't need it.'

'Of course she needs it,' I said.

'I don't want to alarm you, Mr Forman, but the concern with pelvic fracture is massive haemorrhaging into the abdomen and, well, bleeding to death. It can happen very quickly, and—'

'What do you want me to do?'

'We'd like you to talk to her.'

'Of course. Put her on.'

'Unfortunately, she's gone for some additional X-rays. Can you be reached later, on your cellphone? All right. One other thing, Mr Forman, we weren't able to take a psychiatric history from your wife.'

'Why is that?'

'She refuses to talk about it. I'm referring to drugs, any history of behavioural disorders, that kind of thing.'

'She's been under a lot of stress lately,' I said.

'Yes, I am sure that contributes,' Dr Rana said smoothly. 'And she has suffered a severe head injury. But frankly it was the opinion of the psychiatric consultant that your wife was suffering from a bipolar disorder, or a drug disorder, or both.'

'I see . . .'

'And of course such questions naturally arise in the context of a single-car automobile accident . . .'

He meant that the accident might be a suicide attempt. I didn't think that was likely. 'I have no knowledge of my wife taking drugs,' I said. 'But I have been concerned about her behaviour recently.'

Ricky came over and stood by me impatiently. He glanced at his watch. I thought it was pretty odd, that he would push me when I was obviously talking to the hospital about Julia.

The doctor rambled on for a while, but the fact was I didn't have any information that could help him. He said he would have Julia call when she got back, and I flipped the phone closed.

Ricky said, 'OK, fine. Sorry to rush you, Jack, but . . . you know, I've got a lot to show you.'

'Is there a time problem?' I said.

'I don't know. Maybe.'

I started to ask what he meant by that, but he was already leading me out of the residential area, down another passageway. This passage, I noticed, was tightly sealed. We walked along a glass walkway suspended above the floor. The glass had little perforations, and beneath was a series of vacuum ducts for suction. By now I was growing accustomed to the constant hiss of the air handlers.

Midway down the passage was another pair of glass doors. We had to go through them one at a time. Once again, I had the distinct feeling of being in a prison, a high-tech and shiny glass-walled prison—but a prison all the same.

DAY 6: 8.12AM

We came into a large room marked UTILITY and beneath it the words MOLSTOCK/FABSTOCK/FEEDSTOCK. Large containers were stacked on the floor. Off to the right I saw a row of big stainless-steel kettles, sunk below ground with lots of piping and valves surrounding them. It looked exactly like a microbrewery, and I was about to ask Ricky about it when he said, 'So there you are!'

Working at a junction box beneath a monitor screen were three more members of my old team. They looked slightly guilty as we came up, like kids caught with their hands in the cookie jar. At thirty-five, Bobby Lembeck now supervised more code than he wrote. As always, he was wearing faded jeans and a T-shirt.

Then there was Mae Chang, beautiful and delicate. Mae had worked as a field biologist in Sichuan studying the golden snub-nosed monkey before turning to programming. Probably as a result of her time in the field, Mae said very little, moved almost soundlessly, and never raised her voice—but she never lost an argument, either.

And finally Charley Davenport, grumpy, rumpled, and already overweight at thirty. Slow and lumbering, he looked as if he had slept in his clothes, and in fact he often did, after a marathon programming session. Charley was an expert in genetic algorithms, the kind of programming that mimicked natural selection to hone answers. But he was an irritating personality—he hummed, he snorted, talked to himself, and farted with noisy abandon. The group only tolerated him because he was so talented.

'Does it really take three people to do this?' Ricky said.

'Yes, it does,' Bobby said. 'Because it's complicated. I checked the sensors after this morning's episode and it looks to me like they're miscalibrated. Mae knows these sensors, she's used them in China. I'm making code revisions now. And Charley is here because he won't go away and leave us alone.'

'Hey, I have better things to do,' Charley said. 'But I'll have to optimise the sensor code when they've stopped screwing around.' He looked at Bobby. 'None of these guys can optimise worth a damn.'

Mae said, 'Bobby can.'

'Yeah, if you give him six months, maybe.'

'Children,' Ricky said. 'Let's not make a scene in front of our guest.'

I smiled blandly. The truth was, I hadn't been paying attention to what they were saying. I was just watching them. These had been three of my best programmers—and when they had worked for me, they had been self-assured to the point of arrogance. But now I was struck by how nervous and on edge the group was. And thinking back, I realised that Rosie and David had been on edge, too.

'Finish up quickly,' Ricky said, 'and get back to your stations.'

LEAVING THE GROUP behind, Ricky took me across the floor to a small room. 'Everybody's a little uptight right now,' he said, stopping before a small cubicle on the other side of the room.

'And why is that?'

'Because of what's going on here.'

'And what is going on here?'

He touched the door with a keycard, the door latch clicked open, and we went inside. I saw a table, two chairs, a computer monitor and a keyboard. Ricky sat down and immediately started typing.

'The medical imaging project Julia was working on was just an afterthought,' he said, 'a minor commercial application of the technology we are already developing.'

'Uh-huh. Which is?'

'Military.'

'Xymos is doing military work?'

'Yes. Under contract.' He paused. 'Two years ago, the Department of Defense realised from their experience in Bosnia that there was enormous value to robot aircraft that could fly overhead and transmit battlefield images. You could use them to spot the locations of enemy troops, even when they were hidden in jungle or in buildings.'

'OK . . .'

'But obviously,' Ricky said, 'these robot cameras were vulnerable. The Pentagon wanted something that couldn't be shot down, something very small, maybe the size of a dragonfly—a target too small to hit. But there were problems with power supply and with resolution using such a small lens. They needed a bigger lens.'

I nodded. 'And so you thought of a swarm of nanocomponents.'

'That's right. A cloud of components would allow you to make a camera with as large a lens as you wanted. And it couldn't be shot down because a bullet would just pass through the cloud. Also, you could disperse the cloud, the way a flock of birds disperses with a gunshot. Then the camera would be invisible until it re-formed. So it seemed an ideal solution. The Pentagon gave us three years' funding.'

'And?'

'It was of course immediately obvious that we had a problem with distributed intelligence.'

I WAS FAMILIAR with the problem. The nanoparticles in the cloud had to be endowed with a rudimentary intelligence, so that they could interact with each other to form a flock that wheeled in the air. Such coordinated activity might look pretty intelligent, but it occurred even when the individuals making up the flock were rather stupid.

Careful study of flocking behaviour—frame-by-frame video analysis—showed that, unlike humans, birds and fish responded to a few simple stimuli among themselves, rather than following a leader. Flocking simply emerged within the group as a result of simple, low-level rules. Rules like, 'Stay close to the birds nearest you, but don't bump into them.' From these rules, the entire group flocked in smooth coordination. The technical definition of behaviour that occurred in a group, but was not programmed into any member of the group, was emergent behaviour.

I said, 'Your problem was emergent behaviour in the swarm?'

'Exactly.'

'It was unpredictable?'

'To put it mildly.'

This notion of emergent group behaviour had caused a minor revolution in computer science. What that meant for programmers was that you could lay down rules of behaviour for individual agents, but not for the agents acting together. For the first time, a program could produce results that absolutely could not be predicted by the programmer. That excited programmers—but it frustrated them, too.

Because the program's emergent behaviour was erratic. Sometimes agents were so influenced by one another that they lost track of their goal and did something else instead. As one programmer put it, 'Trying to program distributed intelligence is like telling a five-year-old to go to his room and change his clothes. He may do that, but he is equally likely to do something else and never return.'

That was why I began, five years ago, to model predator-prey relationships as a way to keep goals fixed. Because hungry predators—packs of hyenas, African hunting dogs, stalking lionesses—weren't distracted. Circumstances might force them to improvise their methods, but they didn't lose track of their goal. This result was a program module called PREDPREY, which could be used to control any system of agents and make its behaviour purposeful. To make the program seek a goal.

I said, 'You used PREDPREY to program your individual units?'

'Right. We used those rules.'

'So what's the problem?'

'We're not sure.'

'What does that mean?'

'It means we know there's a problem, but we're not sure whether it is a programming problem—or something else.'

'Something else? Like what?' I frowned. 'This is just a cluster of microbots. You can make it do what you want.'

Ricky looked at me uneasily. He pushed his chair away from the table and stood up. 'Let me show you how we manufacture these agents,' he said. 'Then you'll understand the situation better.'

I was curious to see what he showed me next. Because many people I respected thought molecular manufacturing was impossible. One of the major theoretical objections was the time it would take to build a working molecule. Because a typical manufactured molecule consisted of 10,000,000,000,000,000,000,000,000 parts. Calculations showed that even if you could assemble at the rate of a million parts per second, the time to complete one molecule would still be 3,000 trillion years—longer than the known age of the universe. It was known as the build-time problem.

I said to Ricky, 'If you're doing industrial manufacturing then you must have solved the build-time problem.'

'We have.'

'How?'

'Just wait.'

I followed Ricky until we came to a final glass airlock. Stencilled on the glass door was MICROFABRICATION. Ricky waved me in. 'One at a time,' he said. 'That's all the system allows.'

I stepped in. The doors hissed shut behind me. Another blast of air: from below, from the sides, from above. By now I was getting used to it. The second door opened and I walked down another corridor to a large, brightly lit room beyond.

Ricky came after me, talking as we walked, but I don't remember what he said. I couldn't focus on his words. Because by now I was inside the main fab building—a huge windowless space, like a giant hangar. And within this hangar stood a structure of immense complexity that seemed to hang in midair, glowing like a jewel.

AT FIRST, it was hard to understand what I was seeing—it looked like an enormous glowing octopus rising above me, with glinting, faceted arms extending outwards in all directions, throwing complex reflections of colour onto the outer walls. Except this octopus had multiple layers of arms, and they all glowed and sparkled brilliantly.

I blinked, dazzled. I began to make out the details. The octopus was contained within an irregular three-storey framework built entirely of modular glass cubes. Floors, walls, ceilings, staircases—everything was cubes. But the arrangement was haphazard, as if someone had dumped a mound of giant transparent sugar cubes in the centre of the room. Within this cluster of cubes the arms of the octopus snaked off in all directions. The whole thing was held up by a web of struts and connectors, but they were obscured by the reflections, which is why the octopus seemed to hang in midair.

Ricky grinned. 'Neat, huh?'

I nodded slowly. I was seeing more details. What I had seen as an octopus was actually a branching tree structure. A central square conduit ran vertically through the centre of the room, with smaller pipes branching off on all sides. From these branches, even smaller pipes branched off in turn. Everything gleamed as if it were mirrored.

'Why is it so bright?'

'The glass has diamondoid coating,' he said. 'At the molecular level, glass is like Swiss cheese, full of holes. And of course it's a liquid, so atoms just pass right through it.'

'So you coat the glass.'

'Right. Have to.'

Within this shining forest of branching glass, David and Rosie moved, making notes, adjusting valves, consulting handheld computers. I understood that I was looking at a massive assembly line. Small fragments of molecules were introduced into the smallest pipes, and atoms were added to them. Then they moved into the next largest pipes, where more atoms were added. In this way, molecules moved progressively towards the centre of the structure, until assembly was completed and they were discharged into the central pipe.

Ricky said, 'This is just the same as an automobile assembly line, except that it's on a molecular scale. We stick on a protein sequence here, a methyl group there, just the way they stick doors and wheels on a car. At the end of the line, off rolls a new, custom-made molecular structure. Built to our specifications.'

'And the different arms?'

'Make different molecules. That's why the arms look different.'

Ricky led me back outside, glancing at his watch as he did so.

I said, 'Are we late for an appointment?'

'What? No, no. Nothing like that.' Nearby two cubes were actually solid metal rooms, with thick electrical cables running inside. I said, 'Those your magnet rooms?'

'That's right,' Ricky said. 'We've got pulsed field magnets generating sixty Tesla in the core. Something like a million times the earth's magnetic field. Of course we can only pulse them. If we turned them on continuously, they'd explode—ripped apart by the field they generate.'

'Ricky, this is all very impressive,' I said, gesturing to the glowing arms. 'But most of your assembly line is running at room temperature—no vacuum, no cryo, no mag field. How is that possible?'

He shrugged. 'The assemblers don't need any special conditions.'

'The assemblers?' I said. 'Are you telling me you've got molecular assemblers doing your fabrication for you?'

'Of course. I thought you understood that.'

'No, Ricky. I didn't understand that. And I don't like to be lied to.'

He got a wounded look on his face. 'I'm not lying.'

But I was certain that he was.

ONE OF THE FIRST things scientists learned about molecular manufacturing was how phenomenally difficult it was to carry out. Most people believed that nanoengineers would eventually find a way to build 'assemblers'—miniature molecular machines that could turn out specific molecular products. But to my knowledge, no laboratory anywhere in the world had actually been able to do it. But now Ricky was telling me, quite casually, that Xymos could build molecular assemblers that were now turning out molecules for the company.

And I didn't believe him. This kind of giant leap forward just didn't happen. Technologies grew, evolved, matured. Trying to gather my thoughts, I looked down at my feet. And I noticed that some sections of the floor were made of glass. Through the glass I could see steel ducting and pipes below ground level. One set of pipes caught my eye, because it ran from the storage room to a nearby glass cube, at which point it emerged from the floor and headed upwards, branching into the smaller tubes.

That, I assumed, was the feedstock—the raw organic slush that would be transformed on the assembly line into finished molecules.

Looking back down at the floor, I followed the pipes backwards to the place where they entered from the adjacent room. This junction was glass, too. I could see the curved steel underbellies of the big kettles I'd noticed earlier. The tanks that I had thought were a microbrewery. Machinery for controlled microbial growth.

And then I realised what it really was.

I said, 'You son of a bitch.'

Ricky smiled, and shrugged. 'Hey,' he said. 'It gets the job done.'

THOSE KETTLES in the next room were indeed tanks for controlled microbial growth, or fermentation. But Ricky wasn't making beer—he was making microbes, and I had no doubt about the reason why. Unable to construct genuine nanoassemblers, Xymos was using bacteria to crank out their molecules. This was genetic engineering, not nanotechnology.

'Well, not exactly,' Ricky said, when I told him what I thought. 'But I admit we're using a hybrid technology. Not much of a surprise in any case, is it?'

That was true. For at least ten years, observers had been predicting that genetic engineering, computer programming and nanotechnology would eventually merge. They were all involved with similar—and interconnected—activities. There wasn't much difference, for example, between creating a new bacteria to spit out, say, insulin molecules, and creating a man-made, micromechanical assembler to spit out new molecules. It was all happening at the molecular level.

You could think of a molecule as a series of atoms snapped together like Lego blocks, one after another. But the image was misleading. Because unlike a Lego set, atoms couldn't be snapped together in any arrangement you liked. An inserted atom was subject to powerful local forces—magnetic and chemical—with frequently undesirable results. In the face of these difficulties, it was impossible to ignore the fact that there already existed proven molecular factories capable of turning out large numbers of molecules: they were called cells.

'Unfortunately, cellular manufacturing can take us only so far,' Ricky said. 'We harvest the substrate molecules—the raw materials—and then we build on them with nanoengineering procedures.'

I pointed down at the tanks. 'What cells are you growing?'

'Theta-d 5972,' he said. 'A strain of *E. coli.*'

E. coli was a common bacterium, found pretty much everywhere in the natural environment, even in the human intestine. I said, 'So that's how you get your molecules. Bacteria make them for you.'

'Yes,' he said. 'We harvest twenty-seven primary molecules. They fit together in relatively high-temperature settings where the atoms are more active and mix quickly.'

'That's why it's hot in here?'

'Yes. Reaction efficiency has a maxima at one hundred and forty-seven degrees Fahrenheit, so we work there, but you'll get a certain amount of molecular combination at around thirty-five degrees.'

'And you don't need other conditions,' I said. 'Vacuum? Pressure? High magnetic fields?'

Ricky shook his head. 'No, Jack. We maintain those conditions to speed up assembly, but it's not strictly necessary.'

'And these component molecules combine to form your final assembler?'

'Which then assembles the molecules we want. Yes.'

IT WAS A CLEVER solution, creating his assemblers with bacteria. But what, then, was this complex glass building used for?

'Efficiency, and process separation,' Ricky said. 'We can build as many as nine assemblers simultaneously, in the different arms.'

'And where do the assemblers make the final molecules?'

'In this same structure.'

At a nearby work station, Ricky punched up the assembler design on the flat panel display. The assembler looked like a sort of pinwheel, a series of spiral arms going off in different directions, and a dense knot of atoms in the centre. 'It's fractal,' he said. 'So it looks sort of the same at smaller orders of magnitude.'

'And these assemblers make the actual camera units?' I asked.

'Correct.' He typed again. I saw a new image. 'This is our target micromachine, the final camera designed to be airborne. What you're looking at is a molecular helicopter.'

'Where's the propeller?' I said.

'Hasn't got one. The machine uses those little round protrusions you see there, stuck in at angles. Those're motors. The machines actually manoeuvre by climbing the viscosity of the air.'

'Climbing the *what*?'

'Viscosity. Of the air.' He smiled. 'Micromachine level, remember? It's a whole new world, Jack.'

HOWEVER INNOVATIVE the design, Ricky was still bound by the Pentagon's engineering specifications, and the product wasn't performing. Yes, they had built a flying camera that worked perfectly during tests indoors. But outside, even a modest breeze tended to blow it away like the cloud of dust it was.

The engineering team at Xymos was attempting to modify the units to increase mobility, but so far without success. Meanwhile the Department of Defense had backed away from the whole nano concept; the Xymos contract had been cancelled; DOD was going to pull funding in another six weeks.

I said, 'That's why Julia was so desperate for venture capital, these last few weeks?'

'Right,' Ricky said. 'Frankly, this whole company could go belly up before Christmas.'

'Ricky, I'm a programmer. I can't help you with your agent-mobility problems. It's an engineering issue. It's not my area.'

'Um, I know that.' He paused, frowned. 'But actually, we think the program code may be involved in the solution.'

'The code? Involved in the solution to what?'

'Jack, I have to be frank with you. We've made a mistake,' he said. 'But it's not our fault. I swear to you. It was the contractors.'

He explained how the contractors forgot to install the filters in one of the four main vents that exhausts air to the outside. 'In fact, they didn't even cut the slots, so the building inspectors never realised anything was missing. They signed off on the building; we started working here, and for three weeks we vented unfiltered air to the outside environment.'

'And what were the contaminants?'

Ricky bit his lip. 'A little of everything.'

'You vented *E. coli*, assemblers, finished molecules, everything?'

'Correct. About twenty-five kilos of it.'

Ricky was increasingly edgy as he told me all this, avoiding my eyes. I didn't get it. In the annals of industrial pollution, fifty pounds of contamination was trivial. Unless it was highly toxic or radioactive—and it wasn't—such a small quantity simply didn't matter.

I said, 'Ricky, so what? Those particles were scattered by the wind across hundreds of miles of desert. They'll decay from sunlight and cosmic radiation. In a few hours or days, they're gone. Right?'

Ricky shrugged. 'Actually, Jack, that's not what—'

It was at that moment that the alarm went off.

IT WAS A QUIET ALARM, just a soft, insistent pinging, but it made Ricky jump. I said, 'What does that mean?'

'Something set off the perimeter alarms.' He unclipped his radio and said, 'Vince, lock us down.'

The radio crackled. 'We're locked down, Ricky.'

'Raise positive pressure.'

'It's up five pounds above baseline. You want more?'

'No. Leave it there. Do we have visualisation?'

'Not yet.'

'Shit.' Ricky stuck the radio back on his belt, began typing quickly. The work-station screen divided into a half-dozen images from security cameras mounted all around the facility. Some showed the surrounding desert from high up, others were ground views.

I saw nothing. Just desert scrub and occasional clumps of cactus.

'False alarm?' I said.

Ricky shook his head. 'I wish. It'll take a minute to find it.'

'Find what?'

'*That.*'

He pointed to the monitor and bit his lip.

I SAW WHAT APPEARED to be a small, swirling cloud of dark particles. It looked like a dust devil, one of those tiny tornado-like clusters that moved over the ground, spun by convection currents rising from the hot desert floor. Except that this cloud was black and its shape kept shifting, transforming.

'Ricky,' I said. 'What are we looking at?'

'I was hoping you'd tell me.'

'It looks like an agent swarm. Is that your camera swarm?'

'No. It's something else. It doesn't respond to our radio signals. We've tried to make contact with it for almost two weeks,' he said. 'It's generating an electrical field that we can measure, but for some reason we can't interact with it.'

I frowned. 'The swarm's a collection of micro-robotic machines. Why haven't they run out of power? And why exactly can't you control them? Because if they have the ability to swarm, then there's some electrically mediated interaction among them. So you should be able to take control of the swarm—or at least disrupt it.'

'All true,' Ricky said. 'Except we can't.'

'And so you brought me out here . . .'

'To help us get the damn thing back,' Ricky said.

DAY 6: 9.32AM

It was, I thought, a problem no one had ever imagined before. In all the years that I had been programming agents, the focus had been on getting them to interact in a way that produced useful results. It never occurred to us that there might be a larger control issue, or a question of independence. Because the agents had to get their energy from some external source, such as a supplied electrical or microwave field. All you had to do was turn off the field and the agents died.

But Ricky was telling me this cloud had been self-sustaining for days. That just didn't make sense. 'Where is it getting power?'

He sighed. 'We built the units with a small piezo-wafer to generate current from photons. It's only supplementary—we added it as an afterthought—but they seem to be managing with it alone.'

'So the units are solar-powered,' I said.

'Right. And they can store charge for three hours.'

'OK, fine,' I said. Now we were getting somewhere. 'So they have enough power for three hours. What happens at night?'

'They presumably lose power after three hours of darkness and drop to the ground. We go out every night, looking. But we can never find them.'

'You've built in markers?'

'Yes, sure. Every single unit has a fluorescing module in the shell.' Ricky paused. 'We think,' he said, 'that it may hide at night.'

'Hide? You think that swarm is capable of *hiding*?'

'I think it's capable of adapting.' He sighed. 'Anyway, it's more than just one swarm, Jack. There's at least three. Maybe more, by now.'

I felt a momentary blankness washing over me. I suddenly couldn't think, I couldn't put it together. 'What are you saying?'

'I'm saying it reproduces, Jack,' he said. 'The swarm reproduces.'

THE CAMERA now showed a ground-level view of the dust cloud as it swirled towards us. But as I watched, I realised it wasn't swirling like a dust devil. Instead, the particles were twisting one way, then another, in a kind of sinuous, rhythmic movement. Occasionally areas of it caught the sunlight in a way that turned it a shimmering, iridescent silver. That had to be the piezo-panels catching the sun.

'I thought you said the Pentagon was giving up on you, because you couldn't control this swarm in wind.'

'Right. We couldn't.'

'But you must have had strong wind in the last few days.'

'Of course. Usually comes up in late afternoon.'

'Why wasn't the swarm blown away?'

'Because it's figured that one out,' Ricky said gloomily. 'Whenever the wind gusts, the swarm sinks, hangs near the ground until the wind dies down.'

'This is emergent behaviour?'

'Right. Nobody programmed it.' He bit his lip. Was he lying?

'So you're telling me it's learned . . .'

'Right, right.'

'How can it learn? The agents have no memory.'

'Uh . . . well, they have limited memory. We built it in.' Ricky pressed the button on his radio. 'Vince? You see any others?'

'No, Ricky.'

'Where are the others? Guys, speak to me. Anybody hear anything?'

The answers came back, crackling in his handset.

'Not yet.'

'Nothing.'

Ricky shook his head. 'I don't like this. That thing can't be alone.'

'How do you know there are others?'

'Because there always are.' He chewed his lip tensely as he looked at the monitor. 'I wonder what it's up to now . . .'

We didn't have long to wait. In a few moments, the swarm had come within a few yards of the building. Abruptly, it divided in two, and then divided again. Now there were three swarms.

'Son of a bitch,' Ricky said. 'It was hiding the others inside itself.' He pushed his button again. 'Guys, we got all three.' He switched to the overhead views. I saw three black clouds, all moving laterally along the side of the building.

'What're they trying to do?' I said.

'Get inside,' Ricky said.

'Why?'

'You'd have to ask them. But yesterday one of them—'

Suddenly, from a clump of cactus, a cottontail rabbit sprinted away across the desert floor. Immediately, the three swarms pursued it.

Ricky switched the monitor view. We now watched at ground level. The three clouds converged on the terrified creature.

I felt a moment of irrational pride. PREDPREY was working perfectly! Those swarms might as well be lionesses chasing a gazelle, so purposeful was their behaviour. The swarms turned sharply, then split up, cutting off the rabbit's escape to the left and right. The behaviour of the three clouds appeared coordinated. Now they were closing in.

And suddenly one of the swarms sank down, engulfing the rabbit. The other two swarms fell on it moments later. The resulting particle cloud was so dense, it was hard to see the rabbit any more. Apparently it had flipped onto its back, because I saw its hind legs kicking spasmodically in the air, above the cloud itself.

I said, 'They're killing it . . .'

'Yeah,' Ricky said, nodding. 'That's right.'

I frowned. 'So you've seen this before?'

Ricky bit his lip. Didn't answer me, just stared at the screen.

I said, 'Ricky, you've seen this before?'

He gave a long sigh. 'Yeah. Well, the first time was yesterday. They killed a rattlesnake yesterday.'

I thought, *they killed a rattlesnake yesterday*.

The rabbit no longer kicked. A single protruding foot trembled with small convulsions, and then was still. The cloud swirled low to the ground around the animal, rising and falling slightly.

I said, 'It almost looks like they're eating it.'

'I know,' Ricky said.

OF COURSE THAT WAS absurd. PREDPREY was just a biological analogy. As I watched the pulsing cloud, I tried to remember exactly what rules we had written for after the goal was attained. Real predators, of course, would eat their prey, but there was no analogous behaviour for these micro-robots. Perhaps the cloud was just swirling in confusion.

A minute or two later, swarms began to rise up smoothly from the dead rabbit. The three clouds swirled separately for a moment, then merged into one. Sunlight flashed on shimmering silver. And then the swarm moved swiftly off into the desert. In moments, it was gone.

Ricky was watching me. 'What do you think?'

'You've got a breakaway robotic nanoswarm. That some idiot made self-powered and self-sustaining.'

'You think we can get it back?'

'No,' I said. 'From what I've seen, there's not a chance in hell.'

Ricky sighed, and shook his head.

'But you can certainly get rid of it,' I said. 'You can kill it.'

'We can?' His face brightened.

'Absolutely.' And I meant it. I was convinced that Ricky was overstating the problem he faced. I was confident that I could destroy the runaway swarm quickly, that I'd be done with the whole business by dawn tomorrow—at the very latest.

That was how little I understood my adversary.

DAY 6: 10.11 AM

It was ten minutes after the swarms had gone and we were all standing in the storage room. The whole group had gathered there, tense and anxious. They watched me as I clipped a radio transmitter to my belt and pulled a headset over my head. The headset included a video camera, mounted by my left ear.

Ricky said, 'You're really going out there?'

'I am,' I said. 'I want to know what happened to that rabbit.' I turned to the others. 'Who's coming with me?'

Nobody moved. Bobby Lembeck stared at the floor. David Brooks looked away. Ricky inspected his fingernails. I caught Rosie Castro's eye. She shook her head. 'No way, Jack.'

'Why not, Rosie?'

'You saw it yourself. They're hunting.'

'Rosie,' I said, 'I trained you better than this. How can the swarms be hunting?'

'We all saw it.' She stuck her chin out stubbornly. 'The agents can communicate. They can each generate an electrical signal.'

'Right,' I said. 'How big a signal?'

'Well . . .' She shrugged.

'How big, Rosie? It can't be much, can it? The agent is only a hundredth of the thickness of a human hair.'

'True . . .'

'And electromagnetic radiation decays according to the square of the radius, right?' Every high school kid knows that. As you moved away from the electromagnetic source, the strength faded very fast.

And what that meant was the individual agents could only communicate with their immediate neighbours, with agents very close to them. Not to other swarms twenty or thirty yards away.

Rosie's frown deepened.

David Brooks coughed. 'Then what did we see, Jack?'

'You saw an illusion,' I said firmly. 'You saw three swarms acting independently, and you thought they were coordinated. But they're not. And I'm pretty certain that other things you believe about these swarms aren't true, either.'

I HAD TO ADMIT that several unanswered questions nagged at me. The most obvious was why the swarm had escaped the control of Ricky and the others.

But to my mind, all the uncertainties about this and other issues came down to a single, central question—how had the rabbit died? I didn't think it had been killed. I suspected the rabbit's death was accidental, not purposeful.

But we needed to find out.

I adjusted my portable radio headset and picked up a plastic bag.

Ricky said, 'What's the bag for?'

'To bring the rabbit back in.'

'No way,' Ricky said. 'You want to go out there, that's your business. But you're not bringing that rabbit back here.'

I looked at the others. They were all nodding in agreement.

'All right, then. I'll examine it out there.'

'You're really going to go out?'

'Why not?' I looked at them, one after another. 'I have to tell you guys, I think you've all got your knickers in a twist. The cloud's not dangerous. And yes, I'm going out.' I turned to Mae. 'Do you have a dissection kit of some kind that—'

'I'll come with you,' she said quietly.

'OK. Thanks.' I was surprised that Mae was the first to come round to my way of seeing things. But as a field biologist, she was probably better than the others at assessing real-world risk. In any case, her decision seemed to break some tension in the room; the others visibly relaxed. Mae went off to get the dissecting tools. That was when the phone rang. Vince answered it, and turned to me. 'You know somebody named Dr Ellen Forman?'

'Yes.' It was my sister.

'She's on the line.' Vince handed me the phone.

I said, 'Hello? Ellen? Is everything all right?'

'Sure. Fine.' A long sigh. 'I don't know how you do it, is all.'

'Tired?'

'About as tired as I've ever felt.'

'How's Amanda's rash?'

'Better. I'm using the ointment. She's sleeping now. I took her to the park for a while. She was ready to go down.'

'Good, good . . . Ellen, I'm in the middle of something here—'

'Jack? Julia called for you from the hospital a few minutes ago. When I said you'd gone to Nevada, she got pretty upset.'

'Is that right?'

'She said you didn't understand. And you were going to make it worse. Something like that. I think you better call her.'

'OK. I'll call.'

'How are things going out there? You be back tonight?'

'Not tonight,' I said. 'Tomorrow. Ellen, I have to go now—'

'Call the kids at dinnertime, if you can. They'd like to hear from you. Auntie Ellen is fine, but she's not Dad. You know what I mean.'

I told her I'd try to call and I hung up.

MAE AND I were standing by the double glass walls of the outer airlock, just inside the building entrance. Ricky was standing beside us, gloomy and nervous, watching as we made our final preparations. 'You sure this is necessary? To go outside?' he said.

'Ricky, the time we've spent arguing about this, we could have been out and back already,' I said impatiently.

I went through the glass door and stood in the airlock. The door hissed shut behind me. The air handlers whooshed briefly in the now-familiar pattern, and then the far glass slid open. I walked towards the steel fire door that led outside as Mae stepped into the airlock.

I opened the fire door a crack. Harsh, glaring sunlight laid a burning strip on the floor. I felt hot air on my face. Over the intercom, Ricky said, 'Good luck, guys.'

I took a breath, pushed the door wider and stepped into the desert.

The wind had dropped, and the midmorning heat was stifling. Somewhere a bird chittered; otherwise it was silent.

I was certain that the swarms were not dangerous. But now that I was outside, my theoretical inferences seemed to lose force and I felt distinctly uneasy. I scanned the shimmering horizon, looking for black shapes. I saw none.

Mae appeared beside me. 'Ready when you are, Jack.'

'Then let's do it.'

We set off towards the rabbit, which was perhaps fifty yards away. Almost immediately, my heart began to pound and I started to sweat. I knew I had let Ricky spook me, but I couldn't seem to help it. I kept glancing towards the horizon.

Mae was a couple of steps behind me. I said, 'How're you doing?'

'I'll be glad when it's over.'

We were moving through a field of knee-high yellow cholla cactus. Their spines caught the sun. Some small, silent birds hopped on the ground, beneath the cholla. As we approached, they took to the air, wheeling specks against the blue.

At last we came to the rabbit, surrounded by a buzzing black cloud. Startled, I hesitated a step.

'It's just flies,' Mae said. She crouched down beside the carcass, ignoring the flies. She pulled on a pair of rubber gloves and handed me a pair to put on. She placed a square sheet of plastic on the ground and set the rabbit down on it. As she unzipped a little dissection kit I crouched down beside her. The rabbit's carcass had no odour. Externally I could see no sign of what had caused the death.

Mae said, 'Bobby? Are you recording me?'

Over the headset, I heard Bobby say, 'Move your camera down.'

Mae touched the camera mounted on her sunglasses.

'Little more . . . little more . . . Good. That's enough.'

'OK,' Mae said. She turned the rabbit's body over in her hands, inspecting it from all sides. She dictated swiftly: 'On external examination the animal appears entirely normal . . .'

She flipped the animal onto its back and cut down the exposed midsection with a scalpel. A red gash opened; blood flowed. I saw the bones of the rib cage and pinkish coils of intestine. Mae spoke continuously as she cut, noting the tissue colour and texture. All normal. She said to me 'Hold here,' and I moved a hand down, to hold aside the slick intestine. With a stroke of the scalpel she sliced open the stomach. Muddy green liquid spilled out, which Mae again said was normal. She ran her finger around the stomach wall, then paused.

'Umm. Look there,' she said.

'What?'

'There.' She pointed. In several places the stomach was reddish, bleeding slightly as if it had been rubbed raw. I saw black patches in the midst of the bleeding. 'That's not normal,' Mae said. She took a magnifying glass and peered closer, then dictated: 'I observe dark areas approximately four to eight millimetres in diameter, which I presume to be clusters of nanoparticles present in the stomach lining.'

'There are nanoparticles in the stomach?' I said. 'How did they get there? Did the rabbit eat them? Swallow them involuntarily?'

'I doubt it. I would assume they entered actively.'

I frowned. 'You mean they crawled down the—'

'Oesophagus. Yes. At least, I think so.'

She never paused in her swift dissection. She took scissors and cut upwards through the breastbone, then pushed the rib cage open with her fingers. 'Hold here.' I moved my hands to hold the ribs open as she had done. The edges of bone were sharp.

'The lungs are bright pink and firm, normal appearance.' She cut one lobe with the scalpel, then again, and again. Finally she exposed the bronchial tube and cut it open. It was dark black on the inside.

'Bronchi show heavy infestation with nanoparticles consistent with inhalation of swarm elements,' she said, dictating. She continued to cut upwards, into the throat, then opening the mouth . . . I had to turn away for a moment. 'I am observing heavy infiltration of all the nasal passages,' Mae said. 'This is suggestive of partial or full airway obstruction, which in turn may indicate the cause of death.'

I looked back. 'What?'

'Have a look,' she said, 'there seems to be dense particles closing the pharynx, and a response that looks like an allergic reaction or—'

Then Ricky: 'Say, are you guys going to stay out much longer?'

'As long as it takes,' I said.

'You've been out there four minutes already,' Ricky replied.

Mae was shaking her head. 'Ricky, you're not helping here . . .' She looked up then, as if towards the horizon, and while she did so, she uncorked a test tube and slipped a slice of stomach lining into the glass. She put it in her pocket. No one watching the video would have seen what she did. She said, 'All right, we'll take blood samples now.'

'Blood's all you're bringing in here, guys,' Ricky said.

Mae reached for the syringe and drew some blood samples, her pace never slowing. She set the tubes of blood aside. 'Now we will just take a few cultures, and we're done . . .' She flipped over her case, looked. 'Oh, bad luck. The culture swabs aren't here.'

I said, 'Ricky, you see the swabs anywhere?'

'Yes. They're right here by the airlock.'

'You want to bring them out to us?'

He laughed harshly. 'No way I'm going out there in daylight.'

Mae said to me, 'You want to go?'

'No,' I said. I was already holding the animal open; my hands were in position. 'I'll wait here. You go.'

'OK.' She got to her feet and moved off at a light jog.

I heard her footsteps fade, then the clang of the metal door shutting behind her. Then silence. Attracted by the slit-open carcass, the flies came back in force. I swatted the flies away with one hand, keeping busy so I wouldn't think about the fact that I was alone out here.

I kept glancing off in the distance, but I never saw anything. As I brushed away the flies, occasionally my hand touched against the rabbit's fur, and that was when I noticed that beneath the fur, the skin was bright red. Bright red—exactly like a bad sunburn.

I spoke into my headset. 'Bobby?'

Crackle. 'Yes, Jack.'

'Can you see the rabbit?'

'Yes, Jack.'

'The redness of the skin?'

'Uh, just a minute.'

I heard a soft whirr by my temple. Bobby was controlling the camera remotely, zooming in. The whirring stopped.

I said, 'Can you see this? Through my camera?'

There was no answer.

'Bobby, are you there?'

Silence. I heard murmurs, whispers.

'Uh, Jack?' Now it was David Brooks's voice. 'You better go in.'

'Well, I have to wait for Mae, she's going to do cultures—'

'Mae's inside. Come in now, Jack.'

I let go of the rabbit, looked around. 'I don't see anything.'

'They're on the other side of the building, Jack.'

His voice was calm, but I felt a chill. 'They are?'

'Come inside now, Jack.'

I bent over, picked up Mae's samples and started towards the steel door. My feet crunching on the desert floor. I didn't see anything at all.

But I heard something.

It was a peculiar low, thrumming sound. At first I thought I was hearing machinery, but the sound rose and fell, pulsing like a heartbeat. Other beats were superimposed, creating a strange, unworldly quality—like nothing I'd ever heard.

'Jack? You better run.'

'What?'

'*Run.*'

I still couldn't see anything, but the sound was building in intensity, its frequency so low that I felt it as a vibration in my body.

'Run, Jack.'

I ran.

SWIRLING AND GLINTING silver, the first swarm came around the corner of the building, sliding along the exterior wall.

I looked back to see a second swarm as it came around the far end of the building. It, too, was moving towards me.

The headset crackled. David Brooks said: 'Jack, you can't make it.'

'I see that,' I said. The first swarm had already reached the door and was blocking my way. I stopped, uncertain what to do.

It was time for a diversion. I was familiar with the PREDPREY code. I knew the swarms were programmed to pursue moving targets if they seemed to be fleeing from them.

I cocked my arm and threw the black dissection kit high into the air, in the general direction of the second swarm.

Immediately, the second swarm began to go after it.

At the same moment, the first swarm moved away from the door, also pursuing the kit. It was just like a dog chasing a ball. I felt a moment of elation. It was, after all, just a programmed swarm. I thought: *This is child's play*. I hurried towards the door.

That was a mistake. Because apparently my hasty movement triggered the swarm, which immediately stopped and swirled backwards to the door again, blocking my path.

It took me a moment to realise the significance of that. My movement hadn't triggered the swarm to pursue me. Instead it had moved to block my way. It was anticipating my movement. That wasn't in the code. The swarm had gone beyond its programming—way beyond. I couldn't see how that had happened. The individual particles had very little memory, so the intelligence of the swarm was limited. It shouldn't be that difficult to outsmart it.

I tried to feint to the left. The cloud went with me, but only for a moment. Then it dropped back to the door again. As if it knew that my goal was the door, and by staying there it would succeed.

David was saying: 'It's not going to let you get past, Jack.'

Just hearing him say that irritated me. 'You think so? We'll see.'

Because my next step was obvious. Close to the ground like this, the swarm was structurally vulnerable. If I disrupted the cluster then the particles would have to reorganise themselves, just as a scattered flock of birds would re-form in the air. That would give me the few seconds I needed to get through the door.

But how to disrupt it? I needed something with a big flat surface—something to create a disrupting wind . . . My mind was racing.

Behind me, the second cloud was closing in. It moved towards me in an erratic zigzag pattern, to cut off any attempt I might make to run past it. I watched with a kind of horrified fascination. I knew that this was self-organised, emergent behaviour—and its purpose was only too clear. It was stalking me.

Turning in a circle, I looked at the ground all around me. I saw nothing I could use. I was out here with nothing but the shirt on my back, and there was nobody that could help me to—

Of course!

The headset crackled: 'Jack, listen . . .'

But I didn't hear any more after that. As I pulled my shirt over my head, the headset fell to the ground. And then, holding the shirt in my hand, I swung it in broad whooshing arcs through the air. And, screaming like a banshee, I charged the swarm by the door.

THE SWARM VIBRATED with a deep thrumming sound, flattening slightly as I ran towards it. And then I was in the midst of the particles, like being in a dust storm. I couldn't see anything—I groped blindly for the doorknob—and my eyes stung from the particles, but I kept swinging my shirt in broad whooshing arcs, and in a moment the darkness began to fade. I was dispersing the cloud, sending particles spinning off in all directions.

Now I could see the door in front of me. The doorknob was just to my left. I kept swinging my shirt, and suddenly the cloud seemed to clear entirely away, out of range of my disruption. In that instant

I slipped through the door and slammed it shut behind me.

I blinked in sudden darkness. I could hardly see. My throat was dry and my breathing was raspy. I started to feel dizzy.

On the other side of the airlock, Ricky and Mae stood watching me. I heard Ricky shout, 'Come on, Jack! Hurry!'

My eyes burned. My dizziness grew rapidly worse. I leaned against the wall to keep from falling over. My throat felt thick. I was having difficulty breathing. Gasping, I waited for the glass doors to open, but they remained closed. I stared stupidly at the airlock.

'You have to stand in front of the doors! Stand! Stand! Jack!'

I felt like the world was in slow motion. All my strength was gone. My body felt weak and shaky. The stinging was worse. Somehow, I shoved away from the wall, and lurched towards the airlock. With a hiss, the glass doors slid open.

I saw spots before my eyes. I was dizzy and sick to my stomach. I stumbled into the airlock. With every second that passed it was harder to breathe. I knew I was suffocating.

I looked down at my body but could barely see it. My skin appeared black. I was covered in dust. The spray stung me, and then the air handlers started up, whooshing loudly. I saw the dust sucked off my shirt. My vision was clearer, but I still couldn't breathe. I felt a wave of nausea. My knees buckled. I sagged against the wall.

I looked at Mae and Ricky through the second glass doors. As I watched, they receded until they were too far away for me to worry any longer. I closed my eyes and fell to the ground, and the roar of the air handlers faded into cold and total silence.

DAY 6: 11.12AM

'Jack. Don't move. Just for a second, OK?'

Something cold, a cold liquid running up my arm. I opened my eyes. The light was directly overhead, glaring, greenish-bright; I winced. My whole body ached. I was lying on the counter of Mae's biology lab. Squinting in the glare, I saw Mae standing beside me, bent over my left arm. She had an intravenous line in my elbow.

'What's going on?'

'You were in anaphylactic shock, Jack. You had a severe allergic reaction. Your throat almost closed up.'

'It was an allergic reaction to the swarm?'

She hesitated for a moment, then: 'Of course.'

'Would nano-sized particles cause an allergic reaction like that?'

'They certainly could . . .'

I said, 'But you don't think so.'

'No, I don't. I think you reacted to a coliform toxin.'

'A coliform toxin . . .' My throbbing headache came in waves. I tried to figure out what she was saying. 'A toxin from *E. coli* bacteria? Is that what you mean?'

'Right. Proteolytic toxin, probably.'

That made no sense at all. According to Ricky the *E. coli* bacteria were only used to manufacture precursor molecules. 'But bacteria wouldn't be present in the swarm itself,' I said.

'I don't know, Jack. I think they could be.'

Why was she so diffident? I wondered. Ordinarily, Mae was precise, sharp. 'Well,' I said, 'somebody knows. The swarm's been designed. Bacteria's either been designed in, or not.'

I heard her sigh, as if I wasn't getting it. But what wasn't I getting?

'Mae,' I said. 'Somebody has to tell me what's going on here. Not Ricky. I want somebody to really tell me.'

'Good,' she said. 'I think that's a very good idea.'

THAT WAS HOW I found myself sitting in front of a computer work station in one of those small rooms. The project engineer, David Brooks, was sitting beside me. As he talked, David continuously straightened his clothes—he smoothed his tie, shot his cuffs, snugged his collar—and with my headache I might have found it irritating. But I didn't focus on it. Because with every piece of new information David gave me, my headache got worse and worse.

He told me everything, starting from the beginning. Xymos had contracted to make a micro-robotic swarm that would function as an aerial camera. The particles were successfully manufactured, and worked indoors. But when they were tested outside, the swarm was blown away in a strong breeze. That was six weeks ago.

'You tested more swarms after that?' I said.

'Yes, many. Over the next four weeks, or so. But none worked.'

'So those original swarms are all gone—blown away by the wind?'

'Yes.'

'OK. And you saw the first of these desert swarms when?'

'Two weeks ago,' David said, nodding and smoothing his tie.

He explained that, at first, the swarm was so disorganised that when it first appeared, they thought it was a cloud of desert insects, gnats or something. A couple of days later, he said, a swarm appeared again, but it was much better organised. 'It displayed distinctive swarming behaviour, that sort of swirling in the cloud that you've seen. So it was clear that it was our stuff.'

'And what happened then?'

'The swarm swirled around the desert near the installation, like before. It came and went. For the next few days, we tried to gain control of it by radio, but we never could. Then about a week after that we found that none of the cars would start.' He paused. 'I went out there to have a look, and I found that all the onboard computers were dead. In fact, the processor chips themselves were fine. But the memory chips had eroded. They'd literally turned to dust.'

I thought, *Oh shit*. I said, 'Could you figure out why?'

'Sure. It wasn't any big mystery, Jack. The erosion had the characteristic signature of gamma assemblers. You know about that? No? Well, we have nine different assemblers involved in manufacturing and each one has a different function. The gamma assemblers break down carbon material in silicate layers.'

'So these assemblers cut the memory chips in the cars.'

'Right, right, but . . .' David hesitated. He was acting as if I were missing the point. He tugged at his cuffs, fingered his collar. 'The thing you have to keep in mind, Jack, is that these assemblers can work at room temperature, but they're more efficient when its hotter.'

For a moment I didn't understand what he was talking about. What difference did it make about room temperature or desert heat? What did that have to do with memory chips in cars? Then suddenly, finally, the penny dropped.

'Holy shit,' I said.

He nodded. 'Yeah.'

DAVID WAS SAYING that a mixture of components had been vented into the desert, and that these components—which were designed to self-assemble in the fabrication structure—could also self-assemble in the outside world. And that's exactly what was happening.

I ticked the points off to make sure I had it right. 'Basic assembly begins with the bacteria. They've been engineered to eat anything, even garbage, so they can find something in the desert to live off.'

'Right.'

'Which means the bacteria multiply and begin churning out molecules that self-combine, forming larger molecules. Pretty soon you have assemblers, and the assemblers turn out new microagents.'

'Right, right.'

'Which means that the swarms *are* reproducing.'

'Yes. They are.'

'And the individual agents have memory.'

'Yes. A small amount.'

'And they don't need much, that's the whole point of distributed intelligence. It's collective. So they have intelligence, and since they have memory, they can learn from experience.'

'Yes.'

'And the PREDPREY program means they can solve problems.'

'Right. Yes.'

My head throbbed. I was seeing all the implications, now, and they weren't good. 'To all practical purposes, this swarm is alive.'

'Yes.' David nodded. 'At least, it behaves as if it is alive.'

I said, 'This is very bad news.'

Brooks said, 'Tell me.'

'Why wasn't this thing destroyed a long time ago.'

David said nothing. He just looked uncomfortable.

'Because you realise,' I said, 'that you're talking about a mechanical plague. You've got a man-made plague.'

He nodded. 'Yes.'

'That's evolving.'

'Yes.' Brooks sighed. 'It's evolving pretty damn fast. It'll be different this afternoon, when it comes back.'

'Why does it keep coming back?' I said.

'It's trying to get inside.'

'And why is that?'

David shifted uncomfortably. 'We have only theories, Jack.'

'Try me.'

'One possibility is that it's a territorial thing. The swarm may consider the inside of this facility to be a sort of home base.'

I said, 'You believe that?'

'Not really, no.' He hesitated. 'Actually, most of us think that it comes back looking for your wife, Jack. It's looking for Julia.'

DAY 6: 11.42AM

I turned to David. 'What was Julia doing in all this?'

'Helping us, Jack.'

'I'm sure. But how, exactly?'

'In the beginning, she was trying to coax it back,' he said. 'We needed the swarm close to the building to take control again by radio. So Julia helped us keep it close.'

'How?'

'Well, she entertained it.'

'She what?'

'I guess you'd call it that. It was very quickly obvious that the swarm had rudimentary intelligence. It was Julia's idea to treat it like a child. She went outside with bright blocks, toys. Things a kid would like. And the swarm seemed to be responding to her.'

'The swarm was safe to be around at that time?'

'Yes, completely. It was just a particle cloud.' David shrugged. 'Anyway, after the first day or so, she decided to go a step further and formally test it. You know, test it like a child psychologist.'

'David,' I said. 'That swarm's a distributed intelligence. It's a goddamn net. It'll learn from whatever you do. Testing is the same as teaching. What exactly was she doing with it?'

'Just games. She'd lay out three coloured blocks on the ground, two blue and one yellow, see if it would choose the yellow. Stuff like that.'

'But, David,' I said. 'You all knew this was a runaway. Didn't anybody think to just go out and destroy it?'

'Sure. We all wanted to. Julia wouldn't allow it.'

'And nobody argued with her?'

'She's a vice-president of the company, Jack. She kept saying that we had stumbled onto something really big. She was really proud of it. All she wanted to do was "rein it in". Her words.'

'Yeah. Well. How long ago did she say that?'

'Yesterday, Jack.' David shrugged. 'Yesterday afternoon.'

It took me a moment to realise that he was right. Just a single day had passed since Julia had been here, and then had had her accident. And, in that time, the swarms had already advanced enormously.

'How many swarms were there yesterday?'

'Three. But we only saw two. I guess one was hiding.' He shook his head. 'You know, one of the swarms had become like a pet to her. Sometimes when she came out it swirled around her, like it was excited to see her. She'd talk to it, too.'

I pressed my throbbing temples. 'She talked to it,' I repeated. 'Don't tell me the swarms have auditory sensors, too.'

'No. But, well . . . we think the cloud was close enough that her breath deflected some of the particles. In a rhythmic pattern.'

'So the whole cloud was one giant eardrum?'

'In a way, yeah.'

'And it's a net, so it learned. Are you going to tell me it talked back?'

'No, but it had started making weird sounds.'

I nodded. I'd heard those weird sounds.

I was pretty sure that the accelerated behaviour of the swarms was a function of past learning. This was a characteristic of distributed systems—and a characteristic of evolution, which could be considered a kind of learning. In either case, it meant that systems experienced a long, slow starting period, followed by ever-increasing speed.

Teaching made the progression more efficient, and I was sure Julia's teaching had been an important factor in the behaviour of the swarm now. Simply by interacting with it, she had introduced a selection pressure in an organism with emergent behaviour that couldn't be predicted. It was a very foolish thing to do.

So the swarm—already developing rapidly—would develop even more rapidly in the future. Destroying the swarms would be more difficult with each passing hour.

I NEEDED TO TALK to Mae again. I found her in the biology lab, hunched over a computer monitor. I said, 'Mae, listen, I've talked to David and I need to—uh, Mae? Have you got a problem?' She was looking fixedly at the screen.

'I think I do,' she said. 'A problem with the feedstock.'

'What kind of problem?'

'The latest Theta-d stocks aren't growing properly. I'm afraid it's phage contamination.'

'You mean a virus?' I said.

'Yes. Probably a mutant of an existing strain. It's bad news for manufacturing. If we have infected bacterial stocks, we'll have to shut down production.'

'Frankly,' I said, 'shutting down production might be a good idea. Have you told Ricky about this?'

'Not yet.' She shook her head. 'I don't think he needs more bad news right now. And besides . . .'

'Besides what?'

'Ricky has a huge financial stake in the success of this company.' She turned to face me. 'Bobby heard him on the phone the other day, talking about his stock options. And sounding worried. Ricky sees Xymos as his big chance to score. He's really trying to make this happen, really driving himself. He's up all night, working, figuring. He isn't sleeping more than three or four hours. Frankly, I worry it's affecting his judgment. Sometimes I get the feeling he doesn't want to get rid of the swarms at all. Or maybe he's scared.'

'Maybe,' I said.

'Anyway, he's erratic. So if I were you I'd be careful,' she said, 'when you go after the swarms. Because that's what you're going to do, isn't it? Go after them?'

'Yes,' I said. 'That's what I'm going to do.'

DAY 6: 1.12PM

They had all gathered in the lounge, and were watching me with anxious eyes as I explained what we had to do.

The plan was simple enough. Basically, I told them that because the runaway swarm had exhibited self-organising behaviour, meaning it can reassemble itself after an injury or disruption, it had to be totally, physically destroyed. 'That means subjecting the particles to heat, cold, acid, or high magnetic fields. And from what I've seen of its behaviour, I'd say our best chance to destroy it is at night when the swarm loses energy and sinks to the ground.'

Ricky whined, 'But we told you, Jack, we can't find it at night—'

'That's because you didn't tag it. Look, it's a big desert out there. You've got to tag it with something so strong you can follow it back to its hiding place.'

'Tag it with what?'

'That's my next question,' I said. 'What kind of tagging agents have we got here?' I was greeted with blank looks. 'Come on, guys. This is an industrial facility. You must have something that will coat the particles and leave a trail we can follow. A substance that fluoresces intensely, or something radioactive . . . No?'

More blank looks. Shaking their heads.

'Well,' Mae said, 'of course, we have radioisotopes. We use them to check for leaks in the system.'

'OK,' I said. 'Where are the isotopes now?'

Mae smiled bleakly. 'In the storage unit.'

'Where is that?'

'Outside. Next to the parked cars.'

'Right,' I said. 'Then let's go out and get them.'

'Oh, for Christ's sake,' Ricky said, throwing up his hands. 'Are you out of your mind? You nearly died out there this morning, Jack.'

'Would you rather have somebody else do it?' I said.

He frowned. 'What do you mean?'

'You better face facts, Ricky. This is already a disaster. And if we can't get it under control right away, then we have to call for help.'

'Help? What do you mean?'

'I mean, call the Pentagon. Call the Army. We have to call somebody to get these swarms under control.'

'We can't do that, Jack. It would destroy the company. We'd never get funding again.'

'That wouldn't bother me one bit,' I said. I was feeling angry about what had happened in the desert. A chain of bad decisions, errors and screwups extending over months. It seemed as if everyone at Xymos was doing short-term solutions, quick and dirty.

'Look,' I said, 'you've got a runaway swarm that's apparently lethal. You can't screw around with this any more.'

'But, Julia said—'

'I don't care what she said, Ricky. There isn't any choice. This is an organism that is evolving fast. We can't risk delay.'

'Risk it? Jack, you're crazy even to consider it.'

Charley Davenport had been staring at the monitor. Now he turned to the group. 'No, Jack's not crazy.' He grinned at me. 'And I'm going with him.' Charley began to hum 'Born to Be Wild'.

'Me, too,' Mae said. 'I know where the isotopes are stored.'

'We'll need to improvise a spray apparatus of some kind.' David Brooks was rolling up his sleeves carefully. 'Presumably, remotely controlled. That's Rosie's speciality.'

'OK, I'll come, too,' Rosie Castro said, looking at David.

Ricky stared from one to another of us, shaking his head. 'I can't allow you to do this. You guys can't go out there and survive.'

'Sure we can, Ricky,' Charley said, pointing to the monitor. 'Look.'

The monitor showed the desert outside. The early afternoon sun was shining. For a moment I didn't understand what Charley was talking about. Then I saw the sand blowing low on the ground.

'That's right, folks,' Charley Davenport said. 'We got a high wind out there. High wind, no swarms—remember? They have to hug the ground. Time's a-wasting. Let's do it, guys.'

GOING DOWN the hallway to the power station, with the air conditioners roaring full blast, Mae fell into step beside me. I said to her, 'You really don't need to go out there, Mae. You could tell me over the radio how to handle the isotopes.'

'It's not the isotopes I'm concerned with,' she said, her voice low, so it would be buried in the roar. 'It's the rabbit. I need to examine the rabbit again.'

'Why?'

'You remember that tissue sample I cut from the stomach? Well, I looked at it under the microscope a few minutes ago.'

'And?'

'I'm afraid we have big problems, Jack.'

I WAS THE FIRST out of the door, squinting in the desert sunlight. Even though it was almost three o'clock, the sun seemed as bright and fierce as ever. A hot wind ruffled my trousers and shirt. I pulled my headset mouthpiece closer to my lips and said, 'Bobby, you got an image?'

'Yes, Jack.'

Mae came through the door next, followed by Charley. She had a backpack slung over one shoulder.

Then David Brooks came out, with Rosie close behind him.

I was busy scanning the horizon, but I saw nothing. The cars were parked in a corrugated shed about fifty yards away. The shed ended in a square, white, concrete building with narrow windows. That was the storage unit.

We started towards it. Rosie said, 'Is that place air conditioned?'

'Yes,' Mae said. 'But it's still hot. It's poorly insulated.'

'Is it airtight?'

'Not really.'

'That means no,' Davenport said, laughing. He spoke into his headset. 'Bobby, what wind do we have?'

'Seventeen knots,' Bobby Lembeck said. 'Good strong wind.'

'And how long until the wind dies? Sunset?'

'Probably, yeah. Another three hours.'

I said, 'That'll be plenty of time.'

I noticed that David Brooks was not saying anything. He just trudged towards the building. Rosie followed close behind him.

'But you never know,' Davenport said. 'We could all be toast. Any minute now.' He laughed again, in his irritating way.

I said, 'Let's stay focused, Charley.'

'Hey, I'm focused. I'm focused.'

The wind was blowing sand, creating a brownish blur just above the ground. Mae walked beside me. She looked across the desert and said abruptly, 'I want to have a look at the rabbit. You go on ahead.'

She headed off to the right, towards the carcass. I went with her. And the others turned in a group and followed us. It seemed everybody wanted to stay together.

Charley said, 'Why do you want to see it, Mae?'

'I want to check something.'

In a few moments, we were all standing over the carcass.

'Jeez,' Rosie said, as Mae crouched down beside it.

I was startled to see that the exposed flesh was no longer smooth and pink. Instead, it was roughened everywhere. And it was covered all over by a milky white coating.

'Looks like it was dipped in acid,' Charley said.

'Yes, it does,' Mae said. She sounded grim.

All this had occurred in five hours. 'What happened to it?'

Mae had taken out her magnifying glass and was bent close to the animal. She looked here and there, moving the glass quickly. Then she said, 'It's been partially eaten.'

'Eaten? By what?'

'Bacteria.'

'Wait a minute,' Charley Davenport said. 'You think this is caused by Theta-d? You think the *E. coli* is eating it?'

'We'll know soon enough,' she said. She reached into a pouch, and pulled out several glass tubes containing sterile swabs. She daubed the animal with one swab after another, replacing each in a tube.

'Then the Theta-d must be multiplying very aggressively.'

'Bacteria will do that if you give them a good nutrient source. And high temperatures accelerate growth.'

I said, 'But if that's true, it means the swarm—'

'I don't know what it means, Jack,' she said quickly. She looked at me and gave a slight shake of the head, meaning: not now.

But the others weren't put off. Charley Davenport said, 'Are you telling us that the swarms killed the rabbit in order to eat it? In order to grow more *E. coli*? And make more nanoswarms?'

'I didn't say that, Charley.' Her voice was calm, almost soothing.

'But that's what you think,' Charley continued. 'So if we come back in another hour, this white stuff will be gone and we'll see black forming all over the body. New black nanoparticles. And eventually there'll be enough for a new swarm.'

She nodded.

'And that's why the wildlife around here has disappeared?' David Brooks said.

'Yes.' She brushed a strand of her hair back with her hand. 'This has been going on for a while.'

There was a moment of silence. We all stood around the rabbit carcass. It was being consumed so quickly, I imagined I could almost see it happening right before my eyes, in real time.

'We better get rid of those swarms,' Charley said.

We all turned and set off for the shed.

I STEPPED from the sun into the shade of the corrugated shed, and moved along the line of cars towards the door of the storage unit. The door was plastered with warning symbols—for nuclear radiation, biohazard, microwaves, high explosives, laser radiation.

Charley said, 'You can see why we keep this shit outside.'

Mae unlocked the door and went in.

The interior was divided into two large storage rooms, with shelves on all four walls, and freestanding shelves in the middle of the rooms. There was another door in the second room, and a corrugated roll-up door for truck deliveries. Hot sunlight came in through wood-frame windows. I closed the door behind me, and looked at the seal. The shed was definitely not airtight.

I turned to Mae. 'Where are the isotopes?'

'Over here.' She went over to a steel lid set in the concrete floor. The lid lifted with a hiss. I saw a ladder that led down into a circular chamber. The isotopes were stored in metal containers of different sizes. Mae said, 'We have Selenium-172. Shall we use that?'

'Sure.'

Mae started to climb down into the chamber.

'Will you *cut it out*?' In a corner of the room, David Brooks jumped back from Charley Davenport, who was holding a big spray bottle of Windex cleaner. He was testing the squeeze trigger mechanism, and in the process spraying water on David. It didn't look accidental. 'Give me that,' David said, snatching the bottle away.

From the first room, Rosie said, 'Would this work?' She held up a cylinder with wires dangling from it. 'Isn't this a solenoid relay?'

'Yes,' David said. 'But I doubt it can exert enough force to squeeze this bottle. We need something bigger.'

'And don't forget, you also need a remote controller,' Charley said. 'Unless you want to stand there and spray it yourself.'

Mae came up from below, carrying a heavy metal tube. She walked to the sink, and reached for a bottle of straw-coloured liquid. She pulled on heavy rubber-coated gloves, and started to mix the isotope into the glucose liquid, so that it could be sprayed.

Over the headset, Ricky said, 'Aren't you guys forgetting something? Even with a remote, how are you going to get the swarm to come to it? It won't just stand there while you hose it down.'

'We'll find something to attract them,' I said.

'Like what?'

'They were attracted to the rabbit.'

'We don't have any rabbits.'

Charley said, 'You know, Ricky, you are a very negative person.'

Like Mae, Charley was seeing it, too: Ricky had dragged his feet every step of the way. I would have said something to Charley about Ricky, but over our headsets everybody heard everything.

'Hey guys?' It was Bobby Lembeck. 'The wind's dropping.'

'What is it now?' I said.

'Fifteen knots. Down from eighteen.'

'That's still strong,' I said. 'We're OK.'

'I know. I'm just telling you.'

From the next room, Rosie said, 'What's Thermite?' In her hand she held a plastic tray filled with thumb-sized metal tubes.

'Careful with that,' David said. 'It must be left over from construction. Thermite is aluminium and iron oxide. It burns very hot—three thousand degrees—and so bright you can't look directly at it.'

'How much have we got?' I said to Rosie. 'We could use it tonight.'

'I'll look,' she said, and she disappeared around the corner.

A radiation counter was chattering near the sink, where Mae had capped the isotope tube and was pouring the straw-coloured liquid into a Windex bottle.

She was clearly going to be another few minutes, so I went over to a computer work station and turned it on. The screen glowed; there was a menu of options. Aloud, I said, 'Ricky, can I put up the swarm code on this monitor?'

'What do you want the code for?' Ricky sounded alarmed.

'I want to see what you guys have done.'

'Why?'

'Ricky, for Christ's sake, can I see it or not?'

'Sure, of course you can. All the code revisions are in the directory slash code. The password is l-a-n-g-t-o-n, all lower case.'

'OK.'

I entered the password.

'Ricky. Where's the particle code?'

'Isn't it there?'

'Damn it, Ricky. Stop screwing around.'

A pause. 'There should be a subdirectory slash C-D-N. It's kept there.'

I scrolled down. 'I see it.'

Within this directory, I found a list of files, all very small. There was nothing new from the last two weeks.

'Ricky. You haven't changed the code for two weeks?'

'Yeah, about that.'

I clicked on the most recent document and scanned the screen for a while, looking for how they had changed the program structure. Then I scrolled down into the actual code, to see the implementation. But the important code wasn't there.

'Ricky, I want to see that damn module. What's the problem?'

'No problem. I just have to look for it. I'll do it when you get back.'

I glanced over at Mae. 'Have you gone through the code?'

She shook her head. Her expression seemed to say it was never going to happen, that Ricky would keep putting me off. I didn't understand why. I was there to advise them on the code, after all.

In the next room, Rosie and David were poking through the shelves of supplies, looking for radio relays. Across the room, Charley Davenport farted loudly and cried, 'Bingo!'

'Hell, Charley,' Rosie said. 'You make me sick.'

'Oh, sorry.' Charley held up a shiny metal contraption. 'Then I guess you don't want this remote-controlled compression valve.'

'What?' Rosie said, turning.

'Are you kidding?' David said, going over to look.

My headset crackled. 'Hey guys?' It was Bobby Lembeck again. 'Wind's just dropped to six knots.'

I said, 'OK.' I turned to the others. 'Let's finish up, guys.'

I went to the window and looked out. The wind was still ruffling the juniper bushes, but there was no longer a layer of sand blowing across the ground.

Ricky came on the headset: 'Jack, get your team out of there.'

'We're doing it now,' I said.

David Brooks said in a formal tone, 'Guys, there's no point in leaving until we have a valve that we know fits this bottle—'

'I think we better go,' Mae said. 'Finished or not.'

Over the headset, Bobby said, 'Four knots and falling. Fast.'

'Let's go, everybody,' I said. I was herding them towards the door.

Then Ricky came on. 'No. It's too late. They're here.'

Day 6: 3.12pm

Everyone went to the window; we banged heads trying to look out in all directions. As far as I could see, the horizon was clear. I saw nothing at all. 'Where are they?' I said.

'Coming from the south. Four swarms. We have them on screen.'

'Four! Do we have time to run for it?'

'I don't think so.'

David frowned. 'He doesn't *think* so. Jesus.'

And before I could say anything, David had bolted for the far door and stepped into the sunlight. We all spoke at once:

'David, what the hell are you doing?'

'I'm trying to see . . .'

'Get back here!'

'You stupid bastard!'

But Brooks remained where he was, hands shading his eyes from the sun. 'I don't see anything yet,' he said. 'Listen, I think maybe we can make a run for—uh, no we can't.' He sprinted back inside and slammed the door shut, tugging on the doorknob. His voice shook. 'They're coming.'

I went over to him and put my hand on his shoulder. He was still pulling on the doorknob, breathing in ragged gasps. 'David,' I said quietly. 'Let's take it easy now. Let's take a deep breath.'

He was sweating, tense, his shoulders shaking. It was pure panic.

'David,' I said. 'Let's take a deep breath, OK?' I took one, demonstrating. 'That's better. Come on now. Big breath . . . OK, now, let go of the doorknob.'

David shook his head, refusing. Then, finally, he let go and sat back on the ground. He began to cry, head in hands.

'The guy's cracked,' Charley said. 'That's all we need.'

'Shut up, Charley,' Rosie said. She helped David to his feet, nodding to me that she'd take it from here.

I went back to the centre of the room, where the others were standing by the monitor viewing the north face of the main building. The four swarms were there, glinting silver as they moved up and down the length of the building. 'What're they doing?' I said.

'Trying to get in.'

We watched for a moment in silence. Once again I was struck by the purposefulness of their behaviour as they paused at every doorway and closed window, moving up and down along the seals, until finally moving on to the next opening.

'It looks like they don't remember that the doors are sealed.'

'Either that,' he said, 'or this is another generation.'

'You mean these are new swarms since noon?'

Charley shrugged. 'I'm just guessing.'

The possibility that new generations were coming that fast meant that whatever evolutionary mechanism was built into the code was progressing fast, too. If these swarms were reproducing every three hours, it meant they had turned over something like 100 generations in the last two weeks. And with 100 generations, the behaviour would be much sharper.

Mae watched them on the monitor and said, 'At least they're staying by the main building. It seems like they don't know we're here.'

'How would they know?' I said.

'They wouldn't,' Charley said. 'Their main sensory modality is vision. If they don't see it, it doesn't exist for them.'

Rosie came over with David. He said, 'I'm really sorry, guys.'

Charley said, 'Don't worry, David. We understand. You're a psycho and you cracked. No problem.'

Rosie put her arm around David, who blew his nose loudly. She stared at the monitor. 'What's happening now?' she said.

'They don't seem to know we're here.'

'And we're hoping it stays that way.'

'Uh-huh. And if it doesn't?' Rosie said.

I had been thinking about that. 'If it doesn't, we exploit the weaknesses in the PREDPREY assumptions.'

'Which means?'

'We flock,' I said.

Charley gave a horse laugh. 'Yeah, right!'

'I'm serious,' I said.

OVER THE LAST thirty years, scientists had studied predator-prey interactions in everything from the lion to the hyena to the warrior ant. There was now a much better understanding of how prey defended themselves. Animals like zebras and caribou didn't live in herds because they were sociable; herding was a defence against predation. Large numbers of animals provided increased vigilance, and coordinated group movements made it harder for predators to pick out a single individual. Predators were drawn to attack an animal that was distinctive in some way.

So the message was simple. Stay together. Stay the same.

That was our best chance.

But I hoped it wouldn't come to that.

THE SWARMS DISAPPEARED for a while. They had gone around to the other side of the laboratory building. We waited tensely. Eventually they reappeared. They again moved along the side of the building, trying openings one after another.

We all watched the monitor. David Brooks was sweating profusely. 'How long are they going to keep doing that?'

Mae said, 'At least until the wind kicks up again. And it doesn't look like that's going to happen soon.'

Rosie said, 'Come and sit down, David.' Tenderly she walked with him across the room to the sink and sat him on the floor. She put cold water on a paper towel and placed it on the back of his neck.

I was watching the swarms. Their behaviour had subtly changed. They no longer stayed close to the building. Instead, they now moved in a fluid, zigzag pattern away from the wall into the desert, and then back again.

Mae saw it, too. 'New behaviour . . .'

'Yes. Their strategy isn't working, so they're trying something else.'

'They can zigzag all they want,' Charley said. 'It won't open any doors.'

Even so, I was fascinated to see this emergent behaviour, evolving as we watched.

A thought occurred to me. 'How well do the swarms see?'

The headset clicked. It was Ricky. 'They see fabulously,' he said. 'It's what they were made to do, after all.'

I said, 'And how do they do the imaging?' Because they were just a series of individual particles. Like the rods and cones in the eye, central processing was required to form a picture from all the inputs. How was that processing accomplished?

Ricky coughed. 'Uh . . . not sure.'

Charley said, 'It showed up in later generations.'

'You mean they evolved vision on their own?'

'Yeah.'

We watched as the swarm angled away from the wall, moved back near the rabbit, then made for the wall once more. Suddenly, it paused in the desert, not moving, but rising and falling.

I shook my head. 'I think it sees something.'

'Like what?' Charley said.

I was afraid I knew the answer. The swarm represented an extremely high-resolution camera combined with a distributed intelligence network. And one thing distributed networks did particularly well was detect patterns.

'What patterns?' Charley said, when I told him. 'There's nothing out there to detect except sand and cactus thorns.'

Mae said, 'And footprints.'

'What? You mean *our* footprints?'

We watched the swarm hang there, rising and falling for ten or fifteen seconds, like it was breathing. The cloud had turned mostly black now, with just an occasional glint of silver.

Charley bit his lip. 'You really think it sees something?'

'I don't know,' I said. 'Maybe.'

Suddenly, the swarm rose up and began to move again. But it wasn't coming towards us. Instead, it moved on a diagonal over the desert, heading back towards the door in the power building.

'It just tracked us,' Mae said. 'Backward.'

The question was, what would it do next?

THE NEXT FIVE minutes were tense. The swarm retraced its path, going back to the rabbit. It swirled around the rabbit for a while, then once again it retraced the route back to the power station door. It then returned to the rabbit. It repeated this three times.

'It's stuck in a loop,' Charley said.

'Lucky for us,' I said. I was waiting to see if the swarm would modify its behaviour. The original PREDPREY program had a randomising element built into it, to handle situations exactly like this.

'Uh-oh,' Mae said.

The behaviour had changed.

The swarm moved in larger circles, going round and round the rabbit. And almost immediately, it came across another path. It paused a moment and then suddenly rose up and began to move directly towards us, following the path we had taken to the shed.

'Shit,' Charley said. 'I think we're in big trouble.'

MAE AND CHARLEY rushed across the room to look out of the window. I started to shout: 'No, no! Get away from the windows!'

'What?'

'It's visual, remember? Get away from the windows!'

There was no good place to hide in the storage room, not really. Rosie and David crawled under the sink. Charley pushed in beside them, ignoring their protests. Mae slipped into the shadows of one corner of the room, easing herself into the space where two shelves didn't quite meet.

The radio crackled. 'Hey guys?' It was Ricky. 'One's heading for you. And uh . . . No . . . two others are joining it.'

'Ricky,' I said. 'Go off air.'

'What?'

'Off, Ricky.'

I dropped down on my knees behind a cardboard carton of supplies in the main room. The carton wasn't large enough to hide me entirely but someone outside would have to look at an angle through the north window to see me. In any case, it was the best I could do.

Ten or fifteen seconds passed. I could see the sunlight streaming in through the north window above the sink. It made a white rectangle on the floor to my left.

My headset crackled. 'Why no contact?'

'Ricky,' I said, 'these things have auditory capacity, so stay off.'

I reached for the transmitter at my belt, and clicked it off. I signalled the others and they each turned their transmitters off.

Charley mouthed something to me. I thought he mouthed, 'That guy wants us killed.'

We waited.

IT COULDN'T have been more than two or three minutes, but it seemed for ever. My knees began to hurt on the hard concrete floor. Trying to get more comfortable, I shifted my position cautiously; by now I was sure the first swarm was in our vicinity. It hadn't appeared at the windows yet, and I wondered what was taking so long. I was so focused on the pain in my knees that I didn't notice at first that the glaring white rectangle on the floor was turning a dull grey.

The swarm was here.

I wasn't certain, but I fancied that beneath the hum of the air conditioner was a deep thrumming sound. From my position behind the carton, I saw the window above the sink grow progressively darker from swirling black particles, as if there was a dust storm outside.

Underneath the sink, David Brooks began to moan. Charley clapped his hand over his mouth.

And then the swarm vanished from the window, as quickly as it had come. Sunlight poured in again.

Nobody moved.

Moments later, the window in the west wall turned dark, in the same way. I wondered why the swarm didn't enter. The window wasn't airtight. The nanoparticles could slide through the cracks without difficulty. But they didn't even seem to try.

While the west window was still dark, the north window over the sink turned dark again. Now two swarms were looking in at the same time. Ricky had said there were three coming towards the building. I wondered where the third swarm was. A moment later, I knew.

Like a silent black mist, nanoparticles began to come into the room underneath the west door. Soon more particles entered, all around the door frame. Inside the room, the particles spun and swirled aimlessly, but I knew they would self-organise in a few moments.

Then, at the north window, I saw more particles flooding through the cracks and then through the air-conditioning vents in the ceiling.

There was no point in waiting any longer. I got to my feet and stepped from my hiding place. I shouted for everybody to come out of hiding. 'Form up in two rows!'

Charley grabbed the Windex spray bottle and fell into line, grumbling, 'What do you think our chances are?'

'The best they'll ever get,' I said. 'Now form up and stay with me!'

IF WE WEREN'T so frightened, we might have felt ridiculous, shuffling back and forth across the room, trying to coordinate our movements—trying to imitate a flock of birds. We were awkward, but we got better. When we came to a wall, we wheeled and headed back again, moving in unison. I started swinging my arms and clapping with each step. The others did the same. It helped our coordination.

And all the time, we watched the black nanoparticles as they came hissing into the room through cracks in doors and windows. Soon a kind of undifferentiated fog filled the room. I felt pinpricks all over my body, and I was sure the others felt it, too. David started moaning again, but Rosie was right beside him, urging him to keep it together.

Suddenly, with shocking speed the fog cleared, the particles coalescing into two fully formed columns that now stood directly before us, rising and falling in dark ripples.

Seen this close, the swarms exuded an unmistakable sense of menace, almost malevolence. Their deep thrumming sound was clearly audible, and intermittently I heard an angry hiss, like a snake.

But they did not attack us. Just as I had hoped, the programming deficits worked for us. Confronted by a cluster of coordinated prey, these predators were stymied. They did nothing at all.

At least for now. At least until they innovated new behaviour.

I said, 'I suggest we move towards that door—and get the hell out.'

'And then what?' David whined, as we wheeled away from the wall, and moved towards the next room. In his panic he was having trouble staying in sync with the rest of us and kept stumbling.

'We continue this way—flocking this way—back to the lab—and get inside—are you willing to try?'

'Oh jeez,' he moaned. 'I don't know if . . .' He stumbled again. I could almost feel his terror, his overwhelming urge to flee.

'If you go on your own—you'll never make it—are you listening?'

David moaned, 'I don't know . . . I don't know if I can . . .'

The swarm followed us into the next room. But still they did not attack. We were now about twenty feet from the back door, the same door we had come in. I started to feel optimistic. For the first time, I thought it was possible we really might make it.

And then, in an instant, everything went to hell.

DAVID BROOKS BOLTED.

We were well into the back room, and about to work our way around the shelves, when he broke away and headed for the far door.

The swarms instantly spun and chased him.

Rosie was screaming for him to come back, but David was focused on the door. The swarms pursued him with surprising speed. David had almost reached the door when one swarm sank low and spread itself across the floor ahead of him, turning it black.

The moment David Brooks reached the black surface, his feet shot out from under him, as if he had stepped on ice. He howled in pain as he slammed onto the concrete, and immediately tried to scramble to his feet again, but he couldn't get up; he kept slipping and falling, again and again. His glasses shattered. His lips were coated with swirling black residue. He started to have trouble breathing.

Rosie was still screaming as the second swarm descended on David, and the black spread across his face, onto his eyes, into his hair. His movements became increasingly frantic, he moaned pitifully like an animal, as he slid and tumbled on hands and knees towards the door.

Rosie cried, 'We've got to do something!' I grabbed her arm and she struggled in my grip. 'We have to help him!'

'Rosie. There's nothing we can do.'

David was now rolling on the ground, black from head to toe. It looked as though his mouth was a dark hole, as the swarm flowed into his mouth like a black river. His eyeballs were completely black.

His body began to shudder. He clutched at his neck. His feet drummed on the floor. I was sure he was dying.

'Come on, Jack,' Charley said. 'Let's get the hell out of here.'

'You can't leave him! You can't, you can't!' Rosie shouted as she stamped on my foot. In my moment of surprise I let go, and she sprinted across the shed shouting, 'David! David!'

His hand, black as a miner's, stretched towards her. She grabbed his wrist. And in the same moment she fell, slipping on the black floor just as he had done. She kept saying his name, hugging him to her chest, until she began to cough, and a black rim appeared on her lips. David didn't seem to be moving any more.

Charley said, 'Let's go, for Christ's sake. I can't watch.'

I felt unable to move my feet, unable to leave. I turned to Mae. Tears were running down her cheeks. She said: 'Go.'

I nodded slowly and turned towards the door.

And we went outside.

DAY 6: 4.12PM

Beneath the corrugated roof, the air was hot and still. The line of cars stretched away from us. We set off towards the lab building at a brisk jog. We were all thinking about the same thing: in another half a minute we would reach the door, and safety.

But we had forgotten the fourth swarm.

It swirled out from the side of the lab building, and started straight towards us. We stopped, confused.

We were too small a group now to confuse a predator by flocking. We needed a refuge, some kind of shelter before the swarm reached us. I turned full circle, looking in all directions, but there was nothing I could see, except—

'Are the cars locked?'

Charley said, 'No, they shouldn't be.'

We turned and ran.

THE NEAREST CAR was a blue Ford sedan. I opened the driver's door, and Mae opened the passenger side. The swarm was right behind us. I could hear the thrumming sound as I slammed the door shut, as Mae slammed hers. Charley, still holding the Windex spray, was trying to open the rear passenger door, but it was locked. Mae twisted in the seat to unlock it, but Charley had already turned to the next car, a Land Cruiser, and climbed inside.

The inside of the car was like an oven. Mae and I were both sweating. The swarm rushed towards us and swirled over the front windshield, pulsating, shifting back and forth.

Over the headset, a panicked Ricky said, 'Guys? Where are you?'

'We're in the cars.'

The black swarm moved away from our sedan over to the Toyota. We watched as it slid from one window to another, trying to get in. Charley grinned at me through the glass. 'These cars are airtight.'

'What about the air vents?' I said. 'They're not airtight, are they?'

'No,' he said. 'But you'd have to go under the hood to begin to get in. And I'm betting this buzzball can't figure that out.'

Inside our car, Mae was snapping closed the dashboard air ducts one after another. She glanced inside the glove compartment.

I said, 'You find any keys?'

She shook her head, no. Closed the glove compartment.

Over the headset, Ricky said, 'Guys? You got more company.'

I turned to see two additional swarms coming around the shed. They swirled over our car, front and back, and began circling. I felt like we were in a dust storm. From time to time, one of the swarms would rush the windshield and disperse itself over the glass. Then it would coalesce again, back away down the hood, and rush again.

I noticed that with each charge, the swarm would move further back down the hood, taking a longer run. Soon it would back itself up to the grille. And if it started inspecting the grille, it could find the opening to the air vents. Then it would be over.

Over the headset, Bobby Lembeck said, 'Wind's starting to pick up again. Six knots.' He was trying to be encouraging, but six knots wasn't anywhere near enough force.

Charley said, 'Jack? I just lost my buzzball. Where is it?'

I looked over at Charley's car and saw that the third swarm had slid down to the front tyre well and was moving in and out through the holes in the hubcap. 'Checking your hubcaps, Charley,' I said.

'Umm.' He sounded unhappy, and with reason. If the swarm started exploring the car thoroughly, it might stumble on a way in.

I was still looking over my shoulder at Charley's swarm when Mae said quietly, 'Jack. *Look.*'

The swarm outside her window on the passenger side had changed. It was almost entirely silver now, shimmering but pretty stable, and on this silver surface I saw Mae's head and shoulders reflected back. The reflection wasn't perfect, because her eyes and mouth were slightly blurred, but basically it was accurate.

I frowned. 'It's a mirror . . .'

'No,' she said, turning to look at me. The image of her face on the silver surface did not change. Then, after a moment or two, the image dissolved and re-formed to show the back of her head.

'What does that mean?' Mae said.

'I've got a pretty good idea, but—'

The swarm on the front hood was doing the same thing, except that its silver surface showed the two of us sitting side by side in the car, looking very frightened. The swarm was generating the image by the precise positioning of individual particles, which meant—

'Bad news,' Charley said.

'I know,' I said. 'They're innovating.'

Mae shook her head, not understanding.

'The program presets certain strategies to help attain goals. The strategies model what real predators do. One such strategy is to mimic the prey's behaviour—to imitate it.'

She said, 'You think it's trying to make itself appear like us?'

'Yes.'

'This is emergent behaviour? It's evolved on its own?'

'Yes,' I said.

'Bad news,' Charley said mournfully. 'Bad, bad news.'

SITTING THERE, I started to get angry. Because what the mirror imaging meant to me was that I didn't know the real structure of the nanoparticles. I'd been told there was a piezo-wafer that would reflect light.

But this was something entirely different. The swarms were now producing images in colour and holding them fairly stable. Such complexity wasn't possible from the simple nanoparticle I'd been shown. And that meant Ricky had lied to me yet again.

'Jack.' Mae nudged my shoulder and pointed to Charley's car. Her face was grim.

The swarm by the taillight of Charley's car was now a black stream that curved high in the air, and then disappeared in the seam where the red plastic joined the metal.

Over the headset I said, 'Charley . . . I think it's found a way.'

'Yeah, I see it.'

Charley was scrambling into the back seat. Already particles were beginning to fill the inside of the car. Charley coughed. I couldn't see what he was doing, he was down below the window.

'Charley, you better get out.'

And then there was an odd sound, a strange, rhythmic rasping. I turned to Mae, who looked at me questioningly.

'Charley?'

'I'm—spraying these little bastards. Let's see how they do now.'

Mae said, 'You're spraying the isotope?'

He didn't answer. But a moment later he appeared in the window again, spraying in all directions with the Windex bottle. The interior of the car grew darker as more and more particles entered. Soon we couldn't see him at all, but we heard him coughing continuously.

'Charley,' I said, 'run for it.'

Bobby Lembeck said, 'Wind's ten knots. Go for it.'

Ten knots wasn't enough but it was better than nothing.

We heard Charley's voice from the black interior. 'I can't find—door handle, can't feel . . . Where's the goddamn door handle on this—' He broke into a spasm of coughing.

Mae was pointing behind her to the back seat of our car. From the seam where the seat cushion met the back, particles were hissing into the car like black smoke.

I was vaguely aware that the passenger door banged open on the Toyota, and I saw Charley's foot emerge from the black. He was going to try his luck outside. Maybe we should, too, I thought. Already I sensed the particles filling the air. I felt the pinpricks all over my skin.

'Mae, let's run.'

She didn't answer. Probably she knew we'd never make it if we went outside. The swarms would run us down and suffocate us. Just as they did to the others.

The air was thicker. I started to cough. I knew we couldn't survive more than a minute or so, perhaps less. I waved my hand, trying to clear the fog so I could see Mae. It didn't work. I waved my hand again, to try and see what had happened to Charley—all I saw was—

Blowing sand . . . *blowing sand.*

The wind was back up.

'Mae.' I coughed. 'Mae. The door.'

I don't know if she heard me. She was coughing hard. I reached for the door, fumbling for the handle. I felt confused and disorientated and my headset came off. I touched hot metal, jerked it down.

The door swung open beside me. Hot desert air rushed in, swirling the fog. The wind had definitely come up. 'Mae.'

She was racked with coughing. Perhaps she couldn't move. I lunged across to the passenger door. The fog was thinner now, and I saw the handle, twisted it and shoved the door open.

Wind blew through the car.

The black cloud vanished in a few seconds. I crawled out and hauled Mae with me. We were both coughing hard. I threw her arm over my shoulder and half carried her out into the open desert.

EVEN NOW, I don't know how I made it back to the laboratory building. The swarms had vanished; the wind was blowing hard. Mae was a dead weight on my shoulders, her feet dragging over the sand. Her breaths were weak and shallow and I had the feeling she wouldn't survive. I trudged on, putting one foot ahead of the other.

Somehow the door loomed in front of me and I got it open. I took

Mae into the outer room. On the other side of the glass airlock, Ricky and Bobby Lembeck were waiting, cheering us on.

The airlock doors hissed open and I got Mae inside. She managed to stand, though she was doubled over coughing. I stepped away. The wind began to blow her clean.

I watched Bobby help Mae out of the airlock and lead her down the corridor. Ricky was standing waiting for me.

'Your turn, Jack. Come on in,' he said through the intercom.

I didn't move. I stayed leaning against the wall. I said, 'What about Charley? Where is he?'

'He didn't make it, Jack. He never got out of the car.'

'But he's alive.'

'Not for long.'

'Somebody has to go get him,' I said.

'Jack, you know as well as I do what we're up against,' Ricky said. He was doing the voice of reason now, calm and logical. 'We've had terrible losses. We can't risk anybody else. Come on and get in.'

I was taking stock of my body, my breathing, my fatigue. I couldn't go back out right now. Not in the condition I was in.

So I got into the airlock.

WITH A ROAR, the blowers flattened my hair, fluttered my clothes, and cleaned the black particles from my clothes and skin. My vision and breathing improved immediately. I held out my hand and saw it turn from black to pale grey, then to normal flesh colour again. I took another breath. I didn't feel good. But I felt better.

The glass doors opened. Ricky held out his arms. 'Jack. Thank God you're safe.'

I didn't answer. I just turned and went back the way I had come.

'Jack . . . What're you doing?'

The glass doors whished shut, and locked with a thunk. 'I'm not leaving him out there,' I said. 'I'm not leaving him behind.'

DAY 6: 4.22PM

The wind was blowing briskly. There was no sign of the swarms, and I crossed to the shed without incident. I didn't have a headset so I was spared Ricky's commentary.

The back passenger door of the Toyota was open. I found Charley lying on his back, motionless. He was still breathing, although shallowly. With an effort, I managed to pull him into a sitting position.

He stared at me with dull eyes. His lips were blue and his skin was chalky grey. A tear ran down his cheek. His mouth moved.

'Don't try to talk,' I said. 'Save your energy.' Grunting, I swung his legs round so he was facing out. Charley was a big guy, at least twenty pounds heavier than I was. I knew I couldn't carry him back. But behind the back seat of the Toyota I saw the fat tyres of David's dirt bike. That might work.

'OK, Charley . . .' I eased him off the seat and down onto the running board. 'Just stay there, OK?'

I let go of him, and he remained sitting, staring into space.

I went round to the back of the Land Cruiser and popped the trunk. I pulled the dirt bike out of the car and set it on the ground. There was no key in the ignition. I went to the front of the Toyota and opened the glove box. Lip balm, Kleenex, Band-Aids. No keys. Then I noticed that between the seats there was a locked tray. It probably opened with the ignition key.

Where were David's keys? Had Vince taken them on arrival, as he had taken mine? I took a look at Charley's face. Maybe by now he was feeling better. But no, if anything, he appeared weaker. I took his headset off and put it on my head. I heard Ricky and Bobby talking softly. I pulled the mouthpiece near my lips and said, 'Guys? Speak to me.'

A pause. Bobby, surprised: 'Jack?'

'That's right.'

'Jack, you can't stay there. The wind's been falling steadily. It's only ten knots now.'

'OK. Shit, Charley, I can't carry you. And David didn't leave any keys in his car, so we're out of luck—'

I stopped.

What if David were locked out of his car? He was an engineer, he would never be caught unprepared. No, David would have hidden a key. Probably in one of those magnetic key boxes.

I ran my fingers along the inside of the front and back bumpers. Nothing. I felt under the running boards on both sides of the car. Nothing. No magnetic box, no key. I got down and looked under the car. No key. Where else could you hide a key?

I heard the whirr of the video monitor in the corner of the shed. I looked over the ski rack of the car and saw the lens rotate as Bobby and Ricky zoomed in on me. I vaguely wondered why David had a ski rack, because he didn't ski. It must have come with the car as standard equipment and—

I swore. It was so obvious.

There was only one place I hadn't checked. I jumped up on the running board and looked at the roof of the car. I ran my fingers over the ski rack. They touched black tape. I pulled the tape away and saw a silver key. I dropped back down to the ground and went to the locked tray between the front seats. I put the silver key in the lock and twisted it. Inside the tray I found a small yellow key.

'Jack? Nine knots.'

'OK.'

I hurried round to the back of the car and fitted the key into the bike's ignition, straddled the machine and started it up.

'*Jack?* What are you doing?'

I walked the bike round to where Charley was sitting. That was going to be the tricky part. The bike didn't have a kickstand; I moved as close to Charley as I could and then tried to support him enough that he could climb onto the back seat while I still sat on the bike. Fortunately, he seemed to understand what I was doing; I got him in place, with his arms around my waist and his head on my shoulder.

Bobby: 'Jack? They're here. South side. Coming towards you.'

I gunned the motor. And I stayed exactly where I was. I said, 'Hold tight, Charley.' He nodded.

I could see the swarms now, coming around the building. This time there were nine. They headed straight for me in a V-formation. Their own flocking behaviour.

Bobby: 'Jack, do you see them?'

'I see them.' Of course I saw them.

And of course they were different from before. They were denser now, the columns thicker and more substantial.

I waited. I stayed where I was until they were twenty yards away from me, then ten. Were they able to move faster now, or was it my imagination? I waited until they were almost upon me before I twisted the throttle and raced forward. I passed straight through the lead swarm, into the blackness and out again, and then I was gunning for the power station door, not daring to look back over my shoulder. It was a wild ride, and it only lasted a few seconds. As we reached the power station, I dropped the bike, put my shoulder under Charley's arm, and staggered the final step or two to the door.

The swarms were still fifty yards away from the door when I managed to turn the knob, pull, get one foot in the crack, and kick the door open the rest of the way. When I did that I lost my balance, and Charley and I more or less fell through the door onto the concrete.

The door came swinging shut and whanged into our legs. I felt a sharp pain in my ankles—but worse, the door was still open, kept ajar by our legs. I could see the swarms approaching.

I scrambled to my feet and dragged Charley's inert body into the room. The door shut, but I knew it was a fire door, and it wasn't airtight. We wouldn't be safe until we were both in the airlock; until the first set of glass doors had hissed shut.

Grunting and sweating, I hauled Charley into a sitting position, propped up against the side blowers. That cleared his feet of the glass doors. And because only one person could be in the airlock at a time, I stepped back outside and I waited for the doors to close.

But they didn't close.

Bobby Lembeck and Mae came running into the far room, beyond the second set of glass doors. They were waving their arms, making gestures, apparently indicating for me to come back into the airlock. But that didn't make sense. They didn't have headsets on and were waving frantically, come in, come in.

At my feet, I saw the nanoparticles begin to come into the room like black steam. They were coming through the edges of the fire door. I had only five or ten seconds now.

I stepped back in the airlock. Bobby and Mae were nodding, approving. Now they were making other gestures, lifting.

Charley was slumped there in a sitting position, a dead weight. I bent over him, tried to haul him to his feet, but he didn't budge.

'Charley, for God's sake, help.' Groaning, I tried again. Charley kicked his legs and pushed with his arms and I got him a couple of feet off the ground. Then, with a final heave, I got him standing in a kind of crazy lovers' clench. I looked back to the glass doors.

The doors didn't close.

The air was getting blacker all the time. I looked at Mae and Bobby and they were frantic, holding up two fingers, shaking them at me. I didn't get it. What was wrong with the damned doors? Finally, Mae bent over and very deliberately pointed with one finger of each hand to her two shoes. I saw her mouth, 'Two shoes.'

The pinpricks were irritating, making it difficult to think. I felt the old confusion begin to seep over me. My brain felt sluggish. What did she mean, two shoes?

It was beginning to get dark in the airlock. It was becoming harder to see Mae and Bobby. They were pantomiming something else, but I didn't get it. They began to feel distant to me, distant and trivial.

Two shoes. What did she mean?

And then I got it. I turned my back to Charley, leaned against him, and said, 'Put your hands around my neck.' He did, and I grabbed his legs and lifted his feet off the floor.

Instantly, the door hissed shut and the blowers began to blast down on us. From that point on, I don't remember much at all.

Day 6: 6.18pm

I woke up in my bed in the residential module. The air handlers were roaring so loudly the room sounded like an airport. Ricky was sitting watching me, smiling. 'Jack, so you're awake. How do you feel?'

'How's Charley?'

'He seems OK. He's sleeping. I want you to know we're all very grateful for what you've done—I mean, the company is grateful—'

'Screw the company.'

'Jack, please. I feel terrible about what's happened. I really do. If there were any way to go back and change it, believe me, I would.'

I looked at him. 'I don't believe you, Ricky.'

He gave a winning little smile. 'You know that I always valued our friendship, Jack. It was always the most important thing to me.'

I just stared at him. Ricky wasn't listening at all. I thought, Is he on drugs? He was certainly acting bizarrely.

'Well, anyway.' He took a breath, changed the subject. 'Julia's coming out this evening, that's good news.'

'Uh-huh. Why is she coming out?'

'Well, because she's worried about these runaway swarms.'

'How worried is she?' I said. 'Because these swarms could have been killed off weeks ago, when the evolutionary patterns first appeared. But that didn't happen.'

'Yes. Well. The thing is, back then nobody really understood—'

'I think they did, Ricky. When I came out here the pilot told me he'd been told not to get out of the helicopter. The implication was that it was dangerous here.'

He shook his head. 'I don't know what you're talking about.'

THE SHOWER HELPED. I stood under it for about twenty minutes, letting the steaming hot water run over my aching body.

When I came out, I found Ricky there, sitting on a bench. He'd brought me the missing code I had been asking for, as a kind of peace offering.

'Sorry about that,' he said. 'Took me a while to find it. Rosie took a whole subdirectory offline to work on one section. I guess she forgot to put it back. That's why it wasn't in the main directory.'

'Uh-huh.' I scanned the sheet. When I'd finished I said, 'This code looks almost the same as the original.'

'Yeah. The changes are all minor. I don't know why it's such an issue.' He shrugged. 'I mean, as soon as we lost control of the swarm, the precise code seemed a little beside the point to me.'

'And how did you lose control? There's no evolutionary algorithm in this code here.'

He spread his hands. 'Jack,' he said, 'if we knew that, we'd know everything. We wouldn't be in this mess.'

'But I was asked to come here to check problems with the code my team had written. I was told the agents were losing track of their goals.'

'I'd say breaking free of radio control is losing track of goals.'

'But the code's not changed.'

'Yeah well, nobody really cared about the code itself, Jack. It's the behaviour that emerges from the code. That's what we wanted you to help us with. Because I mean, it *is* your code, right?'

'Yeah, and it's your swarm.'

'True enough, Jack.'

He shrugged in his self-deprecating way, and left the room. I stared at the paper for a while, and then crumpled it up and tossed it in the wastebasket. However this problem got solved, it wasn't going to be with computer code. That much was clear.

I DECIDED to go and check on Charley. He was still asleep in his room, sprawled out on the bed. Bobby Lembeck walked by. 'How long has he been asleep?' I asked.

'Since you got back.'

'Do you think we should wake him up, check on him?'

'Nah, let him sleep. We'll check him after dinner.'

'When is that?'

'Quarter of an hour.' Bobby laughed. 'I'm cooking.'

THAT REMINDED ME I was supposed to call home around dinnertime, so I went into my room and dialled.

Ellen answered the phone. 'Hello? What is it!' She sounded harried. I heard Amanda crying and Eric yelling at Nicole in the background.

I said, 'Hi, Ellen.'

'Oh, thank God,' she said. 'You have to speak to your daughter.'

'Nicole, it's your father.' I could tell she was holding out the phone to her.

I looked at the monitor in front of me. It showed views of the desert outside, rotating images from all the security cameras. One camera showed the dirt bike, lying on its side, near the door to the power station. Another showed the outside of the storage shed, with the door swinging open and shut, revealing the outline of Rosie's body inside. I had a nagging feeling about it. Something bothered me.

'It's very simple, Dad,' Nicole was saying in her most reasonable grown-up voice. 'Eric came into my room and knocked all my books on the floor. So I told him to pick them up. He said no and called me the b-word, so I took his G.I. Joe and hid it. That's all.'

Two people had died today. I had almost died. And now my family, which yesterday had been the most important thing in my life, seemed distant and petty.

I said, 'Nicole, you have to listen to Ellen. She's in charge until I get back. So if she says to do something, you do it.'

Then I talked to Ellen. I encouraged her as best I could.

Some time during this conversation, the security camera showing the outside of the shed came up again. And I again saw the swinging door, and the outside of the shed. It all looked the way it should. I did not know what had bothered me.

Then I realised.

David's body wasn't there. Earlier, I had seen his body slide out of the door and disappear from view, so it should be lying outside.

No body.

Perhaps I was mistaken. Or perhaps there were coyotes. In any case, if David's body was gone, there was nothing I could do about it now.

IT WAS ABOUT SEVEN o'clock when we sat down to eat dinner in the little kitchen of the residential module. Bobby brought out plates of ravioli with tomato sauce, and mixed vegetables. I was surprisingly hungry. I ate everything on my plate.

Mae was silent as she ate, as usual. Beside her, Vince Reynolds ate noisily. Ricky was at the far end of the table, looking down at his food and not meeting my eyes. Nobody wanted to talk about Rosie and David, but the empty stools around the table were pretty obvious. Bobby said to me, 'So, you're going to go out tonight?'

'Yes,' I said. 'When is it dark?'

'Sunset should be around seven twenty,' Bobby said.

'So we can go out three hours after that. Some time after ten.'

Bobby said, 'And you think you can track the swarm?'

'We should. Charley sprayed one swarm pretty thoroughly.'

'As a result of which, I glow in the dark,' Charley said, laughing. He came into the room and sat down.

Everyone greeted him enthusiastically. I asked him how he felt.

'OK. A little weak. And I have a headache from hell.'

'I know. Me too.'

'Do you suppose these things get into your brain?' Charley said. 'I mean, that's what everybody's worried about—nanotechnology polluting the environment, right? Nanoparticles are small enough to get places nobody's ever had to worry about before. Maybe we're infected, Jack.'

'You don't seem that worried about it,' Ricky said.

'Hey, what can I do about it now? Hope I give it to you, is about all. Hey, this spaghetti's not bad.'

'Ravioli,' Bobby said.

I said, 'Guys? Are we missing anybody?'

'I don't think so, why?'

I pointed to the monitor. 'Who's that standing out in the desert?'

DAY 6: 7.12PM

'Oh shit,' Bobby said. He jumped up from the table and ran out of the room. Everyone else did, too. I followed the others into the utility room, where there were large wall-mounted screens showing the outside video camera shots.

Ricky was holding his radio as he went: 'Vince, lock us down.'

'We're locked down,' Vince said.

The sun was already below the horizon, but the sky was a bright orange, fading into purple. Silhouetted against this sky was a young man with short hair. He was wearing jeans and a white T-shirt and looked like a surfer. I couldn't see his face clearly in the failing light, but even so, I thought there was something familiar about him.

'We got any floodlights out there?'

'Lights coming up,' Bobby said, and a moment later the young man stood in glaring light. Now I could see him clearly—

And then it hit me. It looked like the same kid who had been in Julia's car last night after dinner, just before her accident. The same blond surfer kid who, now that I saw him again, looked like—

'Jesus, Ricky,' Bobby said. 'He looks like *you*.'

'You're right,' Mae said. 'It's Ricky. He even has your clothes on.'

Ricky was silent for a moment. 'I'll be damned.'

Mae said, 'I can't make out the facial features very well.'

Charley moved closer to the largest of the screens and squinted at the image. 'That's because there aren't any,' he said.

It was as if a sculptor had started to carve a face and had stopped before he was finished.

'You know what we're looking at here, don't you?' Charley said. He sounded worried. 'Pan down. Let's see the rest of him.' Bobby panned down, and we saw white sneakers moving over the desert surface. Except the sneakers didn't seem to be touching the ground, but rather hovering just above it, and they were sort of blurry. Like a sketch rather than an actual sneaker.

'This is very weird,' Mae said.

'Not weird at all,' Charley said. 'The swarm doesn't have enough agents to make high-resolution shoes. So it's approximating.'

'Or else,' I said, 'it's the best it can do with the materials at hand. It must be generating all these colours by tilting its photovoltaic surface at slight angles, catching the light. It's like those flash cards the crowd holds up in football stadiums to make a picture.'

'In which case,' Charley said, 'its behaviour is quite sophisticated.'

'You're acting like this swarm is Einstein,' Ricky said irritably.

'Obviously not,' Charley said, ''cause if it's modelling you, it's certainly no Einstein.'

I glanced at the programmers. They had stricken looks on their faces. They knew exactly how big an advance they were witnessing. Before, the swarm had trouble making a stable 2-D image. Now it was modelling in three dimensions. This transition meant that not only was the swarm now imitating our external appearance, it was also imitating our behaviour. Our walks, our gestures.

Which implied a far more complicated internal model.

Watching the faceless man on the monitor, we saw that the image was now becoming unstable. The swarm had trouble keeping the appearance solid. Instead it fluctuated.

'Running out of power.' Bobby said.

'Yeah, probably,' Charley said. 'It'd take a lot of extra juice to tilt all those particles into exact orientations.'

Indeed, the swarm was reverting back to a cloud appearance again. And as the sky got darker the monitor started to lose definition.

The swarm turned and swirled away.

I watched the swarm disappear into the horizon.

'Three hours,' I said, 'and they're history.'

Day 6: 10.12pm

Charley went back to bed right after dinner. He was still asleep at ten that night, when Mae, Bobby and I were preparing to go out again. We were wearing down vests and jackets, because it was going to be cold. Ricky said he had to wait for Julia, who was flying in any minute now; that was fine with me, I didn't want him anyway. Vince was off somewhere watching TV and drinking beer.

'Let's hit the road,' I said, and we walked in darkness towards the storage shed, a dark outline against the dark sky. I pushed the dirt bike along. Bobby was going to use Vince's All-Terrain Vehicle. None of us talked for a while. Finally, Bobby said, 'We're going to need lights.'

'We're going to need a lot of things,' Mae said. 'I made a list.'

We got to the storage shed and pushed the door open. I saw Bobby hang back in the darkness. I went in, flicked the lights on.

The interior of the storage shed appeared just as we had left it. Mae unzipped her backpack and began walking down the row of shelves. 'We need portable lights . . . flares . . . oxygen . . .'

Bobby said, 'Oxygen? Really?'

'If this site is underground, yes . . . and we need Thermite.'

I said, 'Rosie had it. Maybe she set it down when she . . . I'll look.' I went into the next room. The box of Thermite tubes lay overturned on the floor, the tubes nearby. Rosie must have dropped it when she ran. I looked over at her body by the door.

But Rosie's body was gone.

'Jesus.'

Bobby came running in. 'What is it? What's wrong?'

I pointed to the door. 'Rosie's gone. Her body . . . it's gone.'

'How can that be? An animal?'

'I don't know.' I went over and crouched down at the spot where her body had been just hours before. There were traces of milky secretions on the floor, similar to the coating we had seen on the dead rabbit. By the door there were streaks in the coating.

'It looks like she was dragged out,' Bobby said.

I peered closely at the secretion, looking for footprints. I saw none.

I got up and walked to the door. Bobby stood beside me, looking out into the darkness.

'You see anything?' he said.

'No.'

I returned to Mae. She had found everything. She had coiled magnesium fuse, flare guns, portable flashlights and head-mounted lamps. She had binoculars and night-vision goggles, a field radio, radiation counter, oxygen bottles and clear-plastic gas masks.

As I watched her dividing everything into our three backpacks, I realised that she was the only one of us with actual field experience. I was surprised how dependent on her I felt tonight.

'Let's get started,' I said, hefting a backpack onto my shoulder.

It was 10.43pm.

THE RADIATION COUNTER went crazy when we came to the Toyota. Holding the wand in front of her, Mae left the car and walked into the desert. She turned west and the clicks diminished. She went east and they picked up again. But as she continued east, the clicks slowed. She turned north, and they increased.

'North,' she said.

I got on the bike, gunned the engine. Bobby rumbled out of the shed on Vince's ATV, with its fat rear tyres and bicycle handlebars.

Mae got on the back of my bike and we started off.

The desert that had looked so flat and featureless in daylight was now revealed to have sandy dips, rock-filled beds, and deep arroyos that came up without warning. It took all my attention to keep the bike upright—particularly since Mae was continuously calling directions to me. Sometimes we had to make a full circle until she could be certain of the right path.

We were now several miles from the lab, and I was starting to worry. The counter clicks were becoming less frequent. If we didn't locate the swarm hiding place soon, we'd lose the trail entirely.

Mae was worried, too. She kept bending over closer and closer to the ground, with one hand on the wand and one arm round my waist. And I had to go slower, because the trail was becoming so faint. We lost the trail, found it, went off it again.

And at last I was going round and round in the same spot, three times, then four, but to no avail: the counter in Mae's hand just clicked randomly.

We had lost the trail.

EXHAUSTION HIT ME suddenly, and hard. I had been running on adrenalin all day and now that I was finally defeated a deep weariness came over my body. My eyes drooped. I felt as if I could go to sleep standing on the bike.

Bobby pulled up close to us. 'You guys look behind you?' he said.

'Why?'

'Look back,' he said. 'Look how far we've come.'

I turned and looked over my shoulder. To the south, I saw the bright lights of the fabrication building, surprisingly close. We couldn't be more than a mile or two away. We must have travelled in a big semicircle, eventually turning back towards our starting point.

'That's weird.'

Mae had got off the bike and stepped in front of the headlamp. She was looking at the LCD read-out on the counter. She said, 'Hmm. Take a look at this.'

Bobby leaned over and we both looked at the LCD read-out. It showed a graph of radiation intensity, stepping progressively downward and finally dropping quickly.

Bobby frowned. 'And this is?'

'Time course of tonight's readings,' she said. 'The machine's showing us that ever since we started, the intensity of the radiation has declined arithmetically until the last minute or so, when the decrease suddenly became exponential. It just fell to zero.'

'So?' Bobby looked puzzled. 'That means what? I don't get it.'

'I do.' She turned to me, climbed back on the bike. 'I think I know what happened. Go forward—slowly.'

I let out the clutch and rumbled forward. My headlamp showed a slight rise in the desert, scrubby cactus ahead. We continued up the rise until it flattened, and then the bike began to tilt downwards—

'*Stop!*'

I stopped.

Directly ahead, the desert floor ended. I saw blackness beyond.

'Is that a cliff?'

'No. Just a high ridge.'

I edged the bike forward. We were at the crest of a ridge fifteen feet high, which formed one side of a very wide streambed. Beyond the distant bank, the desert was flat again.

'I understand now,' I said. 'The swarm jumped.'

'Yes,' she said, 'it became airborne. And we lost the trail.'

'But then it must have landed somewhere down there,' Bobby said, pointing to the streambed.

'Maybe,' I said. 'Or it could have gone a quarter-mile beyond.'

Mae was not discouraged. 'Bobby, you stay here,' she said. 'You'll mark the position where it jumped. Jack and I will find a path down, into that plain. Sooner or later, we'll find it.'

'OK,' Bobby said. 'Got you.'

'OK,' I said. We might as well do it. We had nothing to lose. But

I had very little confidence that we would succeed.

Bobby leaned forward over his ATV. 'What's *that*?'

'What?'

'An animal. I saw glowing eyes. In that brush over there.' He pointed to the centre of the streambed.

I frowned. We both had our headlamps trained down the ridge. We were lighting a fairly large arc of desert. I didn't see any animals.

'There!' Mae said.

'I don't see anything.'

She pointed. 'It just went behind that juniper bush.'

'I see the bush,' I said. 'But . . .' I didn't see an animal.

'It's moving left to right. Wait a minute and it'll come out again.'

We waited, and then I saw a pair of bright green, glowing spots. Close to the ground, moving right. I saw a flash of pale white. And almost immediately I knew that something was wrong.

So did Bobby. He twisted his handlebars, moving his headlamp to point directly to the spot. He reached for binoculars. 'Jesus,' he said, staring through the binoculars.

'What? What is it?'

'It's a body being dragged,' he said. And then, in a funny voice, he said, 'It's Rosie.'

DAY 6: 10.58PM

Rosie Castro lay on her back, her head tilted so she appeared to be looking backwards, directly at me, her eyes wide, her arm outstretched towards me, her pale hand open. There was an expression of pleading—or terror—on her face. Rigor mortis had set in, and her body jerked stiffly as it moved over the desert.

She was being dragged away—but no animal was dragging her.

'I don't see what's doing it,' I said. 'There's a shadow below her . . .'

'That's not a shadow,' Mae said. 'It's them. Turn your lights off.'

Bobby and I flicked off our headlamps. 'I thought swarms couldn't maintain power more than three hours?' I said.

'Maybe they've overcome that limitation in the wild.'

The implications were unsettling. If the swarms could now sustain power through the night, they might be active when we reached their hiding place. I had intended to kill them in their sleep, so to speak.

'Where are they taking her?' I said.

Mae unzipped my backpack, and pulled out a set of night goggles. 'Try these.'

I slipped on the headset and flipped the lenses down. Almost immediately, I saw Rosie's body moving farther and farther away, towards what looked like a natural formation—a mound of dark earth about fifteen feet wide and six feet high. Erosion had carved deep, vertical clefts so that the mound looked a little like a huge gear turned on edge. It would be easy to overlook this formation as natural.

But it wasn't natural. And erosion hadn't produced its sculpted look. On the contrary, I was seeing an artificial construction, similar to the huge, intricate nests made by African termites.

Wearing a second pair of goggles, Mae looked for a while in silence, then said, 'This is the product of self-organised behaviour?'

It was indeed difficult to conceive how this construction might have been made. But I was beginning to realise that out here in the desert, asking how something happened was a fool's errand. The swarms were changing fast, almost minute to minute. By the time you figured it out, things would have changed.

We all stood there under the stars. Bobby said, 'What do we do now?'

'Follow Rosie,' I said.

'You mean we follow her into that mound?' he said.

'Yes,' I said.

WE WALKED THE REST of the way. About fifty feet from the mound we became aware of a putrid odour of rotting and decay. It was so strong it made my stomach turn. A faint green glow seemed to be emanating from inside the mound.

Bobby whispered, 'You really want to go in *there*?'

'Not yet,' Mae whispered. She pointed off to one side. Rosie's body was moving up the slope of the mound. As she came to the rim, her rigid legs pointed into the air for a moment. Then her body toppled over, and she vanished into the interior.

Mae whispered, 'OK. Let's go.'

She started forward in her usual noiseless way. Following her, I tried to be as quiet as I could. Bobby crunched and crackled his way along the ground. Mae paused, and gave him a hard look.

Bobby held up his hands as if to say, what can I do?

She whispered, '*Watch where you put your feet.*'

He whispered, 'It's dark, I can't see.'

'You can *if you try*.'

I couldn't recall ever seeing Mae show irritation before, but we were all under pressure now. Mae turned and once again moved forward silently. Bobby followed, making just as much noise as before.

We had only gone a few steps before Mae signalled for him to stop.

He shook his head, no. He clearly didn't want to be left alone.

She gripped his shoulder, pointed firmly to the ground and whispered, 'You stay here. You'll get us all killed. Sit.'

Finally, Bobby sat down.

Mae looked at me. I nodded. We set out again. By now we were twenty feet from the mound itself. The stench was almost overpowering, but more than anything it was the deep thrumming sound that made me want to run away. But Mae kept going.

We inched forward slowly, until we could look over the rim.

It wasn't what I expected at all.

The mound simply narrowed an existing opening that was huge—twenty feet wide or more, revealing a rock slide that sloped downwards from the rim and ended at a gaping hole in the rock to our right.

What I was seeing was the entrance to a very large cave. From our position on the rim, we couldn't see into the cave itself, but the thrumming sound suggested activity within. Mae reached into the side pouch of her pack, and withdrew a small thumb-sized camera on a thin telescoping stick. She opened the telescoping stick to its full length and gently lowered the camera into the hole. On the camera's tiny LCD screen we could now see farther into the cave. It was undoubtedly natural, and perhaps eight feet high, ten feet wide and the rock walls appeared to be covered with milky secretions.

Mae signalled me: Want to go down?

I nodded. I didn't like how this felt, but we really had no choice.

Mae had started very slowly to slide out of her backpack, when suddenly she froze.

I looked at the LCD screen. And I froze, too.

A figure had walked from behind the bend, and now stood alertly at the entrance of the cave, looking around.

It was Ricky.

HE WAS BEHAVING as if he had heard a sound, or had been alerted for some reason. I didn't understand what he was doing here—or even how he had got here. Then another man came around the bend.

He was also Ricky.

I glanced at Mae, but she was utterly still. Only her eyes moved.

I squinted at the screen. Within the limits of video resolution, the two figures appeared to be identical. I couldn't see the faces well, but I had the impression they were more detailed than before.

They didn't seem to notice the camera.

They looked up at the sky, and then at the rock slide for a while. Then they turned their backs on us and returned to the cave.

Still Mae did not move, did not even blink.

Another figure came around the corner. It was David Brooks. He moved awkwardly, stiffly at first, but he quickly became more fluid. I had the feeling I was watching a puppeteer perfect his moves, animating the figure in a more lifelike way. Then David became Ricky. And then David again. And the David figure turned and went away.

Still Mae waited. She waited fully two more minutes, and then finally withdrew the camera. She jerked her thumb, indicating we should go back. Together, we crept silently into the desert night.

WE GATHERED a hundred yards to the west, near our vehicles. Mae was rummaging in her backpack; she pulled out a clipboard with a felt marker. She flicked on her penlight and began to draw.

'This is what you're up against,' she said. 'Past the bend inside the cave we saw, there's a big hole in the floor, and the cave spirals downwards for maybe a hundred yards. That brings you into one large chamber that is maybe a hundred feet high and a couple of hundred feet wide. No passages leading off, at least none that I saw.'

'That you saw?'

'I found that cave a couple of weeks ago, when we first went looking for the swarm's hiding place. I didn't find any indication of a swarm then.' She explained that the cave was filled with bats, packed together in a pink squirming mass, all the way out to the entrance.

'Ugh,' Bobby said. 'I hate bats.'

'I didn't see any bats there tonight.'

'They've all been eaten, probably.'

'Listen, guys,' Bobby said, shaking his head. 'I'm just a programmer. I don't think I can do this. I don't think I can go in there.'

I ignored him. 'We're wasting our time unless we destroy all the swarms and all the assemblers that are making them. Right?'

They both nodded.

'I'm not sure that'll be possible,' I said. 'I thought the swarms would be powered down at night. I thought we could destroy them on the ground. But they're not powered down—at least not all of them. And if just one of them gets past us, if it escapes from the cave . . .' I shrugged. 'Then this has all been a waste of time.'

Mae said, 'We need some way to trap them in the cave.'

'There isn't any way,' Bobby said. 'I mean, they can just fly out, whenever they want.'

Mae said, 'There might be a way.' She started rummaging in her backpack again, looking for something. 'Meanwhile, the three of us better spread out.'

'Why?' Bobby said, alarmed.

'Just do it,' Mae said. 'Now get moving.'

I TIGHTENED my backpack and adjusted the straps so it wouldn't rattle. I locked the night goggles up on my forehead, and I started forward. I was halfway to the mound when I heard the thumping of helicopter blades. That would be Julia coming from the Valley, I thought. I wondered what was so urgent that she had had to leave the hospital against orders and fly out here in the middle of the night.

As the helicopter approached, it switched on its searchlight. I watched the circle of blue-white light as it rippled over the ground. Then it was roaring over me, blinding me for a moment in the halogen light. Almost immediately it banked sharply and circled back.

What the hell was going on?

The helicopter made a slow arc, coming to a stop right above where I was hiding. I rolled onto my back and waved it away repeatedly.

The helicopter descended, and for a moment I thought it was going to land right beside me. Then it abruptly banked again and headed south towards the concrete pad. The sound faded.

I decided I had better change my position fast. I got to my knees and, in a crouch, moved crabwise thirty yards to the left.

When I looked back at the mound I saw three figures coming out of the interior. They all looked like Ricky. I watched as they went down the slope of the mound and out into the brush. One of the figures was going to the place where I had been hiding. My heart began to pound in my chest. I was surrounded by miles of desert and the swarms would hunt me down. In a few moments—

With a roar, the helicopter came back. The three Ricky figures turned and fled, literally flying over the ground, conveying a sense of panic. Did they fear the helicopter? It seemed they did. And as I watched I understood why. Even though the swarms were now heavier and more substantial, they were still vulnerable to strong winds. The helicopter was a hundred feet in the air but the downdraught was powerful enough to deform the running figures, flattening them partially as they fled back to the mound.

I looked over at Mae, who had been standing in the streambed. She yelled, 'Let's go!' and began running towards me. I was dimly aware of Bobby, running away from the mound, back to his ATV. But there was no time to worry about him. The helicopter hung poised right above the mound itself. Dust whipped up, stinging my eyes.

Then Mae was beside me. Removing our goggles, we pulled on our oxygen masks. She turned me, twisted the tank valve behind me. I did the same for her. Then we put the night goggles back on. It seemed like a lot of contraptions jiggling and rattling around my face. She leaned close, shouted: 'Ready?'

'I'm ready!' I shouted, clipping a halogen flashlight to my belt.

Together we clawed our way up the slope of the mound, our clothes whipping around us in the downdraught. We arrived at the edge, barely visible in the thick, swirling dust. We couldn't see anything beyond the rim. We couldn't see what was below.

Mae took my hand and we jumped.

DAY 6: 11.22PM

I landed on loose stones, and half stumbled, half slid down the slope towards the cave entrance. The thumping of the helicopter blades above us was loud. Mae was right beside me, but I could hardly see her in the thick dust. There were no Ricky figures, no swarms, anywhere in sight. We came to the cave entrance and stopped. Mae pulled out the Thermite tubes. She gave me the magnesium fuses and a cigarette lighter. She pointed to the interior of the cave. I nodded.

We rounded the bend and saw nothing but suspended dust and the vague outlines of cave walls. Then from the gloom directly ahead I saw a Ricky figure emerge. He was expressionless, just walking towards us. Then another figure from the left, and another. The three formed a line. They marched towards us at a steady pace.

'First lesson,' Mae said through her headset, holding out one of the Thermite tubes.

'Let's hope they don't learn it,' I said, and I lit the fuse. It sputtered white-hot sparks. She tossed the tube forward. It landed a few feet in front of the advancing group. They ignored it.

Mae said, 'It's a three count . . . two . . . one . . . and *turn away*.'

I twisted away, ducking my head under my arm just as a sphere of blinding white filled the tunnel. Even though my eyes were closed, the glare was so strong that I saw spots when I opened my eyes.

Mae was already moving forward. The dust in the air had a slightly darker tint. I saw no sign of the three figures.

'Did they run?'

'No. Vaporised,' she said. She sounded pleased.

'New situations,' I said. I was feeling encouraged. If the programming assumptions still held, the swarms would be disorganised, chaotic when reacting to genuinely new situations. That was a weakness of distributed intelligence.

'We hope,' Mae said.

We came to the gaping hole in the cave floor she had described. In the night goggles, I saw a sort of sloping ramp. Four or five figures were coming up towards us, and there seemed to be more behind. They all looked like Ricky, but many of them were not so well formed. And those in the rear were just swirling clouds.

'Second lesson.' Mae held out a tube. It sizzled white when I lit it. She rolled it gently down the ramp. The figures hesitated.

'Damn,' I said, but then it was time to duck away, and shield my eyes from the explosive flash. Inside the confined space, there was a roar of expanding gas. I felt a burst of intense heat on my back. When I looked again, most of the swarms beneath us had vanished. But a few hung back, apparently undamaged.

They were learning. Fast.

'Next lesson,' Mae said, holding two tubes this time. I lit both and she rolled one and threw the second one deeper down the ramp. The explosions roared, and a huge gust of hot air rolled past us.

When we looked again, there were no figures in sight, no swarms.

We went down the ramp, heading deeper into the cave.

WE HAD STARTED with twenty Thermite tubes. We had sixteen left, and we had gone only a short distance down the ramp towards the large room at the bottom. Mae moved quickly now—and the few swarms that materialised before us all backed away at our approach. We were herding them into the lower room, moving deeper into the cave. Down here, dust hung suspended in the air, diffusing the infrared beams of the night goggles. The sense of darkness and isolation was frightening. I couldn't tell what was on either side of me unless I turned my head, sweeping my infrared beam back and forth.

We reached level ground. Something crunched underfoot. I looked down and saw the floor was carpeted with thousands of tiny, delicate yellow bones. The bones of bats. Mae was right: they'd all been eaten.

And then at last we came to the large central chamber—a huge space filled from floor to ceiling with an orderly array of dark spheres, about two feet in diameter, and bristling with spiky protrusions. They looked like clusters of enormous sea urchins.

'Is this what I think it is?' Mae's voice was calm, almost scholarly.

'Yeah, I think so,' I said. Unless I was wrong, these spiked clusters were an organic version of the fabrication plant that Xymos had built on the surface. 'This is how they reproduce.' I moved forward.

'You think there's a centre?'

'Maybe.' And if there was, I wanted to drop Thermite on it.

Moving among the clusters was an eerie sensation. Thick mucus-like liquid dripped from the tips of the spikes. And the spheres seemed to be coated with a kind of thick gel that quivered, making the whole cluster seem to be moving, alive. I looked more closely. Then I saw that the surface of the spheres really was alive; crawling within the gel were masses of twisting black worms. 'Jesus!'

'They were here before,' she said calmly.

'What?'

'The worms. They were living in the layer of guano on the cave floor, when I came here before.'

'And now they're involved in swarm synthesis,' I said. 'That didn't take long, just a few days. Co-evolution in action. The spheres probably provide food and collect their excretions in some way.'

'Or collect *them*,' Mae said drily.

'Yeah. Maybe.' It wasn't inconceivable. Ants raised aphids the way we raised cows. Other insects grew fungus in gardens for food.

We moved deeper into the room. The swarms swirled on all sides of us, but they kept their distance. There was a kind of thick muck on the ground. In a few places it glowed streaky green. The streaks went in towards the centre. Suddenly we knew we had reached the centre of the room, because the clusters ended in an open space, and directly ahead I saw what looked like a miniature version of the mound outside. It was about four feet high, perfectly circular, with flat vanes extending outwards on all sides. Pale smoke was coming off the vanes.

We moved closer.

'It's hot,' Mae said. 'What do you think is in there?'

I looked at the floor. I could see now that the streaks of green were running from the clusters down to this central mound. I said, 'Assemblers.' The spiky urchins generated raw organic material. It flowed to the centre, where the assemblers churned out the final molecules. This is where the final assembly occurred.

'Then this is the heart,' Mae said.

'Yeah. You could say.'

The swarms were all around us, hanging back by the clusters. Apparently, they wouldn't come into the centre.

'How many do you want?' she said quietly, taking the Thermite from her pack.

I looked around at all the swarms.

'Five here,' I said. 'We'll need the rest to get out.'

'We can't light five at once . . .'

'It's all right.' I held out my hand and she gave me the five tubes. I tossed them, unlit, into the mound.

'OK,' she said. She understood immediately what I was doing. She was already taking out more tubes.

'Now four,' I said, looking back at the swarms. They were restless, moving back and forth, but still did not approach us. I didn't know how long it would stay that way. 'Three for you, one for me. You do the swarms.'

'Right . . .' She gave me one tube. I lit the others for her. She threw them in the direction we had come. The swarms danced away.

She counted: 'Three . . . two . . . one . . . now!'

We crouched, ducked away from the harsh blast of light. I heard a cracking sound; when I looked again, some of the clusters were breaking up, falling apart. Without hesitating, I lit the next tube, and as it spat white sparks, I tossed it into the central mound.

'Let's go!'

We ran for the entrance, leaping over the crumbling clusters. In my mind I was counting . . . three . . . two . . . one . . .

Now.

There was a kind of high-pitched shriek, and then a terrific blast of hot gas, a booming detonation and stabbing pain in my ears. The shock wave knocked me flat on the ground, sent me skidding forward in the sludge. I felt the spikes sticking into me. My goggles were knocked away and I was surrounded by blackness.

'Mae,' I said. 'Mae . . . where are you? I can't see anything.'

Everything was pitch black. I fought panic.

'It's all right,' Mae said. In the darkness I felt her hand gripping my arm. 'The flashlight's on your belt,' she said.

I fumbled in the darkness, feeling for the clip. I found it, but I couldn't get it open. It was a spring clip and my fingers kept slipping off. I began to hear a thrumming sound, low at first, but starting to build. Finally the clip opened, and I flicked the flashlight on with a sigh of relief. The cave had been transformed by the explosion. Many of the clusters had broken apart and the spikes were all over the floor. Some substance on the floor was beginning to burn. Acrid, foul smoke was billowing up. .

'Come on, Jack,' Mae said, holding out four tubes, and somehow, fumbling with the flashlight, I managed to light them and she flung them in all directions. I threw my hands over my eyes as the hot spheres exploded around me. When I looked again, the swarms were gone. But in only a few moments, they began to re-emerge. First one swarm, then three, then six, then ten—and then too many to count.

I lit the last three tubes and Mae threw them, retracing her steps towards the entrance as she did so. I knew our situation was hopeless. Each blast scattered the swarms for just a moment. They then quickly regrouped.

We came to the foot of the ramp leading back to the surface and I heard the rumble of an engine from somewhere above us. Looking up I saw the ATV poised on the ramp above. Bobby gunned the engine and shouted 'Get outttttt!'

Mae turned and ran up the ramp and I followed. I was vaguely aware of Bobby lighting something that burst into orange flame, and then Mae pushed me against the wall as the riderless ATV roared down the ramp towards the chamber below, with a flaming cloth hanging from its gas tank. It was a motorised Molotov cocktail.

As soon as it passed, Mae shoved me hard in the back. 'Run!'

I sprinted the last few yards up the ramp. Bobby was reaching down for us, hauling us up over the lip to the level above. Then I was running hard towards the cave entrance and had almost reached the opening when a fiery blast knocked us off our feet and I went tumbling through the air and smashed against one of the cave walls. I got to my feet, head ringing.

I looked at Mae and Bobby. They were getting to their feet. With the helicopter still thumping above us, we clambered up the incline and collapsed over the lip of the mound, out into the cool, black, desert night.

The last thing I saw was Mae gesturing for the helicopter to go.

And then the cave exploded into an enormous angry fireball.

Day 7: 12.12am

'Jack.'

Julia rushed towards me as I came down the corridor. Her ankle and wrist were bandaged but in the overhead light her face looked beautiful in a lean, elegant way. She threw her arms round me and buried her head in my shoulder. 'Oh, Jack. Thank God you're all right.'

'Yeah,' I said hoarsely. 'I'm OK.'

'I'm so glad . . . so glad.'

I just stood there, feeling her hug me. Then I hugged her back, not knowing how to react. She was so energised, but I was exhausted, flat.

'I can't tell you,' she said, 'how grateful I am for what you did tonight, Jack. What all of you did,' she added, turning to the others. 'I'm only sorry I wasn't here to help. I know this is all my fault. But we're very grateful. The company is grateful.'

I thought, The company? But all I said was, 'Well, it had to be done.'

'It did, yes. And you did it, Jack. Thank God.'

Ricky was standing in the background, head bobbing up and down.

'I think we should all have a drink,' Julia was saying, as we went down the corridor. 'There must be some champagne here. Ricky? Is there? Yes? I want to celebrate what you guys have done.'

'I just want to sleep,' I said.

'Oh, come on, just one glass.'

It was typical Julia, I thought. Involved in her own world, not noticing how anyone around her was feeling. The last thing any of us wanted to do right now was drink champagne.

'Thanks anyway,' Mae said, shaking her head.

'Maybe tomorrow,' Bobby said.

'Oh well, OK! We'll do it tomorrow, then.'

I noticed how fast she was talking and remembered Ellen's comment about her taking drugs. It certainly seemed like she was on something. But I was so tired I just didn't give a damn.

'I've told the news to Larry Handler, the head of the company,' she said, 'and he's very grateful to you all.'

'That's nice,' I said. 'Is he going to notify the army?'

'Notify the army? About what?'

'About the runaway experiment.'

'Well, Jack, that's all taken care of now. You've taken care of it.'

'I'm not sure we have,' I said. 'Some of the swarms might have escaped. To be safe, I think we should call in the army.'

'The army?' Julia's eyes flicked to Ricky, then back to me. 'Jack, you're right,' she said firmly. 'If there is the slightest chance something was missed, we must notify them at once. In fact, I'll do it right now.'

I glanced back at Ricky. He was still nodding in that mechanical way. It seemed he no longer cared if the experiment was made public.

Julia said, 'You three get some sleep, and I'll call my contacts at the Pentagon.'

'I'll go with you,' I said.

She glanced at me and smiled. 'You don't trust me?'

'It's not that. They might have questions I could answer for them.'

'OK, fine. Good idea. Excellent idea.'

Something was wrong here. I felt as if I were in a play, and everyone was acting a part. Except I didn't know what the play was. I glanced over at Mae. She was frowning slightly. She must have sensed it, too.

We all passed through the airlocks into the residential unit and walked through to the kitchen.

Julia reached for the phone. 'Let's make that call, Jack,' she said.

I went to the refrigerator and got a ginger ale. Mae had an iced tea, Bobby a beer. I noticed a bottle of champagne cooling in the fridge. So she'd already planned the party.

Julia pushed the speakerphone button and punched in a number. But the call didn't go through. The line just went dead. 'That's funny. Ricky, I'm not getting an outside line.'

'Try one more time,' Ricky said.

I sipped my ginger ale and watched them. There was no question that this was all an act for our benefit. Julia dialled a second time. I wondered how she knew the number for the Pentagon by heart.

'Huh,' she said. 'Nothing.'

'Should be OK,' Ricky said, acting puzzled.

'Oh, for Christ's sake,' I said. 'Let me guess. Something has happened and we can't dial out.'

Ricky pushed away from the table. 'I'll check the comm lines.'

'You do that,' I said, glowering.

Julia was staring at me. 'Jack,' she said, 'Why are you angry?'

'I'm being fucked with.'

'I promise you,' she said quietly, meeting my eyes. 'You're not.'

Mae got up from the table, saying she was going to take a shower. Bobby wandered into the lounge to play a video game, his usual way to unwind. Julia and I were alone in the kitchen.

She leaned over the table towards me. She spoke in a low, earnest voice. 'Jack,' she said, 'I think I owe you an explanation.'

She dropped her voice lower, and stretched her hand across the table to cover mine. 'I want to make amends, Jack. I want to make things right.' She paused. 'I hope you do, too,' she said, and suddenly she leaned across the table and tried to kiss me on the lips. I pulled back, turned away. She stared at me, eyes pleading. 'Jack, please.'

'Julia . . .'

The intercom clicked. I heard Ricky's voice. 'Hey, guys? We have a problem with the comm lines. You better come here right away.'

THE COMMUNICATIONS ROOM consisted of a large closet in one corner of the maintenance room. It was sealed with a heavy security door, with a small tempered glass window. Through this window, I could see Charley Davenport slumped with his mouth hanging open and his eyes staring into space. He appeared to be dead. A black buzzing swarm swirled around his head.

'How'd the swarm get there? He went through all the airlocks.'

'I can't imagine,' Ricky said. 'He must have carried it with him, from outside. In his throat or something.' He shrugged. 'Beats me.'

I stared at Ricky, trying to understand his demeanour. He had just discovered that his lab was invaded by a lethal nanoswarm and he didn't appear to be upset at all. He was taking it all very casually.

Mae came hurrying into the room. She took in the situation with a glance. 'Did anyone check the video playback?'

'We can't,' Ricky said. 'The controls are disabled—in there.' It was then I noticed that behind Charley great chunks of wiring had been yanked out.

Mae said, 'Why would Charley go in there?'

I shook my head. I had no idea.

Julia said, 'It's airtight. Maybe he knew he was infected and wanted to seal himself off. I mean, the door's locked from the inside.'

I said, 'Really? How do you know that?'

Julia said, 'Um . . .' She peered through the glass. 'Uh, you can see the lock reflected in that chrome fitting . . . see it?'

I didn't bother to look. But Mae did, and I heard her say, 'Oh yes, Julia. Good observation.' It sounded phoney, but Julia didn't react.

So everybody was play-acting, now. And I didn't understand why.

I said to Ricky, 'Is there a way to unlock the door?'

'I think so. Vince probably has a skeleton key. But nobody's unlocking that door, Jack. Not as long as that swarm is in there.'

'So we can't call anywhere?' I said. 'We're incommunicado?'

'Until tomorrow, yes. Helicopter will be back tomorrow morning.'

I peered through the glass again. The swarm was buzzing around Charley's head and I was starting to see the milky coating form on his body. The usual pattern.

I said, 'Can you turn the air handlers up and suck the particles out?'

'Handlers are going full-bore now,' Ricky said.

'OK, then,' I said, 'let's black out the window and turn the lights out in there. Wait a few hours, until the swarm loses power.'

'Jeez, I don't know,' Ricky said doubtfully.

'What do you mean, Ricky?' Julia said. 'I think it's a great idea. It's certainly worth a try. Let's do it right now.'

'OK, fine,' Ricky said, immediately deferring to her. 'But you're going to have to wait at least six hours.'

I said, 'I thought it was three hours.'

'It is, but I want extra hours before I open that door. If that swarm gets loose in here, we've all had it.'

In the end, that was what we decided to do. We turned out the lights, got black cloth and taped it over the window, and put black cardboard over that. At the end of that time, exhaustion hit me again. 'I have to go to bed,' I said.

'Yes, we all should,' Julia said. 'We can revisit this in the morning.'

We all headed off towards the residence module. Mae sidled up alongside me. 'How are you feeling?' she said.

'OK. My back's starting to hurt a little.'

She nodded. 'You better let me take a look at it.'

'Why?'

'Just let me take a look, before you go to bed.'

'OH, JACK, darling,' Julia cried. 'You poor baby.'

I was sitting on the kitchen table with my shirt off. Mae was applying dressing to the burns I'd received on my back when the cave blew up.

Julia smiled at me. 'Jack, I can't tell you how sorry I am, that you had to go through this.'

I knew that Mae wanted to talk to me in private, but there was no opportunity. Julia was not going to leave us alone for a minute. She had always been jealous of Mae, since I first hired her at Media-Tronics, and now she was competing with her for my attention.

I wasn't flattered.

The dressings were cool at first, as Mae applied them, but within moments they stung bitterly. I winced.

'I don't know what painkillers we have,' Mae said. 'You've got a good area of second-degree burns.'

Julia rummaged frantically through the first-aid kit. 'There's morphine,' she said at last, holding up a bottle. 'That should do it!'

'I don't want morphine,' I said. What I really wanted to say was that I wanted her to go to bed. Julia was annoying me. Her frantic edge was getting on my nerves. And I wanted to talk to Mae alone.

'There's nothing else,' Julia said, 'except aspirin.'

'Aspirin is fine.'

Behind me, Mae said, 'OK. All finished now.' She yawned. 'If you don't mind, I'm going to bed.'

I thanked her, and watched her leave the room. When I turned back, Julia was holding a glass of water and two aspirins for me.

'Thank you,' I said.

'I never liked that woman,' she said.

'Let's get some sleep,' I said.

'There's only single beds here.'

'I know.'

She moved closer. 'I'd like to be with you, Jack.'

'I'm really tired. I'll see you in the morning, Julia.'

Day 7: 4.55am

I slept restlessly, and woke up sweating. The pillow was soaked. I looked over at the work-station monitor. It said 4.55am. I closed my eyes and lay there for a while, but I couldn't go back to sleep. I was wet and uncomfortable. I decided to take a shower.

I walked down the silent corridor to the bathrooms. The doors to all the bedrooms were open and the lights were on, which seemed strange. I could see everybody sleeping as I walked past. I saw Bobby, and I saw Julia, and Vince. Mae's bed was empty. And, of course, Charley's bed was empty.

Ricky's idea that Charley had somehow been carrying the swarm inside his body, in his mouth or something, didn't make a lot of sense to me. Those swarms killed within seconds. So how *did* the swarm get into the comm room with Charley? Why hadn't it attacked Julia and Ricky and Vince?

I forgot about my shower.

I decided to go and look around outside the comm room door. Maybe there was something I had missed. Julia had been talking a lot, interrupting my train of thought. Almost as if she hadn't wanted me to figure something out . . .

As I passed the biology lab I heard the sound of a clicking keyboard. It was Mae at her work station.

'What are you doing?' I asked.

'Checking the video playback.'

'I thought we couldn't do that, because Charley pulled the wires.'

'That's what Ricky said. But it isn't true.'

I started to come around the lab bench. She held up her hand.

'Jack,' she said. 'Maybe you don't want to look at this.'

'What? Why not?'

'It's, uh . . . maybe you don't want to deal with this. Not right now.'

But of course after that, I practically ran round the table to see what was on her monitor. And I stopped. It was an image of an empty corridor. 'Is this what I shouldn't deal with?' I said.

'No. I have to go back a bit . . .' She pressed the BACK button in the corner of the keyboard repeatedly until she came to the place she wanted. Then she ran it forward, the security images jumping from one camera to the next in rapid succession. A corridor. Ricky moving down it. Power station. Outside, looking down on Julia stepping into the floodlight. A corridor. Julia and Ricky together, embracing. There was a clear sense of ease, of familiarity between them. And then they kissed passionately.

'I'M SORRY, JACK,' Mae said. 'I don't know what to say.'

I felt a wave of dizziness, almost as if I might collapse. I sat down on the table, turned away from the screen. I just couldn't look. Mae was saying something more, but I didn't hear her words.

I took a deep breath. I ran my hand through my hair. 'I never would have figured Ricky,' I said. 'He's such a . . . I don't know . . . smarmy kind of guy. Somehow I would have thought she'd pick someone more important, I guess.'

Mae said, 'It may not be what you think, Jack. At least, it may not be exactly what you think.'

'Sorry, Mae,' I said. I felt angry, embarrassed, confused, furious. 'But I don't want to pretend any more. I saw it. I know what it is.'

I THOUGHT I'd be with Julia for ever. We had a family, a life together. And Ricky had a new baby of his own. It didn't make sense. But then, things never turn out the way you think they will.

I heard Mae typing quickly. 'What're you doing?'

'Seeing if I can track what happened to Charley.'

There was nothing I could do about my personal life, at least not right now. I turned round and faced the screen.

'OK,' I said. 'Let's look for Charley.'

We searched for about ten minutes before Charley appeared in any of the images. First we saw him in the residential hallway, walking down the corridor, rubbing his face. He'd obviously just woken up.

'OK,' Mae said. 'We got him.' She froze the image, so we could read it. It was 11.40pm.

I said, 'That's only about half an hour before we got back.'

'Yes.' She ran the images forward. Charley disappeared from the hallway, but we saw him briefly, heading into the bathroom. Then we saw Ricky and Julia in the kitchen. I felt my body tense. But they were just talking.

It was difficult to be sure what happened next, because of the frame rate. Ten frames a second meant that events appeared blurred and jumpy when things moved fast, because too much happened between the frames. But this is what I thought happened:

Charley showed up and began talking to the two of them. He was smiling, cheerful. Then Charley seemed to get angry. Ricky stepped forward. He held his hands up soothingly to Charley: take it easy.

Charley wasn't taking it easy. The two men began to argue. Charley was trying to get round Ricky, but Ricky kept moving to block him, and held his hands up each time, treating Charley in that careful way you do when someone's out of control.

Mae said, 'Is Charley being affected by the swarm? Is that why he's acting that way?'

'I can't tell.' I looked closer at the screen. 'I don't see any swarm.'

'No,' she said. 'But he's pretty angry.'

Suddenly, Charley stepped several paces back. For a moment, he was completely still, as if he had discovered something that stunned him. Then he turned and ran out of the room.

Immediately, Ricky ran after Charley. Julia followed.

We saw Charley in the utility room, dialling the phone. He glanced over his shoulder. A moment later, Ricky came in and Charley hung up. They argued, circling around each other.

Charley picked up a shovel and swung it at Ricky. The first time Ricky dodged away. The second time it caught him on the shoulder and knocked him to the floor. Charley swung the shovel again and Ricky managed to duck away just in time.

'My God . . .' Mae said.

Ricky was getting to his feet, when Charley turned and saw Julia enter the room. Charley looked from one of them to the other. And then Vince entered the room, too. Now that they were all in the room, he seemed to lose his urge to fight.

Suddenly Charley dashed for the comm room, stepped inside and tried to shut the door behind him. Ricky was on him in a flash. He had his foot in the door and Charley couldn't get it closed. Then Vince came right alongside Ricky and the two men forced the door open. The action that came next was swift, blurred on the video, but apparently the three men were fighting, and Ricky managed to get behind Charley and get him in a hammer lock. He stopped fighting. The image was less blurred.

'What's happening?' Mae said. 'They never told us any of this.'

Ricky and Vince were holding Charley from behind. Charley was panting, but he no longer struggled. Julia came into the room. She looked at Charley, and had some conversation with him.

Then she walked up and kissed him full and long on the lips. Charley struggled, tried to wrench away, but Julia continued to kiss him. Then she stepped away, and as she did I saw a river of black between her mouth and Charley's.

'Oh my God,' Mae said.

Julia wiped her lips, and smiled as Charley sagged to the ground. A black cloud came out of his mouth and swirled around his head. Vince patted him on the head and left the room.

Ricky went over to the panels—and pulled out wiring by the handful. Then he turned and walked out.

At once Charley sprang to his feet, closed the door and locked it. But Ricky and Julia just laughed, as if this was a futile gesture. Charley sagged again, and from then on he was out of sight.

Ricky threw his arm round Julia's shoulder and they walked out of the utility room together.

'Well, you two are certainly up bright and early!'

I turned. Julia was standing in the doorway.

SHE CAME FORWARD into the room, smiling. 'You know, Jack,' she said, 'if I didn't trust you so completely, I'd think there was something going on between the two of you.'

'Really?' I said. I stepped away from Mae a little, while she typed quickly. I felt tremendously uneasy.

'Well, you had your heads together about something,' she said. 'What're you looking at, anyway?'

'It's ah, technical.'

'May I see? I have a new interest in technical things.'

By now she had walked round the bench and could see the screen. She frowned at the image, which showed bacterial cultures on a red growth medium. White circles within red circles. 'What's this?'

Mae said, 'Bacterial colonies. We've got some contamination of the coli stock. We're trying to figure out what's wrong.'

'Probably phage, don't you think?' Julia said. 'Isn't that what it usually is with bacterial stocks—a virus?' She glanced at me, and at Mae. 'But surely this isn't what you've been looking at all this time . . .'

'Actually, it is,' I said.

Julia shrugged. 'Do you mind?' Her hand darted forward and hit the BACK key in the corner of the computer keyboard.

The previous screen showed more pictures of bacterial growth.

Julia continued to hit the BACK key half a dozen times more, but all she saw were images of bacteria and viruses, graphs and data tables. She took her hand away from the keyboard. 'You seem to be devoting a lot of time to this. Is it really so important?'

'Well, it's a contaminant,' Mae said. 'I've had to take one tank offline. If we don't control it, we'll have to shut down the entire system.'

'Then by all means keep at it.' She turned to me. 'Want to have breakfast? I'd imagine you must be starving.'

'OK,' I said. I glanced at Mae. 'I'll see you later. Let me know if I can do anything to help.'

I left with Julia. Walking down the corridor next to my wife, I couldn't help but feel as if I was walking with a stranger. Somebody who was immensely dangerous.

I glanced at my watch. The helicopter would be here in less than two hours, now.

As we approached the residential unit, I could smell bacon and eggs cooking. Ricky came round the corner. He smiled heartily when he saw me. 'Hey, Jack. How'd you sleep?'

'I slept OK.'

Inside the kitchen, Bobby was making breakfast. Julia went to the refrigerator, opened the door. The champagne was in there. 'You guys ready to celebrate now?'

'Sure,' Bobby said. 'Sounds great.'

'Absolutely not,' I said. 'Julia, you must take this situation seriously. We have to get the army in here, and we haven't been able to call. It's not time to break out the champagne.'

'Oooh, baby, don't be such a spoilsport, just kiss me, kiss me.' She leaned across the table and puckered her lips.

But it seemed like getting angry was the only move I had. 'Damn it, Julia,' I said, raising my voice, 'the only reason we are in this mess is because you didn't take it seriously in the first place. You had a runaway swarm out there in the desert for what—two weeks? And instead of eradicating it, you played with it. You fooled around until it got out of control, and as a result three people are dead.' I took the bottle to the sink and smashed it, then stomped out of the room. As I left, Vince was coming in.

My stomach flipped. But I kept walking.

There were four of them; I was sure they were all in on it now. And only two of us—unless they had already got to Mae.

MAE WASN'T in the biology laboratory. I looked around and saw that a side door was ajar, leading downstairs to the fermentation chambers. Giant stainless-steel tanks about six feet across.

Mae was standing by the third unit, making notes on a clipboard. She looked at me, then shot a glance towards the ceiling, where a security camera was mounted. She walked round to the other side of the tank and I followed her. Over here, the tank blocked the camera.

She said, 'They slept with the lights on.'

I nodded. I knew what it meant, now.

'They're all infected,' she said. 'And it's not killing them.'

'Yes,' I said, 'but I don't understand why.'

'It must have evolved,' she said, 'to tolerate them.'

'That fast?'

'Evolution can happen fast,' she said. 'I think they're evolved to a milder form, which could be transmitted from one person to another.'

'It's creepy,' I said.

She nodded. 'But what can we do about it?'

And then, to my surprise, she began to cry silently, tears running down her cheeks. Mae was always so strong. Seeing her upset unnerved me now. She was shaking her head. 'Jack, there's nothing we can do. They're going to kill us the way they killed Charley.'

I SHOULD HAVE anticipated that the swarm might evolve in two directions at the same time. I should have looked for it, expected it. If I had, I might be better prepared to deal with the situation now.

I started to wonder what else I had failed to see. What was the first clue I had missed? Probably the fact that my initial contact with a swarm had produced an allergic reaction—a reaction that almost killed me. Mae had called it a coliform reaction. Caused by a toxin that had evolved in the *E. coli* bacteria in the swarm.

'Mae,' I said. 'Wait a minute.'

'What?'

'There might be something we can do to stop them.'

She was sceptical, but she wiped her eyes and listened.

I said, 'The swarm consists of particles and bacteria and the bacteria provide the raw ingredients for the particles to reproduce themselves. Right? OK. So if the bacteria die, the swarm dies too?'

'Probably.' She frowned. 'Are you thinking of an antibiotic? Because you need a lot of antibiotics to clear an *E. coli* infection—'

'No. I'm not thinking of antibiotics.' I tapped the tank in front of me. 'I'm thinking of this. We'll fill the atmosphere with it. They'll breathe it in. Don't shut down this tank. Feed the bacteria into the system. I want the assembly line to start making a lot of virus.'

Mae sighed. 'It won't work, Jack. If I introduce phage into the assembly lines, the virus will rupture a lot of cell membranes, leaving behind all those membranes as a crud. The crud will clog the filters. After about an hour or two, the assembly lines will start to overheat, the safety systems will kick in, and shut everything down. No virus.'

'Can the safety systems be turned off?'

'There's a code,' she said. 'Ricky's the only one who knows it.'

'Oh.'

'It'd be too dangerous to turn off the safeties, Jack. Parts of that system operate at high temperature, and high voltages. And there's a lot of ketones and methane produced in the arms. If that isn't drawn off, you start high voltage sparking . . .' She paused, shrugged.

'What're you saying? It could explode?'

'No, Jack. I'm saying it will explode. In a matter of minutes after the safeties are shut off. Six, maybe eight minutes at most.'

I looked around the room: at the steel tank, curving upwards over my head; at a rack of test tubes at Mae's feet; at a one-gallon plastic bottle of water. I looked at Mae. And I had a plan.

'OK. Do it anyway. Release the virus into the system.'

'What's the point of that? Why, Jack? What good will it do?'

Mae had been a good friend through all this, and now I had a plan and I wasn't going to tell her. I hated to do it this way, but I had to make a distraction for the others. And she had to help me do it—which meant she had to believe in a different plan.

I said, 'Mae, we have to distract them. I want you to release the virus into the assembly line. Let them focus on that. Meanwhile, I'll take some virus up to the maintenance area beneath the roof, and dump it into the sprinkler reservoir. Then I'll set the sprinklers off.'

She nodded. 'It just might work.'

'I can't think of anything better,' I said. 'Now let's draw off some test tubes of virus. I want you to buy me a little time.'

'And how do I do that?'

I told her. She made a face. 'You're kidding! They'll never do it!'

'Of course not. I just need a little time.'

MAE FILLED the test tubes with the thick brown slop. It smelt faecal. It looked faecal.

I picked up a test tube, took a breath and swallowed the contents. It was disgusting. I thought I would vomit, but I didn't. I took another breath, swallowed some water from the bottle, and looked at Mae.

She picked up a test tube, held her nose, and swallowed. I gave her the water bottle, she drank, and poured the rest onto the floor. Then she filled it with brown slop. The last thing she did was twist the handle of a big flow valve. 'There,' she said. 'It's going into the system now.'

'OK,' I said. I took two test tubes and stuck them in my shirt pocket. I took the handle of the water bottle. 'See you later.' And I hurried off.

As I went down the hallway, I figured there was maybe one chance in a thousand that I would succeed.

But I had a chance.

LATER ON, I watched the entire scene on the security camera, so I knew what happened to Mae. She walked into the kitchen, carrying her rack of brown test tubes. The others were all there, eating. Ricky said, 'What've you got there, Mae?'

'Phage,' she said. 'It's from the fermentation tank.'

Julia looked up. 'Ew, no wonder it stinks.'

'Jack just drank one. He made me drink one.'

Ricky snorted. 'Jeez, I'm surprised you didn't puke.'

'I almost did. Jack wants all of you to drink one, too.'

Bobby laughed. 'Yeah? What for?'

'Jack says that Charley was harbouring the swarm inside his body, so maybe the rest of us are, too. So you drink this virus, and it'll kill the bacteria inside you, and kill the swarm.'

Bobby said, 'Are you serious? Drink that crap? No way, Mae!'

Julia frowned. She turned to Mae. 'Where is Jack now?' she said.

'I don't know. The last time I saw him was by the fermentation chamber. I don't know where he is now.'

Julia said to Bobby, 'Check the monitors. Find him.' She came around the table, advancing slowly. 'Tell me the truth, Mae,' she said. 'It will be much better for you if you cooperate.'

From the other side of the room, Bobby said, 'I found him. He's going through the fab room. With a bottle of the crap, looks like.'

'Tell me, Mae,' Julia said, leaning closer. Mae squeezed her eyes and her lips tightly shut. She was shaking with fear. Julia caressed her hair. 'Don't be afraid. Just tell me what he is doing with that bottle.'

Mae began to sob hysterically. 'He took the bottle of virus,' she said, 'and he's putting it in the water sprinklers.'

'Is he?' Julia said. 'How very clever of him. Thank you, sweetie.'

And she kissed Mae on the mouth. Mae squirmed, but Julia was holding her head. When Julia finally stepped back, she said, 'Try and stay calm. It won't hurt you if you don't fight against it.'

And she walked out of the room.

Day 7: 6.12am

Things happened faster than I expected.

I could hear them running towards me down the corridor. I hastily hid the bottle, then ran back and continued crossing the fabrication room. That was when they all came after me. I started to run. Vince tackled me, and I hit the floor hard. Ricky threw himself on top of me, and knocked the wind out of me. Together they dragged me to my feet to face Julia.

'Hi, Jack,' she said, smiling. 'We've just had a nice talk with Mae. So there's no point in beating around the bush. Where is the bottle?'

'What bottle?'

'Jack.' She stepped closer to me and shook her head sadly. I could feel her breath on my face, her lips brushed mine. 'Jack . . . where is the bottle of phage you were going to put in the sprinkler system?'

I stood there.

Ricky said, 'Forget it, Julia. He's not afraid of you. He drank the virus and he thinks it'll protect him.'

'Will it?' Julia said, stepping back.

'Maybe,' Ricky said, 'but I bet he's afraid to die.'

And then he and Vince began dragging me across the fabrication room towards the magnet room. I began to struggle.

'That's right,' Ricky said. 'You know what's coming, don't you?'

This was not in my plan. I didn't know what to do now. I struggled harder, kicking and twisting, but they were both immensely strong.

Julia opened the heavy steel door to the magnet room. Inside, I saw the circular drum of the magnet, six feet in diameter. The two men shoved me in. I sprawled on the ground as the door locked shut.

The intercom clicked. I heard Ricky's voice. 'Ever wonder why these walls are made out of steel, Jack? Pulsed magnets are dangerous. Run them continuously and they blow apart. We got a one-minute load time. So you've got one minute to think it over.'

I had been in this room before, when Ricky showed me around. I remembered there was a knee plate, a safety cut-off. I hit it now.

'Won't work, Jack,' Ricky said laconically. 'I inverted the switching. Now it turns the magnet on, instead of off.'

There was a rumbling as the cooling pumps started up. The air grew swiftly colder. In a moment I could see my breath.

'Sorry if you're uncomfortable, but that's only temporary,' Ricky said. 'Once the pulses get going, the room'll heat up fast.'

The sound was like a muffled jackhammer. *Chunk-chunk-chunk.* The room was starting to get warmer. The noise of the giant pumps filled the room, to make the very air vibrate. It sounded like an enormous MRI. This big terrifying sound, it must have been how Amanda felt, when she was in the MRI. I stared at the magnet, at the heavy bolts that held the plates together. Those bolts would soon become missiles. The load time was the time it took to charge the magnet capacitors, so that pulses of electricity could be delivered. I wondered how long after loading it would take for the pulses to blow the magnet apart. Probably a few seconds at most.

'Ten seconds,' Ricky said. 'Come on, Jack. Don't be a hero. It's not your style. Tell us where it is. Six seconds. Jack, come on . . .'

The *chunk-chunk-chunk* stopped, and there was a *whang!* and a scream of rending metal. The magnet had switched on.

'First pulse,' Ricky said. 'Don't be an arsehole, Jack.'

Another *whang! Whang! Whang!* The pulses were coming faster and faster. I saw the jacketing on the coolant beginning to indent with each pulse. *Whang! Whang!*

I couldn't take it any more. I shouted, 'OK! Ricky! I'll tell you!'

Whang! 'Go ahead, Jack!' *Whang!* 'I'm waiting.'

'No! Turn it off first. And I only tell Julia.'

And then abruptly, silence. The MRI sound had stopped.

The MRI . . .

I stood in the room and waited for Julia to come in. And then, thinking it over, I sat down.

I heard the door unlock. Julia walked in.

'I don't know why you put yourself through it, Jack,' she said. 'It was totally unnecessary. But guess what? The helicopter just arrived. So as soon as you give me the bottle of virus, you can go home.'

I didn't believe her for a second. 'Where is Mae?'

'She's resting, Jack.'

'You've hurt her.'

'No. No, no. Why would I do that?' She shook her head. 'I don't want to hurt anyone, Jack. Not you, not Mae, not anyone. Why can't you accept the new situation?' She held out her hand to me. I took it and she pulled me up. She was stronger than I ever remembered her being. 'After all,' she said, 'you're an integral part of this. You killed the wild type for us, Jack.'

'So the benign type could flourish . . .'

'Exactly, Jack. And create a new synergy with human beings.'

She smiled. It was a creepy smile.

'Julia, this is all bullshit,' I said. 'This is a disease.'

'Well, of course you would say that. Because you don't know any better, yet. You haven't experienced it.' She came forward and hugged me. I let her do it. 'Stop being so stubborn, for once, Jack.' She smiled again. 'Oh, Jack . . . I really have missed you.'

'Me too,' I said. 'I missed you.' I gave her a hug, held her close. She looked beautiful, her lips parted, soft, inviting. I felt her relax.

Then I said, 'Just tell me one thing, Julia. It's been bothering me. Why did you refuse to have an MRI in the hospital?'

She frowned, leaned back to look at me. 'What do you mean?'

'Are you like Amanda?'

'Amanda?'

'Our baby daughter . . . She was cured by the MRI, remember.'

'What are you talking about?'

'Julia, does the swarm have some problem with magnetic fields?'

Her eyes widened. She began to struggle. 'Let go of me! Ricky!'

'Sorry, hon,' I said. I kicked the plate with my knee. There was a loud *whang!* as the magnet pulsed.

Julia screamed.

Her mouth was open as she screamed, a steady continuous sound. I held her hard. The skin of her face began to shiver and vibrate. And then her features seemed to grow, to swell as she screamed. The swelling continued, and began to break up into rivulets and streams.

And then in a sudden rush Julia literally disintegrated before my eyes. The skin of her face and body blew away from her in streams of particles, like sand blown off a sand dune. The particles curved away in the arc of the magnetic field towards the sides of the room.

I felt her body growing lighter and lighter in my arms. Still the particles continued to flow away, with a kind of whooshing sound. And when it was finished, what was left behind—what I still held in my arms—was a pale and cadaverous form. Julia's eyes were sunk deep in her cheeks. Her mouth was thin and cracked, her skin translucent. Her hair was colourless, brittle.

'Jack,' she whispered. 'It's eating me.'

I said, 'I know.'

Her voice was just a whisper. 'You have to do something. The children . . . I . . . kissed them . . .'

I said nothing. I just closed my eyes.

'Jack . . . Save my babies . . . Jack . . .'

I glanced up at the walls and saw, all around me, Julia's face and body stretched and fitted to the room. The particles retained her appearance, but were now flattened onto the walls. And they were still moving, coordinating with the movement of her lips, the blink of her eyes. As I watched, they began to drift back from the walls towards her in a flesh-coloured haze.

Outside the room, I heard Ricky shouting, 'Julia! Julia!' He kicked the door a couple of times, but he didn't come in. I knew he wouldn't dare. Because of the override I could pulse the magnet at will—at least, until the charge ran out.

'Jack,' she said. 'I didn't know . . .'

'It's all right,' I said. The particles were drifting back, reassembling her face before my eyes. Julia was becoming beautiful again.

I kicked the knee plate.

Whang!

The particles shot away, flying back to the walls, though not so swiftly this time. I reached into my pocket and pulled out one of the vials of phage. 'I want you to drink this,' I said.

'No . . . no . . .' She was agitated. 'Too late . . . for . . .'

'Try,' I said. I held the vial to her lips. 'Come on, darling. Try.'

'No . . . Not important . . .' She was breathing shallowly, weakly. She said, 'They have to kill you now. Don't let them . . . Children . . .'

'I won't.'

Her bony hand touched my cheek. She whispered, 'You know I always loved you, Jack. I would never hurt you.'

'I know, Julia. I know.'

The particles on the walls were drifting free once more. Now they seemed to telescope back, returning to her face and body. I kicked the knee plate once again, hoping for more time with her, but there was only a dull mechanical thunk.

The capacitor was drained.

And suddenly, in a *whoosh*, all the particles returned, and Julia was beautiful and strong as before. She pushed me away from her contemptuously. 'I want the bottle of virus, Jack. And I want it now.'

In a way it made everything easier. Because I understood I wasn't dealing with Julia any more. I didn't have to worry about what might happen to her. I just had to worry about Mae—and me.

'OK,' I said. 'OK. I'll get you the virus.' I headed for the door.

'Good. And we'll start with those vials in your shirt pocket.'

'What, these here?' I said, reaching into my pocket. Outside, Ricky and Vince were waiting for me. Seeing my sudden movement, they grabbed me again, one on each side.

'Guys,' I said, 'I can't do this if you—'

'Let him go,' Julia said, coming out of the room.

'Like hell,' Vince said. 'He'll pull something.'

While we struggled, I managed to bring one of the tubes out. I threw it onto the ground. It smashed on the concrete floor, and brown sludge spattered up. They all jumped away, releasing me. They stared at the floor, making sure none of it had touched them.

And in that moment, I ran.

I GRABBED THE BOTTLE from its hiding place, and kept going across the fabrication room. If I could just reach the elevator on the other side of the room and ride it up to the ceiling level, where the tank for the sprinkler system was, then my plan would work.

The elevator was 150 feet away.

I ran hard, vaulting over the lowest arms of the octopus, ducking beneath the chest-high sections. I heard Julia say, 'He's going for the sprinklers!' Ahead, I saw the open cage of the elevator.

I was going to make it, after all.

At that moment, I stumbled over one of the arms and went sprawling. The bottle skidded across the floor. I scrambled quickly to my feet again and retrieved it. I knew they were right behind me. I didn't dare look back.

I ran for the elevator, ducking beneath one final pipe, but when I looked again, Vince was already there, in the cage, grinning. He must have known a short cut through the octopus arms. I looked back and saw Ricky just a few yards behind me, closing fast.

Julia called, 'Give it up, Jack! It's no good.'

She was right about that, it was no good at all. I couldn't get past Vince. And I couldn't outrun Ricky. So I jumped over a pipe, stepped around a standing electrical box, and ducked down. As Ricky jumped the pipe, I slammed my elbow upwards between his legs. He howled and went down, rolling on the floor in agony. I jumped up and kicked him as hard as I could. That was for Charley.

I ran.

At the elevator, Vince stood in a half-crouch, fists bunched. He was relishing a fight. I ran straight towards him and he grinned broadly in anticipation.

And at the last moment, I swerved left. I jumped.

And started climbing the ladder on the wall.

IT WAS DIFFICULT climbing, because I had my thumb hooked through the handle of the bottle, which kept banging painfully against the back of my right hand as I went up. I focused on the pain. I panic at heights and I didn't want to look down. And so I couldn't see what was dragging at my legs, pulling me back towards the floor. I kicked, but whatever it was held on to me.

Finally, I turned to look. I was ten feet above the ground and two rungs beneath me, Ricky had his free arm locked round my legs, his hand clutching my ankle. He jerked at my feet and yanked them off the rung. I slid for an instant and then felt a burst of searing pain in my hands. But I held on.

Ricky was smiling grimly. He had both my legs locked tight against his chest. I kept kicking out until I realised that I could pull one leg up and free. I did, and stomped down on his hand that was holding on to the rung. He yelled, and released my legs to hold on to the ladder with his other hand. I stomped again—and kicked straight back, catching him right under the chin. He slid down five rungs, almost to the bottom of the ladder.

Julia was running across the floor. 'Stop him!' she screamed.

I heard the elevator grind as Vince rode up past me. He would wait for me in the maintenance area under the roof.

I climbed.

I was fifteen feet above the floor. Ricky was still pursuing me but he was far behind. I didn't think he could catch me, but then Julia came swirling up through the air towards me—and grabbed the ladder right alongside me. Except she wasn't Julia, she was the swarm, and for a moment the swarm was disorganised enough that I could see right through her in places. I looked down and saw the real Julia, deathly pale, standing and looking up at me, her face a skull. By now the swarm alongside me became a solid-appearing Julia. The mouth moved and I heard a strange voice say: 'Sorry, Jack.'

I turned to climb again.

The Julia swarm swung back and slammed hard against my body, again and again. I felt like I was hit by a sack of cement, the wind knocked out of me. My grip loosened from the ladder, but I managed to keep going despite the impacts. The swarm had enough mass to hurt me, but not enough to knock me off the ladder.

The swarm must have realised it, too, because now it compressed itself into a sphere and slid smoothly forward to envelop my head in a buzzing cloud. I was totally blind.

I climbed on in darkness.

I was exhausted and defeated and I could feel my energy draining away. And then I felt Ricky pulling at my legs again. I couldn't hold my grip much longer. I knew that all I had to do was release my grip and fall, and it would be over in an instant. I was finished, anyway.

And then I thought of Julia, pale as a ghost and brittle thin, saying in a whisper, 'Save my babies.' I thought of the kids, waiting for me to come back. And I knew I had to go on no matter what.

So I did.

IT'S NOT CLEAR to me what happened to Ricky. But somehow I must have kicked out and caught him in the face.

In that instant Ricky let go of me, and I heard a thump-thump-thumping as his body slid down the ladder to the ground. I heard, 'Ricky, no!' and the cloud vanished from my head. I was completely free again. I looked down and saw the Julia swarm alongside Ricky. He looked up angrily and started towards me, but the Julia swarm said, 'No, Ricky. No, you can't! Let Vince.'

I turned away from them and looked up the ladder.

Vince was standing there, five feet above me.

HIS FEET WERE on the top rungs, and he was leaning over, blocking my way. I paused to take stock, hooking my free arm round the rung nearest my face. And as I shifted my weight, I felt the lump in my pocket. I paused.

I had one more vial of phage.

I reached into my shirt pocket and drew it out. I pulled out the cork with my teeth. Vince didn't move. But his eyes narrowed.

I moved up another rung.

'Better get back, Vince,' I said. 'Before you get wet . . .'

I paused. If I advanced another rung, he could kick me in the head. If I stayed where I was, he would have to come down to me and I could get him. So I stayed.

'What do you say, Vince? Going to stay, or go?'

He frowned. His eyes flicked back and forth, from my face to the vial and back again. And then he stepped away from the ladder.

'Good boy, Vince.'

I came up one rung.

He had stepped back so far that now I couldn't see where he was. I thought he was probably planning to rush me at the top. So I got ready to duck down and swing laterally.

Last rung.

And now I saw him. He wasn't planning anything. He was shaking with panic, huddled in the dark recess of the walkway.

'OK, Vince,' I said. 'I'm coming up.'

I stepped onto the mesh platform. Not twenty paces away, I saw the paired steel tanks for the sprinkler system.

I looked back at Vince, just in time to see him pull a translucent white plastic tarp off a corner box. He wrapped himself from head to foot in the tarp like a shield, and then, with a guttural yell, he charged. I was right at the edge of the ladder. I had no time to get out of the way, I just turned sideways and braced myself against a big three-foot pipe against the coming impact.

Vince slammed into me.

The vial went flying out of my hand, shattering on the mesh. The bottle was knocked from my other hand and tumbled along the walkway, coming to rest ten feet away, at the lip of the mesh path.

Still hiding behind the tarp, Vince smashed into me again and again. I was slammed back against the pipe and slipped on the brown sludge that dripped through holes in the mesh. I fell down on my knees and immediately scrambled towards the bottle. That odd behaviour made Vince stop for a moment; he pulled the tarp away from his face and for the first time he saw the bottle and lunged for it.

But he was too late. I had my hand on the bottle, and yanked it away, just as Vince landed, tarp and all, right where the bottle had been. His head banged hard on the walkway lip. He was momentarily stunned, shaking his head to clear it.

And I grabbed the edge of the tarp and yanked upwards.

Vince yelled, and went over the side.

I WATCHED as he hit the floor. His body didn't move. Then the swarm came off him, sliding into the air like his ghost. The ghost joined Ricky and Julia who were looking up at me. Then they turned away and hurried across the floor of the fabrication room, jumping over the octopus arms as they went.

I got to my feet and headed for the sprinkler tanks. It was easy to figure out the valves. I twisted the inflow, unscrewed the filler cap, waited for the pressurised nitrogen to hiss out, and then dumped in the bottle of phage. Then I screwed the cap back on, twisted the valve, repressurised with nitrogen.

And I was done.

I took a deep breath.

I was going to win this thing, after all.

Day 7: 8.12am

They were all clustered together on the other side of the fabrication room—Julia, Ricky, and now Bobby, as well. Vince was there, too, but I could sometimes see through him, his swarm was slightly transparent. I wondered which of the others were only swarms now. But it didn't matter, anyway.

They were standing with their backs to a bank of computer monitors. They regarded me with puzzlement, and then with increasingly open amusement, as I walked slowly calmly towards them.

'Well, Jack,' Julia said finally. 'How's your day going?'

'Not bad,' I said. 'Things are looking up.'

'You seem very confident.'

I shrugged.

'By the way, where is Mae? We can't find her and we thought we should all be together,' Julia said, 'when we finish our business here.'

'Oh,' I said. 'Is that what happens now? We finish?'

She nodded slowly. 'Yes, Jack. It is.'

I couldn't risk looking at my watch, I had to try and gauge how much time had passed. I was guessing three or four minutes. I said, 'So, what do you have in mind?'

Julia began to pace. 'Well, Jack, I'm very disappointed in how things have gone with you. You've been privileged to witness the birth of something miraculous here. But you are not sympathetic, Jack.'

'No, I'm not.' I reached in my pocket and brought out the plastic cigarette lighter. If Julia or the others noticed, they gave no signs. 'You don't need me,' I said. 'I mean, you're the future, if I remember right. Superior and unstoppable.'

I could see Julia was puzzled by my behaviour. Or appraising. She suspected something. And that made me very nervous.

'Jack,' she said. 'You disappoint me.'

As if on some unspoken cue they all began to move in concentric circles around me. Was this some kind of scanning procedure? 'You said that already,' I said.

I was trying to guess the time. I figured five minutes had elapsed.

'Come, Jack. I want to look more closely.'

She put her arm on my shoulder and led me over to one of the big octopus arms. It was easily six feet across and mirrored on its surface. I could see Julia standing next to me.

'Don't we make a handsome couple? It's a shame. We could have such a future.'

I said, 'Yeah, well . . .'

And the moment I spoke, a river of pale particles streamed off Julia, curved in the air, and came down like a shower all over my body and into my mouth. I clamped my mouth shut, but it didn't matter, because in the mirror my body seemed to dissolve away, to be replaced by Julia's body. I said, 'Cut it out, Julia.'

She laughed. 'Why? I think it's fun.'

'Stop it,' I said. I sounded like me, even though I looked like Julia.

'Jack, you're just no fun any more.'

I pulled at the Julia-image on my face, trying to tear it away like a mask. 'Get it off me,' I said. 'Get it off.' In my panic, I dropped the cigarette lighter on the concrete floor.

I heard a whoosh in my ears, and the Julia-skin was gone, sweeping into the air, then descending onto Julia. Except that she now looked like me. Now there were two Jacks, side by side in the mirror.

'Is this better?' she said.

'I don't know what you are trying to prove.' I took a breath.

I bent over and picked up the lighter.

'I'm not trying to prove anything,' she said. 'I'm just feeling you out, Jack. And you know what I found? You've got a secret, Jack, haven't you? Are you going to tell us why you're so worried about the time?'

Behind Julia, I could see the stacked monitor screens of the control station. I could see that some of the graphs were rising steeply, their lines turning from blue to yellow to red as they climbed.

I did nothing.

Julia turned to the men. 'OK,' she said. 'Make him tell.'

The three men walked towards me. It was time to spring my trap.

'No problem,' I said. I raised my lighter, flicked the flame, and held it under the nearest sprinkler head.

The men stopped in their tracks. They watched me.

But nothing happened.

THE FLAME STARTED melting the soft metal tab beneath the sprinkler head. And still the sprinklers didn't come on.

'Oh shit,' I said.

Julia was watching me thoughtfully. 'It was a nice try. Very inventive, Jack. Good thinking. But you forgot one thing.'

'What's that?'

'There's a safety system for the plant. And when we saw you going for the sprinklers, Ricky turned the system off. Safeties off, sprinklers off.' She shrugged. 'Guess you're out of luck, Jack.'

I flicked the lighter off. There was nothing for me to do. I just stood there, feeling foolish.

'It was a nice try, though,' Julia said. 'But enough is enough.'

She turned to the men and jerked her head. The three of them walked towards me. I said, 'Hey guys, come on . . .' They didn't react. They grabbed me and I started to struggle. 'Hey, come on now . . .'

Ricky said, 'Don't make it any harder for us, Jack.' I spat in his face just as they threw me to the floor. I was hoping the virus would get in his mouth. I was hoping I would delay him, that we would have a fight. Anything for a delay. But they threw me to the floor and then they all fell on me and began to strangle me. I could feel their hands on my neck. Ricky smiled distantly at me, as if he didn't know me, had no feeling for me. They were all strangers, killing me efficiently and quickly. I saw the world start to turn misty before my eyes.

Then there was a faint popping sound, almost like popcorn, or glass cracking, and then Julia screamed, 'What is that?'

The three men released me and got to their feet, as the first of the octopus tubes burst open, high above us. Brown liquid steam hissed out. Another tube popped open, and another. The air was turning dark foggy brown, billowing brown.

Julia screamed 'What is that?'

'It's the assembly line,' Ricky said. 'It's blowing.'

I got to my feet. I said, 'No safety systems, remember? You turned them off. Now it's blowing virus all through this room.'

'Not for long,' Julia said. 'We'll have the safeties back in two seconds.' Ricky was already at the control board, hitting keys.

'Good thinking, Julia,' I said. I lit my cigarette lighter, and held it under the sprinkler head.

Julia screamed, 'Stop! Ricky, stop!'

Ricky stopped.

I SAID, 'Damned if you do, damned if you don't.'

Julia's body was turning shades of grey. So was Ricky, the colour washing out of him. The virus was already affecting their swarms.

There was a brief crackle of sparks, from high in the octopus arms. Then another short lightning arc. Ricky saw it and yelled, 'Forget it, Julia! We take our chances!' He hit the keys and turned the safety system back on. Alarms started to sound. The screens flashed red with the excess concentrations of methane and other gases.

And the sprinklers burst into cones of brown spray.

They screamed as the water touched them. They shrivelled right before my eyes. Julia's face was contorted. She stared at me with pure hatred. But already she was starting to dissolve. The others were rolling on the floor, screaming in pain.

'Come on, Jack.' Someone was tugging at my sleeve. It was Mae. 'Come on,' she said. 'This room is full of methane. You have to go.'

I hesitated, still looking at Julia. Then we turned and ran.

Day 7: 9.11 AM

The helicopter pilot pushed the doors open as we ran across the pad. We jumped in. Mae said, 'Go!'

He said, 'I'll have to insist you get your harnesses on before—'

'Just fly this thing!' I yelled.

Black smoke started to pour out of the power station door we had just come out of. It billowed into the blue desert sky.

The pilot saw it and said, 'Hang on!'

We lifted off and headed north, swinging wide of the building. Now there was smoke coming from all the exhaust vents near the roof. A black haze was rising into the air.

Within minutes the building behind had disappeared below the horizon. Mae was sitting back in her seat, eyes closed.

I said, 'So where were you? Nobody could find you.'

She said, 'I was in the storage shed. Looking for more Thermite.'

'Find any?'

THERE WAS NO SOUND. Just a flash of yellow light that spread across the desert horizon for an instant, and then faded. You could almost believe it never happened. But the helicopter rocked and jolted as the shock wave passed us.

The pilot said, 'Holy Mother of God, what was that?'

'Industrial accident,' I said. 'Very unfortunate.'

He reached for his radio. 'I better report it.'

We flew west, and I saw the green line of the forest and the rolling foothills of the Sierras, as we crossed into California.

Day 7: 11.57 PM

It's late. Almost midnight. The house is silent around me. I am not sure how this will turn out. The kids are all desperately sick, throwing up after I gave them the virus. I haven't told Eric and Nicole about Julia yet. They haven't asked. They're too sick to ask right now.

I'm worried most about Amanda, because I had to give her the virus, too. She has yet to throw up. I don't know whether that's good or bad. Babies react differently.

Ellen's still vomiting, but I think I'm OK, at least for the moment. I'm dead tired. I think I've been dozing on and off. Right now I'm sitting here, waiting for Mae. She thought there was a faint green light coming from the end of my back yard, where the sprinklers are. I told her not to go down there alone, but I'm too tired to go and get her. If she waits until tomorrow, the army can come here with flame throwers and blast the hell out of whatever it is.

The army is acting dumb about this whole thing, but I have Julia's computer here at home, and I removed the hard drive, just to be safe. I duped it and put the original in a safe deposit box in town. I'm not really worried about the army. I'm worried about Larry Handler and the others at Xymos. They know they have horrific lawsuits on their hands. The company will declare bankruptcy some time this week, but they're still liable for criminal charges. Larry especially.

I wouldn't cry if he went to jail.

MAE AND I have managed to put together most of the events of the past few days. Amanda's rash was caused by gamma assemblers—the micromachines that assembled finished molecules from component fragments. The gammas must have been on Julia's clothing when she came home from the lab. Julia worried about that possibility; that was why she always took a shower as soon as she got home. The lab itself had good decontamination procedures, but Julia was interacting with the swarms outside the lab. She knew there was a danger.

Anyway, that night she accidentally let the gammas loose in the nursery and they coated Amanda's skin with tiny biting particles. The magnetic field of the MRI cured her in an instant; all the assemblers were yanked away from her in the first pulse.

Julia knew what was wrong with Amanda, but she didn't tell anybody. Instead she called the Xymos clean-up crew, which showed up in the middle of the night while I was at the hospital. Only Eric saw them, and now I know what he saw. Because the same crew arrived here just a few hours ago to sweep the house.

The lead man wears a silver suit that's antimagnetic, and he does look ghostly. His silvered mask makes him appear faceless. He goes into the environment first to check it out. Then four other men in coveralls follow, to vacuum and clean up. I had told Eric he'd dreamed it, but he hadn't. The crew left behind one of their sensor cubes, under Amanda's bed. That was intentional, to check for residual gammas in case they'd missed any. It wasn't a surge suppressor; it was just constructed to look like one.

Eric's MP3 player was cut by gamma assemblers, the same way the cars in the desert were. Just as the MRI was. And there was a swarm in the convertible with Julia that night. It had come back with her from the desert. I don't know whether she brought it intentionally or not. I wasn't sure of what I saw when she pulled away. In my memory, it looked a little like Ricky, but it was probably too soon for the swarm to be taking on appearances. It hadn't evolved that much, yet. Ellen thinks that in my jealousy I imaged it to be a person.

After her car crashed, Julia called for the clean-up crews. That's why they were there on the road late that night, waiting to go and clean up the site. I don't know what caused the crash itself, whether it was something to do with the swarm or whether it was just an accident. There's no one to ask about it now.

The facility in the desert was entirely destroyed. There was enough methane in the main laboratory to produce a fireball in excess of 2,000 degrees Fahrenheit. Any biological materials would have been incinerated. But I still worry. They never found any bodies in the ruins, not even skeletons.

The last mystery to be cleared up was why the swarms always returned to the laboratory. I kept worrying about it because it didn't fit the PREDPREY formulations.

Of course, in retrospect there was only one possible answer. The swarms were intentionally programmed to return. But why would anybody program in a goal like that?

I didn't know until a few hours ago.

THE CODE that Ricky showed me wasn't the code they had actually used on the particles. He couldn't show me the real code, because I would have known immediately what had been done. Ricky didn't ever tell me. Nobody ever told me.

What bothers me most from reading Julia's email is that they had planned to release a swarm into the environment from the beginning. The story Ricky told me about the missing air filters was just not true.

When they couldn't make the swarm work in high wind, they tried to engineer a solution, and failed. The particles were just too small—and arguably too stupid, too. Their whole multimillion-dollar defence project was going down the drain, and they couldn't solve it.

So they decided to make the swarm solve it for them.

They reconfigured the nanoparticles to add solar power and memory. They rewrote the particle program to include a genetic algorithm. And they released the particles to reproduce and evolve, and see if the swarm could learn to survive on its own.

And they succeeded.

It was so dumb, it was breathtaking. How could they have embarked on this plan without recognising the consequences?

Of course, the technology itself invited the behaviour. Distributed agent systems ran by themselves. That was the whole point: you set them up and let them go. You got in the habit of treating agent networks that way. Autonomy was the point of it all.

But it was one thing to release a population of virtual agents inside a computer's memory to solve a problem. It was another thing to set real agents free in the real world.

They just didn't see the difference.

As far as I know, this was the first time it had ever been done. Maybe it has already happened and we just didn't hear about it. Anyway, I'm sure it'll happen again.

Probably soon.

IT'S TWO IN THE MORNING. The kids finally stopped vomiting. They've gone to sleep. They seem to be peaceful. The baby is asleep, too. I see Mae coming up the hill from behind my house. She's with the guy in the silver suit and the rest of the SSVT team. She's walking towards me. I can see that she's smiling. I hope her news is good.

I could use some good news right now.

Julia's original email says, 'We have nothing to lose.' But in the end they lost everything—their company, their lives, everything. And the ironic thing is, the procedure worked. The swarm actually solved the problem they had set for it. But then it kept going, kept evolving.

And they let it.

They didn't understand what they were doing.

I'm afraid that will be on the tombstone of the human race.

I hope it's not.

We might get lucky.

MICHAEL CRICHTON

When Michael Crichton quit his medical career in the Sixties, in the wake of a lucrative offer for film rights to his thriller *The Andromeda Strain*, his contemporaries thought he was being reckless. But Crichton has never looked back. He has gone on to become one of Hollywood's most successful film-makers and writers and has worked in various roles on many films, including *Coma* (writer/director), *Rising Sun* (co-writer), *Disclosure* (co-producer) and *Twister* (co-writer/co-producer). In 1993 he was in the unique position of having created America's most popular television series, *ER*, its top-grossing film, *Jurassic Park,* and its best-selling book, *Disclosure*.

In *Prey* he returns to a theme he has written about many times: the threat posed to mankind when scientific development goes unchecked. Specifically, he focuses on nanotechnology or the creation of minuscule, artificial machines which have, potentially, the ability to self-reproduce. 'I don't think we have a good sense about what the hazards are,' he says. 'Unfortunately, our species has demonstrated a striking lack of caution in the past. It is hard to imagine that we will behave differently in the future.'

Prey is as disturbing as it is fascinating because some of the science it describes is already in use. 'Pundits predict that these tiny machines will provide everything from miniaturised computer components to new cancer treatments to weapons of war. Nanotechniques are already being used to make sun screens, stain-resistant fabrics, and composite materials in cars. Soon they will be used to make computers and storage devices of extremely small size,' Crichton explains.

Over the years Michael Crichton has received numerous awards, including an Emmy for *ER* and an Oscar for his pioneering work in computerised film production. In 2000 he received his most unusual honour when palaeontologists in China named a newly discovered species of dinosaur after him. Small and armoured, it is called *Bienosaurus crichtoni* and, appropriately enough, dates from the Jurassic period.

STREET BOYS

LORENZO CARCATERRA

Heroes aren't born, they're made.

And in Naples, during four fateful days in 1943, Italy saw the making of the most unlikely heroes of the Second World War—a ragged band of children who fought to save their city from the Nazis.

PREFACE

The German tank stopped in front of the small stone house, its tracks grinding the quarter-acre vegetable garden into pockets of dust. A German officer, young and in full battle gear, stood alongside, a loudhailer in one hand, a lit cigarette in the other. He raised the loudhailer to his lips, staring with crystal blue eyes at the alarmed faces, young and old.

'You must leave now,' he commanded. 'Take no possessions, no food. This is no longer your property. The city is under our rule now. There is always a price to be paid for betrayal. This is yours.'

He saw the old woman out of the corner of his right eye.

She rushed out of the back of the house, her arms wrapped round a three-foot statue of the Virgin Mary. She was dressed in black, with a hand-knitted black shawl draped across her shoulders, her long hair white as an afternoon cloud. The war had cost her all she had once called her own—a husband she loved, sons and daughters who doted on her, grandchildren she had cuddled in her arms. All she had left was the statue that had been in her family for three generations. Gianna Mazella, seventy-eight years old, would rather be found dead than let the statue fall into someone else's hands. So she ran with her head down and her lips pursed against the sculptured marble edges, murmuring a prayer.

The German officer turned to an infantryman at his side. The officer nodded, and the soldier dropped to one knee and brought his rifle up against his shoulder. With one eye squinted shut, he searched for the old woman in his scope.

'Do you have her in range?' the officer asked.

'Yes, sir,' the soldier answered without a shift in position. 'I can graze her in the arm or leg. That will bring her to a stop.'

'We are not here to waste bullets,' the officer said. 'Nor are we here to stop escaping prisoners. We are here to kill them.'

The soldier closed both eyes for a brief moment. 'I have the head shot, sir,' he said softly.

'Then take it,' the officer told him.

The soldier gave the trigger a gentle squeeze, the mild recoil jolting him slightly. He opened both eyes and brought the rifle back against his chest. He saw the old woman spread out, face down, the religious statue inches beyond her grasp.

'Well done,' the officer said. 'Perhaps now the rest of these Italians will realise it doesn't pay to ignore our orders.'

IN THE LATE SUMMER of 1943 Naples was a city under siege.

Italy was once the third and weakest spoke in the Axis wheel forged by Germany and Japan as each nation sought to grab a piece of the world. Now the country's once beloved leader, Benito Mussolini, had been ousted from office and was turning futilely to his ally, Adolf Hitler, for help. This left the Italians, for the most part, leaderless and stripped of any hope for a reasonable peace.

For the first fifteen years of Il Duce's reign, from 1922 to 1937, Italy had thrived. Roads were repaved. Factories were running at full capacity. Crime, once rampant, was shut down. The Italians, who for decades had been treated as the adorable doormats of Europe, revelled in their fresh strength. 'We are the new America,' Italians would brag in long letters sent to relatives in the States. 'We no longer need to leave our land to find fortune.'

The Italians, especially those in the more impoverished southern regions of the country, took to heart Mussolini's words and beliefs. 'It is better to live one day as a lion than a thousand years as a lamb' was a credo that even the youngest schoolboy could recite. Mussolini promised his people riches and glory not seen since the days of the Roman Empire. The Italians would follow him and answer his call to conquer any land.

The arrival of the Second World War brought a vicious and brutal halt to those dreams of power and forced Italians to awaken to a national nightmare. The rebuilt infrastructures were blown to shreds by Allied bombing raids. One hundred and ten thousand Italian soldiers lay dead in the frozen tundra of the Russian front, sent there by

Mussolini to aid Hitler in his maniacal quest. An equal number of bodies was scattered throughout the Italian countryside and in North Africa, all of them victims of their leader's thirst for world domination.

By the summer of 1943 Italy was being attacked on two fronts. American and British troops occupied lands to the south. Sicily, Salerno and Paestum all fell in quick succession. At the same time, what had been an uneasy German friendship now turned into full-blown Nazi rage. Suddenly Hitler's air power and tank divisions throttled the Italian coast, Naples taking the hardest of the hits.

The Nazi high command had deemed Naples a port city that could not be left intact to become a stronghold for Allied forces. They knew that an Anglo-American takeover of the city was inevitable, so a programme was set in motion to ensure that miles of burning buildings, downed electrical wires and bombed-out roads would constitute a welcoming committee. Phase one was to evacuate the city. Phase two involved aerial attacks aimed at destroying any structure that could be used by the enemy. The final phase involved total destruction. 'If the city cannot belong to Hitler,' one German commander fumed, 'then it will belong to no one.'

Any Neapolitan who resisted evacuation would be subject to the whim of the commanding officer in the sector. The few members of the growing Italian resistance fled to surrounding hillsides to await orders. The Neapolitans were not sure of their future, but neither were they foolish enough to believe that the Germans planned to bring them out of Naples into a safe environment. They understood that they were being led to slaughter. It is why all resources were used to hide children from Nazi eyes. The majority of those children who were hidden and left behind were boys. Such thinking reflected a belief that boys would be best able to survive and cope on their own, which easily fed into the southern Italian reluctance ever to leave an unmarried daughter behind, regardless of circumstances.

THE BOY'S NAME was Vincenzo Scolardi. He ran down the narrow streets, dodging cracks in the pavement, as an early-morning mist rested like a large quilt over the city. He had a round brown-crusted loaf of bread under one arm and a string of rosary beads wrapped round the fingers of his left hand. The boy was tall for sixteen, with rich, curly brown hair and olive eyes. He had been a gifted student and a superb soccer player prior to the war. But neither school nor sports were what inspired the boy now. He lived for a life in the military, eager to carry on a family tradition begun by his great-grandfather Giovanni, who held high the banner of a unified Naples, fighting alongside the legendary Giuseppe Garibaldi during his march into the city on September 7, 1860. Vincenzo devoured books on military history and tactics, envisioning the day when he would lead his own troops into battle.

He had spent the night sleeping under an old cot in a deserted apartment off Via Toledo, waiting out the bombing attacks that greeted Naples each night. His mother had sent him out the day before in search of black-market bread, which arrived nightly, carted in by flat-bed trucks and sold in the darkness of quiet alleys.

The trucks had been late. They usually drove into the alleys at nine, but they were delayed by German checkpoints. The boy waited until nearly midnight for the round loaf that would serve as that day's meal for his mother and two sisters. The air-raid alarms sounded seconds after the boy paid for the bread. He dropped his lira into the hands of the black marketer, nodded and turned to leave.

'Don't go home, Vincenzo,' the man whispered.

'My sisters haven't eaten all day,' Vincenzo said.

'Let them have their bread in the morning. Find a warm place and wait out the night.'

The first bombs fell in the piazza off the alley. The area lit up with flames. The black marketer's truck engine kicked over. 'Save yourself,' the man said as he left. 'And the bread, too.'

Vincenzo waited until dawn before he braved the run back home. When he turned the final corner and skidded to a stop, he stood across from where his house had once been and stared at a crumpled mass of pink stucco, cement and wood.

He dropped the bread and fell to his knees. He began to moan, moving back and forth in agony. He lowered his head to the top of his knees. He didn't need to search through the rubble to find out what he already knew to be true. They were dead. His mother and his two sisters were gone from his life.

Vincenzo lifted his head, his face rich with tears and sorrow, and looked to the sky, searching through morning mist for the faces he loved. He let out a series of loud screams, his hands held tight, pounding at the ground around him. No one heard. No one saw. No one came. He was a lost boy now, without a home or a family. He was a victim of the war, joining the ranks of so many Italians who had been stripped of all they held close to their hearts. He was still only a child, but now he was forced to think and fend for himself like a man.

At that moment the boy wanted nothing more than to die. Instead, Vincenzo faced the long and gruelling process of burying his family.

'YOU WANT a marker for the graves?' his friend Franco asked. Franco was fourteen, with a muscular frame, dark eyes and a thick head of hair, long locks easily ruffled by the slightest wind.

Vincenzo shook his head. 'I'm the only one who needs to know where they are,' he said.

'I'm sorry, Vincenzo,' Franco said. 'They did not deserve to die like this.'

Vincenzo stared at the graves and nodded. 'No one does.'

'Maybe if they had left along with the others,' Franco said. He stood next to Vincenzo, his right foot resting against a crumpled stone wall that had once been the older boy's home. 'Maybe today they would still be alive.'

'My mother said that if we were to die, we had earned the right to die in our own city,' Vincenzo said.

'You heard the soldiers with the loudhailers,' Franco said. 'You read the leaflets they dropped. They're coming back. This time with tanks and many more soldiers. They're not going to stop until they destroy all of Naples.'

'I heard them,' Vincenzo said. 'And I believe them.'

'These graves we made won't last very long,' Franco said. 'The bombs will see to that.'

Vincenzo looked past Franco and out across the smoke and ruin of Naples. 'The bombs can't hurt them any more,' he said.

Salerno, Italy: September 25, 1943

Captain Edward Anders of the 45th Thunderbird Infantry Division leaned under the warm shade of a fig tree, a lit Lucky Strike hanging from his lips, and stared down at the beach-head below. His troops had been in the first wave of the attack to capture a city whose name he had never heard before the war. It had taken the American and British troops nine days to advance past the beach and up the side of the sloping mountain where he now stood. Behind him a command post had been set up inside a long series of brown tents. Anders stared at the mountains above him, up towards Cassino, then back towards the city of Naples, and knew there was still a lot of hard fighting left.

'Hey, Cap,' a voice behind him said. 'Word is you want to see me.'

'It was more like an order,' Captain Anders said. 'But let's not stand on formalities.'

Captain Anders turned to look at Corporal Steve Connors as he stood at attention and held his salute, the Gulf of Salerno at his back. Anders brushed away the salute. 'From what I've seen, you have as little patience for that crap as I do. Which probably means neither one of us is going to get far in this army.'

'I just want to get far enough to go home, Cap,' Connors said.

'Will Naples do you in the meantime?' Anders asked.

'What's in Naples?'

'Most likely nothing. From the reports I've seen, the city's nothing more than a ghost town.'

'But still, you want me to go,' Connors said. He removed his helmet and wiped sweat from his brow with the sleeve of his uniform.

Steve Connors was twenty-five years old, a college graduate and second-year law student from Covington, Kentucky. He was just shy of six feet tall with a middleweight fighter's rugged build, topped by thick strands of dark hair, brown eyes and a wide smile that balanced out a hard edge. He had fought under Anders's command for fourteen months, pounding and slashing his way from one blood-drenched beach-head to the next, always the first in line, always the first to fire. He had a street fighter's instincts for battle and survival and was, as far as Ed Anders was concerned, the best soldier for the task at hand.

'It might just be a ghost town with two of our men in it,' Anders said. 'We had a handful of GIs helping the Italian resistance—or whatever was left of it. Most of them slipped out before the evacuation. Two didn't. They could be dead. They could be hiding. But we've got to find out.'

'I go in alone?' Connors asked.

'You'd like that, wouldn't you?' Anders said.

'Very much, sir.'

'But you'll be part of a three-man team. If our soldiers are still in there, they might be hurt. So you'll take one of the medics, Willis. And another good rifle to cover your back. That'll be Scott Taylor.'

Connors winced at the sound of Taylor's name.

'I know you two rub each other the wrong way,' Anders said, 'but this ain't the senior prom. If it gets tight, he's somebody good to have on your side.'

'Yes, sir,' Connors said. 'Anything else I need to know?'

'Not a thing. Just radio back what you see. We'll do the rest.'

'And if we don't find our men? What then, Cap?'

'Enjoy your stay in Naples.'

FIFTEEN MILES outside Rome, eighty Mark IV tanks of the 16th Panzer Division sat in long, silent rows. German soldiers were scattered about, searching out shade and a cool place to doze. Colonel Rudolf von Klaus stood in the open pit of his tank and stared at the note in his hands. The words on the paper had been passed down directly from Adolf Hitler himself. They were as simple and direct as any order he had received in his twenty-five-year military career. 'Allow no stone in Naples to stand' was all it said.

To a precise and proud officer the order read as nothing less than a complete waste of a panzer division that had fought too hard for too long to be reduced to a mop-up unit. It was also a waste of time, of which there was precious little left before this wretched war would reach its ruinous conclusion. Naples had already been contained, its streets emptied. Aerial bombings had destroyed any buildings that could possibly be of use to the enemy.

Von Klaus folded the order and shoved it into his trouser pocket. He gazed around at his troops and took some comfort from the fact that as inane as the order was, its simplicity would at least guarantee that he would not have to leave any more of his men lying dead or wounded on a battlefield. After the Naples mission von Klaus was scheduled to head back home to a wife he had not seen for two years, a daughter who would now be eight and a son too young to remember the last time his father cradled him in his arms. Von Klaus was only forty-six years old but felt decades past that. Nothing, he believed, aged a man more than having to face the reality of inevitable defeat.

'The tanks are repaired and fuelled, sir.' The young officer stood half hidden by the shadows of dangling tree limbs.

'Good,' von Klaus said.

'Sir, if I may, some of the men were wondering when we would be moving on,' the officer said.

'Do you have a girl back home that you care about, Kunnalt?'

'Yes, sir,' Kunnalt said, surprised at the question. 'We plan to marry once the war is over.'

'Then go and find a large rock, sit down and write her a letter,' Von Klaus said. 'I'm in no rush to leave. The empty buildings of Naples will wait for us.'

LATE THAT NIGHT, on the waterfront in Naples, 200 boys and girls were spread out around a large fire, the flames licking the thick, crusty wood, sending sparks and smoke into the starlit sky. Their clothes were dirty and shredded at the sleeves and cuffs, their shoes held together by cardboard and string. All their memories had been scarred by the frightful war. The youngest members of the group, between five and seven years old, stood with their backs to the others, tossing small pebbles into the oil-soaked Bay of Naples. The rest huddled around Vincenzo and Franco.

Vincenzo stepped closer to the fire. He looked down and smiled at two small boys, Giancarlo and Antonio, playing quietly by the edge of the pier. He glanced past them at a girl slowly making her way toward him. She was tall, about fifteen, with rich brown hair rolled up and buried under a cap two sizes too large. She stepped between Vincenzo and the two boys, her arms by her side, an angry look in her soft eyes.

'Where do we go from here?' she asked.

'The hills,' Vincenzo said with a slight shrug.

'And after that?'

'What's your name?' Vincenzo asked.

'Angela,' she said. 'I lived in Forcella with my family. Now I live there alone.'

Forcella was the roughest neighbourhood in Naples. 'Forcella?' Vincenzo said to her. 'Not even a Nazi would be brave enough to set foot in those streets.'

'Especially after dark,' Franco said, laughing.

'But they did,' Angela said, lowering her eyes for a moment.

'What do you want me to do?' Vincenzo said. 'Where do you think we should go? Look around you. This is all that's left of us.'

'So we run,' she said, words laced with sarcasm. 'Like always.'

Vincenzo stepped closer to her, his face red with anger. 'There is nothing else to do,' he said.

Angela glared at Vincenzo for several moments, lowered her head and then turned back into the crowd.

Vincenzo walked in silence around the edges of the fire, the sounds of the crackling wood mixing with the murmurs of the gathered teenagers. 'Naples has always been ruled by outsiders,' he said, stopping alongside Franco. 'But in all that time, the people have never surrendered the streets without a fight. This war, against this enemy, would be the first time that has ever happened.'

'Who are we to stop it?' Franco said, staring into his friend's eyes.

Vincenzo stood for a moment in front of the flames. He then turned and walked away, disappearing into the darkness of the Neapolitan night.

September 26

On a highway twenty-five miles outside Salerno, Steve Connors shifted gears on the Jeep and eased it gently past a large hole in the road and onto a long patch of brown grass. He killed the engine, grabbed a newspaper off the passenger seat and stepped out of the Jeep with his gear. He lit a cigarette as he walked and folded a four-week-old edition of the *Cincinnati Enquirer* over to the sports section, searching for the baseball standings.

'Why we stopping?' Scott Taylor asked, sitting in the front of the Jeep. Taylor was twenty-four, a year younger than Connors. He was tall and muscular with short blond hair, a former high school football star back in Pittsburgh, his home town. The two had known each other since basic training and shared a mutual respect for each other's battle skills and a dislike towards each other for almost everything else.

Connors flopped down under the shade of an old fig tree and leaned his head against its rugged bark. 'Germans mine everything,' he said. 'A road leading into Naples is one they wouldn't miss. Which means we have to drive on grass. Which means before I start, I need a break.'

'I don't need convincing,' Willis, the medic, said, jumping out of the back seat and walking towards Connors and the shade. Willis was still a teenager, though he tried to act older. He was the only child of a single mother, a schoolteacher back in Davenport, Iowa. Willis was slight, had thin brown hair and walked with a farmer's gait. He was a good medic and never panicked in the rush of battle.

'I'll wait here,' Taylor said, lighting a cigarette.

'That's a good idea, Taylor,' Connors said. 'I'd hate to have some sheep-herder come along and drive off with the Jeep.'

Connors rested the Sports Section on his legs and looked out at the silent countryside. The area had been shelled hard, yet the region still retained the core of its beauty. It was a stubborn land, much like the people who lived off it. He glanced at Willis, stretched out under the tree across from his, and at Taylor, stubbornly stewing in the front of the Jeep.

Suddenly he heard the dog's growl.

Connors turned his head and saw a cream-coloured bull mastiff standing a few feet to his left, its thick jowls curled in anger, a wide blotch of blood staining its massive left hind leg. He stared at the dog for several seconds, trying to decide if it was looking for a fight or just on a break from one. He stretched out his fingers and reached for a pack of Necco wafers wedged in the centre of his K rations. The dog caught the hand motion and took two steps forward. Connors pulled the wafers from his pack and tossed them to the dog. The animal sniffed at them and then raised its right front paw and kicked the package away. Connors laughed. 'I can't even get a starving dog to eat this stuff,' he muttered.

Willis turned his head and looked over his shoulder at the dog. 'Cars in my town ain't as big as that dog,' he said.

'He's as scared as he is big,' Connors said. 'So if you're going to move, do it slow.'

He heard the rifle click and turned to see Taylor standing in the front seat of the Jeep, his weapon pointed down at the dog. 'So long as that dog stays in place, you do the same,' Connors told him.

'We're here to find two soldiers,' Taylor said. 'I didn't hear anything about any dog.'

'Pull that trigger and you're going to have to deal with me.'

Connors stood up and, with one hand held out, fingers curled inward, took several slow steps towards the mastiff. The dog lifted its head and crouched down even more, its growl holding steady. 'I'm gonna check your wound,' Connors said in a soft voice. 'See how bad it is.' The dog began to sniff at his knuckles. 'All I ask is you don't take a chunk of my ass.'

The dog licked at Connors's hand, and its nose rubbed the side of the soldier's leg. Connors gently patted the dog's massive neck, searching for a collar. 'Looks like you're out here on your own,' he said. 'Like us.'

Connors squatted down and looked at the wound, still open and raw. 'He might need some stitches,' he said to Willis. 'You up for that?'

Willis moved on hands and knees towards the mastiff, stopping at eye level across from the wound. 'Don't see how I can botch it up any worse than I do on you guys.'

'You're just going to have to trust us,' Connors said to the dog. 'Same as we're doing with you.' He turned to Willis. 'What do you need?' he asked.

'Get me some water from out of that stream,' Willis said.

Connors walked over to a small stream, lowered his helmet into the cool water and brought it back to the dog. 'OK,' he said to Willis. 'Now what?'

'I'll get my pack,' Willis said. 'You run water over the cut, then I'll clean up the area around it.'

'You ever have a dog, Willis?' Connors asked, watching the mastiff flinch as the water fell down the sides of his wound.

'Grew up on a farm,' Willis said, returning with his pack. 'Don't think there was an animal we *didn't* have. How about you?'

'Always wanted one,' Connors said.

Connors cleared away enough blood for Willis to get a good look at the cut. 'He took a hit of shrapnel,' the medic said. 'Nothing too heavy. I'll bandage it up. And if he can stop chasing rabbits for a few days, he should be good as new.'

Connors stood in front of the dog, watching Willis work on its wounds, his back to Taylor's rifle. 'What was the plan?' he asked Taylor. 'Shoot me, then the dog?'

'Only if I had to,' Taylor said. 'And believe me, I wouldn't lose much sleep over either of you.'

'He for real?' Willis asked, gazing past Connors at Taylor.

'We run into trouble, we'll be glad he's with us,' Connors said. 'The rest of the time he's like having a rotting tooth.'

Connors watched Willis work on the mastiff's wound for the better part of the next hour. Willis was careful not to hurt the animal, dabbing at the cut, never pushing or prodding. For its part the dog neither barked nor growled, content to let the young stranger go about his business.

The overhead sun was hot and bright. When he was finished, Willis paused to wipe his forehead and take a long drink from his canteen. Connors walked back to the tree, shoved his newspaper into his pack and then headed for the parked Jeep. He turned to look at the dog. Willis stood across from him, his gear already on his back. Behind them Taylor, his rifle at ease, sat back down in the front seat of the Jeep. 'You be good,' Connors said to the dog. 'If you see any Germans, bite them.'

Connors and Willis walked together towards the Jeep, the dog following slowly. 'Thanks for doing that,' he said to Willis.

'He's the first patient I've had since I've been out here who hasn't bitched and moaned about my medical abilities,' Willis said.

'You two ready?' Taylor asked. 'Or do you want to see if any birds need their wings mended?'

Connors tossed his gear into the Jeep, jumped in behind the wheel and started the engine. The bull mastiff barked loudly and ran towards the Jeep. Connors kept both hands on the steering wheel, his eyes fixed on the empty road leading into Naples. Then he turned to look at the dog, now sitting alongside the Jeep, staring up at Connors with round, pasta-bowl eyes. They stared at each other for several moments, the sun bearing down hard.

'Get in,' Connors said, reaching back to pat the rear seat. 'Take you as far as Naples. After that you're back on your own.'

'Are you nuts?' Taylor asked. 'We can't take a dog with us. It's against any orders anybody would ever give.'

'Give him some space,' Connors said to Willis. 'He'll need room to drool.'

Connors watched as the mastiff jumped into the back seat, its 140-pound girth taking up a sizable portion of the rear, and nestled alongside Willis. 'They grow dogs big around here,' said Connors, looking towards the road. He turned the wheel to the left, ground the clutch into gear and began riding along the tree line. 'I hope the same isn't true about the women.'

THE TWO BOYS KNELT before the main altar of the old church of Santa Caterina a Formiello, their heads bowed in prayer. The church was cool, dark and silent. The whispers of the boys echoed off the stone walls and the shattered windows.

'I can still smell the bowls of Mama's lentils,' said Giancarlo, at twelve the elder by two years, as they rose and sat in straw chairs facing the altar. 'Me eating them with a spoon and you with bread.'

'Is Uncle Mario with us, too?' Antonio asked. He was shivering, huddled close to his brother, the back of his head leaning against the top rung of his chair.

'Always,' Giancarlo said to him with a smile. He stood and looked around the empty, dust-filled church. 'We need to go and join the others. We don't want to be left behind.'

'Just one more prayer,' Antonio said. 'The one I always save for Mama.'

Giancarlo nodded, watching his brother walk the three steps up to the altar. 'You say more prayers than a priest,' he whispered.

Antonio stretched to reach the large, heavy cross resting in the centre of the altar. His small hands gripped the base and slid it closer to him, easing it across the cold marble. As he reached up to kiss the crucified body of Christ, he saw the wires attached to the base of the cross and heard the click of the mechanism that snapped the fuse of the mine. Antonio stepped back and turned to look at Giancarlo for one final time, his wide, frightened eyes telling him what they both already knew.

The explosion rocked the church. Thick shards of marble and wood flew through the air, hurtling towards the ceiling with its painting of St Catherine, her arms spread wide. Below her, buried under mounds of destruction caused by the blast of the German mine, the bodies of Antonio and Giancarlo Bardini lay face down and still.

Their war had finally found its end.

OUTSIDE THE CHURCH, Vincenzo Scolardi and his friend Franco led a slow-moving contingent of more than 200 boys and girls through the empty street. They walked with their heads down, their few belongings bundled inside old shirts and flung over their shoulders.

'When do you think we can come back?' Franco asked, wiping sweat from his brow.

'Maybe never,' Vincenzo said.

The door of the church blasted open. Shards of marble, wood and broken glass embraced the street. Vincenzo and Franco fell to the ground. Behind them the other children scampered for cover.

Vincenzo got to his feet and made his way through the smoke to the front entrance. He stood there for a moment, smoke washing past him, fire licking at his legs, before stepping inside. He walked past piles of wood and stone, then stopped in front of the main altar, its thick marble split in two. He shifted his feet and brushed against a string of rosary beads. He bent down, dropped his hand into a cloud of smoke and picked them up. He stared at them, letting the beads rest against the sides of his fingers. He closed his hands round them, turned and walked out of the church.

He walked past Franco and Angela, ignoring the enquiring faces of the boys and girls who stood now in a large huddle round the front entrance. He began walking back towards the city centre.

'Where are you going?' Franco asked.

'I'm staying,' Vincenzo said.

'To do what?' Franco asked.

Vincenzo stopped, gazed at the faces that surrounded him and took a deep breath. 'Kill as many Germans as I can.'

'You walk into a grave if you do that,' Franco said.

'If I'm going to die, I'll die here,' Vincenzo said. 'In my city. On my streets.' He walked down the centre of the empty street.

Franco and Angela watched him go, then looked at each other, nodded, and started to follow Vincenzo back into the heart of the city. The other children milled nervously about, exchanging glances. Then three boys broke from the pack and followed Franco and Angela. Soon five more trailed them. And then another five.

In all it took less than fifteen minutes for the entire band of street boys and girls to turn and begin a slow walk back to nowhere.

CARLO MALDINI stood against the side of a broken window and stared down at the street below. He took a long drink from a bottle of wine and watched the flames bring down the walls of what had once been his favourite church, too used to violence to be moved by what he saw. Maldini was fifty-six years old, with dark hair tinged white at the sides. He was thin but muscular. His clothes were old and torn. On most days he was too deep into his wine to notice.

The burdens of war had turned Carlo Maldini into a weathered man with a sad face. Benito Mussolini's dream of an Italian empire had cost Maldini a wife and two sons and filled him with an anger that bordered on madness. He gulped down another mouthful of wine. He had spent many a Sunday in that church, side by side with his family, their heads bowed in solemn prayer.

He gazed up the street and watched the large group of children march back down the main road. He turned his head and stared at the young woman standing with her arms folded and her eyes focused on the activity below. She looked beautiful in the morning sunlight that filtered in through the huge holes in what was left of their home. From where he stood, staring at her through the glazed effect of too much wine, the woman looked exactly like her mother. She had long dark strands of hair gently brushing the tops of her shoulders, a round, unlined face filled with the power and passion of her youth, and olive-shaped eyes that could burn a hole through the very soul of a man. Her name was Nunzia. She was twenty years old and his daughter, the only child he had left to lose.

Maldini could not leave Naples when the Germans had ordered the evacuation of the city. He was too drunk, too crammed with rage. He cowered in his basement, hiding, his Nunzia at his side.

'We must go,' she had said to him. 'We'll hide in the mountains and then make our way towards the Americans.'

Maldini could only mumble senseless words about a family he no longer had and happier days. He tried pushing his daughter away.

'I won't leave you here,' Nunzia said.

'There's nothing left for me, little angel,' Maldini said to her, a sad smile crossing his lips. 'I have my wine and my memories. That's all a man like me needs.'

'I'm staying by your side, Papa,' Nunzia said.

'Your mother was stubborn,' Maldini said. 'She wouldn't leave either. And now she's dead. They're all dead. And those that aren't will soon join them.'

'Then we will die here, Papa,' Nunzia said. 'In Naples, where you belong. Where we *both* belong.'

'You don't belong with a drunk,' Maldini said.

'I belong with my father,' Nunzia replied.

Maldini swallowed a long drink of wine and stared at his daughter as she turned her look towards him.

'What will those children do?' Nunzia asked.

'Something foolish, no doubt,' Maldini said.

'I heard a rumour in the piazza yesterday,' Nunzia said. 'From Signora Matturano. She said the Nazis were coming back.'

'Let them come,' Maldini said with a shrug. 'There's nothing left for them to take.' He looked out of the window as the caravan of children began to disappear from view.

'She said there were leaflets dropped from planes,' Nunzia said. 'Her grandson, Franco, showed her one. He's in that group of children down there. I can take you to meet them. I know where they'll sleep tonight.'

Maldini looked away from the window and stared at his daughter. 'Why would I want to do something so crazy?' he asked.

'To help them, Papa,' she said. 'In case the Nazis come back.'

'Help them get *killed*!' Maldini shouted. 'Have I not seen enough blood lost?'

'If they're staying and the Germans are coming back, they'll be forced to fight,' Nunzia said, not backing down. 'With your help or without. If that happens, most of them will die.'

'That's a decision for them to make,' Maldini said. 'Not for me. Take a good look at me, Nunzia. Open your eyes and look beyond your father and see instead the madman who sits in his place. Then tell me, what help can that be to any man or boy?'

'You can tell them what they don't know, Papa. You know about the guns.'

VINCENZO STOOD in the centre of Piazza Plebiscito, the largest square in Naples, surrounded by the Royal Palace and the church of

San Francisco di Paola. Scores of children were spread throughout the square, waiting for someone to tell them what to do. Franco and Angela walked past the crowd and stood across from Vincenzo.

'I counted twenty-three knives and four handguns,' Franco said.

'A map of the city would be good to have,' Vincenzo said.

'So would more guns,' Angela said.

'We need to keep the youngest children out of sight,' Vincenzo said. 'We don't know what's coming and when, but we have to keep them safe. They should have gone to the hills.'

'We can use them as messengers if we need to,' Franco said. 'Nothing more than that.'

Vincenzo walked around the square, staring at the cobblestones, gazing under piles of rubble. 'Not every bomb the Nazis dropped on us exploded. There are at least a dozen here in the square.'

'If we can find some carts, we can gather them up,' Franco said.

'How do you know the bombs will be of any use?' Angela asked. 'They didn't explode when they were dropped from a plane. What are we going to do? *Slide* them towards the Germans?'

'I have no idea,' Vincenzo said with a voice filled with weary irritation. 'All I know is they are bombs and they do explode.'

Angela turned and sat under the shadow of the bronze statue of King Ferdinand I, leaning her back against the cold marble of the base. She looked around her at the boys and girls spread throughout the square. 'How do we keep them alive?' she asked.

Vincenzo stayed silent for several minutes before answering. 'The streets are our best weapon,' he said. 'The dark alleys and the paths through the sewers. Hidden walkways inside churches and museums. Tunnels outside the station. If we use all that, we can fight and never be seen. We'll be an invisible army. One that can beat the Nazis.'

FIFTY MILES OUTSIDE Rome, Colonel Rudolf von Klaus raised his head up to the warm sun, helmet resting on the edge of the tank, goggles loose around his neck. He found the ride down the coastline, dotted with farms and vineyards, a peaceful one and a welcome break from the toils of war. No one, von Klaus believed, could comprehend the cost of war more than a military man. He was relieved it would all soon be at an end.

He caught the movement behind the large bush out of the corner of his eye. Von Klaus tapped one hand on the inside lid of the tank and reached for his revolver with the other. The machine-gun unit shifted under him, moving slowly to its right, the bush in its target sites. 'Draw him out,' von Klaus said in a calm voice.

Six machine-gun rounds pelted at the earth around the bush. Within seconds two small, thin arms were raised up, barely visible beyond the lush leaves of the bush. 'Hold fire,' von Klaus ordered.

He watched as a barefoot boy in shorts and a dirty white T-shirt stepped out from behind the bush and walked towards the tank, arms still raised. The boy stopped, his round face looking up at the colonel. Von Klaus stared down at the boy. 'How old are you?' von Klaus asked him. He spoke fluent Italian.

'Seven,' the boy answered.

'And what were you doing back there?' von Klaus asked.

'Hiding,' the boy said.

'You're not very good at it,' von Klaus said.

The boy nodded.

'Are you a soldier in the Italian army?' von Klaus asked.

'No, signor. I'm too young to be a soldier.'

'Then you're too young for me to take as prisoner,' von Klaus said. 'So bring your arms to rest.'

The boy did as he was told, his eyes darting around at the soldiers gathered next to him, rifles by their sides. 'My brother Marco was a soldier,' the boy said, looking back at von Klaus. 'He was in the war in Africa, fighting the English. He was killed there.'

'Who looks after you?' von Klaus asked.

The boy hesitated. 'I don't need anyone,' he said.

'Your leader would be proud of you,' von Klaus said, his voice soft and sad. 'If he were still in charge. Have you heard the news? About Mussolini?'

'Is he dead?' the boy asked.

'No, but he's no longer in power. And you no longer need to fight.'

'Are you going to kill me?' the boy asked.

'What's your name?' von Klaus asked.

'Massimo,' the boy said.

'Why would you ask such a question, Massimo?'

'You're a Nazi,' he said. 'Nazis killed my mother and father.'

Von Klaus shook his head. 'No. I'm not going to kill you. But I am going to give you an order, and I expect it to be followed.'

'What kind of an order?'

'I want you to go up deeper into the hills,' von Klaus said to him. 'Find a bigger bush to hide behind. And this time stay low enough to the ground that you will not be seen from the road. Can I count on you to follow such an order?'

'Yes,' Massimo said.

'Good,' von Klaus said. 'Spoken like a true soldier.'

The colonel nodded as he and Massimo exchanged a final glance. Then the boy turned and ran back up the sloping hillside.

ONE HUNDRED boys and girls sat around the edge of Castel dell'Ovo in the early morning heat. Carlo Maldini stood to the side. Nunzia was off to his left, her eyes studying the faces of Vincenzo, Franco and Angela.

'Are you the leader?' Maldini asked Vincenzo.

'I don't lead anybody,' Vincenzo said. 'They followed me.'

'That means they're looking for you to lead.' Maldini eased himself past Nunzia and stood towering above Vincenzo. 'And why do they follow you? It's because they heard you talk. But that only gets you so far. Now they need to see you think.'

'We're making a plan,' Angela said. 'Just in case the Nazis do come.'

'Does this plan call for weapons?' Maldini asked. 'Or are you just going to stare at the Nazis until they leave?'

'Many of us have knives. A few have handguns,' Vincenzo said.

Maldini turned away from Vincenzo and stared out at the glimmering waters of the bay. 'Think back,' he said. 'Think to when the Nazis first came to Naples. What is the first thing they did?'

'They took away the guns our fathers kept,' Franco said.

'That's right,' Maldini said, glancing over Franco's shoulder as twenty more boys joined the group. 'And they took them where?'

Vincenzo looked down at the water splashing against the sides of the pier.

'That's right,' Maldini whispered. 'They threw them in the bay.'

'How deep?' Vincenzo asked.

'Fifty feet,' Maldini said. 'Seventy-five at the most.'

'Can they still be used?' Angela asked.

'Once they're dried, cleaned and oiled, they'll be good as new,' Maldini said. 'Maybe a bit rusty, but nothing worse than that.'

'And we get them out how?' Vincenzo asked. 'It would take every free hand we have a full day to dive down and bring up each gun. Then you would need another full day to dry them out. The Nazis might be in the centre of the city before one of us would be able to fire off a single shot.'

'You're not thinking!' Maldini said between clenched teeth. 'My daughter tells me you are a student of history. You should know your religion as well.'

Vincenzo glared into Maldini's eyes, then looked away and glanced at the long row of fishing boats moored to the dock, their oars spread out on the hot ground to dry. 'The boats,' he said.

'That's right,' Maldini said, smiling. 'The boats. You will do as the Apostles once did. Only in place of fish, you pull up guns.'

'Will you stay and help us?' Franco asked.

'It is no longer my war,' Maldini said.

'I will help you,' Nunzia said, arms at her sides, her eyes hard. 'And so will my father. It is better for him to drink his wine in the middle of the bay than behind the window of an empty building.'

Maldini stared at his daughter for several moments, then looked at Vincenzo and shrugged. 'It is easier to fight a Nazi than go against the wishes of a Neapolitan woman,' he said.

STEVE CONNORS LAY PRONE in the warm grass and looked down at Naples from the Camaldoli hill. He rested his binoculars by his side and turned to gaze out across the bay, towards the islands of Ischia and Capri in the distance, and then back down to what had once been a city. The bull mastiff lay next to him, asleep. Taylor and Willis sat behind him, each picking at the contents of a small can of stew with the edges of a cracker.

Connors had come to Naples expecting to see ruin. But he had not been prepared for the level of destruction that stretched out before him. He lay there and stared at the devastation for nearly an hour. Then he stepped back from the bluff and stuffed the small binoculars into the rear of his pack. 'Never seen churches so big,' he said to Willis and Taylor. 'And there are so many. The people who lived on those streets must have given a lot of hours over to prayer.' He turned to take one more look down through the smouldering smoke at the broken buildings below. 'Didn't seem to do them all that much good though, did it?'

'I never used to pray,' Willis said. 'Not until I started eating army rations. Now I pray before every meal.'

'You think we'll ever get a taste of that Italian food we hear about?' Taylor asked.

The first shot rang out and bounced off a rock, missing Connors's leg by less than an inch. The second one clipped the tree where Taylor and Willis were eating, sending both men scurrying for cover.

'You see anything?' Taylor shouted out, rifle at the ready, as he braced himself against the side of a large boulder.

Connors looked at the mastiff and watched as the dog stood, its eyes staring up to the right. 'In the thick bushes,' he said. 'About two o'clock.'

'How many you figure?' Willis asked. He was lying down flat, the tree his only cover.

Connors ran from the edge of the bluff and threw himself to the ground, seeking cover behind a small stone wall. Two bullets rang out, each nicking off a piece of rock. 'So far, I figure it's just the one,' he said. 'But others could be out there.'

Taylor raised his rifle and fired off two quick rounds into the bushes overhead. 'Save your ammo,' Connors said. 'Count on seeing him, not on luck.'

'If he's in there, I'll bring him out,' Taylor said, checking his ammo belt. 'When I do, you take him.'

Connors nodded. 'Willis, you any good with a gun?' he asked.

'I'm better with wounds,' Willis said, his head still down.

'You figure krauts or dagos?' Taylor asked, his knees bent, waiting to make his move.

'Italians have no reason to shoot at us now,' Connors said. 'My guess is a Nazi scout team.'

The mastiff's bark forced Connors to turn to his left, and he fired off two rounds as soon as he saw the glint of another rifle. The second bullet found its mark. He saw a German soldier fall face forwards into a row of hedges. Taylor looked over his shoulder and then waved to Connors. 'The medic covers me,' he said. 'And you take out the other German.'

'He's got the sun to his back,' Connors said. 'You're going to be shooting into glare. He'll have clear sight on you.'

'We can't wait,' Taylor said. 'There might be more than two, or there might be more coming. I'm moving now. Back me.'

Connors took a deep breath and nodded. 'Go,' he said.

Willis and Connors fired into the hedges above them as Taylor made his way up the bluff, running from tree to tree, looking for the hidden soldier. The mastiff stood next to Connors, protected by the row of stones. 'I'm just shooting blind rounds here,' Willis said. 'I'm going to move to that tree to the right.'

'Stay put,' Connors said. 'Let Taylor get to the top of the hill, then we both move.'

'Got an aunt back home like you,' Willis said. 'All worries and no smiles. I'll meet you at the Jeep.'

Willis jumped to his feet and ran for a large tree covered by a thick circle of shrubs. 'Willis!' Connors shouted, watching as the medic stepped into the green patch, the area below his feet too dense for him to see the mine. The explosion sent Willis flying back, his chest and face blown away.

Connors lowered his head and took in several slow, deep breaths. 'Damn it,' he said. 'Damn it!'

He looked back up and saw that Taylor was now directly opposite the German's position. Taylor was well hidden by the trees and took careful aim with his rifle, looking to hit at the ground cover. He fired three quick rounds, the smoke from his rifle giving away his position.

Connors saw the German move from his cover, and raised his rifle. He had the German in his scope lines when he saw Taylor move towards the soldier, firing a steady stream of bullets. Connors held his aim until he had a sure shot, and then he and the German squeezed their triggers at the same time. They both hit their targets.

It took Scott Taylor the rest of that afternoon to die.

Connors lay there and held Taylor in his arms. It was all that was left for him to do. He couldn't radio back to headquarters for help. The transmitter had been blown to bits, along with Willis, but even if he still had it, he couldn't risk giving away his position to any other Germans who were in the area. So instead, Connors just sat and listened to a soldier he had never liked gasp and wheeze his final words. Taylor told him as much as he could about his life in the short hours he had left. Connors promised to let his family back home know how brave he had been.

'Thanks for staying with me,' Taylor said.

'You'd have done the same,' Connors said.

'Don't bet your life on it,' Taylor said, his eyes closing for a final time.

TWELVE ROWING BOATS, in rows of two with four people to a boat, slowly made their way out from the shore of Porto di Santa Lucia.

Maldini and Vincenzo rode in the lead boat, the older man pulling on a set of wooden oars, gliding them through the calm waters. The boats were weighed down with massive fishing nets curled up and running along their centres. The hot sun was now at full boil.

Maldini pulled his oars out of the water and rested them inside the boat. 'We are here,' he said. 'We are floating above the guns.'

'Should we drop the nets?' Vincenzo asked, standing on unsteady legs in the centre of the boat.

'It's what I would do,' Maldini said. 'But I'm not the one in charge.'

Vincenzo cupped his hands around his mouth, balancing himself against the bumps of the small waves. 'Lift your nets,' he shouted to the boys in the other boats. 'And hold them above your heads. Stand as steady as you can.'

The boys grunted and grimaced as they went about a task that normally required the strength of grown men.

'How far do the nets need to be tossed?' Vincenzo asked.

'Enough to stretch them out,' Maldini said. 'Ten feet would be acceptable.'

'They're not strong enough to make that long a throw,' Vincenzo said.

Maldini stared at Vincenzo, the stubble on his face glistening from the spray mist of the waves. He then turned to look back at the boys struggling with the nets. 'Grab that rope from the bow,' he ordered. 'Run it through the ring behind me and then go boat to boat and link them together. It will keep us in tight formation. I'll meet up with you and Franco in the last boat.'

Vincenzo tore off his shirt, ran the thick cord through the circular ring at the nose of the boat and dived into the sea. He swam with one hand, holding the rope above his head with the other.

Maldini was also in the water, swimming towards the last boat on the line. He stopped and turned back towards Vincenzo. 'Have the youngest child swim to shore,' he called out. 'We need more boys. As many as can be found. It will take many hands to lift the nets from the bottom.'

Soon the boats were lined up and tied together, bobbing in unison to the splashing beat of the waves, and more than seventy-five boys swam on either side of the small crafts.

Maldini stood in bare feet in the centre of the first boat, gripping the edge of a rolled-up fishing net in his hands. Vincenzo, Franco and Angela flanked his sides, each holding the same net, waiting for Maldini to give the order. 'The higher we throw it, the further out it will go,' he shouted. 'It should float up and out, unfurl like an old flag. Angela, you tell us when.'

Angela steadied her feet and tightened her grip. '*Forza, Italia*!' she yelled as she reached up with all her strength and, along with the three others, fell back as they let the net go. They sat in the boat and watched the net float in the air, gently spread out and cover the water as if it were a crisply ironed tablecloth.

'Did we do it?' Franco asked. 'Is it out far enough?'

Maldini rubbed the top of the boy's head, watching as the net sank slowly to the bottom of the bay. 'You did well, Franco,' he said. He turned to the others. 'You all did. But we still have four nets to throw. And after that comes the hard part. Pulling them up.'

'We only have three more nets for the guns,' Angela said as she glanced down the sides of the boats.

'That's right,' Maldini said. 'But I asked two of the younger boys to bring out another boat, take it past us to the point and drop their net out there. I can only pray that they come back with enough fish to feed us all. We'll have a hungry group on our hands at the end of the day.'

THE BULL MASTIFF LED the way down the side of the bluff, walking with delicate ease along its narrow path. Connors followed, one hand holding the belt of his shouldered rifle. His uniform was sprinkled with dust and blood. He had buried Willis and Taylor at the top of the bluff, overlooking the Bay of Naples, using their helmets and rifles as markers.

The Jeep was parked under an old pine tree inside a neglected olive grove. There was little wind, but the heat was cooling down with the evening shade.

The bull mastiff saw the boys before Connors did and ran towards them, barking. Connors flipped his rifle from his shoulder to his hands and fast-stepped down the path. He stopped between the dog and the four boys sitting in his Jeep, rifle at his side. One of the boys had his fingers wrapped round the ignition key. They were thin, dirty and dishevelled, and none was older than fourteen. Connors looked at each one, getting only frightened stares in return. The mastiff had now put his paws on the side of the Jeep and was growling, ready to pounce at any sudden movements.

'Do you speak any English?' Connors asked.

'We all do,' the oldest of the four stammered. 'We are taught Neapolitan first. Then Italian and then English.'

'Why are you here?' the boy in the front passenger seat asked.

'I was about to ask the same question,' Connors said. 'And since I'm the one with the rifle, I'd like my answer first.'

'We're looking for Nazis,' the boy said. 'To see if they're really coming to Naples again. And then report back.'

'Report back to who?' Connors asked.

The four shot quick glances at one another and then looked back down at the dog and the soldier. 'The others in our group,' the one holding the ignition key said.

'Let's say that the Nazis *are* coming back,' Connors said. 'What happens then?' He walked closer to the Jeep, rifle slung once again over his shoulder.

'I guess then we fight,' the boy closest to Connors said. The boy's eyes were dark, his face round, sweet and innocent, his hair clipped short.

Connors stared at him. 'Fight the Nazis?'

'That's what you do,' the boy said. 'Why can't we?'

'The Nazis have a habit of shooting back,' Connors said. 'That's one reason to think about.'

The boys stayed silent for several seconds, eyes glancing up towards the ridge where the fight had taken place.

'Does your dog understand Italian?' the boy in the back asked.

'That's *all* he understands,' Connors said.

The boy in the back smiled and snapped his fingers. '*Scendi jou*,' he said in as firm a voice as he could muster. '*E siedati*!'

The bull mastiff lowered his paws, stepped back from the Jeep and sat on the ground, his mouth open, his large tongue dangling.

'It's good to know he listens to *somebody*,' Connors said. 'Tell you his name if I knew it. But I can tell you mine. It's Connors.'

'I am Dante,' the boy in the back said. 'The boy next to me is Claudio. And the two in front are Gaspare and Pepe.'

'How many are there in this group of yours?' Connors asked.

'About two hundred,' Dante said, stepping down from the Jeep. 'Maybe two hundred and fifty.'

'All boys?'

'A few girls,' Gaspare said. 'Just the ones without any family.'

'Any American soldiers down there?' Connors asked, leaning against the side of the Jeep, his helmet off and resting on the bonnet.

'You're the first one any of us have seen,' Dante said.

'What about Italian resistance? Any of them with you?'

'No,' Dante said. 'They left before the evacuation.'

'Are we your prisoners now?' Claudio asked, speaking for the first time. He was the youngest, his brown hair touched with streaks of blond; he looked nervous and ill at ease in the rear of the Jeep.

'Why don't we say that, for the time being, we're working together,' Connors said. 'At least until we see how everything in Naples plays out. Just me, the dog and the four of you.'

'What is it you want us to do?' Dante asked.

'It's not anything that's going to get you into trouble,' Connors said. 'If I'm anywhere in this, it's on your side. Understand?'

'*Sì*,' Dante said, nodding along with the three other boys.

'Good,' Connors said, throwing off his pack and wedging it in the back of the Jeep between Dante and Claudio. He tapped the youngest boy on the knee. 'You're going to have to ride on your friend's lap,' he told him. 'We need to make room for the dog. The same goes for the two of you in front.'

Connors waited for the boys to shift seats and then snapped his fingers and watched as the mastiff hoisted himself into the back.

'What do you call him?' Claudio asked, placing his hand on the top of the mastiff's head.

'I only knew one Italian name before I ran into you guys,' Connors said, shifting into reverse. 'Benito. So that's who he is.'

'You named him after Il Duce?' Gaspare said, his olive eyes flushed wide. 'In Naples that could get you killed.'

'We're not in Naples,' Connors said. 'Yet.'

'You still haven't said what you want us to do,' Pepe said.

'Benito understands you a lot better than he does me,' Connors said. 'Be great if one of you could tell him to stop peeing in the Jeep.'

Santa Lucia Harbour

An orange sun was resting on still water in the distance. A line of boys stood along the stone edges of the shore. In the middle of the bay four wooden boats lurched to starboard, pulled down by the weight of full nets. Around them, boys and girls bobbed like buoys, each holding on to a square of netting or a cord of rope. Vincenzo stood in the centre of the rear boat, staring down at the water and at the fishing nets he had helped pull to the surface, each holding thick piles of rifles and handguns. All around him the boys, on shore and in the water, stared with amazement at their catch of weapons.

'Is this all of it?' Vincenzo asked Maldini.

'It is all you will need,' Maldini said.

'Thank you,' Vincenzo said.

Maldini raised his head and looked over at the boys swimming in the water. 'Look at them,' he said. 'They are so happy. They see the guns and believe that now they can fight the Germans. And most of them will die. You should curse me, not thank me.'

He stared at Vincenzo for several moments, seeing in the boy's brooding eyes the same burden of loss that he himself carried. He turned and looked around him at the joyful faces floating in the water. In time of war, Maldini had learned, life was broken down into a series of moments, each branded into memory. Most of those moments were etched in horror. A few brought a smile and a sense of once again being alive and filled with hope. Maldini knew, as he stared down at the boys and the arsenal of weapons they gleefully embraced, that this was such a moment.

'Death will come when it chooses,' he said to Vincenzo. 'But for today we are alive, and for that we should celebrate.'

Franco looked out at the coastline, at a boat rowing slowly towards them, four small boys struggling with the weight of the oars. 'Fresh fish roasted over an open fire would be a perfect way to start,' he said.

CONNORS EASED THE JEEP to a stop along Via Toledo, gazing through his windscreen at the two boys blocking his path. One of them rested a foot on top of a firm, round ball. They both looked to be about eight years old, wearing threadbare outfits. The smaller of the two smiled at Connors, his bare foot rolling the ball with the edges of his toes. He had golden brown hair and a dark leather tan.

'Move out of the way,' Dante said from his seat in the rear. 'He's an American. Here to help us.'

'Are these two part of your outfit?' Connors asked, keeping his eyes on the smiling boy.

'Yes,' Gaspare said. 'The big one is Roberto. He doesn't trust *anyone*, not even us, and we are his best friends.'

'The other one is Fabrizio,' Dante said. 'He likes everybody. He loves to play football and is very good at it. He may one day have a chance to play for Team Naples.'

Connors jumped from the Jeep and stretched out his arms. 'I didn't even know they played football in Italy,' he said.

'It is *all* we play in Italy,' Pepe said. 'It is the national sport. Every city has a team, and from there the best players are picked to represent Italy against all other countries.'

'You ever played against a team from America?' Connors asked.

'We have never *seen* a team from America,' Gaspare said. 'But if there is one, Italy can beat it. You may be better at winning wars, but you can never beat an Italian in football.'

'And he's the best player in your group?' Connors asked, pointing at Fabrizio as he walked towards him.

'No one is better,' Claudio said. 'He can control the ball and the field. When he runs, he is like a bird—impossible to catch.'

'That sounds to me like one helluva football player,' Connors said, standing across from Fabrizio. 'Are you as good as your friends say?'

Fabrizio nodded, eyes shifting from the American to the mastiff and back. 'Maybe one day we can play a game,' he said.

'That would be fun,' Connors said. 'All we need is a little time and a place to play. And one of you would need to bring a football.'

The boys in the Jeep all laughed, while Fabrizio giggled. 'The sun has played a *trucco* on your eyes, American,' Gaspare said. 'The football is right in front of you. There, under Fabrizio's foot.'

Fabrizio flipped the round white ball from his foot to his knee and then, with his arms spread out, bounced the ball from one leg to the other. Connors took a step back and removed his helmet. 'He's pretty good,' he said to the boys behind him. 'With a *beach* ball.'

'What are you saying, American?' Dante asked. He jumped out of the Jeep, caught the ball and shoved it at Connors. 'This is not a beach ball. It's a football.'

'That's not like any football I've ever seen,' Connors said, shaking his head. 'Maybe what you guys play over here is a whole lot different from what we play back home.'

'What do you like about the football you play, American?' Fabrizio asked, resting the ball against the side of his ankle.

Connors placed a boot on the bumper of the Jeep. 'I like that we play it in the fall. When the weather turns cold and the wind blows down heavy from the hills. I like the smell of the air. I like running on hard ground, the ball held inside my arm, the other fellas rushing in to tackle me and keep me from getting too many yards. In lots of ways, it's not so much the game itself for me. I like baseball a lot more. But I love the time of year football is played.'

Dante said, 'In Italy football is played every day, no matter what month, no matter the weather. But for all the boys here, the best day to play was Sunday. After Mass and before the big family meal.'

'All the squares in the city and all the parks would be filled with people watching their children playing football,' Gaspare said.

'The city was so alive, so happy,' Claudio said. 'I'd look away from the game and find my mother and father in the crowd, always with smiles on their faces. It was everyone's happiest day.'

'Now Sunday is just another day,' Pepe said.

'Have you ever lost anyone, American?' Dante asked Connors. 'Someone close to you?'

'Not the way all of you have,' Connors said, shaking his head. 'The war hasn't cost me family. But you get close to people when you fight a few battles. Then one day a bullet lands or a bomb explodes and those friends are gone. You learn that war isn't the best time to go looking for a new batch of friends.'

Fabrizio stepped up to Connors and tugged at the back of his shirt. 'I will be your friend,' he said. 'And to your dog, too.'

Connors smiled and kneeled down in front of Fabrizio. He picked up the football and held it in his hands. 'He's not my dog,' Connors said. 'We just travel together. But I think having you as a friend is something we both would like.'

'And I will teach you to play football,' Fabrizio said, taking the ball back. 'I will make you the best American player in Naples.'

'Then something good might come out of this war after all,' Connors said, rubbing the top of Fabrizio's head. He glanced over at Roberto. The boy had kept his head down and his eyes to the ground since Connors first pulled up, and had yet to speak a word. 'What about you?' he asked. 'You going to try and make a football player out of me, too?'

'He doesn't speak,' Dante said. 'He listens but never says a word.'

'Why won't he talk?' Connors asked.

'His family was anti-Mussolini,' Pepe said. 'When the Nazis came into Naples, the Fascists pointed them out.'

'The next night the Nazis went to their home,' Dante said. 'Woke them and killed everyone in the family except for Roberto. They left him alone. From that day to this he has not made a sound.'

'We look out for him,' Fabrizio said. 'He is our friend. Just like you.'

Connors put out a hand to touch the boy, thought better of it and then jumped back behind the wheel of the Jeep. 'Pile in, all of you. I think it's time I got a good look at the rest of your squad.'

THE WOOD FIRES SPREAD out across the long stone entrance of the Castel dell'Ovo lit up the cloudless sky. Off in a corner, standing on centuries-old steps, their backs to the sea, three boys sang the words to '*Guarda Un Po*'. Along the far side of the castle walkway, stretched out across the length of the path, handguns and rifles lay in one long row, drying from the heat of the fires and the warm night. Over 100 boys and girls were scattered across the open space, sitting round the four fires, each eating a long meal of fresh fish grilled on wooden sticks and drinking from bottles of wine brought up from the castle basement.

'It's nice to see smiles on their faces again,' Nunzia said. She was sitting opposite the main fire in the centre of the road leading to the castle, a tin cup filled with red wine by her feet. 'At least for one night.'

'A smile goes hand in hand with a stomach full of food,' Franco said. 'It's been a while since many of them have had both.'

'How soon before the guns are ready?' Vincenzo asked. He was resting on the cobblestones, his arms behind his head.

'Maldini said they should be dry by morning,' Franco said. 'Then they'll need to be cleaned. If we could find some oil to coat them, it would be even better.'

Nunzia looked across the square. She saw the Jeep swing its headlights into the piazza and come to a halt in front of a statue. She watched the soldier get out and walk into the centre of the square, a large dog following close behind. He turned to look towards her, their eyes meeting for a brief instant.

'The Americans have finally arrived,' Nunzia said in a calm voice. 'At least one of them.'

Connors and the mastiff slowly weaved their way through the scattered children. As he turned past the edge of a fire, Connors saw an older man walking towards him, a small glass in his hand. 'You in charge here?' Connors asked.

The old man shrugged. 'They don't even trust me to make coffee,' Maldini said.

'Then who?' Connors asked.

Maldini downed the remainder of his drink and turned. 'The boy in the long-sleeved shirt,' he said.

Connors looked past the blaze of flames and down towards the darker end of the waterfront. 'The one next to the girl?' he asked.

'Yes,' Maldini said.

'You're kidding, right?' Connors asked. 'He's only a kid. Where are the others?'

'What others?' Maldini asked, walking with Connors now towards Vincenzo and Nunzia.

'Anyone else,' Connors said. He glanced down at a group of kids drying wet pistols and rifles with rags. 'Resistance fighters. American soldiers. You can't be the only adult here.'

'My daughter would give you an argument about how much of an adult I am. But I'm the only one here old enough to join an army.'

'And what's going on with all this?' Connors said, pointing at the kids with the guns. 'What're all the guns for?'

'They're getting ready,' Maldini said. 'They think the Nazis might be coming back to Naples.'

'They probably are,' Connors said. 'What's it to these kids?'

'They're going to fight them.'

Connors stopped, turned and stared at Maldini. He held the look for several seconds and then said, 'I don't suppose you found a radio while you were digging up rifles. The one I got is pretty banged up.'

'No,' Maldini said, glancing over Connors's shoulder and watching Vincenzo, Franco, Nunzia and Angela come towards them. 'There aren't any radios in Naples.'

'I have to get word to my command,' Connors said. 'See if I can get some trucks sent down here and get these kids out.'

He pulled out a crinkled pack of cigarettes and offered one to Maldini, who shook his head.

'How do you fit into this?' Connors asked. 'Or are you just somebody else that's eager to die?'

'You know me so well, and we only just met,' Maldini said with a chuckle. 'I was drafted, just like you. Except I didn't get a uniform with a fancy patch on the sleeve.'

'You even try to talk them out of it?' Connors asked.

'I no longer try to tell people what to do or what to believe.'

'Our decision was made before you got here,' Vincenzo said, standing behind Connors. 'And it won't change, even after you leave.'

Connors tossed his cigarette into the fire and turned towards the boy. He glanced over at Nunzia and then focused his attention on Vincenzo, who was staring at the Thunderbird patch on his sleeve. 'We need to talk,' Connors said to him. 'Just you and me.'

'We can talk here,' Vincenzo said.

'Yes, we could,' Connors said, 'but we won't.' He grabbed the boy by the arm and led him away from the fire towards the darkness of the silent castle.

THEY WERE in an entrance lit by two hanging torches. Connors was pacing. Vincenzo stood with his back against the cold wall. 'Here's how it's going to work,' Connors said. 'First thing in the morning, you round these kids up and get them to follow me out of the city. If that doesn't happen, then you and me got ourselves a serious problem.'

'What will you do?' Vincenzo asked. 'Shoot me if I don't do as you say?'

'I just might,' Connors said.

'This is our fight,' Vincenzo said. 'Not yours.'

'What makes you so sure there's even going to be a fight?' Connors asked. 'That the Nazis are heading back into the city?'

'Every night their planes dropped leaflets down on us along with the bombs,' Vincenzo said. 'Told us that tanks would be coming in after the air raids ended to destroy what was left of the city.'

'If that's true, then it's all the more reason to get these kids out of here now,' Connors said.

'Everyone we ever trusted has betrayed us,' Vincenzo said. 'Everyone we believed has lied. Your words don't mean anything. You're just another uniform marching through the city.'

'You got a chance to save those kids,' Connors said. 'Instead, you're going to let them stay here and, if the Nazis do show up, watch them die. I can't leave you or these kids here to die. You have to understand that.'

'You have no choice, American,' Vincenzo said. 'And you have to understand that.'

CARLO PETRONI LIT a hand-rolled cigarette and looked around at the barren ornate ballroom of the Villa Pignatelli. The villa was once the site of the finest gardens on the Italian coast. Now the grounds lay scorched by constant aerial attacks. Petroni turned to the curious faces that surrounded him. He was eighteen and a convicted felon, sentenced by an Italian court to two years in the boys' prison at San Enfermo. He was in charge of a small team of thieves who sold their pilfered goods through the black market. Petroni was tall and muscular. He had a small scar below his lower lip. His war had not been against the Nazis or the fascists, but had been fought instead on a daily basis inside the brutal walls of a prison without rules.

When the German evacuation came, the Nazis opened all the prison doors and sent the convicts back to the street. Most of them did as they were told and walked out of Naples. Petroni made sure he and his team of thieves hid and waited. He saw no profit in fleeing. Nor was there any in fighting, as far as he could tell. But Petroni did see a potential opportunity opening up in the next few days. If it evolved as he envisioned, Petroni would end up with the Germans on one side, the Americans on the other and the Italians, as always, stuck in the middle. It was a golden moment to make some money and begin his postwar life with a pocketful of cash. All he needed to do was play one side against the other and stay alive.

'How much longer do we wait?' asked Piero, at thirteen the youngest thief in the group.

'Until we see Nazi uniforms,' Petroni said. 'And then we'll find out if what we heard is true, that some crazy boys are going to try to stop them. If that happens, then we step in.'

Marco, also in the group, asked, 'Step in? What does that mean?'

'It means money in our pockets,' Petroni said. 'We follow all that goes on between the Germans and the boys. We join with both groups and tell each group what they need to hear. Tell the Nazis where the boys are hiding. Tell the boys where the traps are set. Stay back and watch as they all kill each other.'

'I haven't heard anything about money yet,' Piero said.

'The Germans will pay for the information we give,' Petroni said, stomping out the last of his cigarette with the heel of his foot.

'The Germans have money,' Marco said. 'But the boys have nothing to give. So why bother with them?'

'Everyone has something,' Petroni said. 'If these street fighters can't give us money or food, we'll take their weapons.'

'And if we're found out? What if even a few of them suspect us of dealing with the Nazis? What then?'

'If our plans are found out, or even if you *suspect* someone of knowing what we're up to, then that person must die. Whether he is a German soldier or an Italian boy.'

THE 16TH PANZER DIVISION was forty miles outside Naples. Colonel von Klaus stood in the centre of the railway tracks, looking down at the large electrical circuit box by his feet. 'Are these the main power feeds?' he asked.

'Yes, sir,' Kunnalt said. Ernst Kunnalt was tall, with a thick head of red hair buried under his helmet. He relished his role as von Klaus's aide-de-camp. 'These go into all the railway connections. The men discovered another one half a mile further down the road.'

'Destroy them both,' von Klaus said.

'And where would you like the mines placed, sir?' Kunnalt asked. 'We've already buried fifty under the tracks.'

'I want them everywhere you can place them. Side roads, dirt roads, main roads. I want it so no one can follow us into or out of Naples. Once that is completed, we can move into the city.'

'Do you anticipate any resistance?' Kunnalt asked.

'Who is there left to resist?' von Klaus asked. 'The advance scouts reported little movement throughout the city. Children and the elderly mostly. It shouldn't take us more than two, three days on the outside to complete the mission.'

'I've never been sent to destroy a city,' Kunnalt said, gazing up at the bright sky. 'I guess it's not something you think about when you go off to fight a war.'

'Losers destroy,' von Klaus said. 'Winners conquer. To the losers fall the unpleasant chores. Let them have their victory, but let it come at a price. I may be out here on a loser's mission, Kunnalt, but I guarantee you, I'll make it a successful one.'

ANGELA CUT A THIN slab off a week-old hunk of provolone and handed it with the tip of the knife blade to her cousin, Tino. Huddled beside her in the small cemetery, the boy grabbed the cheese with dirty fingers and jammed it into a corner of his mouth.

'Chew slowly,' she warned him. 'This is the last of the food.'

'Are you going to have some?' Tino asked. He was seven, the only relative she had left. He was skinny and had severe asthma. With medicine in short supply Angela felt he was only a frightened breath away from death.

'I had mine for lunch,' she said.

'Thank you for taking me here,' Tino said. 'It's been a while since I got to see them. I was worried the bombs had moved the graves.'

'I told you they wouldn't leave you, didn't I?' Angela said, gazing down at the simply marked graves of Tino's parents, killed during a morning bombing raid.

'Yes, you did,' Tino said.

'I'll leave you alone with them,' Angela said. 'I'll wait for you over by the olive trees.'

Tino nodded. 'I'm going to tell Mama and Papa I caught a fish and that I helped clean it and grill it.'

Angela kissed the top of his head. 'Don't forget to tell them yours was the biggest fish in the net. And you were the youngest one in the boat.'

'I'll also tell them you have been taking good care of me,' he said. 'So they don't worry so much about me.'

ANGELA LEANED against a thin olive tree. She used to love this time of day, cooking smells blending with the odour of wood burning in stone fireplaces, signalling that the afternoon meal was coming to a full boil. Shoeless children crammed the alleys and halls leading into their crowded apartments, the echoes of youthful laughter bouncing off hard walls. Elderly women dressed in widow's black sat on straw chairs, an arm's reach from the kitchen entrance, peeling skin off fresh vegetables.

Angela Rummerta had been born in Forcella and had lived in the tough neighbourhood all her life. She knew full well what the rest of the city thought of the people who prowled its streets. Her people were written off as thieves and ruffians. She was old enough to understand that many of those feelings sprang from truth. She also knew that these five ragged city blocks were the poorest and most neglected in Naples.

But Angela never saw Forcella as a neighbourhood in turmoil. It was her home. Now, standing with her back to a burnt-out olive grove, looking down at a little boy crying over the graves of his parents, she longed for the sights and smells of her old neighbourhood as much as she did for the family she left buried in its ruin.

She took a deep breath, closed her eyes and rested her head against the tree.

She heard the snap of the twig but didn't move. She waited, listening for the next step. She turned her head as soon as she heard a stone roll against the side of a tree, then jumped to her right.

She stood, her arms by her side, her dark shoes firmly planted on brown soil, staring at the thin end of a German soldier's rifle. The soldier was young, tall and gaunt. He motioned with his rifle for her to raise her arms and move back against the tree. Angela moved with careful steps. As the soldier stepped forward, a brown-toothed smile spread across his face. He said something in German, then lowered his rifle and placed it against her dress.

He held the smile as he used the rifle to search her body for weapons, running it slowly around her waist, then down her hips, stopping at her ankles. Angela swallowed hard but held his gaze and didn't flinch when he brought the rifle against her inner thighs and began to move it slowly up. She nodded at the soldier and smiled. The soldier stepped closer, keeping one hand on the rifle, stroking her face with the other. She ran her tongue across her dry lips and rested a hand on top of his. '*Bella*,' the soldier said, using all the Italian he knew, leaning towards Angela's face, his rifle now hanging down against his leg. He brought his mouth down hard against hers, pushing her head against the thin tree. The soldier let the rifle fall to the ground, both his arms now wrapped round his Italian catch.

Angela rested one arm round his shoulders and moved her free hand under the top of her blouse. She gently unsnapped the knife strap she kept round her neck. She brought the knife out of its sheath, still holding the soldier's kiss, feeling him unbutton her blouse. Angela tossed off the soldier's helmet and grabbed the back of his head, pressing her lips tighter against the force of his kiss, and then let the power of the knife take its course.

She plunged the blade deep into his chest, then pulled it out and watched the soldier fall at her feet, face down and dead.

Angela turned her head and saw Tino standing there, staring up at her. The boy walked towards her with outstretched arms, then embraced her, holding her tight round the waist. Angela hugged him back, tears quietly streaming down the sides of her unlined face.

'We should leave,' Angela said.

Tino nodded and began to walk with her, one arm still round Angela, his fingers held against the side of her blood-soaked blouse. They moved down the hill and away from the scorched olive grove.

FIFTEEN MILES OUTSIDE Naples, Colonel von Klaus sat on a folding chair, eyes closed, legs stretched out, the heels of his boots resting on top of an empty crate. He opened his eyes when he heard footsteps.

He stared at the dishevelled boy standing in front of him, Kunnalt by his side. 'Who is your new friend?' he asked.

'A former prisoner of the juvenile jail in Naples,' Kunnalt said. 'He was freed during the evacuation. He walked into camp a short while ago, said he had information we could use before we move our tanks into Naples.'

Von Klaus looked across at the boy. 'Why would you want to help us?'

'I want the war to end,' the boy answered. 'Helping you will make that happen faster.'

'What's your name?' von Klaus asked, lowering his feet and sitting up in the chair.

'Carlo Petroni,' the boy said. 'I lived in Piazza Mercato with my family before the war.'

'Why were you sent to prison?' von Klaus asked.

'I was guilty of the crime of hunger,' Carlo said with a shrug. 'I had no money, so I took what I needed from those who had it.'

'I don't like thieves,' von Klaus said. 'They not only steal, they lie. Which will put into doubt anything you tell me.'

'You'll kill me if I lie,' Carlo said. 'And being found dead is not part of my plan. I wasn't dragged here. I chose to tell *you* what I know, not the Americans and not the resistance fighters.'

'And why are we your chosen ones?' von Klaus asked.

'I stand a better chance to make a profit working with you.'

'And what makes you think I'll be so free with my money?'

'What I have to say is worth more to you than to the others,' Carlo said. 'You and your men are the ones in danger, and if you care about them, you'll pay to save their lives.'

Von Klaus nodded. 'I'll pay for your information,' he said. 'And you'll pay if it turns out to be wrong. And the price I extract will be much higher. Are we clear?'

'Only a fool would refuse such an offer,' Carlo said.

'Tell me what you think is so vital for me to know.'

'The streets of Naples are not as empty as you think,' Carlo said. 'You could be taking your tanks into trouble.'

'Who is there to cause us any trouble?' von Klaus asked. 'Our advance teams speak of nothing other than elderly and children.'

'Some of those boys are staying behind to fight,' Carlo said. 'They may be armed. They'll be fighting you on streets they know well, and they can find places to hide where even your best men will get lost searching them out.'

'How many boys and how heavily armed?' von Klaus asked.

'Last I heard, there were about two hundred,' Carlo said. 'By the time your tanks come into Naples, that number could go up.'

'And their weapons?'

'Hunting rifles, mostly,' Carlo said, sensing the colonel's interest. 'Enough bullets for a few days.'

'Why aren't you with them, getting ready to fight me?'

'I've never been with them,' Carlo said with icy detachment. 'I fight for myself, and only if the price is right.'

'And what price have you placed on your betrayal?'

'Five thousand lire,' Carlo said. 'That will be enough to help me and my friends buy our way out of Naples. And for three rifles and three ammo belts, protection against anyone who tries to stop us.'

'What if the ones trying to stop you are wearing German uniforms?' von Klaus asked. 'Will you kill them, too?'

Carlo smiled and shook his head. 'There would be no need to kill them,' he said. 'Not after I told them that we were friends.'

'It would be a lie,' von Klaus said.

'But one that would help keep me alive.'

'Perhaps. That's all that matters to people like you in time of war, isn't it? Staying alive.'

'It's all that matters at any time,' Carlo said. 'In battle or out. Staying alive is always the final goal.'

'Then you have achieved your goal,' von Klaus told him. 'At least for today. My aide will pay you your money. It's a large sum, enough for you to buy your rifles and ammo from someone other than me. You'll take the same path out of my camp you took in, and there'll be no need for any further contact.'

STEVE CONNORS walked quietly inside the centuries-old catacombs of San Gennaro, the patron saint of Naples, marvelling at the large two-storey web of galleries, which also housed the remains of countless bishops. He stared up at the mosaics and frescoes, impressed with their beauty and intricate design. He rested his pack and rifle against a corner wall and ran a hand against the cold stone. He then settled on a corner step, his back against the smooth, chill carvings of angels and saints.

He had wandered in, looking for a place to clear his head and plan his moves. He was now in the middle of a different mission from the one Captain Anders had sent him on, and he needed time alone. The search mission would turn up empty—that he knew. Any Americans operating in Naples were now either dead or heading towards the safety net of Allied lines.

But now he was stuck with an even bigger issue. What they wanted to do went beyond logic. Those boys wanted to fight. But Connors knew that no matter how valiant the cause, theirs was a hopeless dream whose reality would end with bodies rotting on empty streets.

Connors had no proof the Nazis were coming back to Naples. The leaflets that had been dropped could easily have been a ruse to frighten any strays out of the city. There was simply no reason for them to return.

His initial instinct had been to motor back to Salerno, get a couple of trucks, come back and round up the children. But he could face a delay at headquarters, or even worse, not be given authority to rescue the street kids. He looked around at the dark figures staring down at him and knew he was on a fool's mission.

'Most of what's written on the plaques is not true.'

It was the voice of the young woman he had met by the waterfront. She was standing off to his left, half hidden by the shadows.

'Such as?' Connors asked, standing up from the cool step.

'The body of San Gennaro is not buried here, like the signs say.' Her English was choppy but easy to understand. 'Only his head. It's upstairs, in the rear chapel, up against a back wall.'

'What about this business of the flowing blood?' Connors asked. 'That's not on the level either?'

'Depends on who you ask,' the woman said. 'My grandmother swore on it to the very day she died. My father scoffs and says it is nothing more than the rantings of a silly religion.'

'Which side do you fall on?' Connors asked.

'When I was little, I'd go with my grandmother to church on the three days of the year when San Gennaro's blood would flow,' she said. 'I never saw anything, but the old people acted as if they did. It made them happy. I guess that's all that really matters.'

'It says on one of these that he's the protector of your city,' Connors said. 'Even I know that's a lie.'

'He's a saint,' the woman said. 'Not a saviour.'

'And what about you?' Connors asked. 'What do you do when you're not giving out history lessons?'

The girl stepped out of the shadows and walked closer to Connors. She was tall and thin and as beautiful as any woman he had ever seen. She wore a pale blue dress, and her hair hung thick and loose, resting easily on top of her shoulders. Her lips were full and rich. But it was her eyes that locked Connors in. They were shining, like candles in a darkened harbour. 'I can help you,' she said.

'What's your name?'

'Nunzia.' She smiled and offered him a hand to shake.

Connors reached out and held her hand until Nunzia slowly pulled it free. 'I was named after my father's mother,' she said. 'She was one of the first women in Naples to run her own business. It was a large bakery just outside the city limits. She took it over after my grandfather died and kept it going until the war started.'

'My grandmother had her own business, too, back home,' Connors said. 'My family never liked to talk about it all that much.'

'What kind of business was it?'

'My grandma Helen was a bootlegger. She made illegal whiskey up in the Kentucky hills, sold it to the farm hands and factory workers in the area. Made a lot of money in her time. Most of which she used to put her boys, my father one of them, through school.'

'Your grandma would have done well in Naples,' Nunzia said. 'Here the men give out the commands, but it is the women who enforce the rules.'

'Where does that leave those kids?'

'What do you expect them to do?' Nunzia asked. 'Some will flee and hide. Most will stay and fight if there is someone to fight.'

'I can't let that happen,' Connors said in a firm voice.

'I don't know your name,' she said, her voice soothing and warm in the stillness of the dark room.

'Connors,' he said. 'Steve Connors.'

'And why do you care so much, Steve Connors? We mean nothing to you. We're just another city in another country for you to march through with your tanks and your flag.'

'They're just kids,' Connors said. 'They're not soldiers. And if the Nazis come, they will die.'

'They are close to dead already,' Nunzia said. 'You look into their eyes and you can see it. If there is a battle, it will be more than a chance for them to die. It will be a chance for them to live.'

Connors stared at Nunzia and shook his head, running his hand across the back of his neck. 'How would your patron saint feel about all of this?' he asked.

'If you believe in San Gennaro, then you believe in miracles,' Nunzia said.

THE ZOO AND THE AQUARIUM, once considered the most beautiful and prestigious in all Europe, stood in near ruin, their frescoes and underwater world blasted into mounds of cracked cement and dust piles by the bombing raids. Rivers of dirty water from a burst sewer pipe flowed down the sides of the walls and flooded into the main hall of the aquarium. Prior to the war it had been a favourite visiting place for schoolchildren.

Four Nazi soldiers were sitting on the cold bare cement of a darkened stairwell. They had moved into the city earlier that day, one of the heavily armed advance teams sent in by Colonel von Klaus to assess any trouble brewing on the streets of Naples. The units were to set themselves up in choice locations that would allow them to inflict the most damage in the least time. They were each equipped with three cases of dynamite, six dozen high-impact grenades, scope rifles and two flamethrowers.

'We could look for a drier place to hide,' one of the soldiers, Hans Zimmler, said. He glanced behind him at the water and the large rats swimming in debris. Zimmler, like many of the soldiers under von Klaus, was a young but experienced fighter. 'That water level keeps rising, it could pose a problem for us.'

'That's why no one will look for us here,' a second soldier, Eric Tippler, said. Tippler was in his mid-twenties. 'From this stairwell alone we can cover both the entrance and the exit. Plus we have a clear view of the streets below. We can target anyone in our sights up to three hundred yards.'

The other two soldiers, equally young, experienced and deadly with a weapon, remained silent, their backs against a stone wall, helmets tilted over their eyes.

Zimmler thought for a few moments, then nodded.

Tippler patted Zimmler on the shoulder and smiled as he saw that the other two soldiers were now sound asleep. 'You and I go to the roof,' he said. 'We leave our two lazy friends down here to catch up on their sleep and keep the rats company. We'll set up our target scopes and find the best places to rest our rifles.'

THE TWO BOYS stood in the darkness and watched the soldiers walk past. They slipped out of the emptiness of the large tank, once a watery home to rare species of fish. The two had been living in the barren aquarium for three weeks, finding it a safe refuge from the nightly bombing assaults. Giovanni Malatesta, fifteen, and Frederico Lo Manto, fourteen, had been living on the Naples streets since the early spring.

Giovanni could see the stretched-out legs of the two sleeping soldiers, an open crate of grenades by their feet. The main floor of the aquarium was steeped in shadows. The voices of the other two soldiers echoed down from the upper floors. 'They sleep like the dead,' he whispered to Frederico. 'We can take some of their grenades. They won't even know we were here.'

'We need food,' Frederico said. 'Not grenades.'

Giovanni put a hand on Frederico's thin shoulder. 'Those are worth more than food,' he said. 'Now stay quiet, grab as many as you can hold and then come back to the fish tank.'

'Should we try to grab their rifles, too?' Frederico asked.

'Just the grenades. Only take what they won't miss.'

September 27

As Naples woke to a new day, the glare of the bright orange sun mixed with thick plumes of white smoke, leftover evidence of the predawn bombing raid. The squinting eyes of the city's survivors began to emerge from the cavernous tunnels of the Stazione Centrale that led into and out of the city. The youngest of the children took the lead, running across empty tracks, kicking a soccer ball back and forth, heading towards the main terminals. Soap and clean water were at a premium, making the trickling fountains of the central station a prime gathering place for the tunnel dwellers. Breakfast had long ago become a forgotten meal; the best that could be expected was a small tin of weak coffee and a hard chunk of stale bread. Hunger was now an accepted part of their daily life.

Connors had parked his Jeep a short distance from the tunnels. He slept curled in the back seat, his helmet flat over his face, his rifle within easy reach. The mastiff was stretched out on the ground next to the Jeep, one large paw covering his brow. The sound of thin soles running over hard ground caused them both to stir awake. Connors lifted his helmet and stared up at Maldini.

'What is it?' Connors said, sitting up.

'There's a ship,' the older man said. 'You can see it from the port or from the top of the tunnels. It's heading towards the piers.'

'Ours or theirs?' Connors jumped from the Jeep, reached for his binoculars and followed Maldini up the side of a hill.

'It was too far out for me to see which flag it flew,' Maldini said.

Connors reached the top of the hill and perched himself over the side of a damaged stone wall, lying on his chest, elbows digging into dark earth, staring through the binoculars out towards the horizon. 'It's a Nazi tanker,' Connors said. 'She's running pretty slow, which means she's loaded. I figure she's about a day out of port, maybe a little longer.'

'Loaded with what?'

'Tank fuel, most likely. Those leaflets the kids got were right. The Nazis are coming back. They're coming back for the fuel.'

'How can you be sure?' Maldini asked.

'Tanks are not wind-up toys,' Connors said, getting to his feet. 'Between my guys and the Brits, we got the panzers spread out pretty thin. They're gonna need all that the tankers can hold to get them back up north to Rome.'

'The leaflets also said they would destroy what's left of the city. Will that happen, too?'

Connors didn't answer. He rose and slowly brushed past Maldini and headed back down the hill towards his Jeep.

VINCENZO, FRANCO, FABRIZIO and Gaspare made up one team. Pepe, Dante, Claudio and Angela made up the other. They were playing in Piazza Garibaldi, the large cobblestone square just across from the main railway terminal, morning sun at their backs, relishing the joys of their national game.

Connors pulled the Jeep into the square and inched up slowly to where the kids were playing soccer. 'Look how simple the world would be if left to children,' Maldini said. 'A ball, some boys and a sunny day. Nothing more is needed.'

Connors sat in the Jeep and followed the action for several minutes. His mind was on the tanker. If it was close, so were the Nazi tanks, which meant the roads out of Naples would be a danger to travel. The safer move now might be to keep the boys in the city and hidden, rather than out and running as a group. But that, too, came packed with risks, the least of which was the near-impossible task of keeping 200 children clear of Nazi eyes. Connors looked away from the game and watched as Nunzia walked towards the Jeep, two cups in her hands. 'I thought you both could use some morning coffee,' she said. 'I hope you like it without sugar, Connors. Since we don't have any.'

'This is fine, thanks,' Connors said, taking one cup and passing the other to Maldini.

The older man smiled. 'I see you've met my daughter,' he said.

Connors sipped his coffee and nodded. 'We talked about religion,' he said.

Connors stepped out of the Jeep and walked towards the game. Nunzia and Maldini followed behind. Connors stopped short and followed the ball bouncing along the cobblestones. He stared at the chipped stones, the feet of the children running hard across the damaged surface. Connors tossed his cup to the ground and ran towards the kids. 'Stop moving!' he shouted. 'All of you, stop! Stay still!'

Vincenzo kicked the ball to Franco and turned to look at Connors. 'Keep playing,' he told the others. 'Just ignore what he says.'

Connors ran closer to the group, reaching for the pistol clipped in his holster. 'I said stay still, dammit!' he screamed.

'What we do and what we don't do are none of your business, American,' Vincenzo said, running down the centre of the piazza, angling for Fabrizio's return pass. 'Let us just play our game.'

Connors pulled his gun from the holster, aimed it towards the sky and fired off two rounds. The shots brought all action to a halt. Angela and the boys turned and stared at him. Fabrizio held the ball with his foot, frozen in place.

'You're playing it on a minefield,' Connors said.

Connors got to his knees and filled his hands with a small mound of pebbles. He threw one pebble at a time against the cobblestones, watching intently as they landed.

'What are you doing?' Vincenzo asked.

Connors spoke in a calm voice, eyes focused on the cobblestones. 'Mines are laid down in patterns,' he said. 'Circular or up and down. Once you figure out the pattern, you at least can tell where they are. That's the easy part.'

Connors tossed four more pebbles onto the piazza ground before he heard the clanging sound he needed. The noise came just to the left of Dante's foot. 'There's one,' Connors said.

He crouched down and tossed out a half dozen more pebbles. Connors stood up as soon as a pebble had found its second target, this time close to Angela. 'I'll dig that one out,' he told the group as he stepped gingerly round them. 'Then work my way across until I can dig up enough of them to get you out.'

A large number of boys had gathered in the piazza. 'Keep everyone as far back as you can,' Connors said to Nunzia, catching her eye for a brief second. 'Just in case.'

Connors leaned down on the cobblestones, his face inches from the partially buried mine. Vincenzo crawled up alongside him, a small knife in his hand. 'I'm starting to think that none of you really does understand English,' Connors said.

'You're going to need help,' Vincenzo said.

Connors glared at the boy and then looked down at the knife in his hand. 'I'll lift off the cobblestones,' he said. 'You scrape the dirt away from the edges. But stay away from the top or bottom of the mine. And be gentle. It doesn't take much to set them off.'

Vincenzo inched closer and began to clear away the dirt around the mine, watching as the soldier rested the broken cobblestones off to the side. 'We'll need a place to keep these mines,' Connors said. 'Away from the Germans and away from the kids.'

'I know a place,' Maldini said, standing over Connors and Vincenzo.

'Where?' Vincenzo asked.

'In Parco Virgiliano,' Maldini said. 'There are hundreds of pine trees. It would be easy to keep the mines out of sight.'

'Have you or any of your friends ever transported a mine?' Connors asked, raising his voice.

'We never had to before,' Vincenzo said. 'Now we do.'

'How?' Maldini asked.

'By cart,' Vincenzo said.

Vincenzo looked down at Connors's right hand, the one that was now reaching for the base of the mine, and saw the tremble, the twitching up to his wrist. 'Is it nerves that makes that happen?'

'No,' Connors said with a wry smile. 'And it's not coffee either. It's fear. If I make a mistake, we'll all die.'

Vincenzo took a deep breath and made the sign of the cross. He watched Connors place both his hands under the base, his fingers searching with great care for any trip wire or mechanism. 'It feels clean,' he said. 'The wire's buried right under the lid.'

'What else is left to do?' Vincenzo asked.

'Nothing,' Connors said, 'except lift it out.' He gripped the base of the mine, shut his eyes and gave the mine a tug, lifting it out of the ground. He heard nothing but silence. He rested his head on the ground and took a deep breath. '*Grazia a Dio*,' he heard Vincenzo whisper.

Vincenzo and Maldini helped Connors to his feet, the mine clutched against the soldier's chest. 'How many of these you think are planted?' Connors asked them.

'They put them everywhere they could think of,' Vincenzo said.

'So can we,' Connors said.

'Dig them up and use them against the Nazis?' Vincenzo asked.

'If you really want a shot at them,' Connors said. 'You take everything they gave you and use it against them.'

CONNORS DROVE THE JEEP past Via dei Mille, heading for the high end of the city, hoping to get a gauge on how far away the Nazi tanks were. He stopped in front of the Monument to the Martyrs, its base taken up by the hulking stone statues of four large lions, each blanketed by the warm rays of a late morning sun. He glanced over at Nunzia, sitting casually in the front seat. 'I've never seen a city like this before,' he said. 'Even with all the buildings destroyed, it's still the most beautiful place I'll ever see.'

'It's a stubborn city,' Nunzia said, shielding her eyes and glancing over at him. 'Like its people.'

'You think you'll stay here after the war?' Connors asked.

'I'll go wherever my papa goes,' Nunzia said, shaking her head slowly. 'It's difficult to plan past the next few hours.'

'What do you want to do?' he asked. 'If you could pick something to work at, what would it be?'

She shrugged her thin shoulders. 'I love children,' she said. 'I love to be around them, hear them laugh, argue, shed tears when they can't get their way. It would be nice to spend my days listening to those sounds. It might help take the place of all the other sounds I've had to hear these past few years.'

'You'd be good at that,' Connors told her, a warm smile on his face. 'I'd let you work with my kids any day of the week.'

'You have children?' she asked, a surprised tone to her voice.

'I should have said, if and when I have them,' Connors said with a quick shake of his head. 'No, I don't have any kids or a wife or, for that matter, anyone close to one.'

'What will you do?' she asked. 'When you get back to your home?'

'I was going to be a lawyer before this started,' he said. 'Now I don't really know.'

'You don't look much like a lawyer,' she said, shaking her head in a teasing way. 'Not the kind I've seen, anyway.'

'What kind is that?'

'You have an honest face,' Nunzia said, looking at Connors with eyes that caused him to blush. 'Most of the lawyers that prowled around Naples while Mussolini was in power did not.'

COLONEL VON KLAUS walked alone, head down, shoulders sagging, along an empty stretch of burnt grass fifteen miles north of Naples. He felt a slight twinge of unease over the Naples mission.

His short meeting with young Carlo Petroni had done nothing but amplify his concerns. He had sent word of the meeting back to high command, alerting them to the possibility of a minor counterattack taking shape. Von Klaus never doubted his victory. He only fretted over the manner in which he should battle a force that would clearly be small, poorly armed and hidden.

'A telegram for you, sir.' Kunnalt's voice boomed out from behind him. 'From command headquarters.'

'Read it to me. Let me hear what great wisdom they have to share.' Von Klaus lit a cigarette as Kunnalt rustled open the message. 'Well?' he asked a moment later, turning to face Kunnalt, catching the loss of colour from his face.

'It's their response to our notification of a potential conflict in Naples from children who remained behind. They have scrapped plans for one more night of heavy bombing prior to our arrival tomorrow. But they will send one plane over the city.'

'For what purpose?'

'They will be dropping one hundred thousand pieces of candy onto the city streets, sir. Each one wrapped and laced with poison.'

Von Klaus lowered his eyes to the ground and took the sheet of paper from Kunnalt's trembling fingers. 'Don't speak of this to any of the men,' he told him in hushed tones. 'I don't want my soldiers to feel shame while they fight for their country.'

Von Klaus rested the lit end of his cigarette against the thin sheet of paper and watched it catch fire and burn into black crisps, floating gently upwards into the air.

'What time do you wish us to break camp, sir?' Kunnalt asked, visibly shaken.

'An hour before dawn,' von Klaus said.

'Is there any message you would like me to relay to the men?'

Von Klaus turned and gave a sad smile. 'Yes,' he said. 'Tell them not to accept any candy from strangers.'

VINCENZO ESCORTED the wooden cart through the wrought-iron gates of Parco Virgiliano, his hold on the mule's rein firm but gentle. Franco sat on the mule's back, the rear of the wagon filled with unearthed mines wrapped in children's clothing. The sides of the wagon were weighted down with heavy rocks, helping to give it a smoother ride.

'Is this the last of it?' Vincenzo asked, gazing up at Franco.

Franco jumped to the ground, landing in front of Vincenzo. 'I counted about thirty in all,' he said. 'But there must be several hundred more scattered throughout the main streets.'

'We've been lucky so far, but there's no reason to push it,' Vincenzo said. 'What we have now will have to be enough.'

CONNORS AND NUNZIA stood on the edge of a hill and looked down at the main road leading into Naples. There, spread out before them across a two-mile span, was the full force of the German 16th Panzer Division. Eighty Mark IV tanks paved the way for more than 500 well-armed and well-trained soldiers. Behind them Jeeps pulled anti-aircraft artillery, and two dozen mules ambled along, packed down with bombs and flamethrowers. Connors turned away from the convoy and looked at Nunzia. 'They're heading towards the main road which will lead them to the piers.'

'Will they ever just leave us alone?' she said in a low voice. 'They've taken everything and still aren't satisfied. I don't think they'll be satisfied until we're all dead.'

'We should get back,' Connors said, his eyes still on her. 'Help get those boys ready for a fight.'

'Do you hate them?' she asked, staring down at the convoy.

'Who?'

'The Nazis,' Nunzia said.

'Most of the time,' Connors said. 'A lot of those soldiers are no different from me or the guys in my unit. Same age, pretty much. Same background. Drafted into the army, taken to some country and told to fight. At least you start out thinking that way. Then one night you're sitting in camp, having coffee with some GI from the same part of the country as you, sharing a laugh, and a bullet goes in his head, and he ends up flat on the ground right in front of you. See that happen often enough, you don't think the guy on the other side is like you at all. And all you want to do is kill him.'

'Have you killed many?' she asked.

'Yes,' Connors said. 'But no matter how many you kill, it doesn't erase the image of a guy in the same uniform as you, bleeding in your arms, just waiting to die. It turns you into another kind of person. Or maybe just the kind of person you were all along.'

'You're a good man, Connors,' Nunzia said, 'put in the middle of a horrible war.'

'I'm a good soldier,' Connors said. 'That's different from being a good man.'

LATER THAT DAY Connors stood in the centre of a room at the Castel dell'Ovo and stared down at a crudely drawn map of Naples. 'You guys run out of crayons when you drew this up?' he asked.

'It has everything we need,' Vincenzo said.

'And I need to see and hear everything you know,' Connors said, looking up. 'The sooner the better. We don't have much time.'

'The Nazis know our streets,' Maldini said. 'They've spent enough time here.'

'But they don't know how many of us are here,' Connors said. 'We need to make that work in our favour. And we need to do something else.'

'What?' Vincenzo asked.

'We strip those tanks of fuel,' Connors said, his eyes on everyone in the crowded room. 'We have to blow up that tanker.'

'How many explosives will that take?' Franco asked.

'It's not a question of how many,' Connors said. 'It's how close we can get the explosion to the tanker. The gas will take care of the rest.'

'When?' Vincenzo asked.

'Tomorrow night,' Connors said. 'It has to be hit before the tanks can get to it.'

'And what do we do until the tanker arrives?' Angela asked.

'Get ready for war,' Connors said.

THEY WORKED INTO THE NIGHT.

On the side streets that led into the main piazzas in the centre of the city, a small squadron of boys raised barricades and rested empty rifles on top of them. Maldini led the youngest of the boys through the sewers of Naples, giving each a marked post in the underground passage from which they could view the street above so that they would be able to place objects under the wheels of passing tanks without fear of detection. Several dozen boys were placed on various rooftops and in church steeples, given the best rifles and the most ammunition, free to take aim at the German soldiers who would eventually pass below. Angela and little Tino found kerosene and poured the liquid into empty wine bottles, corking them with shreds of clothing. They left the bottles in church and building entryways, large lit votive candles beside them.

The strongest of the boys were sent out to lug large pots filled with sea water up to the roofs of the highest buildings and rest them on top of thick piles of old wood. When the Germans arrived, wood fires would bring the water to a boil, and the water would be tossed down on the passing soldiers.

'How'd you come up with that idea?' Connors asked Vincenzo as they walked together along the darkened city streets, their eyes on all the activity around them.

'*The Hunchback of Notre-Dame*,' Vincenzo said. 'Only he had oil and much bigger pots.'

In Salerno, Captain Anders sucked on a hard cherry candy as he studied the map on the wooden table before him. He looked across the table at a young officer standing on the other side and nodded. 'The Germans are here,' he said, jabbing a finger at the outskirts of Naples. 'Should be in the city no later than sunup.' He moved his finger to the side. 'Two of my boys were found dead right about here,' he said, 'along with a couple of German soldiers. No Jeep and no equipment left behind. So what's missing from my little puzzle?'

'Corporal Connors,' the officer said. 'We haven't heard one word from him since he left on his mission.'

'That's right, Carlson,' Anders said. 'We haven't heard a damn thing. And how do you read all of that?'

'My hunch is he's either dead or captured, sir,' Carlson said with some assurance. 'If not, we would have heard otherwise by now.'

Anders shifted away from the map and looked up at Carlson. He was newly assigned to Anders's division, transferred over to the Thunderbirds to help the unit cope with the massive losses sustained in the beach landing. 'If we were talking about most soldiers, I would agree with you. But not Connors. I've seen him in action. He's not one to let himself be captured, and he sure as hell acts like he's tough to kill. So I'm betting you're wrong.'

'Then where is he, sir?' Carlson asked.

'He's in that city. And if something's going on there, I'm betting he's right in the middle of it.'

'Then whoever he's with should have access to a radio. Why wouldn't he have made contact?'

'Anything he'd send would be picked up by the Germans.'

'If he's really still alive, we could try and send another team to get him out,' Carlson said.

'Not just yet.' Anders stepped away from the map and folded his arms across his chest. 'Let's give him a little time. Give him a chance to do some damage and get out on his own.'

CONNORS STOOD on a rampart of Castel Sant'Elmo facing the sea, the silent peaks of Mount Vesuvius in the distance. The castle had been built in 1329, its large enclosed walls designed to ward off any attack on the city. Connors thought it a good place to station a few boys so they could follow the tank movements. The entire city was spread out below him, and from such a vantage point nothing could move undetected. He heard Vincenzo step up beside him. 'When the sun is up and the skies are clear,' he told Connors, 'it's easy to see all the islands that surround Naples. But now, with all the smoke and fire, you're lucky if you can see the city.'

'Seeing it is the easy part,' Connors said. 'But how do we get the boys up here to tell us what they see down there? They can't scream it out, and we don't have any signal system set up.'

'I know a way.' Vincenzo glanced at the Thunderbird patch on Connors's sleeve. 'I just don't know how well it will work.'

'I think now would be a real good time to tell me,' Connors said.

'We can use *picciones*. How do you say it in English? They are birds that fly from one place to another and bring you messages.'

'Pigeons,' Connors said. 'You have carrier pigeons?'

'Franco does. He used to race them. Once or twice he sent a bird out with a note from his mamma to a sick old aunt who lived on the other side of the city. She always got the message.'

'We put four boys up here, keep them low and in each corner,' Connors said, walking towards the centre of the castle roof. 'They'll see the tanks before we do.'

'I'll pick the boys. Franco will know if any in our group have handled pigeons before. I'll make sure they're up here.'

'You still want to go ahead with all this?' Connors asked. 'There's still time to get everybody out.'

'We are where we belong,' Vincenzo said. 'All of us. This is a time for Italians to fight.'

Connors stepped closer to Vincenzo and stared down at the boy. 'It's *everybody's* fight,' Connors said. 'I left behind too many dead Americans on your beaches to think of it in any other way.'

'Is that how you got that patch? Fighting here in Italy?'

Connors ran his fingers across the points of the Thunderbird patch. 'This is the symbol of my division,' he said. 'It's a magic bird that American Indians believe brings rain, thunder and lightning down on any enemy.'

'Do you believe that, too?'

'Only when I have a division behind me,' Connors said.

In the distance the low moaning roar of a plane engine could be heard. Connors looked up but could see nothing beyond a cluster of evening clouds. 'That's not a sound you ever get used to hearing,' he said. 'I guess we should head for the tunnels.' He shoved his helmet on his head. 'Make sure everybody else gets there, too.'

Vincenzo walked over to a parapet and pointed down towards the streets at a small huddle of boys scrambling for cover. 'We've done this for a long time,' he said. 'Everyone has their special place to spend the night.'

'Where's yours?'

'Most nights the tunnels of the railway station,' Vincenzo said.

'What about tonight?' Connors asked.

'I think I'll stay here. It's the last night. I won't have the chance again. I want to see with my own eyes what they do to my city.'

'You want to do it alone?' Connors asked. 'Or would you mind some company?'

Vincenzo looked at Connors and smiled. 'It's a big castle,' he said. 'There's enough room for two.'

The two of them sat down, shielded by the castle's thick stone walls, and waited for the nightly destruction to begin.

A NAZI PLANE FLEW low over the city, opened its bomb slots and scattered thousands of chocolate caramels on the abandoned streets below. Vincenzo stared up at the moonlit sky, candy falling around him like snow in a winter storm, his arms spread out, speechless at the eerie sight. Connors didn't move, his eyes frozen on the pieces resting by his boots, his mind awake to a horror he was too frightened to imagine. 'How soon can you get word out to the streets?' he asked Vincenzo.

'They don't need to hear it from me, American,' Vincenzo said, turning to look at Connors. 'They can see for themselves.'

'They can see the candy. But they won't know not to eat it.'

'You think they would poison it?'

'You know them better than I do,' Connors said.

Vincenzo looked down at the candy spread around his feet on the castle roof. 'Are you sure about this?' he asked.

Connors picked up a caramel. 'You want to prove me wrong?'

Vincenzo ran for the door that led down the stairs and out of the castle. 'I'll need help,' he yelled over his shoulder. 'We'll warn the ones hiding in the tunnels first.'

'I'll drive,' Connors said, running past Vincenzo and down a narrow flight of steps. 'You just say where.'

'It should take half an hour to spread the word,' Vincenzo said. 'Maybe less since they're not dropping any bombs.'

'What they're dropping is a lot worse than any bomb,' Connors said, taking the steps two at a clip. 'Remember that now and remember it tomorrow when it really starts to get hot.' He stopped as they entered the large ornate castle hall and grabbed Vincenzo by the shirt. 'In fact, if you're half as smart as you act, you'll never forget what you saw tonight. It might help keep you alive.'

Vincenzo slowly nodded his head, lines of sweat running down his forehead, his upper body shivering, leg muscles tight and weak. He stood in place, watching as Connors ran past him, heading for the Jeep he had left parked in an alley alongside the castle. For the first time in his life, Vincenzo Scolardi had glimpsed the true face of his enemy and was left with a taste of his own fear.

CONNORS AND VINCENZO stood in the centre of the Piazza Bovio, their backs to the dry Fontana del Nettuno, looking at the small army of children, their hands crammed with the candy that had fallen, as if by magic, from the night sky. Connors and Vincenzo had raced through the empty city streets, warning all those in hiding not to eat the candy. Instead, the children were asked to grab all they could and bring it to the Piazza Bovio, where the pile was now high enough to fill Neptune's empty basin. Many of the children pleaded for just one piece, their empty stomachs immune to the harsh warnings. 'How do you know for sure?' one innocent voice pleaded. 'You only think they're poison. You don't really know.'

'They want it to look like kindness,' Vincenzo explained, still shaken by the night's events. 'They know we're hungry and scared.

They want us to think they're our friends. But look around. Look at what's happened to our lives, our homes and our families. Those are not the acts of a friend. Only an enemy would do such things.'

A tall, lean boy in an ill-fitting cotton shirt stepped forward, his hands in his pockets. 'You're wrong,' he said in a loud voice that carried through the huge square. 'You and the American are afraid of the Nazis. I say the candy is safe to eat.'

The boy moved towards the mound of candy lying inside the dry fountain dedicated to the glory of Neptune. Connors brought his rifle up and pointed it at the boy. 'What will you do, American?' the boy asked. 'Shoot me? For wanting some candy? If you do that, then you have to wonder who is the real enemy.'

'This is not a good time to turn stupid,' Connors said. 'Think it through. If you do that and come away still able to tell yourself candy is worth dying for, then don't look for me to stop you.'

Connors lowered his rifle. The boy stepped forward and went past Connors, his eyes fixed only on the sweets. He reached into the fountain and picked up a thick piece of caramel. He smiled and began to peel off the thin wrapping.

'Don't eat that one!'

Connors and Vincenzo looked towards the crowd when they heard Maldini's voice.

'Have what's left of Roberto's candy,' Maldini said. 'He can't finish what he took.'

The boy dropped his caramel and turned to watch the crowd part as Maldini approached the fountain. He was carrying the body of a dark-haired, shirtless boy. The boy's head rested against the older man's chest, his hand still gripping a candy wrapper. Maldini's face was red with anger. He stopped in front of the tall boy and stared deep into his eyes. 'Forget the candy,' he said in a softer voice. 'Come and help me bury our friend.'

San Domenico Maggiore was the church where St Thomas Aquinas once sat and prayed. On its walls, spread through five ornate chapels, hung some of the richest and most beloved artwork in all of Italy. But on this night it was a church filled with boys, their heads bowed in prayer.

Maldini knelt in the front row, the body of the dead boy at rest on the top step of the main altar. Nunzia was next to Maldini. Next to the body a thin boy with an oval face sang the words to the '*Ave Maria*'. Connors and Vincenzo knelt close by, with little Fabrizio gripping the soldier's arm, his eyes frozen on the body of a boy his own age. Next to him the bull mastiff spread out, his massive girth squeezing them all into a tight row.

They stayed there as long as they could. They knelt, prayed and sang until the sun rose and brought a fresh day to a battle-weary city.

The First Day: September 28

The first blast from the tank shattered the weathered walls of a building that had stood on Via Toledo since the sixteenth century. The second sent shards of brick, glass and mortar spilling into the clear morning air. Two German soldiers tossed grenades through the cracked windows of an empty storefront. A young lanky junior officer lifted the lid of his tank, gave a furtive glance down the empty street, and waved on three other tanks that were idling behind his Mark IV.

The tanks motored past and stationed themselves on the right-hand side of the wide boulevard, each surrounded by six armed soldiers, two brandishing flamethrowers. The sunny silence was shaken as they fired one destructive shell after another into the façades of the wobbly buildings that remained. The two soldiers armed with flamethrowers moved inside smouldering homes and offices and torched what little was left. 'Leave them with nothing,' the young officer shouted to his men above the din, his tank slowly moving past them. 'Only when you can see clear through to the next street will you be free to move forward.'

It was eight o'clock on a warm Tuesday morning, and the final destruction of Naples had begun.

CONNORS AND VINCENZO were huddled inside an apartment doorway, a thin curtain separating them from the edge of the smoky street. Connors parted the curtain with the end of his rifle and stared out at the tanks firing shell after shell into the buildings that lined Via Toledo. 'Looks like they're dividing up the division four tanks to a street,' he said.

'How many soldiers?' Vincenzo asked. He was on his knees. By his side were an old hunting rifle and two wine bottles filled with kerosene and topped with rags.

'Thirty-five, maybe forty,' Connors said, sliding his head out for a better look. 'That's counting the ones inside the tanks.'

'Will we have the time we need?' Vincenzo asked.

'It depends on Maldini and Franco,' Connors said. 'If they get there at the right time, we have a good chance.'

'Don't worry,' Vincenzo said. 'They'll be there. They have no other plans for this morning.'

The tanks were now targeting a row of houses several hundred yards down the wide avenue. Connors grabbed one of the wine bottles. 'You wait here,' he said to Vincenzo. 'I'm going to try to get closer. Don't move until you hear the signal.'

Vincenzo nodded as he watched Connors head out onto Via Toledo, running with his head down. Vincenzo sat for a moment with his back against a chipped stone wall. He then looked across at the nearby buildings. There was still no sign of either Maldini or Franco. He looked back down the avenue, peering into the thick smoke. Connors was now a shadow.

Then he heard the church bell ringing—the signal that everyone was in place.

Vincenzo stepped into the street just as Maldini, a wine bottle with a lit fuse in his hand, ran out of a building behind him. Maldini tossed the bottle at an approaching trio of soldiers and then made a jump for Vincenzo, grabbing him round the waist and dragging him back into an alley leading out of Via Toledo. They turned a corner and hid against a cracked stone wall.

From the remaining rooftops above the avenue, two dozen street boys let loose a rainstorm of kerosene cocktails and cylinder tops of unexploded bombs that crashed and exploded on the tanks and soldiers below. Connors came up from the rear and fired two rounds at a German soldier carrying a flamethrower. The soldier landed face down in the dirt. Connors picked up the flamethrower, raced to the tank taking up the rear of the German attack and jumped on its side. He steadied himself and snapped open the lid. He hung the head of the flamethrower in the mouth of the tank and set loose its power, torching those inside. Smoke and screams rose out into the sky.

Connors jumped back to the ground and leaned against the seared tank, assessing the damage. He looked up towards the rooftops and spotted Nunzia. He circled his hand above his head, the signal for everyone above to make a quick retreat. He saw her return the sign, and then he turned his attention back to the street action. A handful of German soldiers were down, and two more of the tanks were disabled. A dozen soldiers walked slowly along the street, searching for targets that were no longer there. Connors quietly backed out of the street, picking up as many weapons as he could hold.

The first battle of the morning was at an end.

MALDINI GRABBED Vincenzo's shoulder and dragged him away from the wall, the German soldiers fast on their heels. 'We can't stay here,' he told him. 'We'll head for the rooftops and then make our way to the waterfront. It's the safest way out.'

They slipped into a darkened hallway as three soldiers ran past. Maldini pointed to a stairwell on the right, and they began the climb up its narrow steps, the older man leading. 'Grab one of those bottles,' Maldini said, pointing at a kerosene cocktail resting by a door jamb. 'Take that candle, too, and use them when you have to.'

When they got to the first-floor landing, they heard the soldiers enter the hall below. 'You go ahead,' Vincenzo said. 'I'll meet you at the waterfront.'

Maldini walked down the two steps that separated them and gripped Vincenzo's arm. 'Are you sure?' he asked.

'I'm sure.' Vincenzo stared into Maldini's eyes.

Maldini took a deep breath and nodded. 'Wait for them to come up the stairs. Light the fuse, hold it above your shoulder and let it go. Then run up these stairs as fast as you've ever run in your life.'

Maldini disappeared round a bend of steps. Vincenzo watched him leave, hearing the heavy pounding of the German soldiers in the stairwell below. He pulled the cloth out of the wine bottle and draped it over the lit candle. He tossed aside the candle and shoved the cloth back into the neck of the bottle. He was now standing a flight above the three soldiers. He stared at them for several seconds, watching as they halted their run and positioned their rifles. He held the bottle up as two bullets hit the wall just above his head.

'*Viva Napoli*!' he shouted.

The explosion shattered part of the wall and demolished the handrail. The soldiers lay dead.

VON KLAUS WATCHED Kunnalt rush up to him, stop and salute. He was always appreciative of the young officer's eagerness to please. The troubled look on the man's face, however, was enough to tell him that the news wasn't good. 'Problems already?' he asked as they stood in the 16th Panzer Division headquarters at the Royal Palace.

'On Via Toledo,' Kunnalt said. 'Nine men are dead. Three are wounded, one critical. And three of the tanks are down.'

Von Klaus stared at Kunnalt. 'Who did this?' he asked, his voice full of anger.

'Boys mostly,' Kunnalt told him. 'They lined the rooftops, armed with rifles and makeshift bombs.'

'Boys plan pranks, not battles,' von Klaus said. 'Someone is leading them. Who?'

'We're not quite sure yet, sir. But the men reported an exchange of gunfire with an American soldier. He came at them from a rear flank and seemed to be in control of the operation.'

'The Americans are firmly entrenched in Salerno,' von Klaus said. 'They won't move until Montgomery moves, and that's at least a week away. They may have sent a small team down to the city, but no one is sent out alone. There may be others scattered throughout the city. We need to find them, and quickly. I don't want any repeats of what happened this morning. This mission will be a success if I have personally to bring down every building myself. Nine dead soldiers and three tanks in ruin. This is insane!'

'Our troops were not expecting resistance,' Kunnalt said.

'They're soldiers,' von Klaus snapped. 'It's time they began to act like it.'

'Do you want me to request aerial assistance?'

Von Klaus shook his head. 'This is our battle. Unless you want me to inform high command that one of the most elite tank troops in the German army can't face down a group of children led by one soldier?'

'Then no changes to the standing orders, sir?'

'The orders hold as given. No mercy in any quarter. Not to the buildings and not to anyone on the streets. That includes children.'

STEVE CONNORS SAT on a thick stone in the dark basement of the San Lorenzo Maggiore church. His hands were on the dials of a broken transmitter, the candle by his feet his only direct light. He moved the dials, slapped at the machine in frustration and then kicked it to the ground. He sat with his back against the wall and looked out into the darkness.

'Does that help make it work?' Vincenzo asked. He stood in a corner of the room, his voice a small echo in the stillness of the basement. He stepped closer to Connors.

'I need to contact my headquarters. I have to get us some help.'

'How much better would your soldiers have done today?'

'We got lucky out there,' Connors said. 'Because the Germans weren't expecting us. That's not going to happen any more, and that means a lot more people are going to die.'

'It was my first fight,' Vincenzo said. 'And I was afraid. More than I thought I would be.'

'All those military books I hear you like to read,' Connors said, looking at Vincenzo. 'They make war sound like a chess game. They don't tell you what it's like to squeeze a trigger and then watch some guy your own age in another uniform fall down dead.'

'Are you always afraid?' Vincenzo asked.

'Never more than the first time. There's no training that can prepare you for that first fight. It gets easier after you've been through a few, but you always get the fear.'

Connors stood and walked towards the steps leading out of the church, stopping in front of a dust-shrouded statue of St Jude.

'He's the patron saint of lost causes,' Vincenzo said. 'Italians pray to him when they have no one else to turn to for help.'

'It do them any good?' Connors asked.

'You've been here long enough to know the answer,' Vincenzo said. 'But Italians never blame the saints. Only themselves. So they pray every day, and once in a while good things happen, and they have a saint to thank for it.' He patted his fingers gently across the statue's bare feet. Then they turned and walked up the narrow steps leading out of the church, leaving behind the peaceful silence.

THREE GERMAN TANKS rumbled around the centre of the Piazza Dante, their engines running hot, officers standing in the open pits. A dozen soldiers were scattered round the tanks, their eyes searching the rooftops. The tanks spread out to designated spots, poised to begin their destructive mission. The action that had taken place earlier in Via Toledo had been radioed to all the units, and they were placed on a full alert.

The sculpture of the poet Dante looked up towards a tolling clock. It was 10.00am.

Two wooden carts were wheeled in and hidden behind the statue. Each cart was loaded with mines and soaked with kerosene. Vincenzo eased past one of the carts, rifle in hand, and crouched down. Franco and Angela stepped in alongside. 'The tanks are right where we need them to be,' Franco said.

'The American needs a few more minutes to get into position,' Vincenzo said. 'Then we can make our move.'

'What if more Nazis come from behind us?' Angela asked.

'We turn the carts on them,' Vincenzo said. 'Which leaves our people in the square out on their own.'

'This is a dangerous plan,' Franco said.

'I'm open to any plans that aren't dangerous,' Vincenzo said.

THE CENTRE TANK shifted gears and ground to a halt. The tanks on either side also came to a quick stop. The square was filled with crouched soldiers aiming weapons at the man and boy standing at ease in the centre of the piazza.

Maldini stood facing three tanks and a dozen foot soldiers, his arms held out, a smile on his face. Next to him, little Fabrizio bounced a soccer ball against the side of his foot.

The officer in the centre tank motioned Maldini closer. 'What are you doing here?' he asked. 'You're not allowed within city limits.'

Maldini walked forward. 'I know, sir,' he said. 'I was set to leave when the Germans first arrived. But then my son ran away. He was afraid of the guns. Ever since, I have spent all my time looking for him. This morning, with the grace of God, I finally found him. He was hiding in one of the large rooms above us.'

Moving the ball from one foot to the other, Fabrizio looked up at the German officer. He then lifted his eyes and saw his target: a mine resting in the centre of a brick column directly above four soldiers with cocked machine guns.

'I could have you shot just for being here,' the officer snarled.

'I know, sir,' Maldini said. 'I beg you, please show us your mercy. We're ready now to go anywhere you want.'

'Were there any others hiding in those buildings?' the officer asked. 'Besides your son.'

'None that I saw, sir,' Maldini said.

Fabrizio lifted the ball from his foot to his knee and balanced it there as he stood on one leg. Maldini turned to the boy and gently rubbed his head. 'It's time to play ball,' he said to him.

Fabrizio nodded, let the soccer ball fall to the ground and began a slow trot, kicking the ball from one foot to the other. The Germans lowered their guns as they watched the boy manoeuvre around the front of the square. Some of them laughed as he kicked the ball upwards and dropped to his knees just as it landed on his forehead. Maldini stood off to the side, his eyes on the mine, his right hand at his back, its fingers wrapped round the hard end of a revolver.

Fabrizio was on his feet again, the ball a blur from foot to chest to head to arm, his hands spread out in front of him, enjoying the nods of approval from the relaxed soldiers. 'Your boy is an excellent player,' the officer said to Maldini, his attention focused on Fabrizio. 'One of the best I've ever seen.'

'Would you care to see him shoot the ball?' Maldini said. 'I swear you'll never live to see a shot like his again.'

The officer glanced round at the happy faces of his men. He looked back to Maldini and nodded his approval.

Fabrizio turned to Maldini, the ball floating in midair, his cherubic face gleaming with thin lines of sweat. 'Score your goal, Fabrizio,' Maldini told him.

The boy moved the ball closer to the soldiers and the tanks. He glanced at his target. He was a short reach away from a soldier's grip when he kicked the ball skywards towards the brick wall next to the centre tank.

The ball landed right on the middle of the mine, sending large pieces of brick, stone and shredded glass cascading down on the tank and the soldiers, its loud blast rocking the piazza. A hot blanket of thick brown smoke engulfed Maldini as he ran towards Fabrizio, clutched the boy in his arms and sprinted across the square to the open door that awaited them. Bullets zinged past them as they ran.

'Was it a good shot?' the little boy asked as they headed towards Connors, who was frantically waving them on.

'It was your best,' Maldini managed to say through gasps of breath as he and Fabrizio rushed past Connors into the immediate safety of the office-building foyer. Connors stared past them, offering cover fire and assessing the damage made by the exploded mine. The centre tank was shrouded in rubble, the officer bent over the open lid, seriously wounded. Three soldiers lay dead. The other two tanks had moved to the centre of the square, raining waste on the empty buildings surrounding them.

Connors looked down at Fabrizio and winked, the mastiff now next to the boy, sniffing and licking at the side of his face. 'I guess you really are a great football player,' Connors said.

Fabrizio patted the top of the mastiff's head and smiled back at Connors. 'But I won't be able to practise any more,' he said. 'That was the only ball I had.'

Nunzia came up behind Connors, resting a hand on the soldier's back. 'They're ready,' she said in a low voice.

Heavy machine-gun fire raked the first floor of the building. 'So are they,' Connors said, staring out at the approaching tanks.

THE TWO WOODEN CARTS were rolled into the shade of the square's archways, four mines in each. Vincenzo bent down against a wall and peered out into the square, heavy gunfire and powerful explosions rocking the foundations of buildings built to last for ever. He wiped his forehead with the sleeve of his shirt, took several deep breaths and closed his eyes. Next to him, crouched down and waiting with weapons cocked, six boys stood ready to move. On the other end of the square Franco waited with a similar group. 'When will we know to go out there?' one of the boys asked Vincenzo.

'You'll know,' Vincenzo assured him.

'I've never fired a rifle before,' the boy said, his voice unable to hide his fragile nerves. 'I hope I shoot something besides myself.'

'Aim it at the uniforms,' Vincenzo said, patting his leg. 'And keep pulling on the trigger. After that it's as much luck as skill.'

The explosion sent them sprawling to the damp ground. It came from the other end of the square, the power of the blast centred in the building where Connors and the others had been positioned, its façade now crumbled, smoke billowing towards the clear sky. The force of the hidden bomb had stretched out into the square, leaving four soldiers dead and a second tank disabled.

Vincenzo stood up and turned to the others. 'It's time,' he said. 'Let's show the Nazis that Naples is still alive.'

They grouped round the back of the cart and pushed it into the open square, aiming it towards the last functioning tank. From the other end of the square Franco and his team did the same. Vincenzo caught Franco's eye and nodded. 'Scatter and fire,' he shouted to the boys behind him. 'Leave the cart to me.'

The boys ran from behind the cart, firing rifle rounds in the direction of the soldiers. Vincenzo rolled the cart with all his might, the mines jiggling. Bullets zinged at him from all directions; a grenade exploded twenty feet to his left. He gave the cart one final push, using the full force of his body, and then he rolled off to his left. Franco released his cart seconds later.

The two carts exploded at the same time. Vincenzo stood up in the midst of all the smoke, waving his arms, signalling the boys out of the square and back into the arches and the safety of the streets. He ran behind them, then turned to check on Franco. The boy was on his knees, a large shard of wood jabbed into the back of his right shoulder. Vincenzo ran to Franco, lifted him to his feet and put an arm round his waist. 'Can you run?' he asked him.

'Faster than you,' Franco said.

Vincenzo gripped him tighter, and both boys ran out of the mangled Piazza Dante, leaving behind three ruined tanks, a dozen dead soldiers and a square erupting in flames.

VON KLAUS TOSSED the map to the ground in anger. 'I am losing men and tanks to children!' he shouted. 'We've been in Naples less than five hours, and I've already lost more men than I did our first morning in North Africa. This is insanity!'

'Our men are like anyone else, sir,' Kunnalt said. 'When they see a child, they tend to let their guard down.'

'They've done more than let their guard down,' von Klaus said. 'They've allowed themselves to be duped by an army of babies.'

'They will be difficult to flush out, sir. We have very little intelligence on them other than what we received from that prison escapee, Petroni. They're scattered and hidden throughout the city. We could make use of Petroni again. He's betrayed them once for money. He might be willing to do so again.'

Von Klaus nodded. 'Find this Petroni and deal with him.'

THE ROOM WAS on the first floor, above the Piazza Trieste e Trento. The blinds were drawn, and a candle in the corner had burned down to a low wick. Franco lay in a small bed, a thin sheet covering him to the waist, his eyes shut, a blood-soaked bandage wrapped round his wounded shoulder. He heard the floorboards creak and opened his eyes. 'Vincenzo?' he said. '*Sei tu*?'

The footsteps came closer, and Franco could make out the image of a boy about his height and weight moving towards the bed. The boy sat on the edge of the mattress.

'Who are you?' Franco asked.

'My name's Carlo,' the boy said in a thick, harsh voice that Franco did not recognise. 'And I can be a friend to you.'

'How did you find me?' Franco asked, wiping drops of fever sweat from his brow. 'No one knows about this place.'

'It wasn't hard,' Carlo said. 'Nothing is if you know who to ask and where to look.'

Franco lifted himself higher in the bed, wincing at the sharp pain in his shoulder. 'You can start telling me what you want,' he said. 'I'm not going anywhere for a few hours.'

'I want to help you and your friends fight the Nazis,' Carlo said. 'Nothing more than that. I have a small group up in the hills. You're going to need all the good people you can find.'

'Why did you wait until now to help us?' Franco asked, still suspicious.

Carlo slid down the edge of the bed, closer to Franco. 'We followed what you all were doing, but from a distance. We wanted to make sure it was going to turn out to be more than just loud talk. And we didn't think you wanted any help from kids like us.'

'You're from the children's prison,' Franco said.

'That's right. Me and everyone from my group.'

'What were you in prison for?' Franco asked.

'That doesn't matter,' Carlo said, shaking off the question. 'We come in with you, or we fight the Nazis out there on our own. I came here thinking that together would be better.'

'Why come to me?'

'The others are scattered and on the move,' Carlo said. 'You're going to be in this bed for a day or two. It just seemed easier.'

'You don't need permission to fight the Nazis. Just go out and disrupt their attack. If you do that, then we'll know you are with us. Until then there's very little for us to say to each other.'

Carlo nodded, stretched his legs and stood up, gazing down at Franco with cold, distant eyes. 'You need what we have,' he said. 'To turn your back on it will be foolish.'

Franco was tired and in pain, and he wished Vincenzo was in the room to help determine if Carlo's words were truthful or a trap. 'What is it you have?' he asked, his throat parched and raw.

'A tank,' Carlo said with genuine glee. 'A panzer tank. And enough shells to deal with an army of problems.'

Franco's eyes widened. 'How did you get a tank?' he asked, intrigued by the possibilities such a weapon offered the street boys.

'The same way we get everything,' Carlo said. 'We stole it. Two nights before the Nazis came into Naples.'

'You have to be trained to drive it,' Franco said.

'If you can drive a car, you can drive a tank.'

Franco pulled aside the sheet and jumped from the bed, his movements startling Carlo, who took two steps back. Franco grabbed Carlo by the centre of his white woollen shirt. 'If you're lying to me, thief,' he said, the strength back in his voice, 'if one word of what you said is not true, I'll find you and I will kill you.'

'You heal quick,' Carlo said, staring deep into Franco's eyes. 'That's a good talent to have during a war.'

Franco released his grip and pushed Carlo away. 'Where's this tank now?' he asked.

'It's wherever you want it to be,' Carlo said, regaining his bravado. 'You name the place and time, and I'll make sure it's there.'

'Can you get it to Via Caracciolo without being spotted?'

'The Nazis will think it's one of their own,' Carlo said. 'We're free to move anywhere we want.'

'Have it there at noon tomorrow,' Franco said. 'Park it along one of the alleys.'

Carlo nodded and headed towards the door. 'Noon it is. Who else will be with you?'

'I was going to ask you the same question,' Franco said.

'Then we should wait until tomorrow,' Carlo said. 'This way we'll both be surprised.'

Franco stood in the centre of the room, watching as Carlo closed the door behind him. He ran his fingers along the sides of his bandage. He grabbed his trousers and put them on. He pulled a torn shirt over his head, wincing as it drew past the cut. Outside, heavy shells pounded at the buildings in a nearby square. Franco took a final look round the room and walked out, once again ready to do battle.

THE LARGE OIL TANKER was moored off the long Beverello wharf, a series of thick ropes wedged around iron pillars keeping it in place. Two overhead spotlights running off a generator cast a glow across its rusty exterior. The tanker had arrived in port earlier that afternoon, its hulk filled with thousands of gallons of fuel, enough to keep the Nazi tanks roaming the streets of Naples until their mission was completed. A dozen guards patrolled its upper railings, submachine guns tucked behind their shoulders, eyes focused on the lapping water beneath them and the dark city streets beyond.

Connors, Maldini and Vincenzo were crouched behind a wooden shack 200 feet from the bow of the tanker. Nunzia and two boys were at the other end of the dock. Connors crawled along the shipside of the dock, a few feet from the glare of the lights. He turned back to Vincenzo and waved him forwards. The boy slid in alongside him, makeshift bomb in his hands, a wristwatch embedded in the centre of the mechanism. 'How much time?' Connors asked.

'Forty-five minutes like you told me,' Vincenzo said. 'Thirty to get there and strap it to the tanker, and fifteen to get away.'

Connors nodded and checked his own watch. 'I'll leave you my pack and rifle. I'll lay the bomb down, and you help the others do what they need to do.'

Vincenzo shook his head. 'I'll put it on the ship,' he said.

'Maybe we should have worked this out before.' Connors's voice was low but his anger apparent. 'Any idiot with wire, tape and explosives can make a bomb. But you need to have some clue about what you're doing to lay it in there.'

'Have you ever done it?' Vincenzo asked. 'Stuck a bomb on the side of an oil tanker in the middle of the night?'

'That's not the point,' Connors said. 'It's a risky move.'

'That's why I should be the one to go,' Vincenzo said. 'You can fight the Nazis off better than me. And after that you can figure out a way to get the others out of the city.'

'It does bother me when what you say starts making sense,' Connors said. 'I'll leave Maldini behind to give you some cover.'

As Vincenzo slithered off towards the cool waters of the bay, Connors crawled back to the shack. He flipped off his pack and handed it to Maldini. 'I filled it up with grenades,' he said. 'First smell of trouble, scatter them across the upper deck of the ship.'

Maldini took the pack and reached inside, pulling out one of the grenades. 'I see our general got his way again,' he said with a grin.

'He should be a lawyer, not a general,' Connors said. 'The kid could argue his way out of a firing squad.'

'He knows those waters and their currents well,' Maldini added. 'And he moves like a ghost.'

VINCENZO SWAM ALONGSIDE the large tanker, holding the device aloft. He swam in next to the rusty hulk, glanced up and saw the muzzle of a machine gun at rest against the top rail. He turned and faced the side of the tanker, placed the bomb in the smoothest area he could find and held it there with thick strips of tape.

There were twenty minutes left on the timer. Vincenzo put an ear up to the watch, making sure it was still ticking. He gave a final look up at the Nazis standing guard and silently swam away.

CONNORS POURED KEROSENE on the rear of the tank, drenching the parked vehicle. He held the five-gallon drum tight against his chest, moving about with quiet steps, eyes on the lid of the tank. Nunzia and the boys were hidden in the darkness behind him. He left the empty drum under the tank and walked backwards to the others. Nunzia waited for him, another drum filled with kerosene in her hand. 'This is the last of it,' she whispered.

'The boys know what they need to do?' Connors asked, nodding over at the two silent teenagers standing beside Nunzia.

'We'll do our job,' one of them said. 'Don't worry about us.'

Connors took the drum from Nunzia, inched back to the tank, uncorked the drum and poured the kerosene out in a straight line, allowing it to follow him as he stepped away from the silent machine. He knew from earlier surveillance that there were only two soldiers inside the tank, both by now asleep. The other three had gone up to the tanker to spend time with those on guard. He paused to look up at the ship, wondering if Vincenzo's handmade bomb would have any impact against such a massive hulk.

Back with the others, Connors rested the now empty drum by his feet, peering down the dark street at the thin line of kerosene he had left behind. He handed his cigarette lighter to the older of the two boys. 'Check the time on your watch,' he told him. 'Wait ten minutes and then drop a light right where I'm standing.'

The boy nodded, clutching the lighter in his right hand.

VINCENZO, STILL WET and chilled from his swim, stood next to Maldini, watching as Connors and Nunzia approached from a side street on their left.

As he ran, Connors looked at his watch and silently ticked down the seconds. 'Now,' he whispered.

The tank explosion lit up the harbour below them, a rich bubble of flames hurtling towards a starless sky. A ship alarm sounded, and lights were turned on up and down the wharf, all working off the single generator the Nazis had activated.

'The ship. It should have gone off already,' Connors said. 'It was timed to go with the tank.'

'Be patient,' Maldini said as they scurried for a nearby hillside.

A dozen soldiers with machine guns lined the perimeter of the wharf, waiting to shoot at the slightest movement. Two tanks came rumbling down Via Acton, and three others were speeding across Via C. Colombo, all primed to protect the port and the oil tanker.

'That bomb doesn't go, we'll never get another shot at that fuel,' Connors said.

'The bomb will work,' Vincenzo said.

'I'll have an easier time believing that, General, after I hear a loud explosion,' Connors said. 'But right now all I see is one tank down and lots of irritated Nazis.'

They reached the hillside in safety. Maldini sat on a large rock and stared at all the activity on the wharf. Off in the distance they heard blasts from Nazi tanks and the rumble of buildings that fell and crumbled. The streets of Naples were now a series of bonfires as the enemy assault continued into the late-night hours. 'No matter what we do to them, they have won,' he said. 'They have defeated Naples.'

'You can't defeat a city, Papa, until you defeat its people,' Nunzia said. 'The Nazis have destroyed Naples, but they haven't destroyed us.'

Connors stood and looked down at the burning streets. 'It makes no military sense, what they're doing,' he said. 'It's not about holding a position or strengthening a defence. The Nazis don't fight to win. They fight to destroy.'

'Get some rest,' Nunzia said, 'all of you. Futile or not, we have more battles to fight tomorrow.'

Vincenzo walked further down the hill and stared at the oil tanker, tears flowing along the sides of his face. In his right hand he held a small statue of San Gennaro, the saint's arms were spread out and there was a peaceful smile on his face.

THE MASSIVE FORCE of the blast knocked Maldini off the rock and sent him rolling down a short hill. Nunzia was tossed next to a pile of stones. Connors jumped to his feet, rifle at the ready. Vincenzo sat on the edge of the hill, the statue at his side, his face lit from the glow of the blast below.

The oil tanker split and rose halfway out of the water, thick plumes of bright orange flames lighting the harbour clear through to the islands that dotted the shoreline. The round cloud that rose from the centre of the tanker billowed high into the night sky.

Vincenzo picked up the statue of San Gennaro and brought it to his lips, giving the patron saint a soft kiss. He stood and turned to Connors, smiling broadly. 'I told you the bomb would work!'

'What the hell took so long?' Connors asked.

'The watch was set on Naples time,' Maldini said. 'It went off when it felt like it.'

The Second Day: September 29

It was just before dawn, the streets a mixture of dark smoke and light mist. Connors, a machine gun hanging over his right shoulder, walked past ruined buildings and smouldering homes, assessing the damage one day's fighting had wrought and anticipating the severity of the Nazi response. Nunzia walked beside him, arms at her sides, her pace relaxed. He looked over at her, her eyes bright and alert, her body shapely and athletic, and wondered if he would ever again be so close to someone as beautiful.

She stopped in front of an ornate double flight of steps leading to the church of San Paolo Maggiore. She gripped a stone railing and stared at a statue of a saint, his arms open, head tilted to the sky.

'It does make you wonder,' Connors said. 'All these bombs falling and tanks blasting away. Most of the buildings fall in a heap. But these churches take the hit, catch a couple of dents here and there, but still stand.' He stepped closer to Nunzia.

Nunzia looked up into his handsome face, her eyes searching beyond the shell of the hardened soldier. She rested a hand on his cheek, and he held it there. He lowered his head; she raised hers, and they kissed, the sun behind them rising over the smouldering city. They held the kiss, letting silence and passion rule the moment, drowning the visions of battles and of friends and family members long since gone. For those sweet brief seconds they were alone and far removed from any war.

'What happens to you after this?' she asked, still only inches from his face. 'Do you get to go home?'

Connors shook his head. 'Not for a while,' he said.

'Do you have a *fidanzata* that waits?' she asked.

Connors smiled. 'That mean a girlfriend?' he asked. 'If it does, the answer's no.'

'It will happen,' she said.

'Why are you so sure of that?' he asked.

'You're a good man,' Nunzia said with a warm smile. 'It's always easy for a good man to find someone to love.'

NAZI SOLDIERS CROWDED into the three-tiered courtyard of the Palazzo Marigliano and sprayed the lower and upper windows with machine-gun bullets and smoke bombs, intending to force out any street boys hiding behind its walls. Two of the soldiers entered a darkened alleyway on the left of the palazzo, walking past floating smoke, their boots crunching down on shattered glass. One of the soldiers saw two small shadows against a pile of stones. He clicked the chamber of his gun and turned it towards the shadows.

Dante and Fabrizio held their breath. They heard the soldier stop. Dante slid a hand to the small of his back and pulled out an old target pistol. He tapped the small boy on the shoulder and pointed to the far side of the alley.

Fabrizio looked up at Dante and shook his head, too afraid to move. Dante grabbed Fabrizio by the arm, and they both came out into the alley. 'Run!' he whispered.

The Nazi fired at the two fleeing boys. He gave chase, trying to zero in on his faraway zigzagging targets. The boys were heading for a bolted iron door at the end of the dark alleyway. Dante was the first to reach the door, but he was unable to move its massive rusty handle. He turned, saw the Nazi in the distance, and grabbed Fabrizio. 'Jump up on my shoulders,' he told the smaller boy. 'And reach for the railing above you. That'll bring you to safety.'

'What will you do?' Fabrizio asked, his lower lip trembling.

'I'll stay and fight the soldier,' Dante said, jamming the gun back into the flat of his back.

'Let me fight with you,' Fabrizio said.

Dante kissed his cheek. 'What kind of an Italian would I be if I let something happen to the best football player in all Naples?' he asked. 'You go, Fabrizio, and let me worry about the Nazi.'

He lifted the boy to his shoulders, clutched his ankles and steered him to the base of the railing. 'Stretch as far as you can,' he said.

Fabrizio's fingers pawed for the railing, missing the bars by inches. He then crouched down on Dante's shoulders and jumped, grabbing onto the black iron rails with both hands. 'I have it,' he said, pulling himself up and over the railing, his back to a shuttered window.

Dante turned and saw the German soldier standing across from him, pointing a machine gun at his chest.

The soldier glanced above and saw Fabrizio pulling up one of the slats on the wooden shutters, struggling to reach the inside handle. The Nazi lifted his gun and aimed it at the small boy. Dante put his hands at his back, grabbing the handle of the target pistol.

The mastiff came from out of the shadows.

It jumped and caught the soldier at chest level, the force of its weight sending them both to the ground and throwing the machine gun up against a wall. The mastiff's sharp teeth closed on the soldier's neck, easily ripping through the collar of his uniform. The soldier lifted his arm to push it off but couldn't budge the mastiff, which shook its powerful grip from side to side, treating the soldier like a large, overstuffed puppet.

Dante ran for the machine gun and tossed it up to Fabrizio. The boy caught it with both hands, his back pressed against the shutter slats. 'Use the end of the gun like a hammer,' Dante said to him. 'Once you get inside, run to the front of the building and head for the sewers. They can't reach you there.'

'Come with me,' Fabrizio said.

'I can't make the jump,' Dante said. 'I'll get to the next alley and make for the tunnels. Don't worry about me.'

'What about Benito?' Fabrizio asked.

'Who?' Dante asked.

'The dog,' Fabrizio said, pointing down at the mastiff, still at the Nazi's neck. 'You have to take him with you and keep him safe.'

Dante reached down and gently pulled the mastiff off the dead soldier. 'He doesn't look like he needs help from anybody.'

MALDINI AND VINCENZO stared up at the long row of silent trams along Via dei Tribunali. The overhead electrical wires were cut.

'We could use these six transit cars to block off the alleys,' Maldini said, looking at the seven dark entrances that led from the heart of the main square. 'That would leave the tanks only one way out, and we can block that with mines.'

'Trams can't move without current,' Vincenzo said.

'We might be able to push them,' Maldini said. He walked round one of the trams, his hand caressing the red-painted side panel, then looked across at Vincenzo. 'We have enough boys, and we have a Jeep. All we need is rope. These trams may be old, but they were built well. The tanks can get over them, but it will take a lot of effort. It will also leave their bellies exposed and give the boys time to jam in either a mine or a grenade.'

'Even with a Jeep and the ropes, it'll be hard to move the trams from the tracks to the alleys,' Vincenzo said, shaking his head.

'We'll push them somehow,' Maldini said in a firm voice.

'That's not much of a plan,' Vincenzo said.

'We're not much of an army,' Maldini said.

SIX PANZER TANKS engulfed the square by the National Archaeological Museum, gun turrets facing the massive two-storey red stone structure. Fifty soldiers were lined along the perimeter. Von Klaus stood in the opening of his tank, looking up to the sky, his cap removed, the sun warming his clear face. 'If nothing else, I'll miss this Italian weather,' he said to Kunnalt, who was across from him, in the next tank.

A LONG LINE of street boys stood along the edges of the museum roof, staring down at the soldiers closing in. Their hands were wrapped in heavy cloths, and there were huge pots of boiling water resting by their feet. 'Wait until they get to the steps,' one of the boys called down the line. 'Then lift the pots.'

A dozen soldiers marched towards the stone steps that led up to the ornate double doors of the museum, three of them lugging flamethrowers. Above them the boys struggled with the cumbersome pots. Two of the younger boys checked on the pots resting above the smouldering fires in the centre of the roof.

'Try and hang on a few more seconds,' the lead boy said, the bulk of his pot teetering on the edge, his eyes focused on the Nazis moving up the steps. 'They're just about where we need them.'

'I can't hold it up any longer,' another boy moaned. 'It's starting to burn through the cloth on my hands.'

'Then let's give them a shower,' the lead boy ordered. 'Keep your feet planted. We only want water to go over—not any of us!'

The boiling water cascaded down in streams, landing in the centre of the walkway just inches beyond the steps, scalding the soldiers caught in the downpour. The boys turned away from the edge and ran to the other side of the roof, where a row of thick ropes lay curled, one end of each tied round the base of a bell tower. They unfurled the ropes and jumped off the side of the museum, leaving behind the pots and the smoking fires.

Three of the soldiers aimed their machine guns at the rooftop, their bullets chipping the curved stone. Three others ran up the steps, heading for the closed front door. Another small unit followed, urged on by the frantic waves of both Kunnalt and von Klaus. The lead soldier stopped in front of the door and riddled the ancient iron design with bullets. Then he reached out for the silver-encrusted door handle and yanked it open.

The explosion sent the door flying out towards the steps, like a large unguided iron missile, landing across the upper bodies of three soldiers. Four others lay dead across the smoke-filled entrance.

Von Klaus pounded at the side of his tank with a closed fist, frustrated at the successful street tactics of the boys. 'They must all be found, Kunnalt,' he said. 'This cannot be allowed to continue.'

THE LONG-ABANDONED PIER along Via Francesco Caracciolo was shuttered and dark, the noon sun unable to crack through the old slabs of wood and thick piles of rock that framed the walls. Carlo Petroni stood in the centre of the high-ceilinged chamber, his shoes resting on the damp floor, his back to the distant sea, his eyes peering into shadow. He turned his head when he heard the footsteps behind him and saw the American uniform.

'A light wouldn't be a bad idea,' Carlo said in heavily accented English. 'I always like to know who I'm talking to.'

'It's wartime,' Connors said, standing less than ten feet away. 'You can't always get what you want.'

'I came like I said I would,' Carlo said. 'At noon, alone and without a gun.'

Connors stepped out of the shadows. 'You also made mention of a tank,' he said. 'And I don't happen to see one here, do you?'

'It would be stupid to bring it here,' Carlo said. He maintained his calm manner, carefully taking note of the soldier. 'It's where we can both get to it. If that's what we decide.'

'It would also be stupid of you to lie about it,' Connors said. 'Franco doesn't trust you. Vincenzo doesn't know you, and from what little I've seen, I don't like you. Which leaves you lots of room to improve your situation.'

'I'm a thief,' Carlo said with a shrug. 'That makes it easy for you and your friends not to trust me or want to know me or even like me. But it doesn't matter what I am. What matters is what I have.'

'Why'd you bother to take the tank in the first place? You don't strike me as a kid who'd risk his life to take on the Nazis.'

'I want the Nazis out of Naples as much as any of your street boys,' Carlo said.

'What do you want for it?' Connors asked.

'I can be a help in what you're trying to do,' Carlo said. 'I can get in to see the Nazi colonel. And I can get in to see you. You have no one on your side who can do both.'

Connors took a deep breath and then several steps back. 'No deal,' he said. 'You can be on our side or theirs, but I'm not going to let you work both. It's a bad game to play, especially in a war. The only one who comes out ahead is you.'

'You're making a poor decision and a big mistake,' Carlo said.

Vincenzo's voice came from the other side of the pier. 'We already have your tank.' He stepped forward, Franco by his side.

Carlo tried to gauge whether what he had just heard was bluff or truth. 'You wouldn't even know where to find it,' he said.

THE DOORS TO THE PIER swung open, and the sun bolted through.

Carlo shielded his eyes from the sunlight, staring out at the German tank parked between the two iron doors, Maldini waving from the open pit. Connors walked past Carlo, heading towards the tank, rifle draped over his shoulder, his helmet hanging on the barrel. He turned and stared at Carlo, who was visibly shaken. 'I'm just a bystander in all this,' Connors said, a sly smile on his face. 'But if I had to guess, I'd say you're not the best thief in Naples.'

CONNORS LEANED against one side of the tank, smoking a cigarette, his rifle and helmet by his feet. He was staring at Dante, who was sitting by the front of the tank, a piece of charcoal in his right hand, sketching on a thin piece of paper. Maldini watched from the mouth of the tank, his eyes filled with admiration.

'Some day, my little friend, your work will hang in galleries,' Maldini said.

The boy looked up at Connors and pointed to his drawing. 'What do you call that in English?' he asked.

'A catapult,' Connors said. 'I used to see them in those Robin Hood movies with Errol Flynn. They caused the Sheriff of Nottingham and his troops a ton of trouble.'

'It will cause the Nazis even more,' Vincenzo said.

'We all know from the movies it can stop men,' Maldini said. 'But can it stop a tank?'

'If you can get your shot off high and at an angle, I suppose it can do some damage,' Connors said. 'But you're going to need something more than rocks.'

'What if there was a bomb in it?' Vincenzo asked, looking from Maldini to Connors. 'We collected one hundred and fifty bombs from the squares. So far we've used about sixty of the cylinders. A few haven't gone off, but most of them have. If we put the right bomb in the catapult, it could destroy a tank.'

'We're forgetting something here,' Connors said. 'We don't have a catapult. Least not one that I've seen.'

'You'll see one soon,' Maldini said. 'We have plenty of wood, rope and wheels, and a dozen boys working to put them all together in a barn behind the Rione Villa. They should be finished by nightfall.'

'Those bombs weigh at least four hundred pounds each,' Connors said. 'You're going to need something in the sling that can hold and release that kind of weight.'

'The Nazis helped us with that,' Maldini said. 'The last night of the bombing they hit the church of Gesù Vecchio and blew out the bell tower. The bells landed in the square. They're more than heavy enough to centre the catapult and release the bomb.'

'First the Nazis went up against our mines, grenades and rifles,'

Franco said. 'Now we add a bomb and a tank. We get stronger as they get weaker.'

'Don't get carried away just yet,' Connors warned. 'Up to now they've been spread out across the city. With the tanker gone, they're going to tighten the units, bring the fight closer to the centre of town. They'll try to squeeze us into a circle, force us to stay in one place and drag the fight out until it's to their advantage. It's easier to handle them in small groups; you can hit quick and run fast. The bigger the units, the tougher it gets to do damage without losing a lot of boys.'

'There is still time to make changes to our plan,' Vincenzo said. 'Franco has the carrier pigeons all in place. They can get word out in less than an hour.'

'We're going to have to move quicker than that,' Connors said. 'We need to react to what they're doing, and we won't know how until we know what they're doing. The plan will have to change on the fly, which means we don't have less than an hour. We have about fifteen minutes.'

'We need more than pigeons to get that done,' Maldini said.

Connors spread his feet apart and looked down at the manhole cover below. 'What we need are these sewers,' he said. 'We use the pigeons in the air and Angela's little crew of sewer rats underground. That'll be our line of communication. Get a rotation set up and never stop it. All the boys will know exactly what's being done and where, every second of this battle. We keep all the surprises on the Nazi end.'

'We can talk to each other, and the Nazis will never see it,' Vincenzo said. 'We'll be above them and below, invisible.'

'Franco, how far can your pigeons go with a message and come back with an answer?' Connors asked.

'A hundred miles,' Franco said.

'Who do they fly to?'

'They head for the closest coop in the area,' Franco said. 'From there, it's up to the messenger.'

'How far do you need them to go?' Maldini asked.

'Salerno,' Connors said.

NUNZIA SAT AT A SMALL TABLE in the shuttered kitchen of a first-floor apartment off Piazza Matteotti, a glass of red wine cupped between her hands. Connors sat across from her, loading an ammo clip into his rifle. There had been more fighting. Gaspare, one of the bravest boys, had died. Nunzia studied his face, the unspoken resolve masking his sadness. 'None of this is new to us,' she said. 'We've lived with death for many years, all of us, young and old.'

'It's not new to me either.' Connors looked up and gazed into her eyes. 'I've seen my share of dying since I put on this uniform. But that's one soldier against another. I can't think of anything that gears a man up to stomach watching an innocent boy, who had no kind of business being in a war, die in front of you. I don't know if I have the kind of courage you need to keep moving and not lose hope. The boys have it. And so do you.'

'We've made it hard for you just to be a soldier,' Nunzia said, reaching a hand out to touch the top of his. 'You've come to mean a lot to us, and I think we've come to mean a great deal to you. That makes your job much more difficult. It's easier if you go into a fight not caring about the people who are involved.'

Connors wrapped his fingers round her hand and leaned across the table, his face inches from hers. He pulled Nunzia gently towards him and kissed her amid the flickering glow of the dwindling candle. She returned the kiss with a fevered passion, and their arms wrapped tightly round each other. 'There's a small bed in the back of the room,' she whispered.

Connors covered her face with his hands, gently stroked her cheeks and neck, and nodded. They went together in silence into the dark emptiness of the room, leaving their guns at rest on the table behind them. They fell on the bed, their bodies entwined, the love that was inside both of them free to escape.

AT THE 45th THUNDERBIRD Division Headquarters in Salerno, the young recruit stood at attention, his nervous eyes scanning the cramped tent filled with maps, chairs and crumpled papers..

Captain Anders cast aside his briefing books and looked up from the table, a cigar jammed into a corner of his mouth. 'All right,' he said impatiently. 'Let's hear it.'

'One of the locals has brought in a pigeon, sir,' the soldier said. 'Actually two of them.'

'What's he want me to do?' Anders asked. 'Eat them?'

'No, sir,' the soldier said. 'They were carrier pigeons, and the messages they were delivering are written in English.'

The soldier opened his shirt pocket and pulled out two rolled-up slivers of white paper. He handed them to Anders, who snatched the sheets from him, unfurled them and read them both. A wide smile spread across the captain's face.

'The man with the pigeons still around?' Anders asked.

'Yes, sir. He asked if it was OK to feed them and give them some water while I was up here with you. I told him I didn't think it would be a problem.'

'He can give them a steam bath and a shave if that's what they need,' Anders said. 'Just so long as they're ready to fly back out again in about ten minutes.'

Anders sat down at the table and tore off two slips of paper from the bottom of a yellow legal pad. He slowly printed out a long series of words on each and rolled them up like cigarettes. He looked up and handed the papers to the young soldier. 'Have him strap these on those pigeons,' Anders told him. 'And tell him to make sure they find their way back to Naples before dark.'

'Yes, sir.'

'And before you go, patch me through to air command.'

'Yes, sir.'

The young soldier saluted and left the tent. Anders looked down at the map spread out across the table. 'We might end up taking that damn city without even seeing it,' he whispered to himself. 'And it would serve those Nazi bastards right. They can't let a Thunderbird come into a town and not expect him to give them more than a handful of trouble.'

ERIC TIPPLER LOWERED his high-powered rifle and stared down from the roof of the aquarium at a group of street boys as they turned a corner and walked in his direction. He then raised the rifle, steadied it against the stone edge of the roof and turned to the soldier next to him. 'Pick one,' he said.

Hans Zimmler stood behind Tippler, arms folded across his chest. 'Tall one on the far right,' he said.

'Head or heart?' Tippler asked.

'Make it more interesting than that,' Zimmler said. 'Arm first, then leg, then head.'

Tippler looked away from the square. 'Two shots are the most I can get off. The others will drag him away before a third.'

'I'll make it worth it for you,' Zimmler said. 'I'll double our usual bet. Two cigarettes instead of the one.'

Tippler peered through his scope, targeting the hit. 'Make it three,' he said. 'One for each shot that I take.'

Zimmler pulled three cigarettes from his shirt pocket and rested them next to Tippler's rifle. 'They're yours if the boy dies.'

Tippler squeezed off the first round. 'Leg first,' he muttered.

Zimmler watched the street boy fall to the ground, both hands clasped around his knee. Two of the boys reached out for him, rushing to drag him to the safety of a brick archway. Tippler's second shot landed at the base of the wounded boy's shoulder and sent him reeling backwards. 'Last shot for the gold,' the Nazi said as he fired the third and fatal bullet.

Tippler released his grip on the rifle, turned and reached for one of the cigarettes. 'Got a light?' he asked.

Zimmler tossed him a lighter, eyes still focused down on the square. 'It seems there'll be no shortage of target practice for you today,' he said, pointing at an array of street boys in the square.

Tippler stood up, cigarette dangling from the centre of his mouth, looked out at the square filled with boys partially hidden in corners and against walls, and nodded. 'Well, we know they're not here to take control of an empty aquarium,' he said. 'They must have heard that panzers are heading into the area.'

'I'll get Zoltan and Glaus from downstairs,' Zimmler said, picking up his rifle and moving from the ledge. 'We can make better use of the box of grenades they're sitting on from up here than they can from down there.'

WILHELM GLAUS STRETCHED his arms towards the ceiling and twisted his neck from side to side, right foot resting on a large box of grenades. The stench of the abandoned aquarium had infiltrated his clothes and gear pack, while the endless army of war-starved water rats parading up and down the stairwell had shoved his patience beyond its normal limits. Glaus looked up when he heard the echo of Zoltan's steps cascade down the empty halls.

Zoltan turned the corner and smiled when he saw Glaus. 'Lots of activity in the square,' he said. 'Boys hiding on all sides. Something big is about to happen, which answers your question as to why they would want us to sit here and do nothing but wait.'

'It's about time,' Glaus said, reaching for his rifle. 'If I had to spend one more day in this hellhole, I was going to let the rats have me for breakfast.'

A different voice responded. 'They're Neapolitan rats,' Maldini said in German, his body shrouded in darkness, a machine gun in his hands. 'They might not have the stomach for Nazi blood.'

Glaus turned, aimed his weapon in the direction of Maldini's voice and fired twice. The return volley came at him from the side, from deep within the empty fish tank, three bullets piercing the side of his neck. He dropped his rifle and fell over backwards, his head resting on top of the crate of grenades. Zoltan stood frozen in place, his eyes on the dead soldier.

'Turn round,' Maldini told him, 'and walk up to the tower.'

Zoltan glanced to his left and saw Giovanni and Frederico step out from behind the slimy terrain of the fish tank, machine guns in their hands, walking towards the crate of grenades.

Maldini came out of the shadows. 'You've done well,' he told the boys. He then turned to Zoltan. 'Now, let's go to the tower. It's time we met your friends.'

Zoltan nodded and began a slow, deliberate walk up the stone stairs.

CONNORS LOOKED UP at the imposing structures surrounding him, at the large square, and at the six tanks positioned in a semicircle around the zoo and aquarium. He checked the dozens of boys scattered round him, lying low, guns poised. Von Klaus had, as Connors had expected, adapted to their continued presence, sending stronger forces into every square.

But the boys had adjusted in their own way. Connors knew that many of them still weren't fit to be in the middle of such fiery fields. There was among them, however, a core group, led by the examples of Vincenzo and Angela, who seemed to be gaining in confidence.

Franco slid up alongside Connors, two machine guns strapped round his neck and a row of grenades clipped across his waist. 'It's here,' he said. 'About fifty yards behind the other tanks. The signal for them to fire will come from Maldini up on the roof.'

Connors nodded, glancing across the square at Nunzia, who was huddled against a stone wall, a machine gun cradled in her hands, four street boys hiding in the shadows with her. She looked over at him and gave him a wave and a warm smile, her face luminous.

MALDINI HELD THE GUN to Zoltan's back, standing with the Nazi in the stairwell. They could both hear the footsteps coming closer, less than one floor above them. Maldini glanced behind him and saw Giovanni and Frederico hovering in a corner of the stairway, rifles hanging across the top of the crate of grenades. 'Remember this,' he whispered into Zoltan's ear. 'No matter what happens, I'll make sure you die before I do. *Capito*?'

The Nazi arched his back. He stiffened when he heard Zimmler's voice. 'Glaus! Zoltan! Time to wake up and join the war. The tanks are in the square. So are some of those boys that have been pestering us. We need you to bring the grenades up.'

'Answer him,' Maldini whispered to Zoltan. 'Tell him you're on your way. And say it loud so he can hear you.'

'We're bringing them up,' Zoltan shouted.

'Have him come down,' Maldini said, moving his gun up against Zoltan's neck. 'Tell him you found some wine, lots of it, and ask what you should do with it.'

'Do you want us to bring the wine up as well?' Zoltan asked, wiping at the sweat coming off his brow. 'Glaus found a case hidden in one of the fish tanks earlier today.'

Maldini heard footsteps and turned to the boys, signalling them to prepare to fire. Giovanni and Frederico took aim up the dark stairway. Zimmler turned a corner, his rifle slung casually over his shoulder. Maldini looked at the two boys and nodded.

Both bullets found their mark.

'Take his rifle and belt and start heading up,' Maldini said to the boys, still holding the gun on Zoltan. 'We still have one more Nazi to deal with.'

'What about him?' Frederico asked, pointing his rifle at Zoltan.

'Don't worry,' Maldini said. 'He'll be bound and gagged. And he won't be alone. We have an army of rats down here who will keep a very close eye on our friend.'

TIPPLER SAW THE AMERICAN soldier running through the square. He double-checked the scope. 'There you are,' the sniper said. 'The ghost of Naples. I wonder how many cigarettes Zimmler would wager on your life?'

Tippler bore down on his target.

Giovanni and Frederico rested the grenade crate on a step and stood inches from the German soldier. The older boy grabbed Frederico's right hand and nodded. They came out of the darkness together, throwing their bodies on the flattened Nazi. They landed on his back just as he squeezed the trigger, sending the shot astray and the rifle cascading over the edge of the roof. Frederico picked up a stone and landed blow after blow on the head and neck of the surprised Tippler. Giovanni gripped the soldier's ammunition belt, leaned down and shoved him forward. Frederico tossed aside the rock and moved next to Giovanni, each boy now pushing with all his strength to get the dazed soldier out of the tower. One final push from both boys and Tippler fell screaming over the side.

Drenched in sweat, Giovanni and Frederico turned and found Maldini standing behind them, the crate of grenades in his hands. He rested the crate next to one of the stone pillars and pulled free a grenade. He peered over the side. The tanks had begun venting their wrath against the old buildings, and soldiers with machine guns were searching for street boys. In the square, wedged in next to the fountain, he spied Connors with Nunzia. Maldini checked his wristwatch. He pulled the pin from the grenade and sent it spiralling down to the battle zone. 'It's time to join our friends,' he said.

CONNORS AIMED his machine gun at an approaching tank and held fire. Looking up, he saw the Nazi soldier flying down out of the aquarium tower. He backed up and reached a hand out for Nunzia. He pulled her along with him as the soldier landed on the other end of the square.

'I was expecting a louder signal,' Connors said, ducking under a fusillade of Nazi bullets.

Nunzia fired off half a dozen rounds and then glanced up at the tower. She saw her father lean over the edge and toss a German grenade. 'That was just an appetiser,' she shouted. 'Here comes the meal now.'

The blast of the first grenade sent three soldiers hurtling to the ground, face down and dead. The next dozen grenades caused a break in the Nazi offensive. Within minutes the square was filled with street boys rising up from the sewers, running out of fiery buildings and jumping down from smoke-filled houses, each firing weapons at the now surrounded German soldiers. Connors ran towards an open manhole, grabbed a sack of grenades from a street boy and jumped on the back of a Nazi tank. He turned to his right and saw kerosene cocktails rain down on two other tanks swinging away from the buildings to bear down on the boys. Connors unpinned two of the grenades and tossed them into an open slot. He jumped off the tank, the explosion hitting while he was in midair.

The remaining tanks were moving in a tight circle, heavily armed soldiers closing in behind them, looking to shoot their way out of a square that just minutes earlier they could claim as their own. Suddenly a panzer tank, its gun turret loaded and in position, blocked their path. Vincenzo stood in the open hole, a pair of goggles hanging off his neck.

'You think they'll be all right?' Nunzia asked, looking through the haze and smoke at the tank.

Connors nodded. 'The Americans have Patton,' he said. 'The Brits have Montgomery and the Neapolitans have Vincenzo. Not a loser in the bunch.'

VINCENZO LOWERED HIS HEAD and looked down into the tank. Dante was pushing buttons and shifting gears, while Claudio and Pepe stood ready to load shells. Fabrizio was huddled in a corner, the bull mastiff at his feet, trying to find comfort inside the tight space.

'How soon do you want us to fire?' Claudio asked.

'They're closing in,' Vincenzo said, staring at the oncoming Nazi tanks and soldiers.

'Do you think they worked out we're not one of theirs?' Pepe asked.

'They're Nazis,' Vincenzo said. 'Not morons.'

Dante took a step back to read the gauges and accidentally stepped on the mastiff's tail. The dog snarled. 'Why is he in here?' Dante asked Fabrizio.

'To protect us,' Fabrizio said with a knowing nod.

'Get ready to fire,' Vincenzo shouted. 'And once you start, Dante, no matter what happens, don't stop.'

Dante was mesmerised by the power of the vehicle. He stood atop a wine crate and looked through the front slot at the square. The Nazis were running towards them, forced out of the square by a firestorm of bullets and grenades. He turned to Claudio and Pepe and nodded. 'Load it,' Dante said. 'And be careful. We want the shells to go out, not come in. Wait for the signal from above.'

'What do you want me to do?' Fabrizio asked.

'Keep an eye on Vincenzo,' Dante told him. 'It's going to get really loud soon, and I may not be able to hear his commands. You listen for me.'

'Fire!' Vincenzo shouted. The first shell came spiralling out of the turret. It exploded against a building, its brutal force sending four Nazi soldiers down to the ground.

The boys applauded; Claudio pumped a small fist in the air and the mastiff barked his approval. Dante shifted a lever and pressed two buttons, smiling when the tank jolted forward. Claudio loaded a fresh shell and waited for the signal to fire again.

The street boys had the Nazis bottled inside the square.

From the tower, Maldini continued his grenade attack. From the rear, Connors and Nunzia fired on the soldiers, directing the boys against the tanks, using flamethrowers and kerosene cocktails. Angela worked the sewers, moving from opening to opening like a frenzied rabbit, tossing out bags of grenades, dragging down wounded boys. Vincenzo and his captured panzer moved into the square, its fiery turret shelling the three remaining tanks. The battle was raging at its fullest and angriest, with boys, girls, women and soldiers all fighting for a piece of a now demolished square.

Connors saw flames shoot out of the rear tracks of one Nazi tank. Three of its soldiers jumped out of the smoky hole and ran down one of the empty side streets. The remaining soldiers were now frantically searching for a way out of the inferno they had initiated. Connors turned to Nunzia and yelled, 'They've had enough. Call everybody back.'

Nunzia jumped to the fountain in the centre of the square and fired her gun into the air, waving one arm in a circular pattern. Within minutes the street boys disappeared as quickly as they had appeared, slipping back into the safety of the sewers, side streets and alleys. The Nazi tanks were by now abandoned, and dead soldiers lined the large square.

Connors and Nunzia turned when they saw Vincenzo's tank approach. Vincenzo and Fabrizio waved at them from the open hole. Fabrizio jumped down from the moving tank, the mastiff fast on his heels, and ran towards them. He stopped when he reached Connors, who reached down and picked the boy up.

'What the hell were you and the dog doing inside that tank?' he asked.

'I was the second in command,' Fabrizio said, smiling. 'I would pass Vincenzo's orders down to Claudio and Dante. Without me victory would have been much more difficult.'

Vincenzo, Claudio and Pepe stepped out of the tank and stared at the bodies and the fires that filled the square. Maldini, Frederico and Giovanni came down the steps of the aquarium. 'The Nazis came here expecting to find Naples,' Maldini said, gazing at the flames and smoke. 'And instead they found a pocket of hell.'

The Third Day: September 30

Connors leaned against the side of a Corinthian column, staring at Castel Nuovo in the predawn darkness. The imposing thirteenth-century castle came complete with a moat, five stone towers and a complex series of archways. An expansive green lawn separated the castle from the main road. 'It'd be hard for the tanks to get up here,' Connors said. 'Most likely they'll decide to fight us out by the grass, leaving their soldiers exposed.'

'Unless it can fly,' Maldini said, 'a tank won't be able to take the castle. Right now it's probably the safest place in all Naples. But things often change faster than we would like.'

'It's like a small city in there,' Connors said. 'You could hide a battalion behind those walls, and no one would have a clue they were in there. The Nazis should have done whatever they needed to keep it out of our hands.'

'The Nazis might have been saving it for last, to bring it down on their way out of the city,' Maldini said with a shrug.

'Maybe.' Connors lit a cigarette. 'But it just doesn't feel right.'

'You're like Vincenzo,' Maldini said. 'You overthink every move and manoeuvre. It's because you're a soldier, and he wants to be one. You ask military questions and expect military answers.'

'Explain it to me, then,' Connors said. 'Tell me why the second most decorated officer in the German command, running with the best tank division they have, can't beat back an army of kids?'

'Because the colonel has a stomach for battle but not for murder,' Maldini said. 'If these were American troops he was fighting, they would have already tasted the full power of that division. But they're children. He sees it and he knows it. He's a fighter who can't give the order that will ensure his victory.'

'But he can't allow himself to lose.'

'You're right. At some point he will have to shove aside the concerns of the man and take on the demands of the soldier.'

'If that's going to happen, it'll be soon. He's low on fuel. He's got to finish here and make a run north, ahead of the Brits and my guys.'

Maldini checked the sky for signs of the rising sun. 'It will be today, tomorrow at the latest. But for now the sun still greets the morning as if the world were at peace.'

'When I first met you,' Connors said, 'I wasn't expecting much. You seemed more interested in your wine than in the kids. But I've seen you fight, and I saw how you helped Vincenzo with the plans. That's not something a drunk usually does.'

'My father was an engineer,' Maldini said. 'He helped design many of the sewer tunnels we now use to run from the Nazis. I used to watch him work. And it was how I made my living, too.'

'That explains the planning,' Connors said. 'But you're also good with a gun. Not many engineers are.'

'This isn't Italy's first world war. It's not mine either.'

THE FOUR BOYS had slept in the tunnels longer than they should have. They were running now towards the castle, hoping to get there before the tanks and soldiers arrived. In the distance behind them they heard the drone of the engines on the street. One of the boys, the tallest and oldest, told the others, 'They must be at least a quarter of a mile behind us. We can make the castle with time to spare.'

'Then why are we running?' the youngest of the quartet asked.

'In case I'm wrong,' the older one said, picking up his pace.

The four turned a corner and saw the imposing castle half a mile further down the wide road. They gave each other relieved glances. 'I told you not to worry,' the tall boy said. 'We should be inside the castle in less than ten minutes.'

They were within the shadows of the castle when the first bullet was fired. It hit the youngest boy in the fleshy part of his shoulder and sent him spiralling to the ground. The other three boys skidded to a stop and rushed to their knees to help their injured friend. Their eyes scanned the empty street for any signs of the shooter. 'Don't waste your time on me, Antonio,' the youngest boy said. 'Get yourselves inside the castle. Don't leave them any more targets.'

'Put your arms round my neck,' Antonio ordered him, shoving his arms under the back and folded legs of the wounded boy. 'We're going to get behind those walls together.'

A second shot bounced off the edge of the pavement just to the left of the crouching boys. 'Then we need to find that sniper,' one of them said.

FROM THE JAGGED ROOFTOP of the castle, Vincenzo, Franco and Angela saw the four street boys running towards the front gates of the castle, led by a tall, lanky teenager.

'That's Antonio Murino and his friends.' Angela couldn't hide her frustration. 'They've never been on time once since I've known them.'

The three of them jumped back when they heard the shot. Then they glanced over the edge of the wall and watched Antonio lift the wounded boy. Franco pointed to a side street across from the castle. 'There's smoke coming from that alley,' he said.

Vincenzo braced himself against the side of the wall and waved an arm at Connors and Maldini. 'One of the boys is down,' he yelled. 'They're close enough to make it, but they'll need help.'

'We'll get them in,' Connors shouted back. 'Meantime, try to spot that shooter and fire down on him.'

Connors checked the clips on his two machine guns and looked over at Maldini. 'You up for an early-morning run?'

Soon they were halfway across the grassy field, heading for the open road and the four boys. The Nazi tanks and soldiers were closing in from the streets above. From the rooftop, Franco and Angela fired a stream of gunfire in the direction of the sheltered alley.

As Connors and Maldini reached the four boys, the Nazi tanks were now visible down the road behind them. Antonio was still holding the wounded boy in his arms. 'The sniper's off to the right,' he told Connors. 'He fired twice and then stopped. Maybe he's just waiting for us to run.'

Maldini checked the wounded boy, lowering the bloody shirt and glancing at the bullet hole. 'What's his name?' he asked Antonio.

'He's my cousin Aldo,' Antonio said. 'The two behind me are Pietro and Giovanni.'

Maldini rubbed the top of Aldo's head and walked over towards Pietro, the young boy shivering in the early morning sun. He leaned down and wrapped his warm hands round his shoulders. 'I need someone strong and brave to protect me when we make our run for the castle,' he told him. 'Would you do that for me?'

Pietro stared back at him, his lower lip trembling, his olive eyes wide with fright, and nodded. '*Sì*,' he said. 'I will protect you.'

'Then I have nothing to fear,' Maldini said.

'We'll run on the sniper's side of the road,' Connors announced. 'That'll make it harder to hit any of us.' He looked at each of the four boys, the rumblings of the approaching tanks echoing in his ears, and gripped the two machine guns in his hands.

They moved in a straight line along the edges of the street, crouching low. Connors led the way. Antonio, with Aldo in his arms, was close behind. Maldini brought up the rear.

They were less than a quarter of a mile from the castle entrance.

Connors skidded to a stop when he saw the tank slam out of the front of a burning building. Seven others soon followed, each with a dozen soldiers in its wake, their rifles and machine guns aimed at the two men and four boys. The tanks spread out and blocked off the road to the castle entrance. Connors turned and looked behind him, where a dozen other tanks and more than sixty soldiers were closing in. He looked over at Maldini. 'If you can think of something clever to get us out of this,' he said, 'now would be the time to tell me.'

'As a matter of fact,' Maldini said, squeezing Pietro closer to him. 'I do have an idea.'

'Share it with me.'

'We're going to surrender,' Maldini said. 'And then let them have everything they want. Including the castle.'

Connors walked over to Maldini, shaking his head. 'That's an insane idea,' he said. 'Even if it works.'

'The insane ones always have a better chance,' Maldini said, moving with Pietro towards the waiting Nazi tanks and soldiers.

CARLO PETRONI WALKED down the centre of Via Taddeo da Sessa, making his way towards the Royal Palace and a meeting with the colonel. He knew he was short on time. The street boys had dismissed him and taken his stolen tank. Von Klaus had grown impatient and wanted results from the money he had invested. Carlo realised his initial plan of playing one side against the other was no longer valid, which left him little choice but to side with the Nazis. It was what he planned to tell von Klaus at their meeting.

He was about to turn a corner when he saw a little boy running towards him, a large dog by his side. 'Don't go down that street,' the boy shouted, his voice barely heard above the barks of the dog.

Carlo ignored the boy and continued walking, turning down a side street that would bring him out closer to Nazi headquarters. The boy's shouting grew louder. 'Stay out of there,' he yelled. 'It's too dangerous.'

Carlo was halfway down the street when he turned and faced the little boy and the dog. 'What do you want?' he asked.

'You can't go down there,' the boy said. 'Come back this way. I'll show you a safer way to go.'

'Who are you to tell me where to go?' Carlo asked.

'My name is Fabrizio,' the boy said.

'Your name means nothing to me. Go play with your dog.'

'The street is mined,' Fabrizio told him. 'Come back this way.'

'Did one of the others send you here?' Carlo asked. 'To tell me some lie and get me to come back with you?'

'No one sent me,' Fabrizio said. 'And I never lie.'

'You live in Naples long enough, you'll learn that the truth is not your friend,' Carlo said with a dismissive wave. He turned and continued his walk down the dank street.

Fabrizio and the mastiff were halfway up a short incline leading towards the railway tunnels when the explosion rocked the street behind them. They ran back and stood, staring through the waves of smoke at the ruined body of Carlo Petroni.

THE LARGE WINDOW SPACES fronting the castle were filled with street boys holding rifles and guns. Their stolen tank was down in the centre of the vast inner courtyard a short distance from the locked front door. The rooftops were a sea of heads and rifles, each poised and aimed at the Nazis below. Nunzia stood next to Vincenzo and Franco. Angela was by her side. She looked down at Connors, her father and the four boys. 'They have no choice. They must give up their weapons.'

'The Nazis aren't interested in prisoners,' Vincenzo said. 'Only in casualties.'

'We can't just stand here and do nothing,' Nunzia said. 'We have to get them out of there.'

'I don't know how,' Vincenzo said. 'If we start shooting, the Nazis will fire on them first before they turn to deal with us.'

'They might be willing to let the others go free,' Franco said, 'in return for the American. He's probably worth more to them than any of the others.'

'The American should betray us,' Angela said. 'It's the smartest move he's got, and the only one.'

'He would never betray us.' Nunzia's voice rose in anger. 'He'd die before he would do anything like that.'

'I know he wouldn't,' Angela said, straining her neck to get a closer look. 'That's why I hope Maldini thinks of it first.'

Vincenzo whirled round and stared down at the younger girl. 'What are you talking about?'

'They're surrounded down there, with no hope for escape. But if they surrender and offer to lead them to us, then the Nazis would be in our circle. That's how we would do it in Forcella. But since I'm not the general, I'll leave the thinking to you.'

Vincenzo looked from Angela to the array of tanks and soldiers lining the street below. Connors, Maldini and the four boys were now standing with their arms raised, their guns tossed to the ground. 'Pull the boys away from the windows,' he said. 'Put them on the other side of the castle, facing the inside, lying low and unseen. Move the tank away from the entrance, at least for now.'

'It's going to take more than that to get it done,' Franco said. 'We haven't gone up against that many tanks and soldiers since this started.'

'I know it will,' Vincenzo agreed. 'While Nunzia gets the boys in position, we'll line the area round the front of the castle with mines. And find Gennaro. Tell him to hide over by the drawbridge, down by the moat. Once the tanks are in, have him break the chains that hold the bridge down.'

'Why do that?' Angela asked.

'Once they're in, I want them to stay in. If they give us too much of a fight, the boys and everyone else can leave by the windows and down the walls.'

Nunzia put her hand on Vincenzo's arm. 'You think the Nazis will fall for it?'

'That all depends,' Vincenzo said, picking up his rifle, 'on how good a traitor your father can be.'

MALDINI, HIS HANDS high above his head, looked at the young German officer standing before him and turned away from Connors. 'I can give you the castle,' he said. 'All I want is for the boys to be safe and the wounded boy to be cared for.'

'And what of the American?' the officer asked. 'Do you wish for his safety as well?'

'The American can look out for himself,' Maldini said.

The officer glanced down at the wounded street boy, now resting on the ground. 'How many are in the castle?' he asked Maldini. His Italian was choppy but clear.

'About a hundred boys,' Maldini told him without hesitating. 'All armed and ready to fight. But with the American out of the way I can get them to put down their weapons. They'll listen to what I have to say. And more important than any of my words, they'll see your tanks and soldiers inside the castle walls. They've grown tired of the battle, and their spirit is already weak. With my help you can take them with few, if any, shots fired.'

Connors glared over at Maldini and shook his head in anger. 'You have no idea what you're doing,' he shouted. 'They'll take the castle and then kill every kid in there. I knew you were a drunk, Maldini. I didn't know you were a coward and a fool.'

Maldini gestured back and forth between Connors and the officer. 'You two still have your war to fight,' he told them. 'Ours is at its end. Let us walk away from it alive.'

The officer stared at Maldini and weighed his options. He could take the castle from the outside, but men and tanks would be lost. It would, he realised, be easier and less costly to take control of the castle from within. That left open the question of trust. He didn't fully believe the older man's instant conversion from street fighter to war-weary saviour, but he'd seen enough battles on this front to appreciate the Italian penchant for switching sides.

'Kill the American,' he said to one of his soldiers. 'Then have the old man and the boys lead us into the castle.'

Maldini stepped in between Connors and the soldier, looking over at the officer and shaking his head. 'Understand, I don't care whether the American lives or dies,' Maldini said. 'In fact, if you wish, I'll kill him myself. But he still has many who follow him hidden behind those stone windows. If we kill him here, on the road, in full view, they'll attack us. But if you let him walk in with us, and he happens to die during a moment of battle, then he will be a casualty of war instead of a martyr.'

The officer stepped up to Maldini. 'I warn you, old man,' he snarled. 'If any of this is a ruse, it'll be your head my bullets will be aimed towards.'

'I'd have it no other way,' Maldini said.

VINCENZO STARED DOWN at Connors, Maldini and the four boys leading the convoy of tanks and soldiers towards the front gates of the castle. 'Let them in,' he said. 'As many as can fit inside the walls. And make sure Gennaro stays low and out of sight.'

'What about the boys and Connors and Papa?' Nunzia asked. 'How do we keep them safe once the shooting starts?'

'I'll be down there with them,' Vincenzo said. 'Somebody needs to greet our guests. Why not me?'

'You'll just be another target,' Angela said. 'They won't let you walk in there with a gun in your hand.'

'I won't need a gun in my hand,' Vincenzo said, turning to leave.

Angela and Franco followed him, but stopped at one of the darkened landings to look down at the street. It was filled with soldiers and tanks heading towards the castle. 'This could be a big mistake,' Angela said. 'Once they're in, they can kill as many of ours as we can of theirs.'

VINCENZO STEPPED into the courtyard through a side door, watching the influx of tanks and soldiers. He had a row of grenades and thin bomb cylinders strapped round his waist, the wires jutting out from each connected to a small device with a red button he held in his right hand. He walked with a quiet purpose towards the young Nazi officer, who was turned away from him, facing Connors and Maldini. Vincenzo nodded to them as he approached. The officer caught the look in their eyes, turned and saw Vincenzo, who gave him a wave, ignoring the Nazi rifles aimed in his direction.

The officer studied the wired mechanism round the boy's waist and raised a hand slightly to hold his men at bay. 'It won't work,' he told Vincenzo, watching as the boy positioned himself next to a tank, his hand at his side, finger pressed on the red button linked to the wires. 'I don't think those bombs are for real, and even if they were, I don't believe you have the courage to set them off.'

'That's not something you'll know until I let go of this button,' Vincenzo said, his voice manifesting a calm, reasonable tone. 'It'd be a waste of many lives if you were wrong.'

The officer reached an arm out for Maldini and dragged the older man closer to him. 'Do you know this boy?' he asked.

'I first met him several days ago,' Maldini said. 'He was the boy most eager to kill the Nazis when they came into the city.'

'How eager?'

'Eager enough to die doing it,' Maldini said.

The officer pushed Maldini aside and glared at Connors. 'What about you?' he asked in English. 'Do you know this boy as well?'

Connors shrugged. 'Dirty shirt, torn pants, dark hair. You spend enough time here, and they all start to blend into one another.'

The courtyard was now filled with twenty tanks, with another fifteen lining the outer perimeter of the castle. One hundred soldiers were inside, guns at their sides, their eyes focused on the large open windows above them. Except for the four prisoners in the middle of the courtyard and Vincenzo standing in front of the tank, none of the other street boys were visible.

The courtyard was silent.

The officer stepped away from Connors and Maldini and approached Vincenzo. The boy had been watching the positioning of the tanks and the deployment of the troops, one squad assigned to each of the interior buildings. The contingent of soldiers outside the castle walls was placed on the edges of the grass, fifty yards beyond the front entrance. The plan in place did not take into account such a large number of tanks and soldiers beyond the walls, which now meant the fleeing boys would be making their drop down the side of the castle under the glare of Nazi rifles.

The officer stood ten feet away from the boy, legs spread slightly apart, a cocked pistol in his hand. 'What is it you want?' he asked.

'Let the prisoners go free. None of them means anything to you. The castle is your prize, and that you already have.'

'But if I don't do as you ask, you'll kill them as well as yourself once you set off your bomb,' the officer said. 'That doesn't seem a wise move.'

'I never said I was wise,' Vincenzo said, stepping away from the tank. 'But I do prefer dying by my own hand, not yours. And I think your prisoners feel the same way.'

'Why only these boys?' the officer asked. 'Why not free the others hiding behind those walls above me as well?'

'I only ask for what I think I can get,' Vincenzo said. 'The boys above us are not here as anyone's prisoners. They're here to fight.'

The officer stood in place for several moments, his eyes shifting from the castle walls to Maldini, who was doing his best to act indifferent. 'The life of just one of my soldiers is more important to me than half a dozen Italians and a vagabond American,' he said finally. 'You can go, and take the rest of them along with you. You may escape death today, but it will come soon enough for you.'

Antonio and Aldo were released, followed by Pietro and Giovanni. Vincenzo and Connors walked in silence beside each other, several feet behind Maldini and the young officer. The Nazi stopped at the front gate and signalled his soldiers to allow the others through.

CONNORS WAITED until they were well out of earshot of the officer before he spoke. 'That's not real, is it?' he asked Vincenzo, pointing towards the bomb wrapped around the boy's waist.

'Neapolitans would rather die than commit suicide,' Vincenzo said. 'The wires aren't even connected to any of the grenades. There was only time enough to make it look real. I found this meter lying next to the boiler in the basement. Without that it wouldn't have worked.'

'How soon before they make their move?' Connors asked.

'We have five minutes to be clear of the gates. The moat gate will be dropped, and the doors will be closed. The Nazis within the walls will have no choice but to hold their position.'

'What about our boys?' Maldini asked. 'How will they get out?'

'They've been told to climb out of the front windows, then to get across the lawn and head down the road to the waterfront.' Vincenzo tried to avoid the hard stares of the Nazi soldiers surrounding them. 'But I didn't count on so many soldiers and tanks stationed outside the walls. I didn't think he'd split his force.'

'You didn't think,' Connors said, angry and frustrated.

'I was busy. I was trying to figure out a way to save your life.'

'We need to think of another way to get the boys out,' Maldini interrupted. 'We have some time. The battle inside will keep the Germans occupied.'

'We need a Plan B, chief, and we needed it five minutes ago,' Connors said to Vincenzo, his anger now coated with sarcasm.

Maldini stopped and looked down at his feet. He was inches from the lid of a manhole cover. He glanced over at Connors and Vincenzo. 'The two of you can go on like an old married couple if you want to,' he said. 'But I have your Plan B.'

THE TANKS WERE PLACED in a circular pattern, their turrets primed and ready to bring down the castle walls, when the first of the ignited wine bottles came crashing down on them. Within seconds the morning sky was obscured by a heavy rain of kerosene cocktails and hand grenades. Soldiers rushed to the sealed doors of the interior buildings only to be blown back by the mines attached to each knob by long wires. Boys stood in open windows, firing down into the crowded courtyard, wounding and killing the Nazis who were now squeezed against the sides of the tanks, the only cover available.

The tanks shelled the buildings, and the soldiers riddled the upper walls with machine-gun spray. Outside the castle walls the Nazi tanks were placed in a straight line to fire fierce volleys against the thick hide of the structure. In the centre of the action the young officer ran along the perimeter of the battle, one of his sleeves streaked with blood, shouting out his commands.

Nunzia fired off the last rounds in her machine gun, clicked in a new ammo clip and turned away from the open window. 'We have to get the boys out soon,' she said to Gennaro.

'We need to wait a few minutes longer,' Gennaro said. 'If we have them climb out of the windows now, they'll be nothing but targets to the soldiers outside.'

'Wait for what? It's time to get them out.'

'Our tank should be in place in the courtyard by now, blocking the front entrance,' Gennaro said. 'The Nazis need to shoot at it and set off the bombs inside. The cover smoke from that should be enough to get some of the boys down unharmed.'

'We don't need to wait for the Nazis,' Nunzia said. 'We can set off the tank ourselves.'

Nunzia and Gennaro ran to the front of the building, each carrying half a dozen grenades in a tied-up woollen shirt. As they turned a dark corner, two Nazi soldiers came up the stairs, guns firing in their direction. Nunzia pushed Gennaro to the ground, braced her back against a wall and fired back. She heard the soldiers fall down the flight of steps. 'Let's go,' she ordered Gennaro.

Together they ran to the open window directly above the tank that barricaded the front entrance to the castle. They rested their hands on the chipped ledge and stared down at the abandoned tank.

'Let me have your grenades,' Nunzia said, reaching out for the boy's knotted-up pack. 'Then make your way down the halls and tell the boys to get ready.'

Gennaro stood and stared out of the window, his dark eyes roaming past the tanks and the soldiers at the front of the castle. 'What are they doing?' he asked, pointing out across the boulevard.

'Who?' Nunzia peered through the smoke, trying to identify the three figures in the distance. Her eyes came alive when she realised who it was huddled over what looked to be an opening in the ground. She turned towards Gennaro. 'Maybe,' she told him, 'we're not as trapped as we think.'

Nunzia pulled the pin on one of the grenades, shoved it back inside the folded garment and dropped the grenades down into the open lip of the tank. She grabbed Gennaro's arm and ran with him, away from the window and down the stairs. The explosion sent a missile-like plume of smoke shooting upwards. Below them the tank had shattered into sharp and deadly pieces that now flew at bullet speed through the courtyard. The bronze door landed against one end of a tank, crushing three soldiers in its path. In the centre of all the destruction the young German officer sat with his back against the side of a tank, tears lining his face. The intensity of the battle had stripped him of his bravado. He sat there, holding an empty gun in one hand, surrendering to a soldier's deadliest enemy: the overwhelming power of fear.

VINCENZO STOOD just beneath the mouth of the open manhole, reaching a hand up for Maldini. Connors was already down below, racing several hundred yards ahead of them, searching out any weapons that had been hidden there by the street boys in the days before the start of the battle. 'Follow the line of water,' Maldini shouted out to him as he climbed down the thin steps. 'It will lead you right under the castle.'

Connors stopped and picked up two kerosene-filled wine bottles.

'You should find another half-dozen or so before we reach the walls,' Maldini said, catching up to him.

'You two move ahead, get Nunzia and those kids out of the castle,' Connors said. 'I'll trail behind and try to do some damage with whatever I find down here.'

'There shouldn't be more than two sewer lids between here and the castle,' Maldini said. 'And be careful. If you're seen, they'll figure out a way to stop us before we can get to the boys.'

The three ran down the dark corridors, Maldini leading the way, moving with subtle grace through the oily darkness of the dank and muddy path. He stopped when they reached the first sewer cover. 'They're right above us,' he said to Connors. 'Grip with your fingers through the holes and slide the cover across. Light the bombs and toss them, close the lid and keep moving.'

'Which way, Columbus?' Connors asked. 'And don't tell me to follow the water again. There's water everywhere down here.'

'You run in a straight line to the second sewer cover,' Maldini said. 'From there take the bend to the right. The walls will start to close in around you. That should put you right under the sub-basement of the castle. From there it's a straight run to the water tunnels and the sea. We'll meet you there.'

'We'll be swimming along the shore and to the west,' Vincenzo said. 'With the current. That gets us away from the Nazis faster.'

'What about the ones who can't swim?' Connors asked. 'How do you plan on getting them through?'

'These boys have been playing in the waters of the bay since they were infants,' Maldini said. 'If there's one thing they know how to do, it's swim.'

'There might be one who can't,' Connors said, avoiding Vincenzo's gaze, his fingers on the sewer cover. 'What do you do with him? Pray he doesn't drown?'

'We won't let you drown, American,' Vincenzo said with a chuckle. 'At least not in front of Nunzia.'

'I guess there isn't a bay where you come from,' Maldini said, shaking his head and moving down the slippery path towards the base of the castle, Vincenzo trailing just behind.

'Just the Ohio River,' Connors mumbled to himself. 'And nobody swims in that, not even fish.'

THE NAZI TANKS now unleashed the full vent of their assault. Shell after shell ripped away at the stone-hard fortress, grenades and bullets flew through the air. The castle had become an inferno.

Gennaro and Franco cowered by Nunzia's side. 'We must get to the sub-basement,' she said. 'It's our only chance to escape.'

'What about the others?' Gennaro asked.

'No one will be left behind,' Nunzia said in a loud, firm voice. 'Angela is getting the children out of the towers on the water side. We'll work our way down and meet up with them underground.'

The three turned a corner, flames licking the sides of the walls. They skidded to a stop and stared down at a large crater at their feet where there had once been a floor. Nunzia looked into the dark void, the eyes of the two boys focused on the fire raging behind them. 'We need to jump,' she said, reaching for their hands. 'It's just one floor down. We can make it.'

'What if the next floor collapses from our weight?' Gennaro asked, his voice cracking.

'It's a chance we have to take,' Nunzia said. 'If we stay here, we'll be dead inside of five minutes.'

'I don't want to go first,' Gennaro said.

'I'll go,' Franco said, stepping in front of Nunzia and Gennaro. 'And then the two of you follow me down one after the other.'

'Aim for the centre,' Nunzia told him, 'and keep your legs bent. It'll help brace your fall.'

Nunzia closed her eyes and waited until she heard the hard landing and Franco's soft voice. 'The floor here is solid,' he yelled up through the smoke. 'But the walls sound like they're going to break apart any minute.'

CONNORS SLID the manhole cover halfway across the opening and lifted his head just above the lip. He stared out at a raging field of thick smoke, explosions and gunfire. There were two tanks off to his left. Soldiers were grouped in tiny clusters, all firing the last of their ammunition towards the open windows above them. Connors stared up at the castle, its thick walls withering and crumbling, huge pockets of fire rising into the sky.

Connors clicked open his cigarette lighter, brushed the flame against the strips of cloth jammed inside the tip of two kerosene-filled wine bottles and tossed them out of the sewer. He watched the bottles land in the centre of a quartet of merging soldiers. The blast sent them all tumbling. He reached down, turning his head away from the action, and picked up two more bottles, the lighter still clutched in his right hand.

Connors never saw the soldier.

The Nazi was on his knees, a thin piece of rope wrapped round his hands, waiting for the American to lift his head again out of the sewer opening. He made a diving lunge towards Connors, twisting the rope round his throat with deadly precision. Connors's head snapped back; his hands dropped the bottles and instinctively reached towards his neck in an attempt to ease the pressure. The Nazi twisted the rope harder. Connors forced his head to turn, the cord cutting through his skin. He then brought his right fist up and landed a stinging blow flush to the centre of the soldier's nose. It stunned him and his grip momentarily loosened.

Connors threw two more punches, one glancing off the Nazi's helmet. He then lowered his aim and directed his hardest punch at the Nazi's Adam's apple. The punch sent the Nazi reeling to his left, inches away from Connors's face, the rope now hanging loose. Connors then pulled the Nazi's head towards him. He coiled his arm round the soldier's neck and snapped it down until he heard the crack of bone.

He pushed the Nazi away from the sewer opening and stepped down slowly back into its dank darkness. He touched the gash across his neck, saw the front of his shirt sopped through with blood, then slid the sewer lid closed. He climbed down the thin steps, stepped into the centre of the unlit corridor and ran towards the sewage tunnels at the furthest end.

MALDINI STOOD with his legs immersed in the cold waters of the bay and his arms inside the end of the sewage tunnel. The tunnel jutted out a dozen feet past the rear of the castle. The water was at low tide and the current was pulling gently to the west as Maldini helped ease the first boy out of the round end of the tunnel. 'Keep your head low,' he said as he placed him in the water. 'So long as you hug the shore, it'll be difficult for the Nazis to see you.'

The boy nodded and began his slow move downstream as Maldini turned back to the tunnel. Inside, the shaft was crammed with two long rows of soot-stained boys. Vincenzo and Nunzia crawled along the tunnel, keeping the boys in line, tending to wounds and calming fears. Franco was at the far end, directing the ones who were still fleeing the burning castle. Maldini did a rough head count. There were fewer than fifty boys waiting to jump into the bay. It meant that at least twenty-five had been lost in the fight.

After he'd eased the last of the boys into the waters of the bay, Maldini jumped back up into the tunnel to join Vincenzo and Nunzia. In the distance he could make out the shadowy forms of

Franco and Angela. 'Call them down,' he said. 'It's time for them to go. Then you two follow. I'll stay back and string together the line of grenades and swim out to meet you as soon as that's done.'

'What about Connors?' Nunzia asked.

'It's going to take me a few minutes to string the line and get the grenades in place. He'll be here by then,' Maldini said.

'What if he isn't, Papa?' Nunzia asked.

Maldini could hear the desperation in her voice. He gently gripped his daughter's arms in his hands. 'It won't take the Nazis long to figure out our escape route. Once they do, if those boys aren't out of the water they will die. I'm not going to let anyone, even a man I've grown to care about and respect, cause that to happen. In my place he would do the same.'

'Your papa is right, Nunzia,' Vincenzo said quietly. 'We wait until the grenade lines are strung. It's the best we can do.'

Nunzia's cheeks were flushed with anger. 'He would never leave any of us,' she said. 'He would fight until he was dead.'

Maldini looked at his only daughter and nodded. 'Get Franco and Angela,' he said. 'The four of you go out there and make sure the children get to safety.'

'And the American?' Nunzia asked.

'I'll get him out of the castle,' Maldini said. 'I promise you. It's the least I can do for the man my daughter loves so much.'

Nunzia embraced her father and held him tight in her arms. 'I love you, Papa,' she whispered.

'And I love you,' Maldini said back to her. 'With all my heart.'

Vincenzo held Nunzia's hand, waiting as Franco and Angela ran up next to them. 'Let's go,' he said. 'The children are waiting.'

Maldini watched each one dive into the cold water and disappear. He then turned away from the water's edge and walked back into the mouth of the storm.

He found Connors in a rear corridor, hunched down on his knees on the sub-basement floor. He was quick to notice the rope-cut across the American's throat. 'I knew you wouldn't be able to find your way alone,' he said. 'I should have left you a compass.'

'It wouldn't have helped,' Connors said. 'I have no sense of direction.'

An explosion just above their heads caused the ground to tremble. 'Then follow me closely,' Maldini said, starting to run down the back end of the sub-basement. 'I won't come back a second time.'

Connors followed Maldini out of the sub-basement into the

sewage tunnel. Above them they heard the heavy footsteps of Nazi soldiers searching for hidden boys or escape routes.

They were both out of breath when they reached the last loop of the sewage tunnel. 'The water's up ahead,' Maldini said. 'Jump in and turn to your right. The current will then take you where you need to go.'

'I'll go in when you go in,' Connors said. 'You don't have the time to put up that grenade line by yourself. The Germans will figure out a way to get down here—it's only a matter of minutes.'

'You don't need to know how to swim,' Maldini said with a knowing smile. 'The bay is kind to all, even Americans. And I'll be right behind you. It won't take me long to get the line ready.'

Maldini walked to a corner of the dark tunnel and picked up a rolled-up wire, a dozen grenades strung through its loops. He turned and looked up at Connors. 'My daughter's waiting for you,' he said. 'And Neapolitan women hate to be kept waiting. Especially the foolish ones who think they're in love.'

Connors gave him a warm look and an easy nod. 'She's waiting for her father, too,' he said. 'I'll see you in the water.'

Maldini started to unspool the wire, walking backwards, carefully laying down a wide zigzag pattern. There were enough grenades on the roll to send a fireball hurtling along the central sewage line and back through the gaping holes in the castle structure.

Maldini had unfurled half the line when he heard the familiar sounds of Nazi machine-gun fire coming towards him. He picked up his pace, placing the last of the grenades down in the centre of the tunnel. He slipped to his knees, reached a hand out for a loose grenade, pulled its pin and dropped it. He got to his feet, bullets zinging past him, and ran for the tunnel exit twenty feet away. His run gave way to a slide as he slipped on a strip of oil. He waved frantically for Connors to stand away from the tunnel exit. 'Worry about my daughter,' Maldini shouted. 'Not about me.'

'Stay low and keep running,' Connors yelled back, watching Maldini get on his feet. 'I hate travelling alone.'

The first bullet ripped into Maldini's shoulder and sent him sprawling to the ground. He lifted himself up to his knees, looked over at Connors less than a dozen feet away and pressed his right hand across his heart.

'Take care of my daughter,' he said to Connors.

The second bullet hit Maldini in the back, but he never felt its sting. The explosion of the grenade line and the loud fireball that followed drowned out all his pain. Connors threw himself under the lapping waves of the bay, the ferocious anger of the fire above warming the murky water. He stayed under, kicking his feet and flapping his arms as he awkwardly moved several feet away, hugging the shoreline and coming up for air under the shade of a hanging tree. He stood up in the shallow water and stared at the lip of the tunnel, expecting somehow to see Maldini miraculously emerge from the firestorm.

The bright morning sky had turned into early afternoon rust as fire and smoke rose high and thick over the empty city. Steve Connors walked back to the open end of the tunnel. He stood in front of the lip, removed his helmet and rested it inside the tunnel. He then took several steps back and saluted.

He held the salute for several silent moments, in memory of the man who had just given him the only gift that would ever matter.

His life.

VON KLAUS STARED DOWN at the map spread out across the front end of his tank. Kunnalt held it down with both hands. The colonel then grabbed the map, tore it in half and tossed it to the ground. 'One hundred men dead!' he shouted. 'More than twenty tanks destroyed! Another fifteen with barely enough fuel to make it out of the city. It's a disaster, and one that should never have happened.'

'The Italians have also sustained a significant number of casualties, sir,' Kunnalt said defensively.

'This Third Reich of ours was to have lasted a thousand years, Kunnalt,' von Klaus said. 'Each one shrouded in glory. And now we can't even defeat an army of children.'

Von Klaus reached over and picked up a bottle of red wine resting on the front end of the tank. 'There is no honour in fighting such a battle,' he said. He poured the wine into a tin cup and handed the bottle to Kunnalt. 'Not like this. Not against children. There will be no victory for us here. No matter the final outcome.'

NUNZIA SAT HUDDLED with her head down, a black sweater draped across her shoulders. Connors leaned against the trunk of a pine tree. A contingent of street boys had gathered round them, building a small fire, boiling small tins of watered-down coffee. Vincenzo handed Nunzia a tin of coffee. She nodded her thanks. He sat down between her and Connors. The mastiff was in front of them, its thick paws stretched out, its head curled to one side.

'We all should try to get some rest,' Connors said in a low voice. 'Both sides have had enough fight for one day.'

'We sent all the boys up into the hills for the night,' Vincenzo said. 'They can take care of their wounds up there and get a night's sleep without any worry.'

'Did Dante and Pepe come back with any information we can use?' Connors was talking to Vincenzo, but his eyes zeroed in on Nunzia, wishing he could will away her sorrow or take the burden of her grief.

'The news isn't good,' Vincenzo said.

'Let me hear it anyway,' Connors said.

'Half the city's been destroyed.' Vincenzo's voice was tired and hoarse. 'Von Klaus is moving his remaining tanks and troops towards the railway tunnels and what we call Spaccanapoli. It's the core of our city.'

'How many tanks does he have left?' Connors asked.

'Dante counted thirty.'

'And soldiers?'

'About two hundred.'

'Where are they going to start? City or tunnel?'

'Pepe saw an advance team moving towards the tunnels,' Vincenzo said. 'It's a short distance between both areas, so they could move quickly from one to the other.'

'So will we,' Connors said. He stepped away from the tree. 'It all ends tomorrow.'

'There are fewer than a hundred boys left,' Vincenzo said. 'About a dozen are wounded, but not enough to keep them out of the fight.'

'Leave the wounded ones in the hills,' Connors said. 'And let them have enough guns and ammo in case some Nazis make their way up there.'

Connors knelt down in front of Nunzia, reaching out a hand to caress the side of her face. 'You might want to sit this one out,' he said. 'Stay up in the hills and help take care of the wounded kids.'

She looked at him and shook her head. 'This is where I belong,' she said. 'It's where we all belong.'

He took a deep breath and nodded. 'Stay here with Vincenzo,' he told her. 'You both need to get some sleep. Have all the boys ready before dawn and be down by the tunnels. I'll meet you there.'

'Where are you going now?' she asked.

'I've never ridden on a tram before.' Connors kissed her on the cheek and held her close. 'I think it's about time I did.'

CONNORS STARED UP at the six large rusty trams along Via dei Tribunali. Thick ropes had been wrapped around their top rows, and down past the cracked windows and then curled up under their bases. He turned and saw that seven wide alleys led out of the square, less than 500 feet of hard cobblestones standing between the alleys and the trams. He walked towards his Jeep, where Dante, Pepe, Claudio and Angela were sitting. The mastiff stood next to the vehicle, its head jammed against Fabrizio. Connors took the keys out of his trouser pocket and flipped them towards Dante, who caught them with his right hand.

Behind them the sun was starting to set, leaving them less than an hour of clear daylight. The surrounding area was barren, buildings torched and crumbled up and down the wide boulevard. 'We probably won't finish before dark,' Connors said. 'If we don't, we'll build some fires along the alley entrances so we can see where we're going. One more fire in this town isn't going to attract any attention.'

'Where do you want me to drive?' Dante asked.

'In front of that first tram, for now,' Connors said. 'Stop about six inches past the front end. Then grab the ropes from underneath and above the trams and tie them to the back of the Jeep.'

'You're going to have the Jeep pull the trams?' Angela asked.

'That was Maldini's plan,' Connors said.

'It will work,' Fabrizio said, stepping up alongside Connors, the dog fast by his side. 'If Maldini said so.'

THEY BEGAN their work at dusk. First they moved the trams across their tracks, the rear wheels of the Jeep kicking up thick pockets of dust as it burned off strips of rubber. Its engines cranked and all cylinders were churning as Dante switched gears.

Connors and Angela went from tram to tram, making sure the gears stayed in neutral. They soaked the insides with kerosene so that they could be used as weapons against the remaining Nazi tanks. Once the trams were across from the mouth of an alley, Dante stopped the Jeep, and Connors slammed down on the tram brake.

Behind the Jeep, Pepe and Claudio quickly undid the ropes. Dante then circled round to the centre of the tram and the ropes were retied. 'We're going to have to topple and drag each one across the mouth of an alley,' Connors said. 'You run that engine as hard as it can run. The rest of you come with me. We'll push from the other side.'

Angela stared up at the imposing old structures. 'I don't think there are enough of us to do what you want.'

Connors looked beyond her shoulders. He nodded his head and smiled. 'There are now,' he said.

They all turned to see Nunzia and Vincenzo walking down the centre of the boulevard, followed by the remaining street boys, numbering fewer than a hundred. Connors walked to meet them, followed by Fabrizio and the mastiff. 'I should have learned by now to give up on giving you people any kind of an order,' he said to Nunzia and Vincenzo.

Nunzia embraced Connors. Vincenzo turned to wave on the ones behind him towards the ropes and the trams. 'I promise you, American,' he said. 'When you give us the right order, we'll follow it.'

IT TOOK THEM most of the night.

They pushed and tugged at each tram, twenty boys linked to a rope, Dante straining the Jeep. As each tram collapsed, it filled the air with dust and chunks of broken glass. After each one fell the boys would stand in a semicircle and pump their small fists towards the sky, eager to move on to the next tram in the line.

Once the half-dozen trams were resting on their sides like tired old animals, the ropes were double-looped round their tops and bottoms. Then, one by one, each was dragged along the cobblestones to the wide end of the alleys.

'What if Maldini was wrong?' Vincenzo asked. 'What if the tanks won't risk going over the trams?'

'They won't be able to help it,' Connors answered with assurance. 'A tank officer's biggest weakness is that he thinks there's nothing he can't run over. And these trams are so old and beat up, those panzers should be able to jump them without any problem. That's why it's important to have mines rigged on the inside.'

Vincenzo looked over at Connors and stared into the soldier's clear, confident eyes. His uniform was reduced to brown smudges, but the patch of the Thunderbird Division was still clean and visible. 'Will it be enough to give us a victory?' he asked.

'You won your fight back on the very first day,' Connors said. 'Just by staying here and standing up to the Nazis. But now you want more than that. Now you want to beat them. That's going to be a little harder.'

'I'm glad you stayed with us,' Vincenzo said. 'I don't know if the boys would have held together without a soldier on their side.'

'You would have thought of something, General,' Connors said, walking towards the alleys and the trams. 'I'd bet my life on it.'

AT THE 45th THUNDERBIRD Infantry Division Headquarters in Salerno, Captain Anders folded a piece of paper in half and slipped it into an envelope. He had written too many of these letters, trying to explain to mothers and fathers why their sons would never come home again.

Anders looked up when he saw a young officer walk into the tent. 'I only want good news,' said Anders. 'And that's an order.'

'Air command has agreed to send a plane to Naples, sir,' the officer said. 'A B-24. It should be there some time today.'

'Just one?'

'It's all they could spare, sir.'

'One might be enough to do the job,' Anders said. 'At the very least it'll give us some idea of what we're looking at down there.'

Anders walked over to the table in the centre of the tent and gazed down at the large map. 'Looks like Patton's making his move,' he said. 'Which means it won't be long before we're on the move, too.'

The Fourth Day: October 1

Nazi soldiers walked in small groups along the empty tracks of the central station, following in the dusty wake of their tanks, ever mindful of the mines that had been placed under the dark rocks. Kunnalt was in the centre tank, standing tall in the open mouth, his binoculars focused on the four wide entrances to the tunnels. 'Fire into them,' he shouted to the tank commanders on either side of him. 'If those boys are in there, I don't just want them blocked in. I want them killed.'

It was eight o'clock in the morning when the first of the Nazi shells exploded inside the train tunnels. Kunnalt waved his soldiers in ahead of the tanks, watching as they riddled the dark tunnels with machine-gun fire and the oppressive power of flamethrowers. The men stopped at the tunnel entrance. Kunnalt surveyed the scene and nodded his approval.

'Check for bodies, then seal the tunnels,' Kunnalt ordered a junior officer. 'Then meet up with us at the next location.'

'What of the wounded, sir?' the officer asked.

'There won't be any wounded,' Kunnalt said. 'At least none that you can find. Have I made myself understood?'

The junior officer snapped a salute. Kunnalt's tank veered away from the tunnels and towards its next destination.

That was when they saw the catapults.

They were 200 feet away, three of them lined up twenty feet apart. They were built of planks of wood, cracked tower bells, burned bricks and rusty chains, held in place by rods and gears pulled off the bodies of disabled tanks. Vincenzo and Nunzia stood behind one of the catapults, heavy wooden mallets in their hands. Two boys were assigned to each one, looking to Vincenzo for the signal to fire. 'Be patient,' Vincenzo said. 'Wait for the American and the boys to get in place and then for the Nazi to make his move.'

'What if he fires on us before we get a shot off?' one of the boys asked.

'Then pray he misses,' Vincenzo said, his eyes looking beyond the boys and past the tanks and soldiers to the smoking tunnels.

THEY WERE CROUCHED down inside the rodent-infested sewers under the train tunnels, fifty boys squeezed into a space suitable for half that number. When the shelling had stopped and the soldiers had ceased firing, Connors popped open the sewer cover and slid it across the grimy rails of the tunnel. He jumped out of the dark hole, checking the tunnel entrance. The Nazi soldiers were all focused on Vincenzo and the catapults. The tunnel was blanketed in smoke, giving the boys a difficult but perfect cover to walk through. 'Let's go,' Connors whispered down into the hole. 'Hold your breath if you have to. You're going to make it through. Don't worry. We'll be coming up onto the soldiers with their backs to us.'

The line of boys streamed out of the tight sewer openings. Their rifles by their sides, they felt their way through the murkiness along both sides of the tunnel. Connors walked down the centre of the tunnel, keeping an eye on the Nazi activity close to the entrance. The soldiers had by now retreated back to the cover of their tanks, firing heavy volleys in the direction of the catapults.

Connors stood by the tunnel entrance, the boys grouped alongside each wall. The Nazis were less than fifty feet away. 'Dante, you and your group move to the right,' he whispered, waving the boys out of the tunnel. 'Claudio, you take your boys to the left. Stay low and don't fire until you see me move out and wave to Vincenzo. And let's hope they don't see us first.'

Connors stayed behind, his two machine guns poised at the Nazi soldiers, watching as the boys made their way out of the tunnel and along the tracks, quietly closing ranks on the enemy. The Nazis were moving forward, closer to the catapults, their tank shells falling short of their intended targets by a good fifty yards.

Connors waved his hand, and he and the boys opened fire. Nazi soldiers fell in a heap, caught unawares by the rear attack. Connors yanked two grenades off his belt, pulled the pins out and threw them towards the tanks. He rolled to the ground and resumed firing, targeting the Nazis closest to the tanks.

'OK, Vincenzo,' he said to himself. 'It's time to ring those bells.'

VINCENZO AND NUNZIA were on their knees in front of the first catapult. Each held a mallet and looked out at Connors and the street boys exchanging heavy fire with the Nazis outside the railway tunnels. Vincenzo rubbed the sides of the old tower bell strapped to the centre of the catapult and got to his feet, his mallet raised high above his head. He pounded down two blows to the left side as Nunzia did the same to the right, and then both stepped back. The chain holding the bell in place snapped and released both the bell and the bomb it held in its well. They watched as the bomb arched high towards the sky, then sank down towards a Nazi tank.

The explosion flung the tank ten feet off the ground. It then bounced across the tracks, crushing several soldiers in its path. Nunzia and the boys jumped in the air and cheered. The boys rushed towards the two remaining catapults, pounding down on the chains holding the bombs and bells, eager to wreak their havoc on the Nazis. 'You did it, Vincenzo,' Nunzia said. 'You really made it work.'

'It wasn't me,' Vincenzo said. 'It was your father. If we win anything at all today, it will be because of what he did and what he showed us could be done.'

THE NAZIS WERE TRAPPED.

Connors and the boys bore down on them, firing their rounds, tossing their grenades and kerosene cocktails. Vincenzo and Nunzia sent their heavy artillery hurtling. Kunnalt surveyed the fiery scene and ordered his tanks and soldiers to swing to the right, to leave the station and head for the centre of the city. There was one unobstructed road open to them, and they moved straight for it, firing wildly at the boys.

'All right,' Connors screamed out, 'everybody move back. Take the wounded and put them in the tunnels. The rest of you get out of sight.'

Dante stepped up next to Connors and watched the retreating tanks and soldiers. Blood ran down the side of his face from a gash above his eye. 'They should be coming up to the spot any second now. Unless we placed them wrong.'

'We'll know soon enough,' Connors said. 'How'd we do on casualties?'

'We lost four boys,' Dante said. 'Six others are wounded. One of them could use a doctor.'

'Have Nunzia look at him,' Connors said. 'See if she can patch him up and keep him together for a couple of days. We should have some help in here by then.'

The loud series of explosions knocked both of them off their feet. The Nazi tanks had driven across the minefield set by the street boys. The heavy blasts sent German soldiers sprawling and hurled armour parts in all directions. Connors got to his knees and wiped a hand across the reopened wound round his neck. He turned to check on Dante. The boy was on his hands and knees. 'How many did you and Franco lay down?' Connors asked.

'All that we had left,' Dante said. 'About a dozen. We laid them about ten feet apart, just like you told us to do.'

'That should be enough to wipe out at least half those tanks.'

'So I did a good job?' Dante asked.

'Yes,' Connors said, getting to his feet. 'A very good job.'

THE FINAL BATTLE for the streets of Naples began in Spaccanapoli, the core of the city, at two in the afternoon.

The sky was as clear as a pane of glass, and the sun burned down on a large piazza dominated by bombed-out houses and dark, imposing office buildings. In the centre of the square was a large church, its three-tiered steeple reaching for the heavens, its curved stone steps leading to shuttered iron doors. Seven wide alleys led into and out of the square like the tentacles of a giant squid.

Four boys were positioned in each of the alleys, hidden against the walls, guns and kerosene cocktails in their hands. Vincenzo peered out from behind a large mound of rubble off one of the main alleys. He saw fifteen Nazi tanks move up and down the square, a large contingent of soldiers following in their wake. Von Klaus stood in the well of a tank in the centre of the square, his eyes on the empty buildings, binoculars at rest, his body calm and at ease.

Von Klaus took a deep breath and tapped against the side of his vehicle. The men in the well below him slammed in the first shell and fired. The first shot of the final battle landed in the middle of an abandoned pharmacy and sent it crumbling to the ground.

Vincenzo lit the fuse of his kerosene bottle and hurled it over his head. He watched it land against the rear of a Nazi tank. The hidden street boys jumped from the alleys and fired at the soldiers in the square. The Nazis whirled and returned fire with a furious volley of their own. The boys emptied their guns and began to back into the alleys, tossing stones at the soldiers who were following them, a tank trailing each small group. Vincenzo monitored the action, running down the centre alley. He then climbed over the driver's end of the collapsed tram blocking his path and emerged from the other end. He moved from one alley to the next, watching the boys lead the pursuing tanks and soldiers towards the trams. 'Remember to climb over the driver's side,' he shouted. 'It's the only place not mined.'

NUNZIA, FRANCO, CLAUDIO, Pepe and Dante were running across the far end of the square, pursued by six Nazi soldiers, both groups firing at each other. The children circled and dived behind a large empty fountain next to a two-storey pink stucco building. Angela bolted out of the shattered front door, tossed a lit kerosene bottle at the soldiers, then jumped in beside the others behind the fountain. 'They're coming at us from both sides,' Angela said. 'We can't let them trap us here.'

Dante secured his last clip into his machine gun. 'I'm tired of running,' he said. 'I'm tired of everything. I think we all are.'

Nunzia looked at each of the children. 'We just need to go a little further,' she pleaded. 'Once I get you out of the square, then you can rest.'

'No,' Dante said, his lips pursed and determined. 'We came here to fight, not to run.'

Nunzia watched as they checked their guns, prepared to step into the teeth of the fight. 'The Nazis have seen our backs for three days,' Angela told her. 'It's time for them to see our faces. See who it is they're fighting.'

Nunzia looked above the rim of the fountain, a dozen soldiers now easing in closer to them, crouched low, machine guns at the ready. She turned back to the children around her. 'Spread out across the base,' she said, 'and fire until your guns are empty. If you need to run, head for the alleys. And God be with you all.'

They rose as one, firing the last of their bullets at the surrounding troops. The return volleys were heavy, landing against the sides of the fountain and in the pink stucco wall behind them. Pepe moved his machine gun from left to right, taking down two Nazi soldiers before the sting of a shoulder wound sent him sprawling to the ground. Angela fired from waist level, shooting her rifle with a sniper's precision. She tossed aside one empty gun, pulled out the blade she kept hidden in the crook of her neck and flung it into the chest of a leaping soldier. Nunzia emptied her pistol, then reached for the machine gun of a fallen soldier. She came up on one knee, ripping bullets into the oncoming Nazis.

Beyond them the piazza had exploded into a vast killing field. Von Klaus worked one end of the square, directing his scattered troops to wreak their havoc on an enemy he had never envisioned being as dangerous or resilient as the street boys. Kunnalt was on the other end, his tanks firing at silent buildings and scampering children.

Connors was on the steps of the church in the centre of a small arsenal of machine guns, flamethrowers, kerosene bottles and grenades, six boys spread out to his left and right. He tossed aside an empty machine gun and reached down for another. He looked across the square and saw Nunzia lead Angela and the boys on their valiant charge. He signalled the boys around him to seek shelter and keep firing as he inched his way forward, separated from the woman he loved by the enemy he loathed.

VINCENZO stood at a distance, surrounded by a cluster of wounded street boys, each watching as the tanks made their move onto the toppled trams. As the front ends of the tanks squeezed down on the rusty hulks, the sound of bending steel and breaking glass vibrated out of the smoky alleys.

The tank in the middle alley went first.

The mines buried inside the tram gave off a violent shudder, splitting the tank and the body of the tram in two. The front end of the tank flew out from the mouth of the alley, flipped over and skidded to a halt. The tram let loose a large gulp of fire.

The next three explosions shook the piazza.

Von Klaus looked at the fire coming out of the alleys, knowing that within the confines of those tight corridors he had lost four tanks and twenty brave men. He slammed his fist against the side of his tank, losing the tight leash he kept on his emotions and finally allowing the hardness of the soldier to overcome the frailties of the man. He saw Kunnalt, fighting on in a corner of the square, his soldiers firing at a woman and a line of street boys. 'You win,' he shouted across the space between them. 'You'll finally get your wish.'

'Which wish is that, sir?' Kunnalt shouted back.
'To see them all dead,' von Klaus said.
His tank moved forward.

VINCENZO PLACED one of the wounded boys under the shade of a large pine tree, resting his head on top of a mound of clothing. Then he turned round and put both hands on Fabrizio's slender arms. 'I want you and the dog to stay here and keep an eye on the wounded. I need someone I can trust to keep them safe.'

Fabrizio nodded, his eyes filled with confidence.

'You should be safe here,' Vincenzo said. 'This street is not one the Nazis will want to take.'

'Where will you be?' Fabrizio asked, staring at Vincenzo and the dozen street boys standing behind him.

'Where I belong,' Vincenzo said.

He ran back towards the fires and the alleys, the rest of the street boys trailing close behind.

NUNZIA, ANGELA and the boys stood in front of the fountain, firing the last bullets in their guns, the bodies of half a dozen soldiers strewn about their feet. A shot fired by Kunnalt, standing in the well of his tank, clipped Claudio in the shoulder and sent him sprawling. Nunzia and Pepe pulled the boy behind the fountain, both still firing their guns. As she emptied the bullets in her chamber, Nunzia saw Connors running across the square towards her, two blazing guns in his hands.

'Nunzia, get down!' Franco shouted.

She turned to catch a rifle tossed to her by Angela. She gave a quick glance at those around her. Franco bled from his leg and arm, holding a machine gun in the crook of his good shoulder. Pepe was shooting from a sitting position, a large gash open on his forehead. Claudio was throwing stones, trying to get to a fallen soldier's gun. Angela stood her ground and fought with a gun and a knife.

Kunnalt was now out of his tank and coming at Nunzia, less than ten feet away. Connors, in the middle of the firefight, inched his way towards her. She turned her head and quickly looked his way, catching his eye and holding the gaze for the briefest of seconds.

Kunnalt's first shot hit her flush in the stomach, knocking her backwards, the gun flying from her hands. The second one landed just below her neckline, its force spinning her round. Angela and the boys held their fire, eyes frozen on Nunzia's fallen body. Connors ripped through the Nazi line in a frenzy, killing all that stood between him and the woman he loved. He rushed to her side, watching as Kunnalt drifted away, enveloped in a veil of smoke. He dropped to his knees and turned her face towards his, desperately aware that the wounds were fatal. 'No,' he mumbled. 'Don't do this. I'm begging you, please, don't die. I'll get you out. We all will. Just please. Hang on for me. Please.'

She placed a hand across his quivering mouth, her warm eyes calm and peaceful. Connors heard and saw nothing else but her, alone in the centre of a brutal storm. 'A good man always finds love,' she said. 'You found it with me, even here, even now.'

'Yes,' Connors said, 'I did find it.'

'And you will again, my American.'

Connors held her closer, kissing the top of her head. '*Ti amo, Nunzia*,' he told her. '*Ti amo*.'

She looked at him and smiled. 'Who taught you to say that?' Her body was giving in to the power of the bullets.

'Your father,' Connors said. 'He told me if I said it twice, the love will last for ever.'

'I think he made that part up,' she said.

'I believed it,' he said, rocking her gently. 'I still believe it.'

Her hand slipped away from his face, and her eyes slowly closed. Connors held her for several minutes, then rested her head back on the ground and turned to the stunned street boys around him. In the corner of the square he saw Kunnalt running back to his tank. He stood and looked at each of the children. 'I want you to stay with her,' he told them.

He picked up a machine gun and ran out into the smoke and haze of the square in search of Kunnalt.

VINCENZO AND THE STREET boys jumped through the thick flames of the exploding trams. They came out of the fire shooting at the Nazis grouped at the far side of the alley. The soldiers turned and quickly returned fire. Several feet behind them von Klaus swung his tank into position to ensure that the boys' charge would be a futile one. The boys moved forward. Bullets found their mark and boys tumbled to the ground. In the centre of the alley Vincenzo lifted his right arm. At the signal the remaining boys dropped their guns and held up two grenades each. They pulled the pins.

'Let them taste it,' Vincenzo shouted out, and watched the arched path of the grenades as they reached the Nazi soldiers.

The explosions rocked the alley and sent them all to the ground. Vincenzo landed hard against a sharp rock, which sliced a deep cut across his cheek. He crawled to his feet. The alley was now empty of Nazis except for von Klaus and his tank. Vincenzo stood, a pistol clutched in his right hand, watching as the tank eased its way into the alley. Von Klaus looked down at the boy from inside the open well. The tank came to a stop twenty feet away from Vincenzo and the street boys. 'I will not allow you a victory,' von Klaus shouted. 'Not today and not ever.'

'It is still our flag that flies here,' Vincenzo said, holding his ground, gripping the trigger of the pistol. 'Not yours.'

'That flag will be the last thing you will live to see,' von Klaus said, poised to give the order to fire. 'Your adventure ends with honour, but in death.'

THE SHOT CAME from an open window just to the right of von Klaus. It caught the colonel in his side, forcing him to double up. Vincenzo looked up and saw a stunned Fabrizio standing in the window. The boy stared at the rifle in his hands.

'I'm sorry I didn't do what you told me to do,' he called out. 'But I didn't want any more of my friends to die.'

Behind Vincenzo two of the street boys had slid open a sewer cover and were scampering into the open hole. Von Klaus held a pistol in his right hand. He lifted his head and looked at Vincenzo. He squeezed off two shaky rounds, one missing the boy, the other grazing his right leg, sending him down to one knee.

Above them a B-24 hovered in the skies.

Vincenzo fired back as he retreated. Two street boys rushed up, grabbed him and dragged him into the sewer hole. Vincenzo and von Klaus exchanged a hard look. As the leader of the street boys disappeared under the sewer cover, a hot shell from the tank turret exploded just above his head.

Vincenzo and the boys raced along the edges of the sewer tunnel and heard the bombs from the B-24 begin to fall on von Klaus and his tank. Vincenzo looked up. 'Enjoy the rest of your time in Naples, Colonel,' he said.

CONNORS AND KUNNALT exchanged gunfire as they both ran. Connors emptied the last bullets in his machine gun, then tossed the gun to the ground and closed in on his target. Kunnalt turned and aimed his pistol directly at Connors, but he was caught at chest level by the American's leap before he could get off another shot. They crashed through the large window of a storefront, the weight of the American knocking the wind from the Nazi. They rolled on the marble floor, over stones and debris, kicking aside thin planks of wood and discarded cardboard boxes. Kunnalt pushed back Connors's head and jabbed several punches into his neck. Connors lifted his right knee and shoved Kunnalt in the chest, sending the Nazi sprawling along the dusty floor, flat on his back.

Kunnalt stretched out his left hand along the dusty floor and wrapped his fingers round a thick hunk of stone.

Connors was on his knees and coming up towards the officer when he caught the blow against the side of his face. A second punch sent him skidding to the front of an old fireplace piled high with ashes. Kunnalt hovered over Connors, yanked him by the hair at the back of his head and then rubbed his face in the ash pile. As Connors struggled to lift his head, the tips of his fingers rubbed against the sharp end of a rusty iron poker. Connors managed to push back his head, his mouth filled with the taste of ash, and slide his body until he could grab the poker with his right hand.

Kunnalt straddled the American, grabbing the back of his shirt and lifting him to his knees. 'A soldier should not have to die this way,' Kunnalt said, a knife held in his right hand. 'Not for a bunch of children.'

Connors whirled round and broke the hold. He got to his feet and jammed the poker deep into Kunnalt's stomach. The knife fell to the floor. Kunnalt gripped the shaft of the poker with his hands, the life ebbing from his face.

Connors stepped back and let the Nazi fall to the cold marble floor. He then walked slowly out of the store.

THE SQUARE WAS a thick mask of smoke.

Four Nazi tanks fired at what was left of the buildings and fleeing children. Connors walked towards the fountain, Angela and the boys still protecting Nunzia's body. Vincenzo, Fabrizio and the mastiff were now with them. Connors stepped between the boys, bent down and gathered Nunzia's body in his arms. He held her close to his chest, his eyes staring at her peaceful face. He turned and placed her gently inside the dry fountain basin. Vincenzo moved alongside him and rested a hand on top of hers. 'You had her love,' Vincenzo said to him.

Connors looked away from Nunzia and stared at the boy, his face and leg bleeding, a machine gun in his left hand. 'Sometimes that's just not enough,' he said in a low voice.

A shell exploded just above their heads, chunks of pink stucco flying down at them, as a Nazi tank advanced on the small group, firing bullets in their direction. 'Up the church steps,' Vincenzo yelled, waving the group away. 'Grab some weapons and hurry. We'll let the tank come to us.'

The group ran towards the steps of the large church, the last building in the square untouched by Nazi bombs, stopping only to pick up guns and grenades from the sides of the fallen. Vincenzo followed, firing his gun at the approaching tank as he moved. Connors, his back to the oncoming vehicle, looked down at Nunzia one more time, then picked up two machine guns and a row of hand grenades and followed Vincenzo towards the steps of the church.

THEY STOOD with their backs against the bronze doors of the medieval structure, the tank inching its way up the stone steps, firing an angry volley of bullets. The ragged army held its place and fired back. Fabrizio threw as many rocks and stones as he could find, the bull mastiff barking angrily by his side. Three other Nazi tanks circled the square and headed in their direction.

The tank bounced from one step to the next, nearly close enough now for the boys to reach out and touch. Angela tossed out her last grenade and ran down the steps, trying to reach an abandoned machine gun. A Nazi soldier leaped out from behind the tank and fired, hitting her in the knee. She fell, grabbed for the machine gun and threw it to Franco. The boy caught it on the run, then he, Connors and Vincenzo jumped on top of the tank and crawled their way towards the lid.

The boys snapped open the lid of the tank and jumped off. Franco fired at the soldiers huddled behind the vehicle. As they all scooted up the stairs, Vincenzo pulling Angela along with them, they watched Connors jam his guns inside the lid of the tank and fire until his bullets were spent. The tank halted inches from the front doors of the shuttered church.

Connors cast aside his guns, jumped off the tank and ran up the steps.

'We only have a few guns left to fight with,' Vincenzo told him. 'They still have three tanks, all heading here.'

'And we're short of bullets and grenades,' Franco said.

The square was a bright blaze of flame and horror. The three tanks rumbled along, closing in on the church. 'You can run,' Connors said. 'They'll get some of you, but not all. It makes no sense for everybody to die.'

'Send Fabrizio and the dog,' Angela said. 'The rest of us will stay.'

Fabrizio stepped out from behind Connors. 'I will never leave my friends,' he said.

Connors reached down and lifted the small boy into his arms. He kissed Fabrizio on the cheek and stared into his gentle eyes.

'It was a miracle we took it this far,' Franco said. 'I thought we would all be dead the first time we tried to fight the Nazis.'

'We were just one miracle short,' Connors said, looking down at the circling tanks. 'That is, if you believe in those things.'

They heard the plane before they saw it.

The B-24 came out of the clouds to bear down on the Nazi tanks. Vincenzo looked up at the American plane, firing at the now fleeing tanks, chasing them into the alleys at the far end of the square. He turned to Connors and shrugged. 'It's getting harder not to believe in miracles,' he said.

The B-24's machine-gun turrets riddled the last remaining Nazi soldiers in the square, then circled back. It swooped down one final time and dropped 300 pounds of bombs on top of the three tanks, sending each to its final destiny.

The streets of Naples were free of Nazi rule.

CONNORS, VINCENZO and the others walked down the steps of the church, out into the burning square, and stopped in front of the fountain and Nunzia's body. 'I want to bury her,' Connors said to Vincenzo. 'Do you know a place she would have liked?'

'Nunzia was like her father,' Vincenzo said. 'She loved the sea and the city. There are places along Piazza Trieste e Trento where she can see both.'

'Take us there,' Connors said.

The American turned and lifted Nunzia's body into his arms and walked with her slowly past each remaining street boy. One by one they gently kissed her folded hands. Then, their hands finally free of guns, they kept their heads bowed in silent prayer as they went off to bury one more of their dead.

THE BONFIRES ALONG the waterfront lit the night sky.

The group sat round the warm flames, drinking from tin cups filled with red wine, their wounds bandaged, staring out at the quiet sea and up towards a blanket of stars. Fabrizio rested his head against the side of the sitting mastiff, both drifting off to sleep.

'No planes, no tanks and no soldiers,' Vincenzo said. 'It's been years since that was true.'

'What happens to us now?' Angela asked, her leg wrapped in cloth, blood still seeping through.

'The Americans should be here in a day or two,' Connors said. 'Some medical units as well. They'll try to find anyone who's left from your families and put you together with them.'

'We won't have to worry about getting killed,' Franco said. 'But now we have to figure out how to live.'

'That's always going to be harder,' Connors told him. 'No matter what side of the war you're on.'

'What about you?' Claudio asked. 'Where will you go?'

'I'll stay here until my unit comes in,' Connors said.

'The Thunderbirds,' Vincenzo said, eyeing the patch once again.

'Right.' Connors gave him a knowing nod. 'Then, wherever they go, I'll go with them.'

'Will you get into trouble for helping us?' Vincenzo asked.

'They don't ever get too mad at you for killing the enemy.'

'I'm happy you stayed with us, American,' Vincenzo said. 'We all are. It's your victory as much as ours.'

'Was it worth it?' Connors asked.

'Yes,' Vincenzo said without hesitation.

'Just for you or for everybody?'

'It means as much to the ones who died as it does to the ones who live,' Vincenzo said, standing now and facing the fire. 'This fight wasn't for us. It was for Naples.'

Franco and Dante threw more wood on the fire, watching it grow bigger. Connors looked past them towards the quiet lapping of the bay. He closed his eyes and smiled when he heard the group begin to sing the first words to their favourite Neapolitan love ballad.

They stayed until early morning, singing the slow and sad lyrical words to '*Parlami d'amore, Mariù*'. Their faces were warm and their cheeks red, their wounded bodies aching from the weight of battle. They lifted their eyes towards the sky and sang out in full voice as they held one another.

They were all that remained of a battered army of children, determined to die for the sake of their freedom. And now they had finally found peace. On the streets of a ruined city they could once again claim as their own.

EPILOGUE

Vincenzo stood on the crowded platform looking up at the train. His shirt and trouser pockets were crammed with official-looking documents, all stamped by both the American forces now in place in Naples and members of a provisional government that had been installed to oversee the rebuilding of the city.

Much had happened since the end of their battle against the Nazi tanks. The Americans had come in several days later and taken control. The boys were given medical attention. Connors came by each day to check on how they were doing. He eventually moved out with the rest of his Thunderbird division, heading up north.

'Will you ever come back to Naples?' Vincenzo had asked.

'Why wouldn't I?' Connors said. 'I have a lot of friends here.'

Angela and the boys were put in temporary quarters as officials sought surviving members of their families. One by one, each member of the group was sent to live in a place he or she would call home. There they could once again be children instead of soldiers.

Vincenzo picked up the suitcase by his side, packed with clothes given him by soldiers, and walked towards the steps of the train.

An American officer blocked his path.

Vincenzo stared up at him and saw that he wore the same patch as Connors. He put down his case and waited.

'Are you Vincenzo?' the officer asked.

'Yes,' the boy said.

'My name's Anders. Do you have a couple of minutes for me?'

'The train doesn't leave for twenty minutes,' Vincenzo said.

'How about we sit on that bench over there?' Anders pointed to a stone slab off to the right. 'You want some coffee or anything?'

'No,' Vincenzo said, walking to the bench and sitting down. 'I have all I need.'

'Where's the train taking you?' he asked. The captain sat down next to the boy and put an unlit cigar into his mouth.

'To my father's sister. She's going to take me in.'

Anders nodded. 'You and your boys gave those Nazis one helluva run,' he said.

'Why are you here?' Vincenzo asked.

Anders gave the boy a slight smile. 'Connors told me you didn't have much patience for bull. As usual, he wasn't lying.'

Anders reached a beefy hand inside his uniform jacket, pulled out a thin yellow envelope and handed it to Vincenzo, who took it.

'After Naples, I sent Connors and some of my Thunderbirds up the coast,' the captain said. 'They teamed up with the Texas Division and some of the Brits and went against the Nazis. Some of those battles got pretty hot, and not all of them went our way.'

'What happened to Connors?' Vincenzo asked, fearing he already knew the answer.

'I lost a lot of good men in those fights,' Anders said, staring hard at the boy by his side. 'Steve Connors was one of them.'

The two sat silently for several minutes. 'Before he went out,' Anders continued, 'he asked me to give you that envelope, just in case anything happened. I don't know what he put in it, but he said whatever it was, you had earned it.'

Vincenzo took a deep breath and wrapped his fingers round the envelope, his throat dry, his lower lip trembling.

'He respected you, kid,' Anders said. 'He respected all of you.'

'One of us he loved,' Vincenzo said in a low voice. 'Nunzia.'

Captain Anders took a deep breath and stood up, then placed his hands on the boy's shoulders. 'I would wish you luck, son,' he said. 'But that would be nothing but a waste of time. You know that better than I do. We just try to live while we can and make the best of it. So you just be well and stay well.'

Vincenzo gripped the envelope tighter and watched as Captain Anders turned and disappeared into the crowd.

VINCENZO SAT in a seat next to a large window. He felt the train inch its way out of the station. He took a deep breath and tore open one side of the yellow envelope. He reached inside and pulled out the Thunderbird patch Connors had worn on his sleeve. He brought the patch up to his chest, lowered his head and cried silent tears.

The train was now chugging along its path, the engine running at full throttle. Vincenzo lifted his head and looked out at the passing scenery, a maze of battered homes, blocked-off roads and military convoys. He caught his reflection in the thick glass and wiped the sides of his face with the palm of his hand.

Outside, white smoke billowed from the front of the train, sending thick clouds streaming through the air.

It was a day of peace in a time of war.

LORENZO CARCATERRA

When writing *Street Boys,* Lorenzo Carcaterra was able to draw on his own experiences of life on the street—not as an orphan in Naples, but as a young boy in one of New York City's toughest neighbourhoods: Hell's Kitchen.

His first book, *A Safe Place* (1993), was a powerful memoir devoted to those difficult early years and his often violent father. His second book, *Sleepers* (1995), was also based on his turbulent coming-of-age in the 1950s and 1960s. It became a best-selling novel and a major motion picture starring Brad Pitt and Robert De Niro.

As for war-torn Naples and the legend of the fearless street boys who stood up to the Nazis, they were an indelible part of Carcaterra's childhood. 'It is a story I have heard many times,' he says. His mother, Raffaela, was born and raised in Italy, and her tales, told in Neapolitan dialect, laid the foundation for *Street Boys*.

'The stories of these boys who took on the Germans became like a folk tale to me, and then as I got older and I visited Naples, more people would tell me about it. And what was interesting is, you'd hear from each person a different version of the story. It's been part of my life since I was a child, I guess it was just a matter of time until I wrote it down.'

A former journalist, Carcaterra is careful to assert that his affecting war saga, soon to be filmed, is heavily fictionalised. 'All the characters are fictional, as are the details of the battles,' he says. 'But at the very heart of this novel, as its deepest centre, there is a simple truth: that a band of children, stripped of all that mattered to their lives, stood up against the most powerful army ever to invade their soil.'

THE VANISHED MAN. Original full-length edition © 2003 by Jeffery Deaver. US condensed edition © The Reader's Digest Association Inc, 2003. British condensed edition © The Reader's Digest Association Limited, 2003.

DON'T LOOK BACK. Original full-length edition © 2002 by Karin Fossum. English translation © 2002 by Felicity David. British condensed edition © The Reader's Digest Association Limited, 2003.

PREY. Original full-length edition © 2002 by Michael Crichton. British condensed edition © The Reader's Digest Association Limited, 2003.

STREET BOYS. Original full-length edition © 2002 by Lorenzo Carcaterra. US condensed edition © The Reader's Digest Association Inc, 2003. British condensed edition © The Reader's Digest Association Limited, 2003.

The right to be identified as authors has been asserted by the following in accordance with sections 77 and 78 of the Copyright, Designs and Patents Act, 1988: Jeffery Deaver, Karin Fossum, Michael Crichton and Lorenzo Carcaterra.

ACKNOWLEDGMENTS AND PICTURE CREDITS: *The Vanished Man*: pages 6–8: Getty Images/Stone; page 147 © Jerry Bauer. *Don't Look Back*: pages 148–150: Getty Images/Stone; page 277 © Bo-Aje Mellin. *Prey*: pages 278–280: Getty Images/Stone; design by Claire Rankin; page 419 © Jonathan Exley. *Street Boys*: pages 420–422: Hulton Archive.

DUSTJACKET CREDITS: Spine from top: Getty Images/Stone; Getty Images/Stone; Getty Images/Stone; design by Claire Rankin; Hulton Archive.

Printed by Maury Imprimeur SA, Malesherbes, France
Bound by Reliures Brun SA, Malesherbes, France

224AU